The Collected Stories of
ISAAC BASHEVIS SINGER

THE
COLLECTED
STORIES
OF
ISAAC
BASHEVIS
SINGER

The Noonday Press
FARRAR · STRAUS · GIROUX
NEW YORK

Copyright © 1953, 1954, 1957, 1961, 1962, 1963, 1964, 1965,
1966, 1967, 1968, 1970, 1971, 1972, 1973, 1974, 1975,
1976, 1977, 1978, 1979, 1980, 1982 by Isaac Bashevis Singer;
renewal copyright © 1981, 1982 by Isaac Bashevis Singer
All rights reserved

Tenth printing, 1991

Printed in the United States of America
Published in Canada by HarperCollins*CanadaLtd*
DESIGNED BY HERB JOHNSON

Library of Congress Cataloging in Publication Data
Singer, Isaac Bashevis.
The collected stories of Isaac Bashevis Singer.
Translated from the Yiddish by various hands.
1. Fiction. I. Title.
PJ5129.S49A22   839'.0933   81–12436
AACR2

Many of these stories originally appeared in *The New Yorker*.
"Gimpel the Fool" and "The Little Shoemakers" originally
appeared in *A Treasury of Yiddish Stories*, edited by
Irving Howe and Eliezer Greenberg, reprinted with
the permission of Viking Penguin Inc.

I · B · S

Contents

Author's Note

It is difficult for me to comment on the choice of the forty-seven stories in this collection, selected from more than a hundred. Like some Oriental father with a harem full of women and children, I cherish them all.

In the process of creating them, I have become aware of the many dangers that lurk behind the writer of fiction. The worst of them are: 1. The idea that the writer must be a sociologist and a politician, adjusting himself to what are called social dialectics. 2. Greed for money and quick recognition. 3. Forced originality—namely, the illusion that pretentious rhetoric, precious innovations in style, and playing with artificial symbols can express the basic and ever-changing nature of human relations, or reflect the combinations and complications of heredity and environment. These verbal pitfalls of so-called "experimental" writing have done damage even to genuine talent; they have destroyed much of modern poetry by making it obscure, esoteric, and charmless. Imagination is one thing, and the distortion of what Spinoza called "the order of things" is something else entirely. Literature can very well describe the absurd, but it should never become absurd itself.

Although the short story is not in vogue nowadays, I still believe that it constitutes the utmost challenge to the creative writer. Unlike the novel, which can absorb and even forgive lengthy digressions, flashbacks, and loose construction, the short story must aim directly at its climax. It must possess uninterrupted tension and suspense. Also, brevity is its very essence. The short story must have a definite plan; it cannot be what in literary jargon is called "a slice of life." The masters of the short story, Chekhov, Maupassant, as well as the sublime scribe of the Joseph story in the Book of Genesis, knew exactly where they were going. One can read them over and over again and never get bored. Fiction in general should never become analytic. As a matter of fact, the writer of fiction should not even try to dabble in psychology and its various isms. Genuine literature informs while it entertains. It manages to be both clear and profound. It has the magical power of merging causality with purpose, doubt with faith, the passions of the flesh with the yearnings of the soul. It is unique and general, national and universal, realistic and mystical. While it tolerates commentary by others, it should never try to explain itself. These obvious truths must be emphasized, because false criticism and pseudo-originality have created a state of literary amnesia in our generation. The zeal for messages has made many writers forget that storytelling is the raison d'être of artistic prose.

For readers who would like me to say something "more personal," I quote here a few passages (though not in the order in which they were written) from a recent memoir of mine: "My isolation from everything remained the same. I had surrendered myself to melancholy and it had taken me prisoner. I had presented Creation with an ultimatum: 'Tell me your secret, or let me perish.' I had to run away from myself. But how? And where? I dreamed of a humanism and ethics the basis of which would be a refusal to justify all the evils the Almighty has sent us and is preparing to bestow upon us in the future. At its best, art can be nothing more than a means of forgetting the human disaster for a while."

I am still working hard to make this "while" worthwhile.

I have had the good fortune to work with three highly talented and true editors, Robert Giroux, Cecil Hemlcy, and Rachel MacKenzie. I dedicate this collection to Rachel MacKenzie's sacred memory. She was blessed with wisdom, charm, and humility, and embued with a perfect understanding of literature—a great editor and, more than that, a great person.

I.B.S.

July 6, 1981

The Collected Stories of
ISAAC BASHEVIS SINGER

Gimpel the Fool

I

I am Gimpel the fool. I don't think myself a fool. On the contrary. But that's what folks call me. They gave me the name while I was still in school. I had seven names in all: imbecile, donkey, flax-head, dope, glump, ninny, and fool. The last name stuck. What did my foolishness consist of? I was easy to take in. They said, "Gimpel, you know the rabbi's wife has been brought to childbed?" So I skipped school. Well, it turned out to be a lie. How was I supposed to know? She hadn't had a big belly. But I never looked at her belly. Was that really so foolish? The gang laughed and hee-hawed, stomped and danced and chanted a good-night prayer. And instead of the raisins they give when a woman's lying in, they stuffed my hand full of goat turds. I was no weakling. If I slapped someone he'd see all the way to Cracow. But I'm really not a slugger by nature. I think to myself: Let it pass. So they take advantage of me.

I was coming home from school and heard a dog barking. I'm not afraid of dogs, but of course I never want to start up with them. One of them may be mad, and if he bites there's not a Tartar in the world who can help you. So I made tracks. Then I looked around and saw the whole market place wild with laughter. It was no dog at all but Wolf-Leib the thief. How was I supposed to know it was he? It sounded like a howling bitch.

When the pranksters and leg-pullers found that I was easy to fool, every one of them tried his luck with me. "Gimpel, the czar is coming to Frampol; Gimpel, the moon fell down in Turbeen; Gimpel, little Hodel Furpiece found a treasure behind the bathhouse." And I like a golem believed everyone. In the first place, everything is possible, as it is written in *The Wisdom of the Fathers*, I've forgotten just how. Second,

---

Translated by Saul Bellow

I had to believe when the whole town came down on me! If I ever dared to say, "Ah, you're kidding!" there was trouble. People got angry. "What do you mean! You want to call everyone a liar?" What was I to do? I believed them, and I hope at least that did them some good.

I was an orphan. My grandfather who brought me up was already bent toward the grave. So they turned me over to a baker, and what a time they gave me there! Every woman or girl who came to bake a batch of noodles had to fool me at least once. "Gimpel, there's a fair in Heaven; Gimpel, the rabbi gave birth to a calf in the seventh month; Gimpel, a cow flew over the roof and laid brass eggs." A student from the yeshiva came once to buy a roll, and he said, "You, Gimpel, while you stand here scraping with your baker's shovel the Messiah has come. The dead have arisen." "What do you mean?" I said. "I heard no one blowing the ram's horn!" He said, "Are you deaf?" And all began to cry, "We heard it, we heard!" Then in came Rietze the candle-dipper and called out in her hoarse voice, "Gimpel, your father and mother have stood up from the grave. They're looking for you."

To tell the truth, I knew very well that nothing of the sort had happened, but all the same, as folks were talking, I threw on my wool vest and went out. Maybe something had happened. What did I stand to lose by looking? Well, what a cat music went up! And then I took a vow to believe nothing more. But that was no go either. They confused me so that I didn't know the big end from the small.

I went to the rabbi to get some advice. He said, "It is written, better to be a fool all your days than for one hour to be evil. You are not a fool. They are the fools. For he who causes his neighbor to feel shame loses Paradise himself." Nevertheless, the rabbi's daughter took me in. As I left the rabbinical court she said, "Have you kissed the wall yet?" I said, "No; what for?" She answered, "It's the law; you've got to do it after every visit." Well, there didn't seem to be any harm in it. And she burst out laughing. It was a fine trick. She put one over on me, all right.

I wanted to go off to another town, but then everyone got busy matchmaking, and they were after me so they nearly tore my coat tails off. They talked at me and talked until I got water on the ear. She was no chaste maiden, but they told me she was virgin pure. She had a limp, and they said it was deliberate, from coyness. She had a bastard, and they told me the child was her little brother. I cried, "You're wasting your time. I'll never marry that whore." But they said indignantly, "What a way to talk! Aren't you ashamed of yourself? We can take you to the rabbi and have you fined for giving her a bad name." I saw then that I wouldn't escape them so easily and I thought: They're set on making me their butt. But when you're married the husband's the master, and if that's all right with her it's agreeable to me too. Besides, you can't pass through life unscathed, nor expect to.

I went to her clay house, which was built on the sand, and the whole gang, hollering and chorusing, came after me. They acted like bear-baiters. When we came to the well they stopped all the same. They were afraid to start anything with Elka. Her mouth would open as if it were on a hinge, and she had a fierce tongue. I entered the house. Lines were strung from wall to wall and clothes were drying. Barefoot she stood by the tub, doing the wash. She was dressed in a worn hand-me-down gown of plush. She had her hair put up in braids and pinned across her head. It took my breath away, almost, the reek of it all.

Evidently she knew who I was. She took a look at me and said, "Look who's here! He's come, the drip. Grab a seat."

I told her all; I denied nothing. "Tell me the truth," I said, "are you really a virgin, and is that mischievous Yechiel actually your little brother? Don't be deceitful with me, for I'm an orphan."

"I'm an orphan myself," she answered, "and whoever tries to twist you up, may the end of his nose take a twist. But don't let them think they can take advantage of me. I want a dowry of fifty guilders, and let them take up a collection besides. Otherwise they can kiss my you-know-what." She was very plainspoken. I said, "It's the bride and not the groom who gives a dowry." Then she said, "Don't bargain with me. Either a flat yes or a flat no. Go back where you came from."

I thought: No bread will ever be baked from *this* dough. But ours is not a poor town. They consented to everything and proceeded with the wedding. It so happened that there was a dysentery epidemic at the time. The ceremony was held at the cemetery gates, near the little corpse-washing hut. The fellows got drunk. While the marriage contract was being drawn up I heard the most pious high rabbi ask, "Is the bride a widow or a divorced woman?" And the sexton's wife answered for her, "Both a widow and divorced." It was a black moment for me. But what was I to do, run away from under the marriage canopy?

There was singing and dancing. An old granny danced opposite me, hugging a braided white hallah. The master of revels made a "God 'a mercy" in memory of the bride's parents. The schoolboys threw burrs, as on Tishe b'Av fast day. There were a lot of gifts after the sermon: a noodle board, a kneading trough, a bucket, brooms, ladles, household articles galore. Then I took a look and saw two strapping young men carrying a crib. "What do we need this for?" I asked. So they said, "Don't rack your brains about it. It's all right, it'll come in handy." I realized I was going to be rooked. Take it another way though, what did

I stand to lose? I reflected: I'll see what comes of it. A whole town can't go altogether crazy.

II

At night I came where my wife lay, but she wouldn't let me in. "Say, look here, is this what they married us for?" I said. And she said, "My monthly has come." "But yesterday they took you to the ritual bath, and that's afterwards, isn't it supposed to be?" "Today isn't yesterday," said she, "and yesterday's not today. You can beat it if you don't like it." In short, I waited.

Not four months later, she was in childbed. The townsfolk hid their laughter with their knuckles. But what could I do? She suffered intolerable pains and clawed at the walls. "Gimpel," she cried, "I'm going. Forgive me!" The house filled with women. They were boiling pans of water. The screams rose to the welkin.

The thing to do was to go to the house of prayer to repeat psalms, and that was what I did.

The townsfolk liked that, all right. I stood in a corner saying psalms and prayers, and they shook their heads at me. "Pray, pray!" they told me. "Prayer never made any woman pregnant." One of the congregation put a straw to my mouth and said, "Hay for the cows." There was something to that too, by God!

She gave birth to a boy. Friday at the synagogue the sexton stood up before the Ark, pounded on the reading table, and announced, "The wealthy Reb Gimpel invites the congregation to a feast in honor of the birth of a son." The whole house of prayer rang with laughter. My face was flaming. But there was nothing I could do. After all, I *was* the one responsible for the circumcision honors and rituals.

Half the town came running. You couldn't wedge another soul in. Women brought peppered chick-peas, and there was a keg of beer from the tavern. I ate and drank as much as anyone, and they all congratulated me. Then there was a circumcision, and I named the boy after my father, may he rest in peace. When all were gone and I was left with my wife alone, she thrust her head through the bed-curtain and called me to her.

"Gimpel," said she, "why are you silent? Has your ship gone and sunk?"

"What shall I say?" I answered. "A fine thing you've done to me! If my mother had known of it she'd have died a second time."

She said, "Are you crazy, or what?"

"How can you make such a fool," I said, "of one who should be the lord and master?"

"What's the matter with you?" she said. "What have you taken it into your head to imagine?"

I saw that I must speak bluntly and openly. "Do you think this is the way to use an orphan?" I said. "You have borne a bastard."

She answered, "Drive this foolishness out of your head. The child is yours."

"How can he be mine?" I argued. "He was born seventeen weeks after the wedding."

She told me then that he was premature. I said, "Isn't he a little too premature?" She said, she had had a grandmother who carried just as short a time and she resembled this grandmother of hers as one drop of water does another. She swore to it with such oaths that you would have believed a peasant at the fair if he had used them. To tell the plain truth, I didn't believe her; but when I talked it over next day with the schoolmaster, he told me that the very same thing had happened to Adam and Eve. Two they went up to bed, and four they descended.

"There isn't a woman in the world who is not the granddaughter of Eve," he said.

That was how it was; they argued me dumb. But then, who really knows how such things are?

I began to forget my sorrow. I loved the child madly, and he loved me too. As soon as he saw me he'd wave his little hands and want me to pick him up, and when he was colicky I was the only one who could pacify him. I bought him a little bone teething ring and a little gilded cap. He was forever catching the evil eye from someone, and then I had to run to get one of those abracadabras for him that would get him out of it. I worked like an ox. You know how expenses go up when there's an infant in the house. I don't want to lie about it; I didn't dislike Elka either, for that matter. She swore at me and cursed, and I couldn't get enough of her. What strength she had! One of her looks could rob you of the power of speech. And her orations! Pitch and sulphur, that's what they were full of, and yet somehow also full of charm. I adored her every word. She gave me bloody wounds though.

In the evening I brought her a white loaf as well as a dark one, and also poppyseed rolls I baked myself. I thieved because of her and swiped everything I could lay hands on: macaroons, raisins, almonds, cakes. I hope I may be forgiven for stealing from the Saturday pots the women left to warm in the baker's oven. I would take out scraps of meat, a chunk of pudding, a chicken leg or head, a piece of tripe, whatever I could nip quickly. She ate and became fat and handsome.

I had to sleep away from home all during the week, at the bakery. On Friday nights when I got home she always made an excuse of some sort. Either she had heartburn, or a stitch in the side, or hiccups, or headaches. You know what women's excuses are. I had a bitter time of it. It was rough. To add to it, this little brother of hers, the bastard, was growing bigger. He'd put lumps on me, and when I wanted to hit back she'd open her mouth and curse so powerfully I saw a green haze floating before my eyes. Ten times a day she threatened to divorce me. Another man in my place would have taken French leave and disappeared. But I'm the type that bears it and says nothing. What's one to do? Shoulders are from God, and burdens too.

One night there was a calamity in the bakery; the oven burst, and we almost had a fire. There was nothing to do but go home, so I went home. Let me, I thought, also taste the joy of sleeping in bed in midweek. I didn't want to wake the sleeping mite and tiptoed into the house. Coming in, it seemed to me that I heard not the snoring of one but, as it were, a double snore, one a thin enough snore and the other like the snoring of a slaughtered ox. Oh, I didn't like that! I didn't like it at all. I went up to the bed, and things suddenly turned black. Next to Elka lay a man's form. Another in my place would have made an uproar, and enough noise to rouse the whole town, but the thought occurred to me that I might wake the child. A little thing like that—why frighten a little swallow, I thought. All right then, I went back to the bakery and stretched out on a sack of flour and till morning I never shut an eye. I shivered as if I had had malaria. "Enough of being a donkey," I said to myself. "Gimpel isn't going to be a sucker all his life. There's a limit even to the foolishness of a fool like Gimpel."

In the morning I went to the rabbi to get advice, and it made a great commotion in the town. They sent the beadle for Elka right away. She came, carrying the child. And what do you think she did? She denied it, denied everything, bone and stone! "He's out of his head," she said. "I know nothing of dreams or divinations." They yelled at her, warned her, hammered on the table, but she stuck to her guns: it was a false accusation, she said.

The butchers and the horse-traders took her part. One of the lads from the slaughterhouse came by and said to me, "We've got our eye on you, you're a marked man." Meanwhile, the child started to bear down and soiled itself. In the rabbinical court there was an Ark of the Covenant, and they couldn't allow that, so they sent Elka away.

I said to the rabbi, "What shall I do?"

"You must divorce her at once," said he.

"And what if she refuses?" I asked.

He said, "You must serve the divorce. That's all you'll have to do."

I said, "Well, all right, Rabbi. Let me think about it."

"There's nothing to think about," said he. "You mustn't remain under the same roof with her."

"And if I want to see the child?" I asked.

"Let her go, the harlot," said he, "and her brood of bastards with her."

The verdict he gave was that I mustn't even cross her threshold— never again, as long as I should live.

During the day it didn't bother me so much. I thought: It was bound to happen, the abscess had to burst. But at night when I stretched out upon the sacks I felt it all very bitterly. A longing took me, for her and for the child. I wanted to be angry, but that's my misfortune exactly, I don't have it in me to be really angry. In the first place—this was how my thoughts went—there's bound to be a slip sometimes. You can't live without errors. Probably that lad who was with her led her on and gave her presents and what not, and women are often long on hair and short on sense, and so he got around her. And then since she denies it so, maybe I was only seeing things? Hallucinations do happen. You see a figure or a mannikin or something, but when you come up closer it's nothing, there's not a thing there. And if that's so, I'm doing her an injustice. And when I got so far in my thoughts I started to weep. I sobbed so that I wet the flour where I lay. In the morning I went to the rabbi and told him that I had made a mistake. The rabbi wrote on with his quill, and he said that if that were so he would have to reconsider the whole case. Until he had finished I wasn't to go near my wife, but I might send her bread and money by messenger.

III

Nine months passed before all the rabbis could come to an agreement. Letters went back and forth. I hadn't realized that there could be so much erudition about a matter like this.

Meanwhile, Elka gave birth to still another child, a girl this time. On the Sabbath I went to the synagogue and invoked a blessing on her. They called me up to the Torah, and I named the child for my mother-in-law—may she rest in peace. The louts and loudmouths of the town who came into the bakery gave me a going over. All Frampol refreshed its spirits because of my trouble and grief. However, I resolved that I would always believe what I was told. What's the good of *not* believing? Today it's your wife you don't believe; tomorrow it's God Himself you won't take stock in.

By an apprentice who was her neighbor I sent her daily a corn or a wheat loaf, or a piece of pastry, rolls or bagels, or, when I got the

chance, a slab of pudding, a slice of honeycake, or wedding strudel—
whatever came my way. The apprentice was a goodhearted lad, and
more than once he added something on his own. He had formerly annoyed me a lot, plucking my nose and digging me in the ribs, but when
he started to be a visitor to my house he became kind and friendly.
"Hey, you, Gimpel," he said to me, "you have a very decent little wife
and two fine kids. You don't deserve them."

"But the things people say about her," I said.

"Well, they have long tongues," he said, "and nothing to do with
them but babble. Ignore it as you ignore the cold of last winter."

One day the rabbi sent for me and said, "Are you certain, Gimpel,
that you were wrong about your wife?"

I said, "I'm certain."

"Why, but look here! You yourself saw it."

"It must have been a shadow," I said.

"The shadow of what?"

"Just of one of the beams, I think."

"You can go home then. You owe thanks to the Yanover rabbi. He
found an obscure reference in Maimonides that favored you."

I seized the rabbi's hand and kissed it.

I wanted to run home immediately. It's no small thing to be separated for so long a time from wife and child. Then I reflected: I'd
better go back to work now, and go home in the evening. I said nothing
to anyone, although as far as my heart was concerned it was like one of
the Holy Days. The women teased and twitted me as they did every day,
but my thought was: Go on, with your loose talk. The truth is out, like
the oil upon the water. Maimonides says it's right, and therefore it is
right!

At night, when I had covered the dough to let it rise, I took my share
of bread and a little sack of flour and started homeward. The moon was
full and the stars were glistening, something to terrify the soul. I hurried
onward, and before me darted a long shadow. It was winter, and a
fresh snow had fallen. I had a mind to sing, but it was growing late and I
didn't want to wake the householders. Then I felt like whistling, but I
remembered that you don't whistle at night because it brings the demons
out. So I was silent and walked as fast as I could.

Dogs in the Christian yards barked at me when I passed, but I
thought: Bark your teeth out! What are you but mere dogs? Whereas I
am a man, the husband of a fine wife, the father of promising children.

As I approached the house my heart started to pound as though it
were the heart of a criminal. I felt no fear, but my heart went thump!
thump! Well, no drawing back. I quietly lifted the latch and went in.
Elka was asleep. I looked at the infant's cradle. The shutter was closed,

but the moon forced its way through the cracks. I saw the newborn child's face and loved it as soon as I saw it—immediately—each tiny bone.

Then I came nearer to the bed. And what did I see but the apprentice lying there beside Elka. The moon went out all at once. It was utterly black, and I trembled. My teeth chattered. The bread fell from my hands, and my wife waked and said, "Who is that, ah?"

I muttered, "It's me."

"Gimpel?" she asked. "How come you're here? I thought it was forbidden."

"The rabbi said," I answered and shook as with a fever.

"Listen to me, Gimpel," she said, "go out to the shed and see if the goat's all right. It seems she's been sick." I have forgotten to say that we had a goat. When I heard she was unwell I went into the yard. The nannygoat was a good little creature. I had a nearly human feeling for her.

With hesitant steps I went up to the shed and opened the door. The goat stood there on her four feet. I felt her everywhere, drew her by the horns, examined her udders, and found nothing wrong. She had probably eaten too much bark. "Good night, little goat," I said. "Keep well." And the little beast answered with a "Maa" as though to thank me for the good will.

I went back. The apprentice had vanished.

"Where," I asked, "is the lad?"

"What lad?" my wife answered.

"What do you mean?" I said. "The apprentice. You were sleeping with him."

"The things I have dreamed this night and the night before," she said, "may they come true and lay you low, body and soul! An evil spirit has taken root in you and dazzles your sight." She screamed out, "You hateful creature! You moon calf! You spook! You uncouth man! Get out, or I'll scream all Frampol out of bed!"

Before I could move, her brother sprang out from behind the oven and struck me a blow on the back of the head. I thought he had broken my neck. I felt that something about me was deeply wrong, and I said, "Don't make a scandal. All that's needed now is that people should accuse me of raising spooks and dybbuks." For that was what she had meant. "No one will touch bread of my baking."

In short, I somehow calmed her.

"Well," she said, "that's enough. Lie down, and be shattered by wheels."

Next morning I called the apprentice aside. "Listen here, brother!" I said. And so on and so forth. "What do you say?" He stared at me as though I had dropped from the roof or something.

"I swear," he said, "you'd better go to an herb doctor or some healer. I'm afraid you have a screw loose, but I'll hush it up for you." And that's how the thing stood.

To make a long story short, I lived twenty years with my wife. She bore me six children, four daughters and two sons. All kinds of things happened, but I neither saw nor heard. I believed, and that's all. The rabbi recently said to me, "Belief in itself is beneficial. It is written that a good man lives by his faith."

Suddenly my wife took sick. It began with a trifle, a little growth upon the breast. But she evidently was not destined to live long; she had no years. I spent a fortune on her. I have forgotten to say that by this time I had a bakery of my own and in Frampol was considered to be something of a rich man. Daily the healer came, and every witch doctor in the neighborhood was brought. They decided to use leeches, and after that to try cupping. They even called a doctor from Lublin, but it was too late. Before she died she called me to her bed and said, "Forgive me, Gimpel."

I said, "What is there to forgive? You have been a good and faithful wife."

"Woe, Gimpel!" she said. "It was ugly how I deceived you all these years. I want to go clean to my Maker, and so I have to tell you that the children are not yours."

If I had been clouted on the head with a piece of wood it couldn't have bewildered me more.

"Whose are they?" I asked.

"I don't know," she said. "There were a lot . . . but they're not yours." And as she spoke she tossed her head to the side, her eyes turned glassy, and it was all up with Elka. On her whitened lips there remained a smile.

I imagined that, dead as she was, she was saying, "I deceived Gimpel. That was the meaning of my brief life."

I V

One night, when the period of mourning was done, as I lay dreaming on the flour sacks, there came the Spirit of Evil himself and said to me, "Gimpel, why do you sleep?"

I said, "What should I be doing? Eating kreplech?"

"The whole world deceives you," he said, "and you ought to deceive the world in your turn."

"How can I deceive all the world?" I asked him.

He answered, "You might accumulate a bucket of urine every day and at night pour it into the dough. Let the sages of Frampol eat filth."

"What about the judgment in the world to come?" I said.

"There is no world to come," he said. "They've sold you a bill of goods and talked you into believing you carried a cat in your belly. What nonsense!"

"Well then," I said, "and is there a God?"

He answered, "There is no God either."

"What," I said, "*is* there, then?"

"A thick mire."

He stood before my eyes with a goatish beard and horn, long-toothed, and with a tail. Hearing such words, I wanted to snatch him by the tail, but I tumbled from the flour sacks and nearly broke a rib. Then it happened that I had to answer the call of nature, and, passing, I saw the risen dough, which seemed to say to me, "Do it!" In brief, I let myself be persuaded.

At dawn the apprentice came. We kneaded the bread, scattered caraway seeds on it, and set it to bake. Then the apprentice went away, and I was left sitting in the little trench by the oven, on a pile of rags. Well, Gimpel, I thought, you've revenged yourself on them for all the shame they've put on you. Outside the frost glittered, but it was warm beside the oven. The flames heated my face. I bent my head and fell into a doze.

I saw in a dream, at once, Elka in her shroud. She called to me, "What have you done, Gimpel?"

I said to her, "It's all your fault," and started to cry.

"You fool!" she said. "You fool! Because I was false is everything false too? I never deceived anyone but myself. I'm paying for it all, Gimpel. They spare you nothing here."

I looked at her face. It was black; I was startled and waked, and remained sitting dumb. I sensed that everything hung in the balance. A false step now and I'd lose eternal life. But God gave me His help. I seized the long shovel and took out the loaves, carried them into the yard, and started to dig a hole in the frozen earth.

My apprentice came back as I was doing it. "What are you doing boss?" he said, and grew pale as a corpse.

"I know what I'm doing," I said, and I buried it all before his very eyes.

Then I went home, took my hoard from its hiding place, and divided it among the children. "I saw your mother tonight," I said. "She's turning black, poor thing."

They were so astounded they couldn't speak a word.

"Be well," I said, "and forget that such a one as Gimpel ever existed." I put on my short coat, a pair of boots, took the bag that held my prayer shawl in one hand, my stock in the other, and kissed the mezuzah. When people saw me in the street they were greatly surprised.

"Where are you going?" they said.

I answered, "Into the world." And so I departed from Frampol.

I wandered over the land, and good people did not neglect me. After many years I became old and white; I heard a great deal, many lies and falsehoods, but the longer I lived the more I understood that there were really no lies. Whatever doesn't really happen is dreamed at night. It happens to one if it doesn't happen to another, tomorrow if not today, or a century hence if not next year. What difference can it make? Often I heard tales of which I said, "Now this is a thing that cannot happen." But before a year had elapsed I heard that it actually had come to pass somewhere.

Going from place to place, eating at strange tables, it often happens that I spin yarns—improbable things that could never have happened—about devils, magicians, windmills, and the like. The children run after me, calling, "Grandfather, tell us a story." Sometimes they ask for particular stories, and I try to please them. A fat young boy once said to me, "Grandfather, it's the same story you told us before." The little rogue, he was right.

So it is with dreams too. It is many years since I left Frampol, but as soon as I shut my eyes I am there again. And whom do you think I see? Elka. She is standing by the washtub, as at our first encounter, but her face is shining and her eyes are as radiant as the eyes of a saint, and she speaks outlandish words to me, strange things. When I wake I have forgotten it all. But while the dream lasts I am comforted. She answers all my queries, and what comes out is that all is right. I weep and implore, "Let me be with you." And she consoles me and tells me to be patient. The time is nearer than it is far. Sometimes she strokes and kisses me and weeps upon my face. When I awaken I feel her lips and taste the salt of her tears.

No doubt the world is entirely an imaginary world, but it is only once removed from the true world. At the door of the hovel where I lie, there stands the plank on which the dead are taken away. The gravedigger Jew has his spade ready. The grave waits and the worms are hungry; the shrouds are prepared—I carry them in my beggar's sack. Another *shnorrer* is waiting to inherit my bed of straw. When the time comes I will go joyfully. Whatever may be there, it will be real, without complication, without ridicule, without deception. God be praised: there even Gimpel cannot be deceived.

The Gentleman from Cracow

I

AMID thick forests and deep swamps, on the slope of a hill, level at the summit, lay the village of Frampol. Nobody knew who had founded it, or why just there. Goats grazed among the tombstones which were already sunk in the ground of the cemetery. In the community house there was a parchment with a chronicle on it, but the first page was missing and the writing had faded. Legends were current among the people, tales of wicked intrigue concerning a mad nobleman, a lascivious lady, a Jewish scholar, and a wild dog. But their true origin was lost in the past.

Peasants who tilled the surrounding countryside were poor; the land was stubborn. In the village, the Jews were impoverished; their roofs were straw, their floors dirt. In summer many of them wore no shoes, and in cold weather they wrapped their feet in rags or wore sandals made of straw.

Rabbi Ozer, although renowned for his erudition, received a salary of only eighteen groszy a week. The assistant rabbi, besides being ritual slaughterer, was teacher, matchmaker, bath attendant, and poorhouse nurse as well. Even those villagers who were considered wealthy knew little of luxury. They wore cotton gabardines, tied about their waists with string, and tasted meat only on the Sabbath. Gold coin was rarely seen in Frampol.

But the inhabitants of Frampol had been blessed with fine children. The boys grew tall and strong, the girls handsome. It was a mixed blessing, however, for the young men left to marry girls from other towns, while their sisters, who had no dowries, remained unwed. Yet despite everything, inexplicably, though the food was scarce and the water foul, the children continued to thrive.

Translated by Martha Glicklich and Elaine Gottlieb

Then, one summer, there was a drought. Even the oldest peasants could not recall a calamity such as this one. No rain fell. The corn was parched and stunted. There was scarcely anything worth harvesting. Not until the few sheaves of wheat had been cut and gathered did the rain come, and with it hail which destroyed whatever grain the drought had spared. Locusts huge as birds came in the wake of the storm; human voices were said to issue from their throats. They flew at the eyes of the peasants who tried to drive them away. That year there was no fair, for everything had been lost. Neither the peasants nor the Jews of Frampol had food. Although there was grain in the large towns, no one could buy it.

Just when all hope had been abandoned and the entire town was about to go begging, a miracle occurred. A carriage drawn by eight spirited horses came into Frampol. The villagers expected its occupant to be a Christian gentleman, but it was a Jew, a young man between the ages of twenty and thirty, who alighted. Tall and pale, with a round black beard and fiery dark eyes, he wore a sable hat, silver-buckled shoes, and a beaver-trimmed caftan. Around his waist was a green silk sash. Aroused, the entire town rushed to get a glimpse of the stranger. This is the story he told: He was a doctor, a widower from Cracow. His wife, the daughter of a wealthy merchant, had died with their baby in childbirth.

Overwhelmed, the villagers asked why he had come to Frampol. It was on the advice of a Wonder Rabbi, he told them. The melancholy he had known after his wife's death, would, the rabbi assured him, disappear in Frampol. From the poorhouse the beggars came, crowding about him as he distributed alms—three groszy, six groszy, half-gulden pieces. The stranger was clearly a gift from Heaven, and Frampol was not destined to vanish. The beggars hurried to the baker for bread, and the baker sent to Zamosc for a sack of flour.

"One sack?" the young doctor asked. "Why that won't last a single day. I will order a wagonload, and not only flour, but cornmeal also."

"But we have no money," the village elders explained.

"God willing, you will repay me when times are good," and saying this, the stranger produced a purse crammed with golden ducats. Frampol rejoiced as he counted out the coins.

The next day, wagons filled with flour, buckwheat, barley, millet, and beans, drove into Frampol. News of the village's good fortune reached the ears of the peasants, and they came to the Jews, to buy goods, as the Egyptians had once come to Joseph. Being without money, they paid in kind; as a result, there was meat in town. Now the ovens burned once more; the pots were full. Smoke rose from the chimneys, sending the odors of roast chicken and goose, onion and garlic, fresh bread and pastry, into the evening air. The villagers returned to their occupations; shoemakers mended shoes; tailors picked up their rusted shears and irons.

The evenings were warm and the sky clear, though the Feast of the Tabernacles had already passed. The stars seemed unusually large. Even the birds were awake, and they chirped and warbled as though in mid-summer. The stranger from Cracow had taken the best room at the inn, and his dinner consisted of broiled duck, marchpane, and twisted bread. Apricots and Hungarian wine were his dessert. Six candles adorned the table. One evening after dinner, the doctor from Cracow entered the large public room where some of the more inquisitive townspeople had gathered and asked,

"Would anyone care for a game of cards?"

"But it isn't Hanukkah yet," they answered in surprise.

"Why wait for Hanukkah? I'll put up a gulden for every groszy."

A few of the more frivolous men were willing to try their luck, and it turned out to be good. A groszy meant a gulden, and one gulden became thirty. Anyone played who wished to do so. Everybody won. But the stranger did not seem distressed. Banknotes and coins of silver and gold covered the table. Women and girls crowded into the room, and it seemed as though the gleam of the gold before them was reflected in their eyes. They gasped in wonderment. Never before in Frampol had such things happened. Mothers cautioned their daughters to take pains with their hair, and allowed them to dress in holiday clothes. The girl who found favor in the eyes of the young doctor would be fortunate; he was not one to require a dowry.

II

The next morning, matchmakers called on him, each extolling the virtues of the girl he represented. The doctor invited them to be seated, served them honey cake, macaroons, nuts, and mead, and announced:

"From each of you I get exactly the same story: Your client is beautiful and clever and possesses every possible distinction. But how can I know which of you is telling the truth? I want the finest of them all as my wife. Here is what I suggest: Let there be a ball to which all the eligible young women are invited. By observing their appearance and behavior, I shall be able to choose among them. Then the marriage contract will be drawn and the wedding arranged."

The matchmakers were astounded. Old Mendel was the first to find words. "A ball? That sort of thing is all right for rich Gentiles, but we Jews have not indulged in such festivities since the destruction of the Temple—except when the Law prescribes it for certain holidays."

"Isn't every Jew obliged to marry off his daughters?" asked the doctor.

"But the girls have no appropriate clothes," another matchmaker protested. "Because of the drought they would have to go in rags."

"I will see that they all have clothes. I'll order enough silk, wool, velvet, and linen from Zamosc to outfit every girl. Let the ball take place. Let it be one that Frampol will never forget."

"But where can we hold it?" another matchmaker interjected. "The hall where we used to hold weddings has burned down, and our cottages are too small."

"There's the marketplace," the gentleman from Cracow suggested.

"But it is already the month of Heshvan. Any day now, it will turn cold."

"We'll choose a warm night when the moon is out. Don't worry about it."

To all the numerous objections of the matchmakers, the stranger had an answer ready. Finally they agreed to consult the elders. The doctor said he was in no hurry, he would await their decision. During the entire discussion, he had been carrying on a game of chess with one of the town's cleverest young men, while munching raisins.

The elders were incredulous when they heard what had been proposed. But the young girls were excited. The young men approved also. The mothers pretended to hesitate, but finally gave their consent. When a delegation of the older men sought out Rabbi Ozer for his approval, he was outraged.

"What kind of charlatan is this?" he shouted. "Frampol is not Cracow. All we need is a ball! Heaven forbid that we bring down a plague, and innocent infants be made to pay for our frivolity!"

But the more practical of the men reasoned with the rabbi, saying, "Our daughters walk around barefoot and in tatters now. He will provide them with shoes and clothing. If one of them should please him he would marry her and settle here. Certainly that is to our advantage. The synagogue needs a new roof. The windowpanes of the house of study are broken, the bathhouse is badly in need of repairs. In the poorhouse the sick lie on bundles of rotting straw."

"All this is true. But suppose we sin?"

"Everything will be done according to the Law, Rabbi. You can trust us."

Taking down the book of the Law, Rabbi Ozer leafed through it. Occasionally he stopped to study a page, and then, finally, after sighing and hesitating, he consented. Was there any choice? He himself had received no salary for six months.

As soon as the rabbi had given his consent there was a great display of activity. The dry-goods merchants traveled immediately to Zamosc and Yanev, returning with cloth and leather paid for by the gentleman from Cracow. The tailors and seamstresses worked day and night; the cobblers left their benches only to pray. The young women, all anticipation, were in a feverish state. Vaguely remembered dance steps were tried out. They baked cakes and other pastries, and used up their stores of jams and preserves which they had been keeping in readiness for illness. The Frampol musicians were equally active. Cymbals, fiddles, and bagpipes, long forgotten and neglected, had to be dusted off and tuned. Gaiety infected even the very old, for it was rumored that the elegant doctor planned a banquet for the poor where alms would be distributed.

The eligible girls were wholly concerned with self-improvement. They scrubbed their skin and arranged their hair; a few even visited the ritual bath to bathe among the married women. In the evenings, faces flushed, eyes sparkling, they met at each other's houses, to tell stories and ask riddles. It was difficult for them, and for their mothers as well, to sleep at night. Fathers sighed as they slept. And suddenly the young girls of Frampol seemed so attractive that the young men who had contemplated marrying outside of town fell in love with them. Although the young men still sat in the study house poring over the Talmud, its wisdom no longer penetrated to them. It was the ball alone that they spoke of now, only the ball that occupied their thoughts.

The doctor from Cracow also enjoyed himself. He changed his clothes several times daily. First it was a silk coat worn with pompommed slippers, then a woolen caftan with high boots. At one meal he wore a pelerine trimmed with beaver tails, and at the next a cape embroidered with flowers and leaves. He breakfasted on roast pigeon which he washed down with dry wine. For lunch he ordered egg noodles and blintzes, and he was audacious enough to eat Sabbath pudding on weekdays. He never attended prayer, but instead played all sorts of games: cards, goats and wolves, coin-pitching. Having finished lunch, he would drive through the neighborhood with his coachman. The peasants would lift their hats as he passed, and bow almost to the ground. One day he strolled through Frampol with a gold-headed cane. Women crowded to the windows to observe him, and boys, following after him, picked up the rock candy he tossed them. In the evenings he and his companions, gay young men, drank wine until all hours. Rabbi Ozer constantly warned his flock that they walked a downhill path led by the Evil One, but they paid no attention to him. Their minds and hearts were completely possessed by the ball, which would be held at the marketplace in the middle of that month, at the time of the full moon.

III

At the edge of town, in a small valley close to a swamp, stood a hut no larger than a chicken coop. Its floor was dirt, its window was boarded; and the roof, because it was covered with green and yellow moss, made one think of a bird's nest that had been forsaken. Heaps of garbage were strewn before the hut, and lime ditches furrowed the soggy earth. Amid the refuse there was an occasional chair without a seat, a jug missing an ear, a table without legs. Every type of broom, bone, and rag seemed to be rotting there. This was where Lipa the ragpicker lived with his daughter, Hodle. While his first wife was alive, Lipa had been a respected merchant in Frampol where he occupied a pew at the east wall of the synagogue. But after his wife had drowned herself in the river, his condition declined rapidly. He took to drink, associated with the town's worst element, and soon ended up bankrupt.

His second wife, a beggar woman from Yanev, bore him a daughter whom she left behind when she deserted him for non-support. Unconcerned about his wife's departure, Lipa allowed the child to shift for herself. Each week he spent a few days collecting rags from the garbage. The rest of the time he was in the tavern. Although the innkeeper's wife scolded him, she received only abusive answers in reply. Lipa had his success among the men as a tale-spinner. He attracted business to the place with his fantastic yarns about witches and windmills and devils and goblins. He could also recite Polish and Ukrainian rhymes and had a knack for telling jokes. The innkeeper allowed him to occupy a place near the stove, and from time to time he was given a bowl of soup and a piece of bread. Old friends, remembering Lipa's former affluence, occasionally presented him with a pair of pants, a threadbare coat, or a shirt. He accepted everything ungraciously. He even stuck out his tongue at his benefactors as they turned away from him.

As in the saying, "Like father, like son," Hodle inherited the vices of both parents—her drunken father, her begging mother. By the time she was six, she had won a reputation as a glutton and thief. Barefoot and half naked, she roamed the town, entering houses and raiding the larders of those who were not home. She preyed on chickens and ducks, cut their throats with glass, and ate them. Although the inhabitants of Frampol had often warned her father that he was rearing a wanton, the information did not seem to bother him. He seldom spoke to her and she did not even call him father. When she was twelve, her lasciviousness became a matter for discussion among the women. Gypsies visited her shack, and it was rumored that she devoured the meat of cats and dogs, in fact, every kind of carcass. Tall and lean, with red hair and green eyes, she went barefoot summer and winter, and her skirts were made of colored scraps discarded by the seamstresses. She was feared by mothers who said she wove spells that blighted the young. The village elders who admonished her received brazen answers. She had the shrewdness of a bastard, the quick tongue of an adder, and when attacked by street urchins, did not hesitate to strike back. Particularly skilled in swearing, she had an unlimited repertoire. It was like her to call out, "Pox on your tongue and gangrene in your eyes," or, possibly, "May you rot till the skunks run from your smell."

Occasionally her curses were effective, and the town grew wary of incurring her anger. But as she matured she tended to avoid the town proper, and the time came when she was almost forgotten. But on the day that the Frampol merchants, in preparation for the ball, distributed cloth and leather among the town's young women, Hodle reappeared. She was now about seventeen, fully grown, though still in short skirts; her face was freckled, and her hair disheveled. Beads, such as those worn by gypsies, encircled her throat, and on her wrists were bracelets made from wolves' teeth. Pushing her way through the crowd, she demanded her share. There was nothing left but a few odds and ends, which were given to her. Furious with her allotment, she hastened home with it. Those who had seen what had happened laughed, "Look who's going to the ball! What a pretty picture she'll make!"

At last the shoemakers and tailors were done; every dress fit, every shoe was right. The days were miraculously warm, and the nights as luminous as the evenings of Pentecost. It was the morning star that, on the day of the ball, woke the entire town. Tables and benches lined one side of the market. The cooks had already roasted calves, sheep, goats, geese, ducks, and chicken, and had baked sponge and raisin cakes, braided bread and rolls, onion biscuits and ginger bread. There were mead and beer and a barrel of Hungarian wine that had been brought by the wine dealer. When the children arrived they brought the bows and arrows with which they were accustomed to play at the Omer feast, as well as their Purim rattles and Torah flags. Even the doctor's horses were decorated with willow branches and autumn flowers, and the coachman paraded them through the town. Apprentices left their work, and yeshiva students their volumes of the Talmud. And despite Rabbi Ozer's injunction against the young matrons' attending the ball, they dressed in their wedding gowns and went, arriving with the young girls, who also came in white, each bearing a candle in her hand as though she were a bridesmaid. The band had already begun to play, and the music was lively. Rabbi Ozer alone was not present, having locked himself in his study. His maidservant had gone to the ball, leaving him to himself. He knew no good could come of such behavior, but there was nothing he could do to prevent it.

By late afternoon all the girls had gathered in the marketplace, surrounded by the townspeople. Drums were beaten. Jesters performed. The girls danced; first a quadrille, then a scissor dance. Next it was cossack, and finally the dance of anger. Now the moon appeared, although the sun had not yet set. It was time for the gentleman from Cracow. He entered on a white mare, flanked by bodyguards and his best man. He wore a large-plumed hat, and silver buttons flashed on his green coat. A sword hung at his side, and his shiny boots rested in the stirrups. He resembled a gentleman off to war with his entourage. Silently he sat in his saddle, watching the girls as they danced. How graceful they were, how charmingly they moved! But one who did not dance was the daughter of Lipa the ragpicker. She stood to one side, ignored by them all.

I V

The setting sun, remarkably large, stared down angrily like a heavenly eye upon the Frampol marketplace. Never before had Frampol seen such a sunset. Like rivers of burning sulphur, fiery clouds streamed across the heavens, assuming the shapes of elephants, lions, snakes, and monsters. They seemed to be waging a battle in the sky, devouring one another, spitting, breathing fire. It almost seemed to be the River of Fire they watched, where demons tortured the evildoers amidst glowing coals and heaps of ashes. The moon swelled, became vast, blood-red, spotted, scarred, and gave off little light. The evening grew very dark, dissolving even the stars. The young men fetched torches, and a barrel of burning pitch was prepared. Shadows danced back and forth as though attending a ball of their own. Around the marketplace the houses seemed to vibrate; roofs quivered, chimneys shook. Such gaiety and intoxication had never before been known in Frampol. Everyone, for the first time in months, had eaten and drunk sufficiently. Even the animals participated in the merrymaking. Horses neighed, cows mooed, and the few roosters that had survived the slaughter of the fowl crowed. Flocks of crows and strange birds flew in to pick at the leavings. Fireflies illumined the darkness, and lightning flashed on the horizon. But there was no thunder. A weird circular light glowed in the sky for a few moments and then suddenly plummeted toward the horizon, a crimson tail behind it, resembling a burning rod. Then, as everyone stared in wonder at the sky, the gentleman from Cracow spoke:

"Listen to me. I have wonderful things to tell you, but let no one be overcome by joy. Men, take hold of your wives. Young men, look to your girls. You see in me the wealthiest man in the entire world. Money is sand to me, and diamonds are pebbles. I come from the land of Ophir, where King Solomon found the gold for his temple. I dwell in the palace of the Queen of Sheba. My coach is solid gold, its wheels inlaid with sapphires, with axles of ivory, its lamps studded with rubies and emeralds, opals and amethysts. The Ruler of the Ten Lost Tribes of Israel knows of your miseries, and he has sent me to be your benefactor. But there is one condition. Tonight, every virgin must marry. I will provide a dowry of ten thousand ducats for each maiden, as well as a string of pearls that will hang to her knees. But make haste. Every girl must have a husband before the clocks strike twelve."

The crowd was hushed. It was as quiet as New Year's Day before the blowing of the ram's horn. One could hear the buzzing of a fly.

Then one old man called out, "But that's impossible. The girls are not even engaged!"

"Let them become engaged."

"To whom?"

"We can draw lots," the gentleman from Cracow replied. "Whoever is to be married will have his or her name written on a card. Mine also. And then we shall draw to see who is meant for whom."

"But a girl must wait seven days. She must have the prescribed ablutions."

"Let the sin be on me. She needn't wait."

Despite the protestations of the old men and their wives, a sheet of paper was torn into pieces, and on each piece the name of a young man or young woman was written by a scribe. The town's beadle, now in the service of the gentleman from Cracow, drew from one skullcap the names of the young men, and from another those of the young women, chanting their names to the same tune with which he called up members of the congregation for the reading of the Torah.

"Nahum, son of Katriel, betrothed to Yentel, daughter of Nathan. Solomon, son of Cov Baer, betrothed to Tryna, daughter of Jonah Lieb." The assortment was a strange one, but since in the night all sheep are black, the matches seemed reasonable enough. After each drawing, the newly engaged couple, hand in hand, approached the doctor to collect the dowry and wedding gift. As he had promised, the gentleman from Cracow gave each the stipulated sum of ducats, and on the neck of each bride he hung a strand of pearls. Now the mothers, unable to restrain their joy, began to dance and shout. The fathers stood by, bewildered. When the girls lifted their dresses to catch the gold coins given by the doctor, their legs and underclothing were exposed, which sent the men into paroxysms of lust. Fiddles screeched, drums pounded, trumpets blared. The uproar was deafening. Twelve-year-old boys were mated with "spinsters" of nineteen. The sons of substantial citizens took the daughters of paupers as brides; midgets were coupled with giants, beauties with cripples. On the last two slips appeared the names of the gentleman from Cracow and Hodle, the daughter of Lipa the ragpicker.

The same old man who had called out previously said, "Woe unto us, the girl is a harlot."

"Come to me, Hodle, come to your bridegroom," the doctor bade.

Hodle, her hair in two long braids, dressed in a calico skirt, and with sandals on her feet, did not wait to be asked twice. As soon as she had been called she walked to where the gentleman from Cracow sat on his mare, and fell to her knees. She prostrated herself seven times before him.

"Is it true, what that old fool says?" her prospective husband asked her.

"Yes, my lord, it is so."

"Have you sinned only with Jews or with Gentiles as well?"

"With both."

"Was it for bread?"

"No. For the sheer pleasure."

"How old were you when you started?"

"Not quite ten."

"Are you sorry for what you have done?"

"No."

"Why not?"

"Why should I be?" she answered shamelessly.

"You don't fear the tortures of hell?"

"I fear nothing—not even God. There is no God."

Once more the old man began to scream, "Woe to us, woe to us, Jews! A fire is upon us, burning, Jews, Satan's fire. Save your souls, Jews. Flee, before it is too late!"

"Gag him," the gentleman from Cracow commanded.

The guards seized the old man and gagged him. The doctor, leading Hodle by the hand, began to dance. Now, as though the powers of darkness had been summoned, the rain and hail began to fall; flashes of lightning were accompanied by mighty thunderclaps. But, heedless of the storm, pious men and women embraced without shame, dancing and shouting as though possessed. Even the old were affected. In the furor, dresses were ripped, shoes shaken off, hats, wigs and skullcaps trampled in the mud. Sashes, slipping to the ground, twisted there like snakes. Suddenly there was a terrific crash. A huge bolt of lightning had simultaneously struck the synagogue, the study house, and the ritual bath. The whole town was on fire.

Now at last the deluded people realized that there was no natural origin to these occurrences. Although the rain continued to fall and even increased in intensity, the fire was not extinguished. An eerie light glowed in the marketplace. Those few prudent individuals who tried to disengage themselves from the demented crowd were crushed to earth and trampled.

And then the gentleman from Cracow revealed his true identity. He was no longer the young man the villagers had welcomed, but a creature covered with scales, with an eye in his chest, and on his forehead a horn that rotated at great speed. His arms were covered with hair, thorns, and elflocks, and his tail was a mass of live serpents, for he was none other than Ketev Mriri, Chief of the Devils.

Witches, werewolves, imps, demons, and hobgoblins plummeted from the sky, some on brooms, others on hoops, still others on spiders. Osnath, the daughter of Machlath, her fiery hair loosened in the wind, her breasts bare and thighs exposed, leaped from chimney to chimney, and skated along the eaves. Namah, Hurmizah the daughter of Aff, and many other she-devils did all sorts of somersaults. Satan himself gave away the bridegroom, while four evil spirits held the poles of the canopy, which had turned into writhing pythons. Four dogs escorted the groom. Hodle's dress fell from her and she stood naked. Her breasts hung down to her navel and her feet were webbed. Her hair was a wilderness of worms and caterpillars. The groom held out a triangular ring and, instead of saying, "With this ring be thou consecrated to me according to the laws of Moses and Israel," he said, "With this ring be thou desecrated to me according to the blasphemy of Korah and Ishmael." And instead of wishing the pair good luck, the evil spirits called out, "Bad luck," and they began to chant:

> *The curse of Eve, the Mark of Cain,*
> *The cunning of the snake, unite the twain.*

Screaming for the last time, the old man clutched at his head and died. Ketev Mriri began his eulogy:

> *Devil's dung and Satan's spell*
> *Bring his ghost to roast in hell.*

V

In the middle of the night, old Rabbi Ozer awoke. Since he was a holy man, the fire which was consuming the town had no power over his house. Sitting up in bed he looked about, wondering if dawn were already breaking. But it was neither day nor night without. The sky was a fiery red, and from the distance came a clamor of shouts and songs that resembled the howling of wild beasts. At first, recalling nothing, the old man wondered what was going on. "Has the world come to an end? Or have I failed to hear the ram's horn heralding the Messiah? Has He arrived?" Washing his hands, he put on his slippers and overcoat and went out.

The town was unrecognizable. Where houses had been, only chimneys stood. Mounds of coal smoldered here and there. He called the beadle, but there was no answer. With his cane, the rabbi went searching for his flock.

"Where are you, Jews, where are you?" he called piteously.

The earth scorched his feet, but he did not slacken his pace. Mad dogs and strange beings attacked him, but he wielded his cane against them. His sorrow was so great that he felt no fear. Where the marketplace used to be, a terrible sight met him. There was nothing but one great swamp, full of mud, slime, and ashes. Floundering in mud up to their waists, a crowd of naked people went through the movements of dance. At first, the rabbi mistook the weirdly moving figures for devils, and was about to recite the chapter, "Let there be contentment," and other passages dealing with exorcism, when he recognized the men of his town. Only then did he remember the doctor from Cracow, and the rabbi cried out bitterly, "Jews, for the sake of God, save your souls! You are in the hands of Satan!"

But the townspeople, too entranced to heed his cries, continued their frenzied movements for a long time, jumping like frogs, shaking as though with fever. With hair uncovered and breasts bare, the women laughed, cried, and swayed. Catching a yeshiva boy by his sidelocks, a girl pulled him to her lap. A woman tugged at the beard of a strange man. Old men and women were immersed in slime up to their loins. They scarcely looked alive.

Relentlessly, the rabbi urged the people to resist evil. Reciting the Torah and other holy books, as well as incantations and the several names of God, he succeeded in rousing some of them. Soon others responded. The rabbi had helped the first man from the mire, then that one assisted the next, and so on. Most of them had recovered by the time the morning star appeared. Perhaps the spirits of their forbears had interceded, for although many had sinned, only one man had died this night in the marketplace square.

Now the men were appalled, realizing that the devil had bewitched them, had dragged them through muck; and they wept.

"Where is our money?" the girls wailed. "And our gold and our jewelry? Where is our clothing? What happened to the wine, the mead, the wedding gifts?"

But everything had turned to mud; the town of Frampol, stripped and ruined, had become a swamp. Its inhabitants were mud-splashed, denuded, monstrous. For a moment, forgetting their grief, they laughed at each other. The hair of the girls had turned into elflocks, and bats were entangled there. The young men had grown gray and wrinkled; the old were yellow as corpses. In their midst lay the old man who had died. Crimson with shame, the sun rose.

"Let us rend our clothes in mourning," one man called, but his words evoked laughter, for all were naked.

"We are doomed, my sisters," lamented a woman.

"Let us drown ourselves in the river," a girl shrieked. "Why go on living?"

One of the yeshiva boys said, "Let us strangle ourselves with our sashes."

"Brothers, we are lost. Let us blaspheme God," said a horse dealer.

"Have you lost your minds, Jews?" cried Rabbi Ozer. "Repent, before it is too late. You have fallen into Satan's snare, but it is my fault, I take the sin upon myself. I am the guilty one. I will be your scapegoat, and you shall remain clean."

"This is madness!" one of the scholars protested. "God forbid that there be so many sins on your holy head!"

"Do not worry about that. My shoulders are broad. I should have had more foresight. I was blind not to realize that the Cracow doctor was the Evil One. And when the shepherd is blind, the flock goes astray. It is I who deserve the punishment, the curses."

"Rabbi, what shall we do? We have no homes, no bedclothes, nothing. Woe to us, to our bodies and to our souls."

"Our babies!" cried the young matrons. "Let us hurry to them!"

But it was the infants who had been the real victims of the passion for gold that had caused the inhabitants of Frampol to transgress. The infants' cribs were burned, their little bones were charred. The mothers stooped to pick up little hands, feet, skulls. The wailing and crying lasted long, but how long can a whole town weep? The gravedigger gathered the bones and carried them to the cemetery. Half the town began the prescribed seven days of mourning. But all fasted, for there was no food anywhere.

But the compassion of the Jews is well known, and when the neighboring town of Yanev learned what had happened, clothing, bed linen, bread, cheese, and dishes were collected and sent to Frampol. Timber merchants brought logs for building. A rich man offered credit. The next day the reconstruction of the town was begun. Although work is forbidden to those in mourning, Rabbi Ozer issued a verdict that this was an exceptional case: the lives of the people were in danger. Miraculously, the weather remained mild; no snow fell. Never before had there been such diligence in Frampol. The inhabitants built and prayed, mixed lime with sand, and recited psalms. The women worked with the men, while girls, forgetting their fastidiousness, helped also. Scholars and men of high position assisted. Peasants from the surrounding villages, hearing of the catastrophe, took the old and infirm into their homes. They also brought wood, potatoes, cabbages, onions and other food. Priests and bishops from Lublin, hearing of events that suggested witchcraft, came to examine witnesses. As the scribe recorded the names of those living in Frampol, Hodle, the daughter of Lipa the ragpicker, was suddenly remembered. But when the townspeople went to where her hut had been, they found the hill covered with weeds and bramble, silent save for the cries of crows and cats; there was no indication that human beings had ever dwelt there.

Then it was understood that Hodle was in truth Lilith, and that the host of the netherworld had come to Frampol because of her. After their investigations, the clergymen from Lublin, greatly astonished at what they had seen and heard, returned home. A few days later, the day before the Sabbath, Rabbi Ozer died. The entire town attended his funeral, and the town preacher said a eulogy for him.

In time, a new rabbi came to the community, and a new town arose. The old people died, the mounds in the cemetery sifted down, and the monuments slowly sank. But the story, signed by trustworthy witnesses, can still be read in the parchment chronicle.

And the events in the story brought their epilogue: the lust for gold had been stifled in Frampol; it was never rekindled. From generation to generation the people remained paupers. A gold coin became an abomination in Frampol, and even silver was looked at askance. Whenever a shoemaker or tailor asked too high a price for his work he was told, "Go to the gentleman from Cracow and he will give you buckets of gold."

And on the grave of Rabbi Ozer, in the memorial chapel, there burns an eternal light. A white pigeon is often seen on the roof: the sainted spirit of Rabbi Ozer.

Joy

I

RABBI BAINISH of Komarov, having buried Bunem, his third son, stopped praying for his ailing children. Only one son and two daughters remained, and all of them spat blood. His wife, frequently breaking into the solitude of his study would scream, "Why are you so silent? Why don't you move heaven and earth?" With clenched fists raised, she would wail, "What good are your knowledge, your prayers, the merits of your ancestors, your prolonged fasts? What does He have against you— our Father in Heaven? Why must all His anger be directed against you?" In her despair she once snatched a sacred book and threw it on the floor. Silently, Rabbi Bainish picked it up. His invariable answer was, "Leave me alone!"

Though he was not yet fifty, the rabbi's beard, so thin that the hairs could be numbered, had turned white as the beard of an old man. His tall body stooped. His stern black eyes looked past everyone. No longer did he comment on the Torah nor preside over meals. For weeks now he had not appeared at the house of study. Though his followers came from other towns to visit him, they had to return without being allowed even a greeting. Behind his bolted door he sat, silent; it was a pregnant silence. The crowd, his "bread and butter" Hasidim, gradually dispersed among other rabbis. Only his intimate circle, the old Hasidim, the wise ones, stayed. When Rebecca, his youngest daughter, died, the rabbi did not even follow her hearse. He gave orders to his sexton, Avigdor, to close the shutters, and they remained closed. Through a heart-shaped aperture in the shutters, came the meager light whereby the rabbi looked through books. He no longer recited the texts out loud; he merely thumbed the pages, opening a book at one place and then at another, and with one eye closed, stared vacantly beyond the pages and the walls. Dipping his

Translated by Norbert Guterman and Elaine Gottlieb

pen in the inkwell, he would move a sheet of paper close to him, but he could not write. He would fill a pipe, but it remained unlit. There was no indication that he had touched the breakfast and supper that had been brought to his study. Weeks, months, went by like this.

One summer day the rabbi appeared at the house of study. Several boys and young men were studying there, while a couple of old men, hangers-on, were meditating. Since their rabbi had been absent for so long, all of them were frightened at the sight of him. Taking a step in one direction, and then a step back, the rabbi asked, "Where is Abraham Moshe of Borisov?"

"At the inn," said a young man who had not yet been struck dumb.

"Would you ask him to come to me, please?"

"I will, Rabbi."

The young man left immediately for the inn. Walking to the bookshelves, the rabbi drew out a book at random, glanced at a page, and then replaced the book. In his unbuttoned robe, his long fringed garment, his short trousers, white stockings, with hat pushed back on his head, his earlocks unkempt, his eyebrows contracted, he stood there. The house of study was so still that water could be heard dripping in the basin, and flies humming around the candlesticks. The grandfather clock, with its long chains and pomegranates on the dial, creaked and struck three. Through the open windows peeped the fruit trees in the orchard; one heard the chirping of birds. In the slanting pillars of dust, tiny particles vibrated, no longer matter, and not yet spirit, reflecting rainbow hues. The rabbi beckoned to a boy who had only recently left the Hebrew school and had begun to read the Talmud on his own.

"What's your name, eh?"

"Moshe."

"What are you studying?"

"The first treatise."

"What chapter?"

"*Shur Shenagah ath haparah.*"

"How do you translate that?"

"A bull gored a cow."

The rabbi stamped his slippered foot. "Why did the bull gore the cow? What had the cow done to him?"

"A bull does not reason."

"But He who created the bull can reason."

The boy did not know the answer to that one. The rabbi pinched his cheek.

"Well, go study," he said, returning to his room.

Reb Abraham Moshe came to him shortly afterwards. He was a small, youthful-faced man, with white beard and earlocks, wearing a floor-length robe, a thick, moss-green sash, and carrying a long pipe that reached to his knees. Over his skullcap he wore a high cap. His eccentricities were well known. He would recite the morning prayer in the afternoon, and the afternoon prayer long after others had returned from the evening service. He chanted psalms at Purim, and during the Kol Nidre prayer, he slept. On Passover eve when everyone celebrated at the Passover feast, he would study a commentary of the Talmudic Treatises on Damages and Compensations. It was rumored that once, at the tavern, he had won a game of chess from a general, and that the general had rewarded him with a license to sell brandy. His wife ran the business; he himself spent more time at Komarov than at home. He would say that living at Komarov was like standing at the foot of Mount Sinai; the air itself purified one. In a more jocular mood, he would comment that there was no need to study at Komarov; it was sufficient to loiter on a bench in the house of study and inhale the Torah as one breathed. The Hasidim knew that the rabbi held Reb Abraham Moshe in the highest esteem, discussed esoteric doctrine with him, and asked his advice. Reb Abraham Moshe was always seated at the head of the table. Nevertheless, each time he visited the rabbi, he spruced up like a young man. He would wash his hands, button his caftan, curl his earlocks, and comb his beard. He would enter with reverence, as one enters the house of a saint.

The rabbi had not sent for him since Rebecca's death; this in itself was an indication of the depth of the rabbi's grief. Reb Abraham Moshe did not shuffle now, as customarily, but walked briskly, almost running. When he had reached the rabbi's door he halted for a moment, touched his cap, his chest, wiped his brow with his handkerchief, and then walked in mincingly. The rabbi, having opened one of the shutters, sat smoking his pipe in the grandfather's chair with the ivory armrests. A half-full glass of tea stood on the table, a roll beside it. Apparently, the rabbi had recovered.

"Rabbi, I'm here," said Reb Abraham Moshe.

"So I see. Be seated."

"Thank you."

The rabbi remained silent a while. Placing his narrow hand on the table edge, he stared at the white nails of his long fingers. Then he said, "Abraham Moshe, it's bad."

"What's bad?"

"Abraham Moshe, it's worse than you think."

"What could be worse?" asked Abraham Moshe, ironically.

"Abraham Moshe, the atheists are right. There is no justice, no Judge."

Reb Abraham Moshe was accustomed to the rabbi's harsh words.

At Komarov, even the Lord of the Universe would not be spared. But to be rebellious is one thing; to deny God, another. Reb Abraham Moshe turned pale. His knees shook.

"Then who rules the world, Rabbi?"

"It's not ruled."

"Who then?"

"A total lie!"

"Come, come . . ."

"A heap of dung . . ."

"Where did the dung come from?"

"In the beginning was the dung."

Reb Abraham Moshe froze. He wanted to speak, but his arguments caught in his throat. Well, it's his grief that talks, he thought. Nevertheless, he marveled. If Job could endure it, so should the rabbi.

"What should we do, then, Rabbi?" Reb Abraham Moshe asked hoarsely.

"We should worship idols."

To keep from falling, Reb Abraham Moshe gripped the table edge.

"What idols?" he asked. Everything inside him seemed to tighten.

The rabbi laughed briefly. "Don't be frightened; I won't send you to the priest. If the atheists are right, what's the difference between Terah and Abraham? Each served a different idol. Terah, who was simpleminded, invented a clay god. Abraham invented a Creator. It is what one invents that matters. Even a lie must have some truth in it."

"You are merely being facetious," Reb Abraham Moshe stammered. His palate felt dry, his throat contracted.

"Well, stop trembling! Sit down!"

Reb Abraham Moshe sat down. The rabbi rose from his seat, walked to the window, and stood there a long time, staring into space. Then he walked to the book cabinet. The cabinet, which smelled of wine and snuffed-out valedictory candles, contained a spice box, and citron box, and a Hanukkah candelabra. The rabbi, taking out a Zohar, opened it at random, stared at the page, nodded, and then, smacking his lips, exclaimed, "A nice invention, very nice!"

II

More and more Hasidim departed. In the house of study, on Saturdays, scarcely a quorum remained. The sextons, all but Avigdor, had left. Finding her solitude unbearable, the rabbi's wife went for a long visit to her brother, the rabbi of Biala. Reb Abraham Moshe stayed at Komarov. He spent one Sabbath each month with his family in his native town. If a man were not to be deserted when his body was sick, he reasoned, then he certainly should not be left alone during the sickness of his soul. If their rabbi were committing sins, God forbid, then one would be interdicted from associating with him, but actually, his piety was now greater than before. He prayed, studied, visited the ritual bathhouse. And he was so ardent in his charity, that he sold his dearest possessions —the silver candlesticks, the large Hanukkah candelabra, his gold watch, and Passover tray—and gave the proceeds to the poor. Reb Abraham Moshe told him reproachfully he was squandering his inheritance, but the rabbi replied, "Poor men *do* exist. That's one thing of which we can be certain."

The summer went by and the month of Elul came. On week days, Avigdor, the sexton, blew the ram's horn at the house of study. Komarov used to be crowded to capacity during the month of Elul; there were not enough beds at the inns, and young people would sleep in storerooms, barns, attics. But this year, it was quiet at Komarov. The shutters remained closed at the inns. Grass grew wild in the rabbi's courtyard; there was no one to trample it. Gossamer threads floated through the air. The apples, pears, and plums ripened on the trees in the orchard, because the boys who used to pick them were gone. The chirping of birds sounded louder than ever. Moles dug up numerous mounds of earth. Certain bushes sprouted berries of a poisonous sort. One day, the rabbi, on his way to the bathhouse, plucked one such berry. "If a thing like this can turn one into a corpse," he thought, "what is a corpse?" He sniffed it and threw it away. "If everything hinges on a berry, then all our affairs are berries." The rabbi entered the bathhouse. "Well, demons, where are you?" he said aloud, and his words were thrown back at him by the echo, "At least let there be devils." He sat on the bench, undressed, removed his fringed garment, and examined it. "Threads and knots and nothing else . . ."

The water was cold, but it made no difference to him. "Who is cold? And if one is cold, what of it?" The coldness cut his breath, and he clung to the railing. Then he plunged and stayed for a long while under the water. Something within him was laughing. "As long as you breathe, you must breathe." The rabbi dried himself and dressed. Returning to his study, he opened a Cabala book, The Two Tablets of the Covenant. Here it was written that "the rigor of the law should be sweetened to deprive Satan of his nourishment." "Well, and what if it's a fairy tale?" The rabbi squinted one eye while the other kept staring. "The sun? Close your eyes and there is no sun. The birds? Stuff your ears and there are no birds. Pain? Swallow a wild berry, and the pain is gone. What is left, then? Nothing at all. The past no longer exists and the future has yet to come. The conclusion is that nothing exists beyond the moment. Well, if so, we really have nothing to worry about."

No more than thirty Hasidim gathered at Komarov for Rosh Hashanah. Although the rabbi appeared at the service in his cloak and shawl, one could not tell if he prayed, for he was silent. After the service the Hasidim sat at the table, but their rabbi's seat was vacant. An old man chanted a little song and the others gave him a rattling accompaniment. Reb Abraham Moshe repeated a comment the rabbi had made on the Torah twenty years ago. Thank God, the rabbi was alive, though for all practical purposes, he was dead.

Avigdor brought to the rabbi's room a decanter of wine, apples with honey, the head of a carp, two hallahs, a quarter of a chicken with stewed carrots, and a slice of pineapple for the blessing of the first fruit. But although it was already evening, the rabbi had touched nothing.

During the month of Elul he had fasted. His body felt as though it had been hollowed. Hunger still gnawed somewhere in his stomach, but it was a hunger unrelated to him. What had he, Bainish of Komarov, to do with food? Must one yield to the body's lusts? If one resists, what does it do—die? "Let it die, if that's what it wants. I am satisfied." A golden-green fly flew in through the open window from the other side of the curtain, and settled on the glazed eye of the carp. The rabbi murmured, "Well, what are you waiting for? Eat . . ."

As the rabbi sat half-awake, half-slumbering in his old chair, his arms on the arm rests, engrossed in thoughts he did not know he was thinking, divested of all external things, he suddenly caught sight of his youngest daughter, Rebecca. Through the closed door she had entered and stood there, erect, pale, her hair plaited in two tresses, wearing her best gold-embroidered dress, a prayer book in one hand, a handkerchief in the other. Forgetting that she had died, the rabbi looked at her, half-surprised. "See, she's a grown girl, how come she's not a bride?" An extraordinary nobility spread over her features; she looked as though she had just recovered from an illness; the pearls of her necklace shone with an unearthly light, with the aura of the Days of Awe. With an expression of modesty and love she gazed at the rabbi.

"Happy holiday, Father."

"Happy holiday, happy new year," the rabbi said.

"Father, say grace."

"What? Of course, of course."

"Father, join the guests at table," she said, half-commanding, half-imploring.

An icy shudder ran through the rabbi's spine. "But she's dead!" At once his eyes were drenched with tears, and he jumped to his feet as though to rush toward her. Through the mist of tears Rebecca's form became distorted, grew longer and partly blurred, but she still loomed before him. The rabbi noticed the silver clasp of her prayer book and the lace of her handkerchief. Her left pigtail was tied with a white ribbon. But her face, as though veiled, dissolved into a blotch. The rabbi's voice broke.

"My daughter, are you here?"

"Yes, Father."

"Why have you come?"

"For you."

"When?"

"After the holidays."

She seemed to withdraw. In the whirling mist her form lost its substance, but her dress continued to drag on the floor in folds and waves like a golden train, and a glow arose from it. Soon this too dissolved, and nothing remained but a sense of wonder, a supernatural tang, a touch of heavenly joy. The rabbi did not weep, but luminous drops fell on his white silken robe embroidered with flowers and leaves. There was a fragrance of myrtle, cloves and saffron. He had a cloying sensation in his mouth, as if he had eaten marzipan.

The rabbi remembered what Rebecca had told him. He put on his fur hat, stood up, and opened the door leading to the house of study. It was time for the evening prayer, but the old men had not yet left the table.

"Happy holiday, my friends," the rabbi said in a cheerful voice.

"Happy holiday, Rabbi."

"Avigdor, I want to say grace."

"I'm ready, Rabbi."

Avigdor brought the wine, and the rabbi, chanting a holiday tune, recited the prayer. He washed his hands with the appropriate blessing and said the prayer for bread. After taking some broth, the rabbi commented on the Torah, a thing he had not done in years. His voice was low, though audible. The rabbi took up the question of why the moon is obscured on Rosh Hashanah. The answer is that on Rosh Hashanah one prays for life, and life means free choice, and freedom is Mystery. If one knew the truth how could there be freedom? If hell and paradise were in the middle of the marketplace, everyone would be a saint. Of all the blessings bestowed on man, the greatest lies in the fact that God's face is forever hidden from him. Men are the children of the Highest, and the Almighty plays hide and seek with them. He hides His face, and the children seek Him while they have faith that He exists. But what if, God forbid, one loses faith? The wicked live on denials; denials in themselves are also a faith, faith in evildoing, and from it one can draw strength for the body. But if the pious man loses his faith, the truth is shown to him, and he is recalled. This is the symbolic meaning of the words, "When a man dies in a tent": when the pious man falls from his rank, and becomes, like the wicked, without permanent shelter, then a light shines from above, and all doubts cease . . .

The rabbi's voice gradually grew weaker. The old men leaned toward him, intently listening. The house of study was so still that one could hear the candles flicker. Reb Abraham Moshe paled. He realized the meaning hidden behind all this. The moment Rosh Hashanah was over, he mailed some letters, having sat until daybreak writing them. The rabbi's wife returned from Biala, and for Yom Kippur the Hasidim arrived in great number. The rabbi had returned to his former self. During the Sukkoth holidays he commented on the Torah in his arbor. On Hashanah Raba he prayed all through the night, until dawn, with his Hasidim. On Simchas Torah, he never wearied of dancing around the reading stand. His Hasidim said later that Komarov had not, even under the old rabbi, blessed be his memory, celebrated that holiday with such gusto. To each of his Hasidim the rabbi spoke personally, asking about his family, and carefully reading each petition. He helped the children decorate the arbor with lanterns, ribbons, bunches of grapes. With his own hands, he wove baskets of lulab leaves for the myrtles. He pinched the cheeks of boys who had come with their fathers, and gave them cookies. As a rule, the rabbi prayed late and alone, but on the day following Sukkoth, he prayed in the house of study with the first quorum. After the service he asked for a glass of coffee. Reb Abraham Moshe and a circle of young men stood watching the rabbi drink coffee. Between swallows, he puffed his pipe. He said, "I want you to know that the material world has no substance."

After breakfast, the rabbi said grace. Then he ordered his bed made ready and murmured something about his old prayer shawl. The moment he lay down he became moribund. His face grew as yellow as his fringed garment. His eyelids closed. Covered with wrinkles, his forehead assumed a strange aspect. Life could literally be seen departing from him; his body shrank and altered. The rabbi's wife wanted to call the doctor, but the rabbi signaled her not to do so. Opening his eyes, he looked toward the door. Between the door jambs, beside the mezuzah, all of them were standing—his four sons and two daughters, his father, blessed be his memory, and his grandfather. Reverently, they all looked in his direction, expectantly, with arms outstretched. Each of them emitted a different light. They bent forward as though restrained by an invisible fence. "So that's the way it is," the rabbi thought. "Well, now everything is clear." He heard his wife sob, and wanted to comfort her, but no strength remained in his throat and lips. Suddenly, Reb Abraham Moshe leaned over him, as though realizing that the rabbi wished to speak, and the rabbi murmured, "One should always be joyous."

Those were his final words.

The Little Shoemakers

I

The Shoemakers and Their Family Tree

THE family of the little shoemakers was famous not only in Frampol but in the outlying district—in Yanev, Kreshev, Bilgoray, and even in Zamoshoh. Abba Shuster, the founder of the line, appeared in Frampol some time after Chmielnitzki's pogroms. He brought himself a plot of ground on the stubby hill behind the butcher stalls, and there he built a house that remained standing until just the other day. Not that it was in such fine condition—the stone foundation settled, the small windows warped, and the shingled roof turned a moldy green and was hung with swallows' nests. The door, moreover, sank into the ground; the banisters became bowlegged; and instead of stepping up onto the threshold, one was obliged to step down. All the same, it did survive the innumerable fires that devastated Frampol in the early days. But the rafters were so rotten that mushrooms grew on them, and when wood dust was needed to staunch the blood of a circumcision, one had only to break off a piece of the outer wall and rub it between one's fingers. The roof, pitched so steeply that the chimneysweep was unable to climb onto it to look after the chimney, was always catching fire from the sparks. It was only by the grace of God that the house was not overtaken by disaster.

The name of Abba Shuster is recorded, on parchment, in the annals of the Frampol Jewish community. It was his custom to make six pairs of shoes every year for distribution among widows and orphans; in recognition of his philanthropy the synagogue called him to the reading of the Torah under the honorific title, Murenu, meaning "our teacher."

His stone in the old cemetery had vanished, but the shoemakers knew a sign for the grave—nearby grew a hazelnut tree. According to the old wives, the tree sprang from Reb Abba's beard.

Reb Abba had five sons; they settled, all but one, in the neighboring

Translated by Isaac Rosenfeld

towns; only Getzel remained in Frampol. He continued his father's charitable practice of making shoes for the poor, and he too was active in the gravediggers' brotherhood.

The annals go on to say that Getzel had a son, Godel, and that to Godel was born Treitel, and to Treitel, Gimpel. The shoemaker's art was handed down from one generation to the next. A principle was fast established in the family, requiring the eldest son to remain at home and succeed his father at the workbench.

The shoemakers resembled one another. They were all short, sandy-haired, and sound, honest workmen. The people of Frampol believed that Reb Abba, the head of the line, had learned shoemaking from a master of the craft in Brod, who divulged to him the secret of strengthening leather and making it durable. In the cellar of their house the little shoemakers kept a vat for soaking hides. God knows what strange chemicals they added to the tanning fluid. They did not disclose the formula to outsiders, and it was handed on from father to son.

As it is not our business to deal with all the generations of the little shoemakers, we will confine ourselves to the last three. Reb Lippe remained without heir till his old age, and it was taken for a certainty that the line would end with him. But when he was in his late sixties his wife died and he married an overripe virgin, a milkmaid, who bore him six children. The eldest son, Feivel, was quite well to do. He was prominent in community affairs, attended all the important meetings, and for years served as sexton of the tailors' synagogue. It was the custom in this synagogue to select a new sexton every Simchas Torah. The man so selected was honored by having a pumpkin placed on his head; the pumpkin was set with lighted candles, and the lucky fellow was led about from house to house and refreshed at each stop with wine and strudel or honey cakes. However, Reb Feivel happened to die on Simchas Torah, the day of rejoicing over the Law, while dutifully making these rounds; he fell flat in the marketplace, and there was no reviving him. Because Feivel had been a notable philanthropist, the rabbi who conducted his services declared that the candles he had borne on his head would light his way to Paradise. The will found in his strongbox requested that when he was carried to the cemetery, a hammer, an awl, and a last should be laid on the black cloth over his coffin, in sign of the fact that he was a man of peaceful industry who never cheated his customers. His will was done.

Feivel's eldest son was called Abba, after the founder. Like the rest of his stock, he was short and thickset, with a broad yellow beard, and a high forehead lined with wrinkles, such as only rabbis and shoemakers have. His eyes were also yellow, and the overall impression he created was that of a sulky hen. Nevertheless, he was a clever workman, charitable like his forbears, and unequaled in Frampol as a man of his word. He would never make a promise unless he was sure he could fulfill it; when he was not sure he said: who knows, God willing, or maybe. Furthermore he was a man of some learning. Every day he read a chapter of the Torah in Yiddish translation and occupied his free time with chapbooks. Abba never missed a single sermon of the traveling preachers who came to town, and he was especially fond of the Biblical passages which were read in the synagogue during the winter months. When his wife, Pesha, read to him, of a Sabbath, from the Yiddish translation of the stories in the Book of Genesis, he would imagine that he was Noah, and that his sons were Shem, Ham, and Japheth. Or else he would see himself in the image of Abraham, Isaac, or Jacob. He often thought that if the Almighty were to call on him to sacrifice his eldest son, Gimpel, he would rise early in the morning and carry out his commands without delay. Certainly he would have left Poland and the house of his birth and gone wandering over the earth where God sent him. He knew the story of Joseph and his brothers by heart, but he never tired of reading it over again. He envied the ancients because the King of the Universe revealed Himself to them and performed miracles for their sake, but consoled himself by thinking that from him, Abba, to the Patriarchs, there stretched an unbroken chain of generations—as if he too were part of the Bible. He sprang from Jacob's loins; he and his sons were of the seed whose number had become like the sand and the stars. He was living in exile because the Jews of the Holy Land had sinned, but he awaited the Redemption, and he would be ready when the time came.

Abba was by far the best shoemaker in Frampol. His boots were always a perfect fit, never too tight or too roomy. People who suffered from chilblains, corns, or varicose veins were especially pleased with his work, claiming that his shoes relieved them. He despised the new styles, the gimcrack boots and slippers with fancy heels and poorly stitched soles that fell apart with the first rain. His customers were respectable burgers of Frampol or peasants from the surrounding villages, and they deserved the best. He took their measurements with a knotted string, as in the old days. Most of the Frampol women wore wigs, but his wife, Pesha, covered her head with a bonnet as well. She bore him seven sons, and he named them after his forefathers—Gimpel, Getzel, Treitel, Godel, Feivel, Lippe, and Chananiah. They were all short and sandy-haired like their father. Abba predicted that he would turn them into shoemakers, and as a man of his word he let them look on at the workbench while they were still quite young, and at times taught them the old maxim—good work is never wasted.

He spent sixteen hours a day at the bench, a sack spread on his knees, gouging holes with the awl, sewing with a wire needle, tinting and polishing the leather or scraping it with a piece of glass; and while he worked he hummed snatches from the canticles of the Days of Awe. Usually the cat huddled nearby and watched the proceedings as though she were looking after him. Her mother and grandmother had caught mice, in their time, for the little shoemakers. Abba could look down the hill through the window and see the whole town and a considerable distance beyond, as far as the road to Bilgoray and the pine woods. He observed the groups of matrons who gathered every morning at the butcher stalls and the young men and idlers who went in and out of the courtyard of the synagogue; the girls going to the pump to draw water for tea, and the women hurrying at dusk to the ritual bath.

Evenings, when the sun was setting, the house would be pervaded by a dusky glow. Rays of light danced in the corners, flicked across the ceiling, and set Abba's beard gleaming with the color of spun gold. Pesha, Abba's wife, would be cooking kasha and soup in the kitchen, the children would be playing, neighboring women and girls would go in and out of the house. Abba would rise from his work, wash his hands, put on his long coat, and go off to the tailors' synagogue for evening prayers. He knew that the wide world was full of strange cities and distant lands, that Frampol was actually no bigger than a dot in a small prayer book; but it seemed to him that his little town was the navel of the universe and that his own house stood at the very center. He often thought that when the Messiah came to lead the Jews to the Land of Israel, he, Abba, would stay behind in Frampol, in his own house, on his own hill. Only on the Sabbath and on holy days would he step into a cloud and let himself be flown to Jerusalem.

II
Abba and His Seven Sons

Since Gimpel was the eldest, and therefore destined to succeed his father, he came foremost in Abba's concern. He sent him to the best Hebrew teachers and even hired a tutor who taught him the elements of Yiddish, Polish, Russian, and arithmetic. Abba himself led the boy down into the cellar and showed him the formula for adding chemicals and various kinds of bark to the tanning fluid. He revealed to him that in most cases the right foot is larger than the left, and that the source of all trouble in the fitting of shoes is usually to be found in the big toes. Then he taught Gimpel the principles for cutting soles and inner soles, snub-toed and pointed shoes, high heels and low; and for fitting customers with flat feet, bunions, hammer toes, and calluses.

On Fridays, when there was always a rush to work to get out, the

older boys would leave cheder at ten in the morning and help their
father in the shop. Pesha baked hallah and prepared their lunch. She
would grasp the first loaf and carry it, hot from the oven, blowing on it
all the while and tossing it from hand to hand, to show it to Abba,
holding it up, front and back, till he nodded approval. Then she would
return with a ladle and let him sample the fish soup, or ask him to taste
a crumb of freshly baked cake. Pesha valued his judgment. When she
went to buy cloth for herself or the children she brought home swatches
for him to choose. Even before going to the butcher she asked his
opinion—what should she get, breast or roast, flank or ribs? She consulted him not out of fear or because she had no mind of her own, but
simply because she had learned that he always knew what he was talking
about. Even when she was sure he was wrong, he would turn out to be
right, after all. He never browbeat her, but merely cast a glance to let
her know when she was being a fool. This was also the way he handled
the children. A strap hung on the wall, but he seldom made use of it; he
had his way by kindness. Even strangers respected him. The merchants
sold him hides at a fair price and presented no objections when he asked
for credit. His own customers trusted him and paid his prices without a
murmur. He was always called sixth to the reading of the Torah in the
tailors' synagogue—a considerable honor—and when he pledged or was
assessed for money, it was never neccessary to remind him. He paid up,
without fail, right after the Sabbath. The town soon learned of his
virtues, and though he was nothing but a plain shoemaker and, if the
truth be told, something of an ignoramus, they treated him as they
would a distinguished man.

When Gimpel turned thirteen, Abba girded the boy's loins in sackcloth and put him to work at the bench. After Gimpel, Getzel, Treitel,
Godel, and Feivel became apprentices. Though they were his own sons
and he supported them out of his earnings, he nevertheless paid them a
wage. The two youngest boys, Lippe and Chananiah, were still attending
the elementary cheder, but they too lent a hand at hammering pegs.
Abba and Pesha were proud of them. In the morning the six workers
trooped into the kitchen for breakfast, washed their six pairs of hands
with the appropriate benediction, and their six mouths chewed the
roasted groats and corn bread.

Abba loved to place his two youngest boys one on each knee, and
sing an old Frampol song to them:

> *A mother had*
> *Ten little boys,*
> *Oh, Lord, ten little boys!*
>
> *The first one was Avremele,*

> *The second one was Berele,*
> *The third one was called Gimpele,*
> *The fourth one was called Dovid'l*
> *The fifth one was called Hershele . . .*

And all the boys came in on the chorus:

> *Oh, Lord, Hershele!*

Now that he had apprentices, Abba turned out more work, and his income grew. Living was cheap in Frampol, and since the peasants often made him a present of a measure of corn or a roll of butter, a sack of potatoes or a pot of honey, a hen or a goose, he was able to save some money on food. As their prosperity increased, Pesha began to talk of rebuilding the house. The rooms were too narrow, the ceiling was too low. The floor shook underfoot. Plaster was peeling off the walls, and all sorts of maggots and worms crawled through the woodwork. They lived in constant fear that the ceiling would fall on their heads. Even though they kept a cat, the place was infested with mice. Pesha insisted that they tear down this ruin and build a larger house.

Abba did not immediately say no. He told his wife he would think it over. But after doing so, he expressed the opinion that he would rather keep things as they were. First of all, he was afraid to tear down the house, because this might bring bad luck. Second, he feared the evil eye—people were grudging and envious enough. Third, he found it hard to part with the home in which his parents and grandparents, and the whole family, stretching back for generations, had lived and died. He knew every corner of the house, each crack and wrinkle. When one layer of paint peeled off the wall, another, of a different color, was exposed; and behind this layer, still another. The walls were like an album in which the fortunes of the family had been recorded. The attic was stuffed with heirlooms—tables and chairs, cobbler's benches and lasts, whetstones and knives, old clothes, pots, pans, bedding, salting boards, cradles. Sacks full of torn prayer books lay spilled on the floor.

Abba loved to climb up to the attic on a hot summer's day. Spiders spun great webs, and the sunlight, filtering in through cracks, fell upon the threads in rainbows. Everything lay under a thick coat of dust. When he listened attentively he would hear a whispering, a murmuring and soft scratching, as of some unseen creature engaged in endless activity, conversing in an unearthly tongue. He was sure that the souls of his forefathers kept watch over the house. In much the same way he loved the ground on which it stood. The weeds were as high as a man's head. There was a dense growth of hairy and brambly vegetation all about the place—the very leaves and twigs would catch hold of one's clothing as though with teeth and claws. Flies and midges swarmed in the air and the ground crawled with worms and snakes of all descriptions. Ants had raised their hills in this thicket; field mice had dug their holes. A pear tree grew in the midst of this wilderness; every year, at the time of the Feast of the Tabernacle, it yielded small fruit with the taste and hardness of wood. Birds and bees flew over this jungle, great big golden-bellied flies. Toadstools sprang up after each rain. The ground was unkept, but an unseen hand guarded its fertility.

When Abba stood here looking up at the summer sky, losing himself in contemplation of the clouds, shaped like sailboats, flocks of sheep, brooms, and elephant herds, he felt the presence of God, His providence and His mercy. He could virtually see the Almighty seated on His throne of glory, the earth serving Him as a footstool. Satan was vanquished; the angels sang hymns. The Book of Memory in which were recorded all the deeds of men lay open. From time to time, at sunset, it even seemed to Abba that he saw the river of fire in the nether world. Flames leaped up from the burning coals; a wave of fire rose, flooding the shores. When he listened closely he was sure he heard the muffled cries of sinners and the derisive laughter of the evil host.

No, this was good enough for Abba Shuster. There was nothing to change. Let everything stand as it had stood for ages, until he lived out his allotted time and was buried in the cemetery among his ancestors, who had shod the sacred community and whose good name was preserved not only in Frampol but in the surrounding district.

III
Gimpel Emigrates to America

Therefore the proverb says: Man proposes, God disposes.

One day while Abba was working on a boot, his eldest son, Gimpel, came into the shop. His freckled face was heated, his sandy hair disheveled under the skullcap. Instead of taking his place at the bench, he stopped at his father's side, regarded him hesitantly, and at last said, "Father, I must tell you something."

"Well, I'm not stopping you," replied Abba.

"Father," he cried, "I'm going to America."

Abba dropped his work. This was the last thing he expected to hear, and up went his eyebrows.

"What happened? Did you rob someone? Did you get into a fight?"

"No, Father."

"Then why are you running away?"

"There's no future for me in Frampol."

"Why not? You know a trade. God willing, you'll marry some day. You have everything to look forward to."

"I'm sick of small towns; I'm sick of the people. This is nothing but a stinking swamp."

"When they get around to draining it," said Abba, "there won't be any more swamp."

"No, Father, that's not what I mean."

"Then what do you mean?" cried Abba angrily. "Speak up!"

The boy spoke up, but Abba couldn't understand a word of it. He laid into synagogue and state with such venom, Abba could only imagine that the poor soul was possessed: the Hebrew teachers beat the children; the women empty their slop pails right outside the door; the shopkeepers loiter in the streets; there are no toilets anywhere, and the public relieves itself as it pleases, behind the bathhouse or out in the open, encouraging epidemics and plagues. He made fun of Ezreal the healer and of Mecheles the marriage broker, nor did he spare the rabbinical court and the bath attendant, the washerwoman and the overseer of the poorhouse, the professions and the benevolent societies.

At first Abba was afraid that the boy had lost his mind, but the longer he continued his harangue, the clearer it became that he had strayed from the path of righteousness. Jacob Reifman, the atheist, used to hold forth in Shebreshin, not far from Frampol. A pupil of his, a detractor of Israel, was in the habit of visiting an aunt in Frampol and had gathered quite a following among the good-for-nothings. It had never occurred to Abba that his Gimpel might fall in with this gang.

"What do you say, Father?" asked Gimpel.

Abba thought it over. He knew that there was no use arguing with Gimpel, and he remembered the proverb: A rotten apple spoils the barrel. "Well," he replied, "what can I do? If you want to go, go. I won't stop you."

And he resumed his work.

But Pesha did not give in so easily. She begged Gimpel not to go so far away; she wept and implored him not to bring shame on the family. She even ran to the cemetery, to the graves of her forefathers, to seek the intercession of the dead. But she was finally convinced that Abba was right: it was no use arguing. Gimpel's face had turned hard as leather, and a mean light showed in his yellow eyes. He had become a stranger in his own home. He spent that night out with friends, and returned in the morning to pack his prayer shawl and phylacteries, a few shirts, a blanket, and some hard-boiled eggs—and he was all set to go. He had saved enough money for passage. When his mother saw that it was settled, she urged him to take at least a jar of preserves, a bottle of cherry juice, bedding, pillows. But Gimpel refused. He was going to steal over the border into Germany, and he stood a better chance if he traveled light. In short, he kissed his mother, said goodbye to his brothers and friends, and off he went. Abba, not wanting to part with his son in anger, took him in the wagon to the station at Reivetz. The train arrived in the middle of the night with a hissing and whistling, a racket and din. Abba took the headlights of the locomotive for the eyes of a hideous devil, and shied away from the funnels with their columns of sparks and smoke and their clouds of steam. The blinding lights only intensified the darkness. Gimpel ran around with his baggage like a madman, and his father ran after him. At the last moment the boy kissed his father's hand, and Abba called after him, into the darkness, "Good luck! Don't forsake your religion!"

The train pulled out, leaving a smell of smoke in Abba's nostrils and a ringing in his ears. The earth trembled under his feet. As though the boy had been dragged off by demons! When he returned home and Pesha fell on him, weeping, he said to her, "The Lord gave and the Lord has taken away . . ."

Months passed without word from Gimpel. Abba knew that this was the way with young men when they leave home—they forget their dearest ones. As the proverb says: Out of sight, out of mind. He doubted that he would ever hear from him, but one day a letter came from America. Abba recognized his son's handwriting. Gimpel wrote that he crossed the border safely, that he saw many strange cities and spent four weeks on board ship, living on potatoes and herring because he did not want to touch improper food. The ocean was very deep and the waves as high as the sky. He saw flying fish but no mermaids or mermen, and he did not hear them singing. New York is a big city, the houses reach into the clouds. The trains go over the roofs. The Gentiles speak English. No one walks with his eyes on the ground, everybody holds his head high. He met a lot of his countrymen in New York; they all wear short coats. He too. The trade he learned at home has come in very handy. He is *all right*; he is earning a living. He will write again, a long letter. He kisses his father and mother and his brothers, and sends regards to his friends.

A friendly letter, after all.

In his second letter Gimpel announced that he had fallen in love with a girl and bought her a diamond ring. Her name is Bessie; she comes from Rumania; and she works *at dresses*. Abba put on his spectacles with the brass frames and spent a long time puzzling this out. Where did the boy learn so many English words? The third letter stated that he was married and that *a reverend* had performed the service. He inclosed a snapshot of himself and wife.

Abba could not believe it. His son was wearing a gentleman's coat and a high hat. The bride was dressed like a countess in a white dress, with train and veil; she held a bouquet of flowers in her hand. Pesha took one look at the snapshot and began to cry. Gimpel's brothers gaped. Neighbors came running, and friends from all over town: they could have sworn that Gimpel had been spirited away by magic to a land of gold, where he had taken a princess to wife—just as in the storybooks the pack merchants brought to town.

To make a long story short, Gimpel induced Getzel to come to America, and Getzel brought over Treitel; Godel followed Treitel, and Feivel, Godel; and then all five brothers brought the young Lippe and Chananiah across. Pesha lived only for the mail. She fastened a charity box to the doorpost, and whenever a letter came she dropped a coin through the slot. Abba worked all alone. He no longer needed apprentices because he now had few expenses and could afford to earn less; in fact, he could have given up work altogether, as his sons sent him money from abroad. Nevertheless he rose at his usual early hour and remained at the bench until late in the evening. His hammer sounded away, joined by the cricket on the hearth, the mouse in its hole, the shingles crackling on the roof. But his mind reeled. For generations the little shoemakers had lived in Frampol. Suddenly the birds had flown the coop. Was this a punishment, a judgment, on him? Did it make sense?

Abba bored a hole, stuck in a peg, and murmured, "So—you, Abba know what you're doing and God does not? Shame on you, fool! His will be done. Amen!"

IV
The Sack of Frampol

Almost forty years went by. Pesha had long since died of cholera, during the Austrian occupation. And Abba's sons had grown rich in America. They wrote every week, begging him to come and join them, but he remained in Frampol, in the same old house on the stubby hill. His own grave lay ready, next to Pesha's, among the little shoemakers; the stone had already been raised; only the date was missing. Abba put up a bench by the side of her grave, and on the eve of Rosh Hashanah or during fasts, he went there to pray and read Lamentations. He loved it in the cemetery. The sky was so much clearer and loftier than in town, and a great, meaningful silence rose from the consecrated ground and the old gravestone overgrown with moss. He loved to sit and look at the tall white birches, which trembled even when no breeze blew, and at the crows balancing in the branches, like black fruit. Before she died Pesha made him promise that he would not remarry and that he would come regularly to her grave with news of the children. He kept his promise. He would stretch out alongside the mound and whisper into her ear, as

if she were still alive, "Gimpel has another grandchild. Getzel's youngest daughter is engaged, thank God . . ."

The house on the hill was nearly in ruins. The beams had rotted
away, and the roof had to be supported by stone posts. Two of the three
windows were boarded over because it was no longer possible to fit glass
to the frames. The floor was all but gone, and the bare ground lay
exposed to the feet. The pear tree in the garden had withered; the trunk
and branches were covered with scales. The garden itself was now
overgrown with poisonous berries and grapes, and there was a profusion
of the burrs that children throw about on Tishe b'Av. People swore they
saw strange fires burning there at night, and claimed that the attic was
full of bats which fly into girls' hair. Be that as it may, an owl certainly
did hoot somewhere near the house. The neighbors repeatedly warned
Abba to move out of this ruin before it was too late—the least wind
might knock it over. They pleaded with him to give up working—his
sons were showering him with money. But Abba stubbornly rose at
dawn and continued at the shoemaker's bench. Although yellow hair
does not readily change color, Abba's beard had turned completely
white, and the white, staining, had turned yellow again. His brows had
sprouted like brushes and hid his eyes, and his high forehead was like a
piece of yellow parchment. But he had not lost his touch. He could still
turn out a stout shoe with a broad heel, even if it did take a little longer.
He bored holes with awl, stitched with the needle, hammered his pegs,
and in a hoarse voice sang the old shoemaker's song:

> *A mother bought a billygoat,*
> *The* shochet *killed the billygoat,*
> *Oh, Lord, the billygoat!*
> *Avremele took its ears,*
> *Berele took its lung,*
> *Gimpele took the gullet,*
> *And Dovid'l took the tongue,*
> *Hershele took the neck . . .*

As there was no one to join him, he now sang the chorus alone:

> *Oh, Lord, the billygoat!*

His friends urged him to hire a servant, but he would not take a
strange woman into the house. Occasionally one of the neighbor women
came in to sweep and dust, but even this was too much for him. He got
used to being alone. He learned to cook for himself and would prepare
soup on the tripod, and on Fridays even put up the pudding for the
Sabbath. Best of all, he liked to sit alone at the bench and follow the
course of his thoughts, which had become more and more tangled with
the years. Day and night he carried on conversations with himself. One

voice asked questions, the other answered. Clever words came to his mind, sharp, timely expressions full of the wisdom of age, as though his grandfathers had come to life again and were conducting their endless disputations inside his head on matters pertaining to this world and the next. All his thoughts ran on one theme: What is life and what is death, what is time that goes on without stopping, and how far away is America? His eyes would close; the hammer would fall out of his hand; but he would still hear the cobbler's characteristic rapping—a soft tap, a louder one, and a third, louder still—as if a ghost sat at his side, mending unseen shoes. When one of the neighbors asked him why he did not go to join his sons, he would point to the heap on the bench and say, "*Nu*, and the shoes? Who will mend them?"

Years passed, and he had no idea how or where they vanished. Traveling preachers passed through Frampol with disturbing news of the outside world. In the tailors' synagogue, which Abba still attended, the young men spoke of war and anti-Semitic decrees, of Jews flocking to Palestine. Peasants who had been Abba's customers for years suddenly deserted him and took their trade to Polish shoemakers. And one day the old man heard that a new world war was imminent. Hitler—may his name vanish!—had raised his legions of barbarians and was threatening to grab up Poland. This scourge of Israel had expelled the Jews from Germany, as in the days of Spain. The old man thought of the Messiah and became terribly excited. Who knows? Perhaps this was the battle of Gog and Magog? Maybe the Messiah really was coming and the dead would rise again! He saw the graves opening and the little shoemakers stepping forth—Abba, Getzel, Treitel, Gimpel, his grandfather, his own father. He called them all into his house and set out brandy and cakes. His wife, Pesha, was ashamed to find the house in such condition, but "Never mind," he assured her, "we'll get someone to sweep up. As long as we're all together!" Suddenly a cloud appears, envelops the town of Frampol—synagogue, house of study, ritual bath, all the Jewish homes, his own among them—and carries the whole settlement off to the Holy Land. Imagine his amazement when he encounters his sons from America. They fall at his feet, crying, "Forgive us, Father!"

When Abba pictured this event his hammer quickened in tempo. He saw the little shoemakers dress for the Sabbath in silks and satins, in flowing robes with broad sashes, and go forth rejoicing in Jerusalem. They pray in the Temple of Solomon, drink the wine of Paradise, and eat of the mighty steer and Leviathan. The ancient Jochanan the shoemaker, renowned for his piety and wisdom, greets the family and engages them in a discussion of Torah and shoemaking. Sabbath over, the whole clan returns to Frampol, which has become part of the Land of

Israel, and reenters the old home. Even though the house is as small as ever, it has miraculously grown roomy enough, like the hide of a deer, as it is written in the Book. They all work at one bench, Abbas, Gimpels, Getzels, Godels, the Treitels and the Lippes, sewing golden sandals for the daughters of Zion and lordly boots for the sons. The Messiah himself calls on the little shoemakers and has them take his measure for a pair of silken slippers.

One morning, while Abba was wandering among his thoughts, he heard a tremendous crash. The old man shook in his bones: the blast of the Messiah's trumpet! He dropped the boot he had been working on and ran out in ecstasy. But it was not Elijah the Prophet proclaiming the Messiah. Nazi planes were bombing Frampol. Panic spread through the town. A bomb fell near the synagogue, so loud that Abba felt his brain shudder in his skull. Hell opened before him. There was a blaze of lightning, followed by a blast that illuminated all of Frampol. A black cloud rose over the courtyard of the synagogue. Flocks of birds flapped about in the sky. The forest was burning. Looking down from his hill, Abba saw the orchards under great columns of smoke. The apple trees were blossoming and burning. Several men who stood near him threw themselves down on the ground and shouted to him to do the same. He did not hear them; they were moving their lips in dumbshow. Shaking with fright, his knees knocking together, he reentered the house and packed a sack with his prayer shawl and phylacteries, a shirt, his shoe-maker's tools, and the paper money he had put away in the straw mattress. Then he took up a stick, kissed the mezuzah, and walked out the door. It was a miracle that he was not killed, the house caught fire the moment he left. The roof swung out like a lid, uncovering the attic with its treasures. The walls collapsed. Abba turned about and saw the shelf of sacred books go up in flames. The blackened pages turned in the air, glowing with fiery letters like the Torah given to the Jews on Mount Sinai.

V

Across the Ocean

From that day on, Abba's life was transformed beyond recognition—it was like a story he had read in the Bible, a fantastic tale heard from the lips of a visiting preacher. He had abandoned the house of his fore-fathers and the place of his birth and, staff in hand, gone wandering into the world like the Patriarch Abraham. The havoc in Frampol and the surrounding villages brought Sodom and Gomorrah to mind, burning like a fiery furnace. He spent his nights in the cemetery together with the other Jews, lying with his head on a gravestone—he too, as Jacob did at Beth-El, on the way from Beer Sheba to Haran.

On Rosh Hashanah the Frampol Jews held services in the forest, with Abba leading the most solemn prayer of the Eighteen Benedictions because he was the only one with a prayer shawl. He stood under a pine tree, which served as an altar, and in a hoarse voice intoned the litany of the Days of Awe. A cuckoo and a woodpecker accompanied him, and all the birds roundabout twittered, whistled, and screeched. Late summer gossamers wafted through the air and trailed onto Abba's beard. From time to time a lowing sounded through the forest, like a blast on the ram's horn. As the Day of Atonement drew near, the Jews of Frampol rose at midnight to say the prayer for forgiveness, reciting it in fragments, whatever they could remember. The horses in the surrounding pastures whinnied and neighed, frogs croaked in the cool night. Distant gunfire sounded intermittently; the clouds shone red. Meteors fell; flashes of lightning played across the sky. Half-starved little children, exhausted from crying, took sick and died in their mothers' arms. There were many burials in the open fields. A woman gave birth.

Abba felt he had become his own great-great-grandfather, who had fled Chmielnitzki's pogroms, and whose name is recorded in the annals of Frampol. He was ready to offer himself in Sanctification of the Name. He dreamed of priests and Inquisitions, and when the wind blew among the branches he heard martyred Jews crying out, "Hear, O Israel, the Lord our God, the Lord is One!"

Fortunately Abba was able to help a good many Jews with his money and shoemaker's tools. With the money they hired wagons and fled south, toward Rumania; but often they had to walk long distances, and their shoes gave out. Abba would stop under a tree and take up his tools. With God's help, they surmounted danger and crossed the Rumanian frontier at night. The next morning, the day before Yom Kippur, an old widow took Abba into her house. A telegram was sent to Abba's sons in America, informing them that their father was safe.

You may be sure that Abba's sons moved heaven and earth to rescue the old man. When they learned of his whereabouts they ran to Washington and with great difficulty obtained a visa for him; then they wired a sum of money to the consul in Bucharest, begging him to help their father. The consul sent a courier to Abba, and he was put on the train to Bucharest. There he was held a week, then transferred to an Italian seaport, where he was shorn and deloused and had his clothes steamed. He was put on board the last ship for the United States.

It was a long and severe journey. The train from Rumania to Italy dragged on, uphill and down, for thirty-six hours. He was given food, but for fear of touching anything ritually unclean he ate nothing at all. His phylacteries and prayer shawl got lost, and with them he lost all track of time and could no longer distinguish between Sabbath and weekdays. Apparently he was the only Jewish passenger on board. There was a man on the ship who spoke German, but Abba could not understand him.

It was a stormy crossing. Abba spent almost the whole time lying down, and frequently vomited gall, though he took nothing but dry crusts and water. He would doze off and wake to the sound of the engines throbbing day and night, to the long, threatening signal blasts, which reeked of fire and brimstone. The door of his cabin was constantly slamming to and fro, as though an imp were swinging on it. The glass-ware in the cupboard trembled and danced; the walls shook; the deck rocked like a cradle.

During the day Abba kept watch at the porthole over his bunk. The ship would leap up as if mounting the sky, and the torn sky would fall as though the world were returning to original chaos. Then the ship would plunge back into the ocean, and once again the firmament would be divided from the waters, as in the Book of Genesis. The waves were a sulphurous yellow and black. Now they would saw-tooth out to the horizon like a mountain range, reminding Abba of the psalmist's words: "The mountains skipped like rams, the little hills like lambs." Then they would come heaving back, as in the miraculous Parting of the Waters. Abba had little learning, but Biblical references ran through his mind, and he saw himself as the prophet Jonah, who fled before God. He too lay in the belly of a whale and, like Jonah, prayed to God for deliver-ance. Then it would seem to him that this was not ocean but limitless desert, crawling with serpents, monsters, and dragons, as it is written in Deuteronomy. He hardly slept a wink at night. When he got up to relieve himself, he would feel faint and lose his balance. With great difficulty he would regain his feet and, his knees buckling under, go wandering, lost, down the narrow, winding corridor, groaning and calling for help until a sailor led him back to the cabin. Whenever this happened he was sure that he was dying. He would not even receive decent Jewish burial, but be dumped in the ocean. And he made his confession, beating his knotty fist on his chest and exclaiming, "Forgive me, Father!"

Just as he was unable to remember when he began his voyage, so he was unaware when it came to an end. The ship had already been made fast to the dock in New York Harbor, but Abba hadn't the vaguest notion of this. He saw huge buildings and towers, but mistook them for the pyramids of Egypt. A tall man in a white hat came into the cabin and shouted something at him, but he remained motionless. At last they helped him dress and led him out on deck, where his sons and daughters-in-law and grandchildren were waiting. Abba was bewildered; a crowd of Polish landowners, counts and countesses, Gentile boys and girls, leaped at him, hugged him, and kissed him, crying out in a strange language, which was both Yiddish and not Yiddish. They half-led, half-carried him away, and placed him in a car. Other cars arrived, packed with Abba's kinfolk, and they set out, speeding like shot arrows over bridges, rivers, and roofs. Buildings rose up and receded, as if by magic, some of the buildings touching the sky. Whole cities lay spread out before him; Abba thought of Pithom and Rameses. The car sped so fast, it seemed to him that people in the streets were moving backward. The air was full of thunder and lightning; a banging and trumpeting, it was a wedding and a conflagration at once. The nations had gone wild, a heathen festival . . .

His sons were crowding around him. He saw them as in a fog and did not know them. Short men with white hair. They shouted, as if he were deaf.

"I'm Gimpel!"

"Getzel!"

"Feivel!"

The old man closed his eyes and made no answer. Their voices ran together; everything was turning pell-mell, topsy-turvy. Suddenly he thought of Jacob arriving in Egypt, where he was met by Pharaoh's chariots. He felt, he had lived through the same experience in a previous incarnation. His beard began to tremble; a hoarse sob rose from his chest. A forgotten passage from the Bible stuck in his gullet.

Blindly he embraced one of his sons and sobbed out, "Is this you? Alive?"

He had meant to say: "Now let me die, since I have seen thy face, because thou art yet alive."

VI

The American Heritage

Abba's sons lived on the outskirts of a town in New Jersey. Their seven homes, surrounded by gardens, stood on the shore of a lake. Every day they drove to the shoe factory, owned by Gimpel, but on the day of Abba's arrival they took a holiday and prepared a feast in his honor. It was to be held in Gimpel's house, in full compliance with the dietary laws. Gimpel's wife, Bessie, whose father had been a Hebrew teacher in the old country, remembered all the rituals and observed them carefully, going so far as to cover her head with a kerchief. Her sisters-in-law did the same, and Abba's sons put on the skullcaps they had once worn during holy days. The grandchildren and great-grandchildren, who did not know a word of Yiddish, actually learned a few phrases. They had heard the legends of Frampol and the little shoemakers and the first Abba of the family line. Even the Gentiles in the neighborhood were fairly well acquainted with this history. In the ads Gimpel published in the papers, he had proudly disclosed that his family belonged to the shoemaking aristocracy:

> Our experience dates back three hundred years to the Polish city of Brod, where our ancestor, Abba, learned the craft from a local master. The community of Frampol, in which our family worked at its trade for fifteen generations, bestowed on him the title of Master in recognition of his charitable services. This sense of public responsibility has always gone hand in hand with our devotion to the highest principles of the craft and our strict policy of honest dealing with our customers.

The day Abba arrived, the papers in Elizabeth carried a notice to the effect that the seven brothers of the famous shoe company were welcoming their father from Poland. Gimpel received a mass of congratulatory telegrams from rival manufacturers, relatives, and friends.

It was an extraordinary feast. Three tables were spread in Gimpel's dining room; one for the old man, his sons, and daughters-in-law, another for the grandchildren, and the third for the great-grandchildren. Although it was broad daylight, the tables were set with candles—red, blue, yellow, green—and their flames were reflected from the dishes and silverware, the crystal glasses and the wine cups, the decanters reminiscent of the Passover Seder. There was an abundance of flowers in every available corner. To be sure, the daughters-in-law would have preferred to see Abba properly dressed for the occasion, but Gimpel put his foot down, and Abba was allowed to spend his first day in the familiar long coat, Frampol style. Even so, Gimpel hired a photographer to take pictures of the banquet—for publication in the newspapers—and invited a rabbi and a cantor to the feast to honor the old man with traditional song.

Abba sat in an armchair at the head of the table. Gimpel and Getzel brought in a bowl and poured water over his hands for the benediction before eating. The food was served on silver trays, carried by colored women. All sorts of fruit juices and salads were set before the old man, sweet brandies, cognac, caviar. But Pharaoh, Joseph, Potiphar's wife, the Land of Goshen, the chief baker, and the chief butler spun round and round in his head. His hands trembled so that he was unable to feed himself, and Gimpel had to help him. No matter how often his sons spoke to him, he still could not tell them apart. Whenever the phone rang he jumped—the Nazis were bombing Frampol. The entire house was whirling round and round like a carousel; the tables were standing on the ceiling and everyone sat upside down. His face was sickly pale in the light of the candles and the electric bulbs. He fell asleep soon after the soup course, while the chicken was being served. Quickly they led him to the bedroom, undressed him, and called a doctor.

He spent several weeks in bed, in and out of consciousness, fitfully dozing as in a fever. He even lacked the strength to say his prayers. There was a nurse at his bedside day and night. Eventually he recovered enough to take a few steps outdoors, in front of the house, but his senses remained disordered. He would walk into clothes closets, lock himself into the bathroom and forget how to come out; the doorbell and the radio frightened him; and he suffered constant anxiety because of the cars that raced past the house. One day Gimpel brought him to a synagogue ten miles away, but even here he was bewildered. The sexton was clean-shaven; the candelabra held electric lights; there was no courtyard, no faucet for washing one's hands, no stove to stand around. The cantor, instead of singing like a cantor should, babbled and croaked. The congregation wore tiny little prayer shawls, like scarves around their necks. Abba was sure he had been hauled into church to be converted . . .

When spring came and he was no better, the daughters-in-law began to hint that it wouldn't be such a bad idea to put him in a home. But something unforeseen took place. One day, as he happened to open a closet, he noticed a sack lying on the floor which seemed somehow familiar. He looked again and recognized his shoemaker's equipment from Frampol: last, hammer and nails, his knife and pliers, the file and the awl, even a broken-down shoe. Abba felt a tremor of excitement; he could hardly believe his eyes. He sat down on a footstool and began to poke about with fingers grown clumsy and stale. When Bessie came in and found him playing with a dirty old shoe, she burst out laughing.

"What are you doing, Father? Be careful, you'll cut yourself, God forbid!"

That day Abba did not lie in bed dozing. He worked busily till evening and even ate his usual piece of chicken with greater appetite. He smiled at the grandchildren when they came in to see what he was doing. The next morning, when Gimpel told his brothers how their father had returned to his old habits, they laughed and thought nothing more of it—but the activity soon proved to be the old man's salvation. He kept at it day after day without tiring, hunting up old shoes in the clothes closets and begging his sons to supply him with leather and tools. When they gave in, he mended every last pair of shoes in the house—man, woman, and child's. After the Passover holidays the brothers got together and decided to build a little hut in the yard. They furnished it with a cobbler's bench, a stock of leather soles and hides, nails, dyes, brushes—everything even remotely useful in the craft.

Abba took on new life. His daughters-in-law cried, he looked fifteen years younger. As in the Frampol days, he now rose at dawn, said his prayers, and got right to work. Once again he used a knotted string as a measuring tape. The first pair of shoes, which he made for Bessie, became the talk of the neighborhood. She had always complained of her feet, but this pair, she insisted, were the most comfortable shoes she had ever worn. The other girls soon followed her example and also had themselves fitted. Then came the grandchildren. Even some of the Gentile neighbors came to Abba when they heard that in sheer joy of the work he was turning out custom-made shoes. He had to communicate with them, for the most part, in gestures, but they got along very well. As for the younger grandchildren and the great-grandchildren, they had long been in the habit of standing at the door to watch him work. Now he was earning money, and he plied them with candies and toys. He even whittled a stylus and began to instruct them in the elements of Hebrew and piety.

One Sunday, Gimpel came into the workshop and, no more than half in earnest, rolled up his sleeves and joined Abba at the bench. The other brothers were not to be outdone, and on the following Sunday eight work stools were set up in the hut. Abba's sons spread sackcloth aprons on their knees and went to work, cutting soles and shaping heels, boring holes and hammering pegs, as in the good old days. The women stood outside, laughing, but they took pride in their men, and the children were fascinated. The sun streamed in through the windows, and motes of dust danced in the light. In the high spring sky, lofting over the grass and the water, floated clouds in the form of brooms, sailboats, flocks of sheep, herds of elephants. Birds sang; flies buzzed; butterflies fluttered about.

Abba raised his dense eyebrows, and his sad eyes looked around at his heirs, the seven shoemakers: Gimpel, Getzel, Treitel, Godel, Feivel, Lippe, and Chananiah. Their hair was white, though yellow streaks remained. No, praise God, they had not become idolaters in Egypt. They had not forgotten their heritage, nor had they lost themselves among the unworthy. The old man rattled and bumbled deep in his chest, and suddenly began to sing in a stifled, hoarse voice:

> *A mother had*
> *Ten little boys,*
> *Oh, Lord, ten little boys!*
>
> *The sixth one was called Velvele,*
> *The seventh one was Zeinvele,*
> *The eighth one was called Chenele,*
> *The ninth one was called Tevele,*
> *The tenth one was called Judele . . .*

And Abba's sons came in on the chorus:

> *Oh, Lord, Judele!*

The Unseen

I
Nathan and Temerl

THEY say that I, the Evil Spirit, after descending to earth in order to induce people to sin, will then ascend to Heaven to accuse them. As a matter of fact, I am also the one to give the sinner the first push, but I do this so cleverly that the sin appears to be an act of virtue; thus, other infidels, unable to learn from the example, continue to sink into the abyss.

But let me tell you a story. There once lived a man in the town of Frampol who was known for his wealth and lavish ways. Named Nathan Jozefover, for he was born in Little Jozefov, he had married a Frampol girl and settled there. Reb Nathan, at the time of this story, was sixty, perhaps a bit more. Short and broad-boned, he had, like most rich people, a large paunch. Cheeks red as wine showed between the clumps of short black beard. Over small twinkling eyes his eyebrows were thick and shaggy. All his life, he had eaten, drunk, and made merry. For breakfast, his wife served him cold chicken and raisin bread, which, like a great landowner, he washed down with a glass of mead. He had a preference for dainties such as roast squab, necks stuffed with chopped milt, pancakes with liver, egg noodles with broth, etc. The townspeople whispered that his wife, Roise Temerl, prepared a noodle puddding for him every day, and if he so desired made a Sabbath dinner in the middle of the week. Actually, she too liked to indulge.

Having plenty of money and no children, husband and wife apparently believed that good cheer was in order. Both of them, therefore, became fat and lazy. After their lunch, they would close the bedroom shutters and snore in their featherbeds as though it were midnight. During the winter nights, long as Jewish exile, they would get out of bed to treat themselves to gizzard, chicken livers, and jam, washed down with

Translated by Norbert Guterman and Elaine Gottlieb

beet soup or apple juice. Then, back to their canopied beds they went to resume their dreams of the next day's porridge.

Reb Nathan gave little time to his grain business, which ran itself. A large granary with two oaken doors stood behind the house he had inherited from his father-in-law. In the yard there were also a number of barns, sheds, and other buildings. Many of the old peasants in the surrounding villages would sell their grain and flax to Nathan alone, for, even though others might offer them more, they trusted Nathan's honesty. He never sent anyone away empty-handed, and sometimes even advanced money for the following year's crop. The simple peasants, in gratitude, brought him wood from the forest, while their wives picked mushrooms and berries for him. An elderly servant, widowed in her youth, looked after the house and even assisted in the business. For the entire week, with the exception of market day, Nathan did not have to lift a finger.

He enjoyed wearing fine clothes and telling yarns. In the summer, he would nap on a bed among the trees of his orchard, or read either the Bible in Yiddish, or simply a story book. He liked, on the Sabbath, to listen to the preaching of a magid, and occasionally to invite a poor man to his house. He had many amusements: for example, he loved to have his wife, Roise Temerl, tickle his feet, and she did this whenever he wished. It was rumored that, he and his wife would bathe together in his own bathhouse, which stood in his yard. In a silk dressing gown embroidered with flowers and leaves, and wearing pompommed slippers, he would step out on his porch in the afternoon, smoking a pipe with an amber bowl. Those who passed by greeted him, and he responded in a friendly fashion. Sometimes he would stop a passing girl, ask her this and that, and then send her off with a joke. After the reading of the Perek on Saturday, he would sit with the women on the bench, eating nuts or pumpkin seeds, listening to gossip, and telling of his own encounters with landowners, priests, and rabbis. He had traveled widely in his youth, visiting Cracow, Brod, and Danzig.

Roise Temerl was almost the image of her husband. As the saying goes: when a husband and wife sleep on one pillow finally they have the same head. Small and plump, she had cheeks still full and red despite her age, and a tiny talkative mouth. The smattering of Hebrew, with which she just found her way through the prayer books, gave her the right to a leading role in the women's section of the prayer house. She often led a bride to the synagogue, was sponsor at a circumcision, and occasionally collected money for a poor girl's trousseau. Although a wealthy woman, she could apply cups to the sick, and would adroitly cut out the pip of a chicken. Her skills included embroidery and knitting.

She possessed numerous jewels, dresses, coats, and furs, all of which she kept in oaken chests as protection against moths and thieves.

Because of her gracious manner, she was welcomed at the butcher's, at the ritual bath, and wherever else she went. Her only regret was that she had no children. To make up for this, she gave charitable contributions and engaged a pious scholar to pray in her memory after her death. She took pleasure in a nest-egg she had managed to save over the years, kept it hidden somewhere in a bag, and now and then enjoyed counting the gold pieces. However, since Nathan gave her everything she needed, she had no idea of how to spend the money. Although he knew of her hoard, he pretended ignorance, realizing that "stolen water is sweet to drink," and did not begrudge her this harmless diversion.

I I
Shifra Zirel the Servant

One day their old servant became ill and soon died. Nathan and his wife were deeply grieved, not only because they had grown so accustomed to her that she was almost a blood relative, but she had also been honest, industrious, and loyal, and it would not be easy to replace her. Nathan and Roise Temerl wept over her grave, and Nathan said the first Kaddish. He promised that after the thirty-day mourning period, he would drive to Janov to order the tombstone she deserved. Nathan, actually, did not come out a loser through her death. Having rarely spent any of her earnings, and being without a family, she had left everything to her employers.

Immediately after the funeral, Roise Temerl began to look for a new servant, but could not find any that compared to the first. The Frampol girls were not only lazy, but they could not bake and fry to Roise Temerl's satisfaction. Various widows, divorced women, and deserted wives were offered her, but none had the qualifications that Roise Temerl desired. Of every candidate presented at her house, she would make inquiries on how to prepare fish, marinate borscht, bake pastry, strudel, egg cookies, etc.; what to do when milk and borscht sour, when a chicken is too tough, a broth too fat, a Sabbath pudding overdone, a porridge too thick or too thin, and other tricky questions. The bewildered girl would lose her tongue and leave in embarrassment. Several weeks went by like this, and the pampered Roise Temerl, who had to do all the chores, could clearly see that it was easier to eat a meal than prepare one.

Well, I, the Seducer, could not stand by and watch Nathan and his wife starve; I sent them a servant, a wonder of wonders.

A native of Zamosc, she had even worked for wealthy families in Lublin. Although at first she had refused—even if she were paid her weight in gold—to go to an insignificant spot like Frampol, various people had intervened, Roise Temerl had agreed to pay a few gulden more than she had paid previously, and the girl, Shifra Zirel, decided to take the job.

In the carriage that had to be sent to Zamosc for her and her extensive luggage, she arrived with suitcases, baskets, and knapsacks, like a rich bride. Well along in her twenties, she seemed no more than eighteen or nineteen. Her hair was plaited in two braids coiled at the sides of her head; she wore a checkered shawl with tassels, a cretonne dress, and narrow heeled shoes. Her chin had a wolf-like sharpness, her lips were thin, her eyes shrewd and impudent. She wore rings in her ears and around her throat a coral necklace. Immediately, she found fault with the Frampol mud, the clay taste of the well water, and the lumpy home-made bread. Served over-cooked soup by Roise Temerl on the first day, she took a drop of it with her spoon, made a face, and complained, "It's sour and rancid!"

She demanded a Jewish or Gentile girl as an assistant, and Roise Temerl, after a strenuous search, found a Gentile one, the sturdy daughter of the bath attendant. Shifra Zirel began to give orders. She told the girl to scrub the floors, clean the stove, sweep the cobwebs in corners, and advised Roise Temerl to get rid of the superfluous pieces of furniture, various rickety chairs, stools, tables, and chests. The windows were cleaned, the dusty curtains removed, and the rooms became lighter and more spacious. Roise Temerl and Nathan were amazed by her first meal. Even the emperor could ask for no better cook. An appetizer of calves' liver and lungs, partly fried and partly boiled, was served before the broth, and its aroma titillated their nostrils. The soup was seasoned with herbs unobtainable at Frampol, such as paprika and capers, which the new servant had apparently brought from Zamosc. Dessert was a mixture of applesauce, raisins, and apricots, flavored with cinnamon, saffron, and cloves, whose fragrance filled the house. Then, as in the wealthy homes of Lublin, she served black coffee with chicory. After lunch, Nathan and his wife wanted to nap as usual, but Shifra Zirel warned them that it was unhealthful to sleep immediately after eating, because the vapors mount from the stomach to the brain. She advised her employers to walk back and forth in the garden a few times. Nathan was brimful of good food, and the coffee had gone to his head. He reeled and kept repeating, "Well, my dear wife, isn't she a treasure of a servant?"

"I hope no one will take her away," Roise Temerl said. Knowing how envious people were, she feared the evil eye, or those who might offer the girl better terms.

There is no sense going into detail about the excellent dishes Shifra Zirel prepared, the babkas and macaroons she baked, the appetizers she introduced. The neighbors found Nathan's rooms and his yard unrecognizable. Shifra Zirel had whitewashed the walls, cleaned the sheds and closets, and hired a laborer to weed the garden and repair the fence and railing of the porch. Like the mistress of the house rather than its servant, she supervised everything. When Shifra Zirel, in a woolen dress and pointed shoes, went for a stroll on Saturdays, after the pre-cooked cholent dinner, she was stared at not only by common laborers and poor girls, but by young men and women of good families as well. Daintily holding up her skirt, she walked, her head high. Her assistant, the bathhouse attendant's daughter, followed, carrying a bag of fruit and cookies, for Jews could not carry parcels on the Sabbath. From the benches in front of their houses women observed her and shook their heads. "She's as proud as a landowner's wife!" they would comment, predicting that her stay in Frampol would be brief.

III
Temptation

One Tuesday, when Roise Temerl was in Janov visiting her sister, who was ill, Nathan ordered the Gentile girl to prepare a steam bath for him. His limbs and bones had been aching since morning, and he knew that the only remedy for this was to perspire abundantly. After putting a great deal of wood in the stove around the bricks, the girl lighted the fire, filled the vat with water, and returned to the kitchen.

When the fire had burnt itself out, Nathan undressed and then poured a bucket of water on the red hot bricks. The bathhouse filled with steam. Nathan, climbing the stairs to the high shelf where the steam was hot and dense, whipped himself with a twig broom that he had prepared previously. Usually Roise Temerl helped him with this. When he perspired she poured the buckets of water, and when she perspired he poured. After they had flogged each other with twig brooms, Roise Temerl would bathe him in a wooden tub and comb him. But this time Roise Temerl had had to go to Janov to her sick sister, and Nathan did not think it wise to wait for her return, since his sister-in-law was very old and might die and then Roise Temerl would have to stay there seven days. Never before had he taken his bath alone. The steam, as usual, soon settled. Nathan wanted to go down and pour more water on the bricks, but his legs felt heavy and he was lazy. With his belly protruding upward, he lay on his back, flogging himself with the broom, rubbing his knees and ankles, and staring at the bent beam on the smoke-blackened ceiling. Through the crack, a patch of clear sky stared in. This was the month of Elul, and Nathan was assailed by melancholy. He remembered his sister-in-law as a young woman full of life, and now she was on her deathbed. He too would not eat marchpanes nor sleep on eiderdown forever, it occurred to him, for some day he would be placed in a dark grave, his eyes covered with shards, and worms would consume the body that Roise Temerl had pampered for the nearly fifty years that she had been his wife.

Probing his soul, Nathan lay there, belly upward, when he suddenly heard the chain clank, the door creak. Looking about, he saw to his amazement, that Shifra Zirel had entered. Barefoot, with a white kerchief around her head, she was dressed only in a slip. In a choking voice, he cried out, "No!" and hastened to cover himself. Upset, and shaking his head, he beckoned her to leave, but Shifra Zirel said, "Don't be afraid, master, I won't bite you."

She poured a bucket of water over the hot bricks. A hissing noise filled the room, and white clouds of steam quickly rose, scalding Nathan's limbs. Then Shifra Zirel climbed the steps to Nathan, grabbed the twig broom, and began to flog him. He was so stunned, he became speechless. Choking, he almost rolled off the slippery shelf. Shifra Zirel, meanwhile, continued diligently to whip him and to rub him with a cake of soap she had brought. Finally, having regained his composure, he said, hoarsely, "What's the matter with you? Shame on you!"

"What's there to be ashamed about?" the servant asked airily. "I won't harm the master . . ."

For a long time she occupied herself combing and massaging him, rubbing him with soap, and drenching him with water, and Nathan was compelled to acknowledge that this devilish woman was more accomplished than Roise Temerl. Her hands, too, were smoother; they tickled his body and aroused his desire. He soon forgot that this was the month of Elul, before the Days of Awe, and told the servant to lock the wooden latch of the door. Then, in a wavering voice, he made a proposition.

"Never, uncle!" she said resolutely, pouring a bucket of water on him.

"Why not?" he asked, his neck, belly, head, all his limbs dripping.

"Because I belong to my husband."

"What husband?"

"The one I'll have some day, God willing."

"Come on, Shifra Zirel," he said. "I'll give you something—a coral necklace, or a brooch."

"You're wasting your breath," she said.

"A kiss at least!" he begged.

"A kiss will cost twenty-five coins," Shifra Zirel said.

"Groszy or threepence pieces?" Nathan asked, efficiently, and Shifra Zirel answered, "Gulden."

Nathan reflected. Twenty-five gulden was no trifle. But I, the Old Nick, reminded him that one does not live forever, and that there was no harm in leaving a few gulden less behind. Therefore, he agreed.

Bending over him, placing her arms about his neck, Shifra Zirel kissed him on the mouth. Half kiss and half bite, it cut his breath. Lust arose in him. He could not climb down, for his arms and legs were trembling, and Shifra Zirel had to help him down and even put on his dressing gown. "So that's the kind you are . . ." he murmured.

"Don't insult me, Reb Nathan," she admonished. "I'm pure."

"Pure as a pig's knuckle," Nathan thought. He opened the door for her. After a moment, glancing anxiously about to make sure he was not seen, he left also. "Imagine such a thing happening!" he murmured. "What impudence! A real whore!" He resolved never again to have anything to do with her.

I V
Troubled Nights

Nathan lay at night on his eiderdown mattress, wrapped in a silken blanket, his head propped up by three pillows, but he was robbed of sleep by my wife Lilith and her companions. He had droused off, but was awake; he began to dream something, but the vision frightened him, and he rose with a start. Someone invisible whispered something into his ear. He fancied, for a moment, that he was thirsty. Then his head felt feverish. Leaving his bed, he slipped into his slippers and dressing gown, and went to the kitchen to scoop up a mug of water. Leaning over the barrel, he slipped and almost fell in. Suddenly he realized that he craved Shifra Zirel with the craving of a young man. "What's the matter with me?" he murmured, "This can only be a trick of the devil." He started to walk to his own room, but found himself going to the little room where the servant slept. Halting at the doorway, he listened. A rustling came from behind the stove, and in the dry wood something creaked. The pale glow of a lantern flashed outside; there was a sigh. Nathan recalled that this was Elul, that God-fearing Jews rise at dawn for the Selichot prayers. Just as he was about to turn back, the servant opened the door and asked in an alert tone, "Who's there?"

"I am," Nathan whispered.

"What does the master wish?"

"Don't you know?"

She groaned and was silent, as though wondering what to do. Then she said, "Go back to bed, master. It's no use talking."

"But I can't sleep," Nathan complained in a tone he sometimes used with Roise Temerl. "Don't send me away!"

"Leave, master," Shifra Zirel said in an angry voice, "or I'll scream!"

"Hush. I won't force you, God forbid. I'm fond of you. I love you."

"If the master loves me then let him marry me."

"How can I! I have a wife!" Nathan said, surprised.

"Well, what of it? What do you think divorce is for?" she said and sat up.

"She's not a woman," Nathan thought, "but a demon." Frightened by her and her talk he remained in the doorway, heavy, bewildered, leaning against the jamb. The Good Spirit, who is at the height of his power during the month of Elul, reminded him of *The Measure of Righteousness*—which he had read in Yiddish—stories of pious men, tempted by landowners' wives, she-demons, whores, but who had refused to succumb to the temptation. "I'll send her away at once, tomorrow, even if I must pay her wages for a year," Nathan decided. But he said, "What's wrong with you? I've lived with my wife for almost fifty years! Why should I divorce her now?"

"Fifty years is sufficient," the brazen servant answered.

Her insolence, rather than repelling him, attracted him the more. Walking to her bed, he sat on the edge. A vile warmth arose from her. Seized by a powerful desire, he said, "How can I divorce her? She won't consent."

"You can get one without her consent," said the servant, apparently well informed.

Blandishments and promises would not change her mind. To all Nathan's arguments, she turned a deaf ear. Day was already breaking when he returned to his bed. His bedroom walls were gray as canvas. Like a coal glowing on a heap of ashes, the sun arose in the east, casting a light, scarlet as the fire of hell. A crow, alighting on the windowsill, began to caw with its curved black beak, as though trying to announce a piece of bad news. A shudder went through Nathan's bones. He felt that he was his own master no longer, that the Evil Spirit, having seized the reins, drove him along an iniquitous path, perilous and full of obstacles.

From then on Nathan did not have a moment's respite.

While his wife, Roise Temerl, observed the mourning period for her sister in Janov, he was roused each night, and driven to Shifra Zirel, who, each time, rejected him.

Begging and imploring, he promised valuable gifts, offered a rich dowry and inclusion in his will, but nothing availed him. He vowed not to return to her, but his vow was broken each time. He spoke foolishly, in a manner unbecoming to a respectable man, and disgraced himself.

When he woke her, she not only chased him away, but scolded him. In passing from his room to hers in the darkness, he would stumble against doors, cupboards, stoves, and he was covered with bruises. He ran into a slop basin and spilled it. He shattered glassware. He tried to recite a chapter of the Psalms that he knew by heart and implored God to rescue him from the net I had spread, but the holy words were distorted on his lips and his mind was confused with impure thoughts. In his bedroom there was a constant buzz and hum from the glowworms, flies, moths, and mosquitoes with which I, the Evil One, had filled it. With eyes open and ears intent, Nathan lay wide awake, listening to each rustle. Roosters crowed, frogs croaked in the swamps, crickets chirped, flashes of lightning glowed strangely. A little imp kept reminding him: Don't be a fool, Reb Nathan, she's waiting for you; she wants to see if you're a man or a mouse. And the imp hummed: Elul or no Elul, a woman's a woman, and if you don't enjoy her in this world it's too late in the next. Nathan would call Shifra Zirel and wait for her to answer. It seemed to him that he heard the patter of bare feet, that he saw the whiteness of her body or of her slip in the darkness. Finally, trembling, afire, he would rise from his bed to go to her room. But she remained stubborn. "Either I or the mistress," she would declare. "Go, master!"

And grabbing a broom from the pile of refuse, she would smack him across the back. Then Reb Nathan Jozefover, the richest man in Frampol, respected by young and old, would return defeated and whipped to his canopied bed, to toss feverishly until sunrise.

V

Forest Road

Roise Temerl, when she returned from Janov and saw her husband, was badly frightened. His face was ashen; there were bags under his eyes; his beard, which until recently had been black, was now threaded with white; his stomach had become loose, and hung like a sack. Like one dangerously ill, he could barely drag his feet along. "Woe is me, even finer things than this are put in the grave!" she exclaimed. She began to question him, but since he could not tell her the truth, he said he was suffering from headaches, heartburn, stitches, and similar ailments. Roise Temerl, though she had looked forward to seeing her husband and had hoped to enjoy herself with him, ordered a carriage and horses and told him to see a doctor in Lublin. Filling a suitcase with cookies, jams, juices, and various other refreshments, she urged him not to spare money, but to find the best of doctors and to take all the medication he prescribed. Shifra Zirel, too, saw her master depart, escorting the carriage on foot as far as the bridge, and wishing him a speedy recovery.

Late at night, by the light of the full moon, while the carriage drove along a forest road and shadows ran ahead, I, the Evil Spirit, came to Reb Nathan and asked, "Where are you going?"

"Can't you see? To a doctor."

"Your ailment can't be cured by a doctor," I said.

"What shall I do then? Divorce my old wife?"

"Why not?" I said to him. "Did not Abraham drive his bondwoman, Hagar, into the wilderness, with nothing but a bottle of water, because he preferred Sarah? And later, did he not take Keturah and have six sons with her? Did not Moses, the teacher of all Jews, take, in addition to Zipporah, another wife from the land of Kush; and when Miriam, his sister, spoke against him, did she not become leprous? Know ye, Nathan, you are fated to have sons and daughters, and according to the law, you should have divorced Roise Temerl ten years after marrying her? Well, you may not leave the world without begetting children, and Heaven, therefore, has sent you Shifra Zirel to lie in your lap and become pregnant and bear healthy children, who after your death, will say Kaddish for you and will inherit your possessions. Therefore do not try to resist, Nathan, for such is the decree of Heaven, and if you do not execute it, you will be punished, you will die soon, and Roise Temerl will be a widow anyway and you will inherit hell."

Hearing these words, Nathan became frightened. Shuddering from head to foot, he said, "If so, why do I go to Lublin? I should, rather, order the driver to return to Frampol."

And I replied, "No, Nathan. Why tell your wife what you're about to do? When she learns you plan to divorce her and take the servant in her place, she will be greatly grieved, and may revenge herself on you or the servant. Rather follow the advice Shifra Zirel gave you. Get divorce papers in Lublin and place them secretly in your wife's dresses; this will make the divorce valid. Then tell her that doctors had advised you to go to Vienna for an operation since you have an internal growth. And before leaving, collect all the money and take it along with you, leaving your wife only the house and the furniture and her personal belongings. Only when you are far from home, and Shifra Zirel with you, you may inform Roise Temerl that she is a divorcee. In this way you will avoid scandal. But do not delay, Nathan, For Shifra Zirel won't tarry, and if she leaves you, you might be punished and perish and lose this world as well as the next."

I made more speeches, pious and impious, and at daybreak, when he fell asleep, I brought him Shifra Zirel, naked, and showed him the images of the children she would bear, male and female, with side whiskers and curls, and I made him eat imaginary dishes she had prepared for him: they tasted of Paradise. He awoke from these visions, famished, and consumed with desire. Approaching the city, the carriage stopped at an inn, where Nathan was served breakfast and a soft bed prepared for him. But on his palate there remained the savor of the pancake he had tasted in his dream. And on his lips he could almost feel Shifra Zirel's kisses. Overcome with longing, he put on his coat again, and told his hosts he must hurry to meet merchants.

In a back alley where I led him, he discovered a miserly scribe, who for five gulden, wrote the divorce papers and had them signed by witnesses, as required by law. Then Nathan, after purchasing numerous bottles and pills from an apothecary, returned to Frampol. He told his wife he had been examined by three doctors, that they had all found he had a tumor in his stomach, and that he must go at once to Vienna to be treated by great specialists or he would not last the year. Shaken by the story, Roise Temerl said, "What's money? Your health means far more to me." She wanted to accompany him, but Nathan reasoned with her and argued, "The trip will cost double; moreover, our business here must be looked after. No, stay here, and God willing, if everything goes well, I'll be back, we'll be happy together." To make a long story short, Roise Temerl agreed with him and stayed.

The same night, after Roise Temerl had fallen asleep, Nathan rose from bed and quietly placed the divorce papers in her trunk. He also visited Shifra Zirel in her room to inform her of what he had done. Kissing and embracing him, she promised to be a good wife and faithful mother to his children. But in her heart, jeering, she thought: You old fool, you'll pay dearly for falling in love with a whore.

And now starts the story of how I and my companions forced the old sinner, Nathan Jozefover, to become a man who sees without being seen, so that his bones would never be properly buried, which is the penalty for lechery.

VI
Nathan Returns

A year passed, Roise Temerl now had a second husband, having married a Frampol grain dealer, Moshe Mecheles, who had lost his wife at the same time as she had been divorced. Moshe Mecheles was a small red-bearded man, with heavy red eyebrows and piercing yellow eyes. He often disputed with the Frampol rabbi, put on two pairs of phylacteries while praying, and owned a water mill. He was always covered with white flour dust. He had been rich before, and after his marriage to Roise Temerl, he took over her granaries and customers and became a magnate.

Why had Roise Temerl married him? For one thing, other people intervened. Secondly, she was lonely, and thought that another husband might at least partially replace Nathan. Third, I, the Seducer, had my own reasons for wanting her married. Well, after marrying, she realized she had made a mistake. Moshe Mecheles had odd ways. He was thin, and she tried to fatten him, but he would not touch her dumplings, pancakes, and chickens. He preferred bread with garlic, potatoes in their skins, onions and radishes, and once a day, a piece of lean boiled beef. His stained caftan was never buttoned; he wore a string to hold up his trousers, refused to go to the bath Roise Temerl would heat for him, and had to be forced to change a shirt or a pair of underpants. Moreover he was rarely at home; he either traveled for business or attended community meetings. He went to sleep late, and groaned and snored in his bed. When the sun rose, so did Moshe Mecheles, humming like a bee. Although close to sixty, Roise Temerl still did not disdain what others like, but Moshe Mecheles came to her rarely, and then it was only a question of duty. The woman finally conceded that she had blundered, but what could be done? She swallowed her pride and suffered silently.

One afternoon around Elul time, when Roise Temerl went to the yard to pour out the slops, she saw a strange figure. She cried out; the basin fell from her hands, the slops spilled at her feet. Ten paces away stood Nathan, her former husband. He was dressed like a beggar, his caftan torn, a piece of rope around his loins, his shoes in shreds, and on his head only the lining of a cap. His once pink face was now yellow, and the clumps of his beard were gray; pouches hung from his eyes. From his disheveled eyebrows he stared at Roise Temerl. For a moment it occurred to her that he must have died, and this was his ghost before her. She almost called out: Pure Soul, return to your place of rest! But since this was happening in broad daylight, she soon recovered from her shock and asked in a trembling voice: "Do my eyes deceive me?"

"No," said Nathan. "It is I."

For a long time husband and wife stood silently gazing at each other. Roise Temerl was so stunned that she could not speak. Her legs began to shake, and she had to hold on to a tree to keep from falling.

"Woe is me, what has become of you?" she cried.

"Is your husband at home?" Nathan asked.

"My husband?" she was bewildered, "No . . ."

About to ask him in, Roise Temerl remembered that according to law, she was not permitted to stay under the same roof with him. Also, she feared that the servant might recognize him. Bending, she picked up the slop basin.

"What happened?" she asked.

Haltingly, Nathan told her how he had met Shifra Zirel in Lublin, married her, and been persuaded by her to go to her relatives in Hungary. At an inn near the border, she deserted him, stealing everything, even his clothes. Since then, he had wandered all over the country, slept in poorhouses, and like a beggar, made the rounds of private homes. At first he had thought he would obtain a writ signed by one hundred rabbis, enabling him to remarry, and he had set out for Frampol. Then he had learned that Roise Temerl had married again, and he had come to beg her forgiveness.

Unable to believe her eyes, Roise Temerl kept staring at him. Leaning on his crooked stick, as a beggar might, he never lifted his eyes. From his ears and nostrils, thatches of hair protruded. Through his torn coat, she saw the sackcloth, and through a slit in it, his flesh. He seemed to have grown smaller.

"Have any of the townspeople seen you?" she asked.

"No. I came through the fields."

"Woe is me. What can I do with you now?" she exclaimed. "I am married."

"I don't want anything from you," Nathan said. "Farewell."

"Don't go!" Roise Temerl said. "Oh, how unlucky I am!"

Covering her face with her hands, she began to sob. Nathan moved aside.

"Don't mourn for me," he said. "I haven't died yet."

"I wish you had," she replied. "I'd be happier."

Well, I, the Destroyer, had not yet tried all my insidious tricks. The scale of sins and punishment was not yet balanced. Therefore, in a vigorous move, I spoke to the woman in the language of compassion, for it is known that compassion, like any other sentiment, can serve evil as well as good purposes. Roise Temerl, I said, he is your husband; you lived with him for fifty years, and you cannot repudiate him, now that he has fallen. And when she asked, "What shall I do? After all, I cannot stand here and expose myself to derision," I made a suggestion. She trembled, raised her eyes, and beckoned Nathan to follow her. Submissively, he walked behind her, like any poor visitor who does everything that the lady of the house tells him to do.

VII
The Secret of the Ruin

In the yard, behind the granary, near the bathhouse, stood a ruin in which many years before, Roise Temerl's parents had lived. It was unoccupied now, its ground floor windows boarded, but on the second floor there were still a few well-preserved rooms. Pigeons perched on the roof, and swallows had nested under the gutter. A worn broom had been stuck in the chimney. Nathan had often said the building should be

razed, but Roise Temerl had insisted that while she was alive her parents' home would not be demolished. The attic was littered with old
rubbish and rags. Schoolboys said that a light emanated from the ruin at
midnight, and that demons lived in the cellar. Roise Temerl led Nathan
there now. It was not easy to enter the ruin. Weeds that pricked and
burned obstructed the path. Roise Temerl's skirt caught on thorns sharp
as nails. Little molehills were everywhere. A heavy curtain of cobwebs
barred the open doorway. Roise Temerl swept them away with a rotten
branch. The stairs were rickety. Her legs were heavy and she had to lean
on Nathan's arm. A thick cloud of dust arose, and Nathan began to
sneeze and cough.

"Where are you taking me?" he asked, bewildered.

"Don't be afraid," Roise Temerl said. "It's all right."

Leaving him in the ruin, she returned to the house. She told the
servant to take the rest of the day off, and the servant did not have to be
told twice. When she had gone, Roise Temerl opened the cabinets that
were still filled with Nathan's clothes, took his linen from the chest, and
brought everything to the ruin. Once more she left, and when she returned it was with a basket containing a meal of rice and pot roast, tripe
with calves' feet, white bread, and stewed prunes. After he had gobbled
his supper and licked off the prune plate, Roise Temerl drew a bucket of
water from the well and told him to go to another room to wash. Night
was falling, but the twilight lingered a long time. Nathan did as Roise
Temerl instructed, and she could hear him splash and sigh in the next
room. Then he changed his clothes. When Roise Temerl saw him, tears
streamed from her eyes. The full moon that shone through the window
made the room bright as daylight, and Nathan, in a clean shirt, his
dressing gown embroidered with leaves and flowers, in his silken cap
and velvet slippers, once again seemed his former self.

Moshe Mecheles happened to be out of town, and Roise Temerl was
in no hurry. She went again to the house and returned with bedding. The
bed only needed to be fitted with boards. Not wanting to light a candle,
lest someone notice the glow, Roise Temerl went about in the dark,
climbed to the attic with Nathan, and groped until she found some old
slats for the bed. Then she placed a mattress, sheets, and pillow on it.
She had even remembered to bring some jam and a box of cookies so
that Nathan could refresh himself before going to sleep. Only then did
she sit down on the unsteady stool to rest. Nathan sat on the edge of the
bed.

After a long silence, he said, "What's the use? Tomorrow I must
leave."

"Why tomorrow?" said Roise Temerl. "Rest up. There's always time
to rot in the poorhouse."

Late into the night they sat, talking, murmuring. Roise Temerl cried and stopped crying, began again and was calm again. She insisted that Nathan confess everything to her, without omitting details, and he told her again how he had met Shifra Zirel, how they had married, how she had persuaded him to go with her to Pressburg, and how she had spent the night full of sweet talk and love play with him at an inn. And at daybreak, when he fell asleep, she had arisen and untied the bag from his neck. He also told Roise Temerl how he had been forced to discard all shame, to sleep in beggars' dormitories, and eat at strangers' tables. Although his story angered her, and she called him blockhead, stupid fool, ass, idiot, her heart almost dissolved with pity.

"What is there to do now?" she kept murmuring to herself, over and over again. And I, the Evil Spirit, answered: Don't let him go. The beggar's life is not for him. He might die of grief or shame. And when Roise Temerl argued that because she was a married woman she had no right to stay with him, I said: Can the twelve lines of a bill of divorcement separate two souls who have been fused by fifty years of common life? Can a brother and sister be transformed by law into strangers? Hasn't Nathan become part of you? Don't you see him every night in your dreams? Isn't all your fortune the result of his industry and effort? And what is Moshe Mecheles? A stranger, a lout. Wouldn't it be better to fry with Nathan in Hell, rather than serve as Moshe Mecheles' footstool in Heaven? I also recalled to her an incident in a storybook, where a landowner, whose wife had eloped with a bear tamer, later forgave her and took her back to his manor.

When the clock in the Frampol church chimed eleven, Roise Temerl returned home. In her luxurious, canopied bed, she tossed, like one in a fever. For a long time, Nathan stood beside his window, looking out. The Elul sky was full of stars. The owl on the roof of the synagogue screeched with a human voice. The caterwauling of cats reminded him of women in labor. Crickets chirped, and unseen saws seemed to be buzzing through tree trunks. The neighing of horses that had grazed all night came through the fields with the calls of shepherds. Nathan, because he stood on an upper floor, could see the whole little town at a glance, the synagogue, the church, the slaughterhouse, the public bathhouse, the market, and the side streets where Gentiles lived. He recognized each shed, shack, and board in his own yard. A goat stripped some bark from a tree. A field mouse left the granary to return to its nest. Nathan watched for a long time. Everything about him was familiar and yet strange, real and ghostly, as though he were no longer among the living—only his spirit floated there. He recalled that there was a Hebrew phrase which applied to him, but he could not remember it exactly. Finally, after trying for a long time, he remembered: *one who sees without being seen.*

VIII
One Who Sees without Being Seen

In Frampol the rumor spread that Roise Temerl, having quarreled with her maid, had dismissed her in the middle of her term. This surprised the housewives, because the girl was reputedly industrious and honest. Actually, Roise Temerl had dismissed the girl to keep her from discovering that Nathan lived in the ruin. As always, when I seduce sinners, I persuaded the couple that all this was provisional, that Nathan would stay only until he had recovered from his wandering. But I made certain that Roise Temerl welcomed the presence of her hidden guest and that Nathan enjoyed being where he was. Even though they discussed their future separation each time they were together, Roise Temerl gave Nathan's quarters an air of permanency. She resumed her cooking and frying for him, and once more brought him her tasty dishes. After a few days, Nathan's appearance changed remarkably. From pastries and puddings, his face became pink again, and once more, like that of a man of wealth, his paunch protruded. Once more he wore embroidered shirts, velvet slippers, silken dressing gowns, and carried batiste handkerchiefs. To keep him from being bored by his idleness, Roise Temerl brought him a Bible in Yiddish, a copy of the *Inheritance of the Deer*, and numerous storybooks. She even managed to procure some tobacco for his pipe, for he enjoyed smoking one, and she brought from the cellar bottles of wine and mead that Nathan had stored for years. The divorced couple had banquets in the ruin.

I made certain that Moshe Mecheles was seldom at home; I sent him to all kinds of fairs, and even recommended him as arbiter in disputes. It did not take long for the ruin behind the granary to become Roise Temerl's only comfort. Just as a miser's thoughts constantly dwell on the treasure he has buried far from sight, so Roise Temerl thought only of the ruin and the secret in her heart. Sometimes she thought that Nathan had died and she had magically resurrected him for a while; at other times, she imagined the whole thing a dream. Whenever she looked out of her window at the moss-covered roof of the ruin, she thought: No! It's inconceivable for Nathan to be there; I must be deluded. And immediately, she had to fly there, up the rickety stairs, to be met halfway by Nathan in person, with his familiar smile and his pleasant odor. "Nathan, you're here?" she would ask, and he would respond, "Yes, Roise Temerl, I'm here and waiting for you."

"Have you missed me?" she would ask, and he would answer: "Of course. When I hear your step, it's a holiday for me."

"Nathan, Nathan," she would continue. "Would you have believed a year ago that it would end like this?"

And he would murmur, "No, Roise Temerl, it is like a bad dream."

"Oh Nathan, we have already lost this world, and I'm afraid we'll lose the other also," Roise Temerl said.

And he replied, "Well, that's too bad, but hell too is for people, not for dogs."

Since Moshe Mecheles belonged to the Hasidim, I, Old Rebel, sent him to spend the Days of Awe with his rabbi. Alone, Roise Temerl bought Nathan a prayer shawl, a white robe, a prayer book, and prepared a holiday meal for him. Since on Rosh Hashanah, there is no moon, he ate the evening meal in darkness, blindly dunked a slice of bread in honey, and tasted an apple, a carrot, the head of a carp, and offered a blessing for the first fruit, over a pomegranate. He stood praying during the day in his robe and prayer shawl. The sound of the ram's horn came faintly to his ears from the synagogue. At the intermission between the prayers, Roise Temerl visited him in her golden dress, her white, satin-lined coat, and the shawl embroidered with silver threads, to wish him a happy new year. The golden chain he had given her for their betrothal hung around her neck. A brooch he had brought to her from Danzig quivered on her breast, and from her wrist dangled a bracelet he had bought her at Brod. She exuded an aroma of honey cake and the women's section of the synagogue. On the evening before the Day of Atonement, Roise Temerl brought him a white rooster as a sacrificial victim and prepared for him the meal to be eaten before commencing the fast. Also, she gave the synagogue a wax candle for his soul. Before leaving for the Minchah prayer at the synagogue, she came to bid him goodbye, and she began to lament so loudly that Nathan feared she would be heard. Falling into his arms, she clung to him and would not be torn away. She drenched his face with tears and howled as though possessed. "Nathan, Nathan," she wailed, "may we have no more unhappiness," and other things that are said when a member of a family dies, repeating them many times. Fearing she might faint and fall, Nathan had to escort her downstairs. Then, standing at the window, he watched the people of Frampol on their way to the synagogue. The women walked quickly and vigorously, as though hurrying to pray for someone on his deathbed; they held up their skirts, and when two of them met, they fell into each other's arms and swayed back and forth as if in some mysterious struggle. Wives of prominent citizens knocked at doors of poor people and begged to be forgiven. Mothers, whose children were ill, ran with arms outstretched, as though chasing someone, crying like madwomen. Elderly men, before leaving home, removed their shoes, put on white robes, prayer shawls, and white skullcaps. In the synagogue yard, the poor sat with alms' boxes on benches. A reddish glow spread over the roofs, reflecting in the window panes, and illuminating pale faces. In the west, the sun grew enormous; clouds around it caught fire, until half the sky was suffused with flames. Nathan recalled the River of Fire, in which all souls must cleanse themselves. The sun sank soon below the horizon. Girls, dressed in white, came outside and carefully closed shutters. Little flames played on the high windows of the synagogue, and inside, the entire building seemed to be one great flicker. A muted hum arose from it, and bursts of sobbing. Removing his shoes, Nathan wrapped himself in his shawl and robe. Half reading and half remembering, he chanted the words of Kol Nidre, the song that is recited not only by the living but by the dead in their graves. What was he, Nathan Jozefover, but a dead man, who instead of resting in his grave, wandered about in a world that did not exist?

I X

Footprints in the Snow

The High Holy Days were over. Winter had come. But Nathan was still in the ruin. It could not be heated, not only because the stove had been dismantled, but because smoke, coming from the chimney, would make people suspicious. To keep Nathan from freezing, Roise Temerl provided him with warm clothes and a coal pot. At night he covered himself with two feather quilts. During the day he wore his fox fur and had felt boots on his feet. Roise Temerl also brought him a little barrel of spirits with a straw in it, which he sipped each time he felt cold, while eating a piece of dried mutton. From the rich food with which Roise Temerl plied him, he grew fat and heavy. In the evenings he stood at the window watching with curiosity the women who went to the ritual bath. On market days he never left the window. Carts drove into the yard and peasants unloaded sacks of grain. Moshe Mecheles, in a cotton padded jacket, ran back and forth, crying out hoarsely. Although it pained Nathan to think that this ridiculous fellow disposed of his possessions and lay with his wife, Moshe Mecheles's appearance made him laugh, as though the whole thing were a kind of prank that he, Nathan, had played on his competitor. Sometimes he felt like calling to him: Hey, there, Moshe Mecheles! while throwing him a bit of plaster or a bone.

As long as there was no snow, Nathan had everything he needed. Roise Temerl visited him often. At night Nathan would go out for a walk on a path that led to the river. But one night a great deal of snow fell, and the next day Roise Temerl did not visit him, for she was afraid someone might notice her tracks in the snow. Nor could Nathan go out to satisfy his natural needs. For two days he had nothing warm to eat, and the water in the pail turned to ice. On the third day Roise Temerl hired a peasant to clear the snow between the house and the granary and she also told him to clear the snow between the granary and the ruin. Moshe Mecheles, when he came home, was surprised and asked, "Why?" but she changed the subject, and since he suspected nothing, he soon forgot about it.

Nathan's life, from then on, became increasingly difficult. After each new snowfall, Roise Temerl cleared the path with a shovel. To keep her neighbors from seeing what went on in the yard, she had the fence repaired. And as a pretext for going to the ruin, she had a ditch for refuse dug close to it. Whenever she saw Nathan, he said it was time for him to take his bundle and leave, but Roise Temerl prevailed on him to wait. "Where will you go?" she asked. "You might, God forbid, drop from exhaustion." According to the almanac, she argued, the winter would be a mild one, and summer would begin early, weeks before Purim, and he only had to get through half the month of Kislev, besides Teveth and Shevat. She told him other things. At times, they did not even speak, but sat silently, holding hands and weeping. Both of them were actually losing strength each day. Nathan grew fatter, more blown up; his belly was full of wind; his legs seemed leaden; and his sight was dimming. He could no longer read his storybooks. Roise Temerl grew thin, like a consumptive, lost her appetite, and could not sleep. Some nights she lay awake, sobbing. And when Moshe Mecheles asked her why, she said it was because she had no children to pray for her after she was gone.

One day a downpour washed away the snow. Since Roise Temerl had not visited the ruin for two days, Nathan expected her to arrive at any moment. He had no food left; only a bit of brandy remained at the bottom of the barrel. For hours on end he stood waiting for her at the window, which was misted over with frost, but she did not come. The night was pitch black and icy. Dogs barked, a wind blew. The walls of the ruin shook; a whistling sound ran through the chimney, and the eaves rattled on the roof. In Nathan's house, now the house of Moshe Mecheles, several lamps seemed to have been lighted; it seemed extraordinarily bright, and the light made the surrounding darkness thicker. Nathan thought he heard the rolling of wheels, as though a carriage had driven to the house. In the darkness, someone drew water from the well, and someone poured out the slops. The night wore on, but despite the late hour, the shutters remained open. Seeing shadows run back and forth, Nathan thought important visitors might have come and were being treated to a banquet. He remained staring into the night until his knees grew weak, and with his last bit of strength, he dragged himself to his bed and fell into a deep sleep.

The cold awoke him early next morning. With stiff limbs he arose and barely propelled himself to the window. More snow had fallen during the night, and a heavy frost had set in. To his amazement, Nathan saw a group of men and women standing around his house. He wondered, anxiously, what was going on. But he did not have to wonder long, for suddenly the door swung open, and four men carried out a coffin hearse covered with a black cloth. "Moshe Mecheles is dead!" Nathan thought. But then he saw Moshe Mecheles following the coffin. It was not he, but Roise Temerl who had died.

Nathan could not weep. It was as though the cold had frozen his tears. Trembling and shaking, he watched the men carrying the coffin, watched the beadle rattling his alms box and the mourners wading through deep snowdrifts. The sky, pale as linen, hung low, meeting the blanketed earth. As though drifting on a flood, the trees in the fields seemed to be afloat in whiteness. From his window, Nathan could see all the way to the cemetery. The coffin moved up and down; the crowd, following it, thinned out and at times vanished entirely, seemed to sink into the ground and then emerge again. Nathan fancied for a moment that the cortege had stopped and no longer advanced, and then, that the people, as well as the corpse, were moving backward. The cortege grew gradually smaller, until it became a black dot. Because the dot ceased to move, Nathan realized that the pallbearers had reached the cemetery, and that he was watching his faithful wife being buried. With the remaining brandy, he washed his hands, for the water in his pail had turned to ice, and he began to murmur the prayer for the dead.

X
Two Faces

Nathan had intended to pack his things and leave during the night, but I, the Chief of the Devils, prevented him from carrying out his plan. Before sunrise he was seized with powerful stomach cramps; his head grew hot and his knees so weak that he could not walk. His shoes had grown brittle; he could not put them on; and his legs had become fat. The Good Spirit counseled him to call for help, to shout until people heard and came to rescue him, because no man may cause his own death, but I said to him: Do you remember the words of King David: "Let me rather fall into God's hands, than into the hands of people?" You don't want Moshe Mecheles and his henchmen to have the satisfaction of revenging themselves on you and jeering. Rather die like a dog. In short, he listened to me, first, because he was proud, and second, because he was not fated to be buried according to law.

Gathering together his last remnants of strength, he pushed his bed to the window, to lie there and watch. He fell asleep early and awoke. There was day, and then night. Sometimes he heard cries in the yard. At other times he thought someone called him by name. His head, he fancied, had grown monstrously large and burdensome, like a millstone carried on his neck. His fingers were wooden, his tongue hard; it seemed bigger than the space it occupied. My helpers, goblins, appeared to him in dreams. They screamed, whistled, kindled fires, walked on stilts, and carried on like Purim players. He dreamed of floods, then of fires, imagined the world had been destroyed, and then that he hovered in the void with bats' wings. In his dreams he also saw pancakes, dumplings, broad noodles with cheese, and when he awoke his stomach was as full as though he had actually eaten; he belched and sighed, and touched his belly that was empty and aching all over.

Once, sitting up, he looked out of the window, and saw to his surprise that people were walking backward, and marveled at this. Soon he saw other extraordinary things. Among those who passed, he recognized men who had long been dead. "Do my eyes deceive me?" he wondered, "Or has Messiah come, and has he resurrected the dead?" The more he looked the more astonished he became. Entire generations passed through the town, men and women with packs on their shoulders and staffs in their hands. He recognized, among them, his father and grandfather, his grandmothers and great-aunts. He watched workers build the Frampol synagogue. They carried bricks, sawed wood, mixed plaster, nailed on eaves. Schoolboys stood about, staring upward and calling a strange word he could not understand, like something in a foreign tongue. As in a dance around the Torah, two storks circled the building. Then the building and builders vanished, and he saw a group of people, barefooted, bearded, wild-eyed, with crosses in their hands, lead a Jew to the gallows. Though the black-bearded young man cried heartrendingly, they dragged him on, tied in ropes. Bells were ringing; the people in the streets ran away and hid. It was midday, but it grew dark as the day of an eclipse of the sun. Finally, the young man cried out: "Shema Yisroel, the Lord our God, the Lord is One," and was left hanging, his tongue lolling out. His legs swayed for a long time, and hosts of crows flew overhead, cawing hoarsely.

On his last night, Nathan dreamed that Roise Temerl and Shifra Zirel were one woman with two faces. He was overjoyed at her appearance. "Why have I not noticed this before?" he wondered. "Why did I have to go through this trouble and anxiety?" He kissed the two-faced female, and she returned his kisses with her doubled lips, pressing against him her two pairs of breasts. He spoke words of love to her, and she responded in two voices. In her four arms and two bosoms, all his questions were answered. There was no longer life and death, here nor there, beginning nor end. "The truth is twofold," Nathan exclaimed. "This is the mystery of all mysteries!"

Without a last confession of his sins, Nathan died that night. I at once transported his soul to the nether abyss. He still wanders to this day in desolate spaces, and has not yet been granted admittance to hell. Moshe Mecheles married again, a young woman this time. She made him pay dearly, soon inherited his fortune, and squandered it. Shifra Zirel became a harlot in Pressburg and died in the poorhouse. The ruin still stands as before, and Nathan's bones still lie there. And, who can tell, perhaps another man, who sees without being seen, is hiding in it.

The Spinoza of Market Street

I

DR. NAHUM FISCHELSON paced back and forth in his garret room in Market Street, Warsaw. Dr. Fischelson was a short, hunched man with a grayish beard, and was quite bald except for a few wisps of hair remaining at the nape of the neck. His nose was as crooked as a beak and his eyes were large, dark, and fluttering like those of some huge bird. It was a hot summer evening, but Dr. Fischelson wore a black coat which reached to his knees, and he had on a stiff collar and a bow tie. From the door he paced slowly to the dormer window set high in the slanting room and back again. One had to mount several steps to look out. A candle in a brass holder was burning on the table and a variety of insects buzzed around the flame. Now and again one of the creatures would fly too close to the fire and sear its wings, or one would ignite and glow on the wick for an instant. At such moments Dr. Fischelson grimaced. His wrinkled face would twitch and beneath his disheveled mustache he would bite his lips. Finally he took a handkerchief from his pocket and waved it at the insects.

"Away from there, fools and imbeciles," he scolded. "You won't get warm here; you'll only burn yourself."

The insects scattered but a second later returned and once more circled the trembling flame. Dr. Fischelson wiped the sweat from his wrinkled forehead and sighed, "Like men they desire nothing but the pleasure of the moment." On the table lay an open book written in Latin, and on its broad-margined pages were notes and comments printed in small letters by Dr. Fischelson. The book was Spinoza's *Ethics* and Dr. Fischelson had been studying it for the last thirty years. He knew every proposition, every proof, every corollary, every note by heart. When he wanted to find a particular passage, he generally opened to the place

Translated by Martha Glicklich and Cecil Hemley

immediately without having to search for it. But, nevertheless, he continued to study the *Ethics* for hours every day with a magnifying glass in his bony hand, murmuring and nodding his head in agreement. The truth was that the more Dr. Fischelson studied, the more puzzling sentences, unclear passages, and cryptic remarks he found. Each sentence contained hints unfathomed by any of the students of Spinoza. Actually the philosopher had anticipated all of the criticisms of pure reason made by Kant and his followers. Dr. Fischelson was writing a commentary on the *Ethics*. He had drawers full of notes and drafts, but it didn't seem that he would ever be able to complete his work. The stomach ailment which had plagued him for years was growing worse from day to day. Now he would get pains in his stomach after only a few mouthfuls of oatmeal. "God in Heaven, it's difficult, very difficult," he would say to himself, using the same intonation as had his father, the late Rabbi of Tishevitz. "It's very, very hard."

Dr. Fischelson was not afraid of dying. To begin with, he was no longer a young man. Secondly, it is stated in the fourth part of the *Ethics* that "a free man thinks of nothing less than of death and his wisdom is a meditation not of death, but of life." Thirdly, it is also said that "the human mind cannot be absolutely destroyed with the human body but there is some part of it that remains eternal." And yet Dr. Fischelson's ulcer (or perhaps it was a cancer) continued to bother him. His tongue was always coated. He belched frequently and emitted a different foul-smelling gas each time. He suffered from heartburn and cramps. At times he felt like vomiting and at other times he was hungry for garlic, onions, and fried foods. He had long ago discarded the medicines prescribed for him by the doctors and had sought his own remedies. He found it beneficial to take grated radish after meals and lie on his bed, belly down, with his head hanging over the side. But these home remedies offered only temporary relief. Some of the doctors he consulted insisted there was nothing the matter with him. "It's just nerves," they told him. "You could live to be a hundred."

But on this particular hot summer night, Dr. Fischelson felt his strength ebbing. His knees were shaky, his pulse weak. He sat down to read and his vision blurred. The letters on the page turned from green to gold. The lines became waved and jumped over each other, leaving white gaps as if the text had disappeared in some mysterious way. The heat was unbearable, flowing down directly from the tin roof; Dr. Fischelson felt he was inside of an oven. Several times he climbed the four steps to the window and thrust his head out into the cool of the evening breeze. He would remain in that position for so long his knees would become wobbly. "Oh it's a fine breeze," he would murmur, "really delightful," and he would recall that according to Spinoza, morality and happiness were identical, and that the most moral deed a man could perform was to indulge in some pleasure which was not contrary to reason.

I I

Dr. Fischelson, standing on the top step at the window and looking out, could see into two worlds. Above him were the heavens, thickly strewn with stars. Dr. Fischelson had never seriously studied astronomy but he could differentiate between the planets, those bodies which like the earth, revolve around the sun, and the fixed stars, themselves distant suns, whose light reaches us a hundred or even a thousand years later. He recognized the constellations which mark the path of the earth in space and that nebulous sash, the Milky Way. Dr. Fischelson owned a small telescope he had bought in Switzerland where he had studied and he particularly enjoyed looking at the moon through it. He could clearly make out on the moon's surface the volcanoes bathed in sunlight and the dark, shadowy craters. He never wearied of gazing at these cracks and crevasses. To him they seemed both near and distant, both substantial and insubstantial. Now and then he would see a shooting star trace a wide arc across the sky and disappear, leaving a fiery trail behind it. Dr. Fischelson would know then that a meteorite had reached our atmosphere, and perhaps some unburned fragment of it had fallen into the ocean or had landed in the desert or perhaps even in some inhabited region. Slowly the stars which had appeared from behind Dr. Fischelson's roof rose until they were shining above the house across the street. Yes, when Dr. Fischelson looked up into the heavens, he became aware of that infinite extension which is, according to Spinoza, one of God's attributes. It comforted Dr. Fischelson to think that although he was only a weak, puny man, a changing mode of the absolutely infinite Substance, he was nevertheless a part of the cosmos, made of the same matter as the celestial bodies; to the extent that he was a part of the Godhead, he knew he could not be destroyed. In such moments, Dr. Fischelson experienced the *Amor dei Intellectualis* which is, according to the philosopher of Amsterdam, the highest perfection of the mind. Dr. Fischelson breathed deeply, lifted his head as high as his stiff collar permitted and actually felt he was whirling in company with the earth, the sun, the stars of the Milky Way, and the infinite host of galaxies known only to infinite thought. His legs became light and weightless and he grasped the window frame with both hands as if afraid he would lose his footing and fly out into eternity.

When Dr. Fischelson tired of observing the sky, his glance dropped to Market Street below. He could see a long strip extending from

Yanash's market to Iron Street with the gas lamps lining it merged into a string of fiery dots. Smoke was issuing from the chimneys on the black, tin roofs; the bakers were heating their ovens, and here and there sparks mingled with the black smoke. The street never looked so noisy and crowded as on a summer evening. Thieves, prostitutes, gamblers, and fences loafed in the square which looked from above like a pretzel covered with poppy seeds. The young men laughed coarsely and the girls shrieked. A peddler with a keg of lemonade on his back pierced the general din with his intermittent cries. A watermelon vendor shouted in a savage voice, and the long knife which he used for cutting the fruit dripped with the blood-like juice. Now and again the street became even more agitated. Fire engines, their heavy wheels clanging, sped by; they were drawn by sturdy black horses which had to be tightly curbed to prevent them from running wild. Next came an ambulance, its siren screaming. Then some thugs had a fight among themselves and the police had to be called. A passerby was robbed and ran about shouting for help. Some wagons loaded with firewood sought to get through into the courtyards where the bakeries were located but the horses could not lift the wheels over the steep curbs and the drivers berated the animals and lashed them with their whips. Sparks rose from the clanging hoofs. It was now long after seven, which was the prescribed closing time for stores, but actually business had only begun. Customers were led in stealthily through back doors. The Russian policemen on the street, having been paid off, noticed nothing of this. Merchants continued to hawk their wares, each seeking to outshout the others.

"Gold, gold, gold," a woman who dealt in rotten oranges shrieked.

"Sugar, sugar, sugar," croaked a dealer of overripe plums.

"Heads, heads, heads," a boy who sold fishheads roared.

Through the window of a Hasidic study house across the way, Dr. Fischelson could see boys with long sidelocks swaying over holy volumes, grimacing and studying aloud in sing-song voices. Butchers, porters, and fruit dealers were drinking beer in the tavern below. Vapor drifted from the tavern's open door like steam from a bathhouse, and there was the sound of loud music. Outside of the tavern, streetwalkers snatched at drunken soldiers and at workers on their way home from the factories. Some of the men carried bundles of wood on their shoulders, reminding Dr. Fischelson of the wicked who are condemned to kindle their own fires in Hell. Husky record players poured out their raspings through open windows. The liturgy of the high holidays alternated with vulgar vaudeville songs.

Dr. Fischelson peered into the half-lit bedlam and cocked his ears. He knew that the behavior of this rabble was the very antithesis of reason. These people were immersed in the vainest of passions, were drunk with emotions, and, according to Spinoza, emotion was never good. Instead of the pleasure they ran after, all they succeeded in obtaining was disease and prison, shame and the suffering that resulted from ignorance. Even the cats which loitered on the roofs here seemed more savage and passionate than those in other parts of the town. They caterwauled with the voices of women in labor, and like demons scampered up walls and leaped onto eaves and balconies. One of the toms paused at Dr. Fischelson's window and let out a howl which made Dr. Fischelson shudder. The doctor stepped from the window and, picking up a broom, brandished it in front of the black beast's glowing, green eyes. "Scat, begone, you ignorant savage!"—and he rapped the broom handle against the roof until the tom ran off.

III

When Dr. Fischelson had returned to Warsaw from Zurich, where he had studied philosophy, a great future had been predicted for him. His friends had known that he was writing an important book on Spinoza. A Jewish Polish journal had invited him to be a contributor; he had been a frequent guest at several wealthy households and he had been made head librarian at the Warsaw synagogue. Although even then he had been considered an old bachelor, the matchmakers had proposed several rich girls for him. But Dr. Fischelson had not taken advantage of these opportunities. He had wanted to be as independent as Spinoza himself. And he had been. But because of his heretical ideas he had come into conflict with the rabbi and had had to resign his post as librarian. For years after that, he had supported himself by giving private lessons in Hebrew and German. Then, when he had become sick, the Berlin Jewish community had voted him a subsidy of five hundred marks a year. This had been made possible through the intervention of the famous Dr. Hildesheimer with whom he corresponded about philosophy. In order to get by on so small a pension, Dr. Fischelson had moved into the attic room and had begun cooking his own meals on a kerosene stove. He had a cupboard which had many drawers, and each drawer was labeled with the food it contained—buckwheat, rice, barley, onions, carrots, potatoes, mushrooms. Once a week Dr. Fischelson put on his wide-brimmed black hat, took a basket in one hand and Spinoza's *Ethics* in the other, and went off to the market for his provisions. While he was waiting to be served, he would open the *Ethics*. The merchants knew him and would motion him to their stalls.

"A fine piece of cheese, Doctor—just melts in your mouth."

"Fresh mushrooms, Doctor, straight from the woods."

"Make way for the doctor, ladies," the butcher would shout. "Please don't block the entrance."

During the early years of his sickness, Dr. Fischelson had still gone in the evening to a café which was frequented by Hebrew teachers and other intellectuals. It had been his habit to sit there and play chess while drinking a half a glass of black coffee. Sometimes he would stop at the bookstores on Holy Cross Street where all sorts of old books and magazines could be purchased cheap. On one occasion a former pupil of his had arranged to meet him at a restaurant one evening. When Dr. Fischelson arrived, he had been surprised to find a group of friends and admirers who forced him to sit at the head of the table while they made speeches about him. But these were things that had happened long ago. Now people were no longer interested in him. He had isolated himself completely and had become a forgotten man. The events of 1905 when the boys of Market Street had begun to organize strikes, throw bombs at police stations, and shoot strike breakers so that the stores were closed even on weekdays had greatly increased his isolation. He began to despise everything associated with the modern Jew—Zionism, socialism, anarchism. The young men in question seemed to him nothing but an ignorant rabble intent on destroying society, society without which no reasonable existence was possible. He still read a Hebrew magazine occasionally, but he felt contempt for modern Hebrew, which had no roots in the Bible or the Mishnah. The spelling of Polish words had changed also. Dr. Fischelson concluded that even the so-called spiritual men had abandoned reason and were doing their utmost to pander to the mob. Now and again he still visited a library and browsed through some of the modern histories of philosophy, but he found that the professors did not understand Spinoza, quoted him incorrectly, attributed their own muddled ideas to the philosopher. Although Dr. Fischelson was well aware that anger was an emotion unworthy of those who walk the path of reason, he would become furious, and would quickly close the book and push it from him. "Idiots," he would mutter, "asses, upstarts." And he would vow never again to look at modern philosophy.

IV

Every three months a special mailman who only delivered money orders brought Dr. Fischelson eighty rubles. He expected his quarterly allotment at the beginning of July but as day after day passed and the tall man with the blond mustache and the shiny buttons did not appear, the doctor grew anxious. He had scarcely a groschen left. Who knows— possibly the Berlin community had rescinded his subsidy; perhaps Dr.

Hildesheimer had died, God forbid; the post office might have made a mistake. Every event has its cause, Dr. Fischelson knew. All was determined, all necessary, and a man of reason had no right to worry. Nevertheless, worry invaded his brain, and buzzed about like the flies. If the worst came to the worst, it occurred to him, he could commit suicide, but then he remembered that Spinoza did not approve of suicide and compared those who took their own lives to the insane.

One day when Dr. Fischelson went out to a store to purchase a composition book, he heard people talking about war. In Serbia somewhere, an Austrian prince had been shot and the Austrians had delivered an ultimatum to the Serbs. The owner of the store, a young man with a yellow beard and shifty yellow eyes, announced, "We are about to have a small war," and he advised Dr. Fischelson to store up food because in the near future there was likely to be a shortage.

Everything happened so quickly. Dr. Fischelson had not even decided whether it was worthwhile to spend four groschen on a newspaper, and already posters had been hung up announcing mobilization. Men were to be seen walking on the street with round, metal tags on their lapels, a sign that they were being drafted. They were followed by their crying wives. One Monday when Dr. Fischelson descended to the street to buy some food with his last kopecks, he found the stores closed. The owners and their wives stood outside and explained that merchandise was unobtainable. But certain special customers were pulled to one side and let in through back doors. On the street all was confusion. Policemen with swords unsheathed could be seen riding on horseback. A large crowd had gathered around the tavern where, at the command of the czar, the tavern's stock of whiskey was being poured into the gutter.

Dr. Fischelson went to his old café. Perhaps he would find some acquaintances there who would advise him. But he did not come across a single person he knew. He decided, then, to visit the rabbi of the synagogue where he had once been librarian, but the sexton with the six-sided skullcap informed him that the rabbi and his family had gone off to the spas. Dr. Fischelson had other old friends in town but he found no one at home. His feet ached from so much walking; black and green spots appeared before his eyes and he felt faint. He stopped and waited for the giddiness to pass. The passers-by jostled him. A dark-eyed high-school girl tried to give him a coin. Although the war had just started, soldiers eight abreast were marching in full battle dress —the men were covered with dust and were sunburnt. Canteens were strapped to their sides and they wore rows of bullets across their chests. The bayonets on their rifles gleamed with a cold, green light. They sang with mournful voices. Along with the men came cannons, each pulled by eight horses; their blind muzzles breathed gloomy terror. Dr. Fischelson felt nauseous. His stomach ached; his intestines seemed about to turn themselves inside out. Cold sweat appeared on his face.

"I'm dying," he thought. "This is the end." Nevertheless, he did manage to drag himself home where he lay down on the iron cot and remained, panting and gasping. He must have dozed off because he imagined that he was in his home town, Tishevitz. He had a sore throat and his mother was busy wrapping a stocking stuffed with hot salt around his neck. He could hear talk going on in the house; something about a candle and about how a frog had bitten him. He wanted to go out into the street but they wouldn't let him because a Catholic procession was passing by. Men in long robes, holding double-edged axes in their hands, were intoning in Latin as they sprinkled holy water. Crosses gleamed; sacred pictures waved in the air. There was an odor of incense and corpses. Suddenly the sky turned a burning red and the whole world started to burn. Bells were ringing; people rushed madly about. Flocks of birds flew overhead, screeching. Dr. Fischelson awoke with a start. His body was covered with sweat and his throat was now actually sore. He tried to meditate about his extraordinary dream, to find its rational connection with what was happening to him and to comprehend it *sub specie eternitatis*, but none of it made sense. "Alas, the brain is a receptacle for nonsense," Dr. Fischelson thought. "This earth belongs to the mad."

And he once more closed his eyes; once more he dozed; once more he dreamed.

V

The eternal laws, apparently, had not yet ordained Dr. Fischelson's end.

There was a door to the left of Dr. Fischelson's attic room which opened off a dark corridor, cluttered with boxes and baskets, in which the odor of fried onions and laundry soap was always present. Behind this door lived a spinster whom the neighbors called Black Dobbe. Dobbe was tall and lean, and as black as a baker's shovel. She had a broken nose and there was a mustache on her upper lip. She spoke with the hoarse voice of a man and she wore men's shoes. For years Black Dobbe had sold breads, rolls, and bagels which she had bought from the baker at the gate of the house. But one day she and the baker had quarreled and she had moved her business to the marketplace and now she dealt in what were called "wrinklers," which was a synonym for cracked eggs. Black Dobbe had no luck with men. Twice she had been engaged to baker's apprentices but in both instances they had returned the engagement contract to her. Some time afterwards she had received an engagement contract from an old man, a glazier who claimed that he was divorced, but it had later come to light that he still had a wife. Black Dobbe had a cousin in America, a shoemaker, and repeatedly she boasted that this cousin was sending her passage, but she remained in Warsaw. She was constantly being teased by the women who would say, "There's no hope for you, Dobbe. You're fated to die an old maid." Dobbe always answered, "I don't intend to be a slave for any man. Let them all rot."

That afternoon Dobbe received a letter from America. Generally she would go to Leizer the tailor and have him read it to her. However, that day Leizer was out and so Dobbe thought of Dr. Fischelson, whom the other tenants considered a convert since he never went to prayer. She knocked on the door of the doctor's room but there was no answer. "The heretic is probably out," Dobbe thought but, nevertheless, she knocked once more, and this time the door moved slightly. She pushed her way in and stood there frightened. Dr. Fischelson lay fully clothed on his bed; his face was as yellow as wax; his Adam's apple stuck out prominently; his beard pointed upward. Dobbe screamed; she was certain that he was dead, but—no—his body moved. Dobbe picked up a glass which stood on the table, ran into the corridor, filled the glass with water from the faucet, hurried back, and threw the water into the face of the unconscious man. Dr. Fischelson shook his head and opened his eyes.

"What's wrong with you?" Dobbe asked. "Are you sick?"

"Thank you very much. No."

"Have you a family? I'll call them."

"No family," Dr. Fischelson said.

Dobbe wanted to fetch the barber from across the street but Dr. Fischelson signified that he didn't wish the barber's assistance. Since Dobbe was not going to the market that day, no "wrinklers" being available, she decided to do a good deed. She assisted the sick man to get off the bed and smoothed down the blanket. Then she undressed Dr. Fischelson and prepared some soup for him on the kerosene stove. The sun never entered Dobbe's room, but here squares of sunlight shimmered on the faded walls. The floor was painted red. Over the bed hung a picture of a man who was wearing a broad frill around his neck and had long hair. "Such an old fellow and yet he keeps his place so nice and clean," Dobbe thought approvingly. Dr. Fischelson asked for the *Ethics*, and she gave it to him disapprovingly. She was certain it was a Gentile prayer book. Then she began bustling about, brought in a pail of water, swept the floor. Dr. Fischelson ate; after he had finished, he was much stronger and Dobbe asked him to read her the letter.

He read it slowly, the paper trembling in his hands. It came from

New York, from Dobbe's cousin. Once more he wrote that he was about to send her a "really important letter" and a ticket to America. By now, Dobbe knew the story by heart and she helped the old man decipher her cousin's scrawl. "He's lying," Dobbe said. "He forgot about me a long time ago." In the evening, Dobbe came again. A candle in a brass holder was burning on the chair next to the bed. Reddish shadows trembled on the walls and ceiling. Dr. Fischelson sat propped up in bed, reading a book. The candle threw a golden light on his forehead which seemed as if cleft in two. A bird had flown in through the window and was perched on the table. For a moment Dobbe was frightened. This man made her think of witches, of black mirrors and corpses wandering around at night and terrifying women. Nevertheless, she took a few steps toward him and inquired, "How are you? Any better?"

"A little, thank you."

"Are you really a convert?" she asked although she wasn't quite sure what the word meant.

"Me, a convert? No, I'm a Jew like any other Jew," Dr. Fischelson answered.

The doctor's assurances made Dobbe feel more at home. She found the bottle of kerosene and lit the stove, and after that she fetched a glass of milk from her room and began cooking kasha. Dr. Fischelson continued to study the *Ethics*, but that evening he could make no sense of the theorems and proofs with their many references to axioms and definitions and other theorems. With trembling hand he raised the book to his eyes and read, "The idea of each modification of the human body does not involve adequate knowledge of the human body itself . . . The idea of the idea of each modification of the human mind does not involve adequate knowledge of the human mind."

V I

Dr. Fischelson was certain he would die any day now. He made out his will, leaving all of his books and manuscripts to the synagogue library. His clothing and furniture would go to Dobbe since she had taken care of him. But death did not come. Rather his health improved. Dobbe returned to her business in the market, but she visited the old man several times a day, prepared soup for him, left him a glass of tea, and told him news of the war. The Germans had occupied Kalish, Bendin, and Cestechow, and they were marching on Warsaw. People said that on a quiet morning one could hear the rumblings of the cannon. Dobbe reported that the casualties were heavy. "They're falling like flies," she said. "What a terrible misfortune for the women."

She couldn't explain why, but the old man's attic room attracted her. She liked to remove the gold-rimmed books from the bookcase, dust them, and then air them on the windowsill. She would climb the few steps to the window and look out through the telescope. She also enjoyed talking to Dr. Fischelson. He told her about Switzerland, where he had studied, of the great cities he had passed through, of the high mounains that were covered with snow even in the summer. His father had been a rabbi, he said, and before he, Dr. Fischelson, had become a student, he had attended a yeshiva. She asked him how many languages he knew and it turned out that he could speak and write Hebrew, Russian, German, and French, in addition to Yiddish. He also knew Latin. Dobbe was astonished that such an educated man should live in an attic room on Market Street. But what amazed her most of all was that although he had the title "Doctor," he couldn't write prescriptions. "Why don't you become a real doctor?" she would ask him. "I am a doctor," he would answer. "I'm just not a physician." "What kind of a doctor?" "A doctor of philosophy." Although she had no idea of what this meant, she felt it must be very important. "Oh, my blessed mother," she would say, "where did you get such a brain?"

Then one evening after Dobbe had given him his crackers and his glass of tea with milk, he began questioning her about where she came from, who her parents were, and why she had not married. Dobbe was surprised. No one had ever asked her such questions. She told him her story in a quiet voice and stayed until eleven o'clock. Her father had been a porter at the kosher butcher shops. Her mother had plucked chickens in the slaughterhouse. The family had lived in a cellar at No. 19 Market Street. When she had been ten, she had become a maid. The man she had worked for had been a fence who bought stolen goods from thieves on the square. Dobbe had had a brother who had gone into the Russian army and had never returned. Her sister had married a coachman in Praga and had died in childbirth. Dobbe told of the battles between the underworld and the revolutionaries in 1905, of blind Itche and his gang and how they collected protection money from the stores, of the thugs who attacked young boys and girls out on Saturday afternoon strolls if they were not paid money for security. She also spoke of the pimps who drove about in carriages and abducted women to be sold in Buenos Aires. Dobbe swore that some men had even sought to inveigle her into a brothel, but that she had run away. She complained of a thousand evils done to her. She had been robbed; her boy friend had been stolen; a competitor had once poured a pint of kerosene into her basket of bagels; her own cousin, the shoemaker, had cheated her out of a hundred rubles before he had left for America. Dr. Fischelson listened to her attentively. He asked her questions, shook his head, and grunted.

"Well, do you believe in God?" he finally asked her.

"I don't know," she answered. "Do you?"

"Yes, I believe."

"Then why don't you go to synagogue?" she asked.

"God is everywhere," he replied. "In the synagogue. In the market-place. In this very room. We ourselves are parts of God."

"Don't say such things," Dobbe said. "You frighten me."

She left the room and Dr. Fischelson was certain she had gone to bed. But he wondered why she had not said good night. "I probably drove her away with my philosophy," he thought. The very next moment he heard her footsteps. She came in carrying a pile of clothing like a peddler.

"I wanted to show you these," she said. "They're my trousseau." And she began to spread out, on the chair, dresses—woolen, silk, velvet. Taking each dress up in turn, she held it to her body. She gave him an account of every item in her trousseau—underwear, shoes, stockings.

"I'm not wasteful," she said. "I'm a saver. I have enough money to go to America."

Then she was silent and her face turned brick-red. She looked at Dr. Fischelson out of the corner of her eyes, timidly, inquisitively. Dr. Fischelson's body suddenly began to shake as if he had the chills. He said, "Very nice, beautiful things." His brow furrowed and he pulled at his beard with two fingers. A sad smile appeared on his toothless mouth and his large fluttering eyes, gazing into the distance through the attic window, also smiled sadly.

VII

The day that Black Dobbe came to the rabbi's chambers and announced that she was to marry Dr. Fischelson, the rabbi's wife thought she had gone mad. But the news had already reached Leizer the tailor, and had spread to the bakery, as well as to other shops. There were those who thought that the "old maid" was very lucky; the doctor, they said, had a vast hoard of money. But there were others who took the view that he was a run-down degenerate who would give her syphilis. Although Dr. Fischelson had insisted that the wedding be a small, quiet one, a host of guests assembled in the rabbi's rooms. The baker's apprentices who generally went about barefoot, and in their underwear, with paper bags on the tops of their heads, now put on light-colored suits, straw hats, yellow shoes, gaudy ties, and they brought with them huge cakes and pans filled with cookies. They had even managed to find a bottle of vodka although liquor was forbidden in wartime. When the bride and groom entered the rabbi's chamber, a murmur arose from the crowd.

The women could not believe their eyes. The woman that they saw was not the one they had known. Dobbe wore a wide-brimmed hat which was amply adorned with cherries, grapes, and plumes, and the dress that she had on was of white silk and was equipped with a train; on her feet were high-heeled shoes, gold in color, and from her thin neck hung a string of imitation pearls. Nor was this all: her fingers sparkled with rings and glittering stones. Her face was veiled. She looked almost like one of those rich brides who were married in the Vienna Hall. The bakers' apprentices whistled mockingly. As for Dr. Fischelson, he was wearing his black coat and broad-toed shoes. He was scarcely able to walk; he was leaning on Dobbe. When he saw the crowd from the doorway, he became frightened and began to retreat, but Dobbe's former employer approached him saying, "Come in, come in, bridegroom. Don't be bashful. We are all brethren now."

The ceremony proceeded according to the law. The rabbi, in a worn satin gaberdine, wrote the marriage contract and then had the bride and groom touch his handkerchief as a token of agreement; the rabbi wiped the point of the pen on his skullcap. Several porters who had been called from the street to make up the quorum supported the canopy. Dr. Fischelson put on a white robe as a reminder of the day of his death and Dobbe walked around him seven times as custom required. The light from the braided candles flickered on the walls. The shadows wavered. Having poured wine into a goblet, the rabbi chanted the benedictions in a sad melody. Dobbe uttered only a single cry. As for the other women, they took out their lace handkerchiefs and stood with them in their hands, grimacing. When the bakers' boys began to whisper wisecracks to each other, the rabbi put a finger to his lips and murmured, *"Eh nu oh,"* as a sign that talking was forbidden. The moment came to slip the wedding ring on the bride's finger, but the bridegroom's hand started to tremble and he had trouble locating Dobbe's index finger. The next thing, according to custom, was the smashing of the glass, but though Dr. Fischelson kicked the goblet several times, it remained unbroken. The girls lowered their heads, pinched each other gleefully, and giggled. Finally one of the apprentices struck the goblet with his heel and it shattered. Even the rabbi could not restrain a smile. After the ceremony the guests drank vodka and ate cookies. Dobbe's former employer came up to Dr. Fischelson and said, *"Mazel tov,"* bridegroom. Your luck should be as good as your wife." "Thank you, thank you," Dr. Fischelson murmured, "but I don't look forward to any luck." He was anxious to return as quickly as possible to his attic room. He felt a pressure in his stomach and his chest ached. His face had become greenish. Dobbe had suddenly become angry. She pulled back her veil and called out to the crowd, "What are you laughing at? This isn't a show." And without picking up the cushion cover in which the gifts were wrapped, she returned with her husband to their rooms on the fifth floor.

Dr. Fischelson lay down on the freshly made bed in his room and began reading the *Ethics*. Dobbe had gone back to her own room. The doctor had explained to her that he was an old man, that he was sick and without strength. He had promised her nothing. Nevertheless she returned wearing a silk nightgown, slippers with pompoms, and with her hair hanging down over her shoulders. There was a smile on her face, and she was bashful and hesitant. Dr. Fischelson trembled and the *Ethics* dropped from his hands. The candle went out. Dobbe groped for Dr. Fischelson in the dark and kissed his mouth. "My dear husband," she whispered to him, *"Mazel tov."*

What happened that night could be called a miracle. If Dr. Fischelson hadn't been convinced that every occurrence is in accordance with the laws of nature, he would have thought that Black Dobbe had bewitched him. Powers long dormant awakened in him. Although he had had only a sip of the benediction wine, he was as if intoxicated. He kissed Dobbe and spoke to her of love. Long-forgotten quotations from Klopstock, Lessing, Goethe, rose to his lips. The pressures and aches stopped. He embraced Dobbe, pressed her to himself, was again a man as in his youth. Dobbe was faint with delight; crying, she murmured things to him in a Warsaw slang which he did not understand. Later, Dr. Fischelson slipped off into the deep sleep young men know. He dreamed that he was in Switzerland and that he was climbing mountains— running, falling, flying. At dawn he opened his eyes; it seemed to him that someone had blown into his ears. Dobbe was snoring. Dr. Fischelson quietly got out of bed. In his long nightshirt he approached the window, walked up the steps and looked out in wonder. Market Street was asleep, breathing with a deep stillness. The gas lamps were flickering. The black shutters on the stores were fastened with iron bars. A cool breeze was blowing. Dr. Fischelson looked up at the sky. The black arch was thickly sown with stars—there were green, red, yellow, blue stars; there were large ones and small ones, winking and steady ones. There were those that were clustered in dense groups and those that were alone. In the higher sphere, apparently, little notice was taken of the fact that a certain Dr. Fischelson had in his declining days married someone called Black Dobbe. Seen from above even the Great War was nothing but a temporary play of the modes. The myriads of fixed stars continued to travel their destined courses in unbounded space. The comets, planets, satellites, asteroids kept circling these shining centers. Worlds were born and died in cosmic upheavals. In the chaos of nebulae, primeval matter was being formed. Now and again a star tore loose, and swept across the sky, leaving behind it a fiery streak. It was the month of August when there are showers of meteors. Yes, the divine substance was extended and had neither beginning nor end; it was absolute, indivisible, eternal, without duration, infinite in its attributes. Its waves and bubbles danced in the universal cauldron, seething with change, following the unbroken chain of causes and effects, and he, Dr. Fischelson, with his unavoidable fate, was part of this. The doctor closed his eyelids and allowed the breeze to cool the sweat on his forehead and stir the hair of his beard. He breathed deeply of the midnight air, supported his shaky hands on the windowsill and murmured, "Divine Spinoza, forgive me. I have become a fool."

The Destruction of Kreshev

I

Reb Bunim Comes to Kreshev

I AM the Primeval Snake, the Evil One, Satan. The Cabala refers to me as Samael and the Jews sometimes call me merely "that one."

It is well known that I love to arrange strange marriages, delighting in such mismatings as an old man with a young girl, an unattractive widow with a youth in his prime, a cripple with a great beauty, a cantor with a deaf woman, a mute with a braggart. Let me tell you about one such "interesting" union I contrived in Kreshev, which is a town on the river San, that enabled me to be properly abusive and gave me the opportunity to perform one of those little stunts that forces the forsaking of both this world and the next between the saying of a yes and a no.

Kreshev is about as large as one of the smallest letters in the smallest prayer books. On two sides of the town there is a thick pine forest and on the third the river San. The peasants in the neighboring villages are poorer and more isolated than any others in the Lublin district and the fields are the most barren. During a good part of the year the roads leading to the larger towns are merely broad trenches of water; one travels by wagon at one's peril. Bears and wolves lurk at the edge of the settlement in winter and often attack a stray cow or calf, occasionally even a human being. And, finally, so that the peasants shall never be rid of their wretchedness, I have instilled in them a burning faith. In that part of the country there is a church in every other village, a shrine at every tenth house. The Virgin stands with rusty halo, holding in her arms Jesus, the infant son of the Jewish carpenter Yossel. To her the aged come—and in the depth of winter kneel down, thus acquiring rheumatism. When May comes we have daily processions of the half-starved chanting with hoarse voices for rain. The incense gives off an acrid odor, and a consumptive drummer beats with all his might to

Translated by Elaine Gottlieb and June Ruth Flaum

frighten me away. Nevertheless, the rains don't come. Or if they do, they are never in time. But that doesn't prevent the people from believing. And so it has continued from time immemorial.

The Jews of Kreshev are both somewhat better informed and more prosperous than the peasants. Their wives are shopkeepers and are skilled in giving false weight and measure. The village peddlers know how to get the peasant women to purchase all sorts of trinkets and thus earn for themselves corn, potatoes, flax, chickens, ducks, geese—and sometimes a little extra. What won't a woman give for a string of beads, a decorated feather duster, a flowered calico, or just a kind word from a stranger? So it is not entirely surprising that here and there among the flaxen-haired children one comes across a curly-haired, black-eyed imp with a hooked nose. The peasants are extremely sound sleepers but the devil does not permit their young women to rest but leads them down back paths to barns where the peddlers wait in the day. Dogs bay at the moon, roosters crow, and God himself dozes among the clouds. The Almighty is old; it is no easy task to live forever.

But let us return to the Jews of Kreshev.

All year round, the marketplace is one deep marsh, for the very good reason that the women empty their slops there. The houses don't stand straight; they are half-sunk into the earth and have patched roofs; their windows are stuffed with rags or covered with ox bladders. The homes of the poor have no floors; some even lack chimneys. In such houses the smoke from the stove escapes through a hole in the roof. The women marry when they are fourteen or fifteen and age quickly from too much childbearing. In Kreshev the cobblers at their low benches have only worn-out, scuffed shoes on which to practice their trade. The tailors have no alternative but to turn the ragged furs brought to them to their third side. The brushmakers comb hog bristles with wooden combs and hoarsely sing fragments of ritual chants and wedding tunes. After market day there is nothing for the storekeepers to do and so they hang around the study house, scratching themselves and leafing through the Talmud or else telling each other amazing stories of monsters and ghosts and werewolves. Obviously in such a town there isn't much for me to do. One is just very hard put to come across a real sin thereabouts. The inhabitants lack both the strength and the inclination. Now and again a seamstress gossips about the rabbi's wife or the water bearer's girl grows large with child, but those are not the sort of things that amuse me. That is why I rarely visit Kreshev.

But at the time I am speaking about there were a few rich men in the town and in a prosperous home anything can happen. So whenever I turned my eyes in that direction, I made sure to see how things were going in the household of Reb Bunim Shor, the community's richest

man. It would take too long to explain in detail how Reb Bunim happened to settle in Kreshev. He had originally lived in Zholkve, which is a
town near Lemberg. He had left there for business reasons. His interest
was lumber and for a very small sum he had purchased a nice tract of
woods from the Kreshev squire. In addition, his wife, Shifrah Tammar
(a woman of distinguished family, granddaughter of the famous scholar
Reb Samuel Edels), suffered from a chronic cough which made her
spit blood, and a Lemberg doctor had recommended that she live in a
wooded area. At any rate, Reb Bunim had moved to Kreshev with all his
possessions, bringing along with him also a grown son and Lise, his ten-
year-old daughter. He had built a house set apart from all the other
dwellings at the end of the synagogue street; and several wagonloads of
furniture, crockery, clothing, books and a host of other things had been
crammed into the building. He had also brought with him a couple of
servants, an old woman and a young man called Mendel, who acted as
Reb Bunim's coachman. The arrival of the new inhabitant restored life
to the town. Now there was work for the young men in Reb Bunim's
forests and Kreshev's coachmen had logs to haul. Reb Bunim repaired
the town's bath and he constructed a new roof for the almshouse.

Reb Bunim was a tall, powerful, large-boned man. He had the voice
of a cantor and a pitch-black beard that ended in two points. He wasn't
much of a scholar and could scarcely get through a chapter of the
Midrash, but he always contributed generously to charity. He could sit
down to a meal and finish at one sitting a loaf of bread and a six-egg
omelet, washing it all down with a quart of milk. Fridays at the bath, he
would climb to the highest perch and would have the attendant beat him
with a bundle of twigs until it was time to light the candles. When he
went into the forest he was accompanied by two fierce hounds, and he
carried a gun. It was said that he could tell at a glance whether a tree
was healthy or rotten. When necessary, he could work eighteen hours on
end and walk for miles on foot. His wife, Shifrah Tammar, had once
been very handsome, but between running to doctors and worrying
about herself, she'd managed to become prematurely old. She was tall
and thin, almost flat-chested, and she had a long, pale face and a beak of
a nose. Her thin lips stayed forever closed and her gray eyes looked
belligerently out at the world. Her periods were painful and when they
came she would take to her bed as though she were mortally ill. In fact,
she was a constant sufferer—one moment it would be a headache, the
next an abscessed tooth or pressure on her abdomen. She was not a fit
mate for Reb Bunim but he was not the sort who complained. Very
likely he was convinced that that was the way it was with all women
since he had married when he was fifteen years old.

There isn't very much to say about his son. He was like his father—

a poor scholar, a voracious eater, a powerful swimmer, an aggressive businessman. He had married a girl from Brod before his father had even moved to Kreshev and had immediately immersed himself in business. He very seldom came to Kreshev. Like his father he had no lack of money. Both of the men were born financiers. They seemed to draw money to them. The way it looked, there didn't appear to be any reason why Reb Bunim and his family would not live out their days in peace as so often happens with ordinary people who because of their simplicity are spared bad luck and go through life without any real problems.

II

The Daughter

But Reb Bunim also had a daughter, and women, as it is well known, bring misfortune.

Lise was both beautiful and well brought up. At twelve she was already as tall as her father. She had blond, almost yellow, hair and her skin was as white and smooth as satin. At times her eyes appeared to be blue and at other times green. Her behavior was a mixture, half Polish lady, half pious Jewish maiden. When she was six her father had engaged a governess to instruct her in religion and grammar. Later Reb Bunim had sent her to a regular teacher and from the very beginning she had shown a great interest in books. On her own she had studied the Scriptures in Yiddish, and dipped into her mother's Yiddish commentary on the Pentateuch. She had also been through *The Inheritance of the Deer, The Rod of Punishment, The Good Heart, The Straight Measure*, and other similar books that she had found in the house. After that, she had managed all by herself to pick up a smattering of Hebrew. Her father had told her repeatedly that it was not proper for a girl to study the Torah and her mother cautioned her that she would be left an old maid since no one wanted a learned wife, but these warnings made little impression on the girl. She continued to study, read *The Duty of the Heart*, and Josephus, familiarized herself with the tales of the Talmud, and in addition learned all sorts of proverbs of the Tanaites and Amorites. She put no limit to her thirst for knowledge. Every time a book peddler wandered into Kreshev she would invite him to the house and buy whatever he had in his sack. After the Sabbath meal her contemporaries, the daughters of the best families of Kreshev, would drop in for a visit. The girls would chatter, play odds and evens, set each other riddles to answer and act as giddily as young girls generally do. Lise was always very polite to her friends, would serve them Sabbath fruits, nuts, cookies, cakes, but she never had much to say—her mind was concerned with weightier matters than dresses and shoes. Yet her manner was always friendly, without the slightest trace of haughtiness in it. On holidays Lise went to the women's synagogue although it was not customary for girls of her age to attend services. On more than one occasion, Reb Bunim, who was devoted to her, would say sorrowfully: "It's a shame that she's not a boy. What a man she would have made."

Shifrah Tammar's feelings were otherwise.

"You're just ruining the girl," she would insist. "If this continues, she won't even know how to bake a potato."

Since there was no competent teacher of secular subjects in Kreshev (Yakel, the community's only teacher, could just about write a single line of legible Yiddish), Reb Bunim sent his daughter to study with Kalman the leech. Kalman was highly esteemed in Kreshev. He knew how to burn out elf-locks, apply leeches, and do operations with just an ordinary breadknife. He owned a caseful of books and manufactured his own pills from the herbs in the field. He was a short, squat man with an enormous belly and as he walked his great weight seemed to make him totter. He looked like one of the local gentry in his plush hat, velvet caftan, knee-length trousers and shoes with buckles. It was the custom in Kreshev to have the procession, taking the bride to the ritual bath, stop for a moment in front of Kalman's porch to serenade him gaily. "Such a man," it was said in town, "must be kept in a good humor. All one can hope is that one never needs him."

But Reb Bunim did need Kalman. The leech was in perpetual attendance upon Shifrah Tammar, and not only did he treat the mother's ailments, but he permitted the daughter to borrow books from his library. Lise read through his whole collection: tomes about medicine, travel books describing distant lands and savage peoples, romantic stories of the nobility, how they hunted and made love, the brilliant balls they gave. Nor was this all. In Kalman's library were also marvelous yarns about sorcerers and strange animals, about knights, kings and princes. Yes, every line of all this Lise read.

Well, now it is time for me to speak about Mendel, Mendel the manservant—Mendel the coachman. No one in Kreshev knew quite where this Mendel had come from. One story was that he'd been a love child who'd been abandoned in the streets. Others said he was the child of a convert. Whatever his origins, he was certainly an ignoramus and was famous not only in Kreshev but for miles around. He literally didn't know his Alef Beth, nor had he ever been seen to pray, although he did own a set of phylacteries. On Friday night all the other men would be at the house of prayer but Mendel would be loitering in the marketplace. He would help the servant girls draw water from the well and would hang around the horses in the stables. Mendel shaved, had discarded his fringed garment, offered no benedictions; he had completely emancipated himself from Jewish custom. On his first appearance in Kreshev, several people had interested themselves in him. He'd been offered free instruction. Several pious ladies had warned him that he'd end up reclining on a bed of nails in Gehenna. But the young man had ignored everyone. He just puckered up his lips and whistled impudently. If some woman assailed him too vigorously, he would snarl back arrogantly: "Oh, you cossack of God, you. Anyway, you won't be in my Gehenna."

And he would take the whip that he always carried with him and use it to hike up the woman's skirt. There would be a great deal of commotion and laughter and the pious lady would vow never again to tangle with Mendel the coachman.

Though he was a heretic that didn't prevent him from being handsome. No, he was very good-looking, tall and lithe, with straight legs and narrow hips and dense black hair which was a little bit curly and a little kinky and in which there were always a few stalks of hay and straw. He had heavy eyebrows which joined together over his nose. His eyes were black, his lips thick. As for his clothing, he went around dressed like a Gentile. He wore riding breeches and boots, a short jacket and a Polish hat with a leather visor which he pulled down in the back until it touched the nape of his neck. He carved whistles from twigs and he also played the fiddle. Another of his hobbies was pigeons and he'd built a coop on top of Reb Bunim's house and occasionally he'd be seen scampering up to the roof to exercise the birds with a long stick. Although he had a room of his own and a perfectly adequate bench-bed, he preferred to sleep in the hay loft, and when he was in the mood he was capable of sleeping for fourteen hours at a stretch. Once there had been so bad a fire in Kreshev that the people had decided to flee the town. At Reb Bunim's house everyone had been looking for Mendel so that he might help pack and carry things away. But there had been no Mendel to be found anywhere. Only after the fire had been put out at last and the excitement had died down had he been discovered in the courtyard, snoring under an apple tree as if nothing had happened.

But Mendel the coachman wasn't only a sleeper. It was well known that he chased the women. One thing, however, could be said for him: he didn't go after the Kreshev maidens. His escapades were always with young peasant girls from the neighboring villages. The attraction that he had for these women seemed almost unnatural. The beer drinkers at the local tavern maintained that Mendel had only to gaze at one of these girls and she would immediately come to him. It was known that more than one had visited him in his attic. Naturally the peasants didn't like this and Mendel had been warned that one of these days they would chop off his head, but he ignored these threats and wallowed deeper and deeper in carnality. There wasn't a village that he had visited with

Reb Bunim where he didn't have his "wives" and families. It almost seemed true that a whistle from him was sufficient sorcery to bring some girl flying to his side. Mendel, however, didn't discuss his power over women. He drank no whiskey, avoided fights, and stayed away from the shoemakers, tailors, hoopers and brushmakers that comprised the poorer population of Kreshev. Nor did they regard him as one of them. He didn't even bother much about money. Reb Bunim, it was said, supplied him with room and board only. But when a Kreshev teamster wanted to hire him and pay him real wages, Mendel remained loyal to the house of Reb Bunim. He apparently did not mind being a slave. His horses and his boots, his pigeons and his girls were the only things that concerned him. So the townspeople gave up on Mendel the coachman.

"A lost soul," they commented. "A Jewish Gentile."

And gradually they became accustomed to him and then forgot him.

III
The Articles of Engagement

As soon as Lise turned fifteen, conjecture began about whom she would marry. Shifrah Tammar was sick, and relations between her and Reb Bunim were strained, so Reb Bunim decided to discuss the matter with his daughter. When the subject was mentioned, Lise became shy and would reply that she would do what her father thought best.

"You have two possibilities," Reb Bunim said during one of these conversations. "The first is a young man from Lublin who comes of a very wealthy family but is no scholar. The other is from Warsaw and a real prodigy. But I must warn you that he doesn't have a cent. Now speak up, girl. The decision is up to you. Which would you prefer?"

"Oh, money," Lise said scornfully. "What value does it have? Money can be lost, but not knowledge." And she turned her gaze downward.

"Then, if I understand you correctly, you prefer the boy from Warsaw?" Reb Bunim said, stroking his long, black beard.

"You know best, Father," Lise whispered.

"One thing in addition that I should mention," he went on, "is that the rich man is very handsome—tall and with blond hair. The scholar is extremely short—a full head shorter than you."

Lise grasped both of her braids and her face turned red and then quickly lost all color. She bit her lip.

"Well, what have you decided, daughter?" Reb Bunim demanded. "You mustn't be ashamed to speak."

Lise began to stammer and her knees trembled from shame. "Where is he?" she asked. "I mean, what does he do?" Where is he studying?"

"The Warsaw boy? He is, may God preserve us, an orphan, and he is at present studying at the Zusmir yeshiva. I am told that he knows the entire Talmud by heart and that he is also a philosopher and a student of the Cabala. He has already written a commentary on Maimonides, I believe."

"Yes," Lise mumbled.

"Does that mean that you want him?"

"Only if you approve, Father."

And she covered her face with both of her hands and ran from the room. Reb Bunim followed her with his eyes. She delighted him—her beauty, chastity, intelligence. She was closer to him than to her mother, and although almost fully grown, would cuddle close to him and run her fingers through his beard. Fridays before he went off to the bathhouse she would have a clean shirt ready for him and on his return before the lighting of the candles she would serve him freshly baked cake and plum stew. He never heard her laughing raucously as did the other young girls nor did she ever go barefoot in his presence. After the Sabbath meal, when he napped, she would walk on tiptoe so as not to wake him. When he was ill, she would put her hand on his forehead to see whether he had fever and would bring all sorts of medicine and tidbits. On more than one occasion Reb Bunim had envied the happy young man who would have her as a wife.

Some days later the people of Kreshev learned that Lise's prospective husband had arrived in town. The young man came in a wagon by himself and he stayed at the house of Rabbi Ozer. Everyone was surprised to see what a scrawny fellow he was, small and thin, with black tousled sidelocks, a pale face and a pointed chin which was barely covered by a few sparse whiskers. His long gaberdine reached to below the ankles. His back was bent and he walked rapidly and as if he didn't know where he was going. The young girls crowded to the windows and watched him pass by. When he arrived at the study house, the men came up to greet him and he immediately began to expatiate in the cleverest possible way. There was no mistaking that this man was a born city dweller.

"Well, you really have some metropolis here," the young man observed.

"No one's claiming that it's Warsaw," one of the town boys commented.

The young cosmopolitan smiled. "One place is pretty much like another," he pointed out. "If they're on the face of the earth, they're all the same."

This said, he began to quote literally from the Babylonian Talmud and the Talmud of Jerusalem, and when he was finished with that, he entertained everyone with news about what was going on in the great world beyond Kreshev. He wasn't himself personally acquainted with Radziwill but he had seen him and he did know a follower of Sabbatai Zevi, the false Messiah. He also had met a Jew who came from Shushan, which was the ancient capital of Persia, and another Jew who had become a convert and studied the Talmud in secret. As if this weren't enough, he began to ask those assembled the most difficult of riddles and, when he tired of that, amused himself by repeating anecdotes of Rabbi Heshl. Somehow or other he managed to convey the additional information that he knew how to play chess, could paint murals employing the twelve signs of the zodiac, and write Hebrew verse which could be read either backwards or forwards and said exactly the same thing no matter how you read it. Nor was this all. This young prodigy, in addition, had studied philosophy and the Cabala, and was an adept in mystical mathematics, being able even to work out the fractions which are to be found in the treatise of Kilaim. It goes without saying that he had had a look at the Zohar and *The Tree of Life* and he knew *The Guide to the Perplexed* as well as his own first name.

He had come to Kreshev looking ragged, but several days after his arrival Reb Bunim outfitted him in a new gaberdine, new shoes, and white stockings, and presented him with a gold watch. And now the young man began to comb his beard and curl his sidelocks. It was not until the signing of the contract that Lise saw the bridegroom, but she had received reports of how learned he was and she was happy that she had chosen him and not the rich young man from Lublin.

The festivities to celebrate the signing of the engagement contract were as noisy as a wedding. Half the town had been invited. As always, the men and women were seated separately and Shloimele, the groom-to-be, made an extremely clever speech and then signed his name with a brilliant flourish. Several of the town's most learned men tried to converse with him on weighty subjects, but his rhetoric and wisdom were too much for them. While the celebration was still going on, and before the serving of the banquet, Reb Bunim broke the usual custom that the bride and groom must not meet before the marriage and let Shloimele into Lise's chamber since the true interpretation of the law is that a man not take a wife unless he has seen her. The young man's gaberdine was unbuttoned, exposing his silk vest and gold watch chain. He appeared a man of the world with his brightly polished shoes and velvet skullcap perched on the top of his head. There was moisture on his high forehead and his cheeks were flushed. Inquisitively, bashfully, he gazed about him with his dark eyes, and his index finger kept twining itself nervously around a fringe of his sash. Lise turned a deep red when she saw him. She had been told that he was not at all good-looking but to her he seemed handsome. And this was the view of the other girls who were present. Somehow or other Shloimele had become much more attractive.

"This is the girl you are to marry," Reb Bunim said. "There's no need for you to be bashful."

Lise had on a black silk dress and around her neck was a string of pearls, which was the present she had been given for this occasion. Her hair appeared almost red under the glow of candlelight, and on the finger of her left hand she wore a ring with the letter "M" inscribed upon it, the first letter of the words *mazel tov*. At the moment of Shloimele's entrance she had been holding an embroidered handkerchief in her hand but upon seeing him it had fallen from her fingers. One of the girls in the room walked over and picked it up.

"It's a very fine evening," Shloimele said to Lise.

"And an excellent summer," answered the bride and her two attendants.

"Perhaps it's a trifle hot," Shloimele observed.

"Yes, it is hot," the three girls answered again in unison.

"Do you think the fault is mine?" Shloimele asked in a sort of singsong. "It is said in the Talmud . . ."

But Shloimele didn't get any further as Lise interrupted him. "I know very well what the Talmud says. 'A donkey is cold even in the month of Tammuz.' "

"Oh, a Talmudic scholar!" Shloimele exclaimed in surprise, and the tips of his ears reddened.

Very soon after that, the conversation ended and everyone began to crowd into the room. But Rabbi Ozer did not approve of the bride and groom meeting before the wedding, and he ordered them to be separated. So Shloimele was once more surrounded only by men and the celebration continued until daybreak.

IV
Love

From the very first moment that she saw him Lise loved Shloimele deeply. At times she believed that his face had been shown to her in a dream before the marriage. At other times she was certain that they had been married before in some other existence. The truth was that I, the Evil Spirit, required so great a love for the furtherance of my schemes.

At night when Lise slept I sought out his spirit and brought it to her and the two of them spoke and kissed and exchanged love tokens. All of her waking thoughts were of him. She held his image within her and addressed it, and this fiction within her replied to her words. She bared her soul to it, and it consoled her and uttered the words of love that she longed to hear. When she put on a dress or a nightgown she imagined that Shloimele was present, and she felt shy and was pleased that her skin was pale and smooth. Occasionally she would ask this apparition those questions which had baffled her since childhood: "Shloimele, what is the sky? How deep is the earth? Why is it hot in summer and cold in the winter? Why do corpses gather at night to pray in the synagogue? How can one see a demon? Why does one see one's reflection in a mirror?"

And she even imagined that Shloimele answered each of these questions. There was one other question that she asked the shadow in her mind: "Shloimele, do you really love me?"

Shloimele reassured her that no other girl was equal to her in beauty. And in her daydreams she saw herself drowning in the river San and Shloimele rescued her. She was abducted by evil spirits and he saved her. Indeed, her mind was all daydreams, so confused had love made her.

But as it happened, Reb Bunim postponed the wedding until the Sabbath after Pentecost and so Lise was forced to wait nearly three-quarters of a year longer. Now, through her impatience, she understood what misery Jacob had undergone when he had been forced to wait seven years before marrying Rachel. Shloimele remained at the rabbi's house and would not be able to visit Lise again until Hanukkah. The young girl often stood at the window in a vain attempt to catch a glimpse of him, for the path from the rabbi's to the study house did not pass Reb Bunim's. The only news that Lise received of him was from the girls who came to see her. One reported that he had grown slightly taller and another said that he was studying the Talmud with the other young men at the study house. A third girl observed that obviously the rabbi's wife was not feeding Shloimele properly, as he had become quite thin. But out of modesty Lise refrained from questioning her friends too closely; nevertheless, she blushed each time her beloved's name was mentioned. In order to make the winter pass more quickly, she began to embroider for her husband-to-be a phylactery bag and a cloth to cover the Sabbath loaf. The bag was of black velvet, upon which she sewed in gold thread a star of David along with Shloimele's name and the date of the month and year. She took even greater pains with the tablecloth, on which were stitched two loaves of bread and a goblet. The words "Holy Sabbath" were done in silver thread, and in the four corners the heads of a stag, a lion, a leopard, and an eagle were embroidered. Nor did she forget to line the seams of the cloth with beads of various colors and she decorated the edges with fringes and tassels. The girls of Kreshev were overwhelmed by her skill and begged to copy the pattern she had used.

Her engagement had altered Lise: she had become even more beautiful. Her skin was white and delicate; her eyes gazed off into space. She moved through the house with the silent step of a somnambulist. From time to time she would smile for no reason at all, and she would stand in front of the mirror for hours on end, arranging her hair and speaking to her reflection as though she had been bewitched. Now if a beggar came to the house she received him graciously and gladly offered him alms. After every meal she went to the poorhouse, bringing soup and meat to the ill and indigent. The poor unfortunates would smile and bless her: "May God grant that you soon eat soup at your wedding."

And Lise quietly added her own "Amen."

Since time continued to hang heavy on her hands, she often browsed among the books in her father's library. There she came across one entitled *The Customs of Marriage* in which it was stated that the bride must purify herself before the ceremony, keep track of her periods and attend the ritual bath. The book also enumerated the wedding rites, told of the period of the seven nuptial benedictions, admonished husband and wife on their proper conduct, paying particular attention to the woman and setting forth a myriad of details. Lise found all of this very interesting since she already had some idea of what went on between the sexes and had even witnessed the love-play of birds and animals. She began to meditate carefully on what she had read, and spent several sleepless nights deep in thought. Her modesty became more intense than it had ever been before, and her face grew flushed and she became feverish; her behavior was so strange that the servant thought she had been bewitched by the evil eye, and sang incantations to cure her. Every time the name of Shloimele was mentioned, she blushed—whether she was included in the reference or not; and whenever anyone approached, she concealed the book of instructions she was forever reading. What was more, she became anxious and suspicious and soon she had got herself into such a state that she both looked forward to the day of marriage and turned away in dread. But Shifrah Tammar just went on preparing her daughter's trousseau. Though estranged from her daughter, she nevertheless wanted the wedding to be so magnificent that the event would live on for years in the minds of the people of Kreshev.

V
The Wedding

The wedding was indeed a grand one. Dressmakers from Lublin had made the bride's garments. For weeks there had been seamstresses at Reb Bunim's house, embroidering and stitching lace on nightgowns, lingerie, and shirtwaists. Lise's wedding gown had been made of white satin and its train was a full four cubits in length. As for food, the cooks had baked a Sabbath loaf which was almost the size of a man and was braided at both ends. Never before had such a bread been seen in Kreshev. Reb Bunim had spared no expense; at his order, sheep, calves, hens, geese, ducks, capons had been slaughtered for the wedding feast. There was also fish from the river San and Hungarian wines and mead supplied by the local innkeeper. The day of the wedding Reb Bunim commanded that the poor of Kreshev be fed, and when word got around an assortment of riffraff from the neighboring district drifted into town to surfeit themselves also. Tables and benches were set up in the street and the beggars were served white Sabbath loaves, stuffed carp, meat stewed in vinegar, gingerbread and tankards of ale. Musicians played for the vagrants and the traditional wedding jester entertained them. The tattered multitude formed circles in the center of the marketplace and danced and jigged delightedly. Everyone was singing and bellowing and the noise was deafening. At evening, the wedding guests began to assemble at Reb Bunim's house. The women wore beaded jackets, headbands, furs, all of their jewelry. The girls had on silk dresses and pointed shoes made especially for the occasion, but inevitably the dressmakers and cobblers had been unable to fill all orders and there were quarrels. There was more than one girl who stayed home, huddling close to the stove the night of the wedding and, unlucky one, weeping her eyes out.

That day Lise fasted and when it was prayer time confessed her sins. She beat her breast as though it were the Day of Atonement for she knew that on one's wedding day all one's transgressions are forgiven. Although she was not particularly pious, and at times even wavered in her faith, as is common with those who are reflective, on this occasion she prayed with great fervor. She also offered up prayers for the man who by the end of the day would have become her husband. When Shifrah Tammar came into the room and saw her daughter standing in a corner with tears in her eyes and beating herself with her fists, she blurted out, "Look at the girl! A real saint!"—and she demanded that Lise stop crying or her eyes would look red and puffy when she stood beneath the canopy.

But you can take my word for it, it was not religious fervor that was causing Lise to weep. For days and weeks before the wedding I had been busy applying myself. All sorts of strange and evil thoughts had been tormenting the girl. One moment she feared that she might not be a virgin at all, and the next she would dream about the instant of deflowering and would burst into tears, fearful that she would not be able to stand the pain. At other times she would be torn by shame, and the very next second would fear that on her wedding night she would perspire unduly, or become sick to her stomach, or wet the bed, or suffer worse humiliation. She also had a suspicion that an enemy had bewitched her, and she searched through her clothing, looking for hidden knots. She wanted to be done with these anxieties but she couldn't control them. "Possibly," she said to herself on one occasion, "I am only dreaming this and I am not to be married at all. Or, perhaps, my husband is some sort of a devil who has materialized in human form and the wedding ceremony will be only a fantasy and the guests, spirits of evil."

This was only one of the nightmares she suffered. She lost her appetite, became constipated, and though she was envied by all the girls in Kreshev, none knew the agony she was undergoing.

Since the bridegroom was an orphan, his father-in-law, Reb Bunim, took care of supplying him with a wardrobe. He ordered for his son-in-law two coats made of fox fur, one for everyday and one for the Sabbath, two gaberdines, one of silk and one of satin, a cloth overcoat, a couple of dressing gowns, several pairs of trousers, a thirteen-pointed hat edged with skunk, as well as a Turkish prayer shawl with three ornaments. Included in the gifts to the bridegroom were a silver spice box upon which a picture of the wailing wall was engraved, a golden citron container, a breadknife with a mother-of-pearl handle, a tobacco box with an ivory lid, a silk-bound set of the Talmud, and a prayer book with silver covers. At the bachelor dinner, Shloimele spoke brilliantly. First of all, he propounded ten questions which seemed to be absolutely basic, and then he answered all ten with a single statement. But after having disposed of these essential questions, he turned around and showed that the questions he had asked were not really questions at all, and the enormous façade of erudition he had erected tumbled to nothing. His audience was left amazed and speechless.

I won't linger too long over the actual ceremony. Suffice it to say that the crowd danced, sang and jumped about the way crowds always do at a wedding, particularly when the richest man in town marries off his daughter. A couple of tailors and shoemakers tried to dance with the serving girls, but were chased away. Several of the guests became drunk and started to jig, shouting "Sabbath, Sabbath." Several of the others sang Yiddish songs which began with words like "What does a poor man cook? Borscht and potatoes . . ." The musicians sawed away on their fiddles, blared with their trumpets, clanged their cymbals, pounded their drums, piped on their flutes and bagpipes. Ancient crones lifted their trains, pushed back their bonnets, and danced, facing each other and clapping hands, but then when their faces almost touched they turned away as if in rage, all of which made the onlookers laugh even more heartily. Shifrah Tammar, despite her usual protestations of bad health (she could scarcely lift her foot from the floor), was recruited by one of the bands of merrymakers and forced to perform both a kozotsky and a scissor dance. As is usual at weddings, I the Arch-Fiend arranged the customary number of jealous spats, displays of vanity and outbursts of wantonness and boasting. When the girls performed the water dance they pulled their skirts up over their ankles as though they were actually wading in the water and the idlers peering in through the windows could not help having their imaginations inflamed. And so anxious was the wedding jester to entertain that he sang countless songs of love for the guests, and corrupted the meaning of Scriptures by interpolating obscenities into the midst of sacred phrases as do the clowns on Purim, and hearing all this, the girls and young matrons clapped their hands and squealed with joy. Suddenly the entertainment was interrupted by a woman's scream. She had lost her brooch and had fainted from anxiety. Though everyone searched high and low, the piece could not be found. A moment later there was more excitement when one of the girls claimed that a young man had pricked her thigh with a needle. This outburst over, it was time for the virtue dance, and while this dance was going on, Shifrah Tammar and the bridesmaids led Lise off to the bridal chamber, which was on the ground floor and so heavily draped and curtained that no light could shine through. On their way to the room the women gave her advice on how to conduct herself, and cautioned her not to be afraid when she saw the groom since the first commandments bid us to propagate and multiply. Shortly after that, Reb Bunim and another man escorted the groom to his bride.

Well, this is one instance when I'm not going to satisfy your curiosity and tell you what went on in the wedding chamber. It is enough to say that when Shifrah Tammar entered the room in the morning, she found her daughter hiding under the quilt and too ashamed to speak to her. Shloimele was already out of bed and in his own room. It took a good deal of coaxing before Lise would permit her mother to examine the sheets, and indeed, there was blood on them.

"*Mazel tov*, daughter," Shifrah Tammar exclaimed. "You are now a woman and share with us all the curse of Eve."

And weeping, she threw her arms about Lise's neck and kissed her.

V I
Strange Behavior

Immediately after the wedding Reb Bunim rode off into the woods to tend to some business, and Shifrah Tammar returned to her sickbed and medicines. The young men at the study house had been of the opinion that once Shloimele was married he would become the head of a yeshiva and dedicate himself to the affairs of the community, which seemed appropriate for a prodigy who was also the son-in-law of a wealthy man. But Shloimele did no such thing. He turned out to be a stay-at-home. He couldn't seem to get to the morning services on time and as soon as the concluding "On us" was said, he was out the door and on his way home. Nor did he think of hanging around after evening prayers. The women around town said that Shloimele went to bed right after supper, and there could be no doubt that the green shutter on his bedroom stayed closed until late in the day. There were also reports from Reb Bunim's maid. She said that the young couple carried on in the most scandalous ways. They were always whispering together, telling each other secrets, consulting books together, and calling each other odd nicknames. They also ate from the same dish, drank from the same goblet, and held hands the way young men and women of the Polish aristocracy did. Once the maid had seen Shloimele hitch up Lise with a sash as if she were a dray horse and then proceed to whip her with a twig. Lise had cooperated in this game by simulating the whinny and gait of a mare. Another game the maid had seen them play was one in which the winner pulls the earlobes of the loser, and she swore that they had continued this nonsense until the ears of both of them had been a blood red.

Yes, the couple were in love, and each day only increased their passion. When he went off to pray she stood at the window watching him disappear as if he were off on some long journey; and when she retired to the kitchen to prepare some broth or a dish of oat grits, Shloimele tagged along or else he immediately called, demanding that she hurry out. On Sabbath, Lise forgot to pray at the synagogue but stood behind the lattice and watched Shloimele in his prayer shawl going about his devotions at the eastern wall. And he, in turn, would gaze upwards at the women's section to catch a glimpse of her. This display also set vicious tongues wagging, but none of this bothered Reb Bunim, who was most gratified to learn how well his daughter and son-in-law got on. Each time he returned from a trip he came bearing presents. But, on the other hand, Shifrah Tammar was very far from pleased. She did not approve of this eccentric behavior, these whispered words of endearment, these perpetual kisses and caresses. Nothing like this had ever happened in her father's house, nor had she even seen such goings-on among ordinary people. She felt disgraced and began rebuking both Lise and Shloimele. This was a kind of conduct that she could not tolerate.

"No, I won't stand for it," she would complain. "The mere thought of it makes me sick." Or she would cry out suddenly: "Not even the Polish nobility make such an exhibition of themselves."

But Lise knew how to answer her. "Wasn't Jacob permitted to show his love for Rachel?" the erudite Lise asked her mother. "Didn't Solomon have a thousand wives?"

"Don't you dare to compare yourself to those saints!" Shifrah Tammar shouted back. "You're not fit to mention their names."

Actually, in her youth Shifrah Tammar had not been very strict in her observances but now she watched over her daughter closely and saw to it that she obeyed all the laws of purity, and would even accompany Lise to the ritual bath to make sure that her immersions were conducted in the prescribed manner. Now and again mother and daughter would quarrel on Friday nights because Lise was late lighting the candles. After the wedding ceremony the bride had had her hair shaved off and begun wearing the customary silk kerchief, but Shifrah Tammar discovered that Lise's hair had grown back and that she would often sit before a mirror now, combing and braiding her curling locks. Shifrah Tammar also exchanged sharp words with her son-in-law. She was displeased that he went so seldom to the study house and spent his time strolling through orchards and fields. Then it became apparent that he had a taste for food and was extremely lazy. He wanted stuffed derma with fritters daily and he made Lise add honey to his milk. As if this were not enough, he'd have plum stews and seed cookies along with raisins and cherry juice sent to his bedroom. At night when they retired, Lise would lock and bolt the bedroom door and Shifrah Tammar would hear the young couple laughing. Once she thought she heard the pair running barefoot across the floor; plaster fell from the ceiling; the chandeliers trembled. Shifrah Tammar had been forced to send a maid upstairs to knock on the door and bid the young lovers be quiet.

Shifrah Tammar's wish had been that Lise would become pregnant quickly and endure the agonies of labor. She had hoped that when Lise became a mother she would be so busy nursing the child, changing its diapers, tending it when it became ill, that she would forget her silliness. But months passed and nothing happened. Lise's face grew more wan, and her eyes burned with a strange fire. The gossip in Kreshev was that the couple were studying the Cabala together.

"It's all very strange," people whispered to each other. "Something weird is going on there."

And the old women sitting on their porches and darning socks or spinning flax had a perpetually interesting topic of conversation. And they listened sharply with their half-deafened ears and shook their heads in indignation.

VII
Secrets of the Chamber

It is now time to reveal the secrets of that bedchamber. There are some for whom it is not enough to satisfy their desires; they must, in addition, utter all sorts of vain words and let their minds wallow in passion. Those who pursue this iniquitous path are inevitably led to melancholy and they enter the Forty-nine Gates of Uncleanliness. The wise men long ago pointed out that everyone knows why a bride steps under the wedding canopy but he who dirties this act through words loses his place in the world to come. The clever Shloimele because of his great learning and his interest in philosophy began to delve more and more into the questions of "he and she." For example, he would suddenly ask while caressing his wife, "Suppose you had chosen that man from Lublin instead of me, do you think you would be lying with him here now?" Such remarks first shocked Lise and she would reply, "But I didn't make that choice. I chose you." Shloimele, however, would not be denied an answer and he would go on talking and proposing even more obscene questions until Lise would finally be forced to admit that if indeed she had picked her husband from Lublin she would unquestionably be lying in his arms and not in those of Shloimele. As if this weren't enough he would also nag her about what she would do if he were to die. "Well," he wanted to know, "would you marry again?" No, no other man could possibly interest her, Lise would insist, but Shloimele would slyly argue with her and through skillful sophistry would undermine her convictions.

"Look, you're still young and attractive. Along would come the matchmaker and shower you with proposals and your father would just not hear of your staying single. So there would be another wedding canopy and another celebration and off you'd be to another marriage bed."

It was useless for Lise to beg him not to talk in such a way since she found the whole subject painful and, in addition, of no value, since it was impossible to foresee the future. No matter what she said, Shloimele continued his sinful words, for they stimulated his passion and at length she grew to enjoy them too, and they were soon spending half their nights whispering questions and answers and wrangling over matters that were beyond anyone's knowledge. So Shloimele wanted to know what she would do if she were shipwrecked on a desert island with only the captain, how she would behave herself if she were among African savages. Suppose she were captured by eunuchs and taken to a sultan's harem, what then? Imagine herself Queen Esther brought before Ahasuerus! And these were only a small part of his imaginings. When she reproached him for being so engrossed in frivolous matters, he undertook the study of Cabala with her, the secrets of intimacy between man and woman and the revelation of conjugal union. Found in Reb Bunim's house were the books *The Tree of Life*, *The Angel Raziel*, and still other volumes of the Cabala and Shloimele told Lise how Jacob, Rachel, Leah, Bilhah, and Zilpah copulate in the higher world, face to face and rump to rump, and the matings of the Holy Father and the Holy Mother, and there were words in these books that simply seemed profane.

And if this were not enough, Shloimele began to reveal to Lise the powers possessed by evil spirits—that they were not only satans, phantoms, devils, imps, hobgoblins and harpies, but that they also held sway over the higher worlds, as for example Nogah, a blend of sanctity and impurity. He produced alleged evidence that the Evil Host had some connection with the world of emanations, and one could infer from Shloimele's words that Satan and God were two equal powers and that they waged constant combat and neither could defeat the other. Another claim of his was that there was no such thing as a sin, since a sin, just as a good deed, can be either big or small and if it is elevated it rises to great heights. He assured her that it is preferable for a man to commit a sin with fervor, than a good deed without enthusiasm, and that yea and nay, darkness and light, right and left, heaven and hell, sanctity and degradation were all images of the divinity and no matter where one sank one remained in the shadow of the Almighty, for beside His light, nothing else exists. He proffered all this information with such rhetoric and strengthened his argument with so many examples that it was a delight to hear him. Lise's thirst to share his company and absorb such revelations increased. Occasionally she felt that Shloimele was luring her from the path of righteousness. His words terrified her and she no longer felt mistress of herself; her soul seemed captive and she thought only what he wanted her to think. But she hadn't the will to stand up to him and she said to herself: "I will go where he leads no matter what happens." Soon he gained such mastery over her that she obeyed him implicitly. And he ruled her at will. He commanded her to strip naked before him, crawl on all fours like an animal, dance before him, sing melodies that he composed half in Hebrew, half in Yiddish, and she obeyed him.

By this time it is quite obvious that Shloimele was a secret disciple of Sabbatai Zevi. For even though the False Messiah was long dead, secret cults of his followers remained in many lands. They met at fairs and markets, recognized each other through secret signs and thus remained safe from the wrath of the other Jews who would excommunicate them. Many rabbis, teachers, ritual slaughterers and other ostensibly respectable folk were included in this sect. Some of them posed as miracle workers, wandering from town to town passing out amulets into which they had introduced not the sacred name of God but unclean names of dogs and evil spirits, Lilith and Asmodeus as well as the name of Sabbatai Zevi himself. All this they managed with such cunning that only the members of the brotherhood could appreciate their handiwork. It provided them great satisfaction to deceive the pious and create havoc. Thus, one disciple of Sabbatai Zevi arrived at a settlement, announced that he was a thaumaturgist and soon many people came to him with chits upon which they'd written their pleas for advice, their problems and requests. Before the counterfeit miracle worker left town, he played his joke and scattered the notes all over the marketplace where they were found by the town rogues, causing disgrace to many. Another cultist was a scribe and placed into the phylacteries, not the passages of law on parchment as prescribed, but filth and goat dung as well as a suggestion that the wearer kiss the scribe's behind. Others of the sect tortured themselves, bathed in icy water, rolled in snow in the winter, subjected themselves to poison ivy in the summer and fasted from Sabbath day to Sabbath day. But these were depraved as well, they sought to corrupt the principles of the Torah and of the Cabala and each of them in his own fashion paid homage to the forces of evil—and Shloimele was one of them.

VIII
Shloimele and Mendel the Coachman

One day, Shifrah Tammar, Lise's mother, died. After the seven days of mourning, Reb Bunim returned to his business affairs and Lise and Shloimele were left to themselves. Having purchased a tract of lumber somewhere in Wolhynia, Reb Bunim maintained horses and oxen there as well as peasants to work them, and, when he left, did not take Mendel the coachman with him. The youth remained in Kreshev. It was summertime and Shloimele and Lise often rode through the countryside in the carriage with Mendel driving. When Lise was busy, the two men went out alone. The fresh pine scent invigorated Shloimele. Also, he enjoyed bathing in the river San, and Mendel would wait on him after they drove to a spot where the water was shallow, for eventually Shloimele would be master of the entire estate.

Thus they became friends. Mendel was nearly two heads taller than Shloimele, and Shloimele admired the coachman's worldly knowledge. Mendel could swim face-up or -down, tread water, catch a fish in the stream with his bare hands and climb the highest trees by the riverbank. Shloimele was afraid of a single cow, but Mendel would chase a whole herd of cattle and had no fear of bulls. He boasted that he could spend a whole night in a cemetery and spoke of having overpowered bears and wolves which attacked him. He claimed victory over a highwayman who had accosted him. In addition, he could play all sorts of tunes on a fife, imitate a crow's cawing, a woodpecker's pecking, cattle's lowing, sheep's and goat's bleating, cat's mewling, and the chirping of crickets. His stunts amused Shloimele, who enjoyed his company. Also he promised to teach Shloimele horseback riding. Even Lise, who used to ignore Mendel, treated him amiably now, sent him on all sorts of errands and offered him honey cake and sweet brandy, for she was a kindly young woman.

Once when the two men were bathing in the river, Shloimele noticed Mendel's physique and admired its masculine attractiveness. His long legs, slim hips, and broad chest all exuded power. After dressing, Shloimele conversed with Mendel, who spoke unrestrainedly of his success among the peasant women, bragging of the women he'd had from nearby villages and the many bastards he had sired. He also numbered among his lovers aristocrats, town women, and prostitutes. Shloimele doubted none of this. When he asked Mendel if he had no fear of retribution, the young man asked what could be done to a corpse. He didn't believe in life after death. He went on expressing himself heretically. Then, puckering his lips and whistling shrilly, he scampered agilely up a tree, knocking down cones and birds' nests. While doing this he roared like a lion, so powerfully that the sound carried for miles, echoing from tree to tree as though hundreds of evil spirits responded to his call.

That night Shloimele told Lise everything that had happened. They discussed the incident in such detail that both of them grew aroused. But Shloimele was not equipped to satisfy his wife's passion. His ardor was greater than his capability and they had to content themselves with lewd talk. Suddenly Shloimele blurted: "Tell me the truth, Lise my love, how would you like to go to bed with Mendel the coachman?"

"God save us, what kind of evil talk is this?" she countered. "Have you lost your mind?"

"Well—? He is a strong and handsome young man—the girls are wild about him . . ."

"Shame on you!" Lise cried. "You defile your mouth!"

"I love defilement!" Shloimele cried, his eyes ablaze. "I am going all the way over to the side of the Host!"

"Shloimele, I'm afraid for you!" Lise said after a long pause. "You're sinking deeper and deeper!"

"One dares everything!" Shloimele said, his knees trembling. " 'Since this generation cannot become completely pure, let it grow completely impure!' "

Lise seemed to shrink and for a long while she was silent. Shloimele could scarcely tell whether she slept or was thinking.

"Were you serious, then?" she asked curiously, her voice muffled.

"Yes, serious."

"And it wouldn't anger you at all?" she demanded.

"No . . . If it brought you pleasure, it would please me as well. You could tell me about it afterwards."

"You're an infidel!" Lise cried out. "A heretic!"

"Yes, so I am! Elisha the son of Abijah was also a heretic! Whoever looks into the vineyard must suffer the consequences."

"You quote the Talmud in answer to everything—watch out, Shloimele! Be on your guard! You're playing with fire!"

"I love fire! I love a holocaust . . . I would like the whole world to burn and Asmodeus to take over the rule."

"Be still!" Lise cried. "Or I shall scream for help."

"What are you afraid of, foolish one?" Shloimele soothed her. "The thought is not the deed. I study with you, I unfold to you the secrets of the Torah, and you remain naïve. Why do you suppose God ordered Hosea to marry a harlot? Why did King David take Bathsheba from Uriah the Hittite and Abigail from Nabal? Why did he, in his old age, order Abeishag the Shunammite brought to him? The noblest ancients practiced adultery. Sin is cleansing! Ah, Lise love, I wish you would obey every whim of mind. I think only of your happiness . . . Even while I guide you to the abyss . . . !"

And he embraced her, caressed and kissed her. Lise lay exhausted and confused by his oratory. The bed beneath her vibrated, the walls shook and it seemed to her that she was already swaying in the net that I, the Prince of Darkness, had spread to receive her.

IX
Adonijah, the Son of Hagith

Strange events followed. Usually Lise did not see very much of Mendel the coachman. She paid little attention to him when they did meet. But since the day Shloimele had spoken to her about Mendel, she seemed to run into him everywhere. She'd walk into the kitchen and find him fooling around with the maid. Confronting Lise, he would grow silent. Soon she began to see him everywhere, in the barn, on horseback, riding toward the river San. Erect as a Cossack he sat, disdainful of saddle or reins. Once when Lise needed water and could not find the maid, she took the pitcher and headed for the well. Suddenly, out of nowhere, Mendel the coachman materialized to help her draw water. One evening as Lise strolled through the meadow (Shloimele happened to be at the study house), the old communal billy goat met her. Lise tried to walk past him, but when she turned off to the right, he blocked her path again. When she turned to the left, he leaped to the left also. At the same time he lowered his pointed horns as if to gore her. Suddenly, rising on his hind legs, he leaned his front legs against her. His eyes were a fiery red, blazing with fury, as if possessed. Lise began to struggle to free herself but he was more powerful than she and almost up-ended her. She screamed and was about to faint when suddenly a loud whistle and the crack of a whip were heard. Mendel the coachman had come upon them, and seeing the struggle, slashed the billy goat across its back with his whip. The thickly knotted thong almost broke the animal's spine. With a choking bleat, he ran off haphazardly. His legs were thickly tufted, tangled with hair. He resembled a wild beast more than a billy goat. Lise was left stunned. For a while, she stared at Mendel silently. Then she shook herself as if waking from a nightmare and said: "Many thanks."

"Such a stupid goat!" Mendel exclaimed. "If ever I get my hands on him again I'll tear his guts out!"

"What was he after?" Lise asked.

"Who knows? Sometimes goats will attack a person. But they'll always go after a woman, never a man!"

"Why is that?—you must be joking!"

"No, I'm serious . . . In a village where I went with the master, there was a billy goat who used to wait for the women as they returned from the ritual bath and attack them. The people asked the rabbi what to do and he ordered the goat slaughtered . . ."

"Really? Why did he have to be killed?"

"So he could no longer gore the women . . ."

Lise thanked him again and thought it miraculous that he had come when he did. In his gleaming boots and riding breeches, whip in hand, the young man faced her with knowing and insolent eyes. Lise was uncertain whether to continue her stroll or return home, since by this time she was afraid of the goat and imagined that it plotted revenge. And the young man, as if reading her mind, offered to escort and protect her. He walked behind her like a guard. After a while, Lise decided to return to the house. Her face was burning, and as she sensed Mendel's eyes upon her, her ankles rubbed together and she stumbled. Sparks were dancing in front of her.

Later when Shloimele came home, Lise wanted to tell him every-thing at once, but she restrained herself. Not until that night after put-ting out the light, did she tell him. Shloimele's astonishment was boundless and he questioned Lise in detail. He kissed and caressed her and the incident seemed to please him immensely. Suddenly he said: "That damned billy goat wanted you—" and Lise asked: "How could a goat possibly want a woman?" He explained that beauty as great as hers could arouse even a goat. At the same time he praised the coach-man for his loyalty and argued that his appearance at the propitious moment had been no accident but a manifestation of love, and that he was ready to go through fire for her. When Lise wondered how Shloimele could know all this, he promised to reveal a secret to her. He directed her to place her hand under his thigh in accordance with ancient custom, imploring her never to reveal a word of this.

When she had obliged him, he began, "Both you and the coachman are reincarnations and descended from a common spiritual source. You, Lise, were in your first existence Abeishag the Shunammite, and he was Adonijah, the son of Hagith. He desired you and sent Bathsheba to King Solomon so that he might surrender you to him for a wife, but since according to the law you were David's widow, his wish was punishable by death and the Horns of the Altar could not protect him, for he was taken away and killed. But law applies only to the body, not the soul. Thus, when one soul lusts for another, the heavens decree that they can find no peace until that lust is gratified. It is written that the Messiah will not come until all passions have been consummated, and because of this, the generations before the Messiah will be completely impure! And when a soul cannot consummate its desire in one existence, it is reincarnated again and again and thus it was with you two. Almost three thousand years now your souls have wandered naked and cannot enter the World of Emanations from where they stem. The forces of Satan have not allowed you two to meet, for then redemption would come. So it happened that when he was a prince, you were a handmaiden, and when you were a princess, he was a slave. In addition, you were separated by oceans. When he sailed to you, the Devil created a storm and sank the ship. There were other obstacles too, and your grief was intense. Now you are both in the same house, but since he is an ignoramus, you shun him. Actually, holy spirits inhabit your bodies, crying out in the dark and longing for union. And you are a married woman because there is a kind of cleansing that can be accomplished through adultery alone. Thus Jacob consorted with two sisters and Jehudah lay with Tamar, his daughter-in-law, and Reuben violated the bed of Bilhah, his own father's concubine, and Hosea took a wife from a brothel, and that is how it was with the rest of them. And know also that the goat was no common goat, but a devil, one of Satan's own and if Mendel hadn't come when he did, the beast would have, God forbid, done you injury."

When Lise inquired if he, Shloimele, were also a reincarnation, he said that he was King Solomon and that he'd returned to earth to nullify the error of his earlier existence, that because of the sin of having Adonijah executed, he was not able to enter the Mansion due him in Paradise. When Lise asked what would follow the correction of the error, if they would all then have to leave the earth, Shloimele replied that he and Lise would subsequently enjoy a long life together but he said nothing of Mendel's future, intimating only that the young man's stay on earth would be a short one. And he made all these statements with the dogmatic absoluteness of the Cabalist to whom no secret is inviolate.

When Lise heard his words, a tremor shook her and she lay there numbed. Lise, familiar with the Scriptures, had often felt a compassion for Adonijah, King David's errant son, who'd lusted for his father's concubine and wished to be king and paid with his head for his rebelliousness. More than once she had wept with pity on reading this chapter in the Book of Kings. She had also pitied Abeishag the Shunammite, the fairest maiden in the land of Israel, who although carnally not known to the king was forced to remain a widow for the rest of her life. It was a revelation to hear that she, Lise, was actually Abeishag the Shunammite and that Adonijah's soul dwelt in Mendel's body.

Suddenly it occurred to her that Mendel indeed resembled Adonijah as she had fancied him in her imagination, and she considered this astonishing. She realized now why his eyes were so black and strange, his hair so thick, why he avoided her and kept himself apart from people and why he gazed at her with such desire. She began to imagine that she could remember her earlier existence as Abeishag the Shunammite and how Adonijah had driven past the palace in a chariot, fifty men running before him, and although she served King Solomon, she'd felt a strong desire to give herself to Adonijah . . . It was as if Shloimele's explanation had unfolded a deep riddle to her and released within her the skein of secrets long past.

That night, the couple did not sleep. Shloimele lay next to her and they conversed quietly until morning. Lise asked questions and Shloimele answered them all reasonably, for my people are notoriously glib, and in her innocence, she believed everything. Even a Cabalist could have been fooled into thinking that these were the words of the living God and that Elijah the Prophet revealed himself to Shloimele. Shloimele's words aroused him to such enthusiasm that he tossed and jerked and his teeth chattered as if he were feverish and the bed swayed beneath him and rivulets of sweat coursed from his body. When Lise realized what she was destined to do, and that Shloimele had to be obeyed, she wept bitterly and soaked her pillow with tears. And Shloimele comforted her and caressed her and divulged to her the innermost secrets of the Cabala. At dawn she lay in a stupor, her strength evaporated, more dead than alive. And thus the power of a false Cabalist and the corrupt words of a disciple of Sabbatai Zevi caused a modest woman to stray from the path of righteousness.

In truth, Shloimele, the villain, devised this whim merely to satisfy his own depraved passions, since he had grown perverse from too much thinking, and what gratified him would make the average person suffer intensely. From an overabundance of lust he had become impotent. Those who understand the complexities of human nature know that joy and pain, ugliness and beauty, love and hate, mercy and cruelty and other conflicting emotions often blend and cannot be separated from each other. Thus I am able not only to make people turn away from the Creator, but to damage their own bodies, all in the name of some imaginary cause.

X
The Repentance

That summer was hot and dry. Reaping their meager corn crop, the peasants sang as though they were keening. Corn grew stunted and half-shriveled. I brought in locusts and birds from the other bank of the river San and what the farmers had labored for the insects devoured. Many cows went dry, probably from spells cast by witches. In the village of Lukoff, not far from Kreshev, a witch was seen riding a hoop and brandishing a broom. Before her ran something with black elflocks, a furry hide and a tail. The millers complained that imps scattered devil's dung in their flour. A herder of horses who tended his animals at night near the marshes, saw hovering in the sky a creature with a crown of thorns and Christians considered this an omen that their Day of Judgment was not far off.

It was the month of Elul. A blight struck the leaves which tore loose from the trees and whirled about in circles in the wind. The heat of the sun blended with the frigid breeze from the Congealed Sea. The birds that migrate to distant lands, held a meeting on the rooftop of the synagogue, chirped, twittered and argued in avian language. Bats swooped about at evening and girls feared leaving their homes, for if a bat got tangled in someone's hair, that person would not live out the year. As usual at this season my disciples, the Shades, began to perpetrate their own brand of mischief. Children were struck down by the measles, the pox, diarrhea, croup and rashes, and although the mothers took the usual protections, measured graves and lit memorial candles, their offspring perished. In the prayer house the ram's horn was sounded several times each day. Blowing the ram's horn, is, as is well known, an effort to drive me away, for when I hear the horn I am supposed to imagine that the Messiah is coming and that God, praised be His name, is about to destroy me. But my ears are not that insensitive that I cannot distinguish between the blast of the Great Shofar and the horn of a Kreshev ram . . .

So you can see I remained alert and arranged a treat for the people of Kreshev that they would not forget in a hurry.

It was during services on a Monday morning. The prayer house was crowded. The sexton was about to take out the Scroll of the Law. He had already turned back the curtain before the Holy Ark and opened the door when suddenly a tumult erupted through the entire chamber. The worshippers stared at the place where the noise had come from. Through the opened doors burst Shloimele. His appearance was shocking. He wore a ragged capote, its lining torn, the lapel ripped as if he were in mourning; he was in stockinged feet as if it were the ninth day of Ab, and about his hips was a rope instead of a sash. He was ashen, his beard tousled, his sidelocks askew. The worshippers could not believe their eyes. He moved quickly to the copper laver and washed his hands. Then he stepped to the reading desk, struck it and cried out in a trembling voice: "Men! I bear evil tidings! Something terrible has happened." In the suddenly still prayer house, the flames in the memorial candles crackled loudly. Presently as in a forest before a storm, a rustle passed through the crowd. Everyone surged closer to the lectern. Prayer books fell to the floor and no one bothered to pick them up. Youngsters climbed up on benches and tables, upon which lay the sacred prayer books, but no one ordered them off. In the women's section there was a commotion and a scuffling. The women were crowding the grate to see what went on below amongst the menfolk.

The aged rabbi, Reb Ozer, was still amongst the living and ruled his flock with an iron hand. Although he wasn't inclined to interrupt the services, he now turned from his place along the eastern wall where he worshipped in prayer shawl and phylacteries and shouted angrily: "What do you want? Speak up!"

"Men, I am a transgressor! A sinner who causes others to sin. Like Jerobom, the son of Nebat!" Shloimele exclaimed and pounded his breast with his fist. "Know ye that I forced my wife into adultery. I confess to everything, I bare my soul!"

Although he spoke quietly, his voice echoed as if the hall were now empty. Something like laughter emanated from the women's section of the synagogue and then it turned to the kind of low wailing that is heard at the evening prayers on the eve of the Day of Atonement. The men seemed petrified. Many thought Shloimele had lost his reason. Others had already heard gossip. After a while Reb Ozer, who had long suspected that Shloimele was a secret follower of Sabbatai Zevi, raised the prayer shawl from his head with trembling hands and draped it about his shoulders. His face with its patches of white beard and sidelocks became a corpse-like yellow.

"What did you do?" the patriarch asked with a cracked voice full of foreboding. "With whom did your wife commit this adultery?"

"With my father-in-law's coachman, that Mendel . . . It's all my fault . . . She did not want to do it, but I persuaded her . . ."

"You?" Reb Ozer seemed about to charge at Shloimele.

"Yes, Rabbi—I."

Reb Ozer stretched out his arm for a pinch of snuff as if to fortify his wasted spirit, but his hand trembled and the snuff slipped from between his fingers. Knees shaking, he was forced to support himself on a stand.

"Why did you do this thing?" he asked feebly.

"I don't know, Rabbi . . . Something came over me!" cried Shloimele, and his puny figure seemed to shrink. "I committed a grave error . . . A grave error!"

"An error?" Reb Ozer demanded and raised one eye. It seemed as if the single eye held a laughter not of this world.

"Yes, an error!" Shloimele said, forlorn, bewildered.

"*Oy vey*—Jews, a fire rages, a fire from Gehenna!" a man with a pitch-black beard and long, disheveled sidelocks cried suddenly. "Our children are dying because of them! Innocent infants who knew nothing of sin!"

With the mention of children, a lament arose from the women's synagogue. It was the mothers remembering their babies who had perished. Since Kreshev was a small town the news spread quickly and a terrible excitement followed. Women mingled with the men, phylacteries fell to the ground, prayer shawls were torn loose. When the crowd quieted, Shloimele started his confession again. He told how he had joined the ranks of the cult of Sabbatai Zevi while still a boy, how he had studied with his fellow disciples, how he had been taught that an excess of degradation meant greater sanctity and that the more heinous the wickedness the closer the day of redemption.

"Men, I am a traitor to Israel!" he wailed. "A heretic from sheer perversity and a whoremonger! I secretly desecrated the Sabbath, ate dairy with meat, neglected my prayers, profaned my prayer books and indulged in every possible iniquity . . . I forced my own wife into adultery! I fooled her into thinking that that bum, Mendel the coachman, was in truth Adonijah the son of Hagith and that she was Abeishag the Shunammite and that they could obtain salvation only through union! I even convinced her that, by sinning, she'd commit a good deed! I have trespassed, been faithless, spoken basely, wrought unrighteousness, been presumptuous and counseled evil."

He screamed in a shrill voice and, each time, beat his bosom. "Spit upon me, Jews. Flail me! Tear me to bits! Judge me!" he cried. "Let me pay for my sins with death."

"Jews, I am not the rabbi of Kreshev but of Sodom!" shouted Reb Ozer, "Sodom and Gomorrah!"

"*Oy*—Satan dances in Kreshev!" wailed the black Jew and clapped his head in both hands. "Satan the Destroyer!"

The man was right. All that day and through the following night I ruled over Kreshev. No one prayed or studied that day, no ram's horn was blown. The frogs in the marshes croaked: "Unclean! Unclean! Unclean!" Crows heralded evil tidings. The community goat went berserk and attacked a woman returning from the ritual bath. In every chimney a demon hovered. From every woman a hobgoblin spoke. Lise was still in bed when the mob overran her house. After shattering the windows with rocks, they stormed her bedroom. When Lise saw the crowds she grew white as the sheet beneath her. She asked to be allowed to dress but they tore the bedding and shredded the silk nightgown from her body, and in such disarray, barefoot and in tatters, her head uncovered, she was dragged off to the house of the rabbi. The young man, Mendel, had just arrived from a village where he had spent several days. Before he even knew what was happening, he was set upon by the butcher boys, tied with ropes, beaten severely and spirited away to the community jail in the anteroom of the synagogue. Since Shloimele had confessed voluntarily, he got away with several facial blows, but of his own free will he stretched out on the threshold of the study house and told everyone who entered or left to spit and walk over him, which is the first penance for the sin of adultery.

XI
The Punishment

Late into the night Reb Ozer sat in the chamber of justice with the ritual slaughterer, the trustee, the seven town elders and other esteemed citizens, listening to the sinners' stories. Although the shutters were closed and the door locked, a curious crowd gathered and the beadle had to keep going out to drive them away. It would take too long to tell all about the shame and depravities detailed by Shloimele and Lise. I'll repeat only a few particulars. Although everyone had supposed Lise would weep and protest her innocence, or simply fall into a faint, she maintained her composure. She answered with clarity every question that the rabbi asked her. When she admitted fornicating with the young man, the rabbi asked how it was possible for a good and intelligent Jewish daughter to do such a thing, and she replied that the blame was all hers, she had sinned and was reconciled to any punishment now. "I know that I've forsaken this world and the next," she said, "and there's no hope for me." She said this as calmly as if the entire chain of events had been a common occurrence, thus astonishing everyone. And when the rabbi asked if she were in love with the young man or if she had sinned under duress she replied that she had acted willingly and of her own accord.

"Perhaps an evil spirit bewitched you?" the rabbi suggested. "Or a spell was cast upon you? Or some dark force compelled you? You could have been in a trance and forgotten the teachings of the Torah and that you were a good Jewish daughter? If this is so—do not deny it!"

But Lise maintained that she knew of no evil spirits, nor demons nor magic nor illusions.

The other men probed further, asked if she'd found knots in her clothing or elflocks in her hair or a yellow stain on the mirror, or a black and blue mark on her body, and she announced that she had encountered nothing. When Shloimele insisted that he had spurred her on and that she was pure of heart, she bowed her head and would neither admit nor deny this. And when the rabbi asked if she regretted her trespasses, she was silent at first, then said: "What's the use of regretting?" and added: "I wish to be judged according to the law—unmercifully." Then she grew silent and it was difficult to get another word out of her.

Mendel confessed that he'd lain with Lise, the daughter of his master, many times; that she'd come to him in his garret and in the garden between the flower beds and that he'd also visited her several times in her own bedroom. Although he had been beaten and his clothing was in shreds, he remained defiant—for as it is written: "Sinners do not repent even at the very gates of Gehenna . . ." and he made uncouth remarks. When one well-respected citizen asked him: "How could you possibly do such a thing?" Mendel snarled: "And why not? She is better than your wife."

At the same time he vilified his inquisitors, called them thieves, gluttons and usurers, claimed that they gave false weight and measure. He also spoke derogatorily of their wives and daughters. He told one worthy that his wife left a trail of refuse behind her; another—that he was too smelly even for his wife, who refused to sleep with him; and made similar observations full of arrogance, mockery and ridicule.

When the rabbi asked him: "Have you no fear? Do you expect to live forever?" he replied that there was no difference between a dead man and a dead horse. The men were so infuriated that they whipped him again and the crowds outside heard his curses while Lise, covering her face with both her hands, sobbed.

Since Shloimele had confessed his sins voluntarily and was prepared to do immediate penance, he was spared and some of the people even addressed him with kindness. Again before the court he related how the disciples of Sabbatai Zevi had ensnarled him in their net when he was a boy and how he had secretly studied their books and manuscripts and come to believe that the deeper one sank in the dregs, the closer one came to the End of Days. And when the rabbi asked why he had not chosen another expression of sin rather than adultery and whether even a man steeped in evil would want his wife defiled, he replied that this particular sin gave him pleasure, that after Lise came to him from the arms of Mendel and they made love, he probed for all the details and this gratified him more than if he had participated in the act himself. When a citizen observed that this was unnatural, Shloimele replied that that was the way it was, all the same. He related that only after she'd lain with Mendel many times and had begun to turn away from him, had he realized that he was losing his beloved wife, and his delight had changed to deep sorrow. He had then tried to change her ways but it was already too late, for she had grown to love the youth, yearned for him and spoke of him day and night. Shloimele also divulged that Lise had given Mendel presents and taken money from her dowry for her lover, who had then bought himself a horse, a saddle and all sorts of trappings. And one day, Lise had told him that Mendel had advised her to divorce her husband and suggested that the two of them flee to a foreign land. Shloimele had still more to reveal. He said that before the affair, Lise had always been truthful, but afterwards she began to protect herself with all sorts of lies and deceptions and finally it came to the point where she put off telling Shloimele about being with Mendel. This statement provoked argument and even violence. The citizens were shocked at these revelations; it was difficult to conceive how so small a town as Kreshev could hide such scandalous actions. Many members of the community were afraid the whole town would suffer God's vengeance and that, Heaven forbid, there would be drought, a Tartar attack, or a flood. The rabbi announced that he would decree a general fast immediately.

Afraid that the townspeople might attack the sinners, or even shed blood, the rabbi and town elders kept Mendel in prison until the following day. Lise, in custody of the women of the Burial Society, was led to the almshouse and locked in a separate room for her own safety. Shloimele remained at the rabbi's house. Refusing to lie in bed, he stretched out on the woodshed floor. Having consulted the elders, the rabbi gave his verdict. The sinners would be led through the town the following day to exemplify the humiliation of those who have forsaken God. Shloimele would then be divorced from Lise, who according to the law was now forbidden to him. Nor would she be permitted to marry Mendel the coachman.

Sentence was executed very early the next morning. Men, women, boys and girls began to assemble in the synagogue courtyard. Truant children climbed to the roof of the study house and the balcony of the women's synagogue in order to see better. Pranksters brought stepladders and stilts. Despite the beadle's warning that the spectacle was to be watched gravely, without jostling or mirth, there was no end of clowning. Although this was their busy pre-holiday season, seamstresses left their work to gloat over the downfall of a daughter of the rich. Tailors, cobblers, barrelmakers and hog-bristle combers clustered about, joked, nudged each other and flirted with the women. In the manner of funeral guests, respectable girls draped shawls about their heads. Women wore double aprons, one before, one behind, as if they were present at the exorcizing of a dybbuk or participating in a levirate marriage ceremony. Merchants closed their shops, artisans left their workbenches. Even the Gentiles came to see the Jews punish their sinners. All eyes were fixed upon the old synagogue from which the sinners would be led to suffer public shame.

The oaken door swung open, accompanied by a humming from the spectators. The butchers led out Mendel—with tied hands, a tattered jacket and the lining of a skullcap on his head. A bruise discolored his forehead. A dark stubble covered his unshaven chin. Arrogantly, he faced the mob and puckered his lips as if to whistle. The butchers held him fast by the elbows for he had already attempted to escape. Catcalls greeted him. Although Shloimele had repented willingly and been spared by the tribunal, he demanded that his punishment be the same as the others. Whistling, shouting and laughter arose when he appeared. He had changed beyond recognition. His face was dead-white. Instead of a gaberdine, a fringed garment and trousers—bits of rag hung from him. One cheek was swollen. Shoeless, holes in his stockings, his bare toes showed. They placed him beside Mendel, and he stood there, bent and stiff as a scarecrow. Many women began to weep at the spectacle as if lamenting one who had died. Some complained that the town elders were cruel and that if Reb Bunim were around such a thing could never take place.

Lise did not appear for a long time. The mob's great curiosity about her caused a terrible crush. Women, in the excitement, lost their headbands. When Lise appeared in the doorway escorted by the Burial Society women, the crowd seemed to freeze. A cry was torn from every throat. Lise's attire had not been altered—but a pudding pot sat upon her head, around her neck hung a necklace of garlic cloves and a dead goose; in one hand she held a broom, in the other a goose-wing duster. Her loins were girdled by a rope of straw. It was plain that the ladies of the Burial Society had toiled with diligence to cause the daughter of a noble and wealthy home to suffer the highest degree of shame and degradation. According to the sentence the sinners were to be led through all the streets in town, to halt before each house, where every man and woman was to spit and heap abuse upon them. The procession began at the house of the rabbi and worked its way down to the homes of the lowest members of the community. Many feared that Lise would collapse and spoil their fun but she was apparently determined to accept her punishment in all its bitterness.

For Kreshev it was like the Feast of Omer in the middle of the month of Elul. Armed with pine cones, bows and arrows, the cheder boys brought food from home, ran wild, screamed and bleated like goats all day. Housewives let their stoves grow cold, the study house was empty. Even the ailing and indigent almshouse occupants came out to attend the Black Feast.

Women whose children were sick or those who still observed the seven days of mourning ran outside their houses to berate the sinners with cries, laments, oaths and clenched fists. Being afraid of Mendel the coachman, who could easily exact revenge, and feeling no real hatred against Shloimele, whom they considered addled, they expressed their fury on Lise. Although the beadle had warned against violence, some of the women pinched and mishandled her. One woman doused her with a bucket of slops, another pelted her with chicken entrails, and she was splattered with all sorts of slime. Because Lise had told the story of the goat and it had made her think of Mendel, town wags had snared the goat and with it in tow followed the procession. Some people whistled, others sang mocking songs. Lise was called: "Harlot, whore, strumpet, wanton, tart, streetwalker, stupid ass, doxie, bitch," and similar names. Fiddlers, a drummer, and a cymbalist played a wedding march alongside the procession. One of the young men, pretending to be the wedding jester, declaimed verses, ribald and profane. The women who escorted Lise tried to humor and comfort her, for this march was her atonement and by repenting she could regain her decency—but she made no response. No one saw her shed a single tear. Nor did she loose her hold on the broom and duster. To Mendel's credit, let me state that he did not oppose his tormentors either. Silently, making no reply to all the abuse, he walked on. As for Shloimele, from the faces he made, it was hard to tell whether he laughed or cried. He walked unsteadily, constantly stopping, until he was pushed and had to go on. He began to limp. Since he had only made others sin, but had not done so himself, he was soon allowed to drop out. A guard accompanied him for protection. Mendel was returned to prison that night. At the rabbi's house, Lise and Shloimele were divorced. When Lise raised both her hands and Shloimele placed the Bill of Divorcement in them, the women lamented.

Men had tears in their eyes. Then Lise was led back to her father's house in the company of the women of the Burial Society.

XII
The Destruction of Kreshev

That night a gale blew as if (as the saying goes) seven witches had hanged themselves. Actually, only one young woman hanged herself— Lise. When the old servant came into her mistress's room in the morning, she found an empty bed. She waited, thinking that Lise was attending to her personal needs, but after a long time had gone by without Lise appearing, the maid went looking for her. She soon found Lise in the attic—hanging from a rope with nothing on her head, barefoot and in her nightgown. She had already grown cold.

The town was shocked. The same women who the day previous had thrown stones at Lise and expressed indignation over her mild punishment wailed now that the community elders had killed a decent Jewish daughter. The men split into two factions. The first faction said that Lise had already paid for her transgressions and that her body should be buried in the cemetery beside her mother's and considered respectable; the second faction argued that she be buried outside the cemetery proper, behind the fence—like other suicides. Members of the second faction maintained that from everything Lise said and did at the chamber of justice, she had died rebellious and unrepentant. The rabbi and community elders were members of the second faction, and they were the ones who triumphed. She was buried at night, behind the fence, by the light of a lantern. Women sobbed, choking. The noise wakened crows nesting in the graveyard trees and they began to caw. Some of the elders asked Lise for forgiveness. Shards were placed over her eyes, according to custom, and a rod between her fingers, so that when the Messiah came she would be able to dig a tunnel from Kreshev to the Holy Land. Since she was a young woman, Kalman the leech was summoned to find out if she was pregnant, for it would have been bad luck to bury an unborn child. The gravedigger said what is said at funerals: "The Rock, His work is perfect, for all His ways are judgment: a God of faithfulness and without iniquity, just and right is He." Handfuls of grass were plucked and thrown over shoulders. The attendants each threw a spadeful of earth into the grave. Although Shloimele no longer was Lise's husband, he walked behind the stretcher and said the Kaddish over her grave. After the funeral he flung himself upon the mound of earth and refused to rise and had to be dragged away by force. And although, according to law, he was exempt from observing the seven days of mourning, he retired to his father-in-law's house and observed all the prescribed rites.

During the period of mourning, several of the townspeople came to pray with Shloimele and offer their condolences, but as though he had vowed eternal silence, he made no response. Ragged and threadbare, peering into the Book of Job, he sat on a footstool, his face waxen, his beard and sidelocks disheveled. A candle flickered in a shard of oil. A rag lay soaking in a glass of water. It was for the soul of the deceased, that she might immerse herself therein. The aged servant brought food for Shloimele but he would take no more than a slice of stale bread with salt. After the seven days of mourning, Shloimele, staff in hand and a pack on his back, went into exile. The townspeople trailed him for a while, trying to dissuade him or to make him wait at least until Reb Bunim returned, but he did not speak, merely shook his head and went on until those who had spoken grew weary and turned back. He was never seen again.

Reb Bunim, meanwhile, detained somewhere in Woliny, had been absorbed in business affairs and knew nothing of his misfortune. A few days before Rosh Hashanah he had a peasant with a wagon take him to Kreshev. He carried numerous gifts for his daughter and son-in-law. One night he stopped at an inn. He asked for news of his family, but although everyone knew what had happened, no one had the courage to tell him. They declared they had heard nothing. And when Reb Bunim treated some of them to whiskey and cake, they reluctantly ate and drank, avoiding his eyes as they offered toasts. Reb Bunim was puzzled by so much reticence.

The town seemed abandoned in the morning, when Reb Bunim rode into Kreshev. The residents had actually fled him. Riding to his house, he saw the shutters closed and barred in midday, and he was frightened. He called Lise, Shloimele and Mendel, but no one answered. The maid too had left the house and lay ill at the almshouse. Finally an old woman appeared from nowhere and told Reb Bunim the terrible news.

"Ah, there is no Lise any more!" the old woman cried, wringing her hands.

"When did she die?" Reb Bunim asked, his face white and frowning. She named the day.

"And where is Shloimele?"

"Gone into exile!" the woman said. "Immediately after the seventh day of mourning . . ."

"Praised be the true Judge!" Reb Bunim offered the benediction for the dead. And he added the sentence from the Book of Job: " 'Naked I came from my mother's womb and naked I will return therein.' "

He went to his room, tore a rent in his lapel, removed his boots and seated himself on the floor. The old woman brought bread, a hard-boiled egg and a bit of ash, as the Law decrees. Gradually she explained to him that his only daughter hadn't died a natural death but had hanged herself. She also explained the reason for her suicide. But Reb Bunim was not shattered by the information, for he was a God-fearing man and accepted whatever punishment came from above, as it is written: "Man is obliged to be grateful for the bad as well as the good," and he maintained his faith and held no resentment against the Lord of the Universe.

On Rosh Hashanah Reb Bunim prayed at the prayer house and chanted his prayers vigorously. Afterwards he ate the holiday meal alone. A maid served him the head of a sheep, apples with honey and a carrot, and he chewed and swayed and sang the table chants. I, the Evil Spirit, tried to tempt the grief-stricken father from the path of righteousness and to fill his spirit with melancholy, for that is the purpose for which the Creator sent me down to earth. But Reb Bunim ignored me and fulfilled the phrase from the proverb: "Thou shalt not answer the fool according to his foolishness." Instead of disputing with me, he studied and prayed, and soon after the Day of Atonement began to construct a Sukkoth booth, and thus occupied his time with the Torah and holy deeds. It is known that I have power only over those who question the ways of God, not those who do holy deeds. And so the holy days passed. He also asked that Mendel the coachman be released from prison so that he might go his own way. Thus Reb Bunim left the town like the saint of whom it is written: "When a saint leaves town, gone is its beauty, its splendor, its glory."

Immediately after the Holy Days, Reb Bunim sold his house and other possessions for a pittance and left Kreshev, because the town reminded him too much of his misfortune. The rabbi and everyone else accompanied him to the road and he left a sum for the study house, the poorhouse, and for other charitable purposes.

Mendel the coachman lingered for a while in neighboring villages. The Kreshev peddlers spoke of how the peasants feared him and of how often he quarreled with them. Some said he had become a horse thief, others a highwayman. There was gossip also that he had visited Lise's grave; his boot marks were discovered in the sand. There were other stories about him. Some people feared that he would exact revenge upon the town—and they were correct. One night a fire broke out. It started in several places at once and despite the rain, flames leaped from house to house until nearly three-quarters of Kreshev was destroyed. The community goat lost its life also. Witnesses swore that Mendel the coachman had started the fire. Since it was bitter cold at the time and many people were left without a roof over their heads, quite a few fell ill, a plague followed, men, women and children perished, and Kreshev was truly destroyed. To this day the town has remained small and poor; it has never been rebuilt to its former size. And this was all because of a sin committed by a husband, a wife, and a coachman. And although it is not customary among Jews to make supplications over the grave of a suicide, the young women who came to visit their parents' graves often stretched out on the mound of earth behind the fence and wept and offered prayers, not only for themselves and their families, but for the soul of the fallen Lise, daughter of Shifrah Tammar. And the custom remains to this day.

Taibele and Her Demon

I

IN the town of Lashnik, not far from Lublin, there lived a man and his wife. His name was Chaim Nossen, hers Taibele. They had no children. Not that the marriage was barren; Taibele had borne her husband a son and two daughters, but all three had died in infancy—one of whooping cough, one of scarlet fever, and one of diphtheria. After that Taibele's womb closed up, and nothing availed: neither prayers, nor spells, nor potions. Grief drove Chaim Nossen to withdraw from the world. He kept apart from his wife, stopped eating meat and no longer slept at home, but on a bench in the prayer house. Taibele owned a dry-goods store, inherited from her parents, and she sat there all day, with a yardstick on her right, a pair of shears on her left, and the women's prayer book in Yiddish in front of her. Chaim Nossen, tall, lean, with black eyes and a wedge of a beard, had always been a morose, silent man even at the best of times. Taibele was small and fair, with blue eyes and a round face. Although punished by the Almighty, she still smiled easily, the dimples playing on her cheeks. She had no one else to cook for now, but she lit the stove or the tripod every day and cooked some porridge or soup for herself. She also went on with her knitting—now a pair of stockings, now a vest; or else she would embroider something on canvas. It wasn't in her nature to rail at fate or cling to sorrow.

One day Chaim Nossen put his prayer shawl and phylacteries, a change of underwear, and a loaf of bread into a sack and left the house. Neighbors asked where he was going; he answered: "Wherever my eyes lead me."

When people told Taibele that her husband had left her, it was too late to catch up with him. He was already across the river. It was discovered that he had hired a cart to take him to Lublin. Taibele sent a messenger to seek him out, but neither her husband nor the messenger

Translated by Mirra Ginsburg

was ever seen again. At thirty-three, Taibele found herself a deserted wife.

After a period of searching, she realized that she had nothing more to hope for. God had taken both her children and her husband. She would never be able to marry again; from now on she would have to live alone. All she had left was her house, her store, and her belongings. The townspeople pitied her, for she was a quiet woman, kindhearted and honest in her business dealings. Everyone asked: how did she deserve such misfortunes? But God's ways are hidden from man.

Taibele had several friends among the town matrons whom she had known since childhood. In the daytime housewives are busy with their pots and pans, but in the evening Taibele's friends often dropped in for a chat. In the summer, they would sit on a bench outside the house, gossiping and telling each other stories.

One moonless summer evening when the town was as dark as Egypt, Taibele sat with her friends on the bench, telling them a tale she had read in a book bought from a peddler. It was about a young Jewish woman, and a demon who had ravished her and lived with her as man and wife. Taibele recounted the story in all its details. The women huddled closer together, joined hands, spat to ward off evil, and laughed the kind of laughter that comes from fear.

One of them asked: "Why didn't she exorcise him with an amulet?"

"Not every demon is frightened of amulets," answered Taibele.

"Why didn't she make a journey to a holy rabbi?"

"The demon warned her that he would choke her if she revealed the secret."

"Woe is me, may the Lord protect us, may no one know of such things!" a woman cried out.

"I'll be afraid to go home now," said another.

"I'll walk with you," a third one promised.

While they were talking, Alchonon, the teacher's helper who hoped one day to become a wedding jester, happened to be passing by. Alchonon, five years a widower, had the reputation of being a wag and a prankster, a man with a screw loose. His steps were silent because the soles of his shoes were worn through and he walked on his bare feet. When he heard Taibele telling the story, he halted to listen. The darkness was so thick, and the women so engrossed in the weird tale, that they did not see him. This Alchonon was a dissipated fellow, full of cunning goatish tricks. On the instant, he formed a mischievous plan.

After the women had gone, Alchonon stole into Taibele's yard. He hid behind a tree and watched through the window. When he saw Taibele go to bed and put out the candle, he slipped into the house. Taibele had not bolted the door; thieves were unheard of in that town. In the hallway, he took off his shabby caftan, his fringed garment, his trousers, and stood as naked as his mother bore him. Then he tiptoed to Taibele's bed. She was almost asleep, when suddenly she saw a figure looming in the dark. She was too terrified to utter a sound.

"Who is it?" she whispered, trembling.

Alchonon replied in a hollow voice: "Don't scream, Taibele. If you cry out, I will destroy you. I am the demon Hurmizah, ruler over darkness, rain, hail, thunder, and wild beasts. I am the evil spirit who espoused the young woman you spoke about tonight. And because you told the story with such relish, I heard your words from the abyss and was filled with lust for your body. Do not try to resist, for I drag away those who refuse to do my will beyond the Mountains of Darkness—to Mount Sair, into a wilderness where man's foot is unknown, where no beast dares to tread, where the earth is of iron and the sky of copper. And I roll them in thorns and in fire, among adders and scorpions, until every bone of their body is ground to dust, and they are lost for eternity in the nether depths. But if you comply with my wish, not a hair of your head will be harmed, and I will send you success in every undertaking..."

Hearing these words, Taibele lay motionless as in a swoon. Her heart fluttered and seemed to stop. She thought her end had come. After a while, she gathered courage and murmured: "What do you want of me? I am a married woman!"

"Your husband is dead. I followed in his funeral procession myself." The voice of the teacher's helper boomed out. "It is true that I cannot go to the rabbi to testify and free you to remarry, for the rabbis don't believe our kind. Besides, I don't dare step across the threshold of the rabbi's chamber—I fear the Holy Scrolls. But I am not lying. Your husband died in an epidemic, and the worms have already gnawed away his nose. And even were he alive, you would not be forbidden to lie with me, for the laws of the *Shulchan Aruch* do not apply to us."

Hurmizah the teacher's helper went on with his persuasions, some sweet, some threatening. He invoked the names of angels and devils, of demonic beasts and of vampires. He swore that Asmodeus, King of the Demons, was his step-uncle. He said that Lilith, Queen of the Evil Spirits, danced for him on one foot and did every manner of thing to please him. Shibtah, the she-devil who stole babies from women in childbed, baked poppyseed cakes for him in Hell's ovens and leavened them with the fat of wizards and black dogs. He argued so long, adducing such witty parables and proverbs, that Taibele was finally obliged to smile, in her extremity. Hurmizah vowed that he had loved Taibele for a long time. He described to her the dresses and shawls she had worn that year and the year before; he told her the secret thoughts that came to her as she kneaded dough, prepared her Sabbath meal, washed herself in the bath, and saw to her needs at the outhouse. He also reminded her of the morning when she had wakened with a black and blue mark on her breast. She had thought it was the pinch of a ghoul. But it was really the mark left by a kiss of Hurmizah's lips, he said.

After a while, the demon got into Taibele's bed and had his will of her. He told her that from then on he would visit her twice a week, on Wednesdays and on Sabbath evenings, for those were the nights when the unholy ones were abroad in the world. He warned her, though, not to divulge to anyone what had befallen her, or even hint at it, on pain of dire punishment: he would pluck out the hair from her skull, pierce her eyes, and bite out her navel. He would cast her into a desolate wilderness where bread was dung and water was blood, and where the wailing of Zalmaveth was heard all day and all night. He commanded Taibele to swear by the bones of her mother that she would keep the secret to her last day. Taibele saw that there was no escape for her. She put her hand on his thigh and swore an oath, and did all that the monster bade her.

Before Hurmizah left, he kissed her long and lustfully, and since he was a demon and not a man, Taibele returned his kisses and moistened his beard with her tears. Evil spirit though he was, he had treated her kindly . . .

When Hurmizah was gone, Taibele sobbed into her pillow until sunrise.

Hurmizah came every Wednesday night and every Sabbath night. Taibele was afraid that she might find herself with child and give birth to some monster with tail and horns—an imp or a mooncalf. But Hurmizah promised to protect her against shame. Taibele asked whether she need go to the ritual bath to cleanse herself after her impure days, but Hurmizah said that the laws concerning menstruation did not extend to those who consorted with the unclean host.

As the saying goes, may God preserve us from all that we can get accustomed to. And so it was with Taibele. In the beginning she had feared that her nocturnal visitant might do her harm, give her boils or elflocks, make her bark like a dog or drink urine, and bring disgrace upon her. But Hurmizah did not whip her or pinch her or spit on her. On the contrary, he caressed her, whispered endearments, made puns and rhymes for her. Sometimes he pulled such pranks and babbled such devil's nonsense, that she was forced to laugh. He tugged at the lobe of her ear and gave her love bites on the shoulder, and in the morning she found the marks of his teeth on her skin. He persuaded her to let her hair grow under her cap and he wove it into braids. He taught her charms and spells, told her about his night-brethren, the demons with whom he flew over ruins and fields of toadstools, over the salt marshes of Sodom, and the frozen wastes of the Sea of Ice. He did not deny that he had other wives, but they were all she-devils; Taibele was the only human wife he possessed. When Taibele asked him the names of his wives, he enumerated them: Namah, Machlath, Aff, Chuldah, Zluchah, Nafkah, and Cheimah. Seven altogether.

He told her that Namah was black as pitch and full of rage. When she quarreled with him, she spat venom and blew fire and smoke through her nostrils.

Machlath had the face of a leech, and those whom she touched with her tongue were forever branded.

Aff loved to adorn herself with silver, emeralds, and diamonds. Her braids were of spun gold. On her ankles she wore bells and bracelets; when she danced, all the deserts rang out with their chiming.

Chuldah had the shape of a cat. She meowed instead of speaking. Her eyes were green as gooseberries. When she copulated, she always chewed bear's liver.

Zluchah was the enemy of brides. She robbed bridegrooms of potency. If a bride stepped outside alone at night during the Seven Nuptial Benedictions, Zluchah danced up to her and the bride lost the power of speech or was taken by a seizure.

Nafkah was lecherous, always betraying him with other demons. She retained his affections only by her vile and insolent talk, which delighted his heart.

Cheimah should have, according to her name, been as vicious as Namah should have been mild, but the reverse was true: Cheimah was a she-devil without gall. She was forever doing charitable deeds, kneading dough for housewives when they were ill, or bringing bread to the homes of the poor.

Thus Hurmizah described his wives, and told Taibele how he disported himself with them, playing tag over roofs and engaging in all sorts of pranks. Ordinarily, a woman is jealous when a man consorts with other women, but how can a human be jealous of a female devil? Quite the contrary. Hurmizah's tales amused Taibele, and she was always plying him with questions. Sometimes he revealed to her mysteries no mortal may know—about God, his angels and seraphs, his heavenly mansions, and the seven heavens. He also told her how sinners, male and female, were tortured in barrels of pitch and caldrons of fiery coals, on beds studded with nails and in pits of snow, and how the Black Angels beat the bodies of the sinners with rods of fire.

The greatest punishment in Hell was tickling, Hurmizah said. There was a certain imp in Hell by the name of Lekish. When Lekish tickled an adulteress on her soles or under the arms, her tormented laughter echoed all the way to the island of Madagascar.

In this way, Hurmizah entertained Taibele all through the night, and soon it came about that she began to miss him when he was away. The summer nights seemed too short, for Hurmizah would leave soon after cockcrow. Even winter nights were not long enough. The truth was that she now loved Hurmizah, and though she knew a woman must not lust after a demon, she longed for him day and night.

II

Although Alchonon had been a widower for many years, match-makers still tried to marry him off. The girls they proposed were from mean homes, widows and divorcees, for a teacher's helper was a poor provider, and Alchonon had besides the reputation of being a shiftless ne'er-do-well. Alchonon dismissed the offers on various pretexts: one woman was too ugly, the other had a foul tongue, the third was a slattern. The matchmakers wondered: how could a teacher's helper who earned nine groschen a week presume to be such a picker and chooser? And how long could a man live alone? But no one can be dragged by force to the wedding canopy.

Alchonon knocked around town—long, lean, tattered, with a red disheveled beard, in a crumpled shirt, with his pointed Adam's apple jumping up and down. He waited for the wedding jester Reb Zekele to die, so that he could take over his job. But Reb Zekele was in no hurry to die; he still enlivened weddings with an inexhaustible flow of quips and rhymes, as in his younger days. Alchonon tried to set up on his own as a teacher for beginners, but no householder would entrust his child to him. Mornings and evenings, he took the boys to and from the cheder. During the day he sat in Reb Itchele the teacher's courtyard, idly whittling wooden pointers, or cutting out paper decorations which were used only once a year, at Pentecost, or modeling figurines from clay. Not far from Taibele's store there was a well, and Alchonon came there many times a day, to draw a pail of water or to take a drink, spilling the water over his red beard. At these times, he would throw a quick glance at Taibele. Taibele pitied him: why was the man knock-ing about all by himself? And Alchonon would say to himself each time: "Woe, Taibele, if you knew the truth!"

Alchonon lived in a garret, in the house of an old widow who was deaf and half-blind. The crone often chided him for not going to the synagogue to pray like other Jews. For as soon as Alchonon had taken the children home, he said a hasty evening prayer and went to bed. Sometimes the old woman thought she heard the teacher's helper get up in the middle of the night and go off somewhere. She asked him where he wandered at night, but Alchonon told her that she had been dreaming. The women who sat on benches in the evenings, knitting socks and gossiping, spread the rumor that after midnight Alchonon turned into a werewolf. Some women said he was consorting with a succubus. Otherwise, why should a man remain so many years without a wife? The rich men would not trust their children to him any longer. He now escorted only the children of the poor, and seldom ate a spoonful of hot food, but had to content himself with dry crusts.

Alchonon became thinner and thinner, but his feet remained as nimble as ever. With his lanky legs, he seemed to stride down the street as though on stilts. He must have suffered constant thirst, for he was always coming down to the well. Sometimes he would merely help a dealer or peasant to water his horse. One day, when Taibele noticed from the distance how his caftan was torn and ragged, she called him into her shop. He threw a frightened glance and turned white.

"I see your caftan is torn," said Taibele. "If you wish, I will advance you a few yards of cloth. You can pay it off later, five pennies a week."

"No."

"Why not?" Taibele asked in astonishment. "I won't haul you before the rabbi if you fall behind. You'll pay when you can."

"No."

And he quickly walked out of the store, fearing she might recognize his voice.

In summertime it was easy to visit Taibele in the middle of the night. Alchonon made his way through back lanes, clutching his caftan around his naked body. In winter, the dressing and undressing in Taibele's cold hallway became increasingly painful. But worst of all were the nights after a fresh snowfall. Alchonon was worried that Taibele or one of the neighbors might notice his tracks. He caught cold and began to cough. One night he got into Taibele's bed with his teeth chattering; he could not warm up for a long time. Afraid that she might discover his hoax, he invented explanations and excuses. But Taibele neither probed nor wished to probe too closely. She had long discovered that a devil had all the habits and frailties of a man. Hurmizah perspired, sneezed, hiccuped, yawned. Sometimes his breath smelled of onion, sometimes of garlic. His body felt like the body of her husband, bony and hairy, with an Adam's apple and a navel. At times, Hurmizah was in a jocular mood, at other times a sigh broke from him. His feet were not goose feet, but human, with nails and frost blisters.

Once Taibele asked him the meaning of these things, and Hurmizah explained: "When one of us consorts with a human female, he assumes the shape of a man. Otherwise, she would die of fright."

Yes, Taibele got used to him and loved him. She was no longer terrified of him or his impish antics. His tales were inexhaustible, but Taibele often found contradictions in them. Like all liars, he had a short memory. He had told her at first that devils were immortal. But one night he asked: "What will you do if I die?"

"But devils don't die!"

"They are taken to the lowest abyss . . ."

That winter there was an epidemic in town. Foul winds came from the river, the woods, and the swamps. Not only children, but adults as well were brought down with the ague. It rained and it hailed. Floods broke the dam on the river. The storms blew off an arm of the windmill. On Wednesday night, when Hurmizah came into Taibele's bed, she noticed that his body was burning hot, but his feet were icy. He shivered and moaned. He tried to entertain her with talk of she-devils, of how they seduced young men, how they cavorted with other devils, splashed about in the ritual bath, tied elflocks in old men's beards, but he was weak and unable to possess her.

She had never seen him in such a wretched state. Her heart misgave her. She asked: "Shall I get you some raspberries with milk?"

Hurmizah replied: "Such remedies are not for our kind."

"What do you do when you get sick?"

"We itch and we scratch . . ."

He spoke little after that. When he kissed Taibele, his breath was sour. He always remained with her until cockcrow, but this time he left early. Taibele lay silent, listening to his movements in the hallway. He had sworn to her that he flew out of the window even when it was closed and sealed, but she heard the door creak. Taibele knew that it was sinful to pray for devils, that one must curse them and blot them from memory; yet she prayed to God for Hurmizah.

She cried out in anguish: "There are so many devils, let there be one more . . ."

On the following Sabbath, Taibele waited in vain for Hurmizah until dawn; he never came. She called him inwardly and muttered the spells he had taught her, but the hallway was silent. Taibele lay benumbed. Hurmizah had once boasted that he had danced for Tubal-cain and Enoch, that he had sat on the roof of Noah's Ark, licked the salt from the nose of Lot's wife, and plucked Ahasuerus by the beard. He had prophesied that she would be reincarnated after a hundred years as a princess, and that he, Hurmizah, would capture her, with the help of his slaves Chittim and Tachtim, and carry her off to the palace of Bashe-math, the wife of Esau. But now he was probably lying somewhere ill, a helpless demon, a lonely orphan—without father or mother, without a faithful wife to care for him. Taibele recalled how his breath came rasping like a saw when he had been with her last; when he blew his nose, there was a whistling in his ear. From Sunday to Wednesday, Taibele went about as one in a dream. On Wednesday she could hardly wait until the clock struck midnight, but the night went, and Hurmizah did not appear. Taibele turned her face to the wall.

The day began, dark as evening. Fine snow dust was falling from the murky sky. The smoke could not rise from the chimneys; it spread over the roofs like ragged sheets. The rooks cawed harshly. Dogs barked. After the miserable night, Taibele had no strength to go to her store. Nevertheless, she dressed and went outside. She saw four pallbearers carrying a stretcher. From under the snow-swept coverlet protruded the blue feet of a corpse. Only the sexton followed the dead man.

Taibele asked who it was, and the sexton answered: "Alchonon, the teacher's helper."

A strange idea came to Taibele—to escort Alchonon, the feckless man who had lived alone and died alone, on his last journey. Who would come to the store today? And what did she care for business? Taibele had lost everything. At least, she would be doing a good deed. She followed the dead on the long road to the cemetery. There she waited while the gravedigger swept away the snow and dug a grave in the frozen earth. They wrapped Alchonon the teacher's helper in a prayer shawl and a cowl, placed shards on his eyes, and stuck between his fingers a myrtle twig that he would use to dig his way to the Holy Land when the Messiah came. Then the grave was closed and the gravedigger recited the Kaddish. A cry broke from Taibele. This Alchonon had lived a lonely life, just as she did. Like her, he left no heir. Yes, Alchonon the teacher's helper had danced his last dance. From Hurmizah's tales, Taibele knew that the deceased did not go straight to Heaven. Every sin creates a devil, and these devils are a man's children after his death. They come to demand their share. They call the dead man Father and roll him through forest and wilderness until the measure of his punishment is filled and he is ready for purification in Hell.

From then on, Taibele remained alone, doubly deserted—by an ascetic and by a devil. She aged quickly. Nothing was left to her of the past except a secret that could never be told and would be believed by no one. There are secrets that the heart cannot reveal to the lips. They are carried to the grave. The willows murmur of them, the rooks caw about them, the gravestones converse about them silently, in the language of stone. The dead will awaken one day, but their secrets will abide with the Almighty and His judgment until the end of all generations.

Alone

I

MANY times in the past I have wished the impossible to happen—and then it happened. But though my wish came true, it was in such a topsy-turvy way that it appeared the Hidden Powers were trying to show me I didn't understand my own needs. That's what occurred that summer in Miami Beach. I had been living in a large hotel full of South American tourists who had come to Miami to cool off, as well as with people like myself who suffered from hay fever. I was fed up with the whole business—splashing about in the ocean with those noisy guests; hearing Spanish all day long; eating heavy meals twice each day. If I read a Yiddish newspaper or book, the others looked at me with astonishment. So it happened that taking a walk one day, I said out loud: "I wish I were alone in a hotel." An imp must have overheard me, for immediately he began to set a trap.

When I came down to breakfast the next morning, I found the hotel lobby in confusion. Guests stood about in small groups, their voices louder than usual. Valises were piled all over. Bellboys were running about pushing carts loaded with clothing. I asked someone what was the matter. "Didn't you hear the announcement over the public-address system? They've closed the hotel." "Why?" I asked. "They're bankrupt." The man moved away, annoyed at my ignorance. Here was a riddle: the hotel was closing! Yet so far as I knew, it did a good business. And how could you suddenly close a hotel with hundreds of guests? But in America I had decided it was better not to ask too many questions.

The air conditioning had already been shut off and the air in the lobby was musty. A long line of guests stood at the cashier's desk to pay their bills. Everywhere there was turmoil. People crushed out cigarettes

Translated by Joel Blocker

on the marble floor. Children tore leaves and flowers off the potted tropical plants. Some South Americans, who only yesterday had pretended to be full-blooded Latins, were now talking loudly in Yiddish. I myself had very little to pack, only one valise. Taking it, I went in search of another hotel. Outside, the burning sun reminded me of the Talmudic story of how, on the plains of Mamre, God had removed the sun from its case so that no strangers would bother Abraham. I felt a little giddy. The days of my bachelorhood came back when, carefree, I used to pack all my belongings in one valise, leave, and within five minutes find myself another room. Passing a small hotel, which looked somewhat run-down, I read the sign: "Off-Season Rates from $2 a Day." What could be cheaper? I went inside. There was no air conditioning. A hunchbacked girl with black piercing eyes stood behind the desk. I asked her if I could have a room.

"The whole hotel," she answered.

"No one is here?"

"Nobody." The girl laughed, displaying a broken row of teeth with large gaps between. She spoke with a Spanish accent.

She had come from Cuba, she told me. I took a room. The hunchback led me into a narrow elevator, which took us up to the third floor. There we walked down a long, dark corridor meagerly lit by a single bulb. She opened a door and let me into my room, like a prisoner into his cell. The window, covered by mosquito netting, looked out over the Atlantic. On the walls the paint was peeling, and the rug on the floor was threadbare and colorless. The bathroom smelled of mildew, the closet of moth repellent. The bed linen, though clean, was damp. I unpacked my things and went downstairs. Everything was mine alone: the swimming pool, the beach, the ocean. In the patio stood a group of dilapidated canvas chairs. All around the sun beat down. The sea was yellow, the waves low and lazy, barely moving, as if they too were fatigued by the stifling heat. Only occasionally, out of duty, they tossed up a few specks of foam. A single sea gull stood on the water trying to decide whether or not to catch a fish. Here before me, drenched in sunlight, was a summer melancholy—odd, since melancholy usually suggests autumn. Mankind, it seemed, had perished in some catastrophe, and I was left, like Noah—but in an empty ark, without sons, without a wife, without any animals. I could have swum naked, nevertheless I put on my bathing suit. The water was so warm, the ocean might have been a bathtub. Loose bunches of seaweed floated about. Shyness had held me back in the first hotel—here it was solitude. Who can play games in an empty world? I could swim a little, but who would rescue me if something went wrong? The Hidden Powers had provided me with an empty hotel—but they could just as easily provide me with an undertow, a deep hole, a shark, or a sea serpent. Those who toy with the unknown must be doubly careful.

After a while I came out of the water and lay down on one of the limp canvas beach chairs. My body was pale, my skull bare, and though my eyes were protected by tinted glasses, the sun's rays glared through. The light-blue sky was cloudless. The air smelled of salt, fish, and mangoes. There was no division, I felt, between the organic and the inorganic. Everything around me, each grain of sand, each pebble, was breathing, growing, lusting. Through the heavenly channels, which, says the Cabala, control the flow of Divine Mercy, came truths impossible to grasp in a northern climate. I had lost all ambition; I felt lazy; my few wants were petty and material—a glass of lemonade or orange juice. In my fancy a hot-eyed woman moved into the hotel for a few nights. I hadn't meant I wanted a hotel completely to myself. The imp had either misunderstood or was pretending to. Like all forms of life, I, too, wanted to be fruitful, wanted to multiply—or at least to go through the motions. I was prepared to forget any moral or aesthetic demands. I was ready to cover my guilt with a sheet and to give way wholly, like a blind man, to the sense of touch. At the same time the eternal question tapped in my brain: Who is behind the world of appearance? Is it Substance with its Infinite Attributes? Is it the Monad of all Monads? Is it the Absolute, Blind Will, the Unconscious? Some kind of superior being has to be hidden in back of all these illusions.

On the sea, oily-yellow near the shore, glassy-green farther out, a sail walked over the water like a shrouded corpse. Bent forward, it looked as if it were trying to call something up from the depths. Overhead flew a small airplane trailing a sign: MARGOLIES' RESTAURANT—KOSHER, 7 COURSES, $1.75. So the Creation had not yet returned to primeval chaos. They still served soup with kasha and kneidlach, knishes and stuffed derma at Margolies' restaurant. In that case perhaps tomorrow I would receive a letter. I had been promised my mail would be forwarded. It was my only link, in Miami, with the outside world. I'm always amazed that someone has written me, taken the trouble to stamp and mail the envelope. I look for cryptic meanings, even on the blank side of the paper.

II

When you are alone, how long the day can be! I read a book and two newspapers, drank a cup of coffee in a cafeteria, worked a crossword puzzle. I stopped at a store that auctioned Oriental rugs, went into another where Wall Street stocks were sold. True, I was on Collins Avenue in Miami Beach, but I felt like a ghost, cut off from everything.

I went into the library and asked a question—the librarian grew frightened. I was like a man who had died, whose space had already been filled. I passed many hotels, each with its special decorations and attractions. The palm trees were topped by half-wilted fans of leaves, and their coconuts hung like heavy testicles. Everything seemed motionless, even the shiny new automobiles gliding over the asphalt. Every object continued its existence with that effortless force which is, perhaps, the essence of all being.

I bought a magazine, but was unable to read past the first few lines. Getting on a bus, I let myself be taken aimlessly over causeways, islands with ponds, streets lined with villas. The inhabitants, building on a wasteland, had planted trees and flowering plants from all parts of the world; they had filled up shallow inlets along the shore; they had created architectural wonders and had worked out elaborate schemes for pleasure. A planned hedonism. But the boredom of the desert remained. No loud music could dispel it, no garishness wipe it out. We passed a cactus plant whose blades and dusty needles had brought forth a red flower. We rode near a lake surrounded by groups of flamingos airing their wings, and the water mirrored their long beaks and pink feathers. An assembly of birds. Wild ducks flew about, quacking—the swampland refused to give way.

I looked out the open window of the bus. All that I saw was new, yet it appeared old and weary: grandmothers with dyed hair and rouged cheeks, girls in bikinis barely covering their shame, tanned young men guzzling Coca-Cola on water skis.

An old man lay sprawled on the deck of a yacht, warming his rheumatic legs, his white-haired chest open to the sun. He smiled wanly. Nearby, the mistress to whom he had willed his fortune picked at her toes with red fingernails, as certain of her charms as that the sun would rise tomorrow. A dog stood at the stern, gazing haughtily at the yacht's wake, yawning.

It took a long time to reach the end of the line. Once there, I got on another bus. We rode past a pier where freshly caught fish were being weighed. Their bizarre colors, gory skin wounds, glassy eyes, mouths full of congealed blood, sharp-pointed teeth—all were evidence of a wickedness as deep as the abyss. Men gutted the fishes with an unholy joy. The bus passed a snake farm, a monkey colony. I saw houses eaten up by termites and a pond of brackish water in which the descendants of the primeval snake crawled and slithered. Parrots screeched with strident voices. At times, strange smells blew in through the bus window, stenches so dense they made my head throb.

Thank God the summer day is shorter in the South than in the North. Evening fell suddenly, without any dusk. Over the lagoons and highways, so thick no light could penetrate, hovered a jungle darkness. Automobiles, headlamps on, slid forward. The moon emerged extraordinarily large and red; it hung in the sky like a geographer's globe bearing a map not of this world. The night had an aura of miracle and cosmic change. A hope I had never forsaken awoke in me: Was I destined to witness an upheaval in the solar system? Perhaps the moon was about to fall down. Perhaps the earth, tearing itself out of its orbit around the sun, would wander into new constellations.

The bus meandered through unknown regions until it returned to Lincoln Road and the fancy stores, half-empty in summer but still stocked with whatever a rich tourist might desire—an ermine wrap, a chinchilla collar, a twelve-carat diamond, an original Picasso drawing. The dandified salesmen, sure in their knowledge that beyond nirvana pulses karma, conversed among themselves in their air-conditioned interiors. I wasn't hungry; nevertheless, I went into a restaurant where a waitress with a newly bleached permanent served me a full meal, quietly and without fuss. I gave her a half-dollar. When I left, my stomach ached and my head was heavy. The late-evening air, baked by the sun, choked me as I came out. On a nearby building a neon sign flashed the temperature—it was ninety-six, and the humidity almost as much! I didn't need a weatherman. Already, lightning flared in the glowing sky, although I didn't hear thunder. A huge cloud was descending from above, thick as a mountain, full of fire and of water. Single drops of rain hit my bald head. The palm trees looked petrified, expecting the onslaught. I hurried back toward my empty hotel, wanting to get there before the rain; besides, I hoped some mail had come for me. But I had covered barely half the distance when the storm broke. One gush and I was drenched as if by a huge wave. A fiery rod lit up the sky and, the same moment, I heard the thunder crack—a sign the lightning was near me. I wanted to run inside somewhere, but chairs blown from nearby porches somersaulted in front of me, blocking my way. Signs were falling down. The top of a palm tree, torn off by the wind, careened past my feet. I saw a second palm tree sheathed in sackcloth, bent to the wind, ready to kneel. In my confusion I kept on running. Sinking into puddles so deep I almost drowned, I rushed forward with the lightness of boyhood. The danger had made me daring, and I screamed and sang, shouting to the storm in its own key. By this time all traffic had stopped, even the automobiles had been abandoned. But I ran on, determined to escape such madness or else go under. I had to get that special-delivery letter, which no one had written and I never received.

I still don't know how I recognized my hotel. I entered the lobby and stood motionless for a few moments, dripping water on the rug. In the mirror across the room, my half-dissolved image reflected itself like a figure in a cubist painting. I managed to get to the elevator and ride up to the third floor. The door of my room stood ajar: inside, mosquitoes, moths, fireflies, and gnats fluttered and buzzed about, sheltering from the storm. The wind had torn down the mosquito net and scattered the papers I had left on the table. The rugs were soaked. I walked over to the window and looked at the ocean. The waves rose like mountains in the middle of seas—monstrous billows ready once and for all to over-flow the shores and float the land away. The waters roared with spite and sprayed white foam into the darkness of the night. The waves were barking at the Creator like packs of hounds. With all the strength I had left, I pulled the window down and lowered the blind. I squatted to put my wet books and manuscripts in order. I was hot. Sweat poured from my body, mingling with rivulets of rain water. I peeled off my clothes and they lay near my feet like shells. I felt like a creature who has just emerged from a cocoon.

III

The storm had still not reached its climax. The howling wind knocked and banged as if with mighty hammers. The hotel seemed like a ship floating on the ocean. Something came off and crashed down—the roof, a balcony, part of the foundation. Iron bars broke. Metal groaned. Windows tore loose from their casements. The windowpanes rattled. The heavy blind on my window billowed up as easily as a curtain. The room was lit with the glare of a great conflagration. Then came a clap of thunder so strong I laughed in fear. A white figure materialized from the darkness. My heart plummeted, my brain trembled in its socket. I al-ways knew that sooner or later one of that brood would show himself to me bodily, full of horrors that are never told because no one who has seen them has survived to tell the story. I lay there silently, ready for the end.

Then I heard a voice: "Excuse please, señor, I am much afraid. You are asleep?" It was the Cuban hunchback.

"No, come in," I answered her.

"I shake. I think I die with fear," the woman said. "A hurricane like this never come before. You are the only one in this hotel. Please excuse that I disturb you."

"You aren't disturbing me. I would put on the light but I'm not dressed."

"No, no. It is not necessary . . . I am afraid to be alone. Please let me stay here until the storm is over."

"Certainly. You can lie down if you want. I'll sit on the chair."

"No, I will sit on the chair. Where is the chair, señor? I do not see it."

I got up, found the woman in the darkness, and led her to the armchair. She dragged herself after me, trembling. I wanted to go to the closet and get some clothing. But I stumbled into the bed and fell on top of it. I covered myself quickly with the sheet so that the stranger would not see me naked when the lightning flashed. Soon after, there was another bolt and I saw her sitting in the chair, a deformed creature in an overlarge nightgown, with a hunched back, disheveled hair, long hairy arms, and crooked legs, like a tubercular monkey. Her eyes were wide with an animal's fear.

"Don't be afraid," I said. "The storm will soon be over."

"Yes, yes."

I rested my head on the pillow and lay still with the eerie feeling that the mocking imp was fulfilling my last wish. I had wanted a hotel to myself—and I had it. I had dreamed of a woman coming, like Ruth to Boaz, to my room—a woman had come. Each time the lightning flashed, my eyes met hers. She stared at me intently, as silent as a witch casting a spell. I feared the woman more than I did the hurricane. I had visited Havana once and, there, found the forces of darkness still in possession of their ancient powers. Not even the dead were left in peace —their bones were dug up. At night I had heard the screams of cannibals and the cries of maidens whose blood was sprinkled on the altars of idolaters. She came from there. I wanted to pronounce an incantation against the evil eye and pray to the spirits who have the final word not to let this hag overpower me. Something in me cried out: *Shaddai*, destroy Satan. Meanwhile, the thunder crashed, the seas roared and broke with watery laughter. The walls of my room turned scarlet. In the hellish glare the Cuban witch crouched low like an animal ready to seize its prey—mouth open, showing rotted teeth; matted hair, black on her arms and legs; and feet covered with carbuncles and bunions. Her nightgown had slipped down, and her wrinkled breasts sagged weightlessly. Only the snout and tail were missing.

I must have slept. In my dream I entered a town of steep, narrow streets and barred shutters, under the murky light of an eclipse, in the silence of a Black Sabbath. Catholic funeral processions followed one after the other endlessly, with crosses and coffins, halberds and burning torches. Not one but many corpses were being carried to the graveyard —a complete tribe annihilated. Incense burned. Moaning voices cried a song of utter grief. Swiftly, the coffins changed and took on the form of phylacteries, black and shiny, with knots and thongs. They divided into

many compartments—coffins for twins, triplets, quadruplets, quintup-
lets . . .

I opened my eyes. Somebody was sitting on my bed—the Cuban
woman. She began to talk thickly in her broken English.

"Do not fear. I won't hurt you. I am a human being, not a beast. My
back is broken. But I was not born this way. I fell off a table when I was
a child. My mother was too poor to take me to the doctor. My father, he
no good, always drunk. He go with bad women, and my mother, she
work in a tobacco factory. She cough out her lungs. Why do you shake?
A hunchback is not contagious. You will not catch it from me. I have
a soul like anyone else—men desire me. Even my boss. He trust me and
leave me here in the hotel alone. You are a Jew, eh? He is also a Jew . . .
from Turkey. He can speak—how do you say it?—Arabic. He marry a
German señora, but she is a Nazi. Her first husband was a Nazi. She
curse the boss and try to poison him. He sue her but the judge is on her
side. I think she bribe him—or give him something else. The boss, he
has to pay her—how do you call it?—alimony."

"Why did he marry her in the first place?" I asked, just to say
something.

"Well, he love her. He is very much a man, red blood, you know.
You have been in love?"

"Yes."

"Where is the señora? Did you marry her?"

"No. They shot her."

"Who?"

"Those same Nazis."

"Uh-huh . . . and you were left alone?"

"No, I have a wife."

"Where is your wife?"

"In New York."

"And you are true to her, eh?"

"Yes, I'm faithful."

"Always?"

"Always."

"One time to have fun is all right."

"No, my dear, I want to live out my life honestly."

"Who cares what you do? No one see."

"God sees."

"Well, if you speak of God, I go. But you are a liar. If I not a
cripple, you no speak of God. He punish such lies, you pig!"

She spat on me, then got off the bed, and slammed the door behind
her. I wiped myself off immediately, but her spittle burned me as if it

were hot. I felt my forehead puffing up in the darkness, and my skin itched with a drawing sensation, as if leeches were sucking my blood. I went into the bathroom to wash myself. I wet a towel for a compress and wrapped it around my forehead. I had forgotten about the hurricane. It had stopped without my noticing. I went to sleep, and when I woke up again it was almost noon. My nose was stopped up, my throat was tight, my knees ached. My lower lip was swollen and had broken out in a large cold sore. My clothes were still on the floor, soaking in a huge puddle. The insects that had come in for refuge the night before were clamped to the wall, dead. I opened the window. The air blowing in was cool, though still humid. The sky was an autumn gray and the sea leaden, barely rocking under its own heaviness. I managed to dress and go downstairs. Behind the desk stood the hunchback, pale, thin, with her hair drawn back, and a glint in her black eyes. She wore an old-fashioned blouse edged with yellowed lace. She glanced at me mockingly. "You have to move out," she said. "The boss call and tell me to lock up the hotel."

"Isn't there a letter for me?"

"No letter."

"Please give me my bill."

"No bill."

The Cuban woman looked at me crookedly—a witch who had failed in her witchcraft, a silent partner of the demons surrounding me and of their cunning tricks.

Yentl the Yeshiva Boy

I

AFTER her father's death, Yentl had no reason to remain in Yanev. She was all alone in the house. To be sure, lodgers were willing to move in and pay rent; and the marriage brokers flocked to her door with offers from Lublin, Tomashev, Zamosc. But Yentl didn't want to get married. Inside her, a voice repeated over and over: "No!" What becomes of a girl when the wedding's over? Right away she starts bearing and rearing. And her mother-in-law lords it over her. Yentl knew she wasn't cut out for a woman's life. She couldn't sew, she couldn't knit. She let the food burn and the milk boil over; her Sabbath pudding never turned out right, and her hallah dough didn't rise. Yentl much preferred men's activities to women's. Her father, Reb Todros, may he rest in peace, during many bedridden years had studied Torah with his daughter as if she were a son. He told Yentl to lock the doors and drape the windows, then together they pored over the Pentateuch, the Mishnah, the Gemara, and the Commentaries. She had proved so apt a pupil that her father used to say:

"Yentl—you have the soul of a man."

"So why was I born a woman?"

"Even Heaven makes mistakes."

There was no doubt about it, Yentl was unlike any of the girls in Yanev—tall, thin, bony, with small breasts and narrow hips. On Sabbath afternoons, when her father slept, she would dress up in his trousers, his fringed garment, his silk coat, his skullcap, his velvet hat, and study her reflection in the mirror. She looked like a dark, handsome young man. There was even a slight down on her upper lip. Only her thick braids showed her womanhood—and if it came to that, hair could always be shorn. Yentl conceived a plan and day and night she could

Translated by Marion Magid and Elizabeth Pollet

think of nothing else. No, she had not been created for the noodle board and the pudding dish, for chattering with silly women and pushing for a place at the butcher's block. Her father had told her so many tales of yeshivas, rabbis, men of letters! Her head was full of Talmudic disputations, questions and answers, learned phrases. Secretly, she had even smoked her father's long pipe.

Yentl told the dealers she wanted to sell the house and go to live in Kalish with an aunt. The neighborhood women tried to talk her out of it, and the marriage brokers said she was crazy, that she was more likely to make a good match right here in Yanev. But Yentl was obstinate. She was in such a rush that she sold the house to the first bidder, and let the furniture go for a song. All she realized from her inheritance was one hundred and forty rubles. Then late one night in the month of Av, while Yanev slept, Yentl cut off her braids, arranged sidelocks at her temples, and dressed herself in her father's clothes. Packing underclothes, phylacteries, and a few books into a straw suitcase, she started off on foot for Lublin.

On the main road, Yentl got a ride in a carriage that took her as far as Zamosc. From there, she again set out on foot. She stopped at an inn along the way, and gave her name there as Anshel, after an uncle who had died. The inn was crowded with young men journeying to study with famous rabbis. An argument was in progress over the merits of various yeshivas, some praising those of Lithuania, others claiming that study was more intensive in Poland and the board better. It was the first time Yentl had ever found herself alone in the company of young men. How different their talk was from the jabbering of women, she thought, but she was too shy to join in. One young man discussed a prospective match and the size of the dowry, while another, parodying the manner of a Purim rabbi, declaimed a passage from the Torah, adding all sorts of lewd interpretations. After a while, the company proceeded to contests of strength. One pried open another's fist; a second tried to bend a companion's arm. One student, dining on bread and tea, had no spoon and stirred his cup with his penknife.

Presently, one of the group came over to Yentl and poked her in the shoulder. "Why so quiet? Don't you have a tongue?"

"I have nothing to say."

"What's your name?"

"Anshel."

"You *are* bashful. A violet by the wayside."

And the young man tweaked Yentl's nose. She would have given him a smack in return, but her arm refused to budge. She turned white. Another student, slightly older than the rest, tall and pale, with burning eyes and a black beard, came to her rescue.

"Hey, you, why are you picking on him?"

"If you don't like it, you don't have to look."

"Want me to pull your sidelocks off?"

The bearded young man beckoned to Yentl, then asked where she came from and where she was going. Yentl told him she was looking for a yeshiva, but wanted a quiet one. The young man pulled at his beard.

"Then come with me to Bechev."

He explained that he was returning to Bechev for his fourth year. The yeshiva there was small, with only thirty students, and the people in the town provided board for them all. The food was plentiful and the housewives darned the students' socks and took care of their laundry. The Bechev rabbi, who headed the yeshiva, was a genius. He could pose ten questions and answer all ten with one proof. Most of the students eventually found wives in the town.

"Why did you leave in the middle of the term?" Yentl asked.

"My mother died. Now I'm on my way back."

"What's your name?"

"Avigdor."

"How is it you're not married?"

The young man scratched his beard. "It's a long story."

"Tell me."

Avigdor covered his eyes and thought a moment. "Are you coming to Bechev?"

"Yes."

"Then you'll find out soon enough anyway. I was engaged to the only daughter of Alter Vishkower, the richest man in town. Even the wedding date was set when suddenly they sent back the engagement contract."

"What happened?"

"I don't know. Gossips, I guess, were busy spreading tales. I had the right to ask for half the dowry, but it was against my nature. Now they're trying to talk me into another match, but the girl doesn't appeal to me."

"In Bechev, yeshiva boys look at women?"

"At Alter's house, where I ate once a week, Hadass, his daughter, always brought in the food . . ."

"Is she good-looking?"

"She's blond."

"Brunettes can be good-looking too."

"No."

Yentl gazed at Avigdor. He was lean and bony with sunken cheeks. He had curly sidelocks so black they appeared blue, and his eyebrows met across the bridge of his nose. He looked at her sharply with the regretful shyness of one who has just divulged a secret. His lapel was rent, according to the custom for mourners, and the lining of his gaberdine showed through. He drummed restlessly on the table and hummed a tune. Behind the high furrowed brow his thoughts seemed to race. Suddenly he spoke:

"Well, what of it. I'll become a recluse, that's all."

II

It was strange, but as soon as Yentl—or Anshel—arrived in Bechev, she was allotted one day's board a week at the house of that same rich man, Alter Vishkower, whose daughter had broken off her betrothal to Avigdor.

The students at the yeshiva studied in pairs, and Avigdor chose Anshel for a partner. He helped her with the lessons. He was also an expert swimmer and offered to teach Anshel the breast stroke and how to tread water, but she always found excuses for not going down to the river. Avigdor suggested that they share lodgings, but Anshel found a place to sleep at the house of an elderly widow who was half blind. Tuesdays, Anshel ate at Alter Vishkower's and Hadass waited on her. Avigdor always asked many questions: "How does Hadass look? Is she sad? Is she gay? Are they trying to marry her off? Does she ever mention my name?" Anshel reported that Hadass upset dishes on the tablecloth, forgot to bring the salt, and dipped her fingers into the plate of grits while carrying it. She ordered the servant girl around, was forever engrossed in storybooks, and changed her hairdo every week. Moreover, she must consider herself a beauty, for she was always in front of the mirror, but, in fact, she was not that good-looking.

"Two years after she's married," said Anshel, "she'll be an old bag."

"So she doesn't appeal to you?"

"Not particularly."

"Yet if she wanted you, you wouldn't turn her down."

"I can do without her."

"Don't you have evil impulses?"

The two friends, sharing a lectern in a corner of the study house, spent more time talking than learning. Occasionally Avigdor smoked, and Anshel, taking the cigarette from his lips, would have a puff. Avigdor liked baked flatcakes made with buckwheat, so Anshel stopped at the bakery every morning to buy one, and wouldn't let him pay his share. Often Anshel did things that greatly surprised Avigdor. If a button came off Avigdor's coat, for example, Anshel would arrive at the yeshiva the next day with needle and thread and sew it back on. Anshel bought Avigdor all kinds of presents: a silk handkerchief, a pair of socks, a muffler. Avigdor grew more and more attached to this boy, five years younger than himself, whose beard hadn't even begun to sprout.

Once Avigdor said to Anshel: "I want you to marry Hadass."

"What good would that do *you*?"

"Better you than a total stranger."

"You'd become my enemy."

"Never."

Avigdor liked to go for walks through the town and Anshel frequently joined him. Engrossed in conversation, they would go off to the water mill, or to the pine forest, or to the crossroads where the Christian shrine stood. Sometimes they stretched out on the grass.

"Why can't a woman be like a man?" Avigdor asked once, looking up at the sky.

"How do you mean?"

"Why couldn't Hadass be just like you?"

"How like me?"

"Oh—a good fellow."

Anshel grew playful. She plucked a flower and tore off the petals one by one. She picked up a chestnut and threw it at Avigdor. Avigdor watched a ladybug crawl across the palm of his hand.

After a while he spoke up: "They're trying to marry me off."

Anshel sat up instantly. "To whom?"

"To Feitl's daughter, Peshe."

"The widow?"

"That's the one."

"Why should you marry a widow?"

"No one else will have me."

"That's not true. Someone will turn up for you."

"Never."

Anshel told Avigdor such a match was bad. Peshe was neither good-looking nor clever, only a cow with a pair of eyes. Besides, she was bad luck, for her husband died in the first year of their marriage. Such women were husband-killers. But Avigdor did not answer. He lit a cigarette, took a deep puff, and blew out smoke rings. His face had turned green.

"I need a woman. I can't sleep at night."

Anshel was startled. "Why can't you wait until the right one comes along?"

"Hadass was my destined one."

And Avigdor's eyes grew moist. Abruptly he got to his feet. "Enough lying around. Let's go."

After that, everything happened quickly. One day Avigdor was confiding his problem to Anshel, two days later he became engaged to Peshe, and brought honey cake and brandy to the yeshiva. An early wedding date was set. When the bride-to-be is a widow, there's no need to wait for a trousseau. Everything is ready. The groom, moreover, was an orphan and no one's advice had to be asked. The yeshiva students drank the brandy and offered their congratulations. Anshel also took a sip, but promptly choked on it.

"Oy, it burns!"

"You're not much of a man," Avigdor teased.

After the celebration, Avigdor and Anshel sat down with a volume of the Gemara, but they made little progress, and their conversation was equally slow. Avigdor rocked back and forth, pulled at his beard, muttered under his breath.

"I'm lost," he said abruptly.

"If you don't like her, why are you getting married?"

"I'd marry a she-goat."

The following day Avigdor did not appear at the study house. Feitl the leather dealer belonged to the Hasidim and he wanted his prospective son-in-law to continue his studies at the Hasidic prayer house. The yeshiva students said privately that though there was no denying the widow was short and round as a barrel, her mother the daughter of a dairyman, her father half an ignoramus, still the whole family was filthy with money. Feitl was part-owner of a tannery; Peshe had invested her dowry in a shop that sold herring, tar, pots and pans, and was always crowded with peasants. Father and daughter were outfitting Avigdor and had placed orders for a fur coat, a cloth coat, a silk kapote, and two pair of boots. In addition, he had received many gifts immediately, things that had belonged to Peshe's first husband: the Vilna edition of the Talmud, a gold watch, a Hanukkah candelabra, a spice box. Anshel sat alone at the lectern.

On Tuesday when Anshel arrived for dinner at Alter Vishkower's house, Hadass remarked: "What do you say about your partner—back in clover, isn't he?"

"What did you expect—that no one else would want him?"

Hadass reddened. "It wasn't my fault. My father was against it."

"Why?"

"Because they found out a brother of his had hanged himself."

Anshel looked at her as she stood there—tall, blond, with a long neck, hollow cheeks, and blue eyes, wearing a cotton dress and a calico apron. Her hair, fixed in two braids, was flung back over her shoulders. A pity I'm not a man, Anshel thought.

"Do you regret it now?" Anshel asked.

"Oh, yes!"

Hadass fled from the room. The rest of the food, meat dumplings and tea, was brought in by the servant girl. Not until Anshel had finished eating and was washing her hands for the Final Blessings did Hadass reappear.

She came up to the table and said in a smothered voice: "Swear to me you won't tell him anything. Why should he know what goes on in my heart!"

Then she fled once more, nearly falling over the threshold.

III

The head of the yeshiva asked Anshel to choose another study partner, but weeks went by and still Anshel studied alone. There was no one in the yeshiva who could take Avigdor's place. All the others were small, in body and in spirit. They talked nonsense, bragged about trifles, grinned oafishly, behaved like shnorrers. Without Avigdor the study house seemed empty. At night Anshel lay on her bench at the widow's, unable to sleep. Stripped of gaberdine and trousers, she was once more Yentl, a girl of marriageable age, in love with a young man who was betrothed to another. Perhaps I should have told him the truth, Anshel thought. But it was too late for that. Anshel could not go back to being a girl, could never again do without books and a study house. She lay there thinking outlandish thoughts that brought her close to madness. She fell asleep, then awoke with a start. In her dream she had been at the same time a man and a woman, wearing both a woman's bodice and a man's fringed garment. Yentl's period was late and she was suddenly afraid . . . who knew? In *Medrash Talpioth* she had read of a woman who had conceived merely through desiring a man. Only now did Yentl grasp the meaning of the Torah's prohibition against wearing the clothes of the other sex. By doing so one deceived not only others but also oneself. Even the soul was perplexed, finding itself incarnate in a strange body.

At night Anshel lay awake; by day she could scarcely keep her eyes open. At the houses where she had her meals, the women complained that the youth left everything on his plate. The rabbi noticed that Anshel no longer paid attention to the lectures but stared out the window lost in private thoughts. When Tuesday came, Anshel appeared at the Vishkower house for dinner. Hadass set a bowl of soup before her and waited, but Anshel was so disturbed she did not even say thank you. She reached for a spoon but let it fall.

Hadass ventured a comment: "I hear Avigdor has deserted you."

Anshel awoke from her trance. "What do you mean?"

"He's no longer your partner."

"He's left the yeshiva."

"Do you see him at all?"

"He seems to be hiding."

"Are you at least going to the wedding?"

For a moment Anshel was silent as though missing the meaning of the words. Then she spoke: "He's a big fool."

"Why do you say that?"

"You're beautiful, and the other one looks like a monkey."

Hadass blushed to the roots of her hair. "It's all my father's fault."

"Don't worry. You'll find someone who's worthy of you."

"There's no one I want."

"But everyone wants you . . ."

There was a long silence. Hadass' eyes grew larger, filling with the sadness of one who knows there is no consolation.

"Your soup is getting cold."

"I, too, want you."

Anshel was astonished at what she had said. Hadass stared at her over her shoulder.

"What are you saying!"

"It's the truth."

"Someone might be listening."

"I'm not afraid."

"Eat the soup. I'll bring the meat dumplings in a moment."

Hadass turned to go, her high heels clattering. Anshel began hunting for beans in the soup, fished one up, then let it fall. Her appetite was gone; her throat had closed up. She knew very well she was getting entangled in evil, but some force kept urging her on. Hadass reappeared, carrying a platter with two meat dumplings on it.

"Why aren't you eating?"

"I'm thinking about you."

"What are you thinking?"

"I want to marry you."

Hadass made a face as though she had swallowed something.

"On such matters, you must speak to my father."

"I know."

"The custom is to send a matchmaker."

She ran from the room, letting the door slam behind her. Laughing inwardly, Anshel thought: "With girls I can play as I please!" She sprinkled salt on the soup and then pepper. She sat there lightheaded. What have I done? I must be going mad. There's no other explanation . . . She forced herself to eat, but could taste nothing. Only then did Anshel remember that it was Avigdor who had wanted her to marry Hadass.

From her confusion, a plan emerged; she would exact vengeance for Avigdor, and at the same time, through Hadass, draw him closer to herself. Hadass was a virgin: what did she know about men? A girl like that could be deceived for a long time. To be sure, Anshel too was a virgin but she knew a lot about such matters from the Gemara and from hearing men talk. Anshel was seized by both fear and glee, as a person is who is planning to deceive the whole community. She remembered the saying: "The public are fools." She stood up and said aloud: "Now I'll really start something."

That night Anshel didn't sleep a wink. Every few minutes she got up for a drink of water. Her throat was parched, her forehead burned. Her brain worked away feverishly of its own volition. A quarrel seemed to be going on inside her. Her stomach throbbed and her knees ached. It was as if she had sealed a pact with Satan, the Evil One who plays tricks on human beings, who sets stumbling blocks and traps in their paths. By the time Anshel fell asleep, it was morning. She awoke more exhausted than before. But she could not go on sleeping on the bench at the widow's. With an effort she rose and, taking the bag that held her phylacteries, set out for the study house. On the way whom should she meet but Hadass's father. Anshel bade him a respectful good morning and received a friendly greeting in return. Reb Alter stroked his beard and engaged her in conversation:

"My daughter Hadass must be serving you left-overs. You look starved."

"Your daughter is a fine girl, and very generous."

"So why are you so pale?"

Anshel was silent for a minute. "Reb Alter, there's something I must say to you."

"Well, go ahead, say it."

"Reb Alter, your daughter pleases me."

Alter Vishkower came to a halt. "Oh, does she? I thought yeshiva students didn't talk about such things."

His eyes were full of laughter.

"But it's the truth."

"One doesn't discuss these matters with the young man himself."

"But I'm an orphan."

"Well . . . in that case the custom is to send a marriage broker."

"Yes . . ."

"What do you see in her?"

"She's beautiful . . . fine . . . intelligent . . ."

"Well, well, well . . . Come along, tell me something about your family."

Alter Vishkower put his arm around Anshel and in this fashion the two continued walking until they reached the courtyard of the synagogue.

IV

Once you say "A," you must say "B." Thoughts lead to words, words lead to deeds. Reb Alter Vishkower gave his consent to the match. Hadass's mother Freyda Leah held back for a while. She said she wanted no more Bechev yeshiva students for her daughter and would rather have someone from Lublin or Zamosc; but Hadass gave warning that if she were shamed publicly once more (the way she had been with Avigdor) she would throw herself into the well. As often happens with such ill-advised matches, everyone was strongly in favor of it—the rabbi, the relatives, Hadass's girl friends. For some time the girls of Bechev had been eyeing Anshel longingly, watching from their windows when the youth passed by on the street. Anshel kept his boots well polished and did not drop his eyes in the presence of women. Stopping in at Beila the baker's to buy a *pletzl*, he joked with them in such a worldly fashion that they marveled. The women agreed there was something special about Anshel: his sidelocks curled like nobody else's and he tied his neck scarf differently; his eyes, smiling yet distant, seemed always fixed on some faraway point. And the fact that Avigdor had become betrothed to Feitl's daughter Peshe, forsaking Anshel, had endeared him all the more to the people of the town. Alter Vishkower had a provisional contract drawn up for the betrothal, promising Anshel a bigger dowry, more presents, and an even longer period of maintenance than he had promised Avigdor. The girls of Bechev threw their arms around Hadass and congratulated her. Hadass immediately began crocheting a sack for Anshel's phylacteries, a hallah cloth, a matzoh bag. When Avigdor heard the news of Anshel's betrothal, he came to the study house to offer his congratulations. The past few weeks had aged him. His beard was disheveled, his eyes were red.

He said to Anshel: "I knew it would happen this way. Right from the beginning. As soon as I met you at the inn."

"But it was you who suggested it."

"I know that."

"Why did you desert me? You went away without even saying good-bye."

"I wanted to burn my bridges behind me."

Avigdor asked Anshel to go for a walk. Though it was already past Succoth, the day was bright with sunshine. Avigdor, friendlier than ever, opened his heart to Anshel. Yes, it was true, a brother of his had succumbed to melancholy and hanged himself. Now he too felt himself near the edge of the abyss. Peshe had a lot of money and her father was a rich man, yet he couldn't sleep nights. He didn't want to be a storekeeper. He couldn't forget Hadass. She appeared in his dreams. Sabbath night when her name occurred in the Havdala prayer, he turned dizzy. Still it was good that Anshel and no one else was to marry her . . . At least she would fall into decent hands. Avigdor stooped and tore aimlessly at the shriveled grass. His speech was incoherent, like that of a man possessed.

Suddenly he said: "I have thought of doing what my brother did."

"Do you love her *that* much?"

"She's engraved in my heart."

The two pledged their friendship and promised never again to part. Anshel proposed that, after they were both married, they should live next door or even share the same house. They would study together every day, perhaps even become partners in a shop.

"Do you want to know the truth?" asked Avigdor. "It's like the story of Jacob and Benjamin: my life is bound up in your life."

"Then why did you leave me?"

"Perhaps for that very reason."

Though the day had turned cold and windy, they continued to walk until they reached the pine forest, not turning back until dusk when it was time for the evening prayer. The girls of Bechev, from their posts at the windows, watched them going by with their arms round each other's shoulders and so engrossed in conversation that they walked through puddles and piles of trash without noticing. Avigdor looked pale, disheveled, and the wind whipped one sidelock about; Anshel chewed his fingernails. Hadass, too, ran to the window, took one look, and her eyes filled with tears.

Events followed quickly. Avigdor was the first to marry. Because the bride was a widow, the wedding was a quiet one, with no musicians, no wedding jester, no ceremonial veiling of the bride. One day Peshe stood beneath the marriage canopy, the next she was back at the shop, dispensing tar with greasy hands. Avigdor prayed at the Hasidic assembly house in his new prayer shawl. Afternoons, Anshel went to visit him and the two whispered and talked until evening. The date of Anshel's wedding to Hadass was set for the Sabbath in Hanukkah week, though the prospective father-in-law wanted it sooner. Hadass had already been betrothed once. Besides, the groom was an orphan. Why should he toss about on a makeshift bed at the widow's when he could have a wife and home of his own?

Many times each day Anshel warned herself that what she was about to do was sinful, mad, an act of utter depravity. She was entangling both Hadass and herself in a chain of deception and committing so many transgressions that she would never be able to do penance. One lie followed another. Repeatedly Anshel made up her mind to flee Bechev in time, to put an end to this weird comedy that was more the work of an imp than a human being. But she was in the grip of a power she could not resist. She grew more and more attached to Avigdor, and could not bring herself to destroy Hadass's illusory happiness. Now that he was married, Avigdor's desire to study was greater than ever, and the friends met twice each day: in the mornings they studied the Gemara and the Commentaries, in the afternoons the Legal Codes with their glosses. Alter Vishkower and Feitl the leather dealer were pleased and compared Avigdor and Anshel to David and Jonathan. With all the complications, Anshel went about as though drunk. The tailors took her measurements for a new wardrobe and she was forced into all kinds of subterfuge to keep them from discovering she was not a man. Though the imposture had lasted many weeks, Anshel still could not believe it: How was it possible? Fooling the community had become a game, but how long could it go on? And in what way would the truth come to the surface? Inside, Anshel laughed and wept. She had turned into a sprite brought into the world to mock people and trick them. I'm wicked, a transgressor, a Jeroboam ben Nabat, she told herself. Her only justification was that she had taken all these burdens upon herself because her soul thirsted to study Torah.

Avigdor soon began to complain that Peshe treated him badly. She called him an idler, a shlemiel, just another mouth to feed. She tried to tie him to the store, assigned him tasks for which he hadn't the slightest inclination, begrudged him pocket money. Instead of consoling Avigdor, Anshel goaded him on against Peshe. She called his wife an eyesore, a shrew, a miser, and said that Peshe had no doubt nagged her first husband to death and would Avigdor also. At the same time, Anshel enumerated Avigdor's virtues: his height and manliness, his wit, his erudition.

"If I were a woman and married to you," said Anshel, "I'd know how to appreciate you."

"Well, but you aren't . . ."

Avigdor sighed.

Meanwhile, Anshel's wedding date drew near.

On the Sabbath before Hanukkah, Anshel was called to the pulpit to read from the Torah. The women showered her with raisins and almonds. On the day of the wedding Alter Vishkower gave a feast for the young men. Avigdor sat at Anshel's right hand. The bridegroom delivered a Talmudic discourse, and the rest of the company argued the points, while smoking cigarettes and drinking wine, liqueurs, tea with lemon or raspberry jam. Then followed the ceremony of veiling the bride, after which the bridegroom was led to the wedding canopy that had been set up at the side of the synagogue. The night was frosty and clear, the sky full of stars. The musicians struck up a tune. Two rows of girls held lighted tapers and braided wax candles. After the wedding ceremony the bride and groom broke their fast with golden chicken broth. Then the dancing began and the announcement of the wedding gifts, all according to custom. The gifts were many and costly. The wedding jester depicted the joys and sorrows that were in store for the bride. Avigdor's wife, Peshe, was one of the guests but, though she was bedecked with jewels, she still looked ugly in a wig that sat low on her forehead, wearing an enormous fur cape, and with traces of tar on her hands that no amount of washing could ever remove. After the virtue dance the bride and groom were led separately to the marriage chamber. The wedding attendants instructed the couple in the proper conduct and enjoined them to "be fruitful and multiply."

At daybreak Anshel's mother-in-law and her band descended upon the marriage chamber and tore the bedsheets from beneath Hadass to make sure the marriage had been consummated. When traces of blood were discovered, the company grew merry and began kissing and congratulating the bride. Then, brandishing the sheet, they flocked outside and danced a kosher dance in the newly fallen snow. Anshel had found a way to deflower the bride. Hadass in her innocence was unaware that things weren't quite as they should have been. She was already deeply in love with Anshel. It is commanded that the bride and groom remain apart for seven days after the first intercourse. The next day Anshel and Avigdor took up the study of the Tractate on Menstruous Women. When the other men had departed and the two were left to themselves in the synagogue, Avigdor shyly questioned Anshel about his night with Hadass. Anshel gratified his curiosity and they whispered together until nightfall.

V

Anshel had fallen into good hands. Hadass was a devoted wife and her parents indulged their son-in-law's every wish and boasted of his accomplishments. To be sure, several months went by and Hadass was still not with child, but no one took it to heart. On the other hand, Avigdor's lot grew steadily worse. Peshe tormented him and finally would not give him enough to eat and even refused him a clean shirt. Since he was always penniless, Anshel again brought him a daily buckwheat cake. Because Peshe was too busy to cook and too stingy to hire a servant, Anshel asked Avigdor to dine at his house. Reb Alter Vishkower and his wife disapproved, arguing that it was wrong for the rejected suitor to visit the house of his former fiancée. The town had plenty to talk about. But Anshel cited precedents to show that it was not prohibited by the Law. Most of the townspeople sided with Avigdor and blamed Peshe for everything. Avigdor soon began pressing Peshe for a divorce, and, because he did not want to have a child by such a fury, he acted like Onan, or, as the Gemara translates it: he threshed on the inside and cast his seed without. He confided in Anshel, told him how Peshe came to bed unwashed and snored like a buzz saw, of how she was so occupied with the cash taken in at the store that she babbled about it even in her sleep.

"Oh, Anshel, how I envy you," he said.

"There's no reason for envying me."

"You have everything. I wish your good fortune were mine—with no loss to you, of course."

"Everyone has troubles of his own."

"What sort of troubles do *you* have? Don't tempt Providence."

How could Avigdor have guessed that Anshel could not sleep at night and thought constantly of running away? Lying with Hadass and deceiving her had become more and more painful. Hadass's love and tenderness shamed her. The devotion of her mother- and father-in-law and their hopes for a grandchild were a burden. On Friday afternoons all of the townspeople went to the baths and every week Anshel had to find a new excuse. But this was beginning to awake suspicions. There was talk that Anshel must have an unsightly birthmark, or a rupture, or perhaps was not properly circumcised. Judging by the youth's years, his beard should certainly have begun to sprout, yet his cheeks remained smooth. It was already Purim, and Passover was approaching. Soon it would be summer. Not far from Bechev there was a river where all the yeshiva students and young men went swimming as soon as it was warm enough. The lie was swelling like an abscess and one of these days it must surely burst. Anshel knew she had to find a way to free herself.

It was customary for the young men boarding with their in-laws to travel to nearby cities during the half-holidays in the middle of Passover week. They enjoyed the change, refreshed themselves, looked around for business opportunities, bought books or other things a young man might need. Bechev was not far from Lublin and Anshel persuaded Avigdor to make the journey with her at her expense. Avigdor was delighted at the prospect of being rid for a few days of the shrew he had at home. The trip by carriage was a merry one. The fields were turning green; storks, back from the warm countries, swooped across the sky in great arcs. Streams rushed toward the valleys. The birds chirped. The windmills turned. Spring flowers were beginning to bloom in the fields. Here and there a cow was already grazing. The companions, chatting, ate the fruit and little cakes that Hadass had packed, told each other jokes, and exchanged confidences until they reached Lublin. There they went to an inn and took a room for two. In the journey, Anshel had promised to reveal an astonishing secret to Avigdor in Lublin. Avigdor had joked: what sort of secret could it be? Had Anshel discovered a hidden treasure? Had he written an essay? By studying the Cabala, had he created a dove?

Now they entered the room and while Anshel carefully locked the door, Avigdor said teasingly: "Well, let's hear your great secret."

"Prepare yourself for the most incredible thing that ever was."

"I'm prepared for anything."

"I'm not a man but a woman," said Anshel. "My name isn't Anshel, it's Yentl."

Avigdor burst out laughing. "I knew it was a hoax."

"But it's true."

"Even if I'm a fool, I won't swallow this."

"Do you want me to show you?"

"Yes."

"Then I'll get undressed."

Avigdor's eyes widened. It occurred to him that Anshel might want to practice pederasty. Anshel took off the gaberdine and the fringed garment, and threw off her underclothes. Avigdor took one look and turned first white, then fiery red. Anshel covered herself hastily.

"I've done this only so that you can testify at the courthouse. Otherwise, Hadass will have to stay a grass widow."

Avigdor had lost his tongue. He was seized by a fit of trembling. He wanted to speak, but his lips moved and nothing came out. He sat down quickly, for his legs would not support him.

Finally he murmured: "How is it possible? I don't believe it!"

"Should I get undressed again?"

"No!"

Yentl proceeded to tell the whole story: how her father, bedridden, had studied Torah with her; how she had never had the patience for women and their silly chatter; how she had sold the house and all the furnishings, left the town, made her way disguised as a man to Lublin, and on the road met Avigdor. Avigdor sat speechless, gazing at the storyteller. Yentl was by now wearing men's clothes once more.

Avigdor spoke: "It must be a dream."

He pinched himself on the cheek.

"It isn't a dream."

"That such a thing should happen to me!"

"It's all true."

"Why did you do it? *Nu*, I'd better keep still."

"I didn't want to waste my life on a baking shovel and a kneading trough."

"And what about Hadass—why did you do that?"

"I did it for your sake. I knew that Peshe would torment you and at our house you would have some peace."

Avigdor was silent for a long time. He bowed his head, pressed his hands to his temples, shook his head. "What will you do now?"

"I'll go away to a different yeshiva."

"What? If you had only told me earlier, we could have . . ."

Avigdor broke off in the middle.

"No—it wouldn't have been good."

"Why not?"

"I'm neither one nor the other."

"What a dilemma I'm in!"

"Get a divorce from that horror. Marry Hadass."

"She'll never divorce me and Hadass won't have me."

"Hadass loves you. She won't listen to her father again."

Avigdor stood up suddenly but then sat down. "I won't be able to forget you. Ever . . ."

VI

According to the Law, Avigdor was now forbidden to spend another moment alone with Yentl; yet dressed in the gaberdine and trousers, she was again the familiar Anshel.

They resumed their conversation on the old footing: "How could you bring yourself to violate the commandment every day: 'A woman shall not wear that which pertaineth to a man'?"

"I wasn't created for plucking feathers and chattering with females."

"Would you rather lose your share in the world to come?"

"Perhaps . . ."

Avigdor raised his eyes. Only now did he realize that Anshel's cheeks were too smooth for a man's, the hair too abundant, the hands too small. Even so he could not believe that such a thing could have happened. At any moment he expected to wake up. He bit his lips, pinched his thigh. He was seized by shyness and could not speak without stammering. His friendship with Anshel, their intimate talk, their confidences, had been turned into a sham and delusion. The thought even occurred to him that Anshel might be a demon. He shook himself as if to cast off a nightmare; yet that power which knows the difference between dream and reality told him it was all true. He summoned up his courage. He and Anshel could never be strangers to one another, even though Anshel was in fact Yentl . . .

He ventured a comment: "It seems to me that the witness who testifies for a deserted woman may not marry her, for the Law calls him 'a party to the affair.' "

"What? That didn't occur to me!"

"We must look it up in Eben Ezer."

"I'm not even sure that the rules pertaining to a deserted woman apply in this case," said Anshel in the manner of a scholar.

"If you don't want Hadass to be a grass widow, you must reveal the secret to her directly."

"That I can't do."

"In any event, you must get another witness."

Gradually the two went back to their Talmudic conversation. It seemed strange at first to Avigdor to be disputing holy writ with a woman, yet before long the Torah had reunited them. Though their bodies were different, their souls were of one kind. Anshel spoke in a singsong, gesticulated with her thumb, clutched her sidelocks, plucked at her beardless chin, made all the customary gestures of a yeshiva student. In the heat of argument she even seized Avigdor by the lapel and called him stupid. A great love for Anshel took hold of Avigdor, mixed with shame, remorse, anxiety. If I had only known this before, he said to himself. In his thoughts he likened Anshel (or Yentl) to Bruria, the wife of Reb Meir, and to Yalta, the wife of Reb Nachman. For the first time he saw clearly that this was what he had always wanted: a wife whose mind was not taken up with material things . . . His desire for Hadass was gone now, and he knew he would long for Yentl, but he dared not say so. He felt hot and knew that his face was burning. He could no longer meet Anshel's eyes. He began to enumerate Anshel's sins and saw that he too was implicated, for he had sat next to Yentl and had touched her during her unclean days. *Nu*, and what could be said about her marriage to Hadass? What a multitude of transgressions there! Wilful deception, false vows, misrepresentation!—Heaven knows what else.

He asked suddenly: "Tell the truth, are you a heretic?"

"God forbid!"

"Then how could you bring yourself to do such a thing?"

The longer Anshel talked, the less Avigdor understood. All Anshel's explanations seemed to point to one thing: she had the soul of a man and the body of a woman. Anshel said she had married Hadass only in order to be near Avigdor.

"You could have married me," Avigdor said.

"I wanted to study the Gemara and Commentaries with you, not darn your socks!"

For a long time neither spoke. Then Avigdor broke the silence: "I'm afraid Hadass will get sick from all this, God forbid!"

"I'm afraid of that, too."

"What's going to happen now?"

Dusk fell and the two began to recite the evening prayer. In his confusion Avigdor mixed up the blessings, omitted some and repeated others. He glanced sideways at Anshel, who was rocking back and forth, beating her breast, bowing her head. He saw her, eyes closed, lift her face to Heaven, as though beseeching: You, Father in Heaven, know the truth . . . When their prayers were finished, they sat down on opposite chairs, facing one another yet a good distance apart. The room filled with shadows. Reflections of the sunset, like purple embroidery, shook on the wall opposite the window. Avigdor again wanted to speak but at first the words, trembling on the tip of his tongue, would not come.

Suddenly they burst forth: "Maybe it's still not too late? I can't go on living with that accursed woman . . . You . . ."

"No, Avigdor, it's impossible."

"Why?"

"I'll live out my time as I am . . ."

"I'll miss you. Terribly."

"And I'll miss you."

"What's the sense of all this?"

Anshel did not answer. Night fell and the light faded. In the darkness they seemed to be listening to each other's thoughts. The Law forbade Avigdor to stay in the room alone with Anshel, but he could not think of her just as a woman. What a strange power there is in clothing, he thought.

But he spoke of something else: "I would advise you simply to send Hadass a divorce."

"How can I do that?"

"Since the marriage sacraments weren't valid, what difference does it make?"

"I suppose you're right."

"There'll be time enough later for her to find out the truth."

The maidservant came in with a lamp, but as soon as she had gone, Avigdor put it out. Their predicament and the words which they must speak to one another could not endure light. In the blackness Anshel related all the particulars. She answered all Avigdor's questions. The clock struck two, and still they talked. Anshel told Avigdor that Hadass had never forgotten him. She talked of him frequently, worried about his health, was sorry—though not without a certain satisfaction—about the way things had turned out with Peshe.

"She'll be a good wife," said Anshel. "I don't even know how to bake a pudding."

"Nevertheless, if you're willing . . ."

"No, Avigdor. It wasn't destined to be . . ."

VII

It was all a great riddle to the town: the messenger who arrived bringing Hadass the divorce papers; Avigdor's remaining in Lublin until after the holidays; his return to Bechev with slumping shoulders and lifeless eyes as if he had been ill. Hadass took to her bed and was visited by the doctor three times a day. Avigdor went into seclusion. If someone ran across him by chance and addressed him, he did not answer. Peshe complained to her parents that Avigdor paced back and forth smoking all night long. When he finally collapsed from sheer fatigue, in his sleep he called out the name of an unknown female—Yentl. Peshe began talking of a divorce. The town thought Avigdor wouldn't grant her one or would demand money at the very least, but he agreed to everything.

In Bechev the people were not used to having mysteries stay mysteries for long. How can you keep secrets in a little town where everyone knows what's cooking in everyone else's pots? Yet, though there were plenty of persons who made a practice of looking through keyholes and laying an ear to shutters, what happened remained an enigma. Hadass lay in her bed and wept. Chanina the herb doctor reported that she was wasting away. Anshel had disappeared without a trace. Reb Alter Vishkower sent for Avigdor and he arrived, but those who stood straining beneath the window couldn't catch a word of what passed between them. Those individuals who habitually pry into other people's affairs came up with all sorts of theories, but not one of them was consistent.

One party came to the conclusion that Anshel had fallen into the hands of Catholic priests and had been converted. That might have made sense. But where could Anshel have found time for the priests, since he was always studying in the yeshiva? And apart from that, since when does an apostate send his wife a divorce?

Another group whispered that Anshel had cast an eye on another woman. But who could it be? There were no love affairs conducted in Bechev. And none of the young women had recently left town—neither a Jewish woman nor a Gentile one.

Somebody else offered the suggestion that Anshel had been carried away by evil spirits, or was even one of them himself. As proof he cited the fact that Anshel had never come either to the bathhouse or to the river. It is well known that demons have the feet of geese. Well, but had

Hadass never seen him barefoot? And who ever heard of a demon sending his wife a divorce? When a demon marries a daughter of mortals, he usually lets her remain a grass widow.

It occurred to someone else that Anshel had committed a major transgression and gone into exile in order to do penance. But what sort of transgression could it have been? And why had he not entrusted it to the rabbi? And why did Avigdor wander about like a ghost?

The hypothesis of Tevel the musician was closest to the truth. Tevel maintained that Avigdor had been unable to forget Hadass and that Anshel had divorced her so that his friend would be able to marry her. But was such friendship possible in this world? And in that case, why had Anshel divorced Hadass even before Avigdor divorced Peshe? Furthermore, such a thing can be accomplished only if the wife has been informed of the arrangement and is willing, yet all signs pointed to Hadass's great love for Anshel, and in fact she was ill from sorrow.

One thing was clear to all: Avigdor knew the truth. But it was impossible to get anything out of him. He remained in seclusion and kept silent with an obstinacy that was a reproof to the whole town.

Close friends urged Peshe not to divorce Avigdor, though they had severed all relations and no longer lived as man and wife. He did not even, on Friday night, perform the kiddush blessing for her. He spent his nights either at the study house or at the widow's where Anshel had found lodgings. When Peshe spoke to him he didn't answer, but stood with bowed head. The tradeswoman Peshe had no patience for such goings-on. She needed a young man to help her out in the store, not a yeshiva student who had fallen into melancholy. Someone of that sort might even take it into his head to depart and leave her deserted. Peshe agreed to a divorce.

In the meantime, Hadass had recovered, and Reb Alter Vishkower let it be known that a marriage contract was being drawn up. Hadass was to marry Avigdor. The town was agog. A marriage between a man and a woman who had once been engaged and their betrothal broken off was unheard of. The wedding was held on the first Sabbath after Tishe b'Av, and included all that is customary at the marriage of a virgin: the banquet for the poor, the canopy before the synagogue, the musicians, the wedding jester, the virtue dance. Only one thing was lacking: joy. The bridegroom stood beneath the marriage canopy, a figure of desolation. The bride had recovered from her sickness, but had remained pale and thin. Her tears fell into the golden chicken broth. From all eyes the same question looked out: why had Anshel done it?

After Avigdor's marriage to Hadass, Peshe spread that rumor that Anshel had sold his wife to Avigdor for a price, and that the money had been supplied by Alter Vishkower. One young man pondered the riddle at great length until he finally arrived at the conclusion that Anshel had lost his beloved wife to Avigdor at cards, or even on a spin of the Hanukkah dreidl. It is a general rule that when the grain of truth cannot be found, men will swallow great helpings of falsehood. Truth itself is often concealed in such a way that the harder you look for it, the harder it is to find.

Not long after the wedding, Hadass became pregnant. The child was a boy and those assembled at the circumcision could scarcely believe their ears when they heard the father name his son Anshel.

Zeidlus the Pope

I

IN ancient times there always lived a few men in every generation whom I, the Evil One, could not corrupt in the usual manner. It was impossible to tempt them to murder, lechery, robbery. I could not even get them to cease studying the Law. In one way only could the inner passions of these righteous souls be reached: through their vanity.

Zeidel Cohen was such a man. In the first place, he had the protection of noble ancestors: he was a descendant of Rashi, whose genealogy reached back to King David. In the second place, he was the greatest scholar in the whole province of Lublin. At five he had studied the Gemara and the Commentaries; at seven he had memorized the Laws of Marriage and Divorce; at nine, he had preached a sermon, quoting from so many books that even the oldest among the scholars were confounded. He was completely at home in the Bible; in Hebrew grammar he had no equal. What is more he studied constantly: summer and winter alike he rose with the morning star and began to read. As he seldom left his rooms for air and did no physical labor, he had little appetite and slept lightly. He had neither the desire nor the patience to converse with friends. Zeidel loved only one thing: books. The moment he entered the study house, or his own home for that matter, he ran straight to the shelves and began to leaf through volumes, sucking into his lungs the dust from ancient pages. So strong was his power of memory that one look at some passage in the Talmud, at some new interpretation in a commentary and he could remember it forever.

Nor could I gain power over Zeidel through his body. His limbs were hairless; by seventeen his pointed skull was bald; only a few hairs grew on his chin. His face was long and stiff; three or four drops of perspiration always hung on the high forehead; his crooked nose was

---

Translated by Joel Blocker and Elizabeth Pollet

strangely naked, like that of a man who is accustomed to wearing glasses but has just taken them off. He had reddish eyelids behind which lay a pair of yellow, melancholy eyes. His hands and feet were small and white as a woman's, though as he never visited the ritual bath it was not known if he was a eunuch or an androgyne. But since his father, Reb Sander Cohen, was extremely rich, himself a scholar and a man of some note, he saw to it that his son made a match befitting the family. The bride came from a rich Warsaw family and was a beauty. Until the day of the wedding she had never seen the groom, and when she did set eyes upon him, just before he covered her face with the veil, it was already too late. She married him and was never able to conceive. She spent her time sitting in the rooms her father-in-law had allotted to her, knitting stockings, reading storybooks, listening to the large wall clock with its gilded chains and weights ring out the half-hours—patiently waiting, it seemed, for the minutes to become days, the days years, until the time should come for her to go to sleep in the old Janov cemetery.

Zeidel possessed such intensity that all his surroundings acquired his character. Though a servant took care of his rooms, the furniture was always covered with dust; the windows, hung with heavy drapes, seemed never to have been opened; thick rugs covered the floors muffling his footsteps so that it sounded as if a spirit, not a man, were walking there. Zeidel received regularly an allowance from his father, but he never spent a penny on himself. He hardly knew what a coin looked like, yet he was a miser and never took a poor man home for a Sabbath meal. He never took the trouble to make friends, and since neither he nor his wife ever invited a guest, no one knew what the interior of their house looked like.

Untroubled by passions or the need to make a living, Zeidel studied diligently. He first devoted himself to the Talmud and the Commentaries. Then he delved into the Cabala and soon became an expert on the occult, even writing tracts on *The Angel Raziel* and *The Book of Creation*. Naturally he was well acquainted with *The Guide for the Perplexed*, the *Kuzari*, and other philosophical works. One day he happened to acquire a copy of the Vulgate. Soon he had learned Latin, and he began to read extensively in the forbidden literature, borrowing many books from a scholarly priest who lived in Janov. In short, just as his father had accumulated gold coins all his life, so Zeidel accumulated knowledge. By the time he was thirty-five no one in all Poland could equal him in learning. Just then I was ordered to tempt him to sin.

"Persuade Zeidel to sin?" I asked. "What kind of sin? He doesn't enjoy food, is indifferent to women, and never has anything to do with business." I had tried heresy before, without success. I remembered our last conversation:

"Let's assume that, God forbid, there is no God," he had answered me. "So what? Then His nonbeing itself is divine. Only God, the Cause of all Causes, could have the power not to exist."

"If there is no Creator, why do you pray and study?" I continued.

"What else should I do?" he asked in return. "Drink vodka and dance with Gentile girls?"

To tell the truth, I had no answer to that, so I left him in peace. His father had since died, and now I was ordered to devote myself to him again. With not the slightest idea of how to begin, I descended to Janov with a heavy heart.

II

I discovered after some time that Zeidel possessed one human weakness: haughtiness. He had much more than that sliver of vanity which the Law permits the scholar.

I laid my plans. In the middle of one night, I woke him from his slumber and said: "Do you know, Zeidel, that you are better versed than any rabbi in Poland in the fine print of the Commentaries?"

"Certainly I know it," he replied. "But who else does? Nobody."

"Do you know, Zeidel, that you outshine all other grammarians in your knowledge of Hebrew?" I continued. "Are you aware that you know more of the Cabala than was divulged to Reb Chaim Vital? Do you know that you are a greater philosopher than Maimonides?"

"Why are you telling me these things?" Zeidel asked, wondering.

"I'm telling you because it's not right that a great man such as you, a master of the Torah, an encyclopedia of knowledge, should be buried in a godforsaken village such as this where no one pays the slightest attention to you, where the townspeople are coarse and the rabbi an ignoramus, with a wife who has no understanding of your true worth. You are a pearl lost in sand, Reb Zeidel."

"Well?" he asked. "What can I do? Should I go about singing my own praises?"

"No, Reb Zeidel. That wouldn't help you. The town would only call you a madman."

"What do you advise, then?"

"Promise me not to interrupt and I'll tell you. You know the Jews have never honored their leaders: they grumbled about Moses; rebelled against Samuel; threw Jeremiah into a ditch; and murdered Zacharias. The Chosen People hate greatness. In a great man, they sense a rival to Jehovah, so they love only the petty and mediocre. Their thirty-six saints are all shoemakers and water-carriers. The Jewish laws are concerned mainly with a drop of milk falling into a pot of meat or with an egg laid on a holiday. They have deliberately corrupted Hebrew, degraded the ancient texts. Their Talmud makes King David into a provincial rabbi advising women about menstruation. The way they reason, the smaller the greater, the uglier the prettier. Their rule is: The closer one is to dust, the nearer one is to God. So you can see, Reb Zeidel, why they find you a thumb in the eye—you with your erudition, wealth, fine breeding, brilliant perceptions, and extraordinary memory."

"Why do you tell me all these things?" Zeidel asked.

"Reb Zeidel, listen to me: what you must do is become a Christian. The Gentiles are the antithesis of the Jews. Since their God is a man, a man can be a God to them. Gentiles admire greatness of any kind and love the men who possess it: men of great pity or great cruelty, great builders or great destroyers, great virgins or great harlots, great sages or great fools, great rulers or great rebels, great believers or great infidels. They don't care what else a man is: if he is great, they idolize him. Therefore, Reb Zeidel, if you want honor, you must embrace their faith. And don't worry about God. To One so mighty and sublime the earth and its inhabitants are no more than a swarm of gnats. He doesn't care whether men pray to Him in a synagogue or a church, fast from Sabbath to Sabbath or bloat themselves with pork. He is too exalted to notice these puny creatures who delude themselves thinking that they are the crown of Creation."

"Does that mean God did not give the Torah to Moses at Sinai?" Zeidel asked.

"What? God open His heart to a man born of woman?"

"And Jesus was not His son?"

"Jesus was a bastard from Nazareth."

"Is there no reward or punishment?"

"No."

"Then what is there?" Zeidel asked me, fearful and confused.

"There is something that exists, but it has no existence," I answered in the manner of the philosophers.

"Is there no hope then ever to know the truth?" Zeidel asked in despair.

"The world is not knowable and there is no truth," I replied, turning his question around. "Just as you can't learn the taste of salt with your nose, the smell of balsam with your ear, or the sound of a violin with your tongue, it's impossible for you to grasp the world with your reason."

"With what can you grasp it?"

"With your passions—some small part of it. But you, Reb Zeidel, have only one passion: pride. If you destroy that too, you'll be hollow, a void."

"What should I do?" Zeidel asked, baffled.

"Tomorrow, go to the priest and tell him that you want to become one of them. Then sell your goods and property. Try to convince your wife to change her religion—if she's willing, good; if not, the loss is small. The Gentiles will make you a priest and a priest is not allowed to have a wife. You'll continue to study, to wear a long coat and skullcap. The only difference will be that instead of being stuck away in a remote village among Jews who hate you and your accomplishments, praying in a sunken hole of a study house where beggars scratch themselves behind the stove, you will live in a large city, preach in a luxurious church where an organ will play, and where your congregation will consist of men of stature whose wives will kiss your hand. If you excel and throw together some hodgepodge about Jesus and his mother the Virgin, they will make you a bishop, and later a cardinal—and God willing, if everything goes well, they'll make you Pope one day. Then the Gentiles will carry you on a gilded chair like an idol and burn incense around you; and they'll kneel before your image in Rome, Madrid, and Crakow."

"What will my name be?" asked Zeidel.

"Zeidlus the First."

So great an impression did my words make that Zeidel started violently and sat up in bed. His wife awoke and asked why he wasn't sleeping. With some hidden instinct, she knew he was possessed by a great desire, and thought: Who knows, perhaps a miracle has happened. But Zeidel had already made up his mind to divorce her, so he told her to keep still and not ask any more questions. Putting on his slippers and robe, he went to his study, where he lit a wax candle and sat until dawn rereading the Vulgate.

III

Zeidel did as I advised. He went to the priest and let him know that he wished to speak about matters of faith. Of course the Gentile was more than willing. What better merchandise is there for a priest than a Jewish soul? Anyway, to cut a long story short, priests and noblemen from the entire province promised Zeidel a great career in the Church; he quickly sold all his possessions, divorced his wife, let himself be baptized with holy water, and became a Christian. For the first time in his life, Zeidel was honored: the ecclesiastics made a big fuss over him, the noblemen lavished praise on him, their wives smiled benignly at him, and he was invited to their estates. The Bishop of Zamosc was his godfather. His name was changed from Zeidel son of Sander to Benedictus Janovsky—the surname in honor of the village where he had been born. Although Zeidel was not yet a priest or even a deacon, he ordered a black cassock from a tailor and hung a rosary and cross around his neck. For the time being, he lived in the priest's rectory, seldom venturing out because when he did Jewish schoolboys ran after him in the streets shouting, "Convert! Apostate!"

His Gentile friends had many different plans for him. Some advised him to go to a seminary and study; others recommended that he enter the Dominican priory in Lublin. Still others suggested he marry a wealthy local woman and become a squire. But Zeidel had little inclination to travel the usual road. He wanted greatness immediately. He knew that in the past many Jewish converts to Christianity had become famous by writing polemics against the Talmud—Petrus Alfonzo, Fablo Christiani of Montpelier, Paul de Santa Maria, Johann Baptista, Johann Pfefferkorn, to mention only a few. Zeidel decided to follow in their footsteps. Now that he had converted and Jewish children abused him in the streets, he suddenly discovered that he had never loved the Talmud. Its Hebrew was debased by Aramaic; its pilpul was dull, its legends improbable, and its Biblical commentaries were farfetched and full of sophistries.

Zeidel traveled to the seminary libraries in Lublin and Crakow to study the treatises written by Jewish converts. He soon discovered they were all much alike. The authors were ignorant, plagiarized from one another liberally, and all cited the same few anti-Gentile passages from the Talmud. Some of them had not even used their own words, had copied the work of others and signed their names. The real *Apologia Contra Talmudum* had yet to be written, and no one was better prepared to do such a work than he with his knowledge of philosophy and the Cabalistic mysteries. At the same time, Zeidel undertook to find fresh proofs in the Bible that the prophets had foreseen Jesus' birth, martyrdom, and resurrection; and to discover corroborative evidence for the Christian religion in logic, astronomy, and natural science. Zeidel's treatise would be for Christianity what Maimonides's *The Strong Hand* was for Judaism—and it would carry its author from Janov directly to the Vatican.

Zeidel studied, thought, wrote, sitting all day and half the night in libraries. From time to time he met Christian scholars and conversed with them in Polish and Latin. With the same fervor that he had studied Jewish books, he now studied the Christian texts. Soon he could recite whole chapters of the New Testament. He became an expert Latinist. After a while he was so thoroughly versed in Christian theology that the priests and monks were afraid to talk to him for with his erudition he found mistakes everywhere. Many times he was promised a seminary appointment but somehow he never got one. A post as librarian in Crakow which was to be his went to a relative of the governor instead.

Zeidel began to realize that even among the Gentiles things were far from perfect. The clergy cared more for gold than for their God. Their sermons were full of errors. Most of the priests did not know Latin, but even in Polish their quotations were incorrect.

For years Zeidel worked on his treatise, but still it was not finished. His standards were so high that he was continually finding flaws, yet the more changes he made, the more he found were necessary. He wrote, crossed out, rewrote, threw away. His drawers were stuffed with manuscript pages, notes, references, but he could not bring his work to a conclusion. After years of effort, he was so fatigued that he could no longer distinguish between right and wrong, sense and nonsense, between what would please and what displease the Church. Nor did he believe any more in what is called truth and falsehood. Nevertheless he continued to ponder, to come up occasionally with a few new ideas. He consulted the Talmud so often in his work that once more he delved into its depths, scribbling notes on the margins of the pages, comparing all the different texts, hardly knowing whether he did so to find new accusations or simply out of habit. At times, he read books about witch trials, accounts of young women possessed by the devil, documents of the Inquisitions, whatever manuscripts he could find that described such events in various countries and epochs.

Gradually, the bag of gold coins that hung around his neck became lighter. His face turned yellow as parchment. His eyes dimmed. His hands trembled like an old man's. His cassock was stained and torn. His hope to become famous among the nations vanished. He came to regret his conversion. But the way back was blocked: first because he doubted all faiths now; second because it was the law of the land that a Christian who returned to Judaism should be burned at the stake.

One day, while Zeidel was sitting, studying a faded manuscript in the library in Crakow, everything went dark before his eyes. At first he thought dusk had fallen and asked why the candles had not been lit. But when a monk told him that the day was still bright, he realized he had gone blind. Unable to return home alone, Zeidel had to be led by the monk. From that time on Zeidel lived in darkness. Fearing that his money would soon run out and he would be left without a groschen as well as without eyes, Zeidel decided, after much hesitation, to become a beggar outside the church of Crakow. "I have lost both this world and the world to come," he reasoned, "so why be haughty? If there is no way up, one must go down." Thus Zeidel son of Sander, or Benedictus Janovsky, took his place among the beggars on the steps of the great cathedral of Crakow.

In the beginning the priests and canons tried to help him. They wanted to put him into a cloister. But Zeidel had no wish to become a monk. He wanted to sleep alone in his garret, and to continue to carry his money bag under his shirt. Nor was he inclined to kneel before an altar. Occasionally a seminary student would stop to talk with him for a few minutes on scholarly matters. But in a short while everyone forgot him. Zeidel hired an old woman to lead him to the church in the morning and home at night. She also brought him a bowl of groats each day. Good-hearted Gentiles threw him alms. He was even able to save some money, and the bag around his neck became heavy again. The other mendicants mocked him, but Zeidel never replied. For hours he knelt on the steps, his bald skull uncovered, his eyes closed, his black robe buttoned to the chin. His lips never ceased shaking and murmuring. Passers-by thought he was praying to the Christian saints, but actually he was reciting the Gemara, the Mishnah, and the psalms. The Gentile theology he had forgotten as quickly as he had learned it; what remained was what he had acquired in his youth. The street was full of tumult: wagons rolled by on the cobblestones; horses neighed; coachmen screamed with hoarse voices and cracked their whips; girls laughed and screeched; children cried; women quarreled, called one another names, uttered obscenities. Every once in a while Zeidel stopped murmuring, but only to doze with his head sunken into his chest. He no longer had any earthly desire, but one yearning still plagued him: to know the truth. Was there a Creator or was the world nothing but atoms and their combinations? Did the soul exist or was all thought mere reverberations of the brain? Was there a final accounting with reward and punishment? Was there a Substance or was the whole of existence nothing but imagination? The sun burned down on him, the rains soaked him, pigeons soiled him with their droppings, but he was impervious to everything. Now that he had lost his only passion, pride, nothing material mattered to him. Sometimes he asked himself: Is it possible that I am Zeidel the prodigy? Was my father Reb Sander, the leader of the community? Did I really have a wife once? Are there still some who knew me? It seemed to Zeidel that none of these things could be true. Such events had never happened, and if they had not, reality itself was one great illusion.

One morning when the old woman came to Zeidel's attic room to take him to the church, she found him ill. Waiting until he dozed off, she stealthily cut the bag of money from around his neck and left. In his stupor Zeidel knew he was being robbed, but he didn't care. His head lay as heavy as a stone on the straw pillow. His feet ached. His joints were filled with pain. His emaciated body was hot and hollow. Zeidel fell asleep, awoke, dozed off; then he awoke again with a start, unable to tell whether it was night or day. Out in the streets he heard voices, screams, stamping hoofs, ringing bells. It seemed to him some pagan multitude was celebrating a holiday with trumpets and drums, torches and wild beasts, lascivious dances, idolatrous sacrifices. "Where am I?" he asked himself. He could not remember the name of the city; he had even forgotten he was in Poland. He thought he might be in Athens, or Rome, or perhaps he was in Carthage. "In what age do I live?" he wondered. His fevered brain made him think it was hundreds of years before the Christian era. Soon he tired from too much thought. Only one question remained to perplex him: Are the Epicureans right? Am I really dying without any revelation? Am I about to be extinguished forever?

Suddenly I, the Tempter, materialized. Although blind, he saw me. "Zeidel," I said, "prepare yourself. The last hour has come."

"Is it you, Satan, Angel of Death?" Zeidel exclaimed joyously.

"Yes, Zeidel," I replied, "I have come for you. And it won't help you to repent or confess, so don't try."

"Where are you taking me?" he asked.

"Straight to Gehenna."

"If there is a Gehenna, there is also a God," Zeidel said, his lips trembling.

"This proves nothing," I retorted.

"Yes it does," he said. "If Hell exists, everything exists. If you are real, He is real. Now take me to where I belong. I am ready."

Drawing my sword I finished him off, took hold of his soul in my claws and, accompanied by a band of demons, flew to the nether world. In Gehenna the Angels of Destruction were raking up the coals. Two mocking imps stood at the threshold, half-fire and half-pitch, each with a three-cornered hat on his head, a whipping rod on his loins. They burst out laughing.

"Here comes Zeidlus the First," one said to the other, "the yeshiva boy who wanted to become Pope."

I · B · S

The Last Demon

I

I, a demon, bear witness that there are no more demons left. Why demons, when man himself is a demon? Why persuade to evil someone who is already convinced? I am the last of the persuaders. I board in an attic in Tishevitz and draw my sustenance from a Yiddish storybook, a leftover from the days before the great catastrophe. The stories in the book are pablum and duck milk, but the Hebrew letters have a weight of their own. I don't have to tell you that I am a Jew. What else, a Gentile? I've heard that there are Gentile demons, but I don't know any, nor do I wish to know them. Jacob and Esau don't become in-laws.

I came here from Lublin. Tishevitz is a godforsaken village; Adam didn't even stop to pee there. It's so small that a wagon goes through town and the horse is in the marketplace just as the rear wheels reach the toll gate. There is mud in Tishevitz from Sukkoth until Tishe b'Av. The goats of the town don't need to lift their beards to chew at the thatched roofs of the cottages. Hens roost in the middle of the streets. Birds build nests in the women's bonnets. In the tailor's synagogue a billy goat is the tenth in the quorum.

Don't ask me how I managed to get to this smallest letter in the smallest of all prayer books. But when Asmodeus bids you go, you go. After Lublin the road is familiar as far as Zamosc. From there on you are on your own. I was told to look for an iron weathercock with a crow perched upon its comb on the roof of the study house. Once upon a time the cock turned in the wind, but for years now it hasn't moved, not even in thunder and lightning. In Tishevitz, even iron weathercocks die.

I speak in the present tense as for me time stands still. I arrive. I look around. For the life of me I can't find a single one of our men. The

Translated by Martha Glicklich and Cecil Hemley

cemetery is empty. There is no outhouse. I go to the ritual bathhouse, but I don't hear a sound. I sit down on the highest bench, look down on the stone on which the buckets of water are poured each Friday, and wonder. Why am I needed here? If a little demon is wanted, is it necessary to import one all the way from Lublin? Aren't there enough devils in Zamosc? Outside the sun is shining—it's close to the summer solstice —but inside the bathhouse it's gloomy and cold. Above me is a spider web, and within the web a spider wiggling its legs, seeming to spin but drawing no thread. There's no sign of a fly, not even the shell of a fly. "What does the creature eat?" I ask myself. "Its own insides?" Suddenly I hear it chanting in a Talmudic singsong: "A lion isn't satisfied by a morsel and a ditch isn't filled up with dirt from its own walls."

I burst out laughing.

"Is that so? Why have you disguised yourself as a spider?"

"I've already been a worm, a flea, a frog. I've been sitting here for two hundred years without a stitch of work to do. But you need a permit to leave."

"They don't sin here?"

"Petty men, petty sins. Today someone covets another man's broom; tomorrow he fasts and puts peas in his shoes. Ever since Abraham Zalman was under the illusion that he was Messiah, the son of Joseph, the blood of the people has congealed in their veins. If I were Satan, I wouldn't even send one of our first-graders here."

"How much does it cost him?"

"What's new in the world?" he asks me.

"It's not been so good for our crowd."

"What's happened? The Holy Spirit grows stronger?"

"Stronger? Only in Tishevitz is he powerful. No one's heard of him in the large cities. Even in Lublin he's out of style."

"Well, that should be fine."

"But it isn't," I said. " 'All-Guilty is worse for us than All-Innocent.' It has reached a point where people want to sin beyond their capacities. They martyr themselves for the most trivial of sins. If that's the way it is, what are we needed for? A short while ago I was flying over Levertov Street, and I saw a man dressed in a skunk's coat. He had a black beard and wavy sidelocks; an amber cigar holder was clamped between his lips. Across the street from him an official's wife was walking, so it occurs to me to say, 'That's quite a bargain, don't you think, Uncle?' All I expected from him was a thought. I had my handkerchief ready if he should spit on me. So what does the man do? 'Why waste your breath on me?' he calls out angrily. 'I'm willing. Start working on her.' "

"What sort of a misfortune is this?"

"Enlightenment! In the two hundred years you've been sitting on your tail here, Satan has cooked up a new dish of kasha. The Jews have now developed writers. Yiddish ones, Hebrew ones, and they have taken over our trade. We grow hoarse talking to every adolescent, but they print their kitsch by the thousands and distribute it to Jews everywhere. They know all our tricks—mockery, piety. They have a hundred reasons why a rat must be kosher. All that they want to do is to redeem the world. Why, if you could corrupt nothing, have you been left here for two hundred years? And if you could do nothing in two hundred years, what do they expect from me in two weeks?"

"You know the proverb, 'A guest for a while sees a mile.' "

"What's there to see?"

"A young rabbi has moved here from Modly Bozyc. He's not yet thirty, but he's absolutely stuffed with knowledge, knows the thirty-six tractates of the Talmud by heart. He's the greatest Cabalist in Poland, fasts every Monday and Thursday, and bathes in the ritual bath when the water is ice cold. He won't permit any of us to talk to him. What's more he has a handsome wife, and that's bread in the basket. What do we have to tempt him with? You might as well try to break through an iron wall. If I were asked my opinion, I'd say that Tishevitz should be removed from our files. All I ask is that you get me out of here before I go mad."

"No, first I must have a talk with this rabbi. How do you think I should start?"

"You tell me. He'll start pouring salt on your tail before you open your mouth."

"I'm from Lublin. I'm not so easily frightened."

I I

On the way to the rabbi, I ask the imp, "What have you tried so far?"

"What haven't I tried?" he answers.

"A woman?"

"Won't look at one."

"Heresy?"

"He knows all the answers."

"Money?"

"Doesn't know what a coin looks like."

"Reputation?"

"He runs from it."

"Doesn't he look backwards?"

"Doesn't even move his head."

"He's got to have some angle."

"Where's it hidden?"

The window of the rabbi's study is open, and in we fly. There's the usual paraphernalia around: an ark with the Holy Scroll, bookshelves, a mezuzah in a wooden case. The rabbi, a young man with a blond beard, blue eyes, yellow sidelocks, a high forehead, and a deep widow's peak sits on the rabbinical chair peering in the Gemara. He's fully equipped: yarmulka, sash, and fringed garment with each of the fringes braided eight times. I listen to his skull: pure thoughts! He sways and chants in Hebrew, *"Rachel t'unah v'gazezah,"* and then translates: "A woolly sheep fleeced."

"In Hebrew Rachel is both a sheep and a girl's name," I say.

"So?"

"A sheep has wool and a girl has hair."

"Therefore?"

"If she's not androgynous, a girl has pubic hair."

"Stop babbling and let me study," the rabbi says in anger.

"Wait a second," I say. "Torah won't get cold. It's true that Jacob loved Rachel, but when he was given Leah instead, she wasn't poison. And when Rachel gave him Bilhah as a concubine, what did Leah do to spite her sister? She put Zilpah into his bed."

"That was before the giving of Torah."

"What about King David?"

"That happened before the excommunication by Rabbi Gershom."

"Before or after Rabbi Gershom, a male is a male."

"Rascal. *Shaddai kra Satan,"* the rabbi exclaims. Grabbing both of his sidelocks, he begins to tremble as if assaulted by a bad dream. "What nonsense am I thinking?" He takes his ear lobes and closes his ears. I keep on talking but he doesn't listen; he becomes absorbed in a difficult passage and there's no longer anyone to speak to. The little imp from Tishevitz says, "He's a hard one to hook, isn't he? Tomorrow he'll fast and roll in a bed of thistles. He'll give away his last penny to charity."

"Such a believer nowadays?"

"Strong as a rock."

"And his wife?"

"A sacrificial lamb."

"What of the children?"

"Still infants."

"Perhaps he has a mother-in-law?"

"She's already in the other world."

"Any quarrels?"

"Not even half an enemy."

"Where do you find such a jewel?"

"Once in a while something like that turns up among the Jews."

"This one I've got to get. This is my first job around here. I've been promised that if I succeed, I'll be transferred to Odessa."

"What's so good about that?"

"It's as near paradise as our kind gets. You can sleep twenty-four hours a day. The population sins and you don't lift a finger."

"So what do you do all day?"

"We play with our women."

"Here there's not a single one of our girls." The imp sighs. "There was one old bitch but she expired."

"So what's left?"

"What Onan did."

"That doesn't lead anywhere. Help me and I swear by Asmodeus's beard that I'll get you out of here. We have an opening for a mixer of bitter herbs. You only work Passovers."

"I hope it works out, but don't count your chickens."

"We've taken care of tougher than he."

III

A week goes by and our business has not moved forward; I find myself in a dirty mood. A week in Tishevitz is equal to a year in Lublin. The Tishevitz imp is all right, but when you sit two hundred years in such a hole, you become a yokel. He cracks jokes that didn't amuse Enoch and convulses with laughter; he drops names from the Haggadah. Every one of his stories wears a long beard. I'd like to get the hell out of here, but it doesn't take a magician to return home with nothing. I have enemies among my colleagues and I must beware of intrigue. Perhaps I was sent here just to break my neck. When devils stop warring with people, they start tripping each other.

Experience has taught that of all the snares we use, there are three that work unfailingly—lust, pride, and avarice. No one can evade all three, not even Rabbi Tsots himself. Of the three, pride has the strongest meshes. According to the Talmud a scholar is permitted the eighth part of an eighth part of vanity. But a learned man generally exceeds his quota. When I see that the days are passing and that the rabbi of Tishevitz remains stubborn, I concentrate on vanity.

"Rabbi of Tishevitz," I say, "I wasn't born yesterday. I come from Lublin, where the streets are paved with exegeses of the Talmud. We use manuscripts to heat our ovens. The floors of our attics sag under the weight of Cabala. But not even in Lublin have I met a man of your eminence. How does it happen," I ask, "that no one's heard of you? True saints should hide themselves, perhaps, but silence will not bring redemption. You should be the leader of this generation, and not merely the rabbi of this community, holy though it is. The time has come for you to reveal yourself. Heaven and earth are waiting for you. Messiah himself sits in the Bird Nest looking down in search of an unblemished saint like you. But what are you doing about it? You sit on your rabbinical chair laying down the law on which pots and which pans are kosher. Forgive me the comparison, but it is as if an elephant were put to work hauling a straw."

"Who are you and what do you want?" the rabbi asks in terror. "Why don't you let me study?"

"There is a time when the service of God requires the neglect of Torah," I scream. "Any student can study the Gemara."

"Who sent you here?"

"I was sent; I am here. Do you think they don't know about you up there? The higher-ups are annoyed with you. Broad shoulders must bear their share of the load. To put it in rhyme: the humble can stumble. Hearken to this: Abraham Zalman was Messiah, son of Joseph, and you are ordained to prepare the way for Messiah, son of David, but stop sleeping. Get ready for battle. The world sinks to the forty-ninth gate of uncleanliness, but you have broken through to the seventh firmament. Only one cry is heard in the mansions, the man from Tishevitz. The angel in charge of Edom has marshaled a clan of demons against you. Satan lies in wait also. Asmodeus is undermining you. Lilith and Namah hover at your bedside. You don't see them, but Shabriri and Briri are treading at your heels. If the Angels were not defending you, that unholy crowd would pound you to dust and ashes. But you do not stand alone, Rabbi of Tishevitz. Lord Sandalphon guards your every step. Metratron watches over you from his luminescent sphere. Everything hangs in the balance, man of Tishevitz; you can tip the scales."

"What should I do?"

"Mark well all that I tell you. Even if I command you to break the law, do as I bid."

"Who are you? What is your name?"

"Elijah the Tishbite. I have the ram's horn of the Messiah ready. Whether the redemption comes, or we wander in the darkness of Egypt another 2,689 years is up to you."

The rabbi of Tishevitz remains silent for a long time. His face becomes as white as the slips of paper on which he writes his commentaries.

"How do I know you're speaking the truth?" he asks in a trembling voice. "Forgive me, Holy Angel, but I require a sign."

"You are right. I will give you a sign."

And I raise such a wind in the rabbi's study that the slip of paper on which he is writing rises from the table and starts flying like a pigeon. The pages of the Gemara turn by themselves. The curtain of the Holy Scroll billows. The rabbi's yarmulka jumps from his head, soars to the ceiling, and drops back onto his skull.

"Is that how Nature behaves?" I ask.

"No."

"Do you believe me now?"

The rabbi of Tishevitz hesitates. "What do you want me to do?"

"The leader of this generation must be famous."

"How do you become famous?"

"Go and travel in the world."

"What do I do in the world?"

"Preach and collect money."

"For what do I collect?"

"First of all collect. Later on I'll tell you what to do with the money."

"Who will contribute?"

"When I order, Jews give."

"How will I support myself?"

"A rabbinical emissary is entitled to a part of what he collects."

"And my family?"

"You will get enough for all."

"What am I supposed to do right now?"

"Shut the Gemara."

"Ah, but my soul yearns for Torah," the rabbi of Tishevitz groans. Nevertheless, he lifts the cover of the book, ready to shut it. If he had done that, he would have been through. What did Joseph de la Rinah do? Just hand Samael a pinch of snuff. I am already laughing to myself, "Rabbi of Tishevitz, I have you all wrapped up." The little bathhouse imp, standing in a corner, cocks an ear and turns green with envy. True, I have promised to do him a favor, but the jealousy of our kind is stronger than anything. Suddenly the rabbi says, "Forgive me, my Lord, but I require another sign."

"What do you want me to do? Stop the sun?"

"Just show me your feet."

The moment the rabbi of Tishevitz speaks these words, I know everything is lost. We can disguise all the parts of our body but the feet. From the smallest imp right up to Ketev Meriri we all have the claws of geese. The little imp in the corner bursts out laughing. For the first time in a thousand years I, the master of speech, lose my tongue.

"I don't show my feet," I call out in rage.

"That means you're a devil. *Pik*, get out of here," the rabbi cries. He races to his bookcase, pulls out *The Book of Creation* and waves it menacingly over me. What devil can withstand *The Book of Creation?* I run from the rabbi's study with my spirit in pieces.

To make a long story short, I remain stuck in Tishevitz. No more Lublin, no more Odessa. In one second all my stratagems turn to ashes. An order comes from Asmodeus himself. "Stay in Tishevitz and fry. Don't go further than a man is allowed to walk on the Sabbath."

How long am I here? Eternity plus a Wednesday. I've seen it all, the destruction of Tishevitz, the destruction of Poland. There are no more Jews, no more demons. The women don't pour out water any longer on the night of the winter solstice. They don't avoid giving things in even numbers. They no longer knock at dawn at the antechamber of the synagogue. They don't warn us before emptying the slops. The rabbi was martyred on a Friday in the month of Nisan. The community was slaughtered, the holy books burned, the cemetery desecrated. *The Book of Creation* has been returned to the Creator. Gentiles wash themselves in the ritual bath. Abraham Zalman's chapel has been turned into a pigsty. There is no longer an Angel of Good or an Angel of Evil. No more sins, no more temptations! The generation is already guilty seven times over, but Messiah does not come. To whom should he come? Messiah did not come for the Jews, so the Jews went to Messiah. There is no further need for demons. We have also been annihilated. I am the last, a refugee. I can go anywhere I please, but where should a demon like me go? To the murderers?

I found a Yiddish storybook between two broken barrels in the house which once belonged to Velvel the barrelmaker. I sit there, the last of the demons. I eat dust. I sleep on a feather duster. I keep on reading gibberish. The style of the book is in our manner; Sabbath pudding cooked in pig's fat: blasphemy rolled in piety. The moral of the book is: neither judge, nor judgment. But nevertheless the letters are Jewish. The alphabet they could not squander. I suck on the letters and feed myself. I count the words, make rhymes, and tortuously interpret and reinterpret each dot.

> *Aleph*, the abyss, what else waited?
> *Beth*, the blow, long since fated.
> *Gimel*, God, pretending He knew,
> *Daleth*, death, its shadow grew.
> *Hai*, the hangman, he stood prepared;
> *Vov*, wisdom, ignorance bared.
> *Zayeen*, the zodiac, signs distantly loomed;
> *Chet*, the child, prenatally doomed.
> *Tet*, the thinker, an imprisoned lord;
> *Yud*, the judge, the verdict a fraud.

Yes, as long as a single volume remains, I have something to sustain me. As long as the moths have not destroyed the last page, there is something to play with. What will happen when the last letter is no more, I'd rather not bring to my lips.

> *When the last letter is gone,*
> *The last of the demons is done.*

Short Friday

I

IN the village of Lapschitz lived a tailor named Shmul-Leibele with his wife, Shoshe. Shmul-Leibele was half tailor, half furrier, and a complete pauper. He had never mastered his trade. When filling an order for a jacket or a gaberdine, he inevitably made the garment either too short or too tight. The belt in the back would hang either too high or too low, the lapels never matched, the vent was off center. It was said that he had once sewn a pair of trousers with the fly off to one side. Shmul-Leibele could not count the wealthy citizens among his customers. Common people brought him their shabby garments to have patched and turned, and the peasants gave him their old pelts to reverse. As is usual with bunglers, he was also slow. He would dawdle over a garment for weeks at a time. Yet, despite his shortcomings, it must be said that Shmul-Leibele was an honorable man. He used only strong thread and none of his seams ever gave. If one ordered a lining from Shmul-Leibele, even one of common sackcloth or cotton, he bought only the very best material, and thus lost most of his profit. Unlike other tailors who hoarded every last bit of remaining cloth, he returned all scraps to his customers.

Had it not been for his competent wife, Shmul-Leibele would certainly have starved to death. Shoshe helped him in whatever way she could. On Thursdays she hired herself out to wealthy families to knead dough, and on summer days went off to the forest to gather berries and mushrooms, as well as pinecones and twigs for the stove. In winter she plucked down for brides' featherbeds. She was also a better tailor than her husband, and when he began to sigh, or dally and mumble to himself, an indication that he could no longer muddle through, she would take the chalk from his hand and show him how to continue. Shoshe had no children, but it was common knowledge that it wasn't she who was

Translated by Joseph Singer and Roger Klein

barren, but rather her husband who was sterile, since all of her sisters had borne children, while his only brother was likewise childless. The townswomen repeatedly urged Shoshe to divorce him, but she turned a deaf ear, for the couple loved one another with a great love.

Shmul-Leibele was small and clumsy. His hands and feet were too large for his body, and his forehead bulged on either side as is common in simpletons. His cheeks, red as apples, were bare of whiskers, and but a few hairs sprouted from his chin. He had scarcely any neck at all; his head sat upon his shoulders like a snowman's. When he walked, he scraped his shoes along the ground so that every step could be heard far away. He hummed continuously and there was always an amiable smile on his face. Both winter and summer he wore the same caftan and sheepskin cap and earlaps. Whenever there was any need for a messenger, it was always Shmul-Leibele who was pressed into service, and however far away he was sent, he always went willingly. The wags saddled him with a variety of nicknames and made him the butt of all sorts of pranks, but he never took offense. When others scolded his tormentors, he would merely observe: "What do I care? Let them have their fun. They're only children, after all . . ."

Sometimes he would present one or another of the mischief makers with a piece of candy or a nut. This he did without any ulterior motive, but simply out of good-heartedness.

Shoshe towered over him by a head. In her younger days she had been considered a beauty, and in the households where she worked as a servant they spoke highly of her honesty and diligence. Many young men had vied for her hand, but she had selected Shmul-Leibele because he was quiet and because he never joined the other town boys who gathered on the Lublin road at noon Saturdays to flirt with the girls. His piety and retiring nature pleased her. Even as a girl Shoshe had taken pleasure in studying the Pentateuch, in nursing the infirm at the almshouse, in listening to the tales of the old women who sat before their houses darning stockings. She would fast on the last day of each month, the Minor Day of Atonement, and often attended the services at the women's synagogue. The other servant girls mocked her and thought her old-fashioned. Immediately following her wedding she shaved her head and fastened a kerchief firmly over her ears, never permitting a stray strand of hair from her matron's wig to show as did some of the other young women. The bath attendant praised her because she never frolicked at the ritual bath, but performed her ablutions according to the laws. She purchased only indisputably kosher meat, though it was a half-cent more per pound, and when she was in doubt about the dietary laws she sought out the rabbi's advice. More than once she had not hesitated to throw out all the food and even to smash the earthen crockery. In short, she was a capable, God-fearing woman, and more than one man envied Shmul-Leibele his jewel of a wife.

Above all of life's blessings the couple revered the Sabbath. Every Friday noon Shmul-Leibele would lay aside his tools and cease all work. He was always among the first at the ritual bath, and he immersed himself in the water four times for the four letters of the Holy Name. He also helped the beadle set the candles in the chandeliers and the candelabra. Shoshe scrimped throughout the week, but on the Sabbath she was lavish. Into the heated oven went cakes, cookies and the Sabbath loaf. In winter, she prepared puddings made of chicken's neck stuffed with dough and rendered fat. In summer she made puddings with rice or noodles, greased with chicken fat and sprinkled with sugar or cinnamon. The main dish consisted of potatoes and buckwheat, or pearl barley with beans, in the midst of which she never failed to set a marrow bone. To insure that the dish would be well cooked, she sealed the oven with loose dough. Shmul-Leibele treasured every mouthful, and at every Sabbath meal he would remark: "Ah, Shoshe love, it's food fit for a king! Nothing less than a taste of Paradise!" to which Shoshe replied, "Eat hearty. May it bring you good health."

Although Shmul-Leibele was a poor scholar, unable to memorize a chapter of the Mishnah, he was well versed in all the laws. He and his wife frequently studied *The Good Heart* in Yiddish. On half-holidays, holidays, and on each free day, he studied the Bible in Yiddish. He never missed a sermon, and though a pauper, he bought from peddlers all sorts of books of moral instructions and religious tales, which he then read together with his wife. He never wearied of reciting sacred phrases. As soon as he arose in the morning he washed his hands and began to mouth the preamble to the prayers. Then he would walk over to the study house and worship as one of the quorum. Every day he recited a few chapters of the Psalms, as well as those prayers which the less serious tended to skip over. From his father he had inherited a thick prayer book with wooden covers, which contained the rites and laws pertaining to each day of the year. Shmul-Leibele and his wife heeded each and every one of these. Often he would observe to his wife: "I shall surely end up in Gehenna, since there'll be no one on earth to say Kaddish over me." "Bite your tongue, Shmul-Leibele," she would counter. "For one, everything is possible under God. Secondly, you'll live until the Messiah comes. Thirdly, it's just possible that I will die before you and you will marry a young woman who'll bear you a dozen children." When Shoshe said this, Shmul-Leibele would shout: "God forbid! You must remain in good health. I'd rather rot in Gehenna!"

Although Shmul-Leibele and Shoshe relished every Sabbath, their greatest satisfaction came from the Sabbaths in wintertime. Since the day before the Sabbath evening was a short one, and since Shoshe was busy until late Thursday at her work, the couple usually stayed up all of Thursday night. Shoshe kneaded dough in the trough, covering it with cloth and a pillow so that it might ferment. She heated the oven with kindling wood and dry twigs. The shutters in the room were kept closed, the door shut. The bed and bench-bed remained unmade, for at day-break the couple would take a nap. As long as it was dark Shoshe prepared the Sabbath meal by the light of a candle. She plucked a chicken or a goose (if she had managed to come by one cheaply), soaked it, salted it and scraped the fat from it. She roasted a liver for Shmul-Leibele over the glowing coals and baked a small Sabbath loaf for him. Occasionally she would inscribe her name upon the loaf with letters of dough, and then Shmul-Leibele would tease her: "Shoshe, I am eating you up. Shoshe, I have already swallowed you." Shmul-Liebele loved warmth, and he would climb up on the oven and from there look down as his spouse cooked, baked, washed, rinsed, pounded and carved. The Sabbath loaf would turn out round and brown. Shoshe braided the loaf so swiftly that it seemed to dance before Shmul-Leibele's eyes. She bustled about efficiently with spatulas, pokers, ladles and goosewing dusters, and at times even snatched up a live coal with her bare fingers. The pots perked and bubbled. Occasionally a drop of soup would spill and the hot tin would hiss and squeal. And all the while the cricket continued its chirping. Although Shmul-Leibele had finished his supper by this time, his appetite would be whetted afresh, and Shoshe would throw him a knish, a chicken gizzard, a cookie, a plum from the plum stew or a chunk of the pot roast. At the same time she would chide him, saying that he was a glutton. When he attempted to defend himself she would cry: "Oh, the sin is upon me, I have allowed you to starve . . ."

At dawn they would both lie down in utter exhaustion. But because of their efforts Shoshe would not have to run herself ragged the following day, and she could make the benediction over the candles a quarter of an hour before sunset.

The Friday on which this story took place was the shortest Friday of the year. Outside, the snow had been falling all night and had blanketed the house up to the windows and barricaded the door. As usual, the couple had stayed up until morning, then had lain down to sleep. They had arisen later than usual, for they hadn't heard the rooster's crow, and since the windows were covered with snow and frost, the day seemed as dark as night. After whispering, "I thank Thee," Shmul-Leibele went outside with a broom and shovel to clear a path, after which he took a bucket and fetched water from the well. Then, as he had no pressing work, he decided to lay off for the whole day. He went to the study house for the morning prayers, and after breakfast wended his way to the bathhouse. Because of the cold outside, the patrons kept up an eternal plaint: "A bucket! A bucket!" and the bath attendant poured more and more water over the glowing stones so that the steam grew constantly denser. Shmul-Leibele located a scraggly willow-broom, mounted to the highest bench and whipped himself until his skin glowed red. From the bathhouse, he hurried over to the study house where the beadle had already swept and sprinkled the floor with sand. Shmul-Leibele set the candles and helped spread the tablecloths over the tables. Then he went home again and changed into his Sabbath clothes. His boots, resoled but a few days before, no longer let the wet through. Shoshe had done her washing for the week, and had given him a fresh shirt, underdrawers, a fringed garment, even a clean pair of stockings. She had already performed the benediction over the candles, and the spirit of the Sabbath emanated from every corner of the room. She was wearing her silk kerchief with the silver spangles, a yellow and gray dress, and shoes with gleaming, pointed tips. On her throat hung the chain that Shmul-Leibele's mother, peace be with her, had given her to celebrate the signing of the wedding contract. The marriage band sparkled on her index finger. The candlelight reflected in the windowpanes, and Shmul-Leibele fancied that there was a duplicate of this room outside and that another Shoshe was out there lighting the Sabbath candles. He yearned to tell his wife how full of grace she was, but there was no time for it, since it is specifically stated in the prayer book that it is fitting and proper to be among the first ten worshippers at the synagogue; as it so happened, going off to prayers he was the tenth man to arrive. After the congregation had intoned the Song of Songs, the cantor sang, "Give thanks," and "O come, let us exult." Shmul-Leibele prayed with fervor. The words were sweet upon his tongue, they seemed to fall from his lips with a life of their own, and he felt that they soared to the eastern wall, rose above the embroidered curtain of the Holy Ark, the gilded lions, and the tablets, and floated up to the ceiling with its painting of the twelve constellations. From there, the prayers surely ascended to the Throne of Glory.

II

The cantor chanted, "Come, my beloved," and Shmul-Leibele trumpeted along in accompaniment. Then came the prayers, and the men recited, "It is our duty to praise . . ." to which Shmul-Leibele added a "Lord of the Universe." Afterwards, he wished everyone a good Sabbath: the rabbi, the ritual slaughterer, the head of the community, the assistant rabbi, everyone present. The cheder lads shouted, "Good

Sabbath, Shmul-Leibele," while they mocked him with gestures and grimaces, but Shmul-Leibele answered them all with a smile, even occasionally pinched a boy's cheek affectionately. Then he was off for home. The snow was piled high so that one could barely make out the contours of the roofs, as if the entire settlement had been immersed in white. The sky, which had hung low and overcast all day, now grew clear. From among white clouds a full moon peered down, casting a day-like brilliance over the snow. In the west, the edge of a cloud still held the glint of sunset. The stars on this Friday seemed larger and sharper, and through some miracle Lapschitz seemed to have blended with the sky. Shmul-Leibele's hut, which was situated not far from the synagogue, now hung suspended in space, as it is written: "He suspendeth the earth on nothingness." Shmul-Leibele walked slowly since, according to law, one must not hurry when coming from a holy place. Yet he longed to be home. "Who knows?" he thought. "Perhaps Shoshe has become ill? Maybe she's gone to fetch water and, God forbid, has fallen into the well? Heaven save us, what a lot of troubles can befall a man."

On the threshold he stamped his feet to shake off the snow, then opened the door and saw Shoshe. The room made him think of Paradise. The oven had been freshly whitewashed, the candles in the brass candelabras cast a Sabbath glow. The aromas coming from the sealed oven blended with the scents of the Sabbath supper. Shoshe sat on the bench-bed apparently awaiting him, her cheeks shining with the freshness of a young girl's. Shmul-Leibele wished her a happy Sabbath and she in turn wished him a good year. He began to hum, "Peace upon ye ministering angels . . ." and after he had said his farewells to the invisible angels that accompany each Jew leaving the synagogue, he recited: "The worthy woman." How well he understood the meaning of these words, for he had read them often in Yiddish, and each time reflected anew on how aptly they seemed to fit Shoshe.

Shoshe was aware that these holy sentences were being said in her honor, and thought to herself, "Here am I, a simple woman, an orphan, and yet God has chosen to bless me with a devoted husband who praises me in the holy tongue."

Both of them had eaten sparingly during the day so that they would have an appetite for the Sabbath meal. Shmul-Leibele said the benediction over the raisin wine and gave Shoshe the cup so that she might drink. Afterwards, he rinsed his fingers from a tin dipper, then she washed hers, and they both dried their hands with a single towel, each at either end. Shmul-Leibele lifted the Sabbath loaf and cut it with the bread knife, a slice for himself and one for his wife.

He immediately informed her that the loaf was just right, and she countered: "Go on, you say that every Sabbath."

"But it happens to be the truth," he replied.

Although it was hard to obtain fish during the cold weather, Shoshe had purchased three-fourths of a pound of pike from the fishmonger. She had chopped it with onions, added an egg, salt and pepper, and cooked it with carrots and parsley. It took Shmul-Leibele's breath away, and after it he had to drink a tumbler of whiskey. When he began the table chants, Shoshe accompanied him quietly. Then came the chicken soup with noodles and tiny circlets of fat which glowed on the surface like golden ducats. Between the soup and the main course, Shmul-Leibele again sang Sabbath hymns. Since goose was cheap at this time of year, Shoshe gave Shmul-Leibele an extra leg for good measure. After the dessert, Shmul-Leibele washed for the last time and made a benediction. When he came to the words: "Let us not be in need either of the gifts of flesh and blood nor of their loans," he rolled his eyes upward and brandished his fists. He never stopped praying that he be allowed to continue to earn his own livelihood and not, God forbid, become an object of charity.

After grace, he said yet another chapter of the Mishnah, and all sorts of other prayers which were found in his large prayer book. Then he sat down to read the weekly portion of the Pentateuch twice in Hebrew and once in Aramaic. He enunciated every word and took care to make no mistake in the difficult Aramaic paragraphs of the Onkelos. When he reached the last section, he began to yawn and tears gathered in his eyes. Utter exhaustion overcame him. He could barely keep his eyes open and between one passage and the next he dozed off for a second or two. When Shoshe noticed this, she made up the bench-bed for him and prepared her own featherbed with clean sheets. Shmul-Leibele barely managed to say the retiring prayers and began to undress. When he was already lying on his bench-bed he said: "A good Sabbath, my pious wife. I am very tired . . ." and turning to the wall, he promptly began to snore.

Shoshe sat a while longer gazing at the Sabbath candles which had already begun to smoke and flicker. Before getting into bed, she placed a pitcher of water and a basin at Shmul-Leibele's bedstead so that he would not rise the following morning without water to wash with. Then she, too, lay down and fell asleep.

They had slept an hour or two or possibly three—what does it matter, actually?—when suddenly Shoshe heard Shmul-Leibele's voice. He waked her and whispered her name. She opened one eye and asked, "What is it?"

"Are you clean?" he mumbled.

She thought for a moment and replied, "Yes."

He rose and came to her. Presently he was in bed with her. A desire for her flesh had roused him. His heart pounded rapidly, the blood coursed in his veins. He felt a pressure in his loins. His urge was to mate with her immediately, but he remembered the Law, which admonished a man not to copulate with a woman until he had first spoken affectionately to her, and he now began to speak of his love for her and how this mating could possibly result in a male-child.

"And a girl you wouldn't accept?" Shoshe chided him, and he replied, "Whatever God deigns to bestow would be welcome."

"I fear this privilege isn't mine any more," she said with a sigh.

"Why not?" he demanded. "Our mother Sarah was far older than you."

"How can one compare oneself to Sarah? Far better you divorce me and marry another."

He interrupted her, stopping her mouth with his hand. "Were I sure that I could sire the twelve tribes of Israel with another, I still would not leave you. I cannot even imagine myself with another woman. You are the jewel of my crown."

"And what if I were to die?" she asked.

"God forbid! I would simply perish from sorrow. They would bury us both on the same day."

"Don't speak blasphemy. May you outlive my bones. You are a man. You would find somebody else. But what would I do without you?"

He wanted to answer her, but she sealed his lips with a kiss. He went to her then. He loved her body. Each time she gave herself to him, the wonder of it astonished him anew. How was it possible, he would think, that he, Shmul-Leibele, should have such a treasure all to himself? He knew the law, one dared not surrender to lust for pleasure. But somewhere in a sacred book he had read that it was permissible to kiss and embrace a wife to whom one had been wed according to the laws of Moses and Israel, and he now caressed her face, her throat and her breasts. She warned him that this was frivolity. He replied, "So I'll lie on the torture rack. The great saints also loved their wives." Nevertheless, he promised himself to attend the ritual bath the following morning, to intone psalms and to pledge a sum to charity. Since she loved him also and enjoyed his caresses, she let him do his will.

After he had satiated his desire, he wanted to return to his own bed, but a heavy sleepiness came over him. He felt a pain in his temples. Shoshe's head ached as well. She suddenly said, "I'm afraid something is burning in the oven. Maybe I should open the flue?"

"Go on, you're imagining it," he replied. "It'll become too cold in here."

And so complete was his weariness that he fell asleep, as did she.

That night Shmul-Leibele suffered an eerie dream. He imagined that he had passed away. The Burial Society brethren came by, picked him up, lit candles by his head, opened the windows, intoned the prayer to justify God's ordainment. Afterwards, they washed him on the ablution board, carried him on a stretcher to the cemetery. There they buried him as the gravedigger said Kaddish over his body.

"That's odd," he thought. "I hear nothing of Shoshe lamenting or begging forgiveness. Is it possible that she would so quickly grow unfaithful? Or has she, God forbid, been overcome by grief?"

He wanted to call her name, but he was unable to. He tried to tear free of the grave, but his limbs were powerless. All of a sudden he awoke.

"What a horrible nightmare!" he thought. "I hope I come out of it all right."

At that moment Shoshe also awoke. When he related his dream to her, she did not speak for a while. Then she said, "Woe is me. I had the very same dream."

"Really? You too?" asked Shmul-Leibele, now frightened. "This I don't like."

He tried to sit up, but he could not. It was as if he had been shorn of all his strength. He looked toward the window to see if it were day already, but there was no window visible, nor any windowpane. Darkness loomed everywhere. He cocked his ears. Usually he would be able to hear the chirping of a cricket, the scurrying of a mouse, but this time only a dead silence prevailed. He wanted to reach out to Shoshe, but his hand seemed lifeless.

"Shoshe," he said quietly, "I've grown paralyzed."

"Woe is me, so have I," she said. "I cannot move a limb."

They lay there for a long while, silently, feeling their numbness. Then Shoshe spoke: "I fear that we are already in our graves for good."

"I'm afraid you're right," Shmul-Leibele replied in a voice that was not of the living.

"Pity me, when did it happen? How?" Shoshe asked. "After all, we went to sleep hale and hearty."

"We must have been asphyxiated by the fumes from the stove," Shmul-Leibele said.

"But I said I wanted to open the flue."

"Well, it's too late for that now."

"God have mercy upon us, what do we do now? We were still young people . . ."

"It's no use. Apparently it was fated."

"Why? We arranged a proper Sabbath. I prepared such a tasty meal. An entire chicken neck and tripe."

"We have no further need of food."

Shoshe did not immediately reply. She was trying to sense her own entrails. No, she felt no appetite. Not even for a chicken neck and tripe. She wanted to weep, but she could not.

"Shmul-Leibele, they've buried us already. It's all over."

"Yes, Shoshe, praised be the true Judge! We are in God's hands."

"Will you be able to recite the passage attributed to your name before the Angel Dumah?"

"Yes."

"It's good that we are lying side by side," she muttered.

"Yes, Shoshe," he said, recalling a verse: *Lovely and pleasant in their lives, and in their death they were not divided.*

"And what will become of our hut? You did not even leave a will."

"It will undoubtedly go to your sister."

Shoshe wished to ask something else, but she was ashamed. She was curious about the Sabbath meal. Had it been removed from the oven? Who had eaten it? But she felt that such a query would not be fitting of a corpse. She was no longer Shoshe the dough-kneader, but a pure, shrouded corpse with shards covering her eyes, a cowl over her head, and myrtle twigs between her fingers. The Angel Dumah would appear at any moment with his fiery staff, and she would have to be ready to give an account of herself.

Yes, the brief years of turmoil and temptation had come to an end. Shmul-Leibele and Shoshe had reached the true world. Man and wife grew silent. In the stillness they heard the flapping of wings, a quiet singing. An angel of God had come to guide Shmul-Leibele the tailor and his wife, Shoshe, into Paradise.

The Séance

I

It was during the summer of 1946, in the living room of Mrs. Kopitzky on Central Park West. A single red bulb burned behind a shade adorned with one of Mrs. Kopitzky's automatic drawings—circles with eyes, flowers with mouths, goblets with fingers. The walls were all hung with Lotte Kopitzky's paintings, which she did in a state of trance and at the direction of her control—Bhaghavar Krishna, a Hindu sage supposed to have lived in the fourth century. It was he, Bhaghavar Krishna, who had painted the peacock with the golden tail, in the middle of which appeared the image of Buddha; the otherworldly trees hung with elflocks and fantastic fruits; the young women of the planet Venus with their branch-like arms and their ears from which stretched silver nets—organs of telepathy. Over the pictures, the old furniture, the shelves with books, there hovered reddish shadows. The windows were covered with heavy drapes.

At the round table on which lay a Ouija board, a trumpet, and a withered rose, sat Dr. Zorach Kalisher, small, broad-shouldered, bald in front and with sparse tufts of hair in the back, half yellow, half gray. From behind his yellow bushy brows peered a pair of small, piercing eyes. Dr. Kalisher had almost no neck—his head sat directly on his broad shoulders, making him look like a primitive African statue. His nose was crooked, flat at the top, the tip split in two. On his chin sprouted a tiny growth. It was hard to tell whether this was a remnant of a beard or just a hairy wart. The face was wrinkled, badly shaven, and grimy. He wore a black corduroy jacket, a white shirt covered with ash and coffee stains, and a crooked bow tie.

When conversing with Mrs. Kopitzky, he spoke an odd mixture of Yiddish and German. "What's keeping our friend Bhaghavar Krishna? Did he lose his way in the spheres of Heaven?"

Translated by Roger H. Klein and Cecil Hemley

"Dr. Kalisher, don't rush me," Mrs. Kopitzky answered. "We cannot give them orders . . . They have their motives and their moods. Have a little patience."

"Well, if one must, one must."

Dr. Kalisher drummed his fingers on the table. From each finger sprouted a little red beard. Mrs. Kopitzky leaned her head on the back of the upholstered chair and prepared to fall into a trance. Against the dark glow of the red bulb, one could discern her freshly dyed hair, black without luster, waved into tiny ringlets; her rouged face, the broad nose, high cheekbones, and eyes spread far apart and heavily lined with mascara. Dr. Kalisher often joked that she looked like a painted bulldog. Her husband, Leon Kopitzky, a dentist, had died eighteen years before, leaving no children. The widow supported herself on an annuity from an insurance company. In 1929 she had lost her fortune in the Wall Street crash, but had recently begun to buy securities again on the advice of her Ouija board, planchette, and crystal ball. Mrs. Kopitzky even asked Bhaghavar Krishna for tips on the races. In a few cases, he had divulged in dreams the names of winning horses.

Dr. Kalisher bowed his head and covered his eyes with his hands, muttering to himself as solitary people often do. "Well, I've played the fool enough. This is the last night. Even from kreplech one has enough."

"Did you say something, Doctor?"

"What? Nothing."

"When you rush me, I can't fall into the trance."

"Trance-shmance," Dr. Kalisher grumbled to himself. "The ghost is late, that's all. Who does she think she's fooling? Just crazy—meshugga."

Aloud, he said: "I'm not rushing you, I've plenty of time. If what the Americans say about time is right, I'm a second Rockefeller."

As Mrs. Kopitzky opened her mouth to answer, her double chin, with all its warts, trembled, revealing a set of huge false teeth. Suddenly she threw back her head and sighed. She closed her eyes, and snorted once. Dr. Kalisher gaped at her questioningly, sadly. He had not yet heard the sound of the outside door opening, but Mrs. Kopitzky, who probably had the acute hearing of an animal, might have. Dr. Kalisher began to rub his temples and his nose, and then clutched at his tiny beard.

There was a time when he had tried to understand all things through his reason, but that period of rationalism had long passed. Since then, he had constructed an anti-rationalistic philosophy, a kind of extreme hedonism which saw in eroticism the *Ding an sich*, and in reason the very lowest stage of being, the entropy which led to absolute death. His position had been a curious compound of Hartmann's idea of the Unconscious with the Cabala of Rabbi Isaac Luria, according to which all things, from the smallest grain of sand to the very Godhead itself, are Copulation and Union. It was because of this system that Dr. Kalisher had come from Paris to New York in 1939, leaving behind in Poland his father, a rabbi, a wife who refused to divorce him, and a lover, Nella, with whom he had lived for years in Berlin and later in Paris. It so happened that when Dr. Kalisher left for America, Nella went to visit her parents in Warsaw. He had planned to bring her over to the United States as soon as he found a translator, a publisher, and a chair at one of the American universities.

In those days Dr. Kalisher had still been hopeful. He had been offered a cathedra in the Hebrew University in Jerusalem; a publisher in Palestine was about to issue one of his books; his essays had been printed in Zurich and Paris. But with the outbreak of the Second World War, his life began to deteriorate. His literary agent suddenly died, his translator was inept and, to make matters worse, absconded with a good part of the manuscript, of which there was no copy. In the Yiddish press, for some strange reason, the reviewers turned hostile and hinted that he was a charlatan. The Jewish organizations which arranged lectures for him cancelled his tour. According to his own philosophy, he had believed that all suffering was nothing more than negative expressions of universal eroticism: Hitler, Stalin, the Nazis who sang the Horst Wessel song and made the Jews wear yellow armbands, were actually searching for new forms and variations of sexual salvation. But Dr. Kalisher began to doubt his own system and fell into despair. He had to leave his hotel and move into a cheap furnished room. He wandered about in shabby clothes, sat all day in cafeterias, drank endless cups of coffee, smoked bad cigars, and barely managed to survive on the few dollars that a relief organization gave him each month. The refugees whom he met spread all sorts of rumors about visas for those left behind in Europe, packages of food and medicines that could be sent them through various agencies, ways of bringing over relatives from Poland through Honduras, Cuba, Brazil. But he, Zorach Kalisher, could save no one from the Nazis. He had received only a single letter from Nella.

Only in New York had Dr. Kalisher realized how attached he was to his mistress. Without her, he became impotent.

II

Everything was exactly as it had been yesterday and the day before. Bhaghavar Krishna began to speak in English with his foreign voice that was half male and half female, duplicating Mrs. Kopitzky's errors in pronunciation and grammar. Lotte Kopitzky came from a village in the

Carpathian Mountains. Dr. Kalisher could never discover her nationality
—Hungarian, Rumanian, Galician? She knew no Polish or German, and
little English; even her Yiddish had been corrupted through her long
years in America. Actually she had been left languageless and Bhaghavar Krishna spoke her various jargons. At first Dr. Kalisher had asked
Bhaghavar Krishna the details of his earthly existence but had been told
by Bhaghavar Krishna that he had forgotten everything in the heavenly
mansions in which he dwelt. All he could recall was that he had lived in
the suburbs of Madras. Bhaghavar Krishna did not even know that in
that part of India Tamil was spoken. When Dr. Kalisher tried to converse with him about Sanskrit, the Mahabharata, the Ramayana, the
Sakuntala, Bhaghavar Krishna replied that he was no longer interested
in terrestrial literature. Bhaghavar Krishna knew nothing but a few
theosophic and spiritualistic brochures and magazines which Mrs.
Kopitzky subscribed to.

For Dr. Kalisher it was all one big joke; but if one lived in a bug-
ridden room and had a stomach spoiled by cafeteria food, if one was in
one's sixties and completely without family, one became tolerant of all
kinds of crackpots. He had been introduced to Mrs. Kopitzky in 1942,
took part in scores of her séances, read her automatic writings, admired
her automatic paintings, listened to her automatic symphonies. A few
times he had borrowed money from her which he had been unable to
return. He ate at her house—vegetarian suppers, since Mrs. Kopitzky
touched neither meat, fish, milk, nor eggs, but only fruit and vegetables
which mother earth produces. She specialized in preparing salads with
nuts, almonds, pomegranates, avocados.

In the beginning, Lotte Kopitzky had wanted to draw him into a
romance. The spirits were all of the opinion that Lotte Kopitzky and
Zorach Kalisher derived from the same spiritual origin: *The Great
White Lodge*. Even Bhaghavar Krishna had a taste for matchmaking.
Lotte Kopitzky constantly conveyed to Dr. Kalisher regards from the
Masters, who had connections with Tibet, Atlantis, the Heavenly Hier-
archy, the Shambala, the Fourth Kingdom of Nature and the Council of
Sanat Kumara. In Heaven as on the earth, in the early forties, all kinds
of crises were brewing. The Powers having realigned themselves, the
members of the Ashrams were preparing a war on Cosmic Evil. The
Hierarchy sent out projectors to light up the planet Earth, and to find
esoteric men and women to serve special purposes. Mrs. Kopitzky assured Dr. Kalisher that he was ordained to play a huge part in the
Universal Rebirth. But he had neglected his mission, disappointed the
Masters. He had promised to telephone, but didn't. He spent months in
Philadelphia without dropping her a postcard. He returned without informing her. Mrs. Kopitzky ran into him in an automat on Sixth Avenue

and found him in a torn coat, a dirty shirt, and shoes worn so thin they no longer had heels. He had not even applied for United States citizenship, though refugees were entitled to citizenship without going abroad to get a visa.

Now, in 1946, everything that Lotte Kopitzky had prophesied had come true. All had passed over to the other side—his father, his brothers, his sisters, Nella. Bhaghavar Krishna brought messages from them. The Masters still remembered Dr. Kalisher, and still had plans for him in connection with the Centennial Conference of the Hierarchy. Even the fact that his family had perished in Treblinka, Maidanek, Stutthof was closely connected with the Powers of Light, the Development of Karma, the New Cycle after Lemuria, and with the aim of leading humanity to a new ascent in Love and a new Aquatic Epoch.

During the last few weeks, Mrs. Kopitzky had become dissatisfied with summoning Nella's spirit in the usual way. Dr. Kalisher was given the rare opportunity of coming into contact with Nella's materialized form. It happened in this way: Bhaghavar Krishna would give a sign to Dr. Kalisher that he should walk down the dark corridor to Mrs. Kopitzky's bedroom. There in the darkness, near Mrs. Kopitzky's bureau, an apparition hovered which was supposed to be Nella. She murmured to Dr. Kalisher in Polish, spoke caressing words into his ear, brought him messages from friends and relatives. Bhaghavar Krishna had admonished Dr. Kalisher time and again not to try to touch the phantom, because contact could cause severe injury to both, to him and Mrs. Kopitzky. The few times that he sought to approach her, she deftly eluded him. But confused though Dr. Kalisher was by these episodes, he was aware that they were contrived. This was not Nella, neither her voice nor her manner. The messages he received proved nothing. He had mentioned all these names to Mrs. Kopitzky and had been questioned by her. But Dr. Kalisher remained curious: Who was the apparition? Why did she act the part? Probably for money. But the fact that Lotte Kopitzky was capable of hiring a ghost proved that she was not only a self-deceiver but a swindler of others as well. Every time Dr. Kalisher walked down the dark corridor, he murmured, "Crazy, meshugga, a ridiculous woman."

Tonight Dr. Kalisher could hardly wait for Bhaghavar Krishna's signal. He was tired of these absurdities. For years he had suffered from a prostate condition and now had to urinate every half hour. A Warsaw doctor who was not allowed to practice in America, but did so clandestinely nonetheless, had warned Dr. Kalisher not to postpone an operation, because complications might arise. But Kalisher had neither the money for the hospital nor the will to go there. He sought to cure himself with baths, hot-water bottles, and with pills he had brought with him from France. He even tried to massage his prostate gland himself. As a rule, he went to the bathroom the moment he arrived at Mrs. Kopitzky's, but this evening he had neglected to do so. He felt a pressure on his bladder. The raw vegetables which Mrs. Kopitzky had given him to eat made his intestines twist. "Well, I'm too old for such pleasures," he murmured. As Bhaghavar Krishna spoke, Dr. Kalisher could scarcely listen. "What is she babbling, the idiot? She's not even a decent ventriloquist."

The instant Bhaghavar Krishna gave his usual sign, Dr. Kalisher got up. His legs had been troubling him greatly but had never been as shaky as tonight. "Well, I'll go to the bathroom first," he decided. To reach the bathroom in the dark was not easy. Dr. Kalisher walked hesitantly, his hands outstretched, trying to feel his way. When he had reached the bathroom and opened the door, someone inside pulled the knob back. It is she, the girl, Dr. Kalisher realized. So shaken was he that he forgot why he was there. "She most probably came here to undress." He was embarrassed both for himself and for Mrs. Kopitzky. "What does she need it for, for whom is she playing this comedy?" His eyes had become accustomed to the dark. He had seen the girl's silhouette. The bathroom had a window giving on to the street, and the shimmer of the street lamp had fallen on to it. She was small, broadish, with a high bosom. She appeared to have been in her underwear. Dr. Kalisher stood there hypnotized. He wanted to cry out, "Enough, it's all so obvious," but his tongue was numb. His heart pounded and he could hear his own breathing.

After a while he began to retrace his steps, but he was dazed with blindness. He bumped into a clothes tree and hit a wall, striking his head. He stepped backwards. Something fell and broke. Perhaps one of Mrs. Kopitzky's otherworldly sculptures! At that moment the telephone began to ring, the sound unusually loud and menacing. Dr. Kalisher shivered. He suddenly felt a warmth in his underwear. He had wet himself like a child.

I V

"Well, I've reached the bottom," Dr. Kalisher muttered to himself. "I'm ready for the junkyard." He walked toward the bedroom. Not only his underwear, his pants also had become wet. He expected Mrs. Kopitzky to answer the telephone; it happened more than once that she awakened from her trance to discuss stocks, bonds, and dividends. But the telephone kept on ringing. Only now he realized what he had done—he had closed the living-room door, shutting out the red glow which helped him find his way. "I'm going home," he resolved. He turned toward the street door but found he had lost all sense of direction in that labyrinth of an apartment. He touched a knob and turned it. He heard a muffled scream. He had wandered into the bathroom again. There seemed to be no hook or chain inside. Again he saw the woman in a corset, but this time with her face half in the light. In that split second he knew she was middle-aged.

"Forgive, please." And he moved back.

The telephone stopped ringing, then began anew. Suddenly Dr. Kalisher glimpsed a shaft of red light and heard Mrs. Kopitzky walking toward the telephone. He stopped and said, half statement, half question: "Mrs. Kopitzky!"

Mrs. Kopitzky started. "Already finished?"

"I'm not well, I must go home."

"Not well? Where do you want to go? What's the matter? Your heart?"

"Everything."

"Wait a second."

Mrs. Kopitzky, having approached him, took his arm and led him back to the living room. The telephone continued to ring and then finally fell silent. "Did you get a pressure in your heart, huh?" Mrs. Kopitzky asked. "Lie down on the sofa, I'll get a doctor."

"No, no, not necessary."

"I'll massage you."

"My bladder is not in order, my prostate gland."

"What? I'll put on the light."

He wanted to ask her not to do so, but she had already turned on a number of lamps. The light glared in his eyes. She stood looking at him and at his wet pants. Her head shook from side to side. Then she said, "This is what comes from living alone."

"Really, I'm ashamed of myself."

"What's the shame? We all get older. Nobody gets younger. Were you in the bathroom?"

Dr. Kalisher didn't answer.

"Wait a moment, I still have *his* clothes. I had a premonition I would need them someday."

Mrs. Kopitzky left the room. Dr. Kalisher sat down on the edge of a chair, placing his handkerchief beneath him. He sat there stiff, wet, childishly guilty and helpless, and yet with that inner quiet that comes from illness. For years he had been afraid of doctors, hospitals, and especially nurses, who deny their feminine shyness and treat grownup men like babies. Now he was prepared for the last degradations of the body. "Well, I'm finished, *kaput*." He made a swift summation of his existence. "Philosophy? what philosophy? Eroticism? whose eroticism?"

He had played with phrases for years, had come to no conclusions. What had happened to him, in him, all that had taken place in Poland, in Russia, on the planets, on the faraway galaxies, could not be reduced either to Schopenhauer's blind will or to his, Kalisher's, eroticism. It was explained neither by Spinoza's substance, Leibnitz's monads, Hegel's dialectic, or Heckel's monism. "They all just juggle words like Mrs. Kopitzky. It's better that I didn't publish all that scribbling of mine. What's the good of all these preposterous hypotheses? They don't help at all . . ." He looked up at Mrs. Kopitzky's pictures on the wall, and in the blazing light they resembled the smearings of school children. From the street came the honking of cars, the screams of boys, the thundering echo of the subway as a train passed. The door opened and Mrs. Kopitzky entered with a bundle of clothes: a jacket, pants, and shirt, and underwear. The clothes smelled of mothballs and dust. She said to him, "Have you been in the bedroom?"

"What? No."

"Nella didn't materialize?"

"No, she didn't materialize."

"Well, change your clothes. Don't let me embarrass you."

She put the bundle on the sofa and bent over Dr. Kalisher with the devotion of a relative. She said, "You'll stay here. Tomorrow I'll send for your things."

"No, that's senseless."

"I knew that this would happen the moment we were introduced on Second Avenue."

"How so? Well, it's all the same."

"*They* tell me things in advance. I look at someone, and I know what will happen to him."

"So? When am I going to go?"

"You still have to live many years. You're needed here. You have to finish your work."

"My work has the same value as your ghosts."

"There *are* ghosts, there are! Don't be so cynical. They watch over us from above, they lead us by the hand, they measure our steps. We are much more important to the Cyclic Revival of the Universe than you imagine."

He wanted to ask her: "Why then, did you have to hire a woman to deceive me?" but he remained silent. Mrs. Kopitzky went out again. Dr. Kalisher took off his pants and underwear and dried himself with his handkerchief. For a while he stood with his upper part fully dressed and his pants off like some mad jester. Then he stepped into a pair of loose drawers that were as cool as shrouds. He pulled on a pair of striped pants that were too wide and too long for him. He had to draw the pants up until the hem reached his knees. He gasped and snorted, had to stop every few seconds to rest. Suddenly he remembered! This was exactly how as a boy he had dressed himself in his father's clothes when his father napped after the Sabbath pudding: the old man's white trousers, his satin robe, his fringed garment, his fur hat. Now his father had become a pile of ashes somewhere in Poland, and he, Zorach, put on the musty clothes of a dentist. He walked to the mirror and looked at himself, even stuck out his tongue like a child. Then he lay down on the sofa. The telephone rang again, and Mrs. Kopitzky apparently answered it, because this time the ringing stopped immediately. Dr. Kalisher closed his eyes and lay quietly. He had nothing to hope for. There was not even anything to think about.

He dozed off and found himself in the cafeteria on Forty-second Street, near the Public Library. He was breaking off pieces of an egg cookie. A refugee was telling him how to save relatives in Poland by dressing them up in Nazi uniforms. Later they would be led by ship to the North Pole, the South Pole, and across the Pacific. Agents were prepared to take charge of them in Tierra del Fuego, in Honolulu and Yokohama . . . How strange, but that smuggling had something to do with his, Zorach Kalisher's, philosophic system, not with his former version but with a new one, which blended eroticism with memory. While he was combining all these images, he asked himself in astonishment: "What kind of relationship can there be between sex, memory, and the redemption of the ego? And how will it work in infinite time? It's nothing but casuistry, casuistry. It's a way of explaining my own impotence. And how can I bring over Nella when she has already perished? Unless death itself is nothing but a sexual amnesia." He awoke and saw Mrs. Kopitzky bending over him with a pillow which she was about to put behind his head.

"How do you feel?"

"Has Nella left?" he asked, amazed at his own words. He must still be half asleep.

Mrs. Kopitzky winced. Her double chin shook and trembled. Her dark eyes were filled with motherly reproach.

"You're laughing, huh? There is no death, there isn't any. We live forever, and we love forever. This is the pure truth."

The Slaughterer

I

YOINEH MEIR should have become the Kolomir rabbi. His father and his grandfather had both sat in the rabbinical chair in Kolomir. However, the followers of the Kuzmir court had set up a stubborn opposition: this time they would not allow a Hasid from Trisk to become the town's rabbi. They bribed the district official and sent a petition to the governor. After long wrangling, the Kuzmir Hasidim finally had their way and installed a rabbi of their own. In order not to leave Yoineh Meir without a source of earnings, they appointed him the town's ritual slaughterer.

When Yoineh Meir heard of this, he turned even paler than usual. He protested that slaughtering was not for him. He was softhearted; he could not bear the sight of blood. But everybody banded together to persuade him—the leaders of the community; the members of the Trisk synagogue; his father-in-law, Reb Getz Frampoler; and Reitze Doshe, his wife. The new rabbi, Reb Sholem Levi Halberstam, also pressed him to accept. Reb Sholem Levi, a grandson of the Sondz rabbi, was troubled about the sin of taking away another's livelihood; he did not want the younger man to be without bread. The Trisk rabbi, Reb Yakov Leibele, wrote a letter to Yoineh Meir saying that man may not be more compassionate than the Almighty, the Source of all compassion. When you slaughter an animal with a pure knife and with piety, you liberate the soul that resides in it. For it is well known that the souls of saints often transmigrate into the bodies of cows, fowl, and fish to do penance for some offense.

After the rabbi's letter, Yoineh Meir gave in. He had been ordained a long time ago. Now he set himself to studying the laws of slaughter as expounded in the *Grain of the Ox*, the *Shulchan Aruch*, and the Com-

Translated by Mirra Ginsburg

mentaries. The first paragraph of the *Grain of the Ox* says that the ritual slaughterer must be a God-fearing man, and Yoineh Meir devoted himself to the Law with more zeal than ever.

Yoineh Meir—small, thin, with a pale face, a tiny yellow beard on the tip of his chin, a crooked nose, a sunken mouth, and yellow frightened eyes set too close together—was renowned for his piety. When he prayed, he put on three pairs of phylacteries: those of Rashi, those of Rabbi Tam, and those of Rabbi Sherira Gaon. Soon after he had completed his term of board at the home of his father-in-law, he began to keep all fast days and to get up for midnight service.

His wife, Reitze Doshe, already lamented that Yoineh Meir was not of this world. She complained to her mother that he never spoke a word to her and paid her no attention, even on her clean days. He came to her only on the nights after she had visited the ritual bath, once a month. She said that he did not remember the names of his own daughters.

After he agreed to become the ritual slaughterer, Yoineh Meir imposed new rigors upon himself. He ate less and less. He almost stopped speaking. When a beggar came to the door, Yoineh Meir ran to welcome him and gave him his last groschen. The truth is that becoming a slaughterer plunged Yoineh Meir into melancholy, but he did not dare to oppose the rabbi's will. It was meant to be, Yoineh Meir said to himself; it was his destiny to cause torment and to suffer torment. And only Heaven knew how much Yoineh Meir suffered.

Yoineh Meir was afraid that he might faint as he slaughtered his first fowl, or that his hand might not be steady. At the same time, somewhere in his heart, he hoped that he would commit an error. This would release him from the rabbi's command. However, everything went according to rule.

Many times a day, Yoineh Meir repeated to himself the rabbi's words: "A man may not be more compassionate than the Source of all compassion." The Torah says, "Thou shalt kill of thy herd and thy flock as I have commanded thee." Moses was instructed on Mount Sinai in the ways of slaughtering and of opening the animal in search of impurities. It is all a mystery of mysteries—life, death, man, beast. Those that are not slaughtered die anyway of various diseases, often ailing for weeks or months. In the forest, the beasts devour one another. In the seas, fish swallow fish. The Kolomir poorhouse is full of cripples and paralytics who lie there for years, befouling themselves. No man can escape the sorrows of this world.

And yet Yoineh Meir could find no consolation. Every tremor of the slaughtered fowl was answered by a tremor in Yoineh Meir's own bowels. The killing of every beast, great or small, caused him as much pain as though he were cutting his own throat. Of all the punishments that could have been visited upon him, slaughtering was the worst.

Barely three months had passed since Yoineh Meir had become a slaughterer, but the time seemed to stretch endlessly. He felt as though he were immersed in blood and lymph. His ears were beset by the squawking of hens, the crowing of roosters, the gobbling of geese, the lowing of oxen, the mooing and bleating of calves and goats; wings fluttered, claws tapped on the floor. The bodies refused to know any justification or excuse—every body resisted in its own fashion, tried to escape, and seemed to argue with the Creator to its last breath.

And Yoineh Meir's own mind raged with questions. Verily, in order to create the world, the Infinite One had had to shrink His light; there could be no free choice without pain. But since the beasts were not endowed with free choice, why should they have to suffer? Yoineh Meir watched, trembling, as the butchers chopped the cows with their axes and skinned them before they had heaved their last breath. The women plucked the feathers from the chickens while they were still alive.

It is the custom that the slaughterer receives the spleen and tripe of every cow. Yoineh Meir's house overflowed with meat. Reitze Doshe boiled soups in pots as huge as cauldrons. In the large kitchen there was a constant frenzy of cooking, roasting, frying, baking, stirring, and skimming. Reitze Doshe was pregnant again, and her stomach protruded into a point. Big and stout, she had five sisters, all as bulky as herself. Her sisters came with their children. Every day, his mother-in-law, Reitz Doshe's mother, brought new pastries and delicacies of her own baking. A woman must not let her voice be heard, but Reitze Doshe's maid-servant, the daughter of a water carrier, sang songs, pattered around barefoot, with her hair down, and laughed so loudly that the noise resounded in every room.

Yoineh Meir wanted to escape from the material world, but the material world pursued him. The smell of the slaughterhouse would not leave his nostrils. He tried to forget himself in the Torah, but he found that the Torah itself was full of earthly matters. He took to the Cabala, though he knew that no man may delve into the mysteries until he reaches the age of forty. Nevertheless, he continued to leaf through the *Treatise of the Hasidim, The Orchard, The Book of Creation*, and *The Tree of Life*. There, in the higher spheres, there was no death, no slaughtering, no pain, no stomachs and intestines, no hearts or lungs or livers, no membranes, and no impurities.

This particular night, Yoineh Meir went to the window and looked up into the sky. The moon spread a radiance around it. The stars flashed and twinkled, each with its own heavenly secret. Somewhere above the

World of Deeds, above the constellations, Angels were flying, and Seraphim, and Holy Wheels, and Holy Beasts. In Paradise, the mysteries of the Torah were revealed to souls. Every holy zaddik inherited three hundred and ten worlds and wove crowns for the Divine Presence. The nearer to the Throne of Glory, the brighter the light, the purer the radiance, the fewer the unholy host.

Yoineh Meir knew that man may not ask for death, but deep within himself he longed for the end. He had developed a repugnance for everything that had to do with the body. He could not even bring himself to go to the ritual bath with the other men. Under every skin he saw blood. Every neck reminded Yoineh Meir of the knife. Human beings, like beasts, had loins, veins, guts, buttocks. One slash of the knife and those solid householders would drop like oxen. As the Talmud says, all that is meant to be burned is already as good as burned. If the end of man was corruption, worms, and stench, then he was nothing but a piece of putrid flesh to start with.

Yoineh Meir understood now why the sages of old had likened the body to a cage—a prison where the soul sits captive, longing for the day of its release. It was only now that he truly grasped the meaning of the words of the Talmud: "Very good, this is death." Yet man was forbidden to break out of his prison. He must wait for the jailer to remove the chains, to open the gate.

Yoineh Meir returned to his bed. All his life he had slept on a feather bed, under a feather quilt, resting his head on a pillow; now he was suddenly aware that he was lying on feathers and down plucked from fowl. In the other bed, next to Yoineh Meir's, Reitze Doshe was snoring. From time to time a whistle came from her nostrils and a bubble formed on her lips. Yoineh Meir's daughters kept going to the slop pail, their bare feet pattering on the floor. They slept together, and sometimes they whispered and giggled half the night.

Yoineh Meir had longed for sons who would study the Torah, but Reitze Doshe bore girl after girl. While they were small, Yoineh Meir occasionally gave them a pinch on the cheek. Whenever he attended a circumcision, he would bring them a piece of cake. Sometimes he would even kiss one of the little ones on the head. But now they were grown. They seemed to have taken after their mother. They had spread out in width. Reitze Doshe complained that they ate too much and were getting too fat. They stole tidbits from the pots. The eldest, Bashe, was already sought in marriage. At one moment, the girls quarreled and insulted each other, at the next they combed each other's hair and plaited it into braids. They were forever babbling about dresses, shoes, stockings, jackets, panties. They cried and they laughed. They looked for lice, they fought, they washed, they kissed.

When Yoineh Meir tried to chide them, Reitze Doshe cried, "Don't butt in! Let the children alone!" Or she would scold, "You had better see to it that your daughters shouldn't have to go around barefoot and naked!"

Why did they need so many things? Why was it necessary to clothe and adorn the body so much, Yoineh Meir would wonder to himself.

Before he had become a slaughterer, he was seldom at home and hardly knew what went on there. But now he began to stay at home, and he saw what they were doing. The girls would run off to pick berries and mushrooms; they associated with the daughters of common homes. They brought home baskets of dry twigs. Reitze Doshe made jam. Tailors came for fittings. Shoemakers measured the women's feet. Reitze Doshe and her mother argued about Bashe's dowry. Yoineh Meir heard talk about a silk dress, a velvet dress, all sorts of skirts, cloaks, fur coats.

Now that he lay awake, all those words reechoed in his ears. They were rolling in luxury because he, Yoineh Meir, had begun to earn money. Somewhere in Reitze Doshe's womb a new child was growing, but Yoineh Meir sensed clearly that it would be another girl. "Well, one must welcome whatever heaven sends," he warned himself.

He had covered himself, but now he felt too hot. The pillow under his head became strangely hard, as though there were a stone among the feathers. He, Yoineh Meir, was himself a body: feet, a belly, a chest, elbows. There was a stabbing in his entrails. His palate felt dry.

Yoineh Meir sat up. "Father in heaven, I cannot breathe!"

I I

Elul is a month of repentance. In former years, Elul would bring with it a sense of exalted serenity. Yoineh Meir loved the cool breezes that came from the woods and the harvested fields. He could gaze for a long time at the pale-blue sky with its scattered clouds that reminded him of the flax in which the citrons for the Feast of Tabernacles were wrapped. Gossamer floated in the air. On the trees the leaves turned saffron yellow. In the twittering of the birds he heard the melancholy of the Solemn Days, when man takes an accounting of his soul.

But to a slaughterer Elul is quite another matter. A great many beasts are slaughtered for the New Year. Before the Day of Atonement, everybody offers a sacrificial fowl. In every courtyard, cocks crowed and hens cackled, and all of them had to be put to death. Then comes the Feast of Booths, the Day of the Willow Twigs, the Feast of Azereth, the Day of Rejoicing in the Law, the Sabbath of Genesis. Each holiday brings its own slaughter. Millions of fowl and cattle now alive were doomed to be killed.

Yoineh Meir no longer slept at night. If he dozed off, he was immediately beset by nightmares. Cows assumed human shape, with beards and sidelocks, and skullcaps over their horns. Yoineh Meir would be slaughtering a calf, but it would turn into a girl. Her neck throbbed, and she pleaded to be saved. She ran to the study house and spattered the courtyard with her blood. He even dreamed that he had slaughtered Reitze Doshe instead of a sheep.

In one of his nightmares, he heard a human voice come from a slaughtered goat. The goat, with his throat slit, jumped on Yoineh Meir and tried to butt him, cursing in Hebrew and Aramaic, spitting and foaming at him. Yoineh Meir awakened in a sweat. A cock crowed like a bell. Others answered, like a congregation answering the cantor. It seemed to Yoineh Meir that the fowl were crying out questions, protesting, lamenting in chorus the misfortune that loomed over them.

Yoineh Meir could not rest. He sat up, grasped his sidelocks with both hands, and rocked.

Reitze Doshe woke up. "What's the matter?"

"Nothing, nothing."

"What are you rocking for?"

"Let me be."

"You frighten me!"

After a while Reitze Doshe began to snore again. Yoineh Meir got out of bed, washed his hands, and dressed. He wanted to put ash on his forehead and recite the midnight prayer, but his lips refused to utter the holy words. How could he mourn the destruction of the Temple when a carnage was being readied here in Kolomir, and he, Yoineh Meir, was the Titus, the Nebuchadnezzar!

The air in the house was stifling. It smelled of sweat, fat, dirty underwear, urine. One of his daughters muttered something in her sleep, another one moaned. The beds creaked. A rustling came from the closets. In the coop under the stove were the sacrificial fowls that Reitze Doshe had locked up for the Day of Atonement. Yoineh Meir heard the scratching of a mouse, the chirping of a cricket. It seemed to him that he could hear the worms burrowing through the ceiling and the floor. Innumerable creatures surrounded man, each with its own nature, its own claims on the Creator.

Yoineh Meir went out into the yard. Here everything was cool and fresh. The dew had formed. In the sky, the midnight stars were glittering. Yoineh Meir inhaled deeply. He walked on the wet grass, among the leaves and shrubs. His socks grew damp above his slippers. He came to a tree and stopped. In the branches there seemed to be some nests. He heard the twittering of awakened fledglings. Frogs croaked in the swamp beyond the hill. "Don't they sleep at all, those frogs?" Yoineh Meir asked himself. "They have the voices of men."

Since Yoineh Meir had begun to slaughter, his thoughts were obsessed with living creatures. He grappled with all sorts of questions. Where did flies come from? Were they born out of their mother's womb, or did they hatch from eggs? If all the flies died out in winter, where did the new ones come from in summer? And the owl that nested under the synagogue roof—what did it do when the frosts came? Did it remain there? Did it fly away to warm countries? And how could anything live in the burning frost, when it was scarcely possible to keep warm under the quilt?

An unfamiliar love welled up in Yoineh Meir for all that crawls and flies, breeds and swarms. Even the mice—was it their fault that they were mice? What wrong does a mouse do? All it wants is a crumb of bread or a bit of cheese. Then why is the cat such an enemy to it?

Yoineh Meir rocked back and forth in the dark. The rabbi may be right. Man cannot and must not have more compassion than the Master of the universe. Yet he, Yoineh Meir, was sick with pity. How could one pray for life for the coming year, or for a favorable writ in Heaven, when one was robbing others of the breath of life?

Yoineh Meir thought that the Messiah Himself could not redeem the world as long as injustice was done to beasts. By rights, everything should rise from the dead: every calf, fish, gnat, butterfly. Even in the worm that crawls in the earth there glows a divine spark. When you slaughter a creature, you slaughter God . . .

"Woe is me, I am losing my mind!" Yoineh Meir muttered.

A week before the New Year, there was a rush of slaughtering. All day long, Yoineh Meir stood near a pit, slaughtering hens, roosters, geese, ducks. Women pushed, argued, tried to get to the slaughterer first. Others joked, laughed, bantered. Feathers flew, the yard was full of quacking, gabbling, the screaming of roosters. Now and then a fowl cried out like a human being.

Yoineh Meir was filled with a gripping pain. Until this day he had still hoped that he would get accustomed to slaughtering. But now he knew that if he continued for a hundred years his suffering would not cease. His knees shook. His belly felt distended. His mouth was flooded with bitter fluids. Reitze Doshe and her sisters were also in the yard, talking with the women, wishing each a blessed New Year, and voicing the pious hope that they would meet again next year.

Yoineh Meir feared that he was no longer slaughtering according to the Law. At one moment, a blackness swam before his eyes; at the next, everything turned golden green. He constantly tested the knife blade on the nail of his forefinger to make sure it was not nicked. Every fifteen minutes he had to go to urinate. Mosquitoes bit him. Crows cawed at him from among the branches.

He stood there until sundown, and the pit became filled with blood.

After the evening prayers, Reitze Doshe served Yoineh Meir buckwheat soup with pot roast. But though he had not tasted any food since morning, he could not eat. His throat felt constricted, there was a lump in his gullet, and he could scarcely swallow the first bite. He recited the Shema of Rabbi Isaac Luria, made his confession, and beat his breast like a man who was mortally sick.

Yoineh Meir thought that he would be unable to sleep that night, but his eyes closed as soon as his head was on the pillow and he had recited the last benediction before sleep. It seemed to him that he was examining a slaughtered cow for impurities, slitting open its belly, tearing out the lungs and blowing them up. What did it mean? For this was usually the butcher's task. The lungs grew larger and larger; they covered the whole table and swelled upward toward the ceiling. Yoineh Meir ceased blowing, but the lobes continued to expand by themselves. The smaller lobe, the one that is called "the thief," shook and fluttered, as if trying to break away. Suddenly a whistling, a coughing, a growling lamentation broke from the windpipe. A dybbuk began to speak, shout, sing, pour out a stream of verses, quotations from the Talmud, passages from the Zohar. The lungs rose up and flew, flapping like wings. Yoineh Meir wanted to escape, but the door was barred by a black bull with red eyes and pointed horns. The bull wheezed and opened a maw full of long teeth.

Yoineh Meir shuddered and woke up. His body was bathed in sweat. His skull felt swollen and filled with sand. His feet lay on the straw pallet, inert as logs. He made an effort and sat up. He put on his robe and went out. The night hung heavy and impenetrable, thick with the darkness of the hour before sunrise. From time to time a gust of air came from somewhere, like a sigh of someone unseen.

A tingling ran down Yoineh Meir's spine, as though someone brushed it with a feather. Something in him wept and mocked. "Well, and what if the rabbi said so?" he spoke to himself. "And even if God Almighty had commanded, what of that? I'll do without rewards in the world to come! I want no Paradise, no Leviathan, no Wild Ox! Let them stretch me on a bed of nails. Let them throw me into the Hollow of the Sling. I'll have none of your favors, God! I am no longer afraid of your Judgment! I am a betrayer of Israel, a willful transgressor!" Yoineh Meir cried. "I have more compassion than God Almighty—more, more! He is a cruel God, a Man of War, a God of Vengeance. I will not serve

Him. It is an abandoned world!" Yoineh Meir laughed, but tears ran down his cheeks in scalding drops.

Yoineh Meir went to the pantry where he kept his knives, his whetstone, the circumcision knife. He gathered them all and dropped them into the pit of the outhouse. He knew that he was blaspheming, that he was desecrating the holy instruments, that he was mad, but he no longer wished to be sane.

He went outside and began to walk toward the river, the bridge, the wood. His prayer shawl and phylacteries? He needed none! The parchment was taken from the hide of a cow. The cases of the phylacteries were made of calf's leather. The Torah itself was made of animal skin. "Father in Heaven, Thou art a slaughterer!" a voice cried in Yoineh Meir. "Thou art a slaughterer and the Angel of Death! The whole world is a slaughterhouse!"

A slipper fell off Yoineh Meir's foot, but he let it lie, striding on in one slipper and one sock. He began to call, shout, sing. I am driving myself out of my mind; he thought. But this is itself a mark of madness . . .

He had opened a door to his brain, and madness flowed in, flooding everything. From moment to moment, Yoineh Meir grew more rebellious. He threw away his skullcap, grasped his prayer fringes and ripped them off, tore off pieces of his vest. A strength possessed him, the recklessness of one who had cast away all burdens.

Dogs chased him, barking, but he drove them off. Doors were flung open. Men ran out barefoot, with feathers clinging to their skullcaps. Women came out in their petticoats and nightcaps. All of them shouted, tried to bar his way, but Yoineh Meir evaded them.

The sky turned red as blood, and a round skull pushed up out of the bloody sea as out of the womb of a woman in childbirth.

Someone had gone to tell the butchers that Yoineh Meir had lost his mind. They came running with sticks and rope, but Yoineh Meir was already over the bridge and was hurrying across the harvested fields. He ran and vomited. He fell and rose, bruised by the stubble. Shepherds who take the horses out to graze at night mocked him and threw horse dung at him. The cows at pasture ran after him. Bells tolled as for a fire.

Yoineh Meir heard shouts, screams, the stamping of running feet. The earth began to slope and Yoineh Meir rolled downhill. He reached the wood, leaped over tufts of moss, rocks, running brooks. Yoineh Meir knew the truth: this was not the river before him; it was a bloody swamp. Blood ran from the sun, staining the tree trunks. From the branches hung intestines, livers, kidneys. The forequarters of beasts rose to their feet and sprayed him with gall and slime. Yoineh Meir could not escape. Myriads of cows and fowls encircled him, ready to take revenge for every cut, every wound, every slit gullet, every plucked feather. With bleeding throats, they all chanted, "Everyone may kill, and every killing is permitted."

Yoineh Meir broke into a wail that echoed through the wood in many voices. He raised his fist to Heaven: "Fiend! Murderer! Devouring beast!"

For two days the butchers searched for him, but they did not find him. Then Zeinvel, who owned the watermill, arrived in town with the news that Yoineh Meir's body had turned up in the river by the dam. He had drowned.

The members of the Burial Society immediately went to bring the corpse. There were many witnesses to testify that Yoineh Meir had behaved like a madman, and the rabbi ruled that the deceased was not a suicide. The body of the dead man was cleansed and given burial near the graves of his father and his grandfather. The rabbi himself delivered the eulogy.

Because it was the holiday season and there was danger that Kolomir might remain without meat, the community hastily dispatched two messengers to bring a new slaughterer.

The Dead Fiddler

I

IN the town of Shidlovtse, which lies between Radom and Kielce, not far from the Mountains of the Holy Cross, there lived a man by the name of Reb Sheftel Vengrover. This Reb Sheftel was supposedly a grain merchant, but all the buying and selling was done by his wife, Zise Feige. She bought wheat, corn, barley, and buckwheat from the landowners and the peasants and sent it to Warsaw. She also had some of the grain milled and sold the flour to stores and bakeries. Zise Feige owned a granary and had an assistant, Zalkind, who helped her in the business and did all the work that required a man's hand; he carried sacks, looked after the horses, and served as coachman whenever Zise Feige drove out to a fair or went to visit a landowner.

Reb Sheftel held to the belief that the Torah is the worthiest merchandise of all. He rose at dawn and went to the study house to pore over the Gemara, the Annotations and Commentaries, the Midrash, and the Zohar. In the evenings, he would read a lesson from the Mishnah with the Mishnah Society. Reb Sheftel also devoted himself to community affairs and was an ardent Radzymin Hasid.

Reb Sheftel was not much taller than a midget, but he had the longest beard in Shidlovtse and the surrounding district. His beard reached down to his knees and seemed to contain every color: red, yellow, even the color of hay. At Tishe b'Av, when the mischiefmakers pelted everyone with burs, Reb Sheftel's beard would be full of them. At first Zise Feige had tried to pull them out, but Reb Sheftel would not allow it, for she pulled out the hairs of the beard too, and a man's beard is a mark of his Jewishness and a reminder that he was created in the image of God. The burs remained in his beard until they dropped out by themselves. Reb Sheftel did not curl his sidelocks, considering this a

---

Translated by Mirra Ginsburg

frivolous custom. They hung down to his shoulders. A tuft of hair grew on his nose. As he studied, he smoked a long pipe.

When Reb Sheftel stood at the lectern in the synagogue in his prayer shawl and phylacteries, he looked like one of the ancients. He had a high forehead, and under shaggy eyebrows, eyes that combined the sharp glance of a scholar with the humility of a God-fearing man. Reb Sheftel imposed a variety of penances upon himself. He drank no milk unless he had been present at the milking. He ate no meat except on the Sabbath and on holidays and only if he had examined the slaughtering knife in advance. It was told of him that on the eve of Passover he ordered that the cat wear socklets on its feet, lest it bring into the house the smallest crumb of unleavened bread. Every night, he faithfully performed the midnight prayers. People said that although he had inherited his grain business from his father and grandfather he still could not distinguish between rye and wheat.

Zise Feige was a head taller than her husband and in her younger days had been famous for her good looks. The landlords who sold her grain showered her with compliments, but a good Jewish woman pays no attention to idle talk. Zise Feige loved her husband and considered it an honor to help him serve the Almighty.

She had borne nine children, but only three remained: a married son, Jedidiah, who took board with his father-in-law in Wlodowa; a boy, Tsadock Meyer, who was still in cheder; and a grown daughter, Liebe Yentl. Liebe Yentl had been engaged and about to be married, but her fiancé, Ozer, caught a cold and died. This Ozer had a reputation as a prodigy and a scholar. His father was the president of the community in Opola. Although Liebe Yentl had seen Ozer only during the signing of the betrothal papers, she wept bitterly when she heard the bad news. Almost at once she was besieged with marriage offers, for she was already a ripe girl of seventeen, but Zise Feige felt that it was best to wait until she got over her misfortune.

Liebe Yentl's betrothed, Ozer, departed this world just after Passover. Now it was already the month of Heshvan. Sukkoth is usually followed by rains and snow, but this fall was a mild one. The sun shone. The sky was blue, as after Pentecost. The peasants in the villages complained that the winter crops were beginning to sprout in the fields, which could lead to crop failure. People feared that the warm weather might bring epidemics. In the meantime, grain prices rose by three groschen on the pood, and Zise Feige had higher profits. As was the custom between man and wife, she gave Reb Sheftel an accounting of the week's earnings every Sabbath evening, and he immediately deducted a share—for the study house, the prayer house, the mending of sacred books, for the inmates of the poorhouse, and for itinerant beggars. There was no lack of need for charity.

Since Zise Feige had a servant girl, Dunya, and was herself a fine housekeeper, Liebe Yentl paid little attention to household matters. She had her own room, where she would often sit, reading storybooks. She copied letters from the letter book. When she had read through all the storybooks, she secretly took to borrowing from her father's bookcase. She was also good at sewing and embroidery. She was fond of fine clothes. Liebe Yentl inherited her mother's beauty, but her red hair came from her father's side. Like her father's beard, her hair was uncommonly long—down to her loins. Since the mishap with Ozer, her face, always pale, had grown paler still and more delicate. Her eyes were green.

Reb Sheftel paid little attention to his daughter. He merely prayed to the Lord to send her the right husband. But Zise Feige saw that the girl was growing up as wild as a weed. Her head was full of whims and fancies. She did not allow herring or radishes to be mentioned in her presence. She averted her eyes from slaughtered fowl and from meat on the salting board or in the soaking dish. If she found a fly in her groats, she would eat nothing for the rest of the day. She had no friends in Shidlovtse. She complained that the girls of the town were common and backward; as soon as they were married, they became careless and slovenly. Whenever she had to go among people, she fasted the day before, for fear that she might vomit. Although she was beautiful, clever, and learned, it always seemed to her that people were laughing and pointing at her.

Zise Feige wanted many times to talk to her husband about the troubles she was having with their daughter, but she was reluctant to divert him from his studies. Besides, he might not understand a woman's problems. He had a rule for everything. On the few occasions when Zise Feige had tried to tell him of her fears, his only reply was, "When, God willing, she gets married, she will forget all this foolishness."

After the calamity with Ozer, Liebe Yentl fell ill from grieving. She did not sleep nights. Her mother heard her sobbing in the dark. She was constantly going for a drink of water. She drank whole dippers full, and Zise Feige could not imagine how her stomach could hold so much water. As though, God forbid, a fire were raging inside her, consuming everything.

Sometimes, Liebe Yentl spoke to her mother like one who was altogether unsettled. Zise Feige thought to herself that it was fortunate the girl avoided people. But how long can anything remain a secret? It was already whispered in town that Liebe Yentl was not all there. She played with the cat. She took solitary walks down the Gentile street that led to the cemetery. When anyone addressed her, she turned pale and her answers were quite beside the point. Some people thought that she was deaf. Others hinted that Liebe Yentl might be dabbling in magic. She had been seen on a moonlit night walking in the pasture across the bridge and bending down every now and then to pick flowers or herbs. Women spat to ward off evil when they spoke of her. "Poor thing, unlucky and sick besides."

I I

Liebe Yentl was about to become betrothed again, this time to a young man from Zawiercia. Reb Sheftel had sent an examiner to the prospective bridegroom, and he came back with the report that Shmelke Motl was a scholar. The betrothal contract was drawn up, ready to be signed.

The examiner's wife, Traine, who had visited Zawiercia with her husband (they had a daughter there), told Zise Feige that Shmelke Motl was small and dark. He did not look like much, but he had the head of a genius. Because he was an orphan, the householders provided his meals; he ate at a different home every day of the week. Liebe Yentl listened without a word.

When Traine had gone, Zise Feige brought in her daughter's supper —buckwheat and pot roast with gravy. But Liebe Yentl did not touch the food. She rocked over the plate as though it were a prayer book. Soon afterwards, she retired to her room. Zise Feige sighed and also went to bed. Reb Sheftel had gone to sleep early, for he had to rise for midnight prayers. The house was quiet. Only the cricket sang its night song behind the oven.

Suddenly Zise Feige was wide awake. From Liebe Yentl's room came a muffled gasping, as though someone were choking there. Zise Feige ran into her daughter's room. In the bright moonlight she saw the girl sitting on her bed, her hair disheveled, her face chalk-white, struggling to keep down her sobs. Zise Feige cried out, "My daughter, what is wrong? Woe is me!" She ran to the kitchen, lit a candle, and returned to Liebe Yentl, bringing a cup of water to splash at her if, God forbid, the girl should faint.

But at this moment a man's voice broke from Liebe Yentl's lips. "No need to revive me, Zise Feige," the voice called out. "I'm not in the habit of fainting. You'd better fetch me a drop of vodka."

Zise Feige stood petrified with horror. The water spilled over from the cup.

Reb Sheftel had also wakened. He washed his hands hastily, put on his bathrobe and slippers, and came into his daughter's room.

The man's voice greeted him. "A good awakening to you, Reb Sheftel. Let me have a schnapps—my throat's parched. Or Slivovitz—anything will do, so long as I wet my whistle."

Man and wife knew at once what had happened: a dybbuk had entered Liebe Yentl. Reb Sheftel asked with a shudder: "Who are you? What do you want?"

"Who I am you wouldn't know," the dybbuk answered. "You're a scholar in Shidlovtse, and I'm a fiddler from Pinchev. You squeeze the bench, and I squeezed the wenches. You're still around in the Imaginary World, and I'm past everything. I've kicked the bucket and have already had my taste of what comes after. I've had it cold and hot, and now I'm back on the sinful earth—there's no place for me either in heaven or in hell. Tonight I started out flying to Pinchev, but I lost my way and got to Shidlovtse instead—I'm a musician, not a coachman. One thing I do know, though—my throat's itchy."

Zise Feige was seized by a fit of tembling. The candle in her hand shook so badly it singed Reb Sheftel's beard. She wanted to scream, to call for help, but her voice stuck in her throat. Her knees buckled, and she had to lean against the wall to keep from falling.

Reb Sheftel pulled at his sidelock as he addressed the dybbuk. "What is your name?"

"Getsl."

"Why did you choose to enter my daughter?" he asked in desperation.

"Why not? She's a good-looking girl. I hate the ugly ones—always have, always will." With that, the dybbuk began to shout ribaldries and obscenities, both in ordinary Yiddish and in musician's slang. "Don't make me wait, Feige dear," he called out finally. "Bring me a cup of cheer. I'm dry as a bone. I've got an itching in my gullet, a twitching in my gut."

"Good people, help!" Zise Feige wailed. She dropped the candle and Reb Sheftel picked it up, for it could easily have set the wooden house on fire.

Though it was late, the townsfolk came running. There are people everywhere with something bothering them; they cannot sleep nights. Tevye the night watchman thought a fire had broken out and ran through the street, knocking at the shutters with his stick. It was not long before Reb Sheftel's house was packed.

Liebe Yentl's eyes goggled, her mouth twisted like an epileptic's, and a voice boomed out of her that could not have come from a woman's throat. "Will you bring me a glass of liquor or won't you? What the devil are you waiting for?"

"And what if we don't?" asked Zeinvl the butcher, who was on his way home from the slaughterhouse.

"If you don't, I'll lay you all wide open, you pious hypocrites. And the secrets of your wives—may they burn up with hives."

"Get him liquor! Give him a drink!" voices cried on every side.

Reb Sheftel's son, Tsadock Meyer, a boy of eleven, had also been awakened by the commotion. He knew where his father kept the brandy that he drank on the Sabbath, after the fish. He opened the cupboard, poured out a glass, and brought it to his sister. Reb Sheftel leaned against the chest of drawers, for his legs were giving way. Zise Feige fell into a chair. Neighbors sprinkled her with vinegar against fainting.

Liebe Yentl stretched out her hand, took the glass, and tossed it down. Those who stood nearby could not believe their eyes. The girl didn't even twitch a muscle.

The dybbuk said, "You call that liquor? Water, that's what it is— hey, fellow, bring me the bottle!"

"Don't let her have it! Don't let her have it!" Zise Feige cried. "She'll poison herself, God help us!"

The dybbuk gave a laugh and a snort. "Don't worry, Zise Feige, nothing can kill me again. So far as I'm concerned, your brandy is weaker than candy."

"You won't get a drink until you tell us who you are and how you got in here," Zeinvl the butcher said. Since no one else dared to address the spirit, Zeinvl took it upon himself to be the spokesman.

"What does the meatman want here?" the dybbuk asked. "Go on back to your gizzards and guts!"

"Tell us who you are!"

"Do I have to repeat it? I am Getsl the fiddler from Pinchev. I was fond of things nobody else hates, and when I cashed in, the imps went to work on me. I couldn't get into paradise, and hell was too hot for my taste. The devils were the death of me. So at night, when the watchman dropped off, I made myself scarce. I meant to go to my wife, may she rot alive, but it was dark on the way and I got to Shidlovtse instead. I looked through the wall and saw this girl. My heart jumped in my chest and I crawled into her breast."

"How long do you intend to stay?"

"Forever and a day."

Reb Sheftel was almost speechless with terror, but he remembered God and recovered. He called out, "Evil spirit, I command you to leave the body of my innocent daughter and go where men do not walk and beasts do not tread. If you don't, you shall be driven out by Holy Names, by excommunication, by the blowing of the ram's horn."

"In another minute you'll have me scared!" the dybbuk taunted. "You think you're so strong because your beard's long?"

"Impudent wretch, betrayer of Israel!" Reb Sheftel cried in anger.

"Better an open rake than a sanctimonious fake," the dybbuk answered. "You may have the Shidlovtse schlemiels fooled, but Getsl the fiddler of Pinchev has been around. I'm telling you. Bring me the bottle or I'll make you crawl."

There was an uproar at the door. Someone had wakened the rabbi, and he came with Bendit the beadle. Bendit carried a stick, a ram's horn, and the *Book of the Angel Raziel*.

III

Once in the bedroom, the rabbi, Reb Yeruchim, ordered the ram's horn to be blown. He had the beadle pile hot coals into a brazier, then he poured incense on the coals. As the smoke of the herbs filled the room, he commanded the evil one with holy oaths from the Zohar, *The Book of Creation*, and other books of the Cabala to leave the body of the woman Liebe Yentl, daughter of Zise Feige. But the unholy spirit defied everyone. Instead of leaving, he played out a succession of dances, marches, hops—just with the lips. He boomed like a bass viol, he jingled like a cymbal, he whistled like a flute, and drummed like a drum.

The page is too short for a recital of all that the dybbuk did and said that night and the nights that followed—his brazen tricks, his blasphemies against the Lord, the insults he hurled at the townsfolk, the boasts of all the lecheries he had committed, the mockery, the outbursts of laughing and of crying, the stream of quotations from the Torah and wedding jester's jokes, and all of it in singsong and in rhyme.

The dybbuk made himself heard only after dark. During the day, Liebe Yentl lay exhausted in bed and evidently did not remember what went on at night. She thought that she was sick and occasionally begged her mother to call the doctor or to give her some medicine. Most of the time she dozed, with her eyes and her lips shut tight.

Since the incantations and the amulets of the Shidlovtse rabbi were of no avail, Reb Sheftel went to seek the advice of the Radzymin rabbi. On the very morning he left, the mild weather gave way to wind and snow. The roads were snowed in and it was difficult to reach Radzymin, even in a sleigh. Weeks went by, and no news came from Reb Sheftel. Zise Feige was so hard hit by the calamity that she fell ill, and her assistant Zalkind had to take over the whole business.

Winter nights are long, and idlers look for ways to while away the time. Soon after twilight, they would gather at Zise Feige's house to hear the dybbuk's talk and to marvel at his antics. Zise Feige forbade them to annoy her daughter, but the curiosity of the townspeople was so great that they would break the door open and enter.

The dybbuk knew everyone and had words for each man according to his position and conduct. Most of the time he heaped mud and ashes upon the respected leaders of the community and their wives. He told each one exactly what he was: a miser or a swindler, a sycophant or a beggar, a slattern or a snob, an idler or a grabber. With the horse traders he talked about horses, and with the butchers about oxen. He reminded Chaim the miller that he had hung a weight under the scale on which he weighed the flour milled for the peasants. He questioned Yukele the thief about his latest theft. His jests and his jibes provoked both astonishment and laughter. Even the older folks could not keep from smiling. The dybbuk knew things that no stranger could have known, and it became clear to the visitors that they were dealing with a soul from which nothing could be hidden, for it saw through all their secrets. Although the evil spirit put everyone to shame, each man was willing to suffer his own humiliation for the sake of seeing others humbled.

When the dybbuk tired of exposing the sins of the townsfolk, he would turn to recitals of his own misdeeds. Not an evening passed without revelations of new vices. The dybbuk called everything by its name, denying nothing. When he was asked whether he regretted his abominations, he said with a laugh: "And if I did, could anything be changed? Everything is recorded up above. For eating a single wormy plum, you get six hundred and eighty-nine lashes. For a single moment of lust, you're rolled for a week on a bed of nails." Between one jest and another, he would sing and bleat and play out tunes so skillfully that no one living could vie with him.

One evening the teacher's wife came running to the rabbi and reported that people were dancing to the dybbuk's music. The rabbi put on his robe and his hat and hurried to the house. Yes, the men and women danced together in Zise Feige's kitchen. The rabbi berated them and warned that they were committing a sacrilege. He sternly forbade Zise Feige to allow the rabble into her house. But Zise Feige lay sick in bed, and her boy, Tsadock Meyer, was staying with relatives. As soon as the rabbi left, the idlers resumed their dancing—a scissors dance, a quarrel dance, a cossack, a water dance. It went on till midnight, when the dybbuk gave out a snore, and Liebe Yentl fell asleep.

A few days later there was a new rumor in town: a second dybbuk had entered Liebe Yentl, this time a female one. Once more an avid crowd packed the house. And, indeed, a woman's voice now came from Liebe Yentl—not her own gentle voice but the hoarse croaking of a shrew. People asked the new dybbuk who she was, and she told them that her name was Beyle Tslove and that she came from the town of Plock, where she had been a barmaid in a tavern and had later become a whore.

Beyle Tslove spoke differently from Getsl the fiddler, with the flat accents of her region and a mixture of Germanized words unknown in Shidlovtse. Beyle Tslove's language made even the butchers and the combers of pigs' bristles blush. She sang ribald songs and soldiers' ditties. She said she had wandered for eighty years in waste places. She had been reincarnated as a cat, a turkey, a snake, and a locust. For a long time her soul resided in a turtle. When someone mentioned Getsl the fiddler and asked whether she knew him and whether she knew that he was also lodged in the same woman, she answered, "I neither know him nor want to know him."

"Why not? Have you turned virtuous all of a sudden?" Zeinvl the butcher asked her.

"Who wants a dead fiddler?"

The people began to call to Getsl the fiddler, urging him to speak up. They wanted to hear the two dybbuks talk to each other. But Getsl the fiddler was silent.

Beyle Tslove said, "I see no Getsl here."

"Maybe he's hiding?" someone said.

"Where? I can smell a man a mile away."

In the midst of this excitement, Reb Sheftel returned. He looked older and even smaller than before. His beard was streaked with gray. He had brought talismans and amulets from Radzymin, to hang in the corners of the room and around his daughter's neck.

People expected the dybbuk to resist and fight the amulets, as evil spirits do when touched by a sacred object. But Beyle Tslove was silent while the amulets were hung around Liebe Yentl's neck. Then she asked, "What's this? Sacred toilet paper?"

"These are Holy Names from the Radzymin rabbi!" Reb Sheftel cried out. "If you do not leave my daughter at once, not a spur shall be left of you!"

"Tell the Radzymin rabbi that I spit at his amulets," the woman said brazenly.

"Harlot! Fiend! Harridan!" Reb Sheftel screamed.

"What's he bellowing for, that Short Friday? Some man—nothing but bone and beard!"

Reb Sheftel had brought with him blessed six-groschen coins, a piece of charmed amber, and several other magical objects that the Evil Host is known to shun. But Beyle Tslove, it seemed, was afraid of nothing. She mocked Reb Sheftel and told him she would come at night and tie an elflock in his beard.

That night Reb Sheftel recited the Shema of the Holy Isaac Luria. He slept in his fringed garment with *The Book of Creation* and a knife under his pillow—like a woman in childbirth. But in the middle of the night he woke and felt invisible fingers on his face. An unseen hand was burrowing in his beard. Reb Sheftel wanted to scream, but the hand covered his mouth. In the morning Reb Sheftel got up with his whole beard full of tangled braids, gummy as if stuck together with glue.

Although it was a fearful matter, the Worka Hasidim, who were bitter opponents of the Radzymin rabbi, celebrated that day with honey cake and brandy in their study house. Now they had proof that the Radzymin rabbi did not know the Cabala. The followers of the Worka rabbi had advised Reb Sheftel to make a journey to Worka, but he ignored them, and now they had their revenge.

IV

One evening, as Beyle Tslove was boasting of her former beauty and of all the men who had run after her, the fiddler of Pinchev suddenly raised his voice. "What were they so steamed up about?" he asked her mockingly. "Were you the only female in Plock?"

For a while all was quiet. It looked as though Beyle Tslove had lost her tongue. Then she gave a hoarse laugh. "So he's here—the scraper! Where were you hiding? In the gall?"

"If you're blind, I can be dumb. Go on, Grandma, keep jabbering. Your story had a gray beard when I was still in my diapers. In your place, I'd take such tall tales to the fools of Chelm. In Shidlovtse there are two or three clever men, too."

"A wise guy, eh?" Beyle Tslove said. "Let me tell you something. A live fiddle-scraper's no prize—and when it comes to a dead one! Go back, if you forgive me, to your resting place. They miss you in the Pinchev cemetery. The corpses who pray at night need another skeleton to make up their quorum."

The people who heard the two dybbuks quarrel were so stunned that they forgot to laugh. Now a man's voice came from Liebe Yentl, now a woman's. The Pinchev fiddler's "r"s were soft, the Plock harlot's hard.

Liebe Yentl herself rested against two pillows, her face pale, her hair down, her eyes closed. No one rightly saw her move her lips, though the room was full of people watching. Zise Feige was unable to keep them out, and there was no one to help her. Reb Sheftel no longer came home at night; he slept in the study house. Dunya the servant girl had left her job in the middle of the year. Zalkind, Zise Feige's assistant, went home in the evenings to his wife and children. People wandered in and out of the house as if it did not belong to anyone. Whenever one of the respectable members of the community came to upbraid the merry gang for ridiculing a stricken girl, the two dybbuks hurled curses and insults at him. The dybbuks gave the townspeople new nicknames: Reitse the busybody, Mindl glutton, Yekl tough, Dvoshe the strumpet. On several occasions, Gentiles and members of the local gentry came to see the wonder, and the dybbuks bantered with them in Polish. A landowner said in a tavern afterwards that the best theater in Warsaw could not compete with the scenes played out by the two dead rascals in Shidlovtse.

After a while, Reb Sheftel, who had been unbending in his loyalty to the Radzymin rabbi, gave in and went to see the rabbi of Worka; perhaps he might help.

The two dybbuks, meanwhile, were carrying on their word duel. It is generally thought that women will get the better of men where the tongue is concerned, but the Pinchev fiddler was a match for the Plock whore. The fiddler cried repeatedly that it was beneath his dignity to wrangle with a harlot—a maid with a certificate of rape—but the hoodlums egged him on. "Answer her! Don't let her have the last word!" They whistled, hooted, clapped their hands, stamped their feet.

The battle of wits gradually turned into storytelling. Beyle Tslove related that her mother, a pious and virtuous woman, had borne her husband, a Hasid and a loafer, eight children, all of them girls. When Beyle Tslove made her appearance in the world, her father was so chagrined that he left home. By trickery, he collected the signatures of a hundred rabbis, permitting him to remarry, and her mother became an abandoned wife. To support the family, she went to market every morning to sell hot beans to the yeshiva students. A wicked tutor, with a goat's beard and sidelocks down to his shoulders, came to teach Beyle Tslove to pray, but he raped her. She was not yet eight years old. When Beyle Tslove went on to tell how she had become a barmaid, how the peasants had pinched and cursed her and pulled her hair, and how a bawd, pretending to be a pious woman, had lured her to a distant city and brought her into a brothel, the girls who were listening burst into tears. The young men, too, dabbed their eyes.

Getsl the fiddler questioned her. Who were the guests? How much did they pay? How much did she have to give the procurers and what was left for her to live on? Had she ever gone to bed with a Turk or a blackamoor?

Beyle Tslove answered all the questions. The young rakes had tormented her in their ways, and the old lechers had wearied her with their demands. The bawd took away her last groschen and locked the bread in the cupboard. The pimp whipped her with a wet strap and stuck needles into her buttocks. From fasting and homesickness she contracted consumption and ended by spitting out her lungs at the poorhouse. And because she had been buried behind the fence, without Kaddish, she was immediately seized by multitudes of demons, imps, mockers, and Babuks. The Angel Dumah asked her the verse that went with her name, and when she could not answer he split her grave with a fiery rod. She begged to be allowed into hell, for there the punishment lasts only twelve months, but the Unholy Ones dragged her off to waste places and deserts. She said that in the desert she had come upon a pit that was the door to Gehenna. Day and night, the screams of sinners who were being punished there came from the pit. She was carried to the Congealed Sea, where sailing ships, wrecked by storms, were held immobile, with dead crews and captains turned to stone. Beyle Tslove had also flown to a land inhabited by giants with two heads and single eyes in their foreheads. Few females were born there, and every woman had six husbands.

Getsl the fiddler also began to talk about the events of his life. He told of incidents at the weddings and balls of the gentry where he had played, and of what happened later, in the hereafter. He said that evildoers did not repent, even in the Nether Regions. Although they had already learned the truth of things, their souls still pursued their lusts. Gamblers played with invisible cards, thieves stole, swindlers swindled, and fornicators indulged in their abominations.

The townsfolk who heard the two were amazed, and Zeinvl the butcher asked, "How can anyone sin when he is rotting in the earth?"

Getsl explained that it was, anyway, the soul and not the body that enjoyed sin. This was why the soul was punished. Besides, there were bodies of all kinds—of smoke, of spiderwebs, of shadow—and they could be used for a while, until the Angels of Destruction tore them to pieces. There were castles, inns, and ruins in the deserts and abysses, which provided hiding places from Judgment, and also Avenging Angels who could be bribed with promises or even with the kind of money that has no substance but is used in the taverns and brothels of the Nether World.

When one of the idlers cried out that this was unbelievable, Getsl called on Beyle Tslove to attest to the truth of his words. "Tell us, Beyle Tslove, what did you really do all these years? Did you recite psalms, or did you wander through swamps and wastes, consorting with demons, Zmoras, and Malachais?"

Instead of replying, Beyle Tslove giggled and coughed. "I can't speak—my mouth's dry."

"Yes, let's have a drop," Getsl chimed in, and when somebody brought over a tumbler of brandy, Liebe Yentl downed it like water. She did not open her eyes or even wince. It was clear to everybody that she was entirely in the sway of the dybbuks within her.

When Zeinvl the butcher realized that the two dybbuks had made peace, he asked, "Why don't you two become man and wife? You'd make a good pair."

"And what are we to do after the wedding?" Beyle Tslove answered. "Pray from the same prayer book?"

"You'll do what all married couples do."

"With what? We're past all doing. Anyway, there's no time—we won't be staying here much longer."

"Why not? Liebe Yentl is still young."

"The Worka rabbi is not the Radzymin schlemiel," Beyle Tslove said. "Asmodeus himself is afraid of his talismans."

"The Worka rabbi can kiss me you know where," Getsl boasted. "But I'm not about to become a bridegroom."

"The match isn't good enough for you?" Beyle Tslove cried. "If you knew who wanted to marry me, you'd croak a second time."

"If she's cursing me now, what can I expect later?" Getsl joked. "Besides, she's old enough to be my great-grandmother—seventy years older than I am, anyway you figure it."

"Numskull. I was twenty-seven years old when I kicked in, and I can't get any older. And how old are you, bottle-bum? Close to sixty, if you're a day."

"May you get as many carbuncles on your bloated flesh as the years I was short of fifty."

"Just give me the flesh, I won't argue over the carbuncles."

The two kept up their wrangling and the crowd kept up its urging until finally the dybbuks consented. Those who have not heard the dead bride and groom haggle about the dowry, the trousseau, the presents, will never know what unholy spirits are capable of.

Beyle Tslove said that she had long since paid for all her transgressions and was therefore as pure as a virgin. "Is there such a thing as a virgin, anyway?" she argued. "Every soul has lodged countless times both in men and in women. There are no more new souls in Heaven. A soul is cleansed in a caldron, like dishes before Passover. It is purified and sent back to earth. Yesterday's beggar is today's magnate. A rabbi's wife becomes a coachman. A horse thief returns as a community elder. A slaughterer comes back as an ox. So what's all the fuss about? Everything is kneaded of the same dough—cat and mouse, bear hunter and bear, old man and infant." Beyle Tslove herself had in previous incarnations been a grain merchant, a dairymaid, a rabbi's wife, a teacher of the Talmud.

"Do you remember any Talmud?" Getsl asked.

"If the Angel of Forgetfulness had not tweaked me on the nose, I would surely remember."

"What do you say to my bride?" Getsl bantered. "A whittled tongue. She could convince a stone. If my wife in Pinchev knew what I was exchanging her for, she'd drown herself in a bucket of slops."

"Your wife filled her bed before you were cold . . ."

The strange news spread throughout the town: tomorrow there would be a wedding at Reb Sheftel's house; Getsl the fiddler and Beyle Tslove would become man and wife.

V

When the rabbi heard of the goings on, he issued a proscription forbidding anyone to attend the black wedding. He sent Bendit the beadle to stand guard at the door of Reb Sheftel's house and allow no one to enter. That night, however, there was a heavy snowfall, and by morning it turned bitterly cold. The wind had blown up great drifts and whistled in all the chimneys. Bendit was shrouded in white from head to foot and looked like a snowman made by children. His wife came after him and took him home, half frozen. As soon as dusk began to fall, the rabble gathered at Reb Sheftel's house. Some brought bottles of vodka or brandy; others, dried mutton and honey cake.

As usual, Liebe Yentl had slept all day and did not waken even when the ailing Zise Feige poured a few spoonfuls of broth into her mouth. But once darkness came, the girl sat up. There was such a crush in the house that people could not move.

Zeinvl the butcher took charge. "Bride, did you fast on your wedding day?"

"The way the dead eat, that's how they look," Beyle Tslove replied with a proverb.

"And you, bridegroom, are you ready?"

"Let her first deliver the dowry."

"You can take all I have—a pinch of dust, a moldy crust . . ."

Getsl proved that evening that he was not only an expert musician but could also serve as rabbi, cantor, and wedding jester. First he played a sad tune and recited "God Is Full of Mercy" for the bride and groom. Then he played a merry tune, accompanying it with appropriate jests. He admonished the bride to be a faithful wife, to dress and adorn herself, and to take good care of her household. He warned the couple to be mindful of the day of death, and sang to them:

> *Weep, bride, weep and moan,*
> *Dead men fear to be alone.*
> *In the Sling, beneath the tide,*
> *A groom is waiting for his bride.*
> *Corpse and corpse, wraith and wraith,*
> *Every demon seeks a mate.*

> *Angel Dumah, devil, Shed,*
> *A coffin is a bridal bed.*

Although it was a mock wedding, many a tear fell from the women's eyes. The men sighed. Everything proceeded according to custom. Getsl preached, sang, played. The guests could actually hear the weeping of a fiddle, the piping of a clarinet, the bleating of a trumpet, the wailing of a bagpipe. Getsl pretended to cover the bride with the veil and played a melody appropriate to the veiling ceremony. After the wedding march he recited the words of "Thou Art Sanctified," which accompany the giving of the ring. He delivered the bridegroom's oration, and announced the wedding presents: a shrouded mirror, a little sack of earth from the Holy Land, a burial cleansing spoon, a stopped clock. When the spirits of the guests seemed to droop, Getsl struck up a kozotsky. They tried to dance, but there was scarcely room to take a step. They swayed and gesticulated.

Beyle Tslove suddenly began to wail. "*Oy*, Getsl!"

"What, my dove!"

"Why couldn't this be real? We weren't born dead!"

"Pooh! Reality itself hangs by a thread."

"It's not a game to me, you fool."

"Whatever it is, let's drink and keep cool. May we rejoice and do well until all the fires are extinguished in hell."

A glass of wine was brought, and Liebe Yentl emptied it to the last drop. Then she dashed it against the wall, and Getsl began to recite in the singsong of the cheder boys:

> *Such is Noah's way,*
> *Wash your tears away.*
> *Take a drink instead,*
> *The living and the dead.*
> *Wine will make you strong,*
> *Eternity is long.*

Zise Feige could not endure any more. She rose from her sickbed, wrapped herself in a shawl, and shuffled into her daughter's room in her slippers. She tried to push through the crowd. "Beasts," she cried. "You are torturing my child!"

Beyle Tslove screamed at her, "Don't you worry, old sourpuss! Better a rotten fiddler than a creep from Zawiercia!"

V I

In the middle of the night there were sounds of steps and shouts outside the door. Reb Sheftel had come home from Worka, bringing a bagful of new amulets, charms, and talismans. The Hasidim of the Worka rabbi entered with him, ready to drive out the rabble. They swung their sashes, crying, "Get out, you scum!"

Several young fellows tried to fight off the Worka Hasidim, but the Shidlovtse crowd was tired from standing so long, and they soon began to file out the door. Getsl called after them, "Brothers, don't let the holy schlemiels get you! Give them a taste of your fists! Hey, you, big shot!"

"Cowards! Bastards! Mice!" Beyle Tslove screeched.

A few of the Worka Hasidim got a punch or two, but after a while the riffraff slunk off. The Hasidim burst into the room, panting and threatening the dybbuks with excommunication.

The warden of the Worka synagogue, Reb Avigdor Yavrover, ran up to Liebe Yentl's bed and tried to hang a charm around her neck, but the girl pulled off his hat and skullcap with her right hand, and with her left she seized him by the beard. The other Hasidim tried to pull him away, but Liebe Yentl thrashed out in all directions. She kicked, bit, and scratched. One man got a slap on the cheek, another had his sidelock pulled, a third got a mouthful of spittle on his face, a fourth a punch in the ribs. In order to frighten off the pious, she cried that she was in her unclean days. Then she tore off her shift and exhibited her shame. Those who did not avert their eyes remarked that her belly was distended like a drum. On the right and the left were two bumps as big as heads, and it was clear that the spirits were there. Getsl roared like a lion, howled like a wolf, hissed like a snake. He called the Worka rabbi a eunuch, a clown, a baboon, insulted all the holy sages, and blasphemed against God.

Reb Sheftel sank to the floor and sat there like a mourner. He covered his eyes with both hands and rocked himself as over a corpse. Zise Feige snatched a broom and tried to drive away the men who swarmed around her daughter, but she was dragged aside and fell to the ground. Two neighboring women helped her to get up. Her bonnet fell off, exposing her shaven head with its gray stubble. She raised two fists and screamed, sobbing, "Torturers, you're killing my child! Lord in Heaven, send Pharaoh's curses upon them!"

Finally, several of the younger Hasidim caught Liebe Yentl's hands and feet and tied her to the bed with their sashes. Then they slipped the Worka rabbi's amulets around her neck.

Getsl, who had fallen silent during the struggle, spoke up. "Tell your miracle worker his charms are tripe."

"Wretch, you're in Hell, and you still deny?" Reb Avigdor Yavrover thundered.

"Hell's full of your kind."

"Dog, rascal, degenerate!"

"Why are you cursing, you louses?" Beyle Tslove yelled. "Is it our fault that your holy idiot hands out phony talismans? You'd better leave the girl alone. We aren't doing her any harm. Her good is our good. We're also Jews, remember—not Tartars. Our souls have stood on Mount Sinai, too. If we erred in life, we've paid our debt, with interest."

"Strumpet, hussy, slut, out with you!" one of the Hasidim cried.

"I'll go when I feel like it."

"Todres, blow the ram's horn—a long blast!"

The ram's horn filled the night with its eerie wail.

Beyle Tslove laughed and jeered. "Blow hot, blow cold, who cares!"

"A broken trill now!"

"Don't you have enough breaks under your rupture bands?" Getsl jeered.

"Satan, Amalekite, apostate!"

Hours went by, but the dybbuks remained obdurate. Some of the Worka Hasidim went home. Others leaned against the wall, ready to do battle until the end of their strength. The hoodlums who had run away returned with sticks and knives. The Hasidim of the Radzymin rabbi had heard the news that the Worka talismans had failed, and they came to gloat.

Reb Sheftel rose from the floor and in his anguish began to plead with the dybbuks. "If you are Jews, you should have Jewish hearts. Look what has become of my innocent daughter, lying bound like a sheep prepared for slaughter. My wife is sick. I myself am ready to drop. My business is falling apart. How long will you torture us? Even a murderer has a spark of pity."

"Nobody pities us."

"I'll see to it that you get forgiveness. It says in the Bible, 'His banished be not expelled from Him.' No Jewish soul is rejected forever."

"What will you do for us?" asked Getsl. "Help us moan?"

"I will recite psalms and read the Mishnah for you. I will give alms. I will say Kaddish for you for a full twelve months."

"I'm not one of your peasants. You can't fool me."

"I have never fooled anyone."

"Swear that you will keep your word!" Getsl commanded.

"What's the matter, Getsl? You anxious to leave me already?" Beyle Tslove asked with a laugh.

Getsl yawned. "I'm sorry for the old folks."

"You want to leave me a deserted wife the very first night?"

"Come along if you can."

"Where to? Behind the Mountains of Darkness?"

"Wherever our eyes take us."

"You mean sockets, comedian!"

"Swear, Reb Sheftel, that you will keep all your promises," Getsl the fiddler repeated. "Make a holy vow. If you break your word, I'll be back with the whole Evil Host and scatter your bones to the four winds."

"Don't swear, Reb Sheftel, don't swear!" the Hasidim cried. "Such a vow is a desecration of the Name!"

"Swear, my husband, swear. If you don't, we shall all perish."

Reb Sheftel put his hand on his beard. "Dead souls, I swear that I will faithfully fulfill all that I take upon myself. I will study the Mishnah for you. I will say Kaddish for twelve months. Tell me when you died, and I will burn memorial candles for you. If there are no headstones on your graves, I will journey to the cemeteries and have them erected."

"Our graves have been leveled long since. Come, Beyle Tslove, let's go. Dawn is rising over Pinchev."

"Imp, you made a fool of a Jewish daughter all for nothing!" Beyle Tslove reproached him.

"Hey, men, move aside!" Getsl cried. "Or I shall enter one of you!"

There was such a crush that, though the door stood open, no one could get out. Hats and skullcaps fell off. Caftans caught on nails and ripped. A muffled cry rose from the crowd. Several Hasidim fell, and others trampled them. Liebe Yentl's mouth opened wide and there was a shot as from a pistol. Her eyes rolled and she fell back on the pillow, white as death. A stench swept across the room—a foul breath of the grave. Zise Feige stumbled on weak legs toward her daughter and untied her. The girl's belly was now flat and shrunken like the belly of a woman after childbirth.

Reb Sheftel attested afterward that two balls of fire came out of Liebe Yentl's nostrils and flew to the window. A pane split open, and the two sinful souls returned through the crack to the World of Delusion.

VII

For weeks after the dybbuks had left her, Liebe Yentl lay sick. The doctor applied cups and leeches; he bled her, but Liebe Yentl never opened her eyes. The woman from the Society of Tenders of the Sick who sat with the girl at night related that she heard sad melodies outside the window, and Getsl's voice begging her to remove the amulets from the girl's neck and let him in. The woman also heard Beyle Tslove's giggling.

Gradually Liebe Yentl began to recover, but she had almost stopped speaking. She sat in bed and stared at the window. Winter was over. Swallows returned from the warm countries and were building a nest under the eaves. From her bed Liebe Yentl could see the roof of the synagogue, where a pair of storks were repairing last year's nest.

Reb Sheftel and Zise Feige feared that Liebe Yentl would no longer be accepted in marriage, but Shmelke Motl wrote from Zawiercia that he would keep to his agreement if the dowry were raised by one third. Reb Sheftel and Zise Feige consented at once. After Pentecost, Shmelke Motl made his appearance at the Shidlovtse prayer house—no taller than a cheder boy but with a large head on a thin neck and tightly twisted sidelocks that stood up like a pair of horns. He had thick eyebrows and dark eyes that looked down at the tip of his nose. As soon as he entered the study house, he took out a Gemara and sat down to study. He sat there, swaying and mumbling, until he was taken to the ceremony of betrothal.

Reb Sheftel invited only a selected few to the engagement meal, for during the time that his daughter had been possessed by the dybbuks he had made many enemies both among the Radzymin Hasidim and among those of Worka. According to custom, the men sat at one table, the women at another. The bridegroom delivered an impromptu sermon on the subject of the Stoned Ox. Such sermons usually last half an hour, but two hours went by and the groom still talked on in his high, grating voice, accompanying his words with wild gestures. He grimaced as though gripped with pain, pulled at a sidelock, scratched his chin, which was just beginning to sprout a beard, grasped the lobe of his ear. From time to time his lips stretched in a smile, revealing blackened teeth, pointed as nails.

Liebe Yentl never once took her eyes from him. The women tried to talk to her; they urged her to taste the cookies, the jam, the mead. But Liebe Yentl bit her lips and stared.

The guests began to cough and fidget, hinting in various ways that it was time to bring the oration to an end, and finally the bridegroom broke off his sermon. The betrothal contract was brought to him, but he did not sign it at once. First he read the page from beginning to end. He was evidently nearsighted, for he brought the paper right up to his nose. Then he began to bargain. "The prayer shawl should have silver braid."

"It will have any braid you wish," Reb Sheftel agreed.

"Write it in."

It was written in on the margin. The groom read on, and demanded, "I want a Talmud printed in Slovita."

"Very well, it will be from Slovita."

"Write it in."

After much haggling and writing in, the groom signed the contract: Shmelke Motl son of the late Catriel Godl. The letters of the signature were as tiny as flyspecks.

When Reb Sheftel brought the contract over to Liebe Yentl and handed her the pen, she said in a clear voice, "I will not sign."

"Daughter, you shame me!"

"I will not live with him."

Zise Feige began to pinch her wrinkled cheeks. "People, go home!" she called out. She snuffed the candles in the candlesticks. Some of the women wept with the disgraced mother; others berated the bride. But the girl answered no one. Before long, the house was dark and empty. The servant went out to close the shutters.

Reb Sheftel usually prayed at the synagogue with the first quorum, but that morning he did not show himself at the holy place. Zise Feige did not go out to do her shopping. The door of Reb Sheftel's house stood locked; the windows were shuttered. Shmelke Motl returned at once to Zawiercia.

After a time Reb Sheftel went back to praying at the synagogue, and Zise Feige went again to market with her basket. But Liebe Yentl no longer came out into the street. People thought that her parents had sent her away somewhere, but Liebe Yentl was at home. She kept to her room and refused to speak to anyone. When her mother brought her a plate of soup, she first knocked at the door as though they were gentry. Liebe Yentl scarcely touched the food, and Zise Feige sent it to the poorhouse.

For some months the matchmakers still came with offers, but since a dybbuk had spoken from her and she had shamed a bridegroom Liebe Yentl could no longer make a proper match. Reb Sheftel tried to obtain a pardon from the young man in Zawiercia, but he had gone away to some yeshiva in Lithuania. There was a rumor that he had hanged himself with his sash. Then it became clear that Liebe Yentl would remain an old maid. Her younger brother, Tsadock Meyer, had in the meantime grown up and got married to a girl from Bendin.

Reb Sheftel was the first to die. This happened on a Thursday night in winter. Reb Sheftel had risen for midnight prayers. He stood at the reading desk, with ash on his head, reciting a lament on the Destruction of the Temple. A beggar was spending that night at the prayer house. About three o'clock in the morning, the man awakened and put some potatoes into the stove to bake. Suddenly he heard a thud. He stood up and saw Reb Sheftel on the floor. He sprinkled him with water from the pitcher, but the soul had already departed.

The townspeople mourned Reb Sheftel. The body was not taken home but lay in the prayer house with candles at its head until the time of burial. The rabbi and some of the town's scholars delivered eulogies. On Friday, Liebe Yentl escorted the coffin with her mother. Liebe Yentl was wrapped in a black shawl from head to toe; only a part of her face showed, white as the snow in the cemetery. The two sons lived far from Shidlovtse, and the funeral could not be postponed till after the Sabbath; it is a dishonor for a corpse to wait too long for burial. Reb Sheftel was put to rest near the grave of the old rabbi. It is known that those who are buried on Friday after noon do not suffer the pressure of the grave, for the Angel Dumah puts away his fiery rod on the eve of the Sabbath.

Zise Feige lingered a few years more, but she was fading day by day. Her body bent like a candle. In her last year she no longer attended to the business, relying entirely on her assistant, Zalkind. She began to rise at dawn to pray at the women's synagogue, and she often went to the cemetery and prostrated herself on Reb Sheftel's grave. She died as suddenly as her husband. It happened during evening prayer on Yom Kippur. Zise Feige had stood all day, weeping, at the railing that divided the women's section from the men's in the prayer house. Her neighbors, seeing her waxen-yellow face, urged her to break her fast, for human life takes precedence over all laws, but Zise Feige refused. When the cantor intoned, "The gates of Heaven open," Zise Feige took from her bosom a vial of aromatic drops, which are a remedy against faintness. But the vial slipped from her hand and she fell forward onto the reading desk. There was an outcry and women ran for the doctor, but Zise Feige had already passed into the True World. Her last words were: "My daughter . . ."

This time the funeral was delayed until the arrival of the two sons. They sat in mourning with their sister. But Liebe Yentl avoided all strangers. Those who came to pray with the mourners and to comfort them found only Jedidiah and Tsadock Meyer. Liebe Yentl would lock herself away in her room.

Nothing was left of Reb Sheftel's wealth. People muttered that the assistant had pocketed the money, but it could not be proved. Red Sheftel and Zise Feige had kept no books. All the accounting had been done with a piece of chalk on the wall of a wardrobe. After the seven days of mourning, the sons called Zalkind to the rabbi's court, but he offered to swear before the Holy Scrolls and black candles that he had not touched a groschen of his employers' money. The rabbi forbade such an oath. He said that a man who could break the commandment "Thou Shalt Not Steal" could also violate the commandment "Thou Shalt Not Take the Name of Thy God the Lord in Vain."

After the judgment, the two sons went home. Liebe Yentl remained with the servant. Zalkind took over the business and merely sent Liebe Yentl two gulden a week for food. Soon he refused to give even that and sent only a few groschen. The servant woman left and went to work elsewhere.

Now that Liebe Yentl no longer had a servant, she was compelled to show herself in the street, but she never came out during the day. She would leave the house only after dark, waiting until the streets were empty and the stores without other customers. She would appear suddenly, as though from nowhere. The storekeepers were afraid of her. Dogs barked at her from Christian yards.

Summer and winter she was wrapped from head to toe in a long shawl. She would enter the store and forget what she wanted to buy. She often gave more money than was asked, as though she no longer remembered how to count. A few times she was seen entering the Gentile tavern to buy vodka. Tevye the night watchman had heard Liebe Yentl pacing the house at night, talking to herself.

Zise Feige's good friends tried repeatedly to see the girl, but the door was always bolted. Liebe Yentl never came to the synagogue on holidays to pray for the souls of the deceased. During the months of Nisan and Elul, she never went to visit the graves of her parents. She did not bake Sabbath bread on Fridays, did not set roasts overnight in the oven, and probably did not bless the candles. She did not come to the women's synagogue even on the High Holy Days.

People began to forget Liebe Yentl—as if she were dead—but she lived on. At times, smoke rose from her chimney. Late at night, she was sometimes seen going to the well for a pail of water. Those who caught sight of her swore that she did not look a day older. Her face was becoming even more pale, her hair redder and longer. It was said that Liebe Yentl played with cats. Some whispered that she had dealings with a demon. Others thought that the dybbuk had returned to her. Zalkind still delivered a measure of flour to the house every Thursday, leaving it in the larder in the entrance hall. He also provided Liebe Yentl with firewood.

There had formerly been several other Jewish households on the street, but gradually the owners had sold to Gentiles. A hog butcher had moved into one house and built a high fence around it. Another house was occupied by a deaf old widow who spent her days spinning flax, guarded by a blind dog at her feet.

Years went by. One early morning in Elul, when the rabbi was sitting in his study writing commentary and drinking tea from a samovar, Tevye the night watchman knocked at his door. He told the rabbi that he had seen Liebe Yentl on the road leading to Radom. The girl wore a long white dress; she had no kerchief on her head and walked barefoot. She was accompanied by a man with long hair, carrying a violin case. The full moon shone brightly. Tevye wanted to call out, but since the figures cast no shadow he was seized with fear. When he looked again, the pair had vanished.

The rabbi ordered Tevye to wait until the worshippers assembled for morning prayer in the synagogue. Then Tevye told the people of the apparition, and two men—a driver and a butcher—went to Reb Sheftel's house. They knocked, but no one answered. They broke open the door and found Liebe Yentl dead. She lay in the middle of the room among piles of garbage, in a long shift, barefoot, her red hair loose. It was obvious that she had not been among the living for many days—perhaps a week or even more. The women of the Burial Society hastily carried off the corpse to the hut for the cleansing of the dead. When the shroud-makers opened the wardrobe, a cloud of moths flew out, filling the house like a swarm of locusts. All the clothes were eaten, all the linens moldy and decayed.

Since Liebe Yentl had not taken her own life and since she had exhibited all the signs of madness, the rabbi permitted her to be buried next to her parents. Half the town followed the body to the cemetery. The brothers were notified and came later to sell the house and order a stone for their sister's grave.

It was clear to everyone that the man who had appeared with Liebe Yentl on the road to Radom was the dead fiddler of Pinchev. Dunya, Zise Feige's former servant, told the women that Liebe Yentl had not been able to forget her dead bridegroom Ozer and that Ozer had become a dybbuk in order to prevent the marriage to Shmelke Motl. But where would Ozer, a scholar and the son of a rich man, have learned to play music and to perform like a wedding jester? And why would he appear on the Radom road in the guise of a fiddler? And where was he going with the dead Liebe Yentl that night? And what had become of Beyle Tslove? Heaven and earth have sworn that the truth shall remain forever hidden.

More years went by, but the dead fiddler was not forgotten. He was heard playing at night in the cold synagogue. His fiddle sang faintly in the bathhouse, the poorhouse, the cemetery. It was said in town that he came to weddings. Sometimes, at the end of a wedding after the Shidlovtse band had stopped playing, people still heard a few lingering notes, and they knew that it was the dead fiddler.

In autumn, when leaves fell and winds blew from the Mountains of the Holy Cross, a low melody was often heard in the chimneys, thin as a hair and mournful as the world. Even children would hear it, and they would ask, "Mama, who is playing?" And the mother would answer, "Sleep, child. It's the dead fiddler."

Henne Fire

I

YES, there are people who are demons. God preserve us! Mothers see things when they give birth, but they never tell what they see!

Henne Fire, as she was called, was not a human being but a fire from Gehenna. I know one should not speak evil of the dead and she suffered greatly for her sins. Was it her fault that there was always a blaze within her? One could see it in her eyes: two coals. It was frightening to look at them. She was black as a gypsy, with a narrow face, sunken cheeks, emaciated—skin and bone. Once I saw her bathing in the river. Her ribs protruded like hoops. How could someone like Henne put on fat? Whatever one said to her, no matter how innocently, she immediately took offense. She would begin to scream, shake her fists, and spin around like a crazy person. Her face would turn white with anger. If you tried to defend yourself, she was ready to swallow you alive and she'd start smashing dishes. Every few weeks her husband, Berl Chazkeles, had to buy a new set.

She suspected everybody. The whole town was out to get her. When she flew into a rage, she said things that would not even occur to an insane person. Swear words poured from her mouth like worm-eaten peas. She knew every curse in the holy book by heart. She was not beyond throwing rocks. Once, in the middle of winter, she broke a neighbor's windowpane and the neighbor never learned why.

Henne had children, four girls, but as soon as they grew up they ran away from home. One became a servant in Lublin; one left for America; the most beautiful, Malkeleh, died of scarlet fever; and the fourth married an old man. Anything was better than living with Henne.

Her husband, Berl, must have been a saint. Only a saint could have stood such a shrew for twenty years. He was a sieve-maker. In those

Translated by the author and Dorothea Straus

days, in the wintertime, work started when it was still dark. The sieve-maker had to supply his own candle. He earned only a pittance. Of course, they were poor, but they were not the only ones. A wagonload of chalk would not suffice to write down the complaints she hurled at him. I lived next door to her and once, when he left for work at dawn, I heard her call after him: "Come back feet first!" I can't imagine what she blamed him for. He gave her his last penny, and he loved her too. How could one love such a fiend? Only God knows. In any case, who can understand what goes on in the heart of a man?

My dear people, even he finally ran away from her. One summer morning, a Friday, he left to go to the ritual bath and disappeared like a stone in the water. When Henne heard he was seen leaving the village, she fell down in an epileptic fit right in the gutter. She knocked her head on the stones, hissed like a snake, and foamed at the mouth. Someone pushed a key into her left hand, but it didn't help. Her kerchief fell off and revealed the fact that she did not shave her head. She was carried home. I've never seen such a face, as green as grass, her eyes rolled up. The moment she came to, she began to curse and I think from then on never stopped. It was said that she even swore in her sleep. At Yom Kippur she stood in the women's section of the synagogue and, as the rabbi's wife recited the prayers for those who could not read, Henne berated the rabbi, the cantor, the elders. On her husband she called forth a black judgment, wished him smallpox and gangrene. She also blasphemed against God.

After Berl forsook her, she went completely wild. As a rule, an abandoned woman made a living by kneading dough in other people's houses or by becoming a servant. But who would let a malicious creature like Henne into the house? She tried to sell fish on Thursdays, but when a woman asked the price, Henne would reply, "You are not going to buy anyhow, so why do you come here just to tease me? You'll poke around and buy elsewhere."

One housewife picked up a fish and lifted its gills to see if it was fresh. Henne tore it from her hands, screaming, "Why do you smell it? Is it beneath your dignity to eat rotten fish?" And she sang out a list of sins allegedly committed by the woman's parents, grandparents, and great-grandparents back to the tenth generation. The other fishmongers sold their wares and Henne remained with a tubful. Every few weeks Henne washed her clothes. Don't ask me how she carried on. She quarreled about everything: the washtubs, the clotheslines, the water pump. If she found a speck of dust on a shirt hanging up to dry, she blamed it on her neighbors. She herself tore down the lines of others. One heard her yelling over half the town. People were afraid of her and gave in, but that was no good either. If you answered her she raised a rumpus, and if you kept silent she would scream, "Is it a disgrace to talk to me?" There was no dealing with her without being insulted.

At first her daughters would come home from the big towns for the holidays. They were good girls, and they all took after their father. One moment mother and daughter would kiss and embrace and before you knew it there would be a cat fight in Butcher Alley, where we lived. Plates crashed, windows were broken. The girl would run out of the house as though poisoned and Henne would be after her with a stick, screaming, "Bitch, slut, whore, you should have dissolved in your mother's belly!" After Berl deserted her, Henne suspected that her daughters knew his whereabouts. Although they swore holy oaths that they didn't, Henne would rave, "Your mouths will grow out the back of your heads for swearing falsely!"

What could the poor girls do? They avoided her like the plague. And Henne went to the village teacher and made him write letters for her saying that she disowned them. She was no longer their mother and they were no longer her daughters.

Still, in a small town one is not allowed to starve. Good people took pity on Henne. They brought her soup, garlic borscht, a loaf of bread, potatoes, or whatever they had to offer, and left it on the threshold. Entering her house was like walking into a lion's den. Henne seldom tasted these gifts. She threw them into the garbage ditch. Such people thrive on fighting.

Since the grownups ignored her, Henne began to quarrel with the children. A boy passed by and Henne snatched his cap because she imagined he had stolen pears from her tree. The pears were as hard as wood and tasted the same; a pig wouldn't eat them. She just needed an excuse. She was always lying and she called everybody else a liar. She went to the chief of police and denounced half the town, accusing this one of being a forger and that one of smuggling contraband from Galicia. She reported that the Hasidim were disrespectful to the czar. In the fall, when the recruits were being drafted, Henne announced in the marketplace that the rich boys were being deferred and the poor ones taken. It was true, too. But if they had all been taken, would it have been better? Somebody had to serve. But Henne, good sort that she was, could not suffer injustice. The Russian officials were afraid that she would cause trouble and had her sent to the insane asylum.

I was there when a soldier and a policeman came to get her. She turned on them with a hatchet. She made such a commotion that the whole town came running. But how strong is a female? As she was bound and loaded into a cart, she cursed in Russian, Polish, and Yiddish. She sounded like a pig being slaughtered. She was taken to Lublin and put in a strait jacket.

I don't know how it happened, but she must have been on her good behavior, because in less than half a year she was back in town. A family had moved into her hut, but she drove the whole lot out in the middle of a cold night. The next day Henne announced that she had been robbed. She went to all the neighbors to look for her belongings and humiliated everybody. She was no longer allowed into the women's synagogue and was even refused when she wanted to buy a seat for the Days of Awe. Things came to such a pass that when she went to the well to get water everyone ran away. It was simply dangerous to come near her.

She did not even respect the dead. A hearse passed by and Henne spat at it, screaming that she hoped the dead man's soul would wander in the wastelands forever. The better type of people turned a deaf ear to her, but when the mourners were of the common kind she got beaten up. She liked to be beaten; that is the truth. She would run around showing off a bump given her by this one, a black eye by that one. She ran to the druggist for leeches and salves. She kept summoning everybody to the rabbi, but the beadle would no longer listen to her and the rabbi had issued an order forbidding her to enter his study. She also tried her luck with the Gentiles, but they only laughed at her. Nothing remained to her but God. And according to Henne she and the Almighty were on the best of terms.

Now listen to what happened. There was a coachman called Kopel Klotz who lived near Henne. Once in the middle of the night he was awakened by screams for help. He looked out the window and saw that the house of the shoemaker across the street was on fire. He grabbed a pail of water and went to help put it out. But the fire was not at the shoemaker's; it was at Henne's. It was only the reflection that he had seen in the shoemaker's window. Kopel ran to her house and found everything burning: the table, the bench, the cupboard. It wasn't a usual fire. Little flames flew around like birds. Henne's nightshirt was burning. Kopel tore it off her and she stood there as naked as the day she was born.

A fire in Butcher Alley is no small thing. The wood of the houses is dry even in winter. From one spark the whole alley could turn into ashes. People came to the rescue, but the flames danced and turned somersaults. Every moment something else became ignited. Henne covered her naked body with a shawl and the fringes began to burn like so many candles. The men fought the fire until dawn. Some of them were overcome by the smoke. These were not flames, but goblins from hell.

In the morning there was another outburst. Henne's bed linen began to burn of itself. That day I visited Henne's hut. Her sheet was full of holes; the quilt and feather bed, too. The dough in the trough had been baked into a flat loaf of bread. A fiery broom had swept the floor, igniting the garbage. Tongues of flame licked everything. God save us, these were tricks of the Evil Host. Henne sent everybody to the devil; and now the devil had turned on her.

Somehow the fire was put out. The people of Butcher Alley warned the rabbi that if Henne could not be induced to leave they would take matters into their own hands. Everyone was afraid for his kin and possessions. No one wanted to pay for the sins of another. Henne went to the rabbi's house and wailed, "Where am I to go? Murderers, robbers, beasts!"

She became as hoarse as a crow. As she ranted, her kerchief took fire. Those who weren't there will never know what the demons can do.

As Henne stood in the rabbi's study, pleading with him to let her stay, her house went up in flames. A flame burst from the roof and it had the shape of a man with long hair. It danced and whistled. The church bells rang an alarm. The firemen tried their best, but in a few minutes nothing was left but a chimney and a heap of burning embers.

Later, Henne spread the rumor that her neighbors had set her house on fire. But it was not so. Who would try a thing like that, especially with the wind blowing? There were scores of witnesses to the contrary. The fiery image had waved its arms and laughed madly. Then it had risen into the air and disappeared among the clouds.

It was then that people began to call her Henne Fire. Up to then she had been known as Black Henne.

I I

When Henne found herself without a roof over her head, she tried to move into the poorhouse but the poor and sick would not let her in. Nobody wants to be burned alive. For the first time she became silent. A Gentile woodchopper took her into his house. The moment she crossed the threshold the handle of his ax caught fire and out she went. She would have frozen to death in the cold if the rabbi hadn't taken her in.

The rabbi had a booth not far from his house which was used during the Sukkoth holidays. It had a roof which could be opened and closed by a series of pulleys. The rabbi's son installed a tin stove so that Henne would not freeze. The rabbi's wife supplied a bed with a straw mattress and linen. What else could they do? Jews don't let a person perish. They hoped the demons would respect a Sukkoth booth and that it would not catch fire. True, it had no mezuzah, but the rabbi hung a talisman on the wall instead. Some of the townspeople offered to bring food to Henne, but the rabbi's wife said, "The little she eats I can provide."

The winter cold began immediately after the Sukkoth holiday and it lasted until Purim. Houses were snowed under. In the morning one had to dig oneself out with a shovel. Henne lay in bed all day. She was not the same Henne: she was docile as a sheep. Yet evil looked out of her eyes. The rabbi's son fed her stove every morning. He reported in the study house that Henne lay all day tucked into her feather bed and never uttered a word. The rabbi's wife suggested that she come into the kitchen and perhaps help a little with the housework. Henne refused. "I don't want anything to happen to the rabbi's books," she said. It was whispered in the town that perhaps the Evil One had left her.

Around Purim it suddenly became warm. The ice thawed and the river overflowed. Bridge Street was flooded. The poor are miserable anyway, but when there is a flood at night and the household goods begin to swim around, life becomes unbearable. A raft was used to cross Bridge Street. The bakery had begun preparing matzos for Passover, but water seeped into the sacks and made the flour unusable.

Suddenly a scream was heard from the rabbi's house. The Sukkoth booth had burst into flame like a paper lantern. It happened in the middle of the night. Later Henne related how a fiery hand had reached down from the roof and in a second everything was consumed. She had grabbed a blanket to cover herself and had run into the muddy court-yard without clothes on. Did the rabbi have a choice? He had to take her in. His wife stopped sleeping at night. Henne said to the rabbi, "I shouldn't be allowed to do this to you." Even before the booth had burned down, the rabbi's married daughter, Taube, had packed her trousseau into a sheet so she could save it at a moment's notice in case of fire.

Next day the community elders called a meeting. There was much talk and haggling, but they couldn't come to a decision. Someone proposed that Henne be sent to another town. Henne burst into the rabbi's study, her dress in tatters, a living scarecrow. "Rabbi, I've lived here all my life, and here I want to die. Let them dig me a grave and bury me. The cemetery will not catch fire." She had found her tongue again and everybody was surprised.

Present at the meeting was Reb Zelig, the plumber, a decent man, and he finally made a suggestion. "Rabbi, I will build her a little house of brick. Bricks don't burn."

He asked no pay for his work, just his costs. Then a roofer promised to make the roof. Henne owned the lot in Butcher Alley, and the chim-ney had remained standing.

To put up a house takes months, but this little building was erected between Purim and Passover, everyone lending a hand. Boys from the study house dumped the ashes. Schoolchildren carried bricks. Yeshiva students mixed mortar. Yudel, the glazier, contributed windowpanes. As the proverb goes: a community is never poor. A rich man, Reb Falik, donated tin for the roof. One day there was a ruin and the next day there was the house. Actually it was a shack without a floor, but how much does a single person need? Henne was provided with an iron bed, a pillow, a straw mattress, a feather bed. She didn't even watch the builders. She sat in the rabbi's kitchen on the lookout for fires.

The house was finished just a day before Passover. From the poor fund, Henne was stocked with matzos, potatoes, eggs, horseradish, all that was necessary. She was even presented with a new set of dishes. There was only one thing everybody refused to do, and that was to have her at the Seder. In the evening they looked in at her window: no holiday, no Seder, no candles. She was sitting on a bench, munching a carrot.

One never knows how things will turn out. In the beginning nothing was heard from Henne's daughter, Mindel, who had gone to America. How does the saying go? Across the sea is another world. They go to America and forget father, mother, Jewishness, God. Years passed and there was not a single word from her. But Mindel proved herself a devoted child after all. She got married and her husband became immensely rich.

Our local post office had a letter carrier who was just a simple peasant. One day a strange letter carrier appeared. He had a long mustache, his jacket had gilded buttons, and he wore insignia on his cap. He brought a letter for which the recipient had to sign. For whom do you think it was? For Henne. She could no more sign her name than I can dance a quadrille. She daubed three marks on the receipt and somebody was a witness. To make it short, it was a letter containing money. Lippe, the teacher, came to read it and half the town listened.

"My dear mother, your worries are over. My husband has become rich. New York is a large city where white bread is eaten in the middle of the week. Everybody speaks English, the Jews too. At night it is as bright as day. Trains travel on tracks high up near the roofs. Make peace with Father and I will send you both passage to America."

The townspeople didn't know whether to laugh or cry. Henne listened but didn't say a word. She neither cursed nor blessed.

A month later another letter arrived, and two months after that, another. An American dollar was worth two rubles. There was an agent in town, and when he heard that Henne was getting money from America, he proposed all kinds of deals to her. Would she like to buy a house, or become a partner in a store? There was a man in our town called Leizer the messenger, although nobody ever sent him anywhere. He came to Henne and offered to go in search of her husband. If he was alive, Leizer was sure he would find him and either bring him home or make him send her a bill of divorcement. Henne's reply was: "If you bring him back, bring him back dead, and you should walk on crutches!"

Henne remained Henne, but the neighbors began to make a fuss over her. That is how people are. When they smell a groschen, they get excited. Now they were quick to greet her, called her Hennely, and waited on her. Henne just glowered at them, muttering curses. She went straight to Zrule's tavern, bought a big bottle of vodka, and took it home. To make a long story short, Henne began to drink. That a woman should drink is rare, even among the Gentiles, but that a Jewish woman should drink was unheard of. Henne lay in bed and gulped down the liquor. She sang, cried, and made crazy faces. She strolled over to the marketplace in her undergarments, followed by cat-calling urchins. It is sacrilegious to behave as Henne did, but what could the townspeople do? Nobody went to prison for drinking. The officials themselves were often dead drunk. The neighbors said that Henne got up in the morning and drank a cup of vodka. This was her breakfast. Then she went to sleep and when she awoke she began to drink in earnest. Once in a while, when the whim seized her, she would open the window and throw out some coins. The little ones almost killed themselves trying to pick them up. As they groped on the ground for the money, she would empty the slops over them. The rabbi sent for her but he might just as well have saved his breath. Everyone was sure that she would drink herself to death. Something entirely different happened.

As a rule, Henne would come out of her house in the morning. Sometimes she would go to the well for a pail of water. There were stray dogs in Butcher Alley and occasionally she would throw them a bone. There were no outhouses and the villagers attended to their needs in the open. A few days passed and nobody saw Henne. The neighbors tried to peer into her window, but the curtains were drawn. They knocked on her door and no one opened it. Finally they broke it open and what they saw should never be seen again. Some time before, Henne had bought an upholstered chair from a widow. It was an old piece of furniture. She used to sit in it drinking and babbling to herself. When they got the door open, sitting in the chair was a skeleton as black as coal.

My dear people, Henne had been burned to a crisp. But how? The chair itself was almost intact, only the material at the back was singed. For a person to be so totally consumed, you'd need a fire bigger than the one in the bathhouse on Fridays. Even to roast a goose, a lot of wood is needed. But the chair was untouched. Nor had the linen on the bed caught fire. She had bought a chest of drawers, a table, a wardrobe, and everything was undamaged. Yet Henne was one piece of coal. There was no body to be laid out, to be cleansed, or dressed in a shroud. The officials hurried to Henne's house and they could not believe their own eyes. Nobody had seen a fire, nobody had smelled smoke. Where could such a hell fire have come from? No ashes were to be found in the stove or under the tripod. Henne seldom cooked. The town's doctor, Chapinski, arrived. His eyes popped out of his head and there he stood like a figure of clay.

"How is it possible?" the chief of police asked.

"It's impossible," the doctor replied. "If someone were to tell me such a thing, I would call him a filthy liar."

"But it has happened," the chief of police interrupted.

Chapinski shrugged his shoulders and murmured, "I just don't understand."

Someone suggested that it might have been lightning. But there had been no lightning and thunder for weeks.

The neighboring squires heard of the event and arrived on the scene. Butcher Alley filled with carriages, britskas, and phaetons. The crowd stood and gaped. Everyone tried to find an explanation. It was beyond reason. The upholstery of the chair was filled with flax, dry as pepper.

A rumor spread that the vodka had ignited in Henne's stomach. But who ever heard of a fire in the guts? The doctor shook his head. "It's a riddle."

There was no point in preparing Henne for burial. They put her bones in a sack, carried it to the cemetery, and buried her. The gravedigger recited the Kaddish. Later her daughters came from Lublin, but what could they learn? Fires ran after Henne and a fire had finished her. In her curses she had often used the word "fire": fire in the head, fire in the belly. She would say, "You should burn like a candle." "You should burn in fever." "You should burn like kindling wood." Words have power. The proverb says: "A blow passes, but a word remains."

My dear people, Henne continued to cause trouble even after her death. Kopel the coachman bought her house from her daughters and turned it into a stable. But the horses sweated in the night and caught cold. When a horse catches cold that way, it's the end. Several times the straw caught fire. A neighbor who had quarreled with Henne about the washing swore that Henne's ghost tore the sheets from the line and threw them into the mud. The ghost also overturned a washtub. I wasn't there, but of a person such as Henne anything can be believed. I see her to this day, black, lean, with a flat chest like a man and the wild eyes of a hunted beast. Something was smouldering within her. She must have suffered. I remember my grandmother saying, "A good life never made anyone knock his head against the wall." However, no matter what misfortunes strike I say, "Burst, but keep a good face on things."

Thank God, not everyone can afford constantly to bewail his lot. A rabbi in our town once said: "If people did not have to work for their bread, everyone would spend his time mourning his own death and life would be one big funeral."

The Letter Writer

I

HERMAN GOMBINER opened an eye. This was the way he woke up each morning—gradually, first with one eye, then the other. His glance met a cracked ceiling and part of the building across the street. He had gone to bed in the early hours, at about three. It had taken him a long time to fall asleep. Now it was close to ten o'clock. Lately, Herman Gombiner had been suffering from a kind of amnesia. When he got up during the night, he couldn't remember where he was, who he was, or even his name. It took a few seconds to realize that he was no longer in Kalomin, or in Warsaw, but in New York, uptown on one of the streets between Columbus Avenue and Central Park West.

It was winter. Steam hissed in the radiator. The Second World War was long since over. Herman (or Hayim David, as he was called in Kalomin) had lost his family to the Nazis. He was now an editor, proofreader, and translator in a Hebrew publishing house called Zion. It was situated on Canal Street. He was a bachelor, almost fifty years old, and a sick man.

"What time is it?" he mumbled. His tongue was coated, his lips cracked. His knees ached; his head pounded; there was a bitter taste in his mouth. With an effort he got up, setting his feet down on the worn carpet that covered the floor. "What's this? Snow?" he muttered. "Well, it's winter."

He stood at the window awhile and looked out. The broken-down cars parked on the street jutted from the snow like relics of a long-lost civilization. Usually the street was filled with rubbish, noise, and children—Negro and Puerto Rican. But now the cold kept everyone indoors. The stillness, the whiteness made him think of his old home, of Kalomin. Herman stumbled toward the bathroom.

Translated by Alizah Shevrin and Elizabeth Shub

The bedroom was an alcove, with space only for a bed. The living room was full of books. On one wall there were cabinets from floor to ceiling, and along the other stood two bookcases. Books, newspapers, and magazines lay everywhere, piled in stacks. According to the lease, the landlord was obliged to paint the apartment every three years, but Herman Gombiner had bribed the superintendent to leave him alone. Many of his old books would fall apart if they were moved. Why is new paint better than old? The dust had gathered in layers. A single mouse had found its way into the apartment, and every night Herman set out for her a piece of bread, a small slice of cheese, and a saucer of water to keep her from eating the books. Thank goodness she didn't give birth. Occasionally, she would venture out of her hole even when the light was on. Herman had even given her a Hebrew name: Huldah. Her little bubble eyes stared at him with curiosity. She stopped being afraid of him.

The building in which Herman lived had many faults, but it did not lack heat. The radiators sizzled from early morning till late at night. The owner, himself a Puerto Rican, would never allow his tenants' children to suffer from the cold.

There was no shower in the bathroom, and Herman bathed daily in the tub. A mirror that was cracked down the middle hung inside the door, and Herman caught a glimpse of himself—a short man, in oversize pajamas, emaciated to skin and bone, with a scrawny neck and a large head, on either side of which grew two tufts of gray hair. His forehead was wide and deep, his nose crooked, his cheekbones high. Only in his dark eyes, with long lashes like a girl's, had there remained any trace of youthfulness. At times, they even seemed to twinkle shrewdly. Many years of reading and poring over tiny letters hadn't blurred his vision or made him nearsighted. The remaining strength in Herman Gombiner's body—a body worn out by illnesses and undernourishment—seemed to be concentrated in his gaze.

He shaved slowly and carefully. His hand, with its long fingers, trembled, and he could easily have cut himself. Meanwhile, the tub filled with warm water. He undressed, and was amazed at his thinness—his chest was narrow, his arms and legs bony; there were deep hollows between his neck and shoulders. Getting into the bathtub was a strain, but then lying in the warm water was a relief. Herman always lost the soap. It would slip out of his hands playfully, like a live thing, and he would search for it in the water. "Where are you running?" he would say to it. "You rascal!" He believed there was life in everything, that the so-called inanimate objects had their own whims and caprices.

Herman Gombiner considered himself to be among the select few privileged to see beyond the façade of phenomena. He had seen a blotter raise itself from the desk, slowly and unsteadily float toward the door, and, once there, float gently down, as if suspended by an invisible string held by some unseen hand. The whole thing had been thoroughly sense-less. No matter how much Herman thought about it, he was unable to figure out any reason for what had taken place. It had been one of those extraordinary happenings that cannot be explained by science, or reli-gion, or folklore. Later, Herman had bent down and picked up the blotter, and placed it back on the desk, where it remained to this day, covered with papers, dusty, and dried out—an inanimate object that for one moment had somehow freed itself from physical laws. Herman Gombiner knew that it had been neither a hallucination nor a dream. It had taken place in a well-lit room at eight in the evening. He hadn't been ill or even upset that day. He never drank liquor, and he had been wide awake. He had been standing next to the chest, about to take a handker-chief out of a drawer. Suddenly his gaze had been attracted to the desk and he had seen the blotter rise and float. Nor was this the only such incident. Such things had been happening to him since childhood.

Everything took a long time—his bath, drying himself, putting on his clothes. Hurrying was not for him. His competence was the result of deliberateness. The proofreaders at Zion worked so quickly they missed errors. The translators hardly took the time to check meanings they were unsure of in the dictionary. The majority of American and even Israeli Hebraists knew little of vowel points and the subtleties of grammar. Herman Gombiner had found the time to study all these things. It was true that he worked very slowly, but the old man, Morris Korver, who owned Zion, and even his sons, the half Gentiles, had always appreci-ated the fact that it was Herman Gombiner who had earned the house its reputation. Morris Korver, however, had become old and senile, and Zion was in danger of closing. It was rumored that his sons could hardly wait for the old man to die so they could liquidate the business.

Even if Herman wanted to, it was impossible for him to do anything in a hurry. He took small steps when he walked. It took him half an hour to eat a bowl of soup. Searching for the right word in a dictionary or checking something in an encyclopedia could involve hours of work. The few times that he had tried to hurry had ended in disaster; he had broken his foot, sprained his hand, fallen down the stairs, even been run over. Every trifle had become a trial to him—shaving, dressing, taking the wash to the Chinese laundry, eating a meal in a restaurant. Crossing the street, too, was a problem, because no sooner would the light turn green than it turned red again. Those behind the wheels of cars possessed the speed and morals of automatons. If a person couldn't run fast enough, they were capable of driving right over him. Recently, he had begun to suffer from tremors of the hands and feet. He had once had a meticulous handwriting, but he could no longer write. He used a typewriter, typing with his right index finger. Old Korver insisted that all Gombiner's troubles came from the fact that he was a vegetarian; without a piece of meat, one loses strength. Herman couldn't take a bite of meat if his life depended on it.

Herman put one sock on and rested. He put on the second sock, and rested again. His pulse rate was slow—fifty or so beats a minute. The least strain and he felt dizzy. His soul barely survived in his body. It had happened on occasion, as he lay in bed or sat on a chair, that his disembodied spirit had wandered around the house, or had even gone out the window. He had seen his own body in a faint, apparently dead. Who could enumerate all the apparitions, telepathic incidents, clairvoyant visions, and prophetic dreams he experienced! And who would believe him? As it was, his co-workers derided him. The elder Korver needed only a glass of brandy and he would call Herman a superstitious greenhorn. They treated him like some outlandish character.

Herman Gombiner had long ago arrived at the conclusion that modern man was as fanatic in his non-belief as ancient man had been in his faith. The rationalism of the present generation was in itself an example of preconceived ideas. Communism, psychoanalysis, Fascism, and radicalism were the shibboleths of the twentieth century. Oh, well! What could he, Herman Gombiner, do in the face of all this? He had no choice but to observe and be silent.

"Well, it's winter, winter!" Herman Gombiner said to himself in a voice half chanting, half groaning. "When will it be Hanukkah? Winter has started early this year." Herman was in the habit of talking to himself. He had always done so. The uncle who raised him had been deaf. His grandmother, rest her soul, would wake up in the middle of the night to recite penitential prayers and lamentations found only in outdated prayer books. His father had died before Herman—Hayim David —was born. His mother had remarried in a faraway city and had had children by her second husband. Hayim David had always kept to himself, even when he attended heder or studied at the yeshiva. Now, since Hitler had killed all of his family, he had no relatives to write letters to. He wrote letters to total strangers.

"What time is it?" Herman asked himself again. He dressed in a dark suit, a white shirt, and a black tie, and went out to the kitchenette. An icebox without ice and a stove that he never used stood there. Twice a week the milkman left a bottle of milk at the door. Herman had a few cans of vegetables, which he ate on days when he didn't leave the house. He had discovered that a human being requires very little. A half cup of milk and a pretzel could suffice for a whole day. One pair of shoes served Herman for five years. His suit, coat, and hat never wore out. Only his laundry showed some wear, and not from use but from the chemicals used by the Chinese laundryman. The furniture certainly never wore out. Were it not for his expenditures on cabs and gifts, he could have saved a good deal of money.

He drank a glass of milk and ate a biscuit. Then he carefully put on his black coat, a woolen scarf, rubbers, and a felt hat with a broad brim. He packed his briefcase with books and manuscripts. It became heavier from day to day, not because there was more in it but because his strength diminished. He slipped on a pair of dark glasses to protect his eyes from the glare of the snow. Before he left the apartment, he bade farewell to the bed, the desk piled high with papers (under which the blotter lay), the books, and the mouse in the hole. He had poured out yesterday's stale water, refilled the saucer, and set out a cracker and a small piece of cheese. "Well, Huldah, be well!"

Radios blared in the hallway. Dark-skinned women with uncombed hair and angry eyes spoke in an unusually thick Spanish. Children ran around half naked. The men were apparently all unemployed. They paced idly about in their overcrowded quarters, ate standing up, or strummed mandolins. The odors from the apartments made Herman feel faint. All kinds of meat and fish were fried there. The halls reeked of garlic, onion, smoke, and something pungent and nauseating. At night his neighbors danced and laughed wantonly. Sometimes there was fighting and women screamed for help. Once a woman had come pounding on Herman's door in the middle of the night, seeking protection from a man who was trying to stab her.

II

Herman stopped downstairs at the mailboxes. The other residents seldom received any mail, but Herman Gombiner's box was packed tight every morning. He took his key out, fingers trembling, inserted it in the keyhole, and pulled out the mail. He was able to recognize who had sent the letters by their envelopes. Alice Grayson, of Salt Lake City, used a rose-colored envelope. Mrs. Roberta Hoff, of Pasadena, California, sent all her mail in the business envelopes of the undertaking establishment for which she worked. Miss Bertha Gordon, of Fairbanks, Alaska, apparently had many leftover Christmas-card envelopes. Today Herman found a letter from a new correspondent, a Mrs. Rose Beechman, of Louisville, Kentucky. Her name and address were hand-printed, with flourishes, across the back of the envelope. Besides the letters, there were several magazines on occultism to which Herman Gombiner subscribed—from America, England, and even Australia. There wasn't room in his briefcase for all these letters and periodicals, so Herman stuffed them into his coat pocket. He went outside and waited for a taxi.

It was rare for a taxi, particularly an empty one, to drive down this street, but it was too much of an effort for him to walk the half block to Central Park West or Columbus Avenue. Herman Gombiner fought his weakness with prayer and autosuggestion. Standing in the snow, he muttered a prayer for a taxi. He repeatedly put his hand into his pocket and fingered the letters in their envelopes. These letters and magazines had become the essence of his life. Through them he had established contact with souls. He had acquired the friendship and even the love of women. The accounts he received from them strengthened his belief in psychic powers and in the world beyond. He sent gifts to his unknown correspondents and received gifts from them. They called him by his first name, revealed their thoughts, dreams, hopes, and the messages they received through the Ouija board, automatic writing, table turning, and other supernatural sources.

Herman Gombiner had established correspondences with these women through the periodicals he subscribed to, where not only accounts of readers' experiences were published but their contributors' names and addresses as well. The articles were mainly written by women. Herman Gombiner always selected those who lived far away. He wished to avoid meetings. He could sense from the way an experience was related, from a name or an address, whether the woman would be capable of carrying on a correspondence. He was almost never wrong. A small note from him would call forth a long letter in reply. Sometimes he received entire manuscripts. His correspondence had grown so large that postage cost him several dollars a week. Many of his letters were sent out special delivery or registered.

Miracles were a daily occurrence. No sooner had he finished his prayer than a taxi appeared. The driver pulled up to the house as if he had received a telepathic command. Getting into the taxi exhausted Herman, and he sat a long while resting his head against the window with his eyes shut, praising whatever Power had heard his supplication. One had to be blind not to acknowledge the hand of Providence, or whatever you wanted to call it. Someone was concerned with man's most trivial requirements.

His disembodied spirit apparently roamed to the most distant places. All his correspondents had seen him. In one night he had been in Los Angeles and in Mexico City, in Oregon and in Scotland. It would come to him that one of his faraway friends was ill. Before long, he would receive a letter saying that she had indeed been ill and hospitalized. Over the years, several had died, and he had had a premonition each time.

For the past few weeks, Herman had had a strong feeling that Zion was going to close down. True, this had been predicted for years, but Herman had always known that it was only a rumor. And just recently the employees had become optimistic; business had improved. The old man talked of a deficit, but everybody knew he was lying in order to avoid raising salaries. The house had published a prayer book that was a best-seller. The new Hebrew–English dictionary that Herman Gombiner was completing had every chance of selling tens of thousands of copies. Nevertheless, Herman sensed a calamity just as surely as his rheumatic knees foretold a change in the weather.

The taxi drove down Columbus Avenue. Herman glanced out the window and closed his eyes again. What is there to see on a wintry day in New York? He remained wrapped up in his gloom. No matter how many sweaters he put on, he was always cold. Besides, one is less aware of the spirits, the psychic contacts, during the cold weather. Herman raised his collar higher and put his hands in his pockets. A violent kind of civilization developed in cold countries. He should never have settled in New York. If he were living in southern California, he wouldn't be enslaved by the weather in this way. Oh, well . . . And was there a Jewish publishing house to be found in southern California?

III

The taxi stopped on Canal Street. Herman paid his fare and added a fifty-cent tip. He was frugal with himself, but when it came to cabdrivers, waiters, and elevator men, he was generous. At Christmastime he even bought gifts for his Puerto Rican neighbors. Today Sam, the elevator man, was apparently having a cup of coffee in the cafeteria across the street, and Herman had to wait. Sam did as he pleased. He came from the same city as Morris Korver. He was the only elevator man, so that when he didn't feel like coming in the tenants had to climb the stairs. He was a Communist besides.

Herman waited ten minutes before Sam arrived—a short man, broad-backed, with a face that looked as if it had been put together out of assorted pieces: a short forehead, thick brows, bulging eyes with big bags beneath them, and a bulbous nose covered with cherry-red moles. His walk was unsteady. Herman greeted him, but he grumbled in answer. The Yiddish leftist paper stuck out of his back pocket. He didn't shut the elevator door at once. First he coughed several times, then lit a cigar. Suddenly he spat and called out, "You've heard the news?"

"What's happened?"

"They've sold the building."

"Aha, so that's it!" Herman said to himself. "Sold? How come?" he asked.

"How come? Because the old wise guy is senile and his sonny boys don't give a damn. A garage is what's going up here. They'll knock down the building and throw the books on the garbage dump. Nobody will get a red cent out of these Fascist bastards!"

"When did it happen?"

"It happened, that's all."

Well, I *am* clairvoyant, Herman thought. He remained silent. For years, the editorial staff had talked about joining a union and working out a pension plan, but talk was as far as they had got. The elder Korver had seen to that. Wages were low, but he would slip some of his cronies an occasional five- or ten-dollar bonus. He gave out money at Hanukkah, sent Purim gifts, and in general acted like an old-style European boss. Those who opposed him were fired. The bookkeepers and other workers could perhaps get jobs elsewhere, but the writers and editors would have nowhere to go. Judaica was becoming a vanishing specialty in America. When Jews died, their religious and Hebrew books were donated to libraries or were simply thrown out. Hitlerism and the war had caused a temporary upsurge, but not enough to make publishing religious works in Hebrew profitable.

"Well, the seven fat years are over," Herman muttered to himself. The elevator went up to the third floor. It opened directly into the editorial room—a large room with a low ceiling, furnished with old desks and outmoded typewriters. Even the telephones were old-fashioned. The room smelled of dust, wax, and something stuffy and stale.

Raphael Robbins, Korver's editor-in-chief, sat on a cushioned chair and read a manuscript, his eyeglasses pushed down to the tip of his nose. He suffered from hemorrhoids and had prostate trouble. A man of medium height, he was broad-shouldered, with a round head and a protruding belly. Loose folds of skin hung under his eyes. His face expressed a grandfatherly kindliness and an old woman's shrewdness. For years his chief task had consisted of eating lunch with old Korver. Robbins was known to be a boaster, a liar, and a flatterer. He owned a library of pornographic books—a holdover from his youth. Like Sam, he came from the same city as Morris Korver. Raphael Robbins's son, a physicist, had worked on the atomic bomb. His daughter had married a rich Wall Street broker. Raphael Robbins himself had accumulated some capital and was old enough to receive his Social Security pension. As Robbins read the manuscript, he scratched his bald pate and shook his head. He seldom returned a manuscript, and many of them were lying about gathering dust on the table, in his two bookcases, and on cabinets in the kitchenette where the workers brewed tea.

The man who had made Morris Korver rich and on whose shoulders the publishing house had rested for years was Professor Yohanan Abarbanel, a compiler of dictionaries. No one knew where his title came from. He had never received a degree or even attended a university. It was said that old Korver had made him a professor. In addition to compiling several dictionaries, Abarbanel had edited a collection of sermons with quotations for rabbis, written study books for bar-mitzvah boys, and put together other handbooks, which had run into many editions. A bachelor in his seventies, Yohanan Abarbanel had had a heart attack and had undergone surgery for a hernia. He worked for a pittance, lived in a cheap hotel, and each year worried that he might be laid off. He had several poor relatives whom he supported. He was a small man, with white hair, a white beard, and a small face, red as a frozen apple; his little eyes were hidden by white bushy eyebrows. He sat at a table and wheezed and coughed, and all the while wrote in a tiny handwriting with a steel pen. The last few years, he couldn't be trusted to complete any work by himself. Each word was read over by Herman Gombiner, and whole manuscripts had to be rewritten.

For some reason, no one in the office ever greeted anyone else with a "hello" or a "good morning" on arrival, or said anything at closing time. During the day, they did occasionally exchange a few friendly words. It might even happen that, not having addressed a word to one another for months, one of them might go over to a colleague and pour out his heart, or actually invite him to supper. But then the next morning they would again behave as if they had quarreled. Over the years they had become bored with one another. Complaints and grudges had accumulated and were never quite forgotten.

Miss Lipshitz, the secretary, who had started working at Zion when she was just out of college, was now entirely gray. She sat at her typewriter—small, plump, and pouting, with a short neck and an ample bosom. She had a pug nose and eyes that seemed never to look at the manuscript she was typing but stared far off, past the walls. Days would pass without her voice being heard. She muttered into the telephone. When she ate lunch in the restaurant across the street, she would sit alone at a table, eating, smoking, and reading a newspaper simultaneously. There was a time when everyone in the office—old Mr. Korver included—had either openly or secretly been in love with this clever girl who knew English, Yiddish, Hebrew, stenography, and much more. They used to ask her to the theater and the movies and quarreled over who should take her to lunch. For years now, Miss Lipshitz had isolated herself. Old man Korver said that she had shut herself up behind an invisible wall.

Herman nodded to her, but she didn't respond. He walked past Ben

Melnick's office. Melnick was the business manager—tall, swarthy, with a young face, black bulging eyes, and a head of milky-white hair. He suffered from asthma and played the horses. All sorts of shifty characters came to see him—bookies. He was separated from his wife and was carrying on a love affair with Miss Potter, the chief bookkeeper, another relative of Morris Korver's.

Herman Gombiner went into his own office. Walking through the editorial room, and not being greeted, was a strain for him. Korver employed a man to keep the place clean—Zeinvel Gitzis—but Zeinvel neglected his work; the walls were filthy, the windows unwashed. Packs of dusty manuscripts and newspapers had been lying around for years.

Herman carefully removed his coat and laid it on a stack of books. He sat down on a chair that had horsehair sticking through its upholstery. Work? What was the sense of working when the firm was closing down? He sat shaking his head—half out of weakness, half from regret. "Well, everything has to have an end," he muttered. "It is predestined that no human institution will last forever." He reached over and pulled the mail out of his coat pocket. He inspected the envelopes, without opening any of them. He came back to Rose Beechman's letter from Louisville, Kentucky. In a magazine called the *Message*, Mrs. Beechman had reported her contacts over the last fifteen years with her dead grandmother, Mrs. Eleanor Brush. The grandmother usually materialized during the night, though sometimes she would also appear in the daylight, dressed in her funeral clothes. She was full of advice for her granddaughter, and once she even gave her a recipe for fried chicken. Herman had written to Rose Beechman, but seven weeks had passed without a reply. He had almost given up hope, although he had continued sending her telepathic messages. She had been ill—Herman was certain of it.

Now her letter lay before him in a light-blue envelope. Opening it wasn't easy for him. He had to resort to using his teeth. He finally removed six folded sheets of light-blue stationery and read:

Dear Mr. Gombiner:

I am writing this letter to you a day after my return from the hospital where I spent almost two months. I was operated on for the removal of a spinal tumor. There was danger of paralysis or worse. But fate, it seems, still wants me here . . . Apparently, my little story in the *Message* caused quite a furor. During my illness, I received dozens of letters from all parts of the country and from England.

It so happened that my daughter put your letter at the bottom of the pile, and had I read them in order, it might have taken several weeks more before I came to yours. But a premonition—what else can I call it?—made me open the very last letter first. It was then that I realized, from the postmark, yours had been among the first, if not the very first, to arrive. It seems I always do things not as I intend to but according to a command from someone or something that I am unaware of. All I can say is: this "something" has been with me as long as I can remember, perhaps even since before I was capable of thinking.

Your letter is so logical, so noble and fascinating, that I may say it has brightened my homecoming. My daughter has a job in an office and has neither the time nor the patience to look after the house. When I returned, I found things in a sorry state. I am by nature a meticulous housekeeper who cannot abide disorder, and so you can imagine my feelings. But your profound and truly remarkable thoughts, as well as the friendliness and humanity implicit in them, helped me to forget my troubles. I read your letter three times and thanked God that people with your understanding and faith exist.

You ask for details. My dear Mr. Gombiner, if I were to relate all the facts, no letter would suffice. I could fill a whole book. Don't forget that these experiences have been going on for fifteen years. My saintly grandmother visited me every day in the hospital. She literally took over the work of the nurses, who are not, as you may know, overly devoted to their patients—nor do they have the time to be. Yes, to describe it all "exactly," as you request, would take weeks, months. I can only repeat that everything I wrote in the *Message* was the honest truth. Some of my correspondents call me "crackpot," "crazy," "charlatan." They accuse me of lying and publicity-seeking. Why should I tell lies and why do I need publicity? It was, therefore, especially pleasing to read your wonderful sentiments. I see from the letterhead that you are a Jew and connected with a Hebrew publishing house. I wish to assure you that I have always had the highest regard for Jews, God's chosen people. There are not very many Jews here in Louisville, and my personal contact has been only with Jews who have little interest in their religion. I have always wanted to become acquainted with a real Jew, who reveres the tradition of the Holy Fathers.

Now I come to the main point of my letter, and I beg you to forgive my rambling. The night before I left the hospital, my beloved grandmother, Mrs. Brush, visited with me till dawn. We chatted about various matters, and just before her departure she said to me, "This winter you will go to New York, where you will meet a man who will change the direction of your life." These were her parting words. I must add here that although for the past fifteen years I have been fully convinced that my grandmother never spoke idly and that whatever she said had meaning, at that moment for the first time I felt some doubt. What business did I, a widow living on a small pension, have in far-off New York? And what man in New York could possibly alter my existence?

It is true I am not yet old—just above forty—and considered an attractive woman. (I beg you not to think me vain. I simply wish to clarify the situation.) But when my husband died eight years ago, I decided that was that. I was left with a twelve-year-old daughter and wished to devote all my energies to her upbringing, and I did. She is today good-looking, has gone through business school and has an excellent position with a real-estate firm, and she is engaged to marry an extremely interesting and well-educated man (a government official). I feel she will be very happy.

I have since my husband's death received proposals from men, but I have always rejected them. My grandmother, it seems, must have agreed with me, because I never heard anything to the contrary from her. I mention this because my grandmother's talk of a trip to New York and the man I would meet there seemed so unlikely that I believed she had said it just to cheer me up after my illness. Later, her words actually slipped my mind.

Imagine my surprise when today, on my return from the hospital, I received a registered letter from a Mr. Ginsburg, a New York lawyer, notifying me of the death of my great-aunt Catherine Pennell and telling me that she had left me a sum of almost five thousand dollars. Aunt Catherine was a spinster and had severed her ties with our family over fifty years ago, before I was born. As far as we knew, she had lived on a farm in Pennsylvania. My father had sometimes talked about her and her eccentricities, but I had never met her nor did I know whether she was alive or dead. How she wound up in New York is a mystery to me, as is the reason for her choosing to leave me money. These are the facts, and I must come to New York concerning the bequest. Documents have to be signed and so forth.

When I read the lawyer's letter and then your highly interesting and dear one, I suddenly realized how foolish I had been to doubt my grandmother's words. She has never made a prediction that didn't later prove true, and I will never doubt her again.

This letter is already too long and my fingers are tired from holding the pen. I simply wish to inform you that I will be in New York for several days in January, or at the latest in early February, and I would consider it a privilege and an honor to meet you personally.

I cannot know what the Powers that be have in store for me, but I know that meeting you will be an important event in my life, as I hope meeting me will be for you. I have extraordinary things to tell you. In the meantime, accept my deepest gratitude and my fondest regards.

I am, very truly yours,
Rose Beechman

I V

Everything happened quickly. One day they talked about closing down the publishing house, and the next day it was done. Morris Korver and his sons called a meeting of the staff. Korver himself spoke in Yiddish, pounded his fist on a bookstand, and shouted with the loud voice of a young man. He warned the workers that if they didn't accept the settlement he and his sons had worked out, none of them would get a penny.

One son, Seymour, a lawyer, had a few words to say, in English. In contrast with his father's shouting, Seymour spoke quietly. The older employees who were hard of hearing moved their chairs closer and turned up their hearing aids. Seymour displayed a list of figures. The publishing house, he said, had in the last few years lost several hundred thousand dollars. How much can a business lose? There it all was, written down in black and white.

After the bosses left, the writers and office workers voted whether or not to agree to the proposed terms. The majority voted to accept. It was argued that Korver had secretly bribed some employees to be on his side, but what was the difference? Every worker was to receive his final check the following day. The manuscripts were left lying on the tables. Sam had already brought up men from the demolition company.

Raphael Robbins carefully put into his satchel the little cushion on which he sat, a magnifying glass, and a drawerful of medicine. He took leave of everyone with the shrewd smile of a man who knew everything in advance and therefore was never surprised. Yohanan Abarbanel took a single dictionary home with him. Miss Lipshitz, the secretary, walked around with red, weepy eyes all morning. Ben Melnick brought a huge trunk and packed his private archives, consisting of horse-racing forms.

Herman Gombiner was too feeble to pack the letters and books that had accumulated in his bookcase. He opened a drawer, looked at the dust-covered papers, and immediately started coughing. He said good-bye to Miss Lipshitz, handed Sam a last five-dollar tip, went to the bank to cash the check, and then waited for a taxi.

For many years, Herman Gombiner had lived in fear of the day when he would be without a job. But when he got into the taxi to go home at one o'clock in the afternoon, he felt the calm of resignation. He never turned his head to look back at the place in which he had wasted almost thirty years. A wet snow was falling. The sky was gray. Sitting in the taxi, leaning his head back against the seat, with eyes closed, Herman Gombiner compared himself to a corpse returning from its own funeral. This is probably the way the soul leaves the body and starts its spiritual existence, he thought.

He had figured everything out. With the almost two thousand dollars he had saved in the bank, the money he had received from Morris Korver, and unemployment insurance, he would be able to manage for two years—perhaps even a few months longer. Then he would have to go on relief. There was no sense in even trying to get another job. Herman had from childhood begged God not to make him dependent on charity, but it had evidently been decided differently. Unless, of course, death redeemed him first.

Thank God it was warm in the house. Herman looked at the mouse's hole. In what way was he, Herman, better than she? Huldah also had to depend on someone. He took out a notebook and pencil and started to calculate. He would no longer need to pay for two taxis daily, or have to eat lunch in a restaurant, or leave a tip for the waiter. There would be no more contributions for all kinds of collections—for Palestine, for employees' children or grandchildren who were getting married, for retirement gifts. He certainly wouldn't be paying any more taxes. Herman examined his clothes closet. He had enough shirts and shoes to last him another ten years. He needed money only for rent, bread, milk, magazines, and stamps. There had been a time when he considered getting a telephone in his apartment. Thank God he had not done it. With these six dollars he could manage for a week. Without realizing it would come to this, Herman had for years practiced the art of reducing his expenditures to a minimum, lowering the wick of life, so to speak.

Never before had Herman Gombiner enjoyed his apartment as he did on that winter day when he returned home after the closing of the publishing house. People had often complained to him about their loneliness, but as long as there were books and stationery and as long as he could sit on a chair next to the radiator and meditate, he was never alone. From the neighboring apartments he could hear the laughter of children, women talking, and the loud voices of men. Radios were turned on full blast. In the street, boys and girls were playing noisily.

The short day grew darker and darker, and the house filled with shadows. Outside, the snow took on an unusual blue coloring. Twilight descended. "So, a day has passed," Herman said to himself. This particular day, this very date would never return again, unless Nietzsche was right in his theory about the eternal return. Even if one did believe that time was imaginary, this day was finished, like the flipped page of a book. It had passed into the archives of eternity. But what had he, Herman Gombiner, accomplished? Whom had he helped? Not even the mouse. She had not come out of her hole, not a peep out of her all day. Was she sick? She was no longer young; old age crept up on everyone . . .

As Herman sat in the wintry twilight, he seemed to be waiting for a sign from the Powers on high. Sometimes he received messages from them, but at other times they remained hidden and silent. He found himself thinking about his parents, grandparents, his sisters, brother, aunts, uncles, and cousins. Where were they all? Where were they resting, blessed souls, martyred by the Nazis. Did they ever think of him? Or had they risen into spheres where they were no longer concerned with the lower worlds? He started to pray to them, inviting them to visit him on this winter evening.

The steam in the radiator hissed, singing its one note. The steam seemed to speak in the pipes, consoling Herman: "You are not alone, you are an element of the universe, a child of God, an integral part of Creation. Your suffering is God's suffering, your yearning His yearning. Everything is right. Let the Truth be revealed to you, and you will be filled with joy."

Suddenly Herman heard a squeak. In the dimness, the mouse had crawled out and looked cautiously around, as if afraid that a cat lurked nearby. Herman held his breath. Holy creature, have no fear. No harm will come to you. He watched her as she approached the saucer of water, took one sip, then a second and a third. Slowly she started gnawing the piece of cheese.

Can there be any greater wonder, Herman thought. Here stands a mouse, a daughter of a mouse, a granddaughter of mice, a product of millions, billions of mice who once lived, suffered, reproduced, and are now gone forever, but have left an heir, apparently the last of her line. Here she stands, nourishing herself with food. What does she think about all day in her hole? She must think about something. She does have a mind, a nervous system. She is just as much a part of God's creation as the planets, the stars, the distant galaxies.

The mouse suddenly raised her head and stared at Herman with a human look of love and gratitude. Herman imagined that she was saying thank you.

V

Since Herman Gombiner had stopped working, he realized what an effort it had been for him to wake up in the morning, to wait outside for a cab, to waste his time with dictionaries, writing, editing, and traveling home again each evening. He had apparently been working with the last of his strength. It seemed to him that the publishing house had closed on the very day that he had expended his last bit of remaining energy. This fact in itself was an excellent example of the presence of Godly compassion and the hand of Providence. But thank heaven he still had the will to read and write letters.

Snow had fallen. Herman couldn't recall another New York winter with as much snow as this. Huge drifts had piled up. It was impossible for cars to drive through his street. Herman would have had to plow his way to Columbus Avenue or Central Park West to get a taxi. He would surely have collapsed. Luckily, the delivery boy from the grocery store didn't forget him. Every other day he brought up rolls, sometimes eggs, cheese, and whatever else Herman had ordered. His neighbors would knock on his door and ask him whether he needed anything—coffee, tea, fruit. He thanked them profusely. Poor as he was, he always gave a mother a nickel to buy some chocolate for her child. The women never left at once; they lingered awhile and spoke to him in their broken English, looking at him as if they regretted having to go. Once, a woman stroked Herman's head gently. Women had always been attracted to him.

There had been times when women had fallen desperately in love with him, but marriage and a family were not for Herman. The thought of raising children seemed absurd to him. Why prolong the human tragedy? Besides, he had always sent every last cent to Kalomin.

His thoughts kept returning to the past. He was back in Kalomin. He was going to heder, studying at a yeshiva, secretly teaching himself modern Hebrew, Polish, German, taking lessons, instructing others. He experienced his first love affair, the meetings with girls, strolls in the woods, to the watermill, to the cemetery. He had been drawn to cemeteries even as a youngster, and would spend hours there, meditating among the tombstones and listening to their stony silence. The dead spoke to him from their graves. In the Kalomin cemetery there grew tall, white-barked birch trees. Their silvery leaves trembled in the slightest breeze, chattering their leafy dialect all day. The boughs leaned over each other, whispering secrets.

Later came the trip to America and wandering around New York without a job. Then he went to work for Zion and began studying English. He had been fairly healthy at that time and had had affairs with women. It was difficult to believe the many triumphs he had had. On lonely nights, details of old episodes and never-forgotten words came to him. Memory itself demonstrates that there is no oblivion. Words a woman had uttered to him thirty years before and that he hadn't really understood at the time would suddenly become clear. Thank God he had enough memories to last him a hundred years.

For the first time since he had come to America, his windows froze over. Frost trees like those in Kalomin formed on the windowpanes—upside-down palms, exotic shrubs, and strange flowers. The frost painted like an artist, but its patterns were eternal. Crystals? What were crystals? Who had taught the atoms and molecules to arrange themselves in this or that way? What was the connection between the molecules in New York and the molecules in Kalomin?

The greatest wonders began when Herman dozed off. As soon as he closed his eyes, his dreams came like locusts. He saw everything with clarity and precision. These were not dreams but visions. He flew over Oriental cities, hovered over cupolas, mosques, and castles, lingered in strange gardens, mysterious forests. He came upon undiscovered tribes, spoke foreign languages. Sometimes he was frightened by monsters.

Herman had often thought that one's true life was lived during sleep. Waking was no more than a marginal time assigned for doing things.

Now that he was free, his entire schedule was turned around. It seemed to happen of itself. He stayed awake at night and slept during the day. He ate lunch in the evening and skipped supper altogether. The alarm clock had stopped, but Herman hadn't rewound it. What difference did it make what time it was? Sometimes he was too lazy to turn the lights on in the evening. Instead of reading, he sat on a chair next to the radiator and dozed. He was overcome by a fatigue that never left him. Am I getting sick, he wondered. No matter how little the grocery boy delivered, Herman had too much.

His real sustenance was the letters he received. Herman still made his way down the few flights of stairs to his letter box in the lobby. He had provided himself with a supply of stamps and stationery. There was a mailbox a few feet from the entrance of the house. If he was unable to get through the snow, he would ask a neighbor to mail his letters. Recently, a woman who lived on his floor offered to get his mail every morning, and Herman gave her the key to his box. She was a stamp collector; the stamps were her payment. Herman now spared himself the trouble of climbing stairs. She mailed his letters and slipped the ones he received under the door, and so quietly that he never heard her footsteps.

He often sat all night writing, napping between letters. Occasionally he would take an old letter from the desk drawer and read it through a magnifying glass. Yes, the dead were still with us. They came to advise their relatives on business, debts, the healing of the sick; they comforted the discouraged, made suggestions concerning trips, jobs, love, marriage. Some left bouquets of flowers on bedspreads, and apported articles from distant places. Some revealed themselves only to intimate ones at the moment of death, others returned years after they had passed away. If this were all true, Herman thought, then his relatives, too, were surely living. He sat praying for them to appear to him. The spirit cannot be burned, gassed, hanged, shot. Six million souls must exist somewhere.

One night, having written letters till dawn, Herman inserted them in envelopes, addressed and put stamps on them, then went to bed. When he opened his eyes, it was full daylight. His head was heavy. It lay like a stone on the pillow. He felt hot, yet chills ran across his back. He had dreamed that his dead family came to him, but they had not behaved appropriately for ghosts; they had quarreled, shouted, even come to blows over a straw basket.

Herman looked toward the door and saw the morning mail pushed under it by his neighbor, but he couldn't move. Am I paralyzed, he wondered. He fell asleep again, and the ghosts returned. His mother and sisters were arguing over a metal comb. "Well, this is too ridiculous," he said to himself. "Spirits don't need metal combs." The dream continued. He discovered a cabinet in the wall of his room. He opened it and letters started pouring out—hundreds of letters. What was this cabinet? The letters bore old datemarks; he had never opened them. In his sleep he felt troubled that so many people had written to him and he hadn't answered them. He decided that a postman must have hidden the letters in order to save himself the trouble of delivering them. But if the postman had already bothered to come to his house, what was the sense of hiding the letters in the cabinet?

Herman awoke, and it was evening. "How did the day pass so quickly?" he asked himself. He tried to get up to go to the bathroom, but his head spun and everything turned black. He fell to the floor. Well, it's the end, he thought. What will become of Huldah?

He lay powerless for a long time. Then slowly he pulled himself up, and by moving along the wall he reached the bathroom. His urine was brown and oily, and he felt a burning sensation.

It took him a long time to return to his bed. He lay down again, and the bed seemed to rise and fall. How strange—he no longer needed to tear open the envelopes of his letters. Clairvoyant powers enabled him to read their contents. He had received a reply from a woman in a small town in Colorado. She wrote of a now dead neighbor with whom she had always quarreled, and of how after the neighbor's death her ghost had broken her sewing machine. Her former enemy had poured water on her floors, ripped open a pillow and spilled out all the feathers. The dead can be mischievous. They can also be full of vengeance. If this was so, he thought, then a war between the dead Jews and the dead Nazis was altogether possible.

That night, Herman dozed, twitched convulsively, and woke up again and again. Outside, the wind howled. It blew right through the house. Herman remembered Huldah; the mouse was without food or water. He wanted to get down to help her, but he couldn't move any part of his body. He prayed to God, "I don't need help any more, but don't let that poor creature die of hunger!" He pledged money to charity. Then he fell asleep.

Herman opened his eyes, and the day was just beginning—an overcast wintry day that he could barely make out through the frost-covered windowpanes. It was as cold indoors as out. Herman listened but could hear no tune from the radiator. He tried to cover himself, but his hands lacked the strength. From the hallway he heard sounds of shouting and running feet. Someone knocked on the door, but he couldn't answer. There was more knocking. A man spoke in Spanish, and Herman heard a woman's voice. Suddenly someone pushed the door open and a Puerto Rican man came in, followed by a small woman wearing a knitted coat and matching hat. She carried a huge muff such as Herman had never seen in America.

The woman came up to his bed and said, "Mr. Gombiner?" She pronounced his name so that he hardly recognized it—with the accent on the first syllable. The man left. In her hand the woman held the letters she had picked up from the floor. She had fair skin, dark eyes, and a small nose. She said, "I knew that you were sick. I am Mrs. Beechman—Rose Beechman." She held out a letter she had sent him that was among those she found at the door.

Herman understood, but was unable to speak. He heard her say, "My grandmother made me come to you. I was coming to New York two weeks from now. You are ill and the furnace in your house has exploded. Wait, I'll cover you. Where is your telephone?"

She pulled the blanket over him, but the bedding was like ice. She started to move about, stamping her boots and clapping her hands. "You don't have a telephone? How can I get a doctor?"

He wanted to tell her he didn't want a doctor, but he was too weak. Looking at her made him tired. He shut his eyes and immediately forgot that he had a visitor.

V I

"How can anyone sleep so much?" Herman asked himself. This sleepiness had transformed him into a helpless creature. He opened his eyes, saw the strange woman, knew who she was, and immediately fell asleep again. She had brought a doctor—a tall man, a giant—and this man uncovered him, listened to his heart with a stethoscope, squeezed his stomach, looked down his throat. Herman heard the word "pneumonia"; they told him he would have to go to the hospital, but he amassed enough strength to shake his head. He would rather die. The doctor reprimanded him good-naturedly; the woman tried to persuade him. What's wrong with a hospital? They would make him well there. She would visit him every day, would take care of him.

But Herman was adamant. He broke through his sickness and spoke to the woman. "Every person has the right to determine his own fate." He showed her where he kept his money; he looked at her pleadingly, stretched out his hand to her, begging her to promise that he would not be moved.

One moment he spoke clearly as a healthy man, and the next he returned to his torpor. He dreamed again—whether asleep or awake he himself didn't know. The woman gave him medicine. A girl came and administered an injection. Thank God there was heat again. The radiator sang all day and half the night. Now the sun shone in—the bit of sunlight that reached his window in the morning; now the ceiling light burned. Neighbors came to ask how he was, mostly women. They brought him bowls of grits, warm milk, cups of tea. The strange woman changed her clothes; sometimes she wore a black dress or a yellow dress, sometimes a white blouse or a rose-colored blouse. At times she appeared middle-aged and serious to him, at others girlishly young and playful. She inserted a thermometer in his mouth and brought his bedpan. She undressed him and gave him alcohol rubs. He felt embarrassed because of his emaciated body, but she argued, "What is there to be ashamed of? We are all the way God made us." Sick as he was, he was still aware of the smoothness of her palms. Was she human? Or an angel? He was a child again, whose mother was worrying about him. He knew very well that he could die of his sleepiness, but he had ceased being afraid of death.

Herman was preoccupied with something—an event, a vision that repeated itself with countless variations but whose meaning he couldn't fathom. It seemed to him that his sleeping was like a long book which he read so eagerly he could not stop even for a minute. Drinking tea, taking medicine were merely annoying interruptions. His body, together with its agonies, had detached itself from him.

He awoke. The day was growing pale. The woman had placed an ice pack on his head. She removed it and commented that his pajama top had blood on it. The blood had come from his nose.

"Am I dying? Is this death?" he asked himself. He felt only curiosity.

The woman gave him medicine from a teaspoon, and the fluid had the strength and the smell of cognac. Herman shut his eyes, and when he opened them again he could see the snowy blue of the night. The woman was sitting at a table that had for years been cluttered with books, which she must have removed. She had placed her fingertips at the edge of the table. The table was moving, raising its front legs and then dropping them down with a bang.

For a while he was wide awake and as clearheaded as if he were well. Was the table really moving of its own accord? Or was the woman raising it? He stared in amazement. The woman was mumbling; she asked questions that he couldn't hear. Sometimes she grumbled; once she even laughed, showing a mouthful of small teeth. Suddenly she went over to the bed, leaned over him, and said, "You will live. You will recover."

He listened to her words with an indifference that surprised him.

He closed his eyes and found himself in Kalomin again. They were all living—his father, his mother, his grandfather, his grandmother, his sisters, his brother, all the uncles and aunts and cousins. How odd that Kalomin could be a part of New York. One had only to reach a street that led to Canal Street. The street was on the side of a mountain, and it was necessary to climb up to it. It seemed that he had to go through a cellar or a tunnel, a place he remembered from other dreams. It grew darker and darker, the ground became steeper and full of ditches, the walls lower and lower and the air more stuffy. He had to open a door to a small chamber that was full of the bones of corpses, slimy with decay. He had come upon a subterranean cemetery, and there he met a beadle, or perhaps a warden or a gravedigger who was attending to the bones.

"How can anyone live here?" Herman asked himself. "Who would want such a livelihood?" Herman couldn't see this man now, but he recalled previous dreams in which he had seen him—bearded and shabby. He broke off limbs like so many rotten roots. He laughed with secret glee. Herman tried to escape from this labyrinth, crawling on his belly and slithering like a snake, overexerting himself so that his breathing stopped.

He awakened in a cold sweat. The lamp was not lit, but a faint glow shone from somewhere. Where is this light coming from, Herman wondered, and where is the woman? How miraculous—he felt well.

He sat up slowly and saw the woman asleep on a cot, covered with an unfamiliar blanket. The faint illumination came from a tiny light bulb plugged into a socket near the floor. Herman sat still and let the perspiration dry, feeling cooler as it dried.

"Well, it wasn't destined that I should die yet," he muttered. "But why am I needed here?" He could find no answer.

Herman leaned back on the pillow and lay still. He remembered everything: he had fallen ill, Rose Beechman had arrived, and had brought a doctor to see him. Herman had refused to go to the hospital.

He took stock of himself. He had apparently passed the crisis. He was weak, but no longer sick. All his pains were gone. He could breathe freely. His throat was no longer clogged with phlegm. This woman had saved his life.

Herman knew he should thank Providence, but something inside him felt sad and almost cheated. He had always hoped for a revelation. He had counted on his deep sleep to see things kept from the healthy eye. Even of death he had thought, Let's look at what is on the other side of the curtain. He had often read about people who were ill and whose astral bodies wandered over cities, oceans, and deserts. Others had come in contact with relatives, had had visions; heavenly lights had appeared to them. But in his long sleep Herman had experienced nothing but a lot of tangled dreams. He remembered the little table that had raised and lowered its front legs one night. Where was it? It stood not far from his bed, covered with a pile of letters and magazines, apparently received during his illness.

Herman observed Rose Beechman. Why had she come? When had she had the cot brought in? He saw her face distinctly now—the small nose, hollow cheeks, dark hair, the round forehead a bit too high for a woman. She slept calmly, the blanket over her breast. Her breathing couldn't be heard. It occurred to Herman that she might be dead. He stared at her intently; her nostrils moved slightly.

Herman dozed off again. Suddenly he heard a mumbling. He opened his eyes. The woman was talking in her sleep. He listened carefully but couldn't make out the words. He wasn't certain whether it was English or another language. What did it mean? All at once he knew: she was talking to her grandmother. He held his breath. His whole being became still. He made an effort to distinguish at least one word, but he couldn't catch a single syllable. The woman became silent and then started to whisper again. She didn't move her lips. Her voice seemed to be coming out of her nostrils. Who knows? Perhaps she wasn't speaking a known language, Herman Gombiner thought. He fancied that she was suggesting something to the unseen one and arguing with her. This intensive listening soon tired him. He closed his eyes and fell asleep.

He twitched and woke up. He didn't know how long he had been sleeping—a minute or an hour. Through the window he saw that it was still night. The woman on the cot was sleeping silently. Suddenly Herman remembered. What had become of Huldah? How awful that throughout his long illness he had entirely forgotten her. No one had fed her or given her anything to drink. "She is surely dead," he said to himself. "Dead of hunger and thirst!" He felt a great shame. He had recovered. The Powers that rule the world had sent a woman to him, a merciful sister, but this creature who was dependent on him for its necessities had perished. "I should not have forgotten her! I should not have! I've killed her!"

Despair took hold of Herman. He started to pray for the mouse's soul. "Well, you've had your life. You've served your time in this forsaken world, the worst of all worlds, this bottomless abyss, where Satan, Asmodeus, Hitler, and Stalin prevail. You are no longer confined to your hole—hungry, thirsty, and sick, but at one with the God-filled cosmos, with God Himself . . . Who knows why you had to be a mouse?"

In his thoughts, Herman spoke a eulogy for the mouse who had shared a portion of her life with him and who, because of him, had left this earth. "What do they know—all those scholars, all those philosophers, all the leaders of the world—about such as you? They have convinced themselves that man, the worst transgressor of all the species, is the crown of creation. All other creatures were created merely to provide him with food, pelts, to be tormented, exterminated. In relation to them, all people are Nazis; for the animals it is an eternal Treblinka. And yet man demands compassion from heaven." Herman clapped his hand to his mouth. "I mustn't live, I mustn't! I can no longer be a part of it! God in heaven—take me away!"

For a while his mind was blank. Then he trembled. Perhaps Huldah was still alive? Perhaps she had found something to eat. Maybe she was lying unconscious in her hole and could be revived? He tried to get off the bed. He lifted the blanket and slowly put one foot down. The bed creaked.

The woman opened her eyes as if she hadn't been asleep at all but had been pretending. "Where are you going?"

"There is something I must find out."

"What? Wait one second." She straightened her nightgown underneath the blanket, got out of bed, and went over to him barefooted. Her feet were white, girlishly small, with slender toes. "How are you feeling?"

"I beg you, listen to me!" And in a quiet voice he told her about the mouse.

The woman listened. Her face, hidden in the shadows, expressed no surprise. She said, "Yes, I did hear the mice scratching several times during the night. They are probably eating your books."

"It's only one mouse. A wonderful creature."

"What shall I do?"

"The hole is right here . . . I used to set out a dish of water for her and a piece of cheese."

"I don't have any cheese here."

"Perhaps you can pour some milk in a little dish. I'm not sure that she is alive, but maybe . . ."

"Yes, there is milk. First I'll take your temperature." She took a thermometer from somewhere, shook it down, and put it in his mouth with the authority of a nurse.

Herman watched her as she busied herself in the kitchenette. She poured milk from a bottle into a saucer. Several times she turned her head and gave him an inquiring look, as if she didn't quite believe what she had just heard.

How can this be, Herman wondered. She doesn't look like a woman with a grown daughter. She looks like a girl herself. Her loose hair reached her shoulders. He could make out her figure through her bathrobe: narrow in the waist, not too broad in the hips. Her face had a mildness, a softness that didn't match the earnest, almost severe letter she had written him. Oh, well, where is it written that everything must match? Every person is a new experiment in God's laboratory.

The woman took the dish and carefully set it down where he had indicated. On the way back to the cot, she put on her house slippers. She took the thermometer out of his mouth and went to the bathroom, where a light was burning. She soon returned. "You have no fever. Thank God."

"You have saved my life," Herman said.

"It was my grandmother who told me to come here. I hope you've read my letter."

"Yes, I read it."

"I see that you correspond with half the world."

"I'm interested in psychic research."

"This is your first day without fever."

For a while, both were silent. Then he asked, "How can I repay you?"

The woman frowned. "There's no need to repay me."

VII

Herman fell asleep and found himself in Kalomin. It was a summer evening and he was strolling with a girl across a bridge on the way to the mill and to the Russian Orthodox Cemetery, where the gravestones bear the photographs of those interred. A huge luminous sphere shimmered in the sky, larger than the moon, larger than the sun, a new incomparable heavenly body. It cast a greenish glow over the water, making it transparent, so that fish could be seen as they swam. Not the usual carp and pike but whales and sharks, fish with golden fins, red horns, with skin similar to that on the wings of bats.

"What is all this?" Herman asked. "Has the cosmos changed? Has the earth torn itself away from the sun, from the whole Milky Way? Is it about to become a comet?" He tried to talk to the girl he was with, but she was one of the ladies buried in the graveyard. She replied in Russian, although it was also Hebrew. Herman asked, "Don't Kant's categories of pure reason any longer apply in Kalomin?"

He woke up with a start. On the other side of the window it was still night. The strange woman was asleep on the cot. Herman examined her more carefully now. She no longer mumbled, but her lips trembled occasionally. Her brow wrinkled as she smiled in her sleep. Her hair was spread out over the pillow. The quilt had slid down, and he could see the bunched-up folds of her nightgown and the top of her breast. Herman stared at her, mute with amazement. A woman had come to him from somewhere in the South—not a Jewess, but as Ruth had come to Boaz, sent by some Naomi who was no longer among the living.

Where had she found bedding, Herman wondered. She had already brought order to his apartment—she had hung a curtain over the window, cleaned the newspapers and manuscripts from the large table. How strange, she hadn't moved the blotter, as if she had known that it was the implement of a miracle.

Herman stared, nodding his head in wonder. The books in the book-cases did not look so old and tattered. She had brought some kind of order to them, too. The air he breathed no longer smelled moldy and dusty but had a moist, cool quality. Herman was reminded of a Passover night in Kalomin. Only the matzos hanging in a sheet from the ceiling were lacking. He tried to remember his latest dream, but he could only recall the unearthly light that fell across the lake. "Well, dreams are all lost," Herman said to himself. "Each day begins with amnesia."

He heard a slight noise that sounded like a child sucking. Herman sat up and saw Huldah. She appeared thinner, weak, and her fur looked grayer, as if she had aged.

"God in Heaven! Huldah is alive! There she stands, drinking milk from the dish!" A joy such as he had seldom experienced gripped Herman. He had not as yet thanked God for bringing him back to life. He had even felt some resentment. But for letting the mouse live he had to praise the Higher Powers. Herman was filled with love both for the mouse and for the woman, Rose Beechman, who had understood his feelings and without question had obeyed his request and given the mouse some milk. "I am not worthy, I am not worthy," he muttered. "It is all pure Grace."

Herman was not a man who wept. His eyes had remained dry even when he received the news that his family had perished in the destruction of Kalomin. But now his face became wet and hot. It wasn't fated that he bear the guilt of a murderer. Providence—aware of every molecule, every mite, every speck of dust—had seen to it that the mouse received its nourishment during his long sleep. Or was it perhaps possible that a mouse could fast for that length of time?

Herman watched intently. Even now, after going hungry for so long, the mouse didn't rush. She lapped the milk slowly, pausing occasionally, obviously confident that no one would take away what was rightfully hers. "Little mouse, hallowed creature, saint!" Herman cried to her in his thoughts. He blew her a kiss.

The mouse continued to drink. From time to time, she cocked her head and gave Herman a sidelong glance. He imagined he saw in her eyes an expression of surprise, as if she were silently asking, "Why did you let me go hungry so long? And who is this woman sleeping here?" Soon she went back to her hole.

Rose Beechman opened her eyes. "Oh! You are up? What time is it?"

"Huldah has had her milk," Herman said.

"What? Oh, yes."

"I beg you, don't laugh at me."

"I'm not laughing at anyone."

"You've saved not one life but two."

"Well, we are all God's creatures. I'll make you some tea."

Herman wanted to tell her that it wasn't necessary, but he was thirsty and his throat felt dry. He even felt a pang of hunger. He had come back to life, with all its needs.

The woman immediately busied herself in the kitchenette, and shortly she brought Herman a cup of tea and two biscuits. She had apparently bought new dishes for him. She sat down on the edge of a chair and said, "Well, drink your tea. I don't believe you realize how sick you were."

"I am grateful."

"If I had been just two days later, nothing would have helped."

"Perhaps it would have been better that way."

"No. People like you are needed."

"Today I heard you talking to your grandmother." Herman spoke, not sure if he should be saying this.

She listened and was thoughtfully silent awhile. "Yes, she was with me last night."

"What did she say?"

The woman looked at him oddly. He noticed for the first time that her eyes were light brown. "I hope you won't make fun of me."

"God in heaven, no!"

"She wants me to take care of you; you need me more than my daughter does—those were her words."

A chill ran down Herman's spine. "Yes, that may be true, but—"

"But what? I beg you, be honest with me."

"I have nothing. I am weak. I can only be a burden . . ."

"Burdens are made to be borne."

"Yes. Yes."

"If you want me to, I will stay with you. At least until you recover completely."

"Yes, I do."

"That is what I wanted to hear." She stood up quickly and turned away. She walked toward the bathroom, embarrassed as a young Kalomin bride. She remained standing in the doorway with her back toward him, her head bowed, revealing the small nape of her neck, her uncombed hair.

Through the window a gray light was beginning to appear. Snow was falling—a dawn snow. Patches of day and night blended together outside. Clouds appeared. Windows, roofs, and fire escapes emerged from the dark. Lights went out. The night had ended like a dream and was followed by an obscure reality, self-absorbed, sunk in the perpetual mystery of being. A pigeon was flying through the snowfall, intent on carrying out its mission. In the radiator, the steam was already whistling. From the neighboring apartments were heard the first cries of awakened children, radios playing, and harassed housewives yelling and cursing in Spanish. The globe called Earth had once again revolved on its axis. The windowpanes became rosy—a sign that in the east the sky was not entirely overcast. The books were momentarily bathed in a purplish light, illuminating the old bindings and the last remnants of gold-engraved and half-legible titles. It all had the quality of a revelation.

A Friend of Kafka

I

I HAD heard about Franz Kafka years before I read any of his books from his friend Jacques Kohn, a former actor in the Yiddish theater. I say "former" because by the time I knew him he was no longer on the stage. It was the early thirties, and the Yiddish theater in Warsaw had already begun to lose its audience. Jacques Kohn himself was a sick and broken man. Although he still dressed in the style of a dandy, his clothes were shabby. He wore a monocle in his left eye, a high old-fashioned collar (known as "father-murderer"), patent-leather shoes, and a derby. He had been nicknamed "the lord" by the cynics in the Warsaw Yiddish writers' club that we both frequented. Although he stooped more and more, he worked stubbornly at keeping his shoulders back. What was left of his once yellow hair he combed to form a bridge over his bare skull. In the tradition of the old-time theater, every now and then he would lapse into Germanized Yiddish—particularly when he spoke of his relationship with Kafka. Of late, he had begun writing newspaper articles, but the editors were unanimous in rejecting his manuscripts. He lived in an attic room somewhere on Leszno Street and was constantly ailing. A joke about him made the rounds of the club members: "All day long he lies in an oxygen tent, and at night he emerges a Don Juan."

We always met at the club in the evening. The door would open slowly to admit Jacques Kohn. He had the air of an important European celebrity who was deigning to visit the ghetto. He would look around and grimace, as if to indicate that the smells of herring, garlic, and cheap tobacco were not to his taste. He would glance disdainfully over the tables covered with tattered newspapers, broken chess pieces, and ashtrays filled with cigarette stubs, around which the club members sat

---

Translated by the author and Elizabeth Shub

endlessly discussing literature in their shrill voices. He would shake his head as if to say, "What can you expect from such schlemiels?" The moment I saw him entering, I would put my hand in my pocket and prepare the zloty that he would inevitably borrow from me.

This particular evening, Jacques seemed to be in a better mood than usual. He smiled, displaying his porcelain teeth, which did not fit and moved slightly when he spoke, and swaggered over to me as if he were on-stage. He offered me his bony, long-fingered hand and said, "How's the rising star doing tonight?"

"At it already?"

"I'm serious. Serious. I know talent when I see it, even though I lack it myself. When we played Prague in 1911, no one had ever heard of Kafka. He came backstage, and the moment I saw him I knew that I was in the presence of genius. I could smell it the way a cat smells a mouse. That was how our great friendship began."

I had heard this story many times and in as many variations, but I knew that I would have to listen to it again. He sat down at my table, and Manya, the waitress, brought us glasses of tea and cookies, Jacques Kohn raised his eyebrows over his yellowish eyes, the whites of which were threaded with bloody little veins. His expression seemed to say, "This is what the barbarians call tea?" He put five lumps of sugar into his glass and stirred, rotating the tin spoon outward. With his thumb and index finger, the nail of which was unusually long, he broke off a small piece of cookie, put it into his mouth, and said, *"Nu ja,"* which meant, One cannot fill one's stomach on the past.

It was all play-acting. He himself came from a Hasidic family in one of the small Polish towns. His name was not Jacques but Jankel. However, he had lived for many years in Prague, Vienna, Berlin, Paris. He had not always been an actor in the Yiddish theater but had played on the stage in both France and Germany. He had been friends with many celebrities. He had helped Chagall find a studio in Belleville. He had been a frequent guest at Israel Zangwill's. He had appeared in a Reinhardt production, and had eaten cold cuts with Piscator. He had shown me letters he had received not only from Kafka but from Jakob Wassermann, Stefan Zweig, Romain Rolland, Ilya Ehrenburg, and Martin Buber. They all addressed him by his first name. As we got to know each other better, he had even let me see photographs and letters from famous actresses with whom he had had affairs.

For me, "lending" Jacques Kohn a zloty meant coming into contact with Western Europe. The very way he carried his silver-handled cane seemed exotic to me. He even smoked his cigarettes differently from the way we did in Warsaw. His manners were courtly. On the rare occasion when he reproached me, he always managed to save my feelings with some elegant compliment. More than anything else, I admired Jacques Kohn's way with women. I was shy with girls—blushed, became embarrassed in their presence—but Jacques Kohn had the assurance of a count. He had something nice to say to the most unattractive woman. He flattered them all, but always in a tone of good-natured irony, affecting the blasé attitude of a hedonist who has already tasted everything.

He spoke frankly to me. "My young friend, I'm as good as impotent. It always starts with the development of an overrefined taste—when one is hungry, one does not need marzipan and caviar. I've reached the point where I consider no woman really attractive. No defect can be hidden from me. That is impotence. Dresses, corsets are transparent for me. I can no longer be fooled by paint and perfume. I have lost my own teeth, but a woman has only to open her mouth and I spot her fillings. That, by the way, was Kafka's problem when it came to writing: he saw all the defects—his own and everyone else's. Most of literature is produced by such plebeians and bunglers as Zola and D'Annunzio. In the theater, I saw the same defects that Kafka found in literature, and that brought us together. But, oddly enough, when it came to judging the theater Kafka was completely blind. He praised our cheap Yiddish plays to heaven. He fell madly in love with a ham actress—Madam Tschissik. When I think that Kafka loved this creature, dreamed about her, I am ashamed for man and his illusions. Well, immortality is not choosy. Anyone who happens to come in contact with a great man marches with him into immortality, often in clumsy boots.

"Didn't you once ask what makes me go on, or do I imagine that you did? What gives me the strength to bear poverty, sickness, and, worst of all, hopelessness? That's a good question, my young friend. I asked the same question when I first read the Book of Job. Why did Job continue to live and suffer? So that in the end he would have more daughters, more donkeys, more camels? No. The answer is that it was for the game itself. We all play chess with Fate as partner. He makes a move; we make a move. He tries to checkmate us in three moves; we try to prevent it. We know we can't win, but we're driven to give him a good fight. My opponent is a tough angel. He fights Jacques Kohn with every trick in his bag. It's winter now; it's cold even with the stove on, but my stove hasn't worked for months and the landlord refuses to fix it. Besides, I wouldn't have the money to buy coal. It's as cold inside my room as it is outdoors. If you haven't lived in an attic, you don't know the strength of the wind. My windowpanes rattle even in the summertime. Sometimes a tomcat climbs up on the roof near my window and wails all night like a woman in labor. I lie there freezing under my blankets and he yowls for a cat, though it may be he's merely hungry. I might give him a morsel of food to quiet him, or chase him away, but in order not to freeze to death I wrap myself in all the rags I possess, even old newspapers—the slightest move and the whole works comes apart.

"Still, if you play chess, my dear friend, it's better to play with a worthy adversary than with a botcher. I admire my opponent. Sometimes I'm enchanted with his ingenuity. He sits up there in an office in the third or seventh heaven, in that department of Providence that rules our little planet, and has just one job—to trap Jacques Kohn. His orders are 'Break the keg, but don't let the wine run out.' He's done exactly that. How he manages to keep me alive is a miracle. I'm ashamed to tell you how much medicine I take, how many pills I swallow. I have a friend who is a druggist, or I could never afford it. Before I go to bed, I gulp down one after another—dry. If I drink, I have to urinate. I have prostate trouble, and as it is I must get up several times during the night. In the dark, Kant's categories no longer apply. Time ceases to be time and space is no space. You hold something in your hand and suddenly it isn't there. To light my gas lamp is not a simple matter. My matches are always vanishing. My attic teems with demons. Occasionally, I address one of them: 'Hey, you, Vinegar, son of Wine, how about stopping your nasty tricks!'

"Some time ago, in the middle of the night, I heard a pounding on my door and the sound of a woman's voice. I couldn't tell whether she was laughing or crying. 'Who can it be?' I said to myself. 'Lilith? Namah? Machlath, the daughter of Ketev M'riri?' Out loud, I called, 'Madam, you are making a mistake.' But she continued to bang on the door. Then I heard a groan and someone falling. I did not dare to open the door. I began to look for my matches, only to discover that I was holding them in my hand. Finally, I got out of bed, lit the gas lamp, and put on my dressing gown and slippers. I caught a glimpse of myself in the mirror, and my reflection scared me. My face was green and unshaven. I finally opened a door, and there stood a young woman in bare feet, wearing a sable coat over her nightgown. She was pale and her long blond hair was disheveled. 'Madam, what's the matter?' I said.

" 'Someone just tried to kill me. I beg you, please let me in. I only want to stay in your room until daylight.'

"I wanted to ask who had tried to kill her, but I saw that she was half frozen. Most probably drunk, too. I let her in and noticed a bracelet with huge diamonds on her wrist. 'My room is not heated,' I told her.

" 'It's better than to die in the street.'

"So there we were both of us. But what was I to do with her? I only have one bed. I don't drink—I'm not allowed to—but a friend had given me a bottle of cognac as a gift, and I had some stale cookies. I gave her a drink and one of the cookies. The liquor seemed to revive her. 'Madam, do you live in this building?' I asked.

" 'No,' she said. 'I live on Ujazdowskie Boulevard.'

"I could tell that she was an aristocrat. One word led to another, and I discovered that she was a countess and a widow, and that her lover lived in the building—a wild man, who kept a lion cub as a pet. He, too, was a member of the nobility, but an outcast. He had already served a year in the Citadel, for attempted murder. He could not visit her, because she lived in her mother-in-law's house, so she came to see him. That night, in a jealous fit, he had beaten her and placed his revolver at her temple. To make a long story short, she had managed to grab her coat and run out of his apartment. She had knocked on the doors of the neighbors, but none of them would let her in, and so she had made her way to the attic.

" 'Madam,' I said to her, 'your lover is probably still looking for you. Supposing he finds you? I am no longer what one might call a knight.'

" 'He won't dare make a disturbance,' she said. 'He's on parole. I'm through with him for good. Have pity—please don't put me out in the middle of the night.'

" 'How will you get home tomorrow?' I asked.

" 'I don't know,' she said. 'I'm tired of life anyhow, but I don't want to be killed by him.'

" 'Well, I won't be able to sleep in any case,' I said. 'Take my bed and I will rest here in this chair.'

" 'No. I wouldn't do that. You are not young and you don't look very well. Please, go back to bed and I will sit here.'

"We haggled so long we finally decided to lie down together. 'You have nothing to fear from me,' I assured her. 'I am old and helpless with women.' She seemed completely convinced.

"What was I saying? Yes, suddenly I find myself in bed with a countess whose lover might break down the door at any moment. I covered us both with the two blankets I have and didn't bother to build the usual cocoon of odds and ends. I was so wrought up I forgot about the cold. Besides, I felt her closeness. A strange warmth emanated from her body, different from any I had known—or perhaps I had forgotten it. Was my opponent trying a new gambit? In the past few years he had stopped playing with me in earnest. You know, there is such a thing as humorous chess. I have been told that Nimzowitsch often played jokes on his partners. In the old days, Morphy was known as a chess prankster. 'A fine move,' I said to my adversary. 'A masterpiece.' With that I realized that I knew who her lover was. I had met him on the stairs—a giant of a man, with the face of a murderer. What a funny end for Jacques Kohn—to be finished off by a Polish Othello.

"I began to laugh and she joined in. I embraced her and held her close. She did not resist. Suddenly a miracle happened. I was a man again! Once, on a Thursday evening, I stood near a slaughterhouse in a small village and saw a bull and a cow copulate before they were going to be slaughtered for the Sabbath. Why she consented I will never know. Perhaps it was a way of taking revenge on her lover. She kissed me and whispered endearments. Then we heard heavy footsteps. Someone pounded on the door with his fist. My girl rolled off the bed and lay on the floor. I wanted to recite the prayer for the dying, but I was ashamed before God—and not so much before God as before my mocking opponent. Why grant him this additional pleasure? Even melodrama has its limits.

"The brute behind the door continued beating it, and I was astounded that it did not give way. He kicked it with his foot. The door creaked but held. I was terrified, yet something in me could not help laughing. Then the racket stopped. Othello had left.

"Next morning, I took the countess's bracelet to a pawnshop. With the money I received, I bought my heroine a dress, underwear, and shoes. The dress didn't fit, neither did the shoes, but all she needed to do was get to a taxi—provided, of course, that her lover did not waylay her on the steps. Curious, but the man vanished that night and never reappeared.

"Before she left, she kissed me and urged me to call her, but I'm not that much of a fool. As the Talmud says, 'A miracle doesn't happen every day.'

"And you know, Kafka, young as he was, was possessed by the same inhibitions that plague me in my old age. They impeded him in everything he did—in sex as well as in his writing. He craved love and fled from it. He wrote a sentence and immediately crossed it out. Otto Weininger was like that, too—mad and a genius. I met him in Vienna— he spouted aphorisms and paradoxes. One of his sayings I will never forget: 'God did not create the bedbug.' You have to know Vienna to really understand these words. Yet who did create the bedbug?

"Ah, there's Bamberg! Look at the way he waddles along on his short legs, a corpse refusing to rest in its grave. It might be a good idea to start a club for insomniac corpses. Why does he prowl around all night? What good are the cabarets to him? The doctors gave him up years ago when we were still in Berlin. Not that it prevented him from sitting in the Romanisches Café until four o'clock in the morning, chatting with the prostitutes. Once, Granat, the actor, announced that he was giving a party—a real orgy—at his house, and among others he invited Bamberg. Granat instructed each man to bring a lady—either his wife or a friend. But Bamberg had neither wife nor mistress, and so he paid a harlot to accompany him. He had to buy her an evening dress for the occasion. The company consisted exclusively of writers, professors, philosophers, and the usual intellectual hangers-on. They all had the same idea as Bamberg—they hired prostitutes. I was there, too. I escorted an actress from Prague, whom I had known a long time. Do you know Granat? A savage. He drinks cognac like soda water, and can eat an omelette of ten eggs. As soon as the guests arrived, he stripped and began dancing madly around with the whores, just to impress his highbrow visitors. At first, the intellectuals sat on chairs and stared. After a while, they began to discuss sex. Schopenhauer said this . . . Nietzsche said that. Anyone who hadn't witnessed it would find it difficult to imagine how ridiculous such geniuses can be. In the midst of it all, Bamberg was taken ill. He turned as green as grass and broke out in a sweat. 'Jacques,' he said, 'I'm finished. A good place to die.' He was having a kidney or a gall-bladder attack. I half carried him out and got him to a hospital. By the way, can you lend me a zloty?"

"Two."

"What! Have you robbed Bank Polski?"

"I sold a story."

"Congratulations. Let's have supper together. You will be my guest."

I I

While we were eating, Bamberg came over to our table. He was a little man, emaciated as a consumptive, bent over and bowlegged. He was wearing patent-leather shoes, and spats. On his pointed skull lay a few gray hairs. One eye was larger than the other—red, bulging, frightened by its own vision. He leaned against our table on his bony little hands and said in his cackling voice, "Jacques, yesterday I read your Kafka's *Castle*. Interesting, very interesting, but what is he driving at? It's too long for a dream. Allegories should be short."

Jacques Kohn quickly swallowed the food he was chewing. "Sit down," he said. "A master does not have to follow the rules."

"There are some rules even a master must follow. No novel should be longer than *War and Peace*. Even *War and Peace* is too long. If the Bible consisted of eighteen volumes, it would long since have been forgotten."

"The Talmud has thirty-six volumes, and the Jews have not forgotten it."

"Jews remember too much. That is our misfortune. It is two thousand years since we were driven out of the Holy Land, and now we are trying to get back in. Insane, isn't it? If our literature would only reflect this insanity, it would be great. But our literature is uncannily sane. Well, enough of that."

Bamberg straightened himself, scowling with the effort. With his tiny steps, he shuffled away from the table. He went over to the gramophone and put on a dance record. It was known in the writers' club that he had not written a word in years. In his old age, he was learning to dance, influenced by the philosophy of his friend Dr. Mitzkin, the author of *The Entropy of Reason*. In this book Dr. Mitzkin attempted to prove that the human intellect is bankrupt and that true wisdom can only be reached through passion.

Jacques Kohn shook his head. "Half-pint Hamlet. Kafka was afraid of becoming a Bamberg—that is why he destroyed himself."

"Did the countess ever call you?" I asked.

Jacques Kohn took his monocle out of his pocket and put it in place. "And what if she did? In my life, everything turns into words. All talk, talk. This is actually Dr. Mitzkin's philosophy—man will end up as a word machine. He will eat words, drink words, marry words, poison himself with words. Come to think of it, Dr. Mitzkin was also present at Granat's orgy. He came to practice what he preached, but he could just as well have written *The Entropy of Passion*. Yes, the countess does call me from time to time. She, too, is an intellectual, but without intellect. As a matter of fact, although women do their best to reveal the charms of their bodies, they know just as little about the meaning of sex as they do about the intellect.

"Take Madam Tschissik. What did she ever have, except a body? But just try asking her what a body really is. Now she's ugly. When she was an actress in the Prague days, she still had something. I was her leading man. She was a tiny little talent. We came to Prague to make some money and found a genius waiting for us—*Homo sapiens* in his highest degree of self-torture. Kafka wanted to be a Jew, but he didn't know how. He wanted to live, but he didn't know this, either. 'Franz,' I said to him once, 'you are a young man. Do what we all do.' There was a brothel I knew in Prague, and I persuaded him to go there with me. He was still a virgin. I'd rather not speak about the girl he was engaged to. He was sunk to the neck in the bourgeois swamp. The Jews of his circle had one ideal—to become Gentiles, and not Czech Gentiles but German Gentiles. To make it short, I talked him into the adventure. I took him to a dark alley in the former ghetto and there was the brothel. We went up the crooked steps. I opened the door and it looked like a stage set: the whores, the pimps, the guests, the madam. I will never forget that moment. Kafka began to shake, and pulled at my sleeve. Then he turned and ran down the steps so quickly I was afraid he would break a leg. Once on the street, he stopped and vomited like a schoolboy. On the way back, we passed an old synagogue, and Kafka began to speak about the golem. Kafka believed in the golem, and even that the future might well bring another one. There must be magic words that can turn a piece of clay into a living being. Did not God, according to the Cabala, create the world by uttering holy words? In the beginning was the Logos.

"Yes, it's all one big chess game. All my life I have been afraid of death, but now that I'm on the threshold of the grave I've stopped being afraid. It's clear, my partner wants to play a slow game. He'll go on taking my pieces one by one. First he removed my appeal as an actor and turned me into a so-called writer. He'd no sooner done that than he provided me with writer's cramp. His next move was to deprive me of my potency. Yet I know he's far from checkmate, and this gives me strength. It's cold in my room—let it be cold. I have no supper—I won't die without it. He sabotages me and I sabotage him. Some time ago, I was returning home late at night. The frost burned outside, and suddenly I realized that I had lost my key. I woke up the janitor, but he had no spare key. He stank of vodka, and his dog bit my foot. In former years I would have been desperate, but this time I said to my opponent, 'If you want me to catch pneumonia, it's all right with me.' I left the house and decided to go to the Vienna station. The wind almost carried me away. I would have had to wait at least three-quarters of an hour for the street-car at that time of night. I passed by the actors' union and saw a light in a window. I decided to go in. Perhaps I could spend the night there. On the steps I hit something with my shoe and heard a ringing sound. I bent down and picked up a key. It was mine! The chance of finding a key on the dark stairs of this building is one in a billion, but it seems that my opponent was afraid I might give up the ghost before he was ready. Fatalism? Call it fatalism if you like."

Jacques Kohn rose and excused himself to make a phone call. I sat there and watched Bamberg dancing on his shaky legs with a literary lady. His eyes were closed, and he leaned his head on her bosom as if it were a pillow. He seemed to be dancing and sleeping simultaneously. Jacques Kohn took a long time—much longer than it normally takes to make a phone call. When he returned, the monocle in his eye shone. "Guess who is in the other room?" he said. "Madam Tschissik! Kafka's great love."

"Really."

"I told her about you. Come, I'd like to introduce you to her."

"No."

"Why not? A woman that was loved by Kafka is worth meeting."

"I'm not interested."

"You are shy, that's the truth. Kafka, too, was shy—as shy as a yeshiva student. I was never shy, and that may be the reason I have never amounted to anything. My dear friend, I need another twenty groschen for the janitors—ten for the one in this building, and ten for the one in mine. Without the money I can't go home."

I took some change out of my pocket and gave it to him.

"So much? You certainly must have robbed a bank today. Forty-six groschen! Piff-paff! Well, if there is a God, He will reward you. And if there isn't, who is playing all these games with Jacques Kohn?"

The Cafeteria

I

EVEN though I have reached the point where a great part of my earnings is given away in taxes, I still have the habit of eating in cafeterias when I am by myself. I like to take a tray with a tin knife, fork, spoon, and paper napkin and to choose at the counter the food I enjoy. Besides, I meet there the *landsleit* from Poland, as well as all kinds of literary beginners and readers who know Yiddish. The moment I sit down at a table, they come over. "Hello, Aaron!" they greet me, and we talk about Yiddish literature, the Holocaust, the state of Israel, and often about acquaintances who were eating rice pudding or stewed prunes the last time I was here and are already in their graves. Since I seldom read a paper, I learn this news only later. Each time, I am startled, but at my age one has to be ready for such tidings. The food sticks in the throat; we look at one another in confusion, and our eyes ask mutely, Whose turn is next? Soon we begin to chew again. I am often reminded of a scene in a film about Africa. A lion attacks a herd of zebras and kills one. The frightened zebras run for a while and then they stop and start to graze again. Do they have a choice?

I cannot spend too long with these Yiddishists, because I am always busy. I am writing a novel, a story, an article. I have to lecture today or tomorrow; my datebook is crowded with all kinds of appointments for weeks and months in advance. It can happen that an hour after I leave the cafeteria I am on a train to Chicago or flying to California. But meanwhile we converse in the mother language and I hear of intrigues and pettiness about which, from a moral point of view, it would be better not to be informed. Everyone tries in his own way with all his means to grab as many honors and as much money and prestige as he

Translated by the author and Dorothea Straus

can. None of us learns from all these deaths. Old age does not cleanse us. We don't repent at the gate of hell.

I have been moving around in this neighborhood for over thirty years—as long as I lived in Poland. I know each block, each house. There has been little building here on uptown Broadway in the last decades, and I have the illusion of having put down roots here. I have spoken in most of the synagogues. They know me in some of the stores and in the vegetarian restaurants. Women with whom I have had affairs live on the side streets. Even the pigeons know me; the moment I come out with a bag of feed, they begin to fly toward me from blocks away. It is an area that stretches from Ninety-sixth Street to Seventy-second Street and from Central Park to Riverside Drive. Almost every day on my walk after lunch, I pass the funeral parlor that waits for us and all our ambitions and illusions. Sometimes I imagine that the funeral parlor is also a kind of cafeteria where one gets a quick eulogy or Kaddish on the way to eternity.

The cafeteria people I meet are mostly men: old bachelors like myself, would-be writers, retired teachers, some with dubious doctorate titles, a rabbi without a congregation, a painter of Jewish themes, a few translators—all immigrants from Poland or Russia. I seldom know their names. One of them disappears and I think he is already in the next world; suddenly he reappears and he tells me that he has tried to settle in Tel Aviv or Los Angeles. Again he eats his rice pudding, sweetens his coffee with saccharin. He has a few more wrinkles, but he tells the same stories and makes the same gestures. It may happen that he takes a paper from his pocket and reads me a poem he has written.

It was in the fifties that a woman appeared in the group who looked younger than the rest of us. She must have been in her early thirties; she was short, slim, with a girlish face, brown hair that she wore in a bun, a short nose, and dimples in her cheeks. Her eyes were hazel—actually, of an indefinite color. She dressed in a modest European way. She spoke Polish, Russian, and an idiomatic Yiddish. She always carried Yiddish newspapers and magazines. She had been in a prison camp in Russia and had spent some time in the camps in Germany before she obtained a visa for the United States. The men all hovered around her. They didn't let her pay the check. They gallantly brought her coffee and cheese cake. They listened to her talk and jokes. She had returned from the devastation still gay. She was introduced to me. Her name was Esther. I didn't know if she was unmarried, a widow, a divorcée. She told me she was working in a factory, where she sorted buttons. This fresh young woman did not fit into the group of elderly has-beens. It was also hard to understand why she couldn't find a better job than sorting buttons in New Jersey. But I didn't ask too many questions. She told me that she had read my writing while still in Poland, and later in the camps in Germany after the war. She said to me, "You are my writer."

The moment she uttered those words I imagined I was in love with her. We were sitting alone (the other man at our table had gone to make a telephone call), and I said, "For such words I must kiss you."

"Well, what are you waiting for?"

She gave me both a kiss and a bite.

I said, "You are a ball of fire."

"Yes, fire from Gehenna."

A few days later, she invited me to her home. She lived on a street between Broadway and Riverside Drive with her father, who had no legs and sat in a wheelchair. His legs had been frozen in Siberia. He had tried to run away from one of Stalin's slave camps in the winter of 1944. He looked like a strong man, had a head of thick white hair, a ruddy face, and eyes full of energy. He spoke in a swaggering fashion, with boyish boastfulness and a cheerful laugh. In an hour, he told me his story. He was born in White Russia but he had lived long years in Warsaw, Lodz, and Vilna. In the beginning of the thirties, he became a Communist and soon afterward a functionary in the Party. In 1939 he escaped to Russia with his daughter. His wife and the other children remained in Nazi-occupied Warsaw. In Russia, somebody denounced him as a Trotskyite and he was sent to mine gold in the north. The G.P.U. sent people there to die. Even the strongest could not survive the cold and hunger for more than a year. They were exiled without a sentence. They died together: Zionists, Bundists, members of the Polish Socialist Party, Ukrainian Nationalists, and just refugees, all caught because of the labor shortage. They often died of scurvy or beriberi. Boris Merkin, Esther's father, spoke about this as if it were a big joke. He called the Stalinists outcasts, bandits, sycophants. He assured me that had it not been for the United States Hitler would have overrun all of Russia. He told how prisoners tricked the guards to get an extra piece of bread or a double portion of watery soup, and what methods were used in picking lice.

Esther called out, "Father, enough!"

"What's the matter—am I lying?"

"One can have enough even of kreplaech."

"Daughter, you did it yourself."

When Esther went to the kitchen to make tea, I learned from her father that she had had a husband in Russia—a Polish Jew who had volunteered in the Red Army and perished in the war. Here in New York she was courted by a refugee, a former smuggler in Germany who had opened a bookbinding factory and become rich. "Persuade her to marry him," Boris Merkin said to me. "It would be good for me, too."

"Maybe she doesn't love him."

"There is no such thing as love. Give me a cigarette. In the camp, people climbed on one another like worms."

II

I had invited Esther to supper, but she called to say she had the grippe and must remain in bed. Then in a few days' time a situation arose that made me leave for Israel. On the way back, I stopped over in London and Paris. I wanted to write to Esther, but I had lost her address. When I returned to New York, I tried to call her, but there was no telephone listing for Boris Merkin or Esther Merkin—father and daughter must have been boarders in somebody else's apartment. Weeks passed and she did not show up in the cafeteria I asked the group about her; nobody knew where she was. "She has most probably married that bookbinder," I said to myself. One evening, I went to the cafeteria with the premonition that I would find Esther there. I saw a black wall and boarded windows—the cafeteria had burned. The old bachelors were no doubt meeting in another cafeteria, or an Automat. But where? To search is not in my nature. I had plenty of complications without Esther.

The summer passed; it was winter. Late one day, I walked by the cafeteria and again saw lights, a counter, guests. The owners had rebuilt. I entered, took a check, and saw Esther sitting alone at a table reading a Yiddish newspaper. She did not notice me, and I observed her for a while. She wore a man's fur fez and a jacket trimmed with a faded fur collar. She looked pale, as though recuperating from a sickness. Could that grippe have been the start of a serious illness? I went over to her table and asked, "What's new in buttons?"

She started and smiled. Then she called out, "Miracles do happen!"

"Where have you been?"

"Where did you disappear to?" she replied. "I thought you were still abroad."

"Where are our cafeterianiks?"

"They now go to the cafeteria on Fifty-seventh Street and Eighth Avenue. They only reopened this place yesterday."

"May I bring you a cup of coffee?"

"I drink too much coffee. All right."

I went to get her coffee and a large egg cookie. While I stood at the counter, I turned my head and looked at her. Esther had taken off her mannish fur hat and smoothed her hair. She folded the newspaper, which meant that she was ready to talk. She got up and tilted the other chair against the table as a sign that the seat was taken. When I sat down, Esther said, "You left without saying goodbye, and there I was about to knock at the pearly gates of heaven."

"What happened?"

"Oh, the grippe became pneumonia. They gave me penicillin, and I am one of those who cannot take it. I got a rash all over my body. My father, too, is not well."

"What's the matter with your father?"

"High blood pressure. He had a kind of stroke and his mouth became all crooked."

"Oh, I'm sorry. Do you still work with buttons?"

"Yes, with buttons. At least I don't have to use my head, only my hands. I can think my own thoughts."

"What do you think about?"

"What not. The other workers are all Puerto Ricans. They rattle away in Spanish from morning to night."

"Who takes care of your father?"

"Who? Nobody. I come home in the evening to make supper. He has one desire—to marry me off for my own good and, perhaps, for his comfort, but I can't marry a man I don't love."

"What is love?"

"You ask me! You write novels about it. But you're a man—I assume you really don't know what it is. A woman is a piece of merchandise to you. To me a man who talks nonsense or smiles like an idiot is repulsive. I would rather die than live with him. And a man who goes from one woman to another is not for me. I don't want to share with anybody."

"I'm afraid a time is coming when everybody will."

"That is not for me."

"What kind of person was your husband?"

"How did you know I had a husband? My father, I suppose. The minute I leave the room, he prattles. My husband believed in things and was ready to die for them. He was not exactly my type but I respected him and loved him, too. He wanted to die and he died like a hero. What else can I say?"

"And the others?"

"There were no others. Men were after me. The way people behaved in the war—you will never know. They lost all shame. On the bunks near me one time, a mother lay with one man and her daughter with another. People were like beasts—worse than beasts. In the middle of it all, I dreamed about love. Now I have even stopped dreaming. The men who come here are terrible bores. Most of them are half mad, too. One of them tried to read me a forty-page poem. I almost fainted."

"I wouldn't read you anything I'd written."

"I've been told how you behave—no!"

"No is no. Drink your coffee."

"You don't even try to persuade me. Most men around here plague you and you can't get rid of them. In Russia people suffered, but I have never met as many maniacs there as in New York City. The building where I live is a madhouse. My neighbors are lunatics. They accuse each other of all kinds of things. They sing, cry, break dishes. One of them jumped out of the window and killed herself. She was having an affair with a boy twenty years younger. In Russia the problem was to escape the lice; here you're surrounded by insanity."

We drank coffee and shared the egg cookie. Esther put down her cup. "I can't believe that I'm sitting with you at this table. I read all your articles under all your pen names. You tell so much about yourself I have the feeling I've known you for years. Still, you are a riddle to me."

"Men and women can never understand one another."

"No—I cannot understand my own father. Sometimes he is a complete stranger to me. He won't live long."

"Is he so sick?"

"It's everything together. He's lost the will to live. Why live without legs, without friends, without a family? They have all perished. He sits and reads the newspapers all day long. He acts as though he were interested in what's going on in the world. His ideals are gone, but he still hopes for a just revolution. How can a revolution help him? I myself never put my hopes in any movement or party. How can we hope when everything ends in death?"

"Hope in itself is a proof that there is no death."

"Yes, I know you often write about this. For me, death is the only comfort. What do the dead do? They continue to drink coffee and eat egg cookies? They still read newspapers? A life after death would be nothing but a joke."

III

Some of the cafeterianiks came back to the rebuilt cafeteria. New people appeared—all of them Europeans. They launched into long discussions in Yiddish, Polish, Russian, even Hebrew. Some of those who came from Hungary mixed German, Hungarian, Yiddish-German—then all of a sudden they began to speak plain Galician Yiddish. They asked to have their coffee in glasses, and held lumps of sugar between their teeth when they drank. Many of them were my readers. They introduced themselves and reproached me for all kinds of literary errors: I contradicted myself, went too far in descriptions of sex, described Jews in such a way that anti-Semites could use it for propaganda. They told me their experiences in the ghettos, in the Nazi concentration camps, in Russia. They pointed out one another. "Do you see that fellow—in Russia he immediately became a Stalinist. He denounced his own friends. Here in America he has switched to anti-Bolshevism." The one who was spoken about seemed to sense that he was being maligned, because the moment my informant left he took his cup of coffee and his rice pudding, sat down at my table, and said, "Don't believe a word of what you are told. They invent all kinds of lies. What could you do in a country where the rope was always around your neck? You had to adjust yourself if you wanted to live and not die somewhere in Kazakhstan. To get a bowl of soup or a place to stay you had to sell your soul."

There was a table with a group of refugees who ignored me. They were not interested in literature and journalism but strictly in business. In Germany they had been smugglers. They seemed to be doing shady business here, too; they whispered to one another and winked, counted their money, wrote long lists of numbers. Somebody pointed out one of them. "He had a store in Auschwitz."

"What do you mean, a store?"

"God help us. He kept his merchandise in the straw where he slept —a rotten potato, sometimes a piece of soap, a tin spoon, a little fat. Still, he did business. Later, in Germany, he became such a big smuggler they once took forty thousand dollars away from him."

Sometimes months passed between my visits to the cafeteria. A year or two had gone by (perhaps three or four; I lost count), and Esther did not show up. I asked about her a few times. Someone said that she was going to the cafeteria on Forty-second Street; another had heard that she was married. I learned that some of the cafeterianiks had died. They were beginning to settle down in the United States, had remarried, opened businesses, workshops, even had children again. Then came cancer or a heart attack. The result of the Hitler and Stalin years, it was said.

One day, I entered the cafeteria and saw Esther. She was sitting alone at a table. It was the same Esther. She was even wearing the same fur hat, but a strand of gray hair fell over her forehead. How strange— the fur hat, too, seemed to have grayed. The other cafeterianiks did not appear to be interested in her any more, or they did not know her. Her face told of the time that had passed. There were shadows under her eyes. Her gaze was no longer so clear. Around her mouth was an expression that could be called bitterness, disenchantment. I greeted her. She smiled, but her smile immediately faded away. I asked, "What happened to you?"

"Oh, I'm still alive."

"May I sit down?"

"Please—certainly."

"May I bring you a cup of coffee?"

"No. Well, if you insist."

I noticed that she was smoking, and also that she was reading not the newspaper to which I contribute but a competition paper. She had gone over to the enemy. I brought her coffee and for myself stewed prunes—a remedy for constipation. I sat down. "Where were you all this time? I have asked for you."

"Really? Thank you."

"What happened?"

"Nothing good." She looked at me. I knew that she saw in me what I saw in her: the slow wilting of the flesh. She said, "You have no hair but you are white."

For a while we were silent. Then I said, "Your father—" and as I said it I knew that her father was not alive.

Esther said, "He has been dead for almost a year."

"Do you still sort buttons?"

"No, I became an operator in a dress shop."

"What happened to you personally, may I ask?"

"Oh nothing—absolutely nothing. You will not believe it, but I was sitting here thinking about you. I have fallen into some kind of trap. I don't know what to call it. I thought perhaps you could advise me. Do you still have the patience to listen to the troubles of little people like me? No, I didn't mean to insult you. I even doubted you would remember me. To make it short, I work but work is growing more difficult for me. I suffer from arthritis. I feel as if my bones would crack. I wake up in the morning and can't sit up. One doctor tells me that it's a disc in my back, others try to cure my nerves. One took X-rays and says that I have a tumor. He wanted me to go to the hospital for a few weeks, but I'm in no hurry for an operation. Suddenly a little lawyer showed up. He is a refugee himself and is connected with the German government. You know they're now giving reparation money. It's true that I escaped to Russia, but I'm a victim of the Nazis just the same. Besides, they don't know my biography so exactly. I could get a pension plus a few thousand dollars, but my dislocated disc is no good for the purpose because I got it later—after the camps. This lawyer says my only chance is to convince them that I am ruined psychically. It's the bitter truth, but how can you prove it? The German doctors, the neurologists, the psychiatrists require proof. Everything has to be according to the textbooks —just so and no different. The lawyer wants me to play insane. Naturally, he gets twenty percent of the reparation money—maybe more.

Why he needs so much money I don't understand. He's already in his seventies, an old bachelor. He tried to make love to me and whatnot. He's half meshugga himself. But how can I play insane when actually I *am* insane? The whole thing revolts me and I'm afraid it will really drive me crazy. I hate swindle. But this shyster pursues me. I don't sleep. When the alarm rings in the morning, I wake up as shattered as I used to be in Russia when I had to walk to the forest and saw logs at four in the morning. Naturally, I take sleeping pills—if I didn't, I couldn't sleep at all. That is more or less the situation."

"Why don't you get married? You are still a good-looking woman."

"Well, the old question—there is nobody. It's too late. If you knew how I felt, you wouldn't ask such a question."

I V

A few weeks passed. Snow had been falling. After the snow came rain, then frost. I stood at my window and looked out at Broadway. The passers-by half walked, half slipped. Cars moved slowly. The sky above the roofs shone violet, without a moon, without stars, and even though it was eight o'clock in the evening the light and the emptiness reminded me of dawn. The stores were deserted. For a moment, I had the feeling I was in Warsaw. The telephone rang and I rushed to answer it as I did ten, twenty, thirty years ago—still expecting the good tidings that a telephone call was about to bring me. I said hello, but there was no answer and I was seized by the fear that some evil power was trying to keep back the good news at the last minute. Then I heard a stammering. A woman's voice muttered my name.

"Yes, it is I."

"Excuse me for disturbing you. My name is Esther. We met a few weeks ago in the cafeteria—"

"Esther!" I exclaimed.

"I don't know how I got the courage to phone you. I need to talk to you about something. Naturally, if you have the time and—please forgive my presumption."

"No presumption. Would you like to come to my apartment?"

"If I will not be interrupting. It's difficult to talk in the cafeteria. It's noisy and there are eavesdroppers. What I want to tell you is a secret I wouldn't trust to anyone else."

"Please, come up."

I gave Esther directions. Then I tried to make order in my apartment, but I soon realized this was impossible. Letters, manuscripts lay around on tables and chairs. In the corners books and magazines were piled high. I opened the closets and threw inside whatever was under my hand: jackets, pants, shirts, shoes, slippers. I picked up an envelope and to my amazement saw that it had never been opened. I tore it open and found a check. "What's the matter with me—have I lost my mind?" I said out loud. I tried to read the letter that came with the check, but I had misplaced my glasses; my fountain pen was gone, too. Well—and where were my keys? I heard a bell ring and I didn't know whether it was the door or the telephone. I opened the door and saw Esther. It must have been snowing again, because her hat and the shoulders of her coat were trimmed with white. I asked her in, and my neighbor, the divorcée, who spied on me openly with no shame—and, God knows, with no sense of purpose—opened her door and stared at my guest.

Esther removed her boots and I took her coat and put it on the case of the Encyclopaedia Britannica. I shoved a few manuscripts off the sofa so she could sit down. I said, "In my house there is sheer chaos."

"It doesn't matter."

I sat in an armchair strewn with socks and handkerchiefs. For a while we spoke about the weather, about the danger of being out in New York at night—even early in the evening. Then Esther said, "Do you remember the time I spoke to you about my lawyer—that I had to go to a psychiatrist because of the reparation money?"

"Yes, I remember."

"I didn't tell you everything. It was too wild. It still seems unbelievable, even to me. Don't interrupt me, I implore you. I'm not completely healthy—I may even say that I'm sick—but I know the difference between fact and illusion. I haven't slept for nights, and I kept wondering whether I should call you or not. I decided not to—but this evening it occurred to me that if I couldn't trust you with a thing like this, then there is no one I could talk to. I read you and I know that you have a sense of the great mysteries—" Esther said all this stammering and with pauses. For a moment her eyes smiled, and then they became sad and wavering.

I said, "You can tell me everything."

"I am afraid that you'll think me insane."

"I swear I will not."

Esther bit her lower lip. "I want you to know that I saw Hitler," she said.

Even though I was prepared for something unusual, my throat constricted. "When—where?"

"You see, you are frightened already. It happened three years ago—almost four. I saw him here on Broadway."

"On the street?"

"In the cafeteria."

I tried to swallow the lump in my throat. "Most probably someone resembling him," I said finally.

"I knew you would say that. But remember, you've promised to listen. You recall the fire in the cafeteria?"

"Yes, certainly."

"The fire has to do with it. Since you don't believe me anyhow, why draw it out? It happened this way. That night I didn't sleep. Usually when I can't sleep, I get up and make tea, or I try to read a book, but this time some power commanded me to get dressed and go out. I can't explain to you how I dared walk on Broadway at that late hour. It must have been two or three o'clock. I reached the cafeteria, thinking perhaps it stays open all night. I tried to look in, but the large window was covered by a curtain. There was a pale glow inside. I tried the revolving door and it turned. I went in and saw a scene I will not forget to the last day of my life. The tables were shoved together and around them sat men in white robes, like doctors or orderlies, all with swastikas on their sleeves. At the head sat Hitler. I beg you to hear me out—even a deranged person sometimes deserves to be listened to. They all spoke German. They didn't see me. They were busy with the Führer. It grew quiet and he started to talk. That abominable voice—I heard it many times on the radio. I didn't make out exactly what he said. I was too terrified to take it in. Suddenly one of his henchmen looked back at me and jumped up from his chair. How I came out alive I will never know. I ran with all my strength, and I was trembling all over. When I got home, I said to myself, 'Esther, you are not right in the head.' I still don't know how I lived through that night. The next morning, I didn't go straight to work but walked to the cafeteria to see if it was really there. Such an experience makes a person doubt his own senses. When I arrived, I found the place had burned down. When I saw this, I knew it had to do with what I had seen. Those who were there wanted all traces erased. These are the plain facts. I have no reason to fabricate such queer things."

We were both silent. Then I said, "You had a vision."

"What do you mean, a vision?"

"The past is not lost. An image from years ago remained present somewhere in the fourth dimension and it reached you just at that moment."

"As far as I know, Hitler never wore a long white robe."

"Perhaps he did."

"Why did the cafeteria burn down just that night?" Esther asked.

"It could be that the fire evoked the vision."

"There was no fire then. Somehow I foresaw that you would give me this kind of explanation. If this was a vision, my sitting here with you is also a vision."

"It couldn't have been anything else. Even if Hitler is living and is hiding out in the United States, he is not likely to meet his cronies at a cafeteria on Broadway. Besides, the cafeteria belongs to a Jew."

"I saw him as I am seeing you now."

"You had a glimpse back in time."

"Well, let it be so. But since then I have had no rest. I keep thinking about it. If I am destined to lose my mind, this will drive me to it."

The telephone rang and I jumped up with a start. It was a wrong number. I sat down again. "What about the psychiatrist your lawyer sent you to? Tell it to him and you'll get full compensation."

Esther looked at me sidewise and unfriendly. "I know what you mean. I haven't fallen that low yet."

V

I was afraid that Esther would continue to call me. I even planned to change my telephone number. But weeks and months passed and I never heard from her or saw her. I didn't go to the cafeteria. But I often thought about her. How can the brain produce such nightmares? What goes on in that little marrow behind the skull? And what guarantee do I have that the same sort of thing will not happen to me? And how do we know that the human species will not end like this? I have played with the idea that all of humanity suffers from schizophrenia. Along with the atom, the personality of *Homo sapiens* has been splitting. When it comes to technology, the brain still functions, but in everything else degeneration has begun. They are all insane: the Communists, the Fascists, the preachers of democracy, the writers, the painters, the clergy, the atheists. Soon technology, too, will disintegrate. Buildings will collapse, power plants will stop generating electricity. Generals will drop atomic bombs on their own populations. Mad revolutionaries will run in the streets, crying fantastic slogans. I have often thought that it would begin in New York. This metropolis has all the symptoms of a mind gone berserk.

But since insanity has not yet taken over altogether, one has to act as though there were still order—according to Vaihinger's principle of "as if." I continued with my scribbling. I delivered manuscripts to the publisher. I lectured. Four times a year, I sent checks to the federal government, the state. What was left after my expenses I put in the savings bank. A teller entered some numbers in my bankbook and this meant that I was provided for. Somebody printed a few lines in a magazine or newspaper, and this signified that my value as a writer had gone up. I saw with amazement that all my efforts turned into paper. My apartment was one big wastepaper basket. From day to day, all this paper was getting drier and more parched. I woke up at night fearful that it would ignite. There was not an hour when I did not hear the sirens of fire engines.

A year after I had last seen Esther, I was going to Toronto to read a paper about Yiddish in the second half of the nineteenth century. I put a few shirts in my valise as well as papers of all kinds, among them one that made me a citizen of the United States. I had enough paper money in my pocket to pay for a taxi to Grand Central. But the taxis seemed to be taken. Those that were not refused to stop. Didn't the drivers see me? Had I suddenly become one of those who see and are not seen? I decided to take the subway. On my way, I saw Esther. She was not alone but with someone I had known years ago, soon after I arrived in the United States. He was a frequenter of a cafeteria on East Broadway. He used to sit at a table, express opinions, criticize, grumble. He was a small man, with sunken cheeks the color of brick, and bulging eyes. He was angry at the new writers. He belittled the old ones. He rolled his own cigarettes and dropped ashes into the plates from which we ate. Almost two decades had passed since I had last seen him. Suddenly he appears with Esther. He was even holding her arm. I had never seen Esther look so well. She was wearing a new coat, a new hat. She smiled at me and nodded. I wanted to stop her, but my watch showed that it was late. I barely managed to catch the train. In my bedroom, the bed was already made. I undressed and went to sleep.

In the middle of the night, I awoke. My car was being switched, and I almost fell out of bed. I could not sleep any more and I tried to remember the name of the little man I had seen with Esther. But I was unable to. The thing I did remember was that even thirty years ago he had been far from young. He had come to the United States in 1905 after the revolution in Russia. In Europe, he had a reputation as a speaker and public figure. How old must he be now? According to my calculations, he had to be in the late eighties—perhaps even ninety. Is it possible that Esther could be intimate with such an old man? But this evening he had not looked old. The longer I brooded about it in the darkness, the stranger the encounter seemed to me. I even imagined that somewhere in a newspaper I had read that he had died. Do corpses walk around on Broadway? This would mean that Esther, too, was not living. I raised the window shade and sat up and looked out into the night— black, impenetrable, without a moon. A few stars ran along with the train for a while and then they disappeared. A lighted factory emerged; I saw machines but no operators. Then it was swallowed in the darkness and another group of stars began to follow the train. I was turning with the earth on its axis. I was circling with it around the sun and moving in the direction of a constellation whose name I had forgotten. Is there no death? Or is there no life?

I thought about what Esther had told me of seeing Hitler in the cafeteria. It had seemed utter nonsense, but now I began to reappraise the idea. If time and space are nothing more than forms of perception, as Kant argues, and quality, quantity, causality are only categories of thinking, why shouldn't Hitler confer with his Nazis in a cafeteria on Broadway? Esther didn't sound insane. She had seen a piece of reality that the heavenly censorship prohibits as a rule. She had caught a glimpse behind the curtain of the phenomena. I regretted that I had not asked for more details.

In Toronto, I had little time to ponder these matters, but when I returned to New York I went to the cafeteria for some private investigation. I met only one man I knew: a rabbi who had become an agnostic and given up his job. I asked him about Esther. He said, "The pretty little woman who used to come here?"

"Yes."

"I heard that she committed suicide."

"When—how?"

"I don't know. Perhaps we are not speaking about the same person."

No matter how many questions I asked and how much I described Esther, everything remained vague. Some young woman who used to come here had turned on the gas and made an end of herself—that was all the ex-rabbi could tell me.

I decided not to rest until I knew for certain what had happened to Esther and also to that half writer, half politician I remembered from East Broadway. But I grew busier from day to day. The cafeteria closed. The neighborhood changed. Years have passed and I have never seen Esther again. Yes, corpses do walk on Broadway. But why did Esther choose that particular corpse? She could have got a better bargain even in this world.

The Joke

I

WHY should a Polish Jew in New York publish a literary magazine in German? The magazine, *Das Wort*, was supposed to come out every three months but barely made it three times a year and sometimes only twice—a little volume of ninety-six pages. None of the German writers who appeared there were known to me. Hitler was already in power and these writers were all refugees. Manuscripts came from Paris, Switzerland, London, and even Australia. The stories were ponderous, with sentences whole pages long. No matter how I tried, I could not finish one of them. The poems had neither rhyme nor rhythm, and as far as I could judge they had no content.

The publisher, Liebkind Bendel, came from Galicia, had lived for years in Vienna, and had become rich here in New York on the stock market and in real estate. He had liquidated all his stocks about six months before the 1929 crash, and at a time when money was a rarity he possessed a lot of cash, with which he bought buildings.

We became acquainted because Liebkind Bendel was planning to publish a magazine like *Das Wort* in Yiddish; he wanted me to be his editor. We met many times in restaurants, cafés, and also in Liebkind Bendel's apartment on Riverside Drive. He was a tiny man with a narrow skull without a single hair, a long face, a pointed nose, a longish chin, and small, almost feminine hands and feet. His eyes were yellow, like amber. He seemed to me like a ten-year-old boy on whom someone had put the head of an adult. He wore gaudy clothes—gold brocade ties. Liebkind Bendel had many interests. He collected autographs and manuscripts, bought antiques, belonged to chess clubs, and considered himself a gourmet and a Don Juan. He liked gadgets—watches that were also calendars, fountain pens with flashlights. He bet on the horses,

Translated by the author and Dorothea Straus

drank cognac, had a huge collection of erotic literature. He was always working on a plan—to save humanity, to give Palestine back to the Jews, to reform family life, to turn matchmaking into a science and an art. One pet idea was a lottery for which the prize would be a beautiful girl—a Miss America or a Miss Universe.

Liebkind Bendel had a German wife, Friedel, no taller than he but broad, with black curly hair. She was the daughter of a laundress and a railroad worker in Hamburg; both her parents were Aryan, but Friedel looked Jewish. For years she had been writing a dissertation on Schlegel's translation of Shakespeare. She did all the work at home and in addition was her husband's secretary. He also had a mistress, Sarah, a widow and the mother of an insane daughter. Sarah lived in Brownsville. Liebkind Bendel once introduced me to her.

Liebkind Bendel's only language was Yiddish. To those who didn't know Yiddish he spoke a lingo that combined Yiddish, German, and English. He had a talent for mangling words. It didn't take me long to realize that he had no connection with literature. The real editor of *Das Wort* was Friedel. The Yiddish version never came to be, but something attracted me to that playful little man. Perhaps it was that I could not fathom him. Every time I thought I knew him, some new whim popped up.

Liebkind Bendel often spoke about his correspondence with an old and famous Hebrew writer, Dr. Alexander Walden, a philosopher who had lived for years in Berlin. There he edited a Hebrew encyclopedia, whose early volumes appeared before the First World War. The publication of this encyclopedia dragged on for so many years that it became a joke. It was said that the last volume would appear after the coming of the Messiah and the resurrection of the dead, when the names included in it would have three dates: the day of birth, the day of death, and the day of arising from the grave.

From the beginning, the encyclopedia had been supported by a Berlin Maecenas, Dan Kniaster, now an old man in his eighties. Although Alexander Walden was supported by Dan Kniaster, he acted like a rich man. He had a large apartment around the Kurfürstendamm, owned many paintings, kept a butler. When he was young, a miracle had happened to Alexander Walden: the daughter of a Jewish multimillionaire, a relative of the Tietzs and the Warburgs, Mathilda Oppenheimer, had fallen in love with him. She lived with him only a few months and then divorced him. But the knowledge that Dr. Alexander Walden had for a time been the husband of a German heiress and wrote in German made the Hebraists stand in awe of him. Since he ignored them, they accused him of being a snob. He avoided even speaking Yiddish, though he was the son of a rabbi from a small village in Poland. He was said to be on intimate terms with Einstein, Freud, and Bergson.

Why Liebkind Bendel was eager to correspond with Dr. Alexander Walden is not clear to me to this day. Dr. Walden had the reputation of not answering letters, and Liebkind Bendel liked to show that no one could defy him. He wrote, asking Alexander Walden to contribute to *Das Wort*. His letters were ignored. He sent long cables, but still Dr. Walden kept silent. At this, Liebkind Bendel resolved to get a letter from Dr. Walden at any price.

In New York, Liebkind Bendel met a Hebrew bibliographer, Dov Ben Zev, who had become half blind from too much reading. Dov Ben Zev knew by heart almost every word Dr. Walden had written. Liebkind Bendel invited Dov Ben Zev to his apartment, had Friedel prepare a supper of blintzes and sour cream, and with the two of them worked out an elaborate scheme. A letter was sent to Dr. Walden, supposedly written by a wealthy girl in New York, a connection of the Lehmans' and the Schiffs', an heiress to many millions—Miss Eleanor Seligman-Braude. It was a letter full of love and admiration for Dr. Walden's works and personality. The knowledge of Dr. Walden's writings was Dov Ben Zev's, the classic German was Freidel's, and the flattery was Liebkind Bendel's.

Liebkind Bendel grasped correctly that in spite of his age Dr. Walden still dreamed of a new rich match. What could be better bait than an American millionairess, unmarried and deeply immersed in Dr. Walden's work? Almost immediately came an airmail handwritten letter eight pages long. Dr. Walden answered love with love. He wanted to come to New York.

Friedel never wrote more than the one letter; she protested that the whole business was an ugly trick and would have nothing more to do with it. But Liebkind Bendel got hold of an old refugee from Germany, a Frau Inge Schuldiener, who was willing to collaborate with him. A correspondence began that lasted from 1933 to 1938. During these years, only one thing kept Dr. Walden from arriving in New York—the fact that he suffered severely from seasickness. In 1937, Dan Kniaster, his property in Berlin about to be confiscated, his business taken over by his sons, had moved to London. He took Dr. Walden with him. On the short trip across the Channel, Dr. Walden became so sick that he had to be carried off the boat at Dover on a stretcher.

One morning in the summer of 1938, I was called to the pay telephone downstairs in my rooming house at seven o'clock. I had gone to sleep late, and it took me some time to get into my bathrobe and slippers and to go down the three flights of stairs. Liebkind Bendel was calling.

"Did I wake you, huh?" he screamed. "I'm in a jam. I haven't slept a wink all night. If you won't help me, I'm ruined. Liebkind Bendel is a goner. You can say Kaddish for me."

"What happened?"

"Dr. Walden is arriving by plane. Frau Schuldiener got a telegram for Eleanor from London. He sent her a thousand kisses!"

It took a few seconds for me to realize what was happening. "What do you want me to do?" I asked. "Disguise myself as an heiress?"

"Oy! Have I made a mess of things! If I weren't afraid that war would break out any day, I would run away to Europe. What shall I do? I am crazy. I should be shut up in a madhouse. Somebody has to meet him."

"Eleanor could be in California."

"But she has just assured him she was staying in the city this summer. Anyway, her address is a furnished room in the West Eighties. He will know immediately that this is not the apartment of a millionairess. He has her telephone number, and Frau Schuldiener will answer and all hell will break loose. She is a *Jaecki* and has no sense of humor."

"I doubt if even God could help you."

"What shall I do—kill myself with suicide? Until now he has been afraid to fly. Suddenly the old idiot got courage. I am ready to donate a million dollars to Rabbi Meir, the miracle worker, that his plane should fall into the ocean. But God and I are not pals. The two of us have until eight this evening."

"Please don't make me a partner in your adventures."

"You are the only one of my friends who knows about it. Last night Friedel was so angry she threatened me with divorce. That schlemiel Dov Ben Zev is in the hospital. I telephoned the Hebraists, but Dr. Walden slighted them so long they have become his bloody enemies. He didn't even make hotel reservations. He most probably expects Eleanor to lead him to the wedding canopy straight from the airport."

"Really, I cannot help you."

"At least let's have breakfast together—if I can't talk to someone, I'll lose my mind. What time do you want to eat?"

"I want to sleep, not to eat."

"Me, too. I took three pills last night. I hear that Dan Kniaster left Germany without a pfennig. He's an old has-been of eighty-five. His sons are real Prussians, assimilationists, half converted. If war breaks out, this Dr. Walden will become a burden on my neck. And how can I explain things to him? He may get a stroke."

We left it that we would meet at eleven o'clock in a restaurant on Broadway. I returned to bed but not to sleep. I half dozed, half laughed to myself, playing with a solution—not because of any loyalty to Liebkind Bendel but in the same way that I sometimes tried to solve a puzzle in a newspaper.

I I

At the restaurant, I hardly recognized Liebkind Bendel. Even though he wore a yellow jacket, a red shirt, and a tie with golden dots, his face looked as pale as after an illness. He was twisting a long cigar between his lips and he had already ordered cognac. He sat on the edge of his chair. Before I managed to sit down, he called to me. "I've found a way out, but you must help me. Eleanor has just perished in an airplane crash. I spoke to Frau Schuldiener and she will back me up. All you have to do is wait for that old skirt chaser at the airport and get him into a hotel. Tell him you are Eleanor's friend or nephew. I will take a room for him and pay the bill for a month in advance. After that I am not responsible. Let him go back to London to find himself a daughter of a lord."

"You could pose as Eleanor's friend as well as I."

"I can't do it. He'd cling to me like a leech. What can he get from you—your manuscripts? You will spend a few hours with him and he won't bother you any more. If worst comes to worse, I'll pay his fare back to England. You will be saving my life and I will never forget it. Don't give him your address. Tell him you live in Chicago or Miami. There was a time when I would have given a fortune to be in his company half an hour, but I have lost the appetite. I am afraid of him. I'm sure that the minute I see him and he utters the name Eleanor I'll burst out laughing. As a matter of fact, I have been sitting here laughing to myself. The waiter thought I had gone out of my mind."

"Bendel, I cannot do it."

"Is this your last word?"

"I cannot play such a farce."

"Well, no is no. I will have to do it, then—I'll tell him that I am a distant cousin, a poor relation. She even supported me. What name should I take? Lipman Geiger. I had a partner in Vienna by that name. Wait, I must make a telephone call."

Liebkind Bendel jumped up and ran to a telephone booth. He stayed there about ten minutes. I could see him through the glass door. He was turning the pages of a notebook. He made strange grimaces. When he returned, he said, "I have gotten a hotel and all the rest of it. What did I need the whole meshuggas for? I'm going to close down the magazine. I will go to Palestine and become a Jew. All these writers—empty heads, they have nothing to say. At fifty my grandfather woke up every night for the midnight prayers; Dr. Walden wants to seduce an heiress at sixty-five. His last letter was simply a song—the Song of Songs. And who needs his encyclopedia? That Frau Schuldiener is a fool, and in addition she plays the fool."

"Perhaps he would marry Frau Schuldiener."

"She's over seventy. Already a great-grandmother. She was once a teacher in Frankfurt . . . in Hamburg—I have forgotten where. She copied her phrases from a book of standard love letters. Perhaps what I should do is get hold of a female who could play the role of Eleanor. How about the Yiddish actresses?"

"All they can do is weep."

"Somewhere in New York there may be a true admirer of his—an old spinster who would be eager for such a match. But where do you find her? As for me, I'm tired of everything. That Friedel is educated enough but without any imagination. All she thinks about is Schlegel. Sarah is completely absorbed by her crazy daughter. They have a new custom— they send the patients home from the institutions and then they take them back again. One month she is there and the other with her mother. I sit with them and I begin to feel that I am not all there myself. Why am I telling you all this? Do me a favor and come with me to the airport. I will always remember it. Do you agree? Give me your hand. Together we'll manage somehow. Let's drink to it."

III

I stood behind the glass partition and watched the passengers arriving. Liebkind Bendel was jittery, and the smoke from his cigar almost asphyxiated me. For some reason I was sure that Dr. Walden was a tall man. But he was short, broad, and fat, with a big belly and a huge head. On that hot summer day he wore a long coat, a flowing tie, and a plush hat with a broad brim. He had a thick gray mustache and was smoking a pipe. He carried two leather valises with old-fashioned locks and side pockets. His eyes under his heavy brows were searching for someone.

Liebkind Bendel's nervousness was contagious. He smelled of liquor, he purred like a tomcat. He waved his hands and cried, "Certainly that's he. I recognize him. See how fat he has gotten—broader than he is long. An old billy goat."

When Dr. Walden came up on the escalator, Liebkind Bendel pushed me toward him. I wanted to run away but I couldn't. Instead, I stepped forward. "Dr. Walden?"

Dr. Walden put down his suitcases, removed the pipe from between his blackish teeth and set it, still lighted, in his pocket. "*Ja.*"

"Dr. Walden," I said, in English, "I am a friend of Miss Eleanor

Seligman-Braude. There was an accident. Her plane crashed." I spoke hurriedly. I felt a dryness in my throat and palate.

I expected a scene, but he just looked at me from under his bushy brows. He cupped his ear and answered me in German. "Would you mind repeating that? I cannot understand your American English."

"A misfortune has happened—a great misfortune." Liebkind Bendel began to speak in Yiddish. "Your friend was flying from California and her plane fell down. It fell right into the sea. All passengers were killed —sixty persons."

"When? How?"

"Yesterday—seventy innocent people—mostly mothers of children." Liebkind Bendel spoke with a Galician accent and singsong. "I was her near friend and so was this young man. We had heard that you were arriving. We wanted to telegraph you, but it was already too late, so we came to greet you. It's a great honor for us, but it's heartbreaking to have to bring such terrible tidings." Liebkind Bendel waved his arms; he shook and screamed into Dr. Walden's ear as though he were deaf.

Dr. Walden took off his hat and placed it on top of his luggage. He was bald in the front but at the back of his head he had a shock of graying blond hair. He took out a soiled handkerchief and wiped the sweat from his forehead. I had the feeling that he still did not understand. He seemed to be considering. His face sagged; he looked dusty, crumpled, unshaved. Clumps of hair protruded from his ears and nostrils. He smelled of medicine. After a while he said in German, "I expected her here in New York. Why did she go to California?"

"For business. Fraulein Seligman-Braude was a business lady. It concerned a big sum—millions—and here in America they say, 'Business before and later pleasure.' She was hurrying back to meet you. But it wasn't destined to be." Liebkind Bendel delivered this in one breath and his voice became shrill. "She told me everything. She worshipped you, Dr. Walden, but man proposes and God imposes, as they say. Eighty healthy people—young women and tiny babies—in the primes of their lives—"

"May I ask you who you are?" Dr. Walden said.

"A friend, a friend. This young man is a Yiddish writer." Liebkind Bendel pointed at me. "He writes in Yiddish papers and all the rest of it—*feuilletons* and what have you. Everything in the mother language so that plain people should enjoy. We have many *landsleit* here in New York, and English is a dried-up tongue for them. They want the juiciness from the old country."

"*Ja.*"

"Dr. Walden, we have rented a hotel room for you," Liebkind Bendel said. "My sympathy to you! Really, this is tragic. What was her name?—Fraulein Braude-Seligson was a wonderful woman. Gentle, with nice manners. Beautiful also. She knew Hebrew and ten other languages. Suddenly something breaks in a motor, a screw gets loose, and all this culture is finished. That is what man is—a straw, a speck of dust, a soap bubble."

I was grateful to Dr. Walden for his dignified behavior. He did not weep, he did not cry out. He raised his brows and his watery eyes, full of red veins, stared at us with astonishment and suspicion. He asked, "Where can I find the men's room? The trip has made me sick."

"Right there, right there!" Liebkind Bendel shouted. "There is no lack of toilets in America. Come with us, Dr. Walden—we just passed the washroom."

Liebkind Bendel lifted one valise, I the other, and we led Dr. Walden to the men's room. He looked questioningly at us and at his luggage. Then he entered the washroom and remained there for quite a long time.

I said, "He behaved like a fine man."

"The worst is over. I was afraid that he might faint. I am not going to forsake him. Let him stay in New York as long as he wants. Perhaps he will write for *Das Wort* after all. I would make him the main editor and all of that. Friedel is tired of it. The writers ask for royalties and send angry letters. If they find a misprint or a single line is missing, your life is in danger. I will give him thirty dollars a week and let him sit and scribble. We could publish the magazine half in German, half in Yiddish. You two together could be the editors. Friedel would be satisfied to be the editorial—how do you call it?—superintendent."

"You told me yourself that Dr. Walden hates Yiddish."

"Today he hates it, tomorrow he will love it. For a few pennies and a compliment you can buy all these intellectuals."

"You shouldn't have told him that I am a Yiddish writer."

"There are a lot of things I shouldn't have done. In the first place I shouldn't have been born, in the second place I shouldn't have married Friedel, in the third place I never should have begun this funny comedy, in the fourth place . . . Since I haven't mentioned your name, he will never find you. It's all because of my admiration for great men. I always loved writers. If a man had something printed in a newspaper or a magazine, he was God. I read the *Neue Freie Presse* as if it were the Bible. Every month I received *Haolam*, and there Dr. Walden published his articles. I ran to lectures like a madman. That is how I met Friedel. Here is our Dr. Walden."

Dr. Walden seemed shaky. His face was yellow. He had forgotten to button his fly. He stared at us and muttered. Then he said, "Excuse me," and he went back into the washroom.

IV

Dr. Walden had asked for my address and telephone number, and I gave him both. I could not cheat this learned man. The day after his arrival in New York, Liebkind Bendel left for Mexico City. Lately he was always flying to Mexico. I suspected he had a mistress there, and most probably business, too. In a strange way, Liebkind Bendel combined the roles of merchant and art connoisseur. He went to Washington to try to get a visa for a Jewish writer in Germany, and there he became a partner in a factory that produced airplane parts. The owner was a Jew from Poland who was in the leather business and had not the slightest knowledge of aviation. I had begun to realize that the world of economy, industry, and so-called practical matters was not much more substantial than that of literature and philosophy.

One day when I came home after lunch, I found a message that Dr. Walden had called. I telephoned him and I heard a stammering and a wheezing. He spoke to me in Germanized Yiddish. He mispronounced my name. He said, "Please come over. I am *kaput*."

Liebkind Bendel had put Dr. Walden in an Orthodox Jewish hotel downtown, though the two of us lived uptown. I suspected that he wanted to keep him as far away as possible. I took the subway to Lafayette Street and walked over to the hotel. The lobby was full of rabbis. They seemed to be having a conference. They strolled up and down in their long gaberdines and velvet hats. They gesticulated, clutched at their beards, and all spoke at the same time. The elevator stopped at each floor and through the open doors I saw a bride being photographed in her wedding dress, yeshiva boys packing prayer books and shawls, and waiters in skullcaps cleaning up after a banquet. I knocked on Dr. Walden's door. He appeared in a burgundy-red bathrobe down to his ankles. It was covered with spots. He wore scuffed slippers. The room reeked of tobacco, valerian drops, and the rancid smell of illness. He looked bloated, old, confused. He asked, "Are you Mr.—what is the name—the editor of *Jugend*?"

I told him my name.

"Do you write for that jargon *Tageblatt*?"

I gave him the name of my newspaper.

"Well—*ja*."

After Dr. Walden tried again and again to speak to me in German, he finally changed to Yiddish, with all the inflections and pronunciations of the village he came from. He said, "What kind of calamity is this? Why all of a sudden did she fly to California? For years I could not make up my mind whether to take this trip or not. Like Kant, I suffer from travel phobia. A friend of mine, Professor Mondek, a relative of the famous Mondek, gave me pills but they prevented me from urinating. I was sure my end had come. A fine thing, I thought, if the airplane arrives to New York with me dead. Instead, she is gone. I just cannot grasp it. I asked someone and he had not heard of this plane crash. I called her number and an old woman answered. She must be deaf and senile—she sounded incoherent. Who was the other little man who met me at the airport?"

"Lipman Geiger."

"Geiger—a grandson of Abraham Geiger? The Geigers don't speak Yiddish. Most of them are converted."

"This Geiger comes from Poland."

"What was his connection with Miss Eleanor Seligman-Braude?"

"Friends."

"I am completely bewildered." Dr. Walden spoke half to me, half to himself. "I know English from reading Shakespeare. I have read *The Tempest* in the original a number of times. It is Shakespeare's greatest work. Each line is deeply symbolic. A masterpiece in every way. Caliban is actually Hitler. But here they speak an English that sounds like Chinese. I don't understand a single word they say. Did Miss Eleanor Seligman-Braude have any family?"

"Distant relatives. But as far as I know she kept away from them."

"What will happen to her fortune? Usually rich people leave a will. Not that I have any interest in such matters—absolutely none. And what about the body? Isn't there going to be a funeral in New York?"

"Her body is somewhere in the ocean."

"Do they fly from California to New York over the ocean?"

"It seems that instead of east the plane flew west."

"How could this be? Where was this crash reported? In what newspaper? When?"

"All I know is what Lipman Geiger told me. He was her friend, not I."

"What? A riddle, a riddle. One should not go against one's own nature. Once, Immanuel Kant was about to take a trip from Königsberg to some other town in Prussia. He had traveled only a short distance when there was rain, lightning, and thunder, and he immediately gave orders to turn back. Somewhere I knew all the time that this trip would be a fiasco. I have nothing to do here—absolutely nothing. But I cannot fly back to London in my present condition. To go by ship would be even worse. I will tell you the truth, I brought almost no money with me. My great friend and benefactor, Dan Kniaster, is now a refugee himself. I worked on an encyclopedia, but we left the plates in Berlin—even the manuscripts. The Nazis had placed a time bomb in our office and we just missed being torn to pieces. Does anybody know that I am in New York? I traveled, as they say, incognito. As things are now, perhaps it would be useful to let the newspapers know. I have many enemies here, but perhaps somewhere a friend might be found."

"I think Lipman Geiger notified the newspapers."

"There is no mention of me anywhere. I asked for the papers." Dr. Walden pointed to a pile of Yiddish newspapers on a chair.

"I will do my best."

"At my age one should not undertake such adventures. Where is that Mr. Geiger?"

"He had to fly to Mexico but he will be back soon."

"To Mexico? What is he doing in Mexico? So, this is my end. I am not afraid of death, but I have no desire to be buried in this wild city. True, London is not much quieter but at least I have a few acquaintances there."

"You will live, Dr. Walden," I said. "You will live to see the fall of Hitler."

"What for? Hitler still has something to spoil on this earth. But I have already committed all my blunders. Too many. This unlucky trip is not even a tragedy. Just a joke—well—*ja*, my life is one big joke, from the beginning to the end."

"You have given much to humanity, to the Jewish reader."

"Trifles, rubbish, junk. Did you personally know Miss Seligman-Braude?"

"Yes—no. I just heard of her."

"I didn't like that Geiger—a buffoon. What do you write in the Yiddish newspapers? What is there to write about? We are returning to the jungle. *Homo sapiens* is bankrupt. All values are gone—literature, science, religion. Well, for my part I have given up altogether."

Dr. Walden took a letter from his pocket. It was stained with coffee and ashes. He scrutinized it, closing one eye, wincing and snorting. "I begin to suspect that this Miss Seligman-Braude never existed."

V

Late one evening when I was lying on my bed fully dressed, brooding about my laziness, neglected work, and lack of will power, I got the signal that I was wanted on the pay telephone downstairs. I ran down the three flights of steps, lifted the receiver, which dangled from a cord, and heard an unfamiliar voice saying my name. The voice said, "I am Dr. Linder. Are you a friend of Dr. Alexander Walden?"

"I have met him."

"Dr. Walden has had a heart attack and is in the Beth Aaron Hospital. He gave me your name and telephone number. Are you a relative?"

"No relative."

"Doesn't he have any family here?"

"It seems not."

"He asked me to call Professor Albert Einstein, but nobody answers. I cannot be bothered with such errands. Come tomorrow to the hospital. He is in the ward. That's all we could give him for the time being. I'm sorry."

"What's the situation?"

"Not too good. He has a whole list of complications. You can visit him between twelve and two or six and eight. Goodbye."

I searched for a nickel to call Friedel but found only a fifty-cent piece and two dollar bills. I went out on Broadway to get change. By the time I had it and found a drugstore with an unoccupied telephone booth, more than half an hour had passed. I dialed Friedel's number and the line was busy. For another quarter of an hour I kept on dialing the same number and it was always busy. A woman entered the next booth and lined up her coins. She looked back at me with a smug expression that seemed to say, "You're waiting in vain." As she spoke, she gesticulated with her cigarette. From time to time she twirled a lock of her bleached hair. Her scarlet, pointed claws suggested a rapaciousness as deep as the human tragedy.

I found a penny and weighed myself. According to this scale, I had lost four pounds. A slip of cardboard fell out. It read, "You are a person with gifts but you waste them on nothing."

I will try once more, and if the telephone is still busy I will go home immediately, I vowed to myself. This scale told the bitter truth.

The line wasn't busy. I heard Friedel's mannish voice. At that very moment, the lady with the bleached hair and scarlet nails hurriedly left the booth. She winked at me with her false eyelashes. "Mrs. Bendel," I said, "I am sorry to disturb you. Dr. Walden has had a heart attack. They have taken him to Beth Aaron Hospital. He is in the ward."

"Oh, my God! I knew that nothing good would come of that joke. I warned Liebkind. It was a crime—absolutely a crime. That is the way Liebkind is—a trick occurs to him and he doesn't know when to stop. What can I do? I don't even know where he is now. He was supposed to stop in Cuba. Where are you?"

"In a drugstore on Broadway."

"Perhaps you could come here. This is no trifling matter. I feel guilty myself. I should have refused to write that first letter. Come up, it's still early. I never go to sleep before two o'clock."

"What do you do until two?"

"Oh, I read, I think, I worry."

"Well, this evening is lost already," I mumbled or thought. I had only a few blocks to walk to Liebkind Bendel's apartment on Riverside Drive. The doorman there knew me. I went up to the fourteenth floor, and the moment I touched the bell Friedel opened the door.

Friedel was short, with wide hips and heavy legs. She had a crooked nose and brown eyes under masculine brows. As a rule, she dressed in dark clothes, and I had never noticed a trace of cosmetics on her. Most of the time when I visited Liebkind Bendel, she immediately brought me half a glass of tea, spoke a few words, and returned to her books and manuscripts. Liebkind Bendel used to say jocosely, "What can you expect from a wife who is an editor? It's a miracle that she can prepare a glass of tea."

This time Friedel had on a white sleeveless dress and white shoes. She was wearing lipstick. She invited me into the living room, and on the coffee table stood a bowl of fruit, a pitcher filled with something to drink, and a plate of cookies. Friedel spoke English with a strong German accent. She indicated the sofa for me and sat down on a chair. She said, "I knew it would end badly. From the beginning, it was the Devil's own game. If Dr. Walden dies, Liebkind will be responsible for his death. Old men are romantic. They forget their years and their powers. That imbecile Frau Schuldiener wrote to him in such a way that he had every reason to give himself illusions. One can fool anybody, even a sage." (Friedel used the Yiddish word *chochom*.)

One could even fool Liebkind Bendel, something whispered in my brain—a dybbuk or an imp. Aloud I said, "You should not have permitted things to go so far, Madame Bendel."

Friedel frowned with her thick brows. "Liebkind does as he pleases. He doesn't ask my advice. He goes away, and I really don't know where or for what purpose. He was supposed to go to Mexico. At the last minute he announced that he wanted to stop in Havana. He has no business either in Havana or in Mexico City. You probably know much more about him than I do. I'm sure he boasts to you about his conquests."

"Absolutely not. I haven't the slightest idea why he went and whom he is seeing."

"I do have an idea. But why talk about it? I know all his Galician tricks . . ."

There was silence for a while. Friedel had never spoken to me in such a manner. The few conversations we had had dealt with German literature, Schlegel's translation of Shakespeare, and with certain Yiddish expressions still in use in some German dialects, which Friedel had discovered were derived from Old German. I was about to answer that there were decent people among the Galicians when the telephone rang.

The instrument stood on a little table near the door. Friedel walked over slowly and sat down to answer it. She spoke softly, but I could tell that she was talking to Liebkind Bendel. He was calling from Havana. I expected Friedel to tell him immediately that Dr. Walden was sick and that I was visiting. But she didn't mention either fact. She spoke to him with irony: Business? Certainly. A week? Take as much time as necessary. A bargain? Buy it, why not? I? I do my work as always—what else is there?

As she spoke, she threw sidelong glances at me. She smiled knowingly. I imagined that she winked at me. What kind of crazy night is this, I thought. I got up and moved hesitatingly toward the door in the direction of the bathroom. Suddenly I did something that perplexed even me. I bent down and kissed Friedel's neck. Her left hand clutched mine and pressed with strength. Her face became both youthful and sneering. At the same time, she asked, "Liebkind, how long will you stay in Havana?"

And she got up and mockingly put the receiver to my ear. I heard Liebkind Bendel's nasal voice. He was telling of antiques to be got in Havana and explaining the difference in the exchange. Friedel leaned over to me so that our ears touched. Her hair tickled my cheek. Her ear almost burned mine. I was ashamed—like a boy. In one moment, my need to go to the bathroom became embarrassingly urgent.

Next morning when Friedel called the hospital, they told her that Dr. Walden was dead. He had died in the middle of the night. Friedel said, "Isn't that cruel? My conscience will torture me to my last moment."

The following day the Yiddish papers came out with the news. The same editors who Liebkind Bendel told me had refused to announce Dr. Walden's arrival in New York now wrote at length about his accomplishments in Hebrew literature. Obituaries also appeared in the English-language press. The photographs were at least thirty years old; in them Dr. Walden looked young, gay, with a full head of hair. According to the papers, the New York Hebraists, Dr. Walden's enemies, were making arrangements for the funeral. The Jewish telegraph service must have wired the event all over the world. Liebkind Bendel called Friedel from Havana to say that he was flying home.

Back in New York, he talked to me on the telephone for almost an hour. He kept repeating that Dr. Walden's death was not his fault. He would have died in London, too. What difference does it make where one ends? Liebkind Bendel was especially eager to know whether Dr. Walden had any manuscripts with him. He was planning to bring out a special number of *Das Wort* dedicated to him. Liebkind Bendel had brought from Havana a painting by Chagall that he had bought from a refugee. He admitted to me that it must have been stolen from a gallery. Liebkind Bendel said to me, "Well, if it had been grabbed by the Nazis, would that have been better? The Maginot Line isn't worth a pinch of tobacco. Hitler will be in Paris! Remember my words."

The chapel where the funeral was to take place was only a few blocks from Liebkind Bendel's apartment, and he, Friedel, and I arranged to meet at the chapel entrance. They were all there—the Hebraists, the Yiddishists, the Anglo-Jewish writers. Taxis kept arriving. From somewhere a small woman appeared, leading a girl who looked emaciated, disturbed. She stopped every few seconds and tapped with her foot on the sidewalk; the woman urged her forward and encouraged her. It was Sarah, Liebkind Bendel's mistress. Mother and daughter tried to go into the chapel, but it was already filled.

After a while, Liebkind Bendel and Friedel arrived in a red car. He was wearing a sand-colored suit and a gaudy tie from Havana. He looked fresh and tanned. Friedel was dressed in black, with a broad-brimmed hat. I told Liebkind that the hall was full and he said, "Don't be naïve. You will see how things are done in America." He whispered something in an usher's ear and the usher led us inside and made room for us in one of the front rows. The artificial candles of the Menorah cast a subdued light. The coffin stood near the dais. A young rabbi with a small black mustache and a tiny skullcap that blended with his shiny pomaded hair spoke a eulogy in English. He seemed to know little of Dr. Walden. He confused facts and dates. He made errors in the titles of Dr. Walden's works. Then an old rabbiner with a white goatee, a refugee from Germany, wearing a black hat that looked like a casserole, spoke in German. He stressed his umlauts and quoted long passages in Hebrew. He called Dr. Walden a pillar of Judaism. He claimed that Dr. Walden had come to America so that he could continue publishing the encyclopedia to which he had devoted his best years. "The Nazis maintain that cannons are more important than butter," the rabbiner declaimed solemnly, "but we Jews, the people of the Book, still believe in the power of the word." He appealed for funds to bring out the last volumes of the encyclopedia for which Dr. Walden had sacrificed his life, coming to America in spite of his illness. He took out a handkerchief and with a corner dabbed away a single tear from behind his misty glasses. He called attention to the fact that among the mourners here in the chapel was present the universally beloved Professor Albert Einstein, a close friend of the deceased. A general whispering and looking around began among the crowd. A few even rose to get a glimpse of the world-famous scientist.

After the German rabbiner's sermon, there was a further eulogy given by the editor of a Hebrew magazine in New York. Then a cantor in a hexagonal hat, with the face of a bulldog, recited "God Full of Mercy." He sang in loud and lugubrious tones.

Near me sat a young woman dressed in black. She had yellow hair and red cheeks. I noticed a ring with a huge diamond on her finger. When the young rabbi was speaking in English, she lifted her veil and blew her nose into a lacy handkerchief. When the old rabbiner spoke in German, she clasped her hands and wept. When the cantor cried out, "In Paradise his rest shall be!" the woman sobbed with as much abandon as the women in the old country. She bent over as though about to collapse, her face drenched with tears. Who can she be, I wondered. As far as I knew, Dr. Walden had no relatives here. I remembered Liebkind Bendel's words that somewhere in New York might be found a true admirer of Dr. Walden's who would really love him. I had realized long ago that whatever anybody can invent already exists somewhere.

After the ceremony, everyone rose and filed past the coffin. I saw ahead of me Professor Albert Einstein looking exactly as he did in his pictures, slightly stooped, his hair long. He stood for a moment, murmuring his farewell. Then I got a glimpse of Dr. Walden. The undertakers had applied their cosmetics. His head rested on a silk pillow, his face stiff as wax, closely shaved, with twirled mustache, and in the corners of his eyes a hint of a smile that seemed to say, "Well, ja, my life was one big joke—from the beginning to the end."

Powers

I

As a rule, those who come for advice to the newspaper where I work do not ask for anyone in particular. We have a reporter who turns out a regular column of advice to readers, and anyone dropping around is usually referred to him. But this man asked especially for me. He was shown my room: a tall man—he had to bend his head to come through the door—without a hat, with a shock of black hair mixed with gray. His black eyes, under shaggy brows, had a wild look that rather frightened me. He had on a light raincoat, although it was snowing outside. His square face was red from the cold. He wore no tie, and his shirt was open, showing a chest covered with hair as thick as fur. He had a broad nose and thick lips. When he talked, he revealed large, separated teeth that appeared unusually strong.

He said, "Are you the writer?"

"I am."

He seemed surprised. "This little man who sits at this table?" he said. "I imagined you somewhat different. Well, things don't have to be exactly as we imagined them. I read every word you write—Yiddish and English both. When I hear that you've published something in a magazine, I run right out to buy it."

"Thank you very much. Please sit down."

"I'd rather stand—but—well—I will sit down. May I smoke?"

"Certainly."

"I should tell you I am not an American. I came here after the Second World War. I've been through Hitler's hell, Stalin's hell, and a couple of other hells besides. But that's not why I came to you. Do you have time to listen to me?"

Translated by the author and Dorothea Straus

"Yes, I have."

"Well, everybody in America is busy. How do you have time to write all those things and to see people too?"

"There is time for everything."

"Perhaps. Here in America time disappears—a week is nothing and a month is nothing, and a year passes by between yes and no. In those hells on the other side, a day seemed longer than a year does here. I've been in this country since 1950, and the years have gone like a dream. Now it's summer, now it's winter, the years just roll away. How old do you think I am?"

"In the forties—maybe fifty."

"Add thirteen years more. In April I will be sixty-three."

"You look young—knock on wood."

"That's what everybody says. In our family we don't turn gray. My grandfather died at ninety-three and he had hardly any gray hair. He was a blacksmith. On my mother's side, they were scholars. I studied at a yeshiva I was a student at the yeshiva of Gur, and for a while in Lithuania. Only until I was seventeen, it's true, but I have a good memory. When I learn something, it stays stuck in my brain. I forget nothing, in a sense, and this is my tragedy. Once I was convinced that poring over the Talmud would be useless, I took to studying worldly books. The Russians had left by that time and the Germans had taken over. Then Poland became independent and I was drafted into the army. I helped to drive the Bolsheviks to Kiev. Then they drove us back to the Vistula. The Poles are not too fond of Jews, but I advanced. They made me a top sergeant—*chorázy*—the highest rank you can reach without military school, and after the war they offered to send me to a military academy. I might have become a colonel or something, but the barracks was not my ambition. I read a lot, painted, and tried to become a sculptor. I began to carve all sorts of figures out of wood. I ended up making furniture. Cabinet work—I specialized in repairing furniture, mostly antiques. You know how it is—inlays fall out, bits break off. It takes skill to make the patch invisible. I still don't know why I threw myself into it with such enthusiasm. To find the right grain of wood, the right color, and to fit it in so that the owner himself couldn't spot the place—for this, one needs iron patience, and instinct too.

"Now I'll tell you why I came to you. It's because you write about the mysterious powers: telepathy, spirits, hypnotism, fatalism, and so on—I read it all. I read it because I possess the powers you describe. I didn't come to boast, and don't get the idea I want to become a news-paperman. Here in America I work at my trade and I earn enough. I'm single—no wife, no children. They killed off my family. I take a drink of whiskey, but I'm not a drunkard. I have an apartment here in New

York, and a cottage in Woodstock. I don't need help from anybody.

"But to get back to the powers. You're right when you say a person is born with them. We're born with everything. I was a child of six when I first began to carve. Later I neglected it, but the gift stayed with me. And that's how it is with the powers. I had them but I didn't know what they were. I got up one morning and it came into my mind that someone in our building was going to fall out the window that day. We lived in Warsaw on Twarda Street. I didn't like the thought—it frightened me. I left for cheder, and when I came home the courtyard was black with people. The ambulance was just arriving. A glazier had been replacing a pane in a window on the second floor, and had fallen out. If such things had happened once, twice—even five times—I might have called it coincidence, but they happened so frequently there could be no question of coincidence. Strange, I began to understand that I should conceal this—as if it were an ugly birthmark. And I was right, because powers like this are a misfortune. It's better to be born deaf or lame than to possess them.

"But, no matter how careful you are, you can't hide everything. Once, I was sitting in the kitchen. My mother—peace be with her—was knitting a stocking. My father earned good money, even though he was a laborer. Our apartment was comfortable, and as clean as a rich man's house. We had a lot of copper dishes, which my mother used to scour each week until they shone. I was sitting on a low bench. I wasn't more than seven years old at the time. All of a sudden, I said, 'Mamma, there's money under the floor! There is money!' My mother stopped knitting and looked at me in amazement. 'What sort of money? What are you babbling about?' 'Money,' I said. 'Gold pieces.' My mother said, 'Are you crazy? How do you know what's under the floor?' 'I know,' I said. Already I realized that I shouldn't have said it, but it was too late.

"When my father came home for dinner, my mother told him what I had said. I wasn't there, but my father was so astonished he confessed that he had hidden a number of golden coins under the floor. I had an older sister and my father was saving a dowry for her—putting money into a bank was not the custom for simple people. When I returned from cheder, my father began to question me. 'Are you spying on me?' Actually, my father had hidden the money when I was in cheder and my mother was out marketing. My sister had gone to visit a friend. He had locked and bolted the door, and we lived on the third floor. He had even been careful enough to stuff the keyhole with cotton. I got a beating, but no matter how I tried I could not explain to him how I knew about those coins. 'This boy is a devil!' my father said, and he gave me an extra box on the ear. It was a good lesson to me to keep my mouth shut.

"I could tell you a hundred things like that about my childhood, but I'll add just one. Across the street from our home there was a store that sold dairy products. In those years, you went to the store to buy boiled milk. They boiled it on a gas range. One morning my mother gave me a pan and told me, 'Go to Zelda across the street and buy a quart of boiled milk.' I went over to the store and there was only one customer—a girl who was buying a few ounces of butter. In Warsaw they used to slice the butter from a big chunk with a bow, like the ones children carried at the Feast of Omer when they went picnicking in the Praga forest. I looked up and saw a strange thing: a light was burning over Zelda's head, as if there were a Hanukkah lamp in her wig. I stood and gaped—how was it possible? Nearby, at the counter, the girl spoke to Zelda as though there was nothing out of the way. After Zelda weighed the butter on the scale and the girl left, Zelda said, 'Come in, come in. Why are you standing there on the threshold?' I wanted to ask her, 'Why does a light burn over your head?' But I already had a hunch that I was the only one who saw it.

"The next day, when I came home from cheder, my mother said to me, 'Did you hear what happened? Zelda from the dairy store dropped dead.' You can imagine my fright. I was only about eight. Since then I've seen the same kind of light many times over the heads of those who were about to die. Thank God, I haven't seen it for the last twenty years. At my age, and among those I spend my days with, I could see those lights all the time."

II

"A while ago, you wrote that in every great love there is an element of telepathy. I was struck by this and decided that I had to see you. In my own life this happened not once, not ten times, but over and over again. In my young years I was romantic. I would see a woman and fall in love with her at first sight. In those days you couldn't just approach a woman and tell her you were in love with her. Girls were delicate creatures. A mere word was considered an insult. Also, in my own way, I was shy. Proud, too. It's not in my nature to run after women. To make it short, instead of talking to a girl, I would think about her—day and night. I fancied all kinds of impossible encounters and adventures. Then I began to notice that my thoughts took effect. The girl I had been thinking about so hard would actually come to me. Once, I deliberately waited for a woman on a crowded street in Warsaw until she appeared. I'm no mathematician, but I know the odds that this woman might cross that street at that very time were about one in twenty million. But she came, as though attracted by an invisible magnet.

"I'm not too credulous; even today I have my doubts. We want to believe that everything happens in a rational way and according to order. We're afraid of mysteries—if there are good powers, it's likely there are also evil ones, and who knows what they might do! But so many irrational things happened to me I would have to be an idiot to ignore them.

"Perhaps because I had this kind of magnetism, I never married. Anyway, I'm not the kind of man who is satisfied with one woman. I had other powers, too, but those I'm not going to boast about. I lived, as they say, in a Turkish paradise—often with as many as five or six lovers at the same time. In the drawing rooms where I used to fix furniture, I often made the acquaintance of beautiful women—mostly Gentiles. And I always heard the same song from them—I was different from other Jews, and all that kind of chatter. I had a room with a separate entrance, and that's all a bachelor needs. I kept brandy and liquors and a good supply of delicacies in my cupboard. If I were to tell you what took place in this room on my sofa, you could make a book out of it—but who cares? The older I grew, the clearer it became to me that for modern man marriage is sheer insanity. Without religion, the whole institution is absurd. Naturally, your mother and my mother were faithful women. For them there was one God and one husband.

"Now I come to the main point. In spite of all the women I had in those years, there was one I stayed with for almost thirty years—actually, until the day the Nazis bombed Warsaw. That day thousands of men crossed the bridge to Praga. I wanted to take Manya with me—Manya was her name—but she had the grippe, and I couldn't wait for her. I had plenty of connections in Poland, but in such a catastrophe they are not worth a sniff of tobacco. Later I was told that the house where I lived was hit by a bomb and reduced to a pile of lime and bricks. I never heard from Manya again.

"This Manya might have been considered an ordinary girl. She came from some little village in Greater Poland. When we met, we were both virgins. But no power and no treachery on my part could destroy the love between us. Somehow she knew of all my abominations and kept warning me that she would leave me, get married, and whatnot. But she came to me regularly every week—often more. The other women never spent the night in my room, but when Manya came she stayed. She was not particularly beautiful—dark, not tall, with black eyes. She had curly hair. In her village they called her Manya the Gypsy. She had all the antics of a gypsy. She told fortunes from cards and read palms. She believed in all kinds of witchcraft and superstitions. She even dressed like a gypsy in flowered skirts and shawls, wore large hoop earrings, and red beads around her neck. There was always a cigarette between her lips.

She made a living as a salesgirl in a lingerie shop. The owners were an elderly couple without children, and Manya became almost a daughter to them. She was an excellent saleswoman. She could sew, embroider, and even learned how to make corsets. She managed the whole business. If she had been willing to steal, she could have had a fortune, but she was one hundred percent honest. Anyhow, the old people were going to leave her the store in their will. In later years, the old man had a liver ailment, so they traveled to Carlsbad, Marienbad, and to Piszczany. And they left everything with Manya. Why did she need to get married? What she needed was a man, and I was that man. This girl, who could barely read and write, was, in her way, very refined—especially in sex. In my life I had God knows how many women, but there was never one like Manya. She had her own caprices and peculiarities, and when I think about them I don't know whether to laugh or cry. Sadism is sadism and masochism is masochism—are there names for all this nonsense? Each time we quarreled we were both terribly unhappy, and making peace was a great ceremony. She could cook fit for a king. When her bosses went to the spas, she cooked meals for me in their apartment. I used to say that her food had sex appeal, and there was some truth in it. This was her good side. The bad side was that Manya could never make peace with the idea that I had other women. She did everything she could to spoil my pleasure. By nature I am not a liar, but because of her I became one. Automatically. I didn't have to invent lies—my tongue did it by itself, and I was often astonished at how clever and farsighted a tongue can be. It foresaw events and situations—a matter I realized only later. However, you cannot fool anybody for thirty years. Manya knew my habits and she never stopped spying on me; my telephone used to ring in the middle of the night. At the same time, my business with other women gave her a perverse enjoyment. Now and again I confessed to her and she would ask for details, call me the worst names, cry, laugh, and become wild. I often felt like an animal trainer—like one who puts his head in the mouth of a lion. I always knew that my successes with other women made sense only as long as Manya was in the background. If I had Manya, the Countess Potocka was a bargain. Without Manya, no conquest was worth a groschen.

"It sometimes happened that I returned from one of my adventures, perhaps at an inn or a nobleman's estate, and I would be with Manya that same night. She refreshed me and I would begin all over again as if nothing had happened. But as I grew older I began to worry that too much love might do me some damage. I am something of a hypochondriac. I read medical books and articles in the newspapers. I worried that I might be ruining my health. Once, when I returned completely exhausted and was to meet Manya, the thought ran through my mind:

how good it would be if Manya would get her period and I would not have to spend the night with her. I called her and she said, 'A funny thing happened, I got my holiday'—this is what she called it—'in the middle of the month.' 'So you've turned into a miracle worker,' I said to myself. But I remained skeptical about its really having anything to do with my wish. Only after such things repeated themselves many times did I realize that I had the power to give orders to Manya's body. Every word I'm telling you is pure truth. A few times I willed her to become sick—of course, just for a while, because I loved her very much—and she immediately got a high fever. It became clear that I ruled over her body completely. If I had wanted her to die, she would have died. I had read books and pamphlets about mesmerism, animal magnetism, and such topics, but it never occurred to me that I possessed this power myself, and in such measure.

"Besides being able to do anything I wanted with her, I also knew her thoughts. I could literally read her mind. Once, after a bitter fight, Manya left, slamming the door so hard that the windowpanes trembled. The moment she left, it occurred to me that she was going to the Vistula to drown herself. I grabbed my overcoat and started after her silently. She went from one street to another and I trailed her like a detective. She never looked back. Finally she reached the Vistula and began to move straight toward the water. I ran after her and grabbed her shoulder. She screamed and struggled. I had saved her from death. After that, I ordered her in my mind never to think of suicide again. Later she told me, 'How strange, I often used to think of making an end to myself. Lately these thoughts have stopped completely. Can you explain this?'

"I could have explained everything. Once when she came to me, I told her, 'You have lost money today.' She became pale. It was the truth. She had returned from a savings bank and had lost six hundred zlotys."

III

"I will tell you the story about the dog and one story more and that will be enough. One summer—it must have been 1928 or 1929—I was overcome by a terrible fatigue. Hypochondria, too. I was entangled in so many affairs and complications that I almost fell apart. My telephone rang constantly. There were bitter quarrels between Manya and me that began to take on an uncanny character. At the place where she worked, the old man's wife had died, and Manya kept threatening to marry him. She had a cousin in South Africa who wrote her love letters and offered to send her an affidavit. Her great love suddenly turned to terrible hatred. She talked about poisoning herself and me. She proposed a double suicide. A fire kindled in her black eyes, which made her look like a Tartar. We are all the descendants of God knows what murderers. Did you or someone else write in your newspaper that every man is potentially a Nazi? At night I usually slept like the dead, but now I suffered from insomnia. When I finally fell asleep, I had nightmares. One morning I felt that my end had come. My legs were shaky, everything whirled before my eyes, there was a ringing in my ears. I saw that if I did not make some change, I would be finished. I decided to leave everything and go away. I packed a bag. As I packed, the telephone rang madly, but I did not answer it. I went down the street and took a droshky to the Vienna depot. A train was about to leave for Crakow, and I bought a ticket. I sat down on the second-class bench and I was so tired that I slept through the whole trip. The conductor woke me at Crakow. In Crakow I again took a droshky and told the driver to take me to a hotel. The moment I entered the hotel room, I fell down on the bed in my clothes and dozed until dawn. I say dozed, because my sleep was fitful—I slept and I did not sleep. I went to the toilet and voices screamed in my ears and bells rang. I literally heard Manya crying and calling me back. I was on the verge of a breakdown. But with my last strength I curbed myself. I had fasted for a day and a night, and when I woke at about eleven o'clock in the morning I was more dead than alive. There are no baths in the Crakow hotel rooms—if you wanted a bath, you had to order it from the maid. There was a washstand and a pitcher of water in the room. Somehow I managed to shave, eat breakfast, and get myself to a railroad station. I rode a few stops, and there the rails ended. Of course I wanted to go to the mountains, but it was not the line to Zakopane but a spur. I arrived at a village near Babia Góra. This is a mountain apart from the other mountains—a mountain individualist— and few tourists go there. There was no hotel or rooming house and I got a room with an old peasant couple—*gazdas*. I guess you know the region and I don't have to tell you how beautiful it is. But this particular village was especially beautiful and wild, perhaps because it was so isolated. The old pair had a dog—a huge specimen—I don't know what breed. They warned me that he would bite and one should be careful. I patted him on the head, I tickled his neck, and he immediately became my pal. That's an understatement—the dog fell madly in love with me—and it happened almost at once. He did not leave me for a minute. The old couple rented the room every summer, but the dog had never become attached to any lodger. To make it short, I ran away from human love and fell into canine love. Burek had all the ways of a woman, even though he was a male. He made scenes of jealousy that were worse than Manya's. I took long walks and he ran after me everywhere. There were whole packs of dogs in the village and if I only looked at another dog Burek became wild. He bit them, and me too. At night he insisted upon sleeping on my bed. In those places, dogs have fleas. I tried not to let him into my room, but he howled and wailed so, he woke half the village. I had to let him in and he immediately jumped on the bed. He cried with a human voice. They began to say in the village that I was a sorcerer. I didn't stay long, because you could die there from boredom. I had taken a few books with me, but I soon read them all. I had rested and was ready for new entanglements. But parting from Burek was not an easy business. He had sensed, with God knows what instinct, that I was about to leave. I had telephoned Manya from the post office and had received telegrams and registered letters in that godforsaken village. The dog kept on barking and howling. The last day, he went into some kind of spasm; he foamed at the mouth. The peasants were afraid he was mad. Until then, he hadn't even been tied up, but his owner got a chain and tied him to a stake. His clamor and his tearing at the chain shattered my nerves.

"I returned to Warsaw, sunburned but not really rested. What the dog did to me in that village, Manya and a few other females did in Warsaw. They all clung to me and bit me. I had orders to mend furniture, and the owners kept phoning me. A few days passed—or perhaps a few weeks; I don't remember exactly. After a difficult day, I went to bed early. I put out the lamp. I was so exhausted that I fell asleep immediately. Suddenly I woke up. Waking up in the middle of the night was not unusual for me, but this time I woke with the feeling that someone was in my room. I used to waken with a heaviness in my chest, but this time I felt an actual weight on my feet. I looked up and there was a dog lying on my blanket. The lamp was out, but it wasn't completely dark because a street lamp shone in. I recognized Burek.

"At first I had the idea that the dog had run after the train to Warsaw. But this was sheer nonsense. In the first place, he was tied up; then, no dog could run for so long after an express train. Even if the dog could have found his way to Warsaw by himself—and found my house —he could not have climbed up three flights of stairs. Besides, my door was always locked. I grasped that this was not a real dog, flesh and blood—it was a phantom. I saw his eyes, I felt the heaviness on my feet, but I didn't dare to touch him. I sat there terrified, and he looked me in the eyes with an expression utterly sad—and something else for which I have no name. I wanted to push him off and free my feet, but felt restrained. This was not a dog but a ghost. I lay down again and tried to fall asleep. After a while I succeeded. A nightmare? Call it a nightmare. But it was Burek just the same. I recognized his eyes, ears, his expression, his fur. The next day I wanted to write to the peasant to ask about the dog. But I knew that he couldn't read, and then I was too busy to write letters. I wouldn't have got an answer anyhow. I am absolutely convinced that the dog had died—what had visited me was not of this world.

"That wasn't the only time he came—over a number of years he kept returning, so that I had ample time to observe him even though he never appeared in the light. The dog was old when I left the village, and the way he looked that last day, I knew that he couldn't have lasted long. Astral body, spirit, soul—call it what you like—it is a fact so far as I'm concerned that a ghost of a dog came to me and lay on my legs, not once but dozens of times. Almost every night at first, then rarely. A dream? No, I wasn't dreaming—unless the whole of life is one dream."

I V

"I will tell you one last incident. I have already told you that a number of the women with whom I had affairs I met in the drawing rooms where I went to repair furniture. This plain man who sits here has made love to Polish countesses. What is a countess? We are all made of the same stuff. But once I met a young woman who really made me jump out of my skin. I was hired to go to a noblewoman's house in Vilanov, to mend an old pianoforte decorated with gilded garlands. While I was working, a young woman glided through the drawing room. She stopped for no more than a second, saw what I was doing, and our eyes met. How can I describe to you how she looked? Both Polish aristocrat and strangely Jewish—as if, by some magic, a gentle yeshiva student had turned into a Polish *panienka*. She had a narrow face and black eyes, such deep ones that I became confused. They actually burned me. Everything about this woman was full of spirituality. Never before have I seen such beauty. She disappeared in an instant, and I remained shattered. Later I asked the owner who that beauty was, and she said it was a niece who was visiting. She mentioned the name of some estate or town from which she came. But in my confusion I wasn't able to pay attention. I could easily have learned her name and address if I hadn't been so dazed. I finished my work; she did not show up again. But her image always stood before my eyes. I began to think about her day and night without stopping. My thoughts wore me out, and I decided to make an end of them, no matter what the cost. Manya realized that I wasn't myself and this was the cause of new scenes. I was so mixed up that, even though I knew Warsaw like my ten fingers, I got lost in the streets and made silly mistakes. It went on like this for months. Slowly my obsession weakened —or perhaps it just sank deeper inside me; I could think about someone else and at the same time brood about her. So the summer passed and it was winter, then it was spring again. One late afternoon—almost dusk

—I don't remember if it was April or May—my telephone rang. I said hello, and no one answered. However, somebody was holding the receiver at the end of the line. I called again, 'Hello, hello, hello!' and I heard a crackle and a stammering voice. I said, 'Whoever you are, be so good as to speak up.'

"After a while I heard a voice that was a woman's voice but also the voice of a boy. She said to me, 'You once worked in Vilanov, in such and such a house. Do you happen to remember someone passing through the drawing room?' My throat became tight, and I almost lost the ability to move my tongue. 'Yes, I remember you,' I said. 'Could anyone forget your face?' She was so quiet I thought she had hung up. But she began to speak again—murmur is more like it. She said, 'I have to talk to you. Where can we meet?' 'Wherever you wish,' I said. 'Would you want to come to me?' 'No, out of the question,' she said. 'Perhaps in a café—' 'No, not in a café,' I said. 'Tell me where you could meet me and I will be there.' She became silent; then she mentioned a little street near the city library, way uptown, near Mokotow. 'When do you want it to be?' I asked. And she said, 'As soon as possible.' 'Perhaps now?' 'Yes, if you can make it.' I knew that there was no café, no restaurant, not even a bench to sit on in that little street, but I told her that I was leaving at once. There had been a time when I thought that if this miracle should happen I would jump for joy. But somehow everything was silent in me. I was neither happy nor unhappy—only amazed.

"When I arrived at our meeting place, it was already night. The street had trees on both sides and few lamps. I could see her in the half darkness. She seemed leaner, and her hair was combed up in a bun. She stood near a tree, wrapped in shadow. Except for her, the street was deserted. She started when I approached her. The trees were blooming and the gutter was full of blossoms. I said to her, 'Here I am. Where can we go?' 'What I want to tell you can be said right here,' she replied. 'What do you want to tell me?' I asked. She hesitated. 'I want to ask you to leave me in peace.'

"I was startled, and said, 'I don't know what you mean.' 'You know very well,' she said. 'You don't leave me in peace. I have a husband and I am happy with him. I want to be a faithful wife.' It wasn't talking but stammering. She paused after each word. She said, 'It wasn't easy to learn who you were and your telephone number. I had to invent a story about a broken chest to get the information from my aunt. I am not a liar; my aunt did not believe me. Still, she gave me your name and address.' Then she became silent.

"I asked, 'Why can't we go somewhere to talk it over?' 'I can't go anywhere. I could have told you this on the telephone—it is all so strange, absolutely insane—but now you know the truth.' 'I really don't know what's on your mind,' I said, just to prolong the conversation. She said, 'I beseech you, by whatever is holy to you, to stop tormenting me. What you want I cannot do—I'd rather die.' And her face became as pale as chalk.

"I still played the fool and said, 'I want nothing from you. It is true that when I saw you in your aunt's drawing room you made a strong impression on me—but I haven't done anything that should upset you.' 'Yes, you have. If we weren't living in the twentieth century, I would think you were a sorcerer. Believe me,' she went on, 'I didn't come easily to the decision to call you. I was even afraid that you might not know who I was—but you knew immediately.'

" 'We cannot stand here on the street and talk,' I said. 'We have to go somewhere.' 'Where? If someone who knows me should see me, I am lost.' I said, 'Come with me.' She hesitated for a while, and then she followed me. She seemed to have difficulty walking on her high heels and she took my arm. I noticed, even though she was wearing gloves, that she had most beautiful hands. Her hand fluttered on my arm, and each time a shudder ran through my body. After a while the young woman became more relaxed with me, and she said, 'What kind of powers do you possess? I have heard your voice several times. I have seen you, too. I woke up in the middle of the night and you were standing at the foot of my bed. Instead of eyes, two green beams shone from your sockets. I woke my husband, but in a second you vanished.'

" 'It's a hallucination,' I said. 'No, you wander in the night.' 'If I do, it's without knowing it.'

"We approached the shore of the Vistula and sat down on a log. It's quiet there. It's not completely safe because it's full of drunks and bums. But she sat with me. She said, 'My aunt will not know what has become of me. I told her that I was going for a walk. She even offered to accompany me. Give me a holy promise that you will let me go. Perhaps you have a wife and you wouldn't want anybody to molest her.'

" 'I have no wife,' I said, 'but I promise you that, as far as it depends on me, I will not molest you. That's all I can promise.'

" 'I will be grateful to you until my last breath.'

"That is the story. I never saw the woman again. I don't even know her name. I don't know why, but of all the strange things that have happened to me this made the strongest impression. Well, that's all. I won't disturb you any more."

"You don't disturb me," I said. "It's good to meet a person with such powers. It strengthens my own faith. But how did it happen that Manya had the grippe when you left Warsaw? Why didn't you order her to get well?"

"What? I ask myself this question constantly. It seems that my power is only negative. To heal the sick, one must be a saint and, as you see, I am far from being a saint. Or it may be—who knows—that to have a woman along in those days was dangerous."

The stranger hung his head. He began to drum on the table with his fingers and to hum to himself. Then he got up. It seemed to me that his face had changed; it had become gray and wrinkled. Suddenly he looked his age. He even appeared less tall than before. I noticed that his raincoat was full of spots. He gave me his hand to say goodbye, and I accompanied him to the elevator.

"Do you still think about women?" I asked.

He thought it over as though he hadn't grasped my words. He looked at me sadly, with suspicion. "Only about dead women."

Something Is There

I

As a rule, Rabbi Nechemia from Bechev knew the cunning of the Evil One and how to subdue him, but the last few months he had been plagued by something new and terrifying: wrath against the Creator. A part of the rabbi's brain quarreled with the Lord of the Universe, rebelliously arguing: Yes, you are great, eternal, all mighty, wise, even full of mercy. But with whom do you play hide-and-seek—with flies? What help is your greatness to the fly when it falls into the net of the spider that sucks out its life? Of what avail are all your attributes to the mouse when the cat clamps it in its claws? Rewards in Paradise? The beasts have no use for them. You, Father in heaven, have the time to wait for the End of Days, but they can't wait. When you cause a fire in Feitl the water carrier's hut and he has to sleep with his family in the poorhouse on a cold winter's night, that is an injustice beyond repair. The dimming of your light, free choice, redemption, may serve to explain you, but Feitl the water carrier needs to rest after a day's toil, not to toss about on a bed of rotten straw.

The rabbi knew well that Satan was talking to him. He tried every means to silence him. He submerged himself in the icy water of the ritual bath, fasted, and studied the Torah until his eyes closed from weariness. But the Devil refused to be thwarted. His insolence grew. He screamed from morning till night. Lately, he had begun to defile the rabbi's dreams. The rabbi dreamed of Jews being burned at the stake, of yeshiva boys led to the gallows, of violated virgins, tortured infants. He was shown the cruelties of Chmielnitzki's and Gonta's soldiers and those of the savages who consume the limbs of animals before the beasts expire. Cossacks impaled children with their spears and buried them still alive. A Haydamak with a long mustache and murderous eyes ripped

Translated by the author and Rosanna Gerber

open a woman's belly and sewed a cat inside. In his dream, the rabbi waved his fists toward heaven and shouted, "Is all this for your glory, Heavenly Killer?"

The whole court at Bechev was on the verge of collapse. The old rabbi, Reb Eliezer Tzvi, Rabbi Nechemia's father, had died three years before. He had suffered from cancer of the stomach. Rabbi Nechemia's mother had developed the same disease in her breast. Besides the rabbi, one daughter and a son remained. The rabbi's younger brother, Simcha David, became an "enlightened one" while his parents were alive. He left the court and his wife, the daughter of the Zhilkovka rabbi, and went to Warsaw to study painting. The rabbi's sister, Hinde Shevach, had married the son of the Neustater rabbi, Chaim Mattos, who immediately after the marriage sank into melancholia and returned to his parents. Hinde Shevach became an abandoned wife. Since he was considered insane, Chaim Mattos was not permitted to go through divorce proceedings. Rabbi Nechemia's own wife, a descendant of the rabbi of Kotzk, had died together with her infant at childbirth. The matchmakers proposed various mates for the rabbi, but he gave them all the same answer: "I will think it over."

Actually, no appropriate match was offered. Most of the Bechev Hasidim had deserted Reb Nechemia. In the rabbinical courts, the same laws prevailed as among the fish in the sea: the big ones devoured the little ones. The first to leave were the rich. What could keep them in Bechev? The study house was half ruined. The roof of the ritual bath had caved in. Weeds grew everywhere. Reb Nechemia was left with a single beadle—Reb Sander. The rabbi's house had many rooms, which were seldom cleaned, and a layer of dust covered everything. The wallpaper was peeling. Windowpanes were broken and not replaced. The entire building had settled in such a way that the floors all slanted. Beila Elke, the maid, suffered from rheumatism; her joints became knotted. Reb Nechemia's sister, Hinde Shevach, had no patience for housework. She sat on the couch all day long reading books. When the rabbi lost a button from his coat, there was no one to sew it on.

The rabbi was barely twenty-seven years old, but he appeared older. His tall figure was stooped. He had a yellow beard, yellow eyebrows, yellow sidelocks. He was nearly bald. He had a high forehead, blue eyes, a narrow nose, a long neck with a protruding Adam's apple. He had a consumptive pallor. In his study, Reb Nechemia, wearing a faded housecoat, a wrinkled skullcap, and shoddy slippers, paced back and forth. On the table lay a long pipe and a bag of tobacco. The rabbi would light it, take one puff, and put it down. He would pick up a book, open it, and close it without reading. He even ate impatiently. He bit off a piece of bread and chewed it while walking. He took a sip of his coffee and continued to pace. It was summer, between Pentecost and the Days of Awe, when no Hasidim go forth on pilgrimages, and during the long summer days the rabbi had time enough to brood. All problems blended into one—why the suffering? There was no answer to be found to this question, neither in the Pentateuch, in the books of the Prophets, in the Talmud, in the Zohar, nor in *The Tree of Life.* If the Lord is omnipotent, He could reveal Himself without the aid of the Evil Host. If He is not omnipotent, then He is not really God. The only solution to the riddle was that of the heretics: There is neither a judge nor a judgment. All creation is a blind accident—an inkwell fell on a sheet of paper and the ink wrote a letter by itself, each word a lie, the sentences chaos. In that case, why does he, Rabbi Nechemia, make a fool of himself? What kind of a rabbi is he? To whom does he pray? To whom does he complain? On the other hand, how can spilled ink compose even a single line? And from where does the ink and the sheet of paper come? *Nu,* and from where does God come?

Rabbi Nechemia stood at the open window. Outside, there was a pale blue sky; around a golden-yellow sun, little clouds curled like the flax that is used to protect the ethrog in its case. On the naked branch of a desiccated tree stood a bird. A swallow? A sparrow? Its mother was also a bird, and so, too, its grandmother—generation after generation, thousands of years. If Aristotle was right that the universe always existed, then the chain of generations had no beginning. But how could that be?

The rabbi grimaced as if in pain. He formed a fist. "You want to conceal your face?" He spoke to God. "So be it. You conceal your face and I will conceal mine. Enough is enough." He decided to put into action what he had contemplated for a long time.

II

That Friday night the rabbi slept little. He napped and awoke intermittently. Each time he fell asleep, horrors seized him anew. Blood flowed. Corpses lay strewn in the gutters. Women ran through flames, with singed hair and charred breasts. Bells clanged. A stampede of beasts with ram's horns, pig's snouts, with skins of hedgehogs and pussy udders emerged from burning forests. A cry rose from the earth—a lament of men, women, serpents, demons. In the confusion of his dream, the rabbi imagined that Simchas Torah and Purim had fallen on the same day. Had the calendar been altered, the rabbi wondered, or had the Evil One taken dominion? At dawn an old man with a crooked beard, wearing a torn robe, ranted at him and shook his fists. The rabbi tried to blow the ram's horn to excommunicate him, but instead of a blast the sound was a wheeze that might have come from a deflated lung.

The rabbi trembled and his bed shook. His pillow was wet and twisted, as if it had just been wrung out from the washtub. The rabbi's eyes were half glued together. "Abominations," the rabbi muttered. "Scum of the brain." For the first time since he could remember, the rabbi did not perform the ablutions. "The power of evil? Let's see what evil can do! The sacred can only stay mute." He walked over to the window. The rising sun rolled among the clouds like a severed head. At a pile of garbage, the community he-goat was trying to chew last year's palm leaves. "You are still alive?" the rabbi addressed him. And he remembered the ram whose horns were caught in the thicket which Abraham had sacrificed instead of Isaac. He always had a need of burnt offerings, the rabbi thought of God. His creatures' blood was a sweet savor to Him.

"I will do it, I will do it," the rabbi said aloud.

In Bechev they prayed late. On the summer Sabbaths there was barely a quorum, even counting the few old men who were supported by the court. The night before, the rabbi had resolved not to put on his fringed garment, but he did so anyway out of habit. He had planned to go bareheaded, but reluctantly he placed the skullcap on his head. One sin at a time is enough, he decided. He sat down on his chair and dozed. After a while, he started and got up. Until yesterday the Good Spirit had attempted to reprimand the rabbi and to threaten him with Gehenna or a demeaning transmigration of the soul. But now the voice from Mount Horeb was stifled. All fears had vanished. Only anger remained. "If He does not need the Jews, the Jews don't need Him." The rabbi spoke no longer directly to the Almighty but to some other deity—perhaps to one of those mentioned in the Eighty-second Psalm: "God standeth in the Congregation of the mighty, He judgeth among the Gods." Now the rabbi agreed with every kind of heresy—with those who deny Him entirely and with those who believe in two dominions; with the idolators who serve the stars and the constellations and those who uphold the Trinity; with the Karaaites, who renounced the Talmud; with the Samaritans, who forsook Mount Sinai for Mount Gerizim. Yes, I have known the Lord and I intend to spite Him, the rabbi said. Many matters suddenly became clear: the primeval snake, Cain, the Generation of the Flood, the Sodomites, Ishmael, Esau, Korach, and Jeroboam, the son of Nebat. To a silent torturer one does not speak, and to a persecutor one does not pray.

The rabbi hoped that somehow at the last moment a miracle would occur—God would reveal Himself or some power would restrain him.

But nothing happened. He opened the drawer and took out his pipe, an object forbidden to the touch on the Sabbath. He filled it with tobacco. Before striking the match, the rabbi hesitated. He admonished himself, "Nechemia, son of Eliezer Tzvi, this is one of the thirty-nine tasks prohibited on the Sabbath! For this, one is stoned." He looked around. No wings fluttered; no voice called. He withdrew a match and lit the pipe. His brain rattled in his skull like a kernel in the nutshell. He was plummeting into the abyss.

Usually the rabbi enjoyed smoking, but now the smoke tasted acrid. It scratched his throat. Someone might knock at the door! He poured a few drops of ablution water into the pipe—another major violation, to extinguish a fire. He had a desire for further transgression, but what? He wanted to spit on the mezuzah but refrained. For a while, the rabbi listened to the turmoil within him. Then he went out into the corridor and passed along to Hinde Shevach's room. He pulled at the latch and tried to open the door.

"Who is there?" Hinde Shevach called out.

"It is I."

The rabbi heard her rustling, murmuring. Then she opened the door. She must just have awakened. She wore a house robe with arabesques, slippers, and on her shaven head a silk kerchief. Nechemia was tall, but Hinde Shevach was small. Though she was barely twenty-five years old, she looked older, with dark circles under her eyes and the grieved expression of an abandoned wife. The rabbi rarely came to her room, never so early and on the Sabbath.

She asked, "Has something happened?"

The rabbi's eyes filled with laughter. "The Messiah has come. The moon fell down."

"What kind of talk is that?"

"Hinde Shevach, everything is finished," the rabbi said, astounded by his own words.

"What do you mean?"

"I'm not a rabbi any more. There is no more court unless you want to take over and become the second Virgin of Ludmir."

Hinde Shevach's yellowish eyes measured him crookedly. "What happened?"

"I've had my fill."

"What will become of the court, of me?"

"Sell everything, divorce your schlemiel, or leave for America."

Hinde Shevach stood still. "Sit down, you frighten me."

"I'm tired of all these lies," the rabbi said. "The whole nonsense. I'm not a rabbi and they're not Hasidim. I'm leaving for Warsaw."

"What will you do in Warsaw? Do you want to follow in Simcha David's path?"

"Yes, his path."

Hinde Shevach's pale lips trembled. She looked for a handkerchief among her clothes on a chair. She held it to her mouth. "What about me?" she asked.

"You are still young. You're not a cripple," the rabbi said, baffled by his own words. "The whole world is open to you."

"Open? Chaim Mattos is not allowed to divorce me."

"He's allowed, allowed."

The rabbi wanted to say, "You can do without divorce," but he was afraid that Hinde Shevach might faint. He felt a surge of defiance, the courage and the relief of one who had rid himself of all yokes. For the first time he grasped what it meant to be a nonbeliever. He said, "The Hasidic institution is sheer mendicancy. Nobody needs us. The whole business is a swindle and a falsehood."

III

It all passed smoothly. Hinde Shevach locked herself in her room, apparently crying. Sander the beadle got drunk after Havdalah, the ushering out of the Sabbath, and went to sleep. The old men sat in the study house. One recited the Valedictory Prayers, another read *The Beginning of Wisdom,* a third cleaned his pipe with a wire, a fourth patched a sacred book. A few candles flickered. The rabbi gave a final look at the study house. "A ruin," he murmured. He had packed his satchel himself. Since his wife's death, he had grown accustomed to fetching his own linen from the chest where the maid placed it. He took out several shirts, some underwear, and long white stockings. He didn't even pack his prayer shawl and phylacteries. What for?

The rabbi stole away from the village. How convenient that the moon was not shining. He did not take the highway but walked along the back roads, with which he had been familiar as a boy. He did not wear his velvet hat. He had found a cap and a gaberdine from the days when he was a bachelor.

Actually, the rabbi was no longer the same man. He felt that he was possessed by a demon who thought and chattered in its own peculiar manner. Now he passed through fields and a forest. Even though it was Saturday night, when the Evil Ones run rampant, the rabbi felt bolder and stronger. He no longer feared dogs or robbers. He arrived at the station only to learn that he would have to wait for a train until dawn. He sat down on a bench, near a peasant who lay snoring. The rabbi had recited neither the Evening Prayer nor the Shema. I will shave off my beard, too, he decided. He was aware that his escape could not remain a secret and that his Hasidim might seek him out and find him. Briefly, he considered leaving Poland.

He fell asleep and was awakened by the ringing of a bell. The train had arrived. Earlier, he had bought a fourth-class ticket because in those carriages there is never any illumination; the passengers sit or stand in the dark. He was apprehensive of encountering citizens of Bechev, but the car was full of Gentiles. One of them struck a match, and the rabbi saw peasants wearing four-cornered hats, brown caftans, linen trousers —most of them barefoot or with rags on their feet. There was no window in the car, only a round opening. When the sun rose, it cast a purple light on the bedraggled lot of men, who were smoking cheap tobacco, eating coarse bread with lard, and washing it down with vodka. Their wives reclined on the baggage and dozed.

The rabbi had heard about the pogroms in Russia. Bumpkins such as these killed men, raped women, plundered, and tortured children. The rabbi huddled in a corner. He tried to cover his nose from the stench. "God, is this your world?" he asked. "Did you attempt to give them the Torah on Mount Seir and Mount Paran? Is it among them that you have dispersed your chosen people?" The wheels clammered along the rails. Smoke from the locomotive seeped through the round hole. It reeked of coal, oil, and some indiscernible smoldering substance. "Can I become one of these?" the rabbi asked himself. "If God doesn't exist, neither did Jesus."

The rabbi felt a strong urge to urinate but there were no facilities. These passengers seemed to be flea- and lice-ridden. He felt an itch beneath his shirt. He began to regret having left Bechev. "Who prevented me from being an infidel there?" he asked himself. "At least I had my own bed. And what will I do in Warsaw? I have been impetuous. I forgot that a heretic too needs food and a pillow under his head. My few rubles will not last long. Simcha David is a pauper himself." The rabbi had been informed that Simcha David was starving, wore tattered clothes, and in addition was stubborn and impractical. "Well, and what did he expect? There is no lack of charlatans in Warsaw."

The rabbi's legs ached and he lowered himself to the floor. He shoved the visor of his cap lower on his forehead. Jews boarded the train at various stations; someone might recognize him. Suddenly he heard familiar words. "Oh, my God, the soul which Thou gavest me is pure; Thou didst create it, Thou didst form it, Thou didst breathe it into me; Thou preservest it within me; and Thou wilt take it from me but wilt restore it unto me hereafter . . ." "A lie, a brazen lie," something in the rabbi exclaimed. "All have the same spirit—a man, an animal.

Ecclesiastes himself admitted this; therefore, the sages wanted to censor him. Well, but what is a spirit? Who formed the spirit? What do the worldly books say about that?"

The rabbi slept and dreamed that it was Yom Kippur. He stood in the synagogue yard along with a group of Jews who wore white robes and prayer shawls. Someone had locked the synagogue, but why? The rabbi lifted his eyes to the sky and instead of one moon he saw two, three, five. What was that? The moons seemed to rush toward one another. They became larger and more radiant. Lightning struck, thunder rolled, and the sky blazed in flames. The Jews emitted a howling lament: "Woe, Evil is prevailing!"

Shaken, the rabbi awoke. The train had arrived in Warsaw. He had not been in Warsaw since his father—blessed be his memory—fell ill and went there to see Dr. Frankel a few months before his demise. Father and son had then traveled in a special carriage. Sextons and court members had accompanied them. A crowd of Hasidim had waited at the station. His father was led to the house of a rich follower on Twarda Street. In his living room Father interpreted the Torah. Now Nechemia walked along the platform carrying his own valise. Some of the passengers ran, others dragged their luggage. Porters shouted. A gendarme appeared with a sword on one side, a revolver on the other, his chest covered with medals, his square face red and fat. His tallowy eyes measured the rabbi with suspicion, hatred, and with something that reminded the rabbi of a predatory beast.

The rabbi entered the city. Trolley cars clanged their bells, droshkies converged, the coachmen flicked their whips, the horses galloped over the cobblestones. There was a stench of pitch, refuse, and smoke. "This is the world?" the rabbi asked himself. "Here the Messiah is supposed to come?" He searched in his breast pocket for the scrap of paper bearing Simcha David's address, but it had vanished. "Are the demons playing with me already?" The rabbi returned his hand to the pocket and withdrew the paper he had been searching for. Yes, a demon was mocking him. But if there is no God, how can there be an Evil Host? He stopped a passer-by and asked for directions to Simcha David's street.

The man gave them. "What a distance!" he said.

IV

Each time the rabbi asked how to reach Smotcha Street, where Simcha David lived, he was advised to take a trolley car or a droshky, but the trolley seemed too formidable and a droshky was too expensive. Besides, the driver might be a Gentile. The rabbi spoke no Polish. He stopped to rest every few minutes. He hadn't eaten breakfast; still, he didn't know whether or not he was hungry. His mouth watered and he felt a dryness in his throat. The smell of freshly baked rolls, bagels, boiled milk, and smoked herring drifted from the courtyards. He passed by stores that sold leather, hardware, dry-goods, and ready-made clothes. The salesmen vied for customers, tore at their sleeves, winking and interspersing their Yiddish with Polish. Saleswomen called out in a singsong, "Apples, pears, plums, potato kugel, hot peas and beans." A wagon laden with kindling tried to pass through a narrow gate. A cart piled high with sacks of flour forced its way through another gate. A madman—barefoot, wearing a caftan with one sleeve missing and a torn cap—was being chased by a bevy of boys. They called taunts and threw pebbles at him.

"Mother cooked a kitten," a young boy sang out in a high-pitched voice. Blond sidelocks hung down from his octagonal cap.

The rabbi proceeded to cross the street and was nearly run down by an express wagon drawn by two Belgian horses. Women wrung their hands and scolded him. A man with a dirty gray beard who carried a sack on his shoulders said, "You'll have to recite a thanksgiving benediction this Saturday."

"So, thanksgiving." The rabbi spoke to himself. "And what does he carry in the sack—his portion in Paradise?"

He finally reached Smotcha Street. Someone pointed out the gate number to him. At the gate a girl was selling onion rolls. He entered a courtyard where children were playing tag around a huge, freshly tarred garbage receptacle. Nearby, a dyer dipped a red skirt in a kettle filled with black dye. In an open window a girl was airing a feather bed, beating it with a stick. The first people he asked knew nothing of Simcha David. Then one woman said, "He must live in the attic."

The rabbi was unaccustomed to so many steps. He had to stop to catch his breath. Refuse littered the stairway. Apartment doors stood ajar. A tailor was sewing on a machine. One flat contained a line of weaving looms where girls with bits of cotton in their hair deftly knotted threads. On the higher stories, holes gaped in the plastered walls and the smell became stifling. Suddenly the rabbi saw Simcha David. He had emerged from a dark corridor, capless, in a short jacket spattered with paint and clay. He had yellow hair and yellow eyebrows. He carried a bundle. The rabbi was amazed that he recognized his brother; he looked so much like a Gentile. "Simcha David!" he called.

Simcha David stared. "A familiar face, but—"

"Take a good look."

Simcha David shrugged. "Who are you?"

"Your brother, Nechemia."

Simcha David didn't even blink. His pale blue eyes looked dull, sad, ready for all the bizarre things time might bring. Two deep wrinkles had formed at the corners of his mouth. He was no longer the prodigy of Bechev but a shabby laborer. After a while he said, "Yes, it's you. What's wrong?"

"I've chosen to follow you."

"Well, I can't stop now. I have to meet someone. They're waiting for me. I'm late already. I'll let you into my room so you can rest. We'll talk later."

"So be it."

" 'I had not thought to see thy face,' " Simcha David quoted from Genesis.

"*Nu*, I thought you had already forgotten everything," the rabbi said. He was more embarrassed by his brother's quoting the Bible than by his coolness.

Simcha David opened the door of a room so tiny it reminded the rabbi of a cage. The ceiling hung crookedly. Along the walls leaned canvases, frames, rolls of paper. It smelled of paint and turpentine. There was no bed, only a dilapidated couch.

Simcha David asked, "What do you want to do in Warsaw? These are hard times." He left without waiting for a reply.

Why is he in such a rush, the rabbi wondered. He sat on the couch and looked around. Nearly all the paintings were of females—some nude, some half nude. On a little table lay brushes and a palette. This must be the way he makes a living, the rabbi thought. It was clear to him now that he had acted in folly. He shouldn't have come here. One can suffer pain anywhere.

The rabbi waited for an hour, two, but Simcha David didn't return. Hunger gnawed at him. "Today is a day of fast for me—a heretic's fast," he told himself. A voice inside him teased, "You deserve what you're getting." "I don't repent," the rabbi retorted. He was ready to wrangle with the Angel of God as he once struggled with the Lord of Evil.

The rabbi picked up a book from the floor. It was in Yiddish. He read a story about a saint who, instead of going to the Evening Prayer, gathered kindling for a widow. What is this—morality or mockery? The rabbi had expected to read a denial of God and the Messiah. He picked up a pamphlet whose pages were falling out, and read about colonists in Palestine. Young Jews plowed, sowed, dried swamps, planted eucalyptus trees, fought the Bedouins. One of these pioneers had perished and the writer called him a martyr. The rabbi sat bewildered. If there's no Creator, why go to the Holy Land? And what do they mean by a martyr?

The rabbi grew tired and lay down. "Such Jewishness is not for me," he said. "I'd rather convert!" But where did one convert? Besides, to convert, one had to pretend belief in the Nazarene. It seemed that the world was full of faith. If you didn't believe in one God, you must believe in another. The Cossacks sacrificed themselves for the czar. Those who wanted to dethrone the czar sacrificed themselves for the revolution. But where were the real heretics, those who believed in nothing? He had not come to Warsaw to barter one faith for another.

V

The rabbi waited for three hours, but Simcha David didn't come back. This is how the modern ones are, he brooded. Their promise is not a promise; they have no sense of kinship or friendship. Actually, what they worship is the ego. These thoughts perturbed him—wasn't he one of them now? But how does one curb the brain from thinking? He gazed about the room. What could thieves find of value here? The naked females? He went out the door, closed it, and walked down the stairs. He took his valise with him. He was dizzy and walked unsteadily. On the street, he passed a restaurant but was ashamed to enter. He didn't even know how to order a meal. Did all the patrons sit at the same table? Did men eat together with women? People might ridicule his appearance. He returned to the gate of the house where Simcha David lived and bought two rolls. But where could he eat them? He remembered the proverb "One who eats in the street resembles a dog." He stood in the gateway and bit into the roll.

He had already committed sins that were punishable by death, but eating without washing his hands and without reciting a benediction disturbed him. He found it difficult to swallow. Well, it's a matter of habit, the rabbi comforted himself. One must get accustomed even to being a transgressor. He ate one roll and put the other into his pocket. He walked aimlessly. On one street, three funeral processions drove past him. The first hearse was followed by several men. A few droshkies rode after the second. No one accompanied the third. "Well, it doesn't make any difference to them," the rabbi said to himself. " 'For the dead know not anything, neither have they any more a reward,' " he quoted Ecclesiastes.

He turned right and went by long, narrow dry-goods stores lit up inside by gas lamps although it was midday. From wagons nearly as large as houses, men were unloading rolls of woolens, alpaca, cottons, and prints. A porter walked along with a basket on his shoulders, his back bent under the load. High-school boys in uniforms with gilded buttons and insignias on their caps toted books strapped to their shoulders. The rabbi stopped. If you didn't believe in God, why raise chil-

dren, why support wives? According to logic, a nonbeliever should care
only for his own body and for no one else.

He walked on. In the next block a bookstore displayed books in
Hebrew and Yiddish: *The Generations and Their Interpreters, The
Mysteries of Paris, The Little Man, Masturbation, How to Prevent Consumption.* One book was titled *How the Universe Came into Being.* I'm
going to buy it, the rabbi decided. There were a few customers inside.
The bookseller, a man with gold-rimmed glasses attached to a ribbon,
was talking to a man who had long hair and wore a hat with a wide brim
and a cape on his shoulders. The rabbi stopped at the shelves and
browsed among the books.

A salesgirl approached him and asked, "What do you want—a
prayer book, a benedictor?"

The rabbi blushed. "I noticed a book in the window but I've already
forgotten its name."

"Come out, show it to me," the girl said, winking at the man with
the gold-rimmed glasses. She smiled and dimples formed in her cheeks.

The rabbi had an impulse to run away. He pointed out the book.

"Masturbation?" the girl asked.

"No."

"Vichna Dvosha Goes to America?"

"No, the one in the middle."

"How the Universe Came into Being? Let's go back inside." The girl
whispered to the store owner, who now stood behind the counter. He
scratched his forehead. "It's the last copy."

"Shall I take it from the window?" the girl asked.

"But why do you need that book in particular?" the store owner
said. "It's out of date. The universe didn't come into being the way the
author describes. Nobody was there to tell."

The girl burst out laughing. The man in the cape asked, "Where do
you come from, the provinces?"

"Yes."

"For what did you come to Warsaw? To buy merchandise for your
store?"

"Yes, merchandise."

"What kind of merchandise?"

The rabbi wanted to answer that it was no business of his, but it
wasn't in his nature to be insolent. He said, "I want to know what the
heretics are saying."

The girl laughed again. The merchant took off his glasses. The man
in the cape stared at him with his big black eyes. "That's all you need?"

"I want to know."

"Well, he wants to know. Will they allow you to read it? If they catch you with such a book, they'll throw you out of the study house."

"No one will know," the rabbi replied. He realized that he was speaking like a child, not like an adult.

"Well, I guess the Enlightenment is still alive, the same as fifty years ago," the man in the cape said to the owner. "This is the way they used to come to Vilna and ask, 'How was the world created? Why does the sun shine? Which came first, the chicken or the egg?' " He turned to the rabbi. "We don't know, my dear man, we don't know. We have to live without faith and without knowledge."

"So why are you Jews?" the rabbi asked.

"We have to be Jews. An entire people cannot become assimilated. Besides, the Gentiles don't want us. There are several hundred converts in Warsaw and the Polish press attacks them constantly. And what would conversion accomplish? We have to remain a people."

"Where can I get the book?" the rabbi asked.

"Who knows. It's out of print. Anyway, it only states that the universe evolved. As to how it evolved, how life was created, and all the rest, nobody has an inkling."

"So why are you unbelievers?"

"My dear man, we have no time to engage in discussions with you. I have one copy and I don't want to stir the dust," the owner said. "Come back in a few weeks when we redo the window. The universe won't turn sour in that short a time."

"Please forgive me."

"My dear fellow, there are no unbelievers any more," said the man in the cape. "In my time there were a few, but the old ones have died and the new generation is practical. They want to improve the world but don't know how to go about it. Do you at least earn a living from your store?"

"So-so," the rabbi muttered.

"Do you have a wife and children?"

The rabbi didn't answer.

"What is the name of your village?"

The rabbi remained silent. He felt as timid as a cheder boy. He said, "Thank you," and left.

VI

The rabbi continued to walk the streets. Dusk was falling, and he remembered that it was time for the Evening Prayer, but he was in no mood to flatter the Almighty, to call Him a bestower of knowledge, a reviver of the dead, a healer of the sick, a freer of the imprisoned, or to implore Him to return His holy presence to Zion and to rebuild Jerusalem.

The rabbi passed a jail. A black gate was opened and a man bound in chains was led in. A cripple without legs moved about on a board with wheels. A blind man sang a song about a sunken ship. On a narrow street, the rabbi heard an uproar. Someone had been stabbed—a tall young man with blood gushing from his throat. A woman moaned, "He refused to be robbed, so they attacked with their knives. May hell's fire consume them. God waits long but punishes well."

Why does He wait so long, the rabbi wanted to ask. And whom does He punish? The stricken, not the strikers. Police arrived, and the siren of an ambulance wailed. Young men in torn pants, the visors of their caps covering their eyes, rushed out from the gates, and girls with their hair disheveled, worn-out slippers on their bare feet. The rabbi was afraid of the mob and its noise. He entered a courtyard. A girl with a shawl over her shoulders, her cheeks as red as though painted with beets, said to the rabbi, "Come in, it's twenty groschen."

"Where shall I go?" the rabbi asked uncomprehendingly.

"Come right downstairs."

"I'm looking for a place where I can lodge."

"I will recommend you." The girl took his arm.

The rabbi started. For the first time since he had grown up, a strange woman was touching him. The girl led him down dark steps. They walked through a corridor so narrow that only one person could pass at a time. The girl walked ahead, dragging the rabbi by his sleeve. A subterranean dampness hit his nostrils. What was this—a living grave, the gate to Gehenna? Someone was playing on a harmonica. A woman was ranting. A cat or a rat jumped over his feet. A door opened and the rabbi saw a room without a window, lit by a small kerosene lamp, its chimney black with soot. Near a bare bed that had only a straw mattress stood a washbasin of pink water. The rabbi's feet stuck to the threshold like those of an ox being led into the slaughterhouse. "What's this? Where are you taking me?"

"Don't play dumb. Let's have fun."

"I'm looking for an inn."

"Hand over the twenty groschen."

Could this be a house of ill repute? The rabbi trembled and withdrew a handful of change from his pocket. "Take it yourself."

The girl picked up a ten-groschen coin, a six-groschen coin, and a four-groschen coin. After some hesitation she added a kopeck. She pointed to the bed. The rabbi dropped the remaining coins and ran back through the corridor. The floor was uneven and full of holes. He nearly fell. He bumped into the brick wall. "God in Heaven, save me!" His shirt was drenched. When he reached the courtyard, it was already night. The place stank of garbage, gutter, and rot. Now the rabbi deplored that he had invoked the name of God. His mouth filled with bile. A tremor ran through his spine. These are the pleasures of the world? Is this what Satan has to sell? He took out his handkerchief and wiped his face. Where do I go now? "Whereto shall I flee Thy countenance?" He raised his eyes, and above the walls hovered the sky with a new moon and a few stars. He gazed bewildered, as if viewing it for the first time. Not even twenty-four hours had passed since he had left Bechev, but it seemed to him that he had been wandering for weeks, months, years.

The girl from the cellar stepped out again. "Why did you run away, you silly yokel?"

"Please forgive me," the rabbi said, and he walked out into the street. The crowd was gone. Smoke rose from chimneys. Storekeepers were locking their stores with iron bars and locks. What had happened to the young man who was stabbed, the rabbi wondered. Had the earth swallowed him? Suddenly he realized that he was still carrying his valise. How was this possible? It seemed as if his hand clutched it with a power of its own. Perhaps this was the same power that created the world? Maybe this power was God? The rabbi wanted to laugh and to cry. I'm not even good at sinning—a bungler in every way. Well, it's my end, my end. In that case there's only one way out, to give back the six hundred and thirty limbs and sinews. But how? Hanging? Drowning? Was the Vistula nearby? The rabbi stopped a passer-by. "Excuse me, how do you get to the Vistula?"

The man had a sooty face, like a chimney sweeper. From under his bushy, coal-black eyebrows, he stared at the rabbi. "For what do you need the Vistula? Do you want to fish?" His voice barked like a dog's.

"Fish, no."

"What else, swim to Danzig?"

A jester, the rabbi thought. "I was told there is an inn in the neighborhood."

"An inn near the Vistula? Where do you come from, the provinces? What are you doing here, looking for a teaching job?"

"Teaching? Yes. No."

"Mister, to walk the Warsaw cobblestones, you need strength. Do you have any money?"

"A few rubles."

"For one gulden a night, you can sleep in my place. I live right here in number 14. I have no wife. I will give you her bed."

"Well, so be it. I thank you."

"Have you eaten?"

"Yes, in the morning."

"In the morning, huh? Come with me to the tavern. We'll have a glass of beer. A snack, too. I'm the coal dealer from across the street." The man pointed with a black finger to a store whose doors were barred. He said, "Be careful, they may steal your money. A man from the provinces has just been taken to the hospital in an ambulance. They stabbed him with a knife."

VII

The coal dealer walked up the few steps to the tavern. The rabbi stumbled along after him. The dealer opened a glass door and the rabbi was struck by the odor of beer, vodka, garlic, by the sounds of men's and women's loud voices and of dance music. His eyes blurred. "Why do you stop?" the coal handler asked. "Let's go." He took the rabbi's arm and dragged him.

Through vapor as dense as in the bathhouse of Bechev, the rabbi saw distorted faces, racks of bottles on the wall, a beer barrel with a brass pump, a counter on which sat platters of roasted geese, plates of appetizers. Fiddles screeched, a drum pounded; everyone seemed to be yelling. "Has something happened?" the rabbi asked.

The coal dealer led him to a table and screamed into his ear, "This is not your little village. This is Warsaw. Here you have to know your way around."

"I'm not used to such noise."

"You'll get used to it. What kind of teacher do you want to be? There are more teachers here than pupils. Every schlemiel becomes a teacher. What's the good of all the studying? They forget anyhow. I went to cheder myself. They taught me Rashi and all that. I still remember a few words: 'And the Lord said unto Moses—' "

"A few words of the Torah are also Torah," the rabbi said, aware that he had no right to speak after having violated so many commandments.

"What? None of it's worth a cock's crow. These boys sit in the study house, shaking and making crazy faces. When they're about to be drafted, they rupture themselves. They marry and can't support their wives. They breed dozens of children, who crawl about barefoot and naked . . ."

Perhaps he is the real unbeliever, the rabbi thought. He asked, "Do you believe in God?"

The coal dealer placed a fist on the table. "How do I know? I was never in heaven. Something is there. Who made the world? On the

Sabbath I go to pray with a group called 'The Love of Friends.' It costs a few rubles, but how does the saying go—let it be a mitzvah. We pray with a rabbi who barely has a piece of bread. His wife comes to me to buy ten pounds of coal. What are ten pounds of coal in the winter? I add a piece just for good measure. If there is a God, then why does He allow the Poles to beat up the Jews?"

"I don't know. I wish I did."

"What does the Torah say? You seem to know the fine points."

"The Torah says that the wicked are punished and the righteous rewarded."

"When? Where?"

"In the next world."

"In the grave?"

"In Paradise."

"Where is Paradise?"

A waiter approached. "For me, light beer and chicken livers," the coal dealer ordered. "What do you want?"

The rabbi was at a loss for an answer. He asked, "Can one wash one's hands here?"

The coal dealer snorted. "Here you eat without washing, but it's kosher. They won't serve you pork."

"Perhaps I will have a cookie," the rabbi muttered.

"A cookie? What else? Here you have to wash everything down. What kind of beer do you want? Light? Dark?"

"Let it be light."

"Well, give him a mug of oat beer and an egg cookie." After the waiter left, the coal dealer began to drum the table with his sooty nails. "If you haven't eaten since morning, that isn't enough. Here, if you don't eat you'll drop like a fly. In Warsaw you have to be a glutton. If you want to wash your hands for the benediction, go into the toilet. There's a faucet there, but you'll have to wipe your hands on your coat."

"Why am I so unhappy?" the rabbi asked himself. "I am sunk in iniquity just like the rest of them—even worse. If I don't want to be Jacob, I have to be Esau." To the coal dealer, he said, "I don't want to be a teacher."

"What do you want to be, a count?"

"I would like to learn some trade."

"What trade? If you want to be a tailor or a shoemaker or a furrier, you have to begin young. They take you as an apprentice and the master's wife tells you to pour out the slops and to rock the baby in the cradle. I know. I learned to be a carpenter and my master never let me touch the saw or the plane. I suffered with him for four years and when I left I had learned nothing. Before I knew it, I had to go serve the czar. For three years I ate the soldier's black bread. In the barracks you have to eat pig, otherwise you have no strength to carry the gun. Did I have a choice? When I was discharged, I went to work for a coal dealer and this has been my trade since. Everybody steals. They bring you a wagon of coals that should weigh one hundred pood but it weighs only ninety. Ten pood are stolen along the way. If you ask too many questions, they knife you. So what can I do? I pour water on the coal and that makes it heavier. If I didn't do it, I would go hungry. Do you understand me?"

"Yes, I understand."

"So why chatter about a trade? You most probably warmed the bench in the study house all these years, didn't you?"

"Yes, I studied."

"So you're good for nothing except to be a teacher. But you have to be fit for that also. There's a Talmud Torah on the block where they had a softy of a teacher. The boys who study there are all hoodlums. They played so many tricks on him he ran away. As for the rich, they want a modern teacher who wears a tie and knows how to write Russian. Do you have a wife?"

"No."

"Divorced?"

"A widower."

"Shake hands. I had a good wife. She was a little deaf but did her job. She prepared my meals, we had five children, but three died when they were babies. I have a son in Yekaterinslav. My daughter works in a hardware store. She boards with her employers. She doesn't want to cook for her papa. Her boss is a rich man. Anyhow, I'm alone. How long have you been a widower?"

"A few years."

"What do you do when you need a female?"

The rabbi blushed and then became pale. "What can one do?"

"For money, everything can be had in Warsaw. Not here on this street. Here they're all infected. You go to a girl and she has a little worm in her blood. You get sick and you begin to rot. There's a man in the neighborhood whose whole nose has rotted off. On the better streets the whores have to be inspected every month at the doctor's. It cost you a ruble to be with one of them, but at least they're clean. The matchmakers are after me but I can't make up my mind. All the women want is your rubles. I was sitting with one right here in the tavern and she asked me, 'How much money do you have?' She was an old hag and ugly as sin. I said to her that how much money I had saved up was none of her business. If for one ruble I can get a girl who is young and pretty, why do I need such an old bag? Do you follow me? Here's our beer. What's the matter? You're as pale as death."

VIII

Three weeks had passed, but the rabbi still wandered about in Warsaw. He slept at the coal dealer's. The coal dealer had taken him to the Yiddish theater after the Sabbath meal. He had also taken the rabbi with him to the races at Vilanov.

Every day except Saturday, the rabbi visited Bresler's library. He stood at the bookshelves and browsed. Then there was a table where one could sit and read. The rabbi came in the morning and stayed until closing time. In the afternoon he went out and bought a roll, a bagel, or a piece of potato kugel from a market woman. He ate without a benediction. He read books in Hebrew, in Yiddish. He even tried to read German. In the library he found the book that he had first seen in the shop window, *How the Universe Came into Being*. "Yes, how was it created without a creator?" the rabbi asked himself. He had developed the habit of talking to himself. He tugged at his beard, winced, and shook as he used to in the study house. He muttered, "Yes, a fog, but who made the fog? How did it arise? When did it begin?"

The earth was torn away from the sun, he read—but who formed the sun? Man descended from an ape—but where did the ape come from? And since the author wasn't present when all this happened, how could he be so sure? Their science explained everything away in distance of time and space. The first cell appeared hundreds of millions of years ago, in the slime at the edge of the ocean. The sun will be extinguished billions of years hence. Millions of stars, planets, comets, move in a space with no beginning and no end, without a plan or purpose. In the future all people will be alike, there will be a Kingdom of Freedom without competition, crises, wars, jealousy, or hatred. As the Talmud says, anyone who wants to lie will tell of things that happen far away. In an old copy of the Hebrew magazine, *Haasif*, the rabbi read about Spinoza, Kant, Leibnitz, Schopenhauer. They called God substance, monad, hypothesis, blind will, nature.

The rabbi clutched at one of his sidelocks. Who is this nature? Where did it get so much skill and power? It took care of the most distant star, of a rock in the bottom of the ocean, of the slightest speck of dust, of the food in a fly's stomach. In him, Rabbi Nechemia of Bechev, nature did everything at once. It gave him abdominal cramps, it stuffed his nose, it made his skull tingle, it gnawed at his brain like the gnat that plagued Titus. The rabbi blasphemed God and apologized to Him. One moment he wished death upon himself and the next he feared sickness. He needed to urinate, went to the toilet but couldn't function. As he read, he saw green and golden spots before his eyes and the lines merged, diverged, bent, and passed over one another. "Am I going blind? Is it the end? Have the demons already got hold of me? No, Father of the Universe, I will not recite my confession. I'm ready for all your Gehennas. If you can be silent for an eternity, I at least will remain dumb until I give up my soul. You are not the only man of war," the rabbi spoke to the Almighty. "If I am your son, I too can put up a fight."

The rabbi stopped reading in an orderly fashion. He would take out a book, open it at the middle, run through a few lines, and replace it on the shelf. No matter where he opened, he encountered a lie. All books had one thing in common: they avoided the essential, spoke vaguely, and gave different names to the same object. They knew neither how grass grew nor what light was, how heredity worked, the stomach digested, the brain thought, how weak nations grew strong, nor how the strong perished. Even though these scholars wrote thick books about the distant galaxies, they hadn't yet discovered what went on a mile beneath the crust of the earth.

The rabbi turned pages and gaped. He would lay his forehead on the edge of the table and nap for an instant. "Woe to me, I have no more strength." Every night, the coal dealer tried to persuade the rabbi to return to his own village. He would say, "You will collapse and they won't even know what to write on your headstone."

IX

Late one night when Hinde Shevach slept, she was awakened by steps in the corridor. Who creeps around in the middle of the night, Hinde Shevach wondered. Since her brother had left, it was as silent in the house as in a ruin. Hinde Shevach got up, put on a house coat and slippers. She opened a crack in the door and noticed a light in her brother's room. She walked over and saw the rabbi. His gaberdine was torn, his shirt was unbuttoned, his skullcap was crumpled. The expression on his face was entirely altered. He was bent like an old man. In the middle of the room stood a satchel.

Hinde Shevach wrung her hands. "Are my eyes deceiving me?"

"No."

"Father in Heaven, they're searching for you all over. May the thoughts that I had be scattered over the wastelands. They're already writing about you in the newspapers."

"So, well."

"Where were you? Why did you leave? Why did you hide?"

The rabbi didn't reply.

"Why didn't you say you were leaving?" Hinde Shevach asked despondently.

The rabbi dropped his head and didn't answer.

"We thought you were dead, God forbid. I telegraphed Simcha David but no answer came. I wanted to sit the seven days of mourning for you. Heaven save me! The whole town is in an uproar. They invented the most gruesome things. They even informed the police. A policeman came to ask me for your description and all the rest of it."

"Too bad."

"Did you see Simcha David?" Hinde Shevach asked after a hesitation.

"Yes. No."

"How is he making out?"

"Eh."

Hinde Shevach gulped. "You're as white as chalk, all in tatters. They dreamed up such stories that I was ashamed to show my face. Letters and telegrams came."

"Well . . ."

"You can't just get rid of me like this." Hinde Shevach changed her tone. "Speak clearly. Why did you do it? You're not just a street urchin, you're the rabbi of Bechev."

"No more rabbi."

"God have mercy. There will be bedlam. Wait, I'll bring you a glass of milk."

Hinde Shevach withdrew. The rabbi heard her go down the steps. He seized his beard and swayed. A huge shadow wavered along the wall and ceiling. After a while Hinde Shevach returned. "There is no milk."

"*Nu.*"

"I won't go until you tell me why you left," Hinde Shevach said.

"I wanted to know what the heretics say."

"What do they say?"

"There are no heretics."

"Is that so?"

"The whole world worships idols," the rabbi muttered. "They invent gods and they serve them."

"The Jews also?"

"Everybody."

"Well, you've lost your mind." Hinde Shevach remained standing for a while and stared, then she walked back to her bedroom.

The rabbi lay down on his bed fully clothed. He felt his strength leaving him—not ebbing away but all at once, rapidly. A light he never knew was there flickered in his brain. His hands and feet grew numb.

His head lay heavy on the pillow. After a time, the rabbi lifted an eyelid. The candle had burned out. A pre-dawn moon, jagged and dimmed by fog, shone through the window. In the east, the sky reddened. "Something is there," the rabbi murmured.

The war between the rabbi of Bechev and God had come to an end.

A Crown of Feathers

REB NAFTALI HOLISHITZER, the community leader in Krasnobród, was left in his old age with no children. One daughter had died in childbirth and the other in a cholera epidemic. A son had drowned when he tried to cross the San River on horseback. Reb Naftali had only one grandchild—a girl, Akhsa, an orphan. It was not the custom for a female to study at a yeshiva, because "the King's daughter is all glorious within" and Jewish daughters are all the daughters of kings. But Akhsa studied at home. She dazzled everyone with her beauty, wisdom, and diligence. She had white skin and black hair; her eyes were blue.

Reb Naftali managed an estate that had belonged to the Prince Czartoryski. Since he owed Reb Naftali twenty thousand guldens, the prince's property was a permanent pawn, and Reb Naftali had built for himself a water mill and a brewery and had sown hundreds of acres with hops. His wife, Nesha, came from a wealthy family in Prague. They could afford to hire the finest tutors for Akhsa. One taught her the Bible, another French, still another the pianoforte, and a fourth dancing. She learned everything quickly. At eight, she was playing chess with her grandfather. Reb Naftali didn't need to offer a dowry for her marriage, since she was heir to his entire fortune.

Matches were sought for her early, but her grandmother was hard to please. She would look at a boy proposed by the marriage brokers and say, "He has the shoulders of a fool," or, "He has the narrow forehead of an ignoramus."

One day Nesha died unexpectedly. Reb Naftali was in his late seventies and it was unthinkable that he remarry. Half his day he devoted to religion, the other half to business. He rose at daybreak and pored over the Talmud and the Commentaries and wrote letters to community el-

Translated by the author and Laurie Colwin

ders. When a man was sick, Reb Naftali went to comfort him. Twice a week he visited the poorhouse with Akhsa, who carried a contribution of soup and groats herself. More than once, Akhsa, the pampered and scholarly, rolled up her sleeves and made beds there.

In the summer, after midday sleep, Reb Naftali ordered his britska harnessed and he rode around the fields and village with Akhsa. While they rode, he discussed business, and it was known that he listened to her advice just as he had listened to her grandmother's.

But there was one thing that Akhsa didn't have—a friend. Her grandmother had tried to find friends for her; she had even lowered her standards and invited girls from Krasnobród. But Akhsa had no patience with their chatter about clothes and household matters. Since the tutors were all men, Akhsa was kept away from them, except for lessons. Now her grandfather became her only companion. Reb Naftali had met famous noblemen in his lifetime. He had been to fairs in Warsaw, Crakow, Danzig, and Königsberg. He would sit for hours with Akhsa and tell her about rabbis and miracle workers, about the disciples of the false Messiah Sabbatai Zevi, quarrels in the Sejm, the caprices of the Zamojskis, the Radziwills, and the Czartoryskis—their wives, lovers, courtiers. Sometimes Akhsa would cry out, "I wish you were my fiancé, not my grandfather!" and kiss his eyes and his white beard.

Reb Naftali would answer, "I'm not the only man in Poland. There are plenty like me, and young to boot."

"Where, Grandfather? Where?"

After her grandmother's death, Akhsa refused to rely on anyone else's judgment in the choice of a husband—not even her grandfather's. Just as her grandmother saw only bad, Reb Naftali saw only good. Akhsa demanded that the matchmakers allow her to meet her suitor, and Reb Naftali finally consented. The young pair would be brought together in a room, the door would be left open, and a deaf old woman servant would stand at the threshold to watch that the meeting be brief and without frivolity. As a rule, Akhsa stayed with the young man not more than a few minutes. Most of the suitors seemed dull and silly. Others tried to be clever and made undignified jokes. Akhsa dismissed them abruptly. How strange, but her grandmother still expressed her opinion. Once, Akhsa heard her say clearly, "He has the snout of a pig." Another time, she said, "He talks like the standard letter book."

Akhsa knew quite well that it was not her grandmother speaking. The dead don't return from the other world to comment on prospective fiancés. Just the same, it was her grandmother's voice, her style. Akhsa wanted to talk to her grandfather about it, but she was afraid he would think her crazy. Besides, her grandfather longed for his wife, and Akhsa didn't want to stir up his grief.

When Reb Naftali Holishitzer realized that his granddaughter was driving away the matchmakers, he was troubled. Akhsa was now past her eighteenth year. The people in Krasnobród had begun to gossip— she was demanding a knight on a white horse or the moon in heaven; she would stay a spinster. Reb Naftali decided not to give in to her whims any more but to marry her off. He went to a yeshiva and brought back with him a young man named Zemach, an orphan and a devout scholar. He was dark as a gypsy, small, with broad shoulders. His sidelocks were thick. He was nearsighted and studied eighteen hours a day. The moment he reached Krasnobród, he went to the study house and began to sway in front of an open volume of the Talmud. His sidelocks swayed, too. Students came to talk with him, and he spoke without lifting his gaze from the book. He seemed to know the Talmud by heart, since he caught everyone misquoting.

Akhsa demanded a meeting, but Reb Naftali replied that this was conduct befitting tailors and shoemakers, not a girl of good breeding. He warned Akhsa that if she drove Zemach away he would disinherit her. Since men and women were in separate rooms during the engagement party, Akhsa had no chance of seeing Zemach until the marriage contract was to be signed. She looked at him and heard her grandmother say, "They've sold you shoddy goods."

Her words were so clear it seemed to Akhsa that everyone should have heard them, but no one had. The girls and women crowded around her, congratulating her and praising her beauty, her dress, her jewelry. Her grandfather passed her the contract and a quill, and her grandmother cried out, "Don't sign!" She grabbed Akhsa's elbow and a blot formed on the paper.

Reb Naftali shouted, "What have you done!"

Akhsa tried to sign, but the pen fell from her hand. She burst into tears. "Grandfather, I can't."

"Akhsa, you shame me."

"Grandfather, forgive me." Akhsa covered her face with her hands. There was an outcry. Men hissed and women laughed and wept. Akhsa cried silently. They half led, half carried her to her room and put her on her bed.

Zemach exclaimed, "I don't want to be married to this shrew!"

He pushed through the crowd and ran to get a wagon back to the yeshiva. Reb Naftali went after him, trying to pacify him with words and money, but Zemach threw Reb Naftali's banknotes to the ground. Someone brought his wicker trunk from the inn where he had stayed. Before the wagon pulled away, Zemach cried out, "I don't forgive her, and God won't, either."

For days after that, Akhsa was ill. Reb Naftali Holishitzer, who had been successful all his life, was not accustomed to failure. He became sick; his face took on a yellow pallor. Women and girls tried to comfort Akhsa. Rabbis and elders came to visit Reb Naftali, but he got weaker as the days passed. After a while, Akhsa gained back her strength and left her sickbed. She went to her grandfather's room, bolting the door behind her. The maid who listened and spied through the keyhole reported that she had heard him say, "You are mad!"

Akhsa nursed her grandfather, brought him his medicine and bathed him with a sponge, but the old man developed an inflammation of the lungs. Blood ran from his nose. His urine stopped. Soon he died. He had written his will years before and left one-third of his estate to charity and the rest to Akhsa.

According to the law, one does not sit shivah in mourning after the death of a grandfather, but Akhsa went through the ceremony anyway. She sat on a low stool and read the book of Job. She ordered that no one be let in. She had shamed an orphan—a scholar—and caused the death of her grandfather. She became melancholy. Since she had read the story of Job before, she began to search in her grandfather's library for another book to read. To her amazement, she found a Bible translated into Polish—the New Testament as well as the Old. Akhsa knew it was a forbidden book, but she turned the pages anyway. Had her grandfather read it, Akhsa wondered. No, it couldn't be. She remembered that on the Gentile feast days, when holy icons and pictures were carried in processions near the house, she was not allowed to look out of the window. Her grandfather told her it was idolatry. She wondered if her grandmother had read this Bible. Among the pages she found some pressed cornflowers—a flower her grandmother had often picked. Grandmother came from Bohemia; it was said that her father had belonged to the Sabbatai Zevi sect. Akhsa recalled that Prince Czartoryski used to spend time with her grandmother when he visited the estate, and praised the way she spoke Polish. If she hadn't been a Jewish girl, he said, he would have married her—a great compliment.

That night Akhsa read the New Testament to the last page. It was difficult for her to accept that Jesus was God's only begotten son and that He rose from the grave, but she found this book more comforting to her tortured spirit than the castigating words of the prophets, who never mentioned the Kingdom of Heaven or the resurrection of the dead. All they promised was a good harvest for good deeds and starvation and plague for bad ones.

On the seventh night of shivah, Akhsa went to bed. The light was out and she was dozing when she heard footsteps that she recognized as her grandfather's. In the darkness, her grandfather's figure emerged: the light face, the white beard, the mild features, even the skullcap on his high forehead. He said in a quiet voice, "Akhsa, you have committed an injustice."

Akhsa began to cry. "Grandfather, what should I do?"

"Everything can be corrected."

"How?"

"Apologize to Zemach. Become his wife."

"Grandfather, I hate him."

"He is your destined one."

He lingered for a moment, and Akhsa could smell his snuff, which he used to mix with cloves and smelling salts. Then he vanished and an empty space remained in the darkness. She was too amazed to be frightened. She leaned against the headboard, and after some time she slept.

She woke with a start. She heard her grandmother's voice. This was not a murmuring like Grandfather's but the strong voice of a living person. "Akhsa, my daughter."

Akhsa burst into tears. "Grandmother, where are you?"

"I'm here."

"What should I do?"

"Whatever your heart desires."

"What, Grandmother?"

"Go to the priest. He will advise you."

Akhsa became numb. Fear constricted her throat. She managed to say, "You're not my grandmother. You're a demon."

"I am your grandmother. Do you remember how we went wading in the pond that summer night near the flat hill and you found a gulden in the water?"

"Yes, Grandmother."

"I could give you other proof. Be it known that the Gentiles are right. Jesus of Nazareth is the Son of God. He was born of the Holy Spirit as prophesied. The rebellious Jews refused to accept the truth and therefore they are punished. The Messiah will not come to them because He is here already."

"Grandmother, I'm afraid."

"Akhsa, don't listen!" her grandfather suddenly shouted into her right ear. "This isn't your grandmother. It's an evil spirit disguised to trick you. Don't give in to his blasphemies. He will drag you into perdition."

"Akhsa, that is not your grandfather but a goblin from behind the bathhouse," Grandmother interrupted. "Zemach is a ne'er-do-well, and vengeful to boot. He will torment you, and the children he begets will be vermin like him. Save yourself while there is time. God is with the Gentiles."

"Lilith! She-demon! Daughter of Ketev M'riri!" Grandfather growled.

"Liar!"

Grandfather became silent, but Grandmother continued to talk, although her voice faded. She said, "Your real grandfather learned the truth in Heaven and converted. They baptized him with heavenly water and he rests in Paradise. The saints are all bishops and cardinals. Those who remain stubborn are roasted in the fires of Gehenna. If you don't believe me, ask for a sign."

"What sign?"

"Unbutton your pillowcase, rip open the seams of the pillow, and there you will find a crown of feathers. No human hand could make a crown like this."

Her grandmother disappeared, and Akhsa fell into a heavy sleep. At dawn, she awoke and lit a candle. She remembered her grandmother's words, unbuttoned the pillowcase, and ripped open the pillow. What she saw was so extraordinary she could scarcely believe her eyes: down and feathers entwined into a crown, with little ornaments and complex designs no worldly master could have duplicated. On the top of the crown was a tiny cross. It was all so airy that Akhsa's breath made it flutter. Akhsa gasped. Whoever had made this crown—an angel or a demon— had done his work in darkness, in the inside of a pillow. She was beholding a miracle. She extinguished the candle and stretched out on the bed. For a long time she lay without any thoughts. Then she went back to sleep.

In the morning when she awoke, Akhsa thought she had had a dream, but on the night table she saw the crown of feathers. The sun made it sparkle with the colors of the rainbow. It looked as if it were set with the smallest of gems. She sat and contemplated the wonder. Then she put on a black dress and a black shawl and asked that the carriage be brought round for her. She rode to the house where Koscik, the priest, resided. The housekeeper answered her knock. The priest was nearing seventy and he knew Akhsa. He had often come to the estate to bless the peasants' bread at Easter time and to give rites to the dying and conduct weddings and funerals. One of Akhsa's teachers had borrowed a Latin–Polish dictionary from him. Whenever the priest visited, Akhsa's grandmother invited him to her parlor and they conversed over cake and vishniak.

The priest offered Akhsa a chair. She sat down and told him everything. He said, "Don't go back to the Jews. Come to us. We will see to it that your fortune remains intact."

"I forgot to take the crown. I want to have it with me."

"Yes, my daughter, go and bring it."

Akhsa went home, but a maid had cleaned her bedroom and dusted the night table; the crown had vanished. Akhsa searched in the garbage ditch, in the slops, but not a trace could she find.

Soon after that, the terrible news was abroad in Krasnobród that Akhsa had converted.

Six years passed. Akhsa married and became the Squiress Maria Malkowska. The old squire, Wladyslaw Malkowski, had died without direct heir and had left his estate to his nephew Ludwik. Ludwik had remained a bachelor until he was forty-five, and it seemed he would never marry. He lived in his uncle's castle with his spinster sister, Gloria. His love affairs were with peasant girls, and he had sired a number of bastards. He was small and light, with a blond goatee. Ludwik kept to himself, reading old books of history, religion, and genealogy. He smoked a porcelain pipe, drank alone, hunted by himself, and avoided the noblemen's dances. The business of the estate he handled with a strong hand, and he made sure his bailiff never stole from him. His neighbors thought he was a pedant, and some considered him half mad. When Akhsa accepted the Christian faith, he asked her—now Maria—to marry him. Gossips said that Ludwik, the miser, had fallen in love with Maria's inheritance. The priests and others persuaded Akhsa to accept Ludwik's proposal. He was a descendant of the Polish king Leszczyński. Gloria, who was ten years older than Ludwik, opposed the match, but Ludwik for once did not listen to her.

The Jews of Krasnobród were afraid that Akhsa would become their enemy and instigate Ludwik against them, as happened with so many converts, but Ludwik continued to trade with the Jews, selling them fish, grain, and cattle. Zelig Frampoler, a court Jew, delivered all kinds of merchandise to the estate. Gloria remained the lady of the castle.

In the first weeks of their marriage, Akhsa and Ludwik took trips together in a surrey. Ludwik even began to pay visits to neighboring squires, and he talked of giving a ball. He confessed all his past adventures with women to Maria and promised to behave like a God-fearing Christian. But before long he fell back into his old ways; he withdrew from his neighbors, started up his affairs with peasant girls, and began to drink again. An angry silence hung between man and wife. Ludwik ceased coming to Maria's bedroom, and she did not conceive. In time, they stopped dining at the same table, and when Ludwik needed to tell Maria something he sent a note with a servant. Gloria, who managed the finances, allowed her sister-in-law a gulden a week; Maria's fortune now belonged to her husband. It became clear to Akhsa that God was punishing her and that nothing remained but to wait for death. But what would happen to her after she died? Would she be roasted on a bed of needles and be thrown into the waste of the netherworld? Would she be reincarnated as a dog, a mouse, a millstone?

Because she had nothing to occupy her time with, Akhsa spent all day and part of the night in her husband's library. Ludwik had not added to it, and the books were old, bound in leather, in wood, or in moth-eaten velvet and silk. The pages were yellow and foxed. Akhsa read stories of ancient kings, faraway countries, of all sorts of battles and intrigues among princes, cardinals, dukes. She pored over tales of the Crusades and the Black Plague. The world crawled with wickedness, but it was also full of wonders. Stars in the sky warred and swallowed one another. Comets foretold catastrophes. A child was born with a tail; a woman grew scales and fins. In India, fakirs stepped barefooted on red-hot coals without being burned. Others let themselves be buried alive, and then rose from their graves.

It was strange, but after the night Akhsa found the crown of feathers in her pillow she was not given another sign from the powers that rule the universe. She never heard from her grandfather or grandmother. There were times when Akhsa desired to call out to her grandfather, but she did not dare mention his name with her unclean lips. She had betrayed the Jewish God and she no longer believed in the Gentile one, so she refrained from praying. Often when Zelig Frampoler came to the estate and Akhsa saw him from the window, she wanted to ask him about the Jewish community, but she was afraid that he might hold it a sin to speak to her, and that Gloria would denounce her for associating with Jews.

Years rolled by. Gloria's hair turned white and her head shook. Ludwik's goatee became gray. The servants grew old, deaf, and half blind. Akhsa, or Maria, was in her thirties, but she often imagined herself an old woman. With the years she became more and more convinced that it was the Devil who had persuaded her to convert and that it was he who had fashioned the crown of feathers. But the road back was blocked. The Russian law forbade a convert to return to his faith. The bit of information that reached her about the Jews was bad: the synagogue in Krasnobród had burned down, as well as the stores in the marketplace. Dignified householders and community elders hung bags on their shoulders and went begging. Every few months there was an epidemic. There was nowhere to return to. She often contemplated suicide, but how? She lacked the courage to hang herself or cut her veins; she had no poison.

Slowly, Akhsa came to the conclusion that the universe was ruled by the black powers. It was not God holding dominion but Satan. She

found a thick book about witchcraft that contained detailed descriptions
of spells and incantations, talismans, the conjuring up of demons and
goblins, the sacrifices to Asmodeus, Lucifer, and Beelzebub. There were
accounts of the Black Mass; and of how the witches anointed their
bodies, gathered in the forest, partook of human flesh, and flew in the
air riding on brooms, shovels, and hoops, accompanied by bevies of
devils and other creatures of the night that had horns and tails, bat's
wings, and the snouts of pigs. Often these monsters lay with the witches,
who gave birth to freaks.

Akhsa reminded herself of the Yiddish proverb "If you cannot go
over, go under." She had lost the world to come; therefore, she decided
to enjoy some revelry while she had this life. At night she began to call
the Devil, prepared to make a covenant with him as many neglected
women had done before.

Once in the middle of the night, after Akhsa had swallowed a potion
of mead, spittle, human blood, crow's egg spiced with galbanum and
mandrake, she felt a cold kiss on her lips. In the shine of the late-night
moon she saw a naked male figure—tall and black, with long elflocks,
the horns of a buck, and two protruding teeth, like a boar's. He bent
down over her, whispering, "What is your command, my mistress? You
may ask for half my kingdom."

His body was as translucent as a spider web. He stank of pitch.
Akhsa had been about to reply, "You, my slave, come and have me."
Instead, she murmured, "My grandparents."

The Devil burst into laughter. "They are dust!"

"Did you braid the crown of feathers?" Akhsa asked.

"Who else?"

"You deceived me?"

"I am a deceiver," the Devil answered with a giggle.

"Where is the truth?" Akhsa asked.

"The truth is that there is no truth."

The Devil lingered for a while and then disappeared. For the remainder of the night, Akhsa was neither asleep nor awake. Voices spoke
to her. Her breasts became swollen, her nipples hard, her belly distended. Pain bored into her skull. Her teeth were on edge, and her
tongue enlarged so that she feared it would split her palate. Her eyes
bulged from their sockets. There was a knocking in her ears as loud as a
hammer on an anvil. Then she felt as if she were in the throes of labor.
"I'm giving birth to a demon!" Akhsa cried out. She began to pray to the
God she had forsaken. Finally she fell asleep, and when she awoke in
the pre-dawn darkness all her pains had ceased. She saw her grandfather
standing at the foot of her bed. He wore a white robe and cowl, such as

he used to wear on the eve of Yom Kippur when he blessed Akhsa before going to the Kol Nidre prayer. A light shone from his eyes and lit up Akhsa's quilt. "Grandfather," Akhsa murmured.

"Yes, Akhsa. I am here."

"Grandfather, what shall I do?"

"Run away. Repent."

"I'm lost."

"It is never too late. Find the man you shamed. Become a Jewish daughter."

Later, Akhsa did not remember whether her grandfather had actually spoken to her or she had understood him without words. The night was over. Daybreak reddened the window. Birds were twittering. Akhsa examined her sheet. There was no blood. She had not given birth to a demon. For the first time in years, she recited the Hebrew prayer of thanksgiving.

She got out of bed, washed at the basin, and covered her hair with a shawl. Ludwik and Gloria had robbed her of her inheritance, but she still possessed her grandmother's jewelry. She wrapped it in a handkerchief and put it in a basket, together with a shirt and underwear. Ludwik had either stayed the night with one of his mistresses or he had left at dawn to hunt. Gloria lay sick in her boudoir. The maid brought Akhsa her breakfast, but she ate little. Then she left the estate. Dogs barked at her as if she were a stranger. The old servants looked in amazement as the squiress passed through the gates with a basket on her arm and a kerchief on her head like a peasant woman.

Although Malkowski's property was not far from Krasnobród, Akhsa spent most of the day on the road. She sat down to rest and washed her hands in a stream. She recited grace and ate the slice of bread she had brought with her.

Near the Krasnobród cemetery stood the hut of Eber, the gravedigger. Outside, his wife was washing linen in a tub. Akhsa asked her, "Is this the way to Krasnobród?"

"Yes, straight ahead."

"What's the news from the village?"

"Who are you?"

"I'm a relative of Reb Naftali Holishitzer."

The woman wiped her hands on her apron. "Not a soul is left of that family."

"Where is Akhsa?"

The old woman trembled. "She should have been buried head first, Father in Heaven." And she told about Akhsa's conversion. "She's had her punishment already in this world."

"What became of the yeshiva boy she was betrothed to?"

"Who knows? He isn't from around here."

Akhsa asked about the graves of her grandparents, and the old woman pointed to two headstones bent one toward the other, overgrown with moss and weeds. Akhsa prostrated herself in front of them and lay there until nightfall.

For three months, Akhsa wandered from yeshiva to yeshiva, but she did not find Zemach. She searched in community record books, questioned elders and rabbis—without result. Since not every town had an inn, she often slept in the poorhouse. She lay on a pallet of straw, covered with a mat, praying silently that her grandfather would appear and tell her where to find Zemach. He gave no sign. In the darkness, the old and the sick coughed and muttered. Children cried. Mothers cursed. Although Akhsa accepted this as part of her punishment, she could not overcome her sense of indignity. Community leaders scolded her. They made her wait for days to see them. Women were suspicious of her—why was she looking for a man who no doubt had a wife and children, or might even be in his grave? "Grandfather, why did you drive me to this?" Akhsa cried. "Either show me the way or send death to take me."

On a wintry afternoon, while Akhsa was sitting in an inn in Lublin, she asked the innkeeper if he had ever heard of a man called Zemach—small in stature, swarthy, a former yeshiva boy and scholar. One of the other guests said, "You mean Zemach, the teacher from Izbica?"

He described Zemach, and Akhsa knew she had found the one she was looking for. "He was engaged to marry a girl in Krasnobród," she said.

"I know. The convert. Who are you?"

"A relative."

"What do you want with him?" the guest asked. "He's poor, and stubborn to boot. All his pupils have been taken away from him. He's a wild and contrary man."

"Does he have a wife?"

"He's had two already. One he tortured to death and the other left him."

"Does he have children?"

"No, he's sterile."

The guest was about to say more, but a servant came to call for him.

Akhsa's eyes filled with tears. Her grandfather had not forsaken her. He had led her in the right direction. She went to arrange conveyance to Izbica, and in front of the inn stood a covered wagon ready to leave.

"No, I am not alone," she said to herself. "Every step is known in Heaven."

In the beginning, the roads were paved, but soon they became dirt trails full of holes and ditches. The night was wet and dark. Often the passengers had to climb down and help the coachman push the wagon out of the mud. The others scolded him, but Akhsa accepted her discomfort with grace. Wet snow was falling and a cold wind blew. Every time she got out of the wagon she sank over her ankles in mud. They arrived in Izbica late in the evening. The whole village was a swamp. The huts were dilapidated. Someone showed Akhsa the way to Zemach the teacher's house—it was on a hill near the butcher shops. Even though it was winter, there was a stench of decay in the air. Butcher-shop dogs were slinking around.

Akhsa looked into the window of Zemach's hut and saw peeling walls, a dirt floor, and shelves of worn books. A wick in a dish of oil gave the only light. At the table sat a little man with a black beard, bushy brows, a yellow face, and a pointed nose. He was bending myopically over a large volume. He wore the lining of a skullcap and a quilted jacket that showed the dirty batting. As Akhsa stood watching, a mouse came out of its hole and scurried over to the bed, which had a pallet of rotting straw, a pillow without a case, and a moth-eaten sheepskin for a blanket. Even though Zemach had aged, Akhsa recognized him. He scratched himself. He spat on his fingertips and wiped them on his forehead. Yes, that was he. Akhsa wanted to laugh and cry at the same time. In a moment she turned her face toward the darkness. For the first time in years, she heard her grandmother's voice. "Akhsa, run away."

"Where to?"

"Back to Esau."

Then she heard her grandfather's voice. "Akhsa, he will save you from the abyss."

Akhsa had never heard her grandfather speak with such fervor. She felt the emptiness that comes before fainting. She leaned against the door and it opened.

Zemach lifted one bushy brow. His eyes were bulging and jaundiced. "What do you want?" he rasped.

"Are you Reb Zemach?"

"Yes, who are you?"

"Akhsa, from Krasnobród. Once your fiancée . . ."

Zemach was silent. He opened his crooked mouth, revealing a single tooth, black as a hook. "The convert?"

"I have come back to Jewishness."

Zemach jumped up. A terrible cry tore from him. "Get out of my house! Blotted be your name!"

"Reb Zemach, please hear me!"

He ran toward her with clenched fists. The dish of oil fell and the light was extinguished. "Filth!"

The study house in Holishitz was packed. It was the day before the new moon, and a crowd had gathered to recite the supplications. From the women's section came the sound of pious recitation. Suddenly the door opened, and a black-bearded man wearing tattered clothes strode in. A bag was slung over his shoulder. He was leading a woman on a rope as if she were a cow. She wore a black kerchief on her head, a dress made of sackcloth, and rags on her feet. Around her neck hung a wreath of garlic. The worshippers stopped their prayers. The stranger gave a sign to the woman and she prostrated herself on the threshold. "Jews, step on me!" she called. "Jews, spit on me!"

Turmoil rose in the study house. The stranger went up to the reading table, tapped for silence, and intoned, "This woman's family comes from your town. Her grandfather was Reb Naftali Holishitzer. She is the Akhsa who converted and married a squire. She has seen the truth now and wants to atone for her abominations."

Though Holishitz was in the part of Poland that belonged to Austria, the story of Akhsa had been heard there. Some of the worshippers protested that this was not the way of repentance; a human being should not be dragged by a rope, like cattle. Others threatened the stranger with their fists. It was true that in Austria a convert could return to Jewishness according to the law of the land. But if the Gentiles were to learn that one who went over to their faith had been humiliated in such a fashion, harsh edicts and recriminations might result. The old rabbi, Reb Bezalel, approached Akhsa with quick little steps. "Get up, my daughter. Since you have repented, you are one of us."

Akhsa rose. "Rabbi, I have disgraced my people."

"Since you repent, the Almighty will forgive you."

When the worshippers in the women's section heard what was going on, they rushed into the room with the men, the rabbi's wife among them. Reb Bezalel said to her, "Take her home and dress her in decent clothing. Man was created in God's image."

"Rabbi," Akhsa said, "I want to atone for my iniquities."

"I will prescribe a penance for you. Don't torture yourself."

Some of the women began to cry. The rabbi's wife took off her shawl and hung it over Akhsa's shoulders. Another matron offered Akhsa a cape. They led her into the chamber where in olden times they had kept captive those who sinned against the community—it still contained a block and chain. The women dressed Akhsa there. Someone brought her a skirt and shoes. As they busied themselves about her, Akhsa beat her breast with her fist and recounted her sins: she had spited God, served idols, copulated with a Gentile. She sobbed, "I practiced witchcraft. I conjured up Satan. He braided me a crown of feathers." When Akhsa was dressed, the rabbi's wife took her home.

After prayers, the men began to question the stranger as to who he was and how he was connected with Reb Naftali's granddaughter.

He replied, "My name is Zemach. I was supposed to become her husband, but she refused me. Now she has come to ask my forgiveness."

"A Jew should forgive."

"I forgive her, but the Almighty is a God of vengeance."

"He is also a God of mercy."

Zemach began a debate with the scholars, and his erudition was obvious at once. He quoted the Talmud, the Commentaries, and the Responsa. He even corrected the rabbi when he misquoted.

Reb Bezalel asked him, "Do you have a family?"

"I am divorced."

"In that case, everything can be set right."

The rabbi invited Zemach to go home with him. The women sat with Akhsa out in the kitchen. They urged her to eat bread with chicory. She had been fasting for three days. In the rabbi's study the men looked after Zemach. They brought him trousers, shoes, a coat, and a hat. Since he was infested with lice, they took him to the baths.

In the evening, the seven outstanding citizens of the town and all the important elders gathered. The wives brought Akhsa. The rabbi pronounced that, according to the law, Akhsa was not married. Her union with the squire was nothing but an act of lechery. The rabbi asked, "Zemach, do you desire Akhsa for a wife?"

"I do."

"Akhsa, will you take Zemach for a husband?"

"Yes, Rabbi, but I am not worthy."

The rabbi outlined Akhsa's penance. She must fast each Monday and Thursday, abstain from meat and fish on the weekdays, recite psalms, and rise at dawn for prayers. The rabbi said to her, "The chief thing is not the punishment but the remorse. 'And he will return and be healed,' the prophet says."

"Rabbi, excuse," Zemach interrupted. "This kind of penance is for common sins, not for conversion."

"What do you want her to do?"

"There are more severe forms of contrition."

"What, for example?"

"Wearing pebbles in the shoes. Rolling naked in the snow in winter —in nettles in summer. Fasting from Sabbath to Sabbath."

"Nowadays, people do not have the strength for such rigors," the rabbi said after some hesitation.

"If they have the strength to sin, they should have the strength to expiate."

"Holy Rabbi," said Akhsa, "do not let me off lightly. Let the rabbi give me a harsh penance."

"I have said what is right."

All kept silent. Then Akhsa said, "Zemach, give me my bundle." Zemach had put her bag in a corner. He brought it to the table and she took out a little sack. A sigh could be heard from the group as she poured out settings of pearls, diamonds, and rubies. "Rabbi, this is my jewelry," Akhsa said. "I do not deserve to own it. Let the rabbi dispose of it as he wishes."

"Is it yours or the squire's?"

"Mine, Rabbi, inherited from my sacred grandmother."

"It is written that even the most charitable should never give up more than a fifth part."

Zemach shook his head. "Again I am in disagreement. She disgraced her grandmother in Paradise. She should not be permitted to inherit her jewels."

The rabbi clutched his beard. "If you know better, you become the rabbi." He rose from his chair and then sat down again. "How will you sustain yourselves?"

"I will be a water carrier," Zemach said.

"Rabbi, I can knead dough and wash linen," Akhsa said.

"Well, do as you choose. I believe in the mercy, not in the rigor, of the law."

In the middle of the night Akhsa opened her eyes. Husband and wife lived in a hut with a dirt floor, not far from the cemetery. All day long Zemach carried water. Akhsa washed linen. Except for Saturday and holidays, both fasted every day and ate only in the evening. Akhsa had put sand and pebbles into her shoes and wore a rough woolen shirt next to her skin. At night they slept separately on the floor—he on a mat by the window, she on a straw pallet by the oven. On a rope that stretched from wall to wall hung shrouds she had made for them.

They had been married for three years, but Zemach still had not approached her. He had confessed that he, too, was dipped in sin. While he had a wife, he had lusted for Akhsa. He had spilled his seed like Onan. He had craved revenge upon her, had railed against the Almighty, and had taken out his wrath on his wives, one of whom died. How could he be more defiled?

Even though the hut was near a forest and they could get wood for nothing, Zemach would not allow the stove to be heated at night. They slept in their clothes, covered with sacks and rags. The people of Holishitz maintained that Zemach was a madman; the rabbi had called for man and wife and explained that it is as cruel to torture oneself as it is to torture others, but Zemach quoted from *The Beginning of Wisdom* that repentance without mortification is meaningless.

Akhsa made a confession every night before sleep, and still her dreams were not pure. Satan came to her in the image of her grand-mother and described dazzling cities, elegant balls, passionate squires, lusty women. Her grandfather had become silent again.

In Akhsa's dreams, Grandmother was young and beautiful. She sang bawdy songs, drank wine, and danced with charlatans. Some nights she led Akhsa into temples where priests chanted and idolators kneeled before golden statues. Naked courtesans drank wine from horns and gave themselves over to licentiousness.

One night Akhsa dreamed that she stood naked in a round hole. Midgets danced around her in circles. They sang obscene dirges. There was a blast of trumpets and the drumming of drums. When she awoke, the black singing still rang in her ears. "I am lost forever," she said to herself.

Zemach had also wakened. For a time he looked out through the one windowpane he had not boarded up. Then he asked, "Akhsa, are you awake? A new snow has fallen."

Akhsa knew too well what he meant. She said, "I have no strength."

"You had the strength to give yourself to the wicked."

"My bones ache."

"Tell that to the Avenging Angel."

The snow and the late-night moon cast a bright glare into the room. Zemach had let his hair grow long, like an ancient ascetic. His beard was wild and his eyes glowed in the night. Akhsa could never understand how he had the power to carry water all day long and still study half the night. He scarcely partook of the evening meal. To keep himself from enjoying the food, he swallowed his bread without chewing it, he over-salted and -peppered the soup she cooked for him. Akhsa herself had become emaciated. Often she looked at her reflection in the slops and saw a thin face, sunken cheeks, a sickly pallor. She coughed frequently and spat phlegm with blood. Now she said, "Forgive me, Zemach, I can't get up."

"Get up, adulteress. This may be your last night."

"I wish it were."

"Confess! Tell the truth."

"I have told you everything."

"Did you enjoy the lechery?"

"No, Zemach, no."

"Last time you admitted that you did."

Akhsa was silent for a long time. "Very rarely. Perhaps for a second."

"And you forgot God?"

"Not altogether."

"You knew God's law, but you defied Him willfully."

"I thought the truth was with the Gentiles."

"All because Satan braided you a crown of feathers?"

"I thought it was a miracle."

"Harlot, don't defend yourself!"

"I do not defend myself. He spoke with Grandmother's voice."

"Why did you listen to your grandmother and not to your grandfather?"

"I was foolish."

"Foolish? For years you wallowed in utter desecration."

After a while man and wife went out barefoot into the night. Zemach threw himself into the snow first. He rolled over and over with great speed. His skullcap fell off. His body was covered with black hair, like fur. Akhsa waited a minute, and then she too threw herself down. She turned in the snow slowly and in silence while Zemach recited, "We have sinned, we have betrayed, we have robbed, we have lied, we have mocked, we have rebelled." And then he added, "Let it be Thy will that my death shall be the redemption for all my iniquities."

Akhsa had heard this lamentation often, but it made her tremble every time. This was the way the peasants had wailed when her husband, Squire Malkowski, whipped them. She was more afraid of Zemach's wailing than of the cold in winter and the nettles in summer. Occasionally, when he was in a gentler temper, Zemach promised that he would come to her as husband to wife. He even said that he would like to be the father of her children. But when? He kept on searching for new misdeeds in both of them. Akhsa grew weaker from day to day. The shrouds on the rope and the headstones in the graveyard seemed to beckon her. She made Zemach vow that he would recite the Kaddish over her grave.

On a hot day in the month of Tammuz, Akhsa went to gather sorrel leaves from the pasture that bordered the river. She had fasted all day long and she wanted to cook schav for herself and Zemach for their evening meal. In the middle of her gathering she was overcome by exhaustion. She stretched out on the grass and dozed off, intending to rest only a quarter of an hour. But her mind went blank and her legs turned to stone. She fell into a deep sleep. When she opened her eyes, night had fallen. The sky was overcast, the air heavy with humidity. There was a storm coming. The earth steamed with the scent of grass and herbs, and it made Akhsa's head reel. In the darkness she found her basket, but it was empty. A goat or cow had eaten her sorrel. Suddenly she remembered her childhood, when she was pampered by her grandparents, dressed in velvet and silk, and served by maids and butlers. Now coughing choked her, her forehead was hot, and chills flashed through her spine. Since the moon did not shine and the stars were obscured, she scarcely knew her way. Her bare feet stepped on thorns and cow pats. "What a trap I have fallen into!" something cried out in her. She came to a tree and stopped to rest. At that moment she saw her grandfather. His white beard glowed in the darkness. She recognized his high forehead, his benign smile, and the loving kindness of his gaze. She called out, "Grandfather!" And in a second her face was washed with tears.

"I know everything," her grandfather said. "Your tribulations and your grief."

"Grandfather, what shall I do?"

"My daughter, your ordeal is over. We are waiting for you—I, Grandmother, all who love you. Holy angels will come to meet you."

"When, Grandfather?"

In that instant the image dissolved. Only the darkness remained. Akhsa felt her way home like someone blind. Finally, she reached her hut. As she opened the door she could feel that Zemach was there. He sat on the floor and his eyes were like two coals. He called out, "It's you?"

"Yes, Zemach."

"Why were you so long? Because of you I couldn't say my evening prayers in peace. You confused my thoughts."

"Forgive me, Zemach. I was tired and I fell asleep in the pasture."

"Liar! Convert! Scum!" Zemach screeched. "I searched for you in the pasture. You were whoring with a shepherd."

"What are you saying? God forbid!"

"Tell me the truth!" He jumped up and began to shake her. "Bitch! Demon! Lilith!"

Zemach had never acted so wildly. Akhsa said to him, "Zemach, my husband, I am faithful to you. I fell asleep on the grass. On the way home I saw my grandfather. My time is up." She was seized with such weakness that she sank to the floor.

Zemach's wrath vanished immediately. A mournful wail broke from him. "Sacred soul, where will I be without you? You are a saint. Forgive me my harshness. It was because of my love. I wanted to cleanse you so that you could sit in Paradise with the Holy Mothers."

"As I deserve, so shall I sit."

"Why should this happen to you? Is there no justice in Heaven?" And Zemach wailed in the voice that terrified her. He beat his head against the wall.

The next morning Akhsa did not rise from her bed. Zemach brought porridge he had cooked for her on the tripod. When he fed it to her, it spilled out of her mouth. Zemach fetched the town healer, but the healer did not know what to do. The women of the Burial Society came. Akhsa lay in a state of utter weakness. Her life was draining away. In the middle of the day Zemach went on foot to the town of Jaroslaw to bring a doctor. Evening came and he had not returned. That morning the rabbi's wife had sent a pillow to Akhsa. It was the first time in years she had slept on a pillow. Toward evening, the Burial Society women went home to their families and Akhsa remained alone. A wick burned in a dish of oil. A tepid breeze came through the open window. The moon did not shine, but the stars glittered. Crickets chirped, and frogs croaked with human voices. Once in a while a shadow passed the wall across from her bed. Akhsa knew that her end was near, but she had no fear of death. She took stock of her soul. She had been born rich and beautiful, with more gifts than all the others around her. Bad luck had made everything turn to the opposite. Did she suffer for her own sins or was she a reincarnation of someone who had sinned in a former generation? Akhsa knew that she should be spending her last hours in repentance and prayer. But such was her fate that doubt did not leave her even now. Her grandfather had told her one thing, her grandmother another. Akhsa had read in an old book about the Apostates who denied God, considering the world a random combination of atoms. She had now one desire—that a sign should be given, the pure truth revealed. She lay and prayed for a miracle. She fell into a light sleep and dreamed she was falling into depths that were tight and dark. Each time it seemed that she had reached the bottom, the foundation collapsed under her and she began to sink again with greater speed. The dark became heavier and the abyss even deeper.

She opened her eyes and knew what to do. With her last strength she got up and found a knife. She took off the pillowcase and with numb fingers ripped open the seams of the pillow. From the down stuffing she pulled out a crown of feathers. A hidden hand had braided in its top the four letters of God's name.

Akhsa put the crown beside her bed. In the wavering light of the wick, she could see each letter clearly: the *Yud*, the *Hai*, the *Vov*, and the other *Hai*. But, she wondered, in what way was this crown more a revelation of truth than the other? Was it possible that there were different faiths in Heaven? Akhsa began to pray for a new miracle. In her dismay she remembered the Devil's words: "The truth is that there is no truth."

Late at night, one of the Burial Society women returned. Akhsa wanted to implore her not to step on the crown, but she was too weak. The woman stepped on the crown, and its delicate structure dissolved. Akhsa closed her eyes and never opened them again. At dawn she sighed and gave up her soul.

One of the women lifted a feather and put it to her nostrils, but it did not flutter.

Later in the day, the Burial Society women cleansed Akhsa and dressed her in the shroud that she had sewn for herself. Zemach still had not returned from Jaroslaw and he was never heard of again. There was talk in Holishitz that he had been killed on the road. Some surmised that Zemach was not a man but a demon. Akhsa was buried near the chapel of a holy man, and the rabbi spoke a eulogy for her.

One thing remained a riddle. In her last hours Akhsa had ripped open the pillow that the rabbi's wife had sent her. The women who washed her body found bits of down between her fingers. How could a dying woman have the strength to do this? And what had she been searching for? No matter how much the townspeople pondered and how many explanations they tried to find, they never discovered the truth.

Because if there is such a thing as truth it is as intricate and hidden as a crown of feathers.

I · B · S

A Day in Coney Island

TODAY I know exactly what I should have done that summer—my work. But then I wrote almost nothing. "Who needs Yiddish in America?" I asked myself. Though the editor of a Yiddish paper published a sketch of mine from time to time in the Sunday edition, he told me frankly that no one gave a hoot about demons, dybbuks, and imps of two hundred years ago. At thirty, a refugee from Poland, I had become an anachronism. As if that were not enough, Washington had refused to extend my tourist visa. Lieberman, my lawyer, was trying to get me a permanent visa, but for that I needed my birth certificate, a certificate of morality, a letter saying that I was employed and would not become a public charge, and other papers I could not obtain. I sent alarmed letters to my friends in Poland. They never replied. The newspapers were predicting that Hitler would invade Poland any day.

I opened my eyes after a fitful sleep, full of nightmares. My Warsaw wristwatch showed a quarter to eleven. Through the cracks in the shade a golden light poured in. I could hear the sound of the ocean. For a year and a half I had been renting a furnished room in an old house in Sea Gate, not far from Esther (that's what I'll call her here), and I paid sixteen dollars a month for it. Mrs. Berger, the landlady, gave me breakfast at cost.

Until they deported me to Poland, I was enjoying American comfort. I took a bath in the bathroom down the hall (at that time of day, it was not occupied), and I could see a huge boat arriving from Europe—either the *Queen Mary* or the *Normandie*. What a luxury to look out my bathroom window and see the Atlantic Ocean and one of the newest and fastest ships in the world! While shaving, I made a decision: I would not

Translated by the author and Laurie Colwin

let them deport me to Poland. I would not fall into Hitler's paws. I would stay illegally. I had been told that if war broke out I had a good chance of becoming a citizen automatically. I grimaced at my reflection in the mirror. Already, my red hair was gone. I had watery blue eyes, inflamed eyelids, sunken cheeks, a protruding Adam's apple. Although people came from Manhattan to Sea Gate to get sunburned, my skin remained sickly white. My nose was thin and pale, my chin pointed, my chest flat. I often thought that I looked not unlike the imps I described in my stories. I stuck out my tongue and called myself a crazy *batlan*, which means an unworldly ne'er-do-well.

I expected Mrs. Berger's kitchen to be empty so late in the morning, but they were all there: Mr. Chaikowitz; his third wife; the old writer Lemkin, who used to be an anarchist; and Sylvia, who had taken me to a movie on Mermaid Avenue a few days before (until five o'clock the price of a ticket was only ten cents) and translated for me in broken Yiddish what the gangsters in the film were saying. In the darkness, she had taken my hand, which made me feel guilty. First, I had vowed to myself to keep the Ten Commandments. Second, I was betraying Esther. Third, I had a bad conscience about Anna, who still wrote me from Warsaw. But I didn't want to insult Sylvia.

When I entered the kitchen, Mrs. Berger cried out, "Here's our writer! How can a man sleep so long? I've been on my feet since six this morning." I looked at her thick legs, at her crooked toes and protruding bunions. Everyone teased me. Old Chaikowitz said, "Do you realize that you've missed the hour of morning prayer? You must be one of the Kotzker Hasids who pray late." His face was white and so was his goatee. His third wife, a fat woman with a thick nose and fleshy lips, joined in. "I bet this greenhorn hasn't even got phylacteries." As for Lemkin, he said, "If you ask me, he was up writing a best-seller the whole night."

"I'm hungry for the second time," Sylvia announced.

"What are you going to eat today?" Mrs. Berger asked me. "Two rolls with one egg, or two eggs with one roll?"

"Whatever you give me."

"I'm ready to give you the moon on a plate. I'm scared of what you may write about me in your Yiddish paper."

She brought me a large roll with two scrambled eggs and a big cup of coffee. The price of the breakfast was a quarter, but I owed Mrs. Berger six weeks' rent and for six weeks of breakfasts.

While I ate, Mrs. Chaikowitz talked about her oldest daughter, who had been widowed a year ago and was now remarried. "Have you ever heard of a thing like this?" she said. "He hiccupped once and dropped dead. It seems something ruptured in his brain. God forbid the misfortunes that can happen. He left her over $50,000 insurance. How long can a young woman wait? The other one was a doctor, this one is a lawyer—the biggest lawyer in America. He took one look at her and said, 'This is the woman I've been waiting for.' After six weeks they got married and went to Bermuda on the honeymoon. He bought her a ring for $10,000."

"Was he a bachelor?" Sylvia asked.

"He had a wife before, but she was not his type and he divorced her. She gets plenty of alimony from him—$200 a week. May she spend it all on medicine."

I ate my breakfast quickly and left. Outside, I looked in the letter box, but there was nothing for me. Only two blocks away I could see the house Esther had rented the winter before last. She let rooms to people who wanted to spend their vacations near New York. I couldn't visit her during the daytime; I used to steal over late at night. A lot of Yiddish writers and journalists lived there that summer, and they were not to know about my love affair with Esther. Since I didn't intend to marry her, why jeopardize her reputation? Esther was almost ten years older than I. She had divorced her husband—a Yiddish poet, a modernist, a Communist, a charlatan. He took off for California and never sent a penny for their two little daughters. He was living with an artist who painted abstract pictures. Esther needed a husband to support her and the girls, not a Yiddish writer who specialized in werewolves and sprites.

I had been in America for eighteen months, but Coney Island still surprised me. The sun poured down like fire. From the beach came a roar even louder than the ocean. On the boardwalk, an Italian watermelon vender pounded on a sheet of tin with his knife and called for customers in a wild voice. Everyone bellowed in his own way: sellers of popcorn and hot dogs, ice cream and peanuts, cotton candy and corn on the cob. I passed a sideshow displaying a creature that was half woman, half fish; a wax museum with figures of Marie Antoinette, Buffalo Bill, and John Wilkes Booth; a store where a turbanned astrologer sat in the dark surrounded by maps and globes of the heavenly constellations, casting horoscopes. Pygmies danced in front of a little circus, their black faces painted white, all of them bound loosely with a long rope. A mechanical ape puffed its belly like a bellows and laughed with raucous laughter. Negro boys aimed guns at metal ducklings. A half-naked man with a black beard and hair to his shoulders hawked potions that strengthened the muscles, beautified the skin, and brought back lost potency. He tore heavy chains with his hands and bent coins between his fingers. A little farther along, a medium advertised that she was calling back spirits from the dead, prophesying the future, and giving advice on love and marriage. I had taken with me a copy of Payot's *The Educa-*

tion of the Will in Polish. This book, which taught how to overcome laziness and do systematic spiritual work, had become my second Bible. But I did the opposite of what the book preached. I wasted my days with dreams, worries, empty fantasies, and locked myself in affairs that had no future.

At the end of the boardwalk, I sat down on a bench. Every day, the same group of old men was gathered there discussing Communism. A little man with a round red face and white hair like foam shook his head violently and yelled, "Who's going to save the workers—Hitler? Mussolini? That social Fascist Léon Blum? That opportunist Norman Thomas? Long live Comrade Stalin! Blessed be his hands!"

A man whose nose was etched with broken veins yelled back, "What about the Moscow trials? The millions of workers and peasants Stalin exiled to Siberia? What about the Soviet generals your Comrade Stalin executed?" His body was short and broad, as if his midsection had been sawed out. He spat into his handkerchief and shrieked, "Is Bukharin truly a German spy? Does Trotsky take money from Rockefeller? Was Kamenev an enemy of the proletariat? And how about yourself and the proletariat—you slum landlord!"

I often imagined that these men didn't stop to eat or sleep but waged their debate without interruption. They jumped against one another like he-goats ready to lunge. I had taken out a notebook and a fountain pen to write down a topic (perhaps about these debaters), but instead I began to draw a little man with long ears, a nose like a ram's horn, goose feet, and two horns on his head. After a while, I covered his body with scales and attached wings. I looked down at *The Education of the Will*. Discipline? Concentration? What help would that be if I was doomed to perish in Hitler's camps? And even if I survived, how would another novel or story help humanity? The metaphysicians had given up too soon, I decided. Reality is neither solipsism nor materialism. One should begin from the beginning: What is time? What is space? Here was the key to the whole riddle. Who knows, maybe I was destined to solve it.

I closed my eyes and determined once and forever to break through the fence between idea and being, the categories of pure reason and the thing in itself. Through my eyelids the sun shone red. The pounding of the waves and the din of the people merged. I felt, almost palpably, that I was one step from truth. "Time is nothing, space is nothing," I murmured. But that nothingness is the background of the world picture. Then what is the world picture? Is it matter? Spirit? Is it magnetism or gravitation? And what is life? What is suffering? What is consciousness? And if there is a God, what is He? Substance with infinite attributes?

The Monad of Monads? Blind will? The Unconscious? Can He be sex, as the cabalists hint? Is God an orgasm that never ceases? Is the universal nothingness the principle of femininity? I wouldn't come to any decision now, I decided. Maybe at night, in bed . . .

I opened my eyes and walked toward Brighton. The girders of the el threw a net of sun and shade on the pavements. A train from Manhattan zoomed by with a deafening clatter. No matter how time and space are defined, I thought, it is impossible to be simultaneously in Brooklyn and Manhattan. I passed by windows displaying mattresses, samples of roofing shingles, kosher chickens. I stopped at a Chinese restaurant. Should I go eat lunch? No, in the cafeteria it might be a nickel cheaper. I was down to almost my last cent. If my sketch, "After the Divorce," didn't appear in the Sunday edition, nothing remained but suicide.

Walking back, I marveled at myself. How could I have allowed my finances to dwindle this way? It was true that a tourist wasn't permitted to work, but how would the Immigration and Naturalization Service know if I washed dishes in a restaurant, or if I got a job as a messenger, or as a Hebrew teacher? It was crazy to wait until you were completely broke. True, I had convinced myself that I could be sustained by the leftovers on cafeteria tables. But sooner or later the manager or cashier would notice a human scavenger. The Americans would rather throw food into the garbage can than let it be eaten without payment. Thinking of food made me hungry. I remembered what I had read about fasting. With water to drink, a man can live for sixty days or so. I had read somewhere else that on an expedition to the South or North Pole Amundsen had eaten one of his boots. My present hunger, I told myself, was nothing but hysteria. Two eggs and a roll contain enough starch, fat, and protein for days to come. Just the same, I felt a gnawing in my stomach. My knees were weak. I was going to meet Esther that night, and starvation leads to impotence. I barely reached the cafeteria. I entered, took a check, and approached the buffet counter. I knew that those who are condemned to death order last meals; people don't even want to be executed on an empty stomach. This, I thought, was proof that life and death have no connection. Since death has no substance, it cannot end life. It is only a frame for living processes that are eternal.

I had not yet become a vegetarian, but I was brooding about vegetarianism. Nevertheless, I picked out flanken in horseradish with boiled potatoes and lima beans, a cup of noodle soup, a large roll, a cup of coffee, and a piece of cake—all for sixty cents. Holding my tray, I passed tables littered with the remains of meals, but I stopped at a clean one. On a chair lay the afternoon tabloid. Although I wanted to read it, I remembered Payot's words: intellectuals should eat slowly, chew each bite thoroughly, and not read. I glanced at the headlines just the same.

Hitler had again demanded the Polish Corridor. Smigly-Rydz had announced in the Sejm that Poland would fight for every inch of territory. The German ambassador in Tokyo had had an audience with the Mikado. A retired general in England had criticized the Maginot Line and predicted that it would be broken at the first attack. The powers that rule the universe were preparing the catastrophe.

After I finished eating, I counted my money, and I remembered that I had to call the newspaper and ask about my sketch. I knew that a call from Coney Island to Manhattan cost ten cents, and the Sunday editor, Leon Diamond, rarely came to the office. Still, I couldn't leave everything to fate. One dime wouldn't change the situation. I got up resolutely, found an empty telephone booth, and made the call. I prayed to the same powers preparing the world catastrophe that the operator wouldn't give me a wrong number. I pronounced my number as clearly as I could in my accent, and she told me to put in my dime. The girl at the switchboard answered and I asked for Leon Diamond. I was almost sure she would tell me he wasn't in the office, but I heard his voice on the line. I began to stutter and excuse myself. When I told him who I was, he said brusquely, "Your story will be in on Sunday."

"Thank you. Thank you very much."

"Send me a new story. Goodbye."

"A miracle! A miracle of Heaven!" I shouted to myself. The moment I hung up, another miracle occurred; money began to pour from the telephone—dimes, nickels, quarters. For a second I hesitated; to take it would be theft. But the Telephone Company would never get it back anyway, and someone who needed it less than I might find it. How many times had I put dimes into the telephone without getting a connection! I looked around and saw a fat woman in a bathing suit and a wide-brimmed straw hat waiting for the booth. I grabbed all the coins, shoved them into my pocket, and left, feeling like a new person. In my thoughts I apologized to the powers that know everything. I walked out of the cafeteria and strode toward Sea Gate. I calculated: if I got fifty dollars for the sketch, I would give Mrs. Berger thirty to cover my rent and breakfasts and I would still have twenty dollars to spend. Besides, I would re-establish credit with her and could stay on. In that case, I should call Lieberman, the lawyer. Who knows, maybe he had news from the consul in Toronto. A tourist could not get a permanent visa while in the United States. I would have to go to Cuba or Canada. The trip to Cuba was too expensive to consider, but would Canada allow me to enter? Lieberman had warned me that I would have to be smuggled from Detroit to Windsor, and whoever took me across the bridge would ask a fee of a hundred dollars.

Suddenly I realized that I had committed not one theft but two. In my elation, I had forgotten to pay for my lunch. I still held the check in my hand. This was certainly the work of Satan. Heaven was tempting me. I decided to go back and pay the sixty cents. I walked briskly, almost running. In the cafeteria, a man in a white uniform was standing next to the cashier. They spoke English. I wanted to wait until they were finished, but they kept on talking. The cashier threw a sidelong glance at me and asked, "What do you want?"

I answered in Yiddish, "I forgot to pay for my meal."

He grimaced and muttered, "Never mind, get out of here."

"But—"

"Get out of here, you," he growled, and then he winked.

With that, I understood what was going on. The man in the white uniform must have been the owner, or the manager, and the cashier didn't want him to see that he had let a customer get by without paying. The powers were conspiring to provide me with one stroke of luck after another. I went out, and through the glass door I saw the cashier and the man in the white uniform laughing. They were laughing at me, the greenhorn, with my Yiddish. But I knew that Heaven was trying me out, weighing my merits and iniquities on a scale: did I deserve to stay in America or must I perish in Poland. I was ashamed at having so much faith after calling myself an agnostic or unbeliever, and I said to my invisible critics, "After all, even according to Spinoza everything is determined. In the universe there are no large and small events. To eternity, a grain of sand is as important as a galaxy."

I didn't know what to do with the check. Should I keep it till tomorrow or throw it away? I decided I would give the money to the cashier without it. I tore it to bits and threw them into the trash can.

At home, I collapsed on my bed and fell into a heavy sleep, where I found the secret of time, space, and causality. It seemed unbelievably simple, but the moment I opened my eyes it was all forgotten. What remained was the taste of something otherworldly and marvelous. In my dream I gave my philosophic discovery a name that might have been Latin, Hebrew, Aramaic, or a combination of all three. I remembered myself saying, "Being is nothing but . . ." and there came the word that answered all questions. Outside, it was dusk. The bathers and swimmers had all gone. The sun sank into the ocean, leaving a fiery streak. A breeze brought the smell of underwater decay. A cloud in the form of a huge fish appeared out of nowhere, and the moon crept behind its scales. The weather was changing; the lighthouse fog bell rang sharply. A tugboat pulled three dark barges. It seemed unmovable, as if the Atlantic had turned into the Congealed Sea I used to read about in storybooks.

I no longer needed to scrimp, and I went to the café in Sea Gate and ordered cheesecake and coffee. A Yiddish journalist, a contributor to the paper that printed my sketches, came over and sat at my table. He had white hair and a ruddy face.

"Where have you been hiding these days? Nobody sees you. I was told you live here in Sea Gate."

"Yes, I live here."

"I've rented a room at Esther's. You know who she is—the crazy poet's ex-wife. Why don't you come over? The whole Yiddish press is there. They mentioned you a few times."

"Really? Who?"

"Oh, the writers. Even Esther praises you. I think myself that you have talent, but you choose themes no one cares about and nobody believes in. There are no demons. There is no God."

"Are you sure?"

"Absolutely sure."

"Who created the world?"

"Oh, well. The old question. It's all nature. Evolution. Who created God? Are you really religious?"

"Sometimes I am."

"Just to be spiteful. If there is a God, why does He allow Hitler to drag innocent people to Dachau? And how about your visa? Have you done anything about it? If you haven't, you'll be deported and your God will worry very little about it."

I told him my complications, and he said, "There's only one way out for you—marry a woman who's an American citizen. That'll make you legal. Later, you can get the papers and become a citizen yourself."

"I would never do that," I said.

"Why not?"

"It's an insult to both the woman and to me."

"And to fall into Hitler's hands is better? It's nothing but silly pride. You write like a ripe man, but you behave like a boy. How old are you?"

I told him.

"At your age, I was exiled to Siberia for revolutionary activities."

The waiter came over, and I was about to pay when the writer grabbed my check. I'm too lucky today, I thought.

I looked toward the door and saw Esther. She often dropped in here in the evening, which was the reason I avoided the café. Esther and I had conspired to keep our affair a secret. Besides, I had become pathologically bashful in America. My boyish blushing had returned. In Poland, I never thought of myself as short, but among the American giants I became small. My Warsaw suit looked outlandish, with its broad lapels and padded shoulders. In addition, it was too heavy for the New York heat. Esther kept reproaching me for wearing a stiff collar, a vest, and a hat in the hot weather. She saw me now and seemed embarrassed, like a provincial girl from Poland. We had never been together in public. We spent our time in the dark, like two bats. She made a move to leave, but my companion at the table called out to her. She approached unsteadily. She was wearing a white dress and a straw hat with a green ribbon. She was brown from the sun, and her black eyes had a girlish sparkle. She didn't look like a woman approaching forty, but slim and youthful. She came over and greeted me as if I were a stranger. In the European fashion, she shook my hand. She smiled self-consciously and said "you" to me instead of "thou."

"How are you? I haven't seen you for a long time," she said.

"He's hiding." The writer denounced me. "He's not doing anything about his visa and they'll send him back to Poland. The war is going to break out soon. I advised him to marry an American woman because he'd get a visa that way, but he won't listen."

"Why not?" Esther asked. Her cheeks were glowing. She smiled a loving, wistful smile. She sat down on the edge of a chair.

I would have liked to make a clever, sharp reply. Instead, I said sheepishly, "I wouldn't marry to get a visa."

The writer smiled and winked. "I'm not a matchmaker, but you two would make a fitting pair."

Esther looked at me questioningly, pleading and reproachful. I knew I had to answer right then, either seriously or with a joke, but not a word came out. I felt hot. My shirt was wet and I was stuck to my seat. I had the painful feeling that my chair was tipping over. The floor heaved up and the lights on the ceiling intertwined, elongated and foggy. The café began to circle like a carrousel.

Esther got up abruptly. "I have to meet someone," she said, and turned away. I watched her hurry toward the door. The writer smiled knowingly, nodded, and went over to another table to chat with a colleague. I remained sitting, baffled by the sudden shift in my luck. In my consternation I took the coins from my pocket and began to count and recount them, identifying more by touch than by sight, doing intricate calculations. Every time, the figures came out different. As my game with the powers on high stood now, I seemed to have won a dollar and some cents and to have lost refuge in America and a woman I really loved.

The Cabalist of East Broadway

As happens so often in New York, the neighborhood changed. The synagogues became churches, the yeshivas restaurants or garages. Here and there one could still see a Jewish old people's home, a shop selling Hebrew books, a meeting place for *landsleit* from some village in Rumania or Hungary. I had to come downtown a few times a week, because the Yiddish newspaper to which I contributed was still there. In the cafeteria on the corner, in former times one could meet Yiddish writers, journalists, teachers, fund raisers for Israel, and the like. Blintzes, borscht, kreplech, chopped liver, rice pudding, and egg cookies were the standard dishes. Now the place catered mainly to Negroes and Puerto Ricans. The voices were different, the smells were different. Still, I used to go there occasionally to eat a quick lunch or to drink a cup of coffee. Each time I entered the cafeteria, I would immediately see a man I'll call Joel Yabloner, an old Yiddish writer who specialized in the Cabala. He had published books about Holy Isaac Luria, Rabbi Moshe of Cordova, the Baal Shem, Rabbi Nachman of Bratslav. Yabloner had translated part of the Zohar into Yiddish. He also wrote in Hebrew. According to my calculations, he must have been in his early seventies.

Joel Yabloner, tall, lean, his face sallow and wrinkled, had a shiny skull without a single hair, a sharp nose, sunken cheeks, a throat with a prominent Adam's apple. His eyes bulged and were the color of amber. He wore a shabby suit and an unbuttoned shirt that revealed the white hair on his chest. Yabloner had never married. In his youth he suffered from consumption, and the doctors had sent him to a santorium in Colorado. Someone told me that there he was forced to eat pork, and as a result he fell into melancholy. I seldom heard him utter a word. When

Translated by Alma Singer and Herbert Lottman

I greeted him, he barely nodded and often averted his eyes. He lived on the few dollars a week the Yiddish Writers' Union could spare him. His apartment on Broome Street had no bath, telephone, central heating. He ate neither fish nor meat, not even eggs or milk—only bread, vegetables, and fruit. In the cafeteria he always ordered a cup of black coffee and a dish of prunes. He would sit for hours staring at the revolving door, at the cashier's desk, or the wall where, years ago, a commercial artist had painted the market on Orchard Street, with its pushcarts and peddlers. The paint was peeling now.

The president of the Writers' Union told me that although all of Joel Yabloner's friends and admirers had died out here in New York, he still had relatives and disciples in the land of Israel. They had often invited him to come there to live. They would publish his works, they promised (he had trunks filled with manuscripts), find an apartment for him, and see that he was taken care of in every way. Yabloner had a nephew in Jerusalem who was a professor at the university. There were still some Zionist leaders who considered Joel Yabloner their spiritual father. So why should he sit here on East Broadway, a silent and forgotten man? The Writers' Union would have sent his pension to him in Israel, and he could also have received Social Security, which he had never bothered to claim. Here in New York he had already been burglarized a few times. A mugger had knocked out his last three teeth. Eiserman, the dentist who had translated Shakespeare's sonnets into Yiddish, told me that he had offered to make Yabloner a set of false teeth, but Yabloner had said to him, "There is only one step from false teeth to a false brain."

"A great man, but a queer one," Eiserman said to me while he drilled and filled my own teeth. "Or perhaps he wants to atone for his sins this way. I've heard that he had love affairs in his youth."

"Yabloner—love affairs?"

"Yes, love affairs. I myself knew a Hebrew teacher, Deborah Soltis, who was madly in love with him. She was my patient. She died about ten years ago."

In connection with this, Eiserman told me of a curious episode. Joel Yabloner and Deborah Soltis saw each other over a period of twenty years, indulging in long conversations, often discussing Hebrew literature, the fine points of grammar, Maimonides, and Rabbi Judah ha-Levi, but the pair never went so far as to kiss. The closest they came was once when both of them were looking up the meaning of a word or an idiom in Ben-Yahudah's great dictionary and their heads met accidentally. Yabloner fell into a playful mood and said, "Deborah, let's trade eyeglasses."

"What for?" Deborah Soltis asked.

"Oh, just like that. Only for a little while."

The two lovers exchanged reading glasses, but he couldn't read with hers and she couldn't read with his. So they replaced their own glasses on their own noses—and that was the most intimate contact the two ever achieved.

Eventually, I stopped going down to East Broadway. I sent my articles to the newspaper by mail. I forgot Joel Yabloner. I didn't even know that he was still alive. Then one day when I walked into a hotel lobby in Tel Aviv I heard applause in an adjoining hall. The door to the hall was half open and I looked in. There was Joel Yabloner behind a lectern, making a speech. He wore an alpaca suit, a white shirt, a silk skullcap, and his face appeared fresh, rosy, young. He had a full set of new teeth and had sprouted a white goatee. I happened not to be especially busy, so I found an empty chair and sat down.

Yabloner did not speak modern Hebrew but the old holy tongue with the Ashkenazi pronunciation. When he gesticulated, I noticed the sparkling links in his immaculate shirt cuffs. I heard him say in a Talmudic singsong, "Since the Infinite One filled all space and, as the Zohar expresses it, 'No space is empty of Him,' how did He create the universe? Rabbi Chaim Vital gave the answer: 'Before creation, the attributes of the Almighty were all potential, not actual. How can one be a king without subjects, and how can there be mercy without anyone to receive it?' "

Yabloner clutched his beard, glanced at his notes. Once in a while, he took a sip from a glass of tea. I observed quite a number of women and even young girls in the audience. A few students took notes. How strange—there was also a nun. She must have understood Hebrew. "The Jewish state has resuscitated Joel Yabloner," I said to myself. One seldom has a chance to enjoy someone else's good fortune, and for me Yabloner's triumph was a symbol of the Eternal Jew. He had spent decades as a lonely, neglected man. Now he seemed to have come into his own. I listened to the rest of the lecture, which was followed by a question period. Unbelievable, but that sad man had a sense of humor. I learned that the lecture had been organized by a committee which had undertaken to publish Yabloner's work. One of the members of the committee knew me, and asked if I wished to attend a banquet in Yabloner's honor. "Since you are a vegetarian," he added, "here is your chance. They will serve only vegetables, fruits, nuts. When do they ever have a vegetarian banquet? Once in a lifetime."

Between the lecture and the banquet, Joel Yabloner went out on the terrace for a rest. The day had been hot, and now in the late afternoon a breeze was blowing from the sea. I approached him, saying, "You don't remember me, but I know you."

"I know you very well. I read everything you write," he replied. "Even here I try not to miss your stories."

"Really, it is a great honor for me to hear you say so."

"Please sit down," he said, indicating a chair.

God in Heaven, that silent man had become talkative. He asked me all kinds of questions about America, East Broadway, Yiddish literature. A woman came over to us. She wore a turban over her white hair, a satin cape, and men's shoes with low, wide heels. She had a large head, high cheekbones, the complexion of a gypsy, black eyes that blazed with anger. The beginnings of a beard could be seen on her chin. In a strong, mannish voice she said to me, "*Adoni* [Sir], my husband just finished an important lecture. He must speak at the banquet, and I want him to rest for a while. Be so good as to leave him alone. He is not a young man any more and he should not exert himself."

"Oh, excuse me."

Yabloner frowned. "Abigail, this man is a Yiddish writer and my friend."

"He may be a writer and a friend, but your throat is overstrained. If you argue with him, you will be hoarse later."

"Abigail, we aren't arguing."

"*Adoni*, please listen to me. He doesn't know how to take care of himself."

"Well, we shall talk later," I said. "You have a devoted wife."

"So they tell me."

I took part in the banquet—ate the nuts, almonds, avocados, cheese, bananas that were served. Yabloner again made a speech, this time about the author of the cabalistic book *The Treatise of the Hasidim*. His wife sat near him on the stage. Each time his voice became scratchy she handed him a glass of white fluid—some variety of yogurt. After the speech, in the course of which Yabloner demonstrated much erudition, the chairman announced that an assistant professor at the Hebrew University was writing Yabloner's biography and that funds were being raised to publish it. The author was called out on the stage. He was a young man with a round face, shining eyes, and the tiniest of skullcaps, which blended into his pomaded hair. In his closing words, Yabloner thanked his old friends, his students, all those who came to honor him. He paid tribute to his wife, Abigail, saying that without her help he would never have been able to put his manuscripts in order. He mentioned her first husband, whom he referred to as a genius, a saint, a pillar of wisdom. From a huge handbag that resembled a valise more than a lady's purse, Mrs. Yabloner took out a red kerchief like the ones used by old-fashioned rabbis and blew her nose with a blast that reverberated throughout the hall. "Let him intercede for us at the Throne of Glory!" she called out.

After the banquet I went over to Yabloner and said, "Often when I saw you sitting all alone in the cafeteria I was tempted to ask you why you didn't go to Israel. What was your reason for waiting so long?"

He paused, closing his eyes as if the question required pondering, and finally shrugged his shoulders. "Man does not live according to reason."

Again a few years passed. The typesetter on the newspaper for which I worked had lost a page of my most recent article, and since the article had to appear the next day—Saturday—there wasn't time to send the copy by mail. I had to take a cab to deliver it to the composing room myself. I gave the missing page to the foreman and went down to the editorial department to see the editor and some of my old colleagues. The winter day was short, and when I came back onto the street I felt the long-forgotten hustle and bustle of the oncoming Sabbath. Even though the neighborhood was no longer predominantly Jewish, some synagogues, yeshivas, and Hasidic study houses had refused to leave. Here and there I saw in a window a woman lighting her Sabbath candles. Men in wide-brimmed velvet or fur hats were going to prayers, accompanied by boys with long sidelocks. My father's words came to my mind: "The Almighty will always have His quorum." I remembered the chants of the Sabbath-eve liturgy: "Let us exalt," "Come my bridegroom," "The temple of the King."

I was not in a hurry any more, and I decided to have a cup of coffee in the cafeteria before I took the subway home. I pushed the revolving door. For a moment I imagined that nothing had changed, and I thought I could hear those voices of my first years in America—the cafeteria filled with Old World intellectuals shouting their opinions of Zionism, Jewish Socialism, the life and culture in America. But the faces were not familiar. Spanish was the language I heard. The walls had been painted over, and the scenes of Orchard Street with its pushcarts and peddlers had disappeared. Suddenly I saw something I could not believe. At a table in the middle of the room sat Joel Yabloner—without a beard, in a shabby suit and an unbuttoned shirt. He was emaciated, wrinkled, and disheveled, and his mouth again appeared sunken and empty. His bulging eyes stared at the empty wall opposite. Was I mistaken? No, it was Yabloner, all right. In his expression there was the desperation of a man caught in a dilemma from which there is no escape. With the cup of coffee in my hand, I stopped. Should I approach him to greet him, should I ask permission to sit down at his table?

Someone pushed me, and half of my coffee spilled over. The spoon fell on the floor with a clang. Yabloner turned around and our eyes met for a second. I nodded to him, but he did not respond. Then he turned his face away. Yes, he recognized me, but he was not in a mood for conversation. I even imagined that he had shaken his head in refusal. I found a table against the wall and sat down. I drank what was left of my coffee, all the while looking at him sideways. Why had he left Israel? Did he miss something here? Was he running away from someone? I had a strong desire to go over and ask him, but I knew that I would not get anything out of him.

A power stronger than man and his calculations has driven him out of Paradise, back to Hell, I decided. He did not even go to the Friday-night services. He was hostile not only to people but to the Sabbath itself. I finished the coffee and left.

A few weeks later, I read among the obituaries that Joel Yabloner had died. He was buried somewhere in Brooklyn. That night I lay awake until three o'clock, thinking about him. Why did he return? Had he not atoned enough for the sins of his youth? Had his return to East Broadway some explanation in the lore of the Cabala? Had some holy sparks strayed from the World of Emanation into the Evil Host? And could they have been found and brought back to their sacred origin only in this cafeteria? Another idea came into my head—perhaps he wanted to lie near that teacher with whom he exchanged eyeglasses? I remembered the last words I heard from him: "Man does not live according to reason."

A Quotation from Klopstock

THOSE who have to do with women must boast. In literary circles in Warsaw, Max Persky was known as a woman chaser. His followers contended that if he hadn't spent so much of his time on females, he might have become a second Sholem Aleichem or a Yiddish Maupassant. Although he was twenty years older than I, we became friends. I had read his work and listened to all his stories. That summer evening we sat in a little garden café, drinking coffee and eating blueberry cookies. The sun had already set and a pale September moon hung in the sky above the tin roofs. But remnants of the sunset were still reflected in the glass door which led to the interior of the café. The air was warm and smelled of the Praga forest, freshly baked babkas, and the manure that peasants gathered from the stables to dump into the fields. Max Persky smoked one cigarette after another. The tray filled with ashes and butts. Even though he was already in his forties—some maintained he was nearly fifty—Max Persky looked young. He had a boyish figure, a head of black shiny hair, a brown-complexioned face, full lips, and the penetrating eyes of a hypnotist. The two lines at the sides of his mouth gave him an air of fatalistic awareness. His enemies gossiped that he took money from wealthy women. It was also said that a woman had committed suicide over him. Our waitress, middle-aged, with a young figure, kept staring at him. From time to time she smiled guiltily at me as if to say, I can't help it. She had a short nose, sunken cheeks, and a pointed chin. I noticed that the middle finger was missing from her left hand.

Max Persky suddenly asked me, "What happened to that woman who was twelve years older than you? Do you still see her?"

I wanted to answer him but he shook his head. He said, "There is something about older women that the younger ones cannot supply. I,

Translated by the author and Dorothea Straus

myself, had one, not twelve years older than I but thirty. I was a young man of about twenty-seven and she must have been in her fifties. She was a spinster, a teacher of German literature. She also knew Hebrew. In those years the rich Jews in Warsaw wanted their daughters to be versed in Goethe, Schiller, and Lessing. If they weren't, they lacked *kultur*. A pinch of Hebrew did no harm either. Theresa Stein made a living teaching these subjects. You most probably have never heard of her, but in my time she was well known in Warsaw. This was a woman who took poetry very seriously, which proves that she was not too clever. She certainly was no beauty. To enter her small apartment on Nowolipki Street was an experience. Poverty hovered all around it, but she had turned her rooms into a kind of old maid's temple. She spent half of her earnings on books, mostly gold-embossed with velvet bindings. She bought paintings also. When I was introduced to her she was still a kosher virgin. I needed a quotation from Klopstock's *Messiah* for one of my stories, and I telephoned and she asked me to visit her that evening. When I arrived, she had already found the quotation I needed and many others. I brought her my first book, which had just been published. She knew Yiddish quite well. She worshipped Peretz. Whom did she not worship? She spoke the word 'talent' as solemnly as a pious Jew mentions God. She was small and roundish with brown eyes, from which radiated goodness and naïveté. Women like that don't exist any more. Since I was young and played the part of a cynic, I immediately did everything I could to shock her. I denounced all poets as imbeciles and told her I was having affairs with four women at the same time. Her eyes filled with tears. She said to me, 'You are so young, so talented, and already so unhappy. You don't know yet what real love is, and therefore you torture your immortal soul. True love will come to you and you will find treasures that will open the gates of Heaven to you.' To comfort me for being so misled, she offered me tea with jam cake she had baked herself and a glass of cherry brandy. I did not wait long before I began to kiss her—almost out of habit. I will never forget her expression at the first kiss. Her eyes lit up with a strange light. She clutched both my wrists and said, 'Don't do it! I take such things seriously!' She trembled and stuttered and tried to quote Goethe. Her body became unusually hot. I practically raped her, although not exactly. I spent the night at her house, and if someone could convey in a book all she said that night, it would be a work of genius. She promptly fell in love with me—with a love that endured to her last minute. I am far from being holy even today, but in those years I didn't have a trace of conscience. I considered the whole thing a joke.

"She began to telephone me every day—three times a day—but I had no time for her and invented countless excuses. Nevertheless, I used to visit her from time to time—mostly on rainy nights when I had no other engagements. Every visit was literally a holiday for her. If she could manage it, she prepared a festive supper, bought flowers in my honor, and dressed in fancy gowns or kimonos. She showered me with gifts. She tried to persuade me to read the German classics with her. But I tore them all to pieces and confessed to her brazenly all my sins, even about the brothels I had visited in my youth. There are some women who can be shocked constantly, and for her I never lacked material. Just because she spoke gently, with flowery phrases and noble quotations, I used the language of the streets and called everything by its name. She used to say, 'God will forgive you. Since He bestowed talent upon you, you are His favorite.' The truth is that it was impossible to spoil her. Figuratively speaking, she remained a virgin to the end. She possessed a purity and love for humanity not to be erased. She defended everyone, even that famous anti-Semite, Purish-kevitch. She said, 'The poor man is deluded. There are souls who sink in darkness because they never have the chance to see the divine light.' I did not realize it then but I slept with a saint, like the Saint Theresa whose namesake she was.

"She was so pure that the things I forced her to do shattered her. I have a large bundle of her letters and they are stained with her tears— not false ones but true. A time is coming when no one will believe that such women existed. Meanwhile, years passed, she grew older and her hair became white, but her face remained young and her eyes shone with all the illusions of romanticism. I had less and less time for her. The rich Jews of Warsaw slowly lost their interest in German culture and Theresa earned less and less. But I could not completely sever our relationship. I always had the feeling that, if everything went wrong and I was forsaken by everyone, I could depend on Theresa to be my mother, my wife, my protector. She had developed the tolerance characteristic of such natures. I was allowed to do anything. I never had to defend myself. In my situation one has to be a chronic liar, but to Theresa I could tell the truth no matter how brutal. She always had the same answer, 'You poor boy! You great artist!'

"The years, meanwhile, did their job. Theresa became bent and wrinkled. She began to suffer from rheumatism. She had to lean on a cane. I was ashamed of myself for my charity, if it could be called that, but to leave her completely meant killing her. She clung to me with her last strength. At night in bed she became young again. Sometimes in the dark, words escaped her which astounded me. Among other things she promised me that after her death she would appear to me, if it were possible. I don't want to disappoint you, so I am telling you in advance that she never kept that promise. But my story is just beginning."

Max Persky signaled the waitress and she came over at once, as though she had been waiting impatiently for this call. He spoke to her with caressing familiarity, "Panna Helena, I am beginning to get hungry."

"My God, today we have what you like—tomato soup."

"What are you going to have?" he asked me.

"Tomato soup, also."

"Panna Helena, make it two." He winked at her and I understood that he had the same conspiratorial relationship with her that he had had with Theresa Stein. Max Persky was in his own way a philanthropist—not with money but with love.

After the soup Max Persky lit a cigarette and asked, "Where did I stop? Yes, she grew old. She had to move out of her apartment and become a boarder with other people. This was a real tragedy, but I could not help her. You know, I never had a penny. I could not even lend a hand with the packing and moving, because Theresa Stein had a spotless reputation in Warsaw and the slightest gossip would have caused her to lose her last lessons. To tell the truth, no one would have really believed that Theresa was capable of doing what she actually did. The older she became the more guilty she felt about it and, nevertheless, shamefully asked for her due. As long as she had her private apartment, it was not difficult to keep the conspiracy. I always came to her early in the evening, and never failed to carry a book with me to pretend I was her pupil. If the neighbors ever saw me, they certainly did not suspect that I was Theresa's lover. But when she boarded with other people, I could not visit her any more. This should have been the end, but with women such as Theresa it's as difficult to end as to begin. She kept calling me and writing me long letters. We began to meet in cafés in the faraway Gentile streets. Every time I met her she brought me some kind of present—a book, a tie, even handkerchiefs and socks.

At this time I was having an affair with a niece of the Biala Rabbi whose name was Nina. I think I've told you already about this Nina. She ran away from the rabbi's court and tried to become a painter in Warsaw. She kept threatening her uncle the rabbi that if he refused to help her with money, she would convert. She was half crazy. The love between us was what pulp novels call stormy. She burned with jealousy and always suspected the women who were most innocent. Every few weeks she attempted suicide. Until then I had never hit a woman, but Nina's hysteria was the kind that could be quieted only with blows. She admitted it herself. When she began her wild antics, tearing her hair, crying, laughing, and trying to throw herself out the window, there was no other remedy but to give her a few fiery slaps in the face. It worked like a charm. After the slaps she usually started to kiss. Until then

I knew well how to manage my women. But Nina harassed me with her jealous behavior. If she caught me with another woman, she grabbed her hair and tore at it like a fishwife. She drove all my girls away. To get rid of Nina was impossible. She carried poison with her. I fell into such despair that I began to write a play—the one they ruined later in the Central Theater.

"One night, it was in the winter, Nina had to go to Biala to see her uncle. Whenever she went on a trip, she waited to let me know at the last minute to prevent me from making other rendezvous. The insane are very sly. This evening when she told me she was leaving, I began to telephone all my victims. But it was one of those nights when everyone was either busy or sick. There was an epidemic of grippe. Since I had been promising Theresa for weeks and months that I would meet her, it occurred to me that this was the right opportunity. I telephoned her and invited her for supper in a Gentile restaurant. Then I took her to my home. Even though we had been lovers for years, each time she behaved like a frightened virgin. She had to find an explanation for her landlord about not coming home to sleep. She was so alarmed and she stammered and sighed so on the telephone that I regretted the whole business. She was never much of an eater, but that evening she could not swallow a bite. A withered old woman sat opposite me at the table. The waiter thought she was my mother and asked, 'Why isn't your mother eating?' I felt awful. After supper she wanted to go home. But I knew that if I consented she would be bitterly disappointed. I also noticed that she had a nightgown in her bag. To make it short, I persuaded her to go to my apartment. When a young girl fusses too much it's bad enough, but when an old woman behaves like a frightened virgin, it's both comical and tragic. We climbed up the three flights of stairs and a few times she stopped to rest. She had brought me a present, a suit of woolen underwear. I made tea. I tried to cheer her up with a glass of cognac. But she refused to drink. After much hesitation, many apologies, and quotations from Faust and Heine's *Buch der Lieder*, she went to bed with me. I was sure that I wouldn't have the slightest desire for her but sex is full of caprices. After a while we both fell asleep. I had already decided that this night was the end of our miserable affair. Even she had hinted that we shouldn't make fools of ourselves any more.

"I was tired and fell asleep soundly. I awoke with an uncanny feeling. At first I did not remember with whom I was in bed. For a moment I thought it was Nina. I stretched out my hand and touched her. At that instant I knew the truth: Theresa was dead. To this day I don't know if she became sick and tried to wake me, or simply died in her sleep. I have gone through many tragedies, but what I experienced that night was sheer terror. My first impulse was to call an ambulance, but all Warsaw would immediately have known that Theresa Stein had died in Max Persky's bed. If the Pope had been caught stealing from an attic in Krochmalna Street, it would not have created a greater sensation. A man fears nothing as much as ridicule. Half of Warsaw would have cursed me, and the other half jeered. When I lit the lamp and looked at her face, I was frozen with horror. She appeared not sixty but ninety. I wanted to run to the end of the earth so that no one would ever learn what had happened to me. But I had spent all my money in the restaurant and for the droshky. I realized that coming home with me and walking up all those steps had killed her. I had actually committed a murder and I had done it out of pity.

"I lit all the lamps, covered the corpse with a blanket, and began to look for a way to end my own idiotic life. To die near her would create the impression that it was a double suicide. One is ashamed of what people will say and think even after one has gone. Prestige, not love, is stronger than death. I looked at my watch and it was ten minutes after three. As I stood there bewildered, cursing the day of my birth, the doorbell rang. I was sure it was the police. They could easily have accused me of murder. I did not answer, but the ringing soon became insistent and loud. I was sure that the next step would be breaking down the door. I did not ask who it was and opened. It was Nina.

"She had missed her train. Nina was an expert at being late for trains, theaters, rendezvous. She said there was no other train that night and she had gone home. But in the middle of the night she was assailed by the desire to be with me. Or perhaps she thought she would catch me with someone else and scratch out her eyes. How strange that I felt overjoyed to see Nina. To be alone with a corpse in such circumstances is so painful that all other suffering and shame is pallid by comparison. Nina said, 'Why are all the lamps burning?' She looked at the bed and exclaimed, 'There is no use hiding her!' She ran to the bed and wanted to tear off the blanket, but I held her hands and said, 'Nina, a corpse is lying there.' She saw from my face that I was not lying. I expected her to make a terrible rumpus and to wake the neighbors. Nina could be thrown into a panic at the sight of a little mouse or a beetle. But at this moment she became calm and seemed cured of all her madness. She said, 'A corpse? Who is it?' When I told her it was Theresa Stein, she began to laugh, not hysterically but in the way a healthy person would break out laughing at a good joke. I said, 'Nina, this is no joke. Theresa Stein died in my bed.'

"Nina knew Theresa Stein. The whole of intellectual Warsaw knew her. She still did not believe it, until I opened Theresa's pocketbook and showed Nina her passport. With the Russians everyone had to carry a passport, even women."

"How does it happen that you never wrote about this?" I asked Max Persky.

"No one has heard the truth until now. There are still too many people who knew Theresa Stein."

He lit another cigarette. It was now night. The moon was as yellow as brass.

"What a story it would make," I said.

"Perhaps I will write it someday, but only in my old age, when no one in Warsaw remembers Theresa Stein. It's still too soon. But let me tell you the rest. Nina was ready to help me, and even had a plan. We could easily have ended up in Siberia or on the gallows, but at such moments one becomes strangely courageous. We dressed the corpse in all her clothes. We decided to tell the janitor that the woman had had an attack of gallstones and we were taking her to the hospital. This janitor was an old drunkard and he never turned on the light when he opened the gate. Taking off Theresa Stein's nightgown and dressing her in her bloomers and other things almost killed us. Her body was a ruin. When she was dressed I lifted her and carried her down three dark flights of stairs. She did not weigh much but still I almost ruptured myself carrying her. Nina helped me by holding her feet. How Nina the hysteric could do all this is still a riddle to me. Never before or since was she so normal—or perhaps I should say supernormal. In the dark passageway to the gate, I stood Theresa up, propping her against the wall. Her head fell on my shoulder and for a moment I imagined she was alive! Nina knocked on the janitor's window and we heard a squeaking door and the typical growling of a man awakened in the middle of the night. He opened the gate, sighing and cursing, as Nina and I dragged the corpse along upright, holding her under the arms. I even managed to tip the janitor. He asked no questions and we told him nothing. If a policeman had happened to come along, I wouldn't be sitting here with you. But the street was empty. We pulled the corpse to the nearest corner and set her carefully on the pavement. I put her pocketbook near her. The whole business did not last longer than a few minutes. I was so dazed that I didn't know what to do next. But Nina took me to her home.

"There is an old saying that there is no such thing as a perfect murder. What we did that night had all the elements of a perfect crime. If we had actually strangled Theresa, the whole thing could not have gone more smoothly. It's true we probably left fingerprints, but the technique of discovering fingerprints was not known then in Warsaw. Little the Russian police cared that an old woman had been found dead in the street. She was taken to the morgue. When the Jews learned that Theresa Stein had been found dead, the community leaders arranged for her to be taken to the cleansing room at the Gęsia Street cemetery without an autopsy. Of course I learned all this later. You will not believe it, but that night—or what was left of the night—I slept with Nina and everything went as usual. At that time I still had good nerves. I also drank half a bottle of vodka. There is really no rule about how nerves will react.

"I don't have to tell you that Warsaw was shocked at the details of Theresa's death. Our Yiddish newspapers gave the event full coverage. Theresa had told her landlady that she was spending the night with a sick relative. But who was that relative? No one ever learned. My janitor could have told the police we carried out a woman in the middle of the night, but he was half blind and never read the newspapers. Since her pocketbook was found near her, it was assumed that she had dropped dead from natural causes. I remember that the feuilletonist of *Today* developed a theory that Theresa Stein went out to help the poor and the sick. He compared her to the saint in Peretz's story who, instead of going to night prayers, went to heat the oven of a sick widow.

"Our Warsaw Jews adore funerals. But such a funeral as Theresa Stein had, I never saw before. Hundreds of droshkies followed the hearse. Women and girls cried as if it were Yom Kippur. Countless eulogies were spoken. The rabbi of the German synagogue preached that the spirits of Goethe, Schiller, and Lessing were hovering over Theresa's grave, as well as the souls of Judah ha-Levi and Solomon Ibn Gabriol. I wasn't too sure about Nina's power to keep a secret. Hysteria and denunciation often go together. I was afraid that at our first quarrel Nina would go to the police. But a real change had taken place in her. She stopped bothering me with her jealousy. We actually never again spoke of that night. It became our great secret.

"Not long afterward the war began. Then Nina developed consumption, which she had really had for years before. Her family put her in a sanatorium at Otwock. I often visited her. Something in her character seemed to have altered. I never needed to stifle her hysteria with a slap again. She died in 1918."

"She never tried to appear to you?" I asked.

"You mean Nina or Theresa? Both had promised, but neither kept her word. Even if such an entity as a soul exists, I don't believe it cares to come down with messages from the other world. I really hope that death is the end of all our nonsense.

"I forgot to add one fact. It has no real connection with my story but it is interesting just the same. During all these years Nina had threatened her uncle, the Biala Rabbi, with conversion. The rabbi was terribly afraid of having a convert in his family and sent her money. After her death, when the family was going to bury her and documents were necessary, they learned that she had been a Catholic for years. It created a commotion among the Hasidim. Warsaw was already under German occupation. They bribed the authorities and buried her in the Jewish cemetery. As a matter of fact, she is lying not too far from Theresa Stein, in the first row. Why she converted I will never know. She often spoke about the Jewish God and mentioned her holy ancestors."

Max Persky became silent. The night grew cool. Around the lamp above the door flies, moths, butterflies, and all kinds of gnats had a summer night's orgy. Max Persky nodded his head over a truth that hung on his lips. "In love you don't do favors," he said. "You have to be an egotist or else you destroy yourself and your lover."

He hesitated awhile and then he looked at the waitress. She came to the table at once. "More coffee?"

"Yes, Helena. Tell me, how late are you working today?"

"As usual we close at twelve."

"I will wait for you outside."

A Dance and a Hop

HOUSES sometimes bear a strange resemblance to those who inhabit them. Leizer, my uncle Jekhiel's former brother-in-law, owned such a house. Beila, Leizer's sister, was Uncle Jekhiel's second wife. She was no longer alive and my uncle had married for the third time after my parents brought me to Shebrin.

A man in his sixties, Leizer was tall and broad-boned. In his youth he was a giant, but in his later years he became bent and broken from troubles. His wife was dead. He was plagued by a hernia, and a bad leg caused him to walk with a limp. The granary he possessed had burned down and his grain business was gone. His two older daughters baked bread and flatcakes, and from their meager earnings he maintained himself. Actually, all his misfortunes stemmed from his three daughters, Rachel, Leah, and Feigel, who remained spinsters. How was it possible for three girls in a Jewish village not to be married? Everyone in Shebrin asked the same question, and I think that Leizer and his daughters were as baffled as the others, perhaps more so.

But let us go back to the house. Its brick walls were unusually thick, its roof green from moss, and the chimney, no matter how often it was swept, always spewed forth a mixture of smoke and flames. Grzymak, the chimney sweep, swore that he once saw an imp in the chimney: a creature black as soot, hunched both in front and in back, with an elflock in the middle of his skull and a nose that reached to his belly. He seemed to live there. A neighbor's daughter had also seen this monster. In the middle of the night, when she went to pour out the slops, she heard him giggling. As she glanced up at Leizer's roof, the creature, crouching on the tip of the chimney, beckoned her to come to him and stretched out his tongue that was the length of a shovel.

Translated by the author and Ruth Schachner Finkel

Why did the builder who constructed this house make the walls almost a yard thick, with no windows facing the front and with a long entranceway that was dark even in broad daylight? Why were the ceilings low and heavily beamed and the attic unproportionately high? No one knew the answer, as the building was about two hundred years old. The small, crooked windows looked out over a swamp which led to the river. On murky summer nights, mysterious lights hovered over the swamp and it was said that those who went toward the lights never returned.

Leizer's rupture caused his intestines to drop and there was one woman in Shebrin who could manipulate them back. If not for her, people said, Leizer would have died long ago. It was a disgrace for Leizer that a strange female should touch his private parts, but when it's a question of saving a life, such things must be overlooked. This woman refused payment. It was her good deed. She also specialized in warding off the evil eye and removing the pips from chickens, thus enabling them to eat again.

Leah was already past forty when my parents and I arrived in Shebrin. Tall and broad like her father, she had the hands of a man and a face that was as wide and as brown as the pumpernickel loaves she baked. It was difficult to get a word out of her. Her strength, too, was that of a man. She chopped wood, brought water from the well, and carried sacks of flour from the mill on her back. In spite of all this, one could see that she was quite good-looking, with regular features and black, fiery eyes.

I heard it told that one day when she carried a sack of grain to the mill, she was attacked by two brigands. One of them held a rifle to her chest. Leah grabbed the gun, broke it in two, and with the butt hit the brigands until they passed out. The culprits were caught, taken to the hospital, and later jailed.

Rachel, who was younger than Leah, resembled her physically; but all that was hard, strong, and resolute in Leah appeared weak, soft, and indecisive in her sister. No one dared ask Leah why she had never married but everybody asked Rachel. Her reply was always the same: "When you serve dinner, you serve the soup first, then the meat."

I remember my mother once said to her, "Is it so terrible if one serves the meat first? There's no law against this."

Rachel listened and replied, "It is the custom, first you serve the soup and then the meat."

Leah kneaded the dough, shaped the loaves, shoveled them into the oven, and then removed the finished baked goods. Selling was Rachel's job. On Thursdays she stood in the marketplace with a basket of loaves, flatcakes, bagels, and rolls. Fridays she sold hallah and Sabbath cookies.

Feigel, the youngest, was only twenty-nine years old at that time and the matchmakers had not yet given up on her. Her mother had died at her birth. Unlike her sisters, Feigel was fair, small statured, and bore no resemblance to the rest of the family. She was supposed to have taken after a great-aunt from Janov. Three times she was engaged. Her first fiancé died, she returned the engagement contract to the second, and the third one went to war and was never heard from again.

Leah and Feigel were not on speaking terms for more than ten years. They even avoided looking at each other. Feigel liked to sing. She had a cat. Her father bought her a sewing machine and she became a seamstress, making shirts, men's underwear, and brassières. She had long discussions with the matchmakers. From time to time introductions and meetings were arranged with a potential suitor, but somehow nothing came of them. Feigel often visited my mother. She told horror stories about the 1915 cholera epidemic and gossiped about the girls and young women in Shebrin who became smugglers during the war. The Austrian gendarmes frequently made them undress when they searched them, and they touched intimate parts of their bodies, where no decent woman allows herself to be touched by a strange man. My mother nodded her bewigged head. "It's all a result of our long exile."

Feigel accused Leah of witchcraft, saying that Leah didn't desire marriage herself and that she had prevented Rachel from getting a husband. Every time Feigel became engaged, Leah cast an evil spell. Feigel would say to my mother, "My dear aunt, that Leah is a male, not a female."

"What are you talking about?" My mother winced. "She has breasts."

"She has the feet of a Cossack. God made a mistake."

"How can you say this? The Almighty doesn't make any mistakes."

"If so, she's a mooncalf."

This family did not come up to our standards. My uncle Jekhiel had fallen in love with his second wife, though she was much beneath him, and when Feigel called my mother "aunt" it was like a slap in the face. But my mother had compassion for Leizer's daughters because they were orphans. She sent me to buy baked farfel from them and ordered my shirts to be sewn by Feigel. Her fingers tickled me when she took the measurements and I had to laugh. My mother's comment about Leah having breasts preyed on my mind. Until then I thought that only women who nurse children have breasts. Yes, Leah had a huge bosom, but she had the deep voice of a man. Could she be what the Talmud called androgynous? I was as fearful of her as of the dark gateways that was full of holes and ditches. From reading storybooks I knew that there existed sinful females who copulated with demons and gave birth to sprites and succubi. Perhaps Leah was having an affair with the demon who dwelt in her chimney. I was close to bar mitzvah age and kept thinking more and more about what I had studied in the Gemara concerning relations between men and women. Novels, too, began to interest me. It was at about this time that my mother asked Feigel to make me several pairs of drawers and shirts.

I brought the linen to Feigel, and as I approached the house I noticed a thick black smoke issuing from the chimney. I pondered about the devil who lurked in his sooty lair. When I passed the bakery I saw Leah standing in a shabby skirt and huge boots. As she sprinkled water on the freshly baked loaves, the steam rose into the air.

The threshold of the gate was high and I tripped over it. It was a hot day and the door of Leizer's room was ajar. His white beard had turned brown in spots from the snuff tobacco he used. The thought that a female rummaged around with his genitals invoked in me feelings of curiosity and disgust. He had a workshop equipped with hammers, saws, pliers, screwdrivers, and knives. Boards and metal rods were stacked in the corner. I remembered my mother saying that when he was young he tried to invent a cradle that would be self-rocking with the force of weights and springs. This was the reason that his business went to pieces.

After a while I entered Feigel's room. It was the brightest in the house. Father and daughters did not live as a family. They were rather like neighbors. Some of the rooms were ruined and remained locked. Feigel had a mannequin in her room—a female without a head but with hips and breasts. Pieces of thread caught in Feigel's hair gave her a special charm in my eyes. It was hard to believe that she was nearing thirty, as her appearance was that of a young girl. She deftly stepped on the treadle of her sewing machine with her small foot and quickly moved her index finger out of the way of the needle.

"You are here, huh?" She smiled at me invitingly.

"Yes, my mother sent me."

"You love your mother?"

I stood there embarrassed. "Yes, why not?"

"Is a Hasid allowed to love a female?" she asked.

"A mother is not a female."

"What else?"

Feigel rose to take my measurements, being most careful as my mother had pointed out to her that my neck had gotten thicker. Her knuckles touched my chin and I felt that her fingers were warm and soft. Suddenly she bent her head, and her hair brushed my cheek as she kissed me on the lips. I was so perplexed that I could not utter a word. "Don't mention this to anyone," she admonished me.

How peculiar: days in advance I knew that I was about to commit some transgression. My brain teemed with sinful thoughts. Several nights earlier I had dreamed about my cousin Taube, naked, her body enveloped in a net. The following day I fasted until noon.

In Shebrin word got around that Feigel was about to be engaged again. The new suitor, a droshky driver from Warsaw, had a relative in Shebrin, Chaim Kalch, and it was through him that the match was arranged. Everything went quickly. One day we heard about it and two days later we were invited to the engagement party. The affair was a quiet one, the guests were few. Leibush, the bridegroom-to-be, seemed like a man in his late thirties or perhaps early forties, big, with a reddish-blue complexion, a large nose, thick lips, and a deeply creviced and pimpled neck. I imagined that he smelled of horse manure and axle grease. Under flaxen eyebrows, his watery blue eyes had a look that suggested anger and mockery, as if the whole event were nothing but a sham. Rachel served chopped herring, freshly baked kaiser rolls, and vodka. Leah put in an appearance just for a minute, not even bothering to change her clothes. Leibush had the coarse voice of one who customarily shouts. I heard him say, "I'm tired of the Warsaw cobblestones." He drank three-quarters of the vodka and ate almost all the rolls while discussing business. He had had enough of the Warsaw tumult and stench, and he intended to buy a horse and wagon in Shebrin to carry freight to Lublin. People in Warsaw didn't know how to cross the streets, and when an accident occurred, the driver got the blame. From his words I understood that he most probably ran over someone, with a resulting lawsuit, or perhaps he went to jail. Feigel, too, helped with the refreshments. My father drew up the engagement papers. He asked Leibush, "What is your full name?"

"Leibush Motl."

"Aryeh Mordecai." My father translated the name into Hebrew.

"What are you?" my father asked. "A Cohen, a Levi, or an Israelite?"

"Who knows what I am."

"Don't you attend synagogue? Aren't you called up to the reading of the Torah?"

"Once in a while."

"Here you will have to attend the synagogue. In a small town you must behave," Feigel interrupted.

"Well . . ."

Feigel's father, Leizer, appeared peeved, impatient, and barely able to wait until he could return to his hammers, saws, files, and screws. To everything that was said, he nodded in silence. Feigel smiled, joked, and even winked at me. She shrugged. "Marriage and death are unavoidable."

"What makes you say such things?" my mother asked. "You're still young and you will live till 120."

"Not so young. No one knows what the next day will bring."

"Exactly my words," Leibush agreed. "Last week as I sat drinking a mug of beer with my friend, his head suddenly fell to one side and he was a goner."

"God forbid the misfortunes that can happen."

"People creep right under the wheels."

The wedding date was set for a month later. Leizer and Leah wanted the wedding to be a quiet one, but Feigel demanded a ceremony with musicians and a jester. I heard her say to my mother, "What does a girl get out of life? A dance and a hop."

At the wedding, Feigel danced with her sister Rachel and then with another girl. She looked lovely in the bridal gown she had made herself. The gown opened out like an umbrella as she whirled around and I saw her lace-trimmed panties. After the virtue dance, two women led Feigel into a darkened bedroom. A few minutes later Leizer and one of the other men escorted Leibush to his bride.

Leah came to the wedding dressed in her Sabbath dress and high-heeled shoes. Under her heavy, masculine brows her black eyes were sad and resentful. When my mother went to wish Rachel *mazel tov*, she replied, "Whoever heard of serving the dessert before the main dish?"

"You and Leah will also bring joy to the father one day."

"Maybe."

The morning after the wedding, the whispering began. A boy who had hidden behind the window of the bridal chamber announced that Feigel and Leibush quarreled half the night. There was scolding, and blows were struck. In order to reach the window he had crept through the swamp, and he showed the mud and moss that still clung to his pants and boots. Feigel soon called on my mother to unburden herself. I was most eager to listen to Feigel's secret but she dismissed me. "Do me a favor," she said, "and leave the room. It's not for your ears."

From the other side of the door I heard muttering and stifled crying. When Feigel left, my mother's face had red blotches. I inquired as to what was wrong with the couple, and my mother said, "God spare us, how many madmen there are."

"They don't get along?"

"She has bad luck."

But the boys in the study house spoke clear words: "Feigel does not allow her husband into her bed."

Leibush came to my uncle Jekhiel to press charges, and they locked themselves in the study. Just as Leibush had previously maligned Warsaw and praised Shebrin, he now reversed himself. He stood in the marketplace surrounded by boys and men and kept repeating, "How can anyone live in this godforsaken village? One can lose one's mind just from seeing so much mud. Whatever else can be said about Warsaw, at least it's lively."

"For money you can get everything here also," called out a newly married young man.

"What can you get? There's not even a place to drink a decent glass of beer."

People tried to make peace between Feigel and Leibush. Horse dealers offered to sell Leibush a team of horses for a song. Merchants promised they would hire him to carry their merchandise to Lublin and Lemberg. But Leibush shook his head. Feigel didn't show herself. A girl who went to her shop to be fitted for a dress found the door locked. My aunt Yentl came to talk it over with my mother. They murmured and the ribbons of Yentl's bonnet shook. "I'm afraid there'll be no bread from this dough," Yentl said.

"A crazy ignoramus," my mother agreed.

The marriage was quickly dissolved. Divorce in Shebrin was not permitted because the river had two names and there was some doubt as to which name to use in the divorce papers. The pair went to Lublin to obtain the divorce. I watched both of them mount the wagon for the trip. Leibush seated himself near the driver and Feigel sat in the rear on a bundle of hay. She wore the same hat with the feather which she had worn on the Sabbath after the wedding when she was led into the women's section of the synagogue. She looked drawn and older. Rachel came out and handed her sister a package of food. Girls and women watched from behind drawn curtains.

Though Feigel was supposed to return soon afterward, weeks passed and she still remained in Lublin. When she did get back, winter had set in. Rachel paid us a visit and said, "Never serve the third course before the first."

"Forgive me, Rachel, but you talk nonsense."

"Men are wild beasts," Rachel spoke, half to my mother and half to herself.

"What's the matter with you? The greatest saints were men."

"Maybe in ancient times."

One afternoon Feigel appeared at our house. "It's all Leah," she confided to my mother. "She bewitched us. When she learned I was about to marry, hell broke loose. She put a curse on me. This is the truth."

"If one trusts in God, one need not fear evil."

"It doesn't help. She's got Rachel under her spell. Rachel repeats Leah's every word like a parrot. She would stand on her head if Leah told her to. The reason she's my enemy is because I refused to do her bidding."

"God will send you the right match."

"No, Auntie, my bridegroom will be the Angel of Death."

Feigel spoke the truth. Not long after this conversation, we heard that she was mortally ill. Though a doctor was summoned, he could not help her. Women reported that she was as emaciated as a consumptive and was failing more and more each day. When I went to buy farfel I no longer heard the sound of Feigel's sewing machine. One time I noticed that the door to Feigel's workshop was open and I looked in. She sat basting a seam. When she saw me, she smiled weakly and said, "Look at him, he's grown up."

"Feigel, I wish you a speedy recovery."

"If wishes were horses, beggars would ride. I'm already beyond help, but it's nice that you came to visit me. Come in, sit down."

When I sat on the stool she began to reminisce. "Only yesterday you were a child. Now you're an adult. There's one thing I want you to remember: never torture the woman who will fall into your hands!"

"God forbid."

"We are all God's children."

"The main thing is that you should be healthy."

"No, my darling. I'm not long for this world," and a knowing smile appeared on her lips.

A few weeks later Feigel died. She had sent for my uncle Jekhiel, recited her confession to him, and requested that her trousseau be given to poor brides. The village women said she died like a saint. I followed her hearse. Rachel wailed and pounded her head with both fists, but Leah walked silently. Leizer recited the Kaddish. Father and daughters sat together for the seven days of mourning.

After Feigel's death the family fell apart. Leizer contracted pneumonia several months later and passed away. Now the rumors spread that Rachel was losing her mind. She gave the customers more change than they paid for the items. It reached the stage where Leah no longer trusted her to sell. Leah herself wasn't good at selling. She had no patience with the peasants and their haggling. Her baking was limited to those who came to the shop—a few girls and matrons who liked her baked goods. The two sisters could not earn a living any more. Rachel, who used to make the household purchases, no longer came to the butcher shop. She became senile. When she visited with my mother, dates and facts were confused in her stories. As a rule she brought us bread and rolls every second weekday. One Sabbath the door opened and Rachel entered in workday clothes, carrying a bakery basket. My mother began to pinch her cheeks. "Rachel, what is the matter with you? It's the Sabbath!"

"Sabbath? I thought it was Sunday."

"But all the stores are closed. Carrying is forbidden."

"Shall I take the bread back home?"

"No, leave it. Didn't you prepare a Sabbath stew?"

"Maybe I did. I will go home."

Not long after this incident Rachel developed cancer of the breast. She lay in bed and Leah took care of her. Dr. Katz, the Shebrin physician, maintained that if Rachel went to Warsaw they might be able to operate and save her. Though the community was ready to pay her expenses, Rachel refused to go, saying, "Here I was born and here I will die."

In her pain and delirium she began to sing songs. Fragments of the Rosh Hashanah and Yom Kippur liturgies remained in her memory. It became obvious that she had a singing voice, though no one had ever heard her sing before. She even improvised words and melodies, as well as threnodies for her father and her long-dead mother—all in the plaintive tones inherited from generations. She now openly complained that Leah prevented Feigel and herself from marrying.

After Rachel's death Leah stopped baking. She rented out two rooms and was somehow able to manage from the income. Her seclusion was complete. She went nowhere and didn't even come on Rosh Hashanah to the women's section of the synagogue to hear the blowing of the ram's horn. The chimney stopped spewing smoke and sparks, and in Shebrin it was said the imp now lived behind Leah's stove and slept with her in her bench bed. Although she was past her sixtieth year, her hair remained black as pitch.

When I left Shebrin, Leah was still alive. I heard that she died just before the Nazi invasion. For a long time I hadn't thought about the sisters, but yesterday when I dozed off for a minute at my desk, I dreamed about Feigel. I saw her in a bridal gown, silken shoes, her hair streaming down to her waist, her face pale, and her eyes alight with an other-worldly joy. She was waving a palm branch and a citron fruit as though it were Sukkoth and saying to my mother, "What has a girl from her life? Nothing but a dance and a hop."

Grandfather and Grandson

AFTER Beyle Teme's death Reb Mordecai Meir sold his store and began to live on his capital. Someone figured out for him with a pencil on paper that if he spent eight rubles a week it would last him seven years—and how much longer could he live? He had reached the age at which his parents had died. Every minute after that was a gift.

His only daughter had died of typhus several years ago and he had a few grandchildren somewhere in Slonim, but they would have to get along without his inheritance. Reb Mordecai Meir's daughter had married a Litvak, an opponent of Hasidism, an enlightened Jew, and her father had virtually cut her off as his child.

Reb Mordecai Meir was a small man with a yellowish-white beard, a broad forehead, bushy eyebrows beneath which peeped a pair of yellow eyes, like a chicken's. On the tip of his nose there grew a little beard. Wisps of hair stuck out of his ears and nostrils. In the course of time his back had become bowed and he always looked as if he were searching for something on the floor. He didn't walk but shuffled his feet. All year round he wore a cotton caftan with a sash, low shoes, and a velvet hat over two skullcaps. He spoke in half sentences, only to the initiated Hasidim.

Even among Hasidim, Reb Mordecai Meir was known as an impractical man. Though he had lived in Warsaw for years, he was not at all acquainted with the streets of Warsaw. The only road he knew was from his home to the Hasidic house of prayer and back. During the year, he occasionally traveled to the Rabbi of Alexandrow, but he always had difficulty finding the trolley to the railway station, changing cars, and buying tickets. In all this he had to be assisted by young men who knew

Translated by Evelyn Torton Beck and Ruth Schachner Finkel

their way around. He had neither the time nor the patience for such externals.

At midnight he arose for study and prayer. Very early each morning he recited the Gemara and the Tosephot commentary. After that came psalms, more prayers, delving into Hasidic books, and discussing Hasidic matters. The winter days were short. Before one had a bite to eat and a nap, it was time to return to the study house for evening prayers. Even though the summer days were long, there were not enough of them. First it was Passover, then the Feast of Omer, and before you could turn around it was Shevuoth. After that came the seventeenth of Tammuz, the three weeks of mourning for the destruction of the Temple, the nine days of refraining from meat, and then Tishe b'Av, the Sabbath of Comfort. These were followed by the month of Elul, when even fish in water tremble. Later there was Rosh Hashanah, the ten days of Penitence, Yom Kippur, Sukkoth, the Day of Rejoicing in the Law, and then, Sabbath of Genesis.

As a boy, Reb Mordecai Meir had already realized that if one wanted to be a real Jew there was no time for anything else. Praised be God, his wife, Beyle Teme, had understood this. She never asked him to assist in the store, to concern himself with business, to carry the burden of earning a living. He seldom had any money with him except for the few guldens which she gave him each week for alms, the ritual bath, books, snuff, and pipe tobacco. Reb Mordecai Meir wasn't even certain of the exact location of the store and the merchandise sold there. A shopkeeper had to talk to women customers and he knew well that it was only one short step from talking, to looking, to lecherous thoughts.

The street on which Reb Mordecai Meir lived teemed with unbelievers, loose women. Boys peddled Yiddish newspapers which were full of mockery and atheism. The saloons swarmed with ruffians. In his library, Reb Mordecai Meir kept the windows shut, even during the summer. As soon as he opened the transom of the window, he immediately heard the playing of frivolous songs on the gramophone and female laughter. In the courtyard, bareheaded jugglers often performed their tricks, which he felt might be black magic. Reb Mordecai Meir was told that Jewish boys and girls went to the Yiddish theater where they made fun of Jewishness. There emerged worldly writers, writing in Hebrew and Yiddish. They incited the readers to sin. At every turn the Evil Spirit lay in wait. There was only one way to defeat him: with Torah, prayer, Hasidism.

The years passed and Reb Mordecai Meir did not know where or how. Overnight his yellow beard turned gray. Because he did not want to go to the barber shop and sit among the shaven transgressors, Beyle Teme used to cut his hair. She took off his skullcaps and he quickly replaced them. She would argue, "How can I cut your hair with the skullcaps on your head?"

In later years he became bald and only his sidelocks remained. When Beyle Teme stopped having children (five of the children had died and they were left with just the one daughter, Zelda Rayzel), Reb Mordecai Meir separated himself from his wife. What more was needed after he had fulfilled the commandment "Be fruitful and multiply"? To be sure, according to the Law a man was permitted to have relations with his wife when she could no longer bear children. Some were even of the opinion that one must not become a recluse. But when was this said? Only when one could copulate without any desire for the flesh. If a person had intercourse for the sake of pleasure, this could lead to temptations and lust. Besides, in recent years Beyle Teme was not in good health. She used to return home from the shop exhausted, smelling of herring and valerian drops.

After Zelda Rayzel's death, Beyle Teme became melancholy. She wept almost every night and kept repeating the same words: "Why did this happen to me?" Reb Mordecai Meir reminded her that it was forbidden to complain against God. "All God does is good." The reason there was such a thing as death was because the body was only a garment. The soul is sent to be cleansed in Gehenna for a short time and after that it goes to Paradise and learns the secrets of the Torah. Were eating, drinking, urinating, and sweating such a bargain?

But Beyle Teme became sicker from day to day. She passed away on a Wednesday and was buried on Friday afternoon. Since it was just before the Sabbath she was spared the pressure of the grave, which those who are buried on weekdays suffer. Reb Mordecai Meir recited Kaddish for the repose of her soul, prayed before the congregation, studied Mishnah. When the thirty days of mourning had passed, a relative took over the shop for four thousand rubles. Pesha, a neighbor who was a widow, came to Reb Mordecai Meir every day to clean and cook some food. For the Sabbath she prepared stew and a pudding for him. The Hasidim tried to arrange a match but he refused to remarry.

One summer morning, while reading *The Generations of Jacob Joseph*, he dozed off and was awakened by the sound of knocking. He opened the door and saw a young man without a beard, a head of long hair over which he wore a broad-brimmed black hat, in a black blouse tied with a sash, and checkered pants. In one hand he carried a satchel and in the other a book. His face was pale and he had a short nose.

Reb Mordecai Meir asked, "What do you want?"

Blinking his widely separated eyes, he stammered, "I am Fulie . . . You are my grandfather."

Reb Mordecai Meir stood dumfounded. He had never heard the name Fulie. Then he realized that this was most probably the modern variation of the old Jewish name Raphael. It was Zelda Rayzel's eldest son. Reb Mordecai Meir felt both pain and shame. He had a grandson who tried to imitate the Gentiles. He said, "So come in." After hesitating a moment, the boy came in and put his suitcase down. Reb Mordecai Meir asked, "What kind—is that—?" and pointed to the book.

"Economics."

"Of what use is that to you?"

"Well . . ."

"What's new in Slonim?" Reb Mordecai Meir asked. He didn't want to mention the name of his former son-in-law, who was an anti-Hasid. Fulie made a face as if to indicate that he did not fully comprehend his grandfather's question.

"In Slonim? Just like everywhere else. The rich get richer and the workers have nothing to eat. I had to leave because . . ." and Fulie stopped himself.

"What will you do here?"

"Here—I'll look around—I'll . . ."

Well, a stutterer, Reb Mordecai Meir thought. His throat scratched and his stomach started to turn. It was his daughter Zelda Rayzel's son, but as long as he shaved his beard and dressed like a Gentile, what would he, Reb Mordecai Meir, do with him? He nodded his head and gaped. It seemed that the boy took after the other side of the family with his high cheekbones, narrow forehead, and wide mouth. His bedraggled and famished appearance reminded Reb Mordecai Meir of the recruits who starve themselves to avoid conscription.

"Wash your hands. Eat something. Don't forget that you are a Jew."

"Grandfather, they don't let you forget."

In the kitchen the boy sat down at the table and began to leaf through his book. Reb Mordecai Meir opened the kitchen closet but found no bread there; only onions, a string of dried mushrooms, a package of chicory, a few heads of garlic.

He said to Fulie, "I'll give you money, go to the store and buy a loaf of bread or something else you might like to eat."

"Grandfather, I'm not hungry. And besides, the less I'm outside the better," the boy answered.

"Why? You're not sick, God forbid, are you?"

"All of Russia has the same sickness. Everywhere it is full of denouncers and secret agents. Grandfather, I am not altogether 'clean.' "

"Have you been called by the military?"

"That too."

"Maybe you can be saved?"

"All mankind needs to be saved, not only I."

Reb Mordecai Meir had decided not to get angry, no matter what his grandson did or said. Anger won't win anyone over to piety. There were moments when Reb Mordecai Meir wanted to spit on the impudent fellow and drive him out of his house. But he restrained himself with all his might. Even though Fulie spoke in Yiddish, Reb Mordecai Meir did not fully comprehend what he was saying. All of his talk boiled down to one complaint: the rich live in luxury, the poor suffer deprivation. He continuously mentioned the workers in the factories, the peasants who tilled the fields. He spoke against the czar. "He resides in a palace and lets others rot in cellars. Millions die of hunger, consumption. The people must wake up. There must be a revolution . . ."

Reb Mordecai Meir clutched his beard and asked, "How do you know that a new czar would be better?"

"If we have our way, there will be no new czar."

"Who will rule?"

"The people."

"All the people can't sit in the ruling chair," Reb Mordecai Meir answered.

"Representatives will be chosen from the workers and peasants."

"When they get power, they may also become villains," Reb Mordecai Meir argued.

"Then they'll be made one head shorter."

"It is written: 'For the poor shall never cease out of the land,' " Reb Mordecai Meir spoke. "To whom would one give charity if there were no paupers? Besides, everything is ordained in Heaven. On Rosh Hashanah it is decreed in Heaven who shall be rich and who shall be poor."

"The Heavens are nothing but air," Fulie said. "No one decrees anything."

"What? The world created itself?"

"It evolved."

"What does that mean?"

The boy began to say something, then got stuck. He mentioned names which Reb Mordecai Meir had never heard. He mixed Polish, Russian, and German words. The sum total of his talk was that everything was accident, chance. He babbled about a mist, gravitation, the earth tearing away from the sun and cooling off. He denied the exodus from Egypt, that the Red Sea was split, that the Jews received the Torah on Mount Sinai. It was all a legend. Each of Fulie's words pained Reb Mordecai Meir's insides, as if he had swallowed the molten lead which, in ancient times, was given to those who were condemned to be burned. A cry tore from his throat. He wanted to shout, "Blackguard, Jeroboam, son of Nebat, get out of my house, go to the devil!" But he remembered that the boy was an orphan, a stranger in the city, without means. He could, God forbid, become a convert, or commit suicide.

"May God forgive you. You are deluded," he said.

"You asked, Grandfather, so I answered."

From then on, grandfather and grandson stopped debating. They actually didn't speak. Reb Mordecai Meir sat in the living room, Fulie stayed in the kitchen and slept there on the cot. When Pesha cooked something, she also gave him a plate of food. She bought him bread, butter, cheese. She washed his shirt. Fulie was given a key to the outer door. Though he was not registered, the janitor let him in at night. Each time Fulie gave him ten groschen. Some nights he didn't come home at all.

Reb Mordecai Meir slept little. Right after evening prayers fatigue overcame him and he went to bed, but after an hour or two he awoke. In the morning Fulie was gone before Reb Mordecai Meir began to recite the Shema. "One must not estrange them," Reb Mordecai Meir said to himself. "The birth throes of the Messiah have begun."

In the kitchen, in a box of books, Reb Mordecai Meir found a Yiddish pamphlet with frayed pages. He tried to read it but could understand little of what was written there. The writer seemed to argue with another writer of his kind. He mentioned such strange names as Zhelyabov, Kilbatchitch, Perovskaya. One, it said, was a martyr. A bitter taste came to Reb Mordecai Meir's mouth. In his old age he had to room with a heretic who was his grandchild. In the Alexandrow study house he asked what was going on in the world and was told things which utterly amazed him. Those who, years before, had murdered the czar had begun to arouse the populace anew. Among them were many Jews. Somewhere in Russia a bomb had been thrown, a train derailed, sacks of gold robbed. In some faraway city a governor had been shot. The jails were full. Many rebels were sent to Siberia. The Hasid who recounted these events said, "They kill and are killed. It is each man's sword in his neighbor!"

"What do they want?" Reb Mordecai Meir asked.

"That all should be equal."

"How is this possible?"

"Sons of the rich have joined their group."

The Hasid reported that the daughter of a wine dealer, a Hasid of the Rabbi of Gur, got mixed up with these instigators and was imprisoned in the Citadel. There she fasted for eighteen days and had to be fed by force.

Reb Mordecai Meir was stunned. The Redemption must be near! He asked, "If they don't believe in the world to come, why do they torment themselves so?"

"They want justice."

That evening, when Reb Mordecai Meir returned home after evening prayers, he saw Fulie seated at the kitchen table, his black blouse unbuttoned, his hair unkempt, chewing on a piece of bread and reading a book.

"Why do you eat dry bread? The woman cooks for you too."

"Pesha? She was taken to the hospital."

"Really? We must pray for her."

"She had an attack of gallstones. If you like I can make something."

"You?"

"I'll make sure it's kosher."

"You believe in it?"

"For your sake."

"Well, no."

From that day on grandfather and grandson ate only dry food. Fulie brought rolls, sugar, cheese from the store. He brewed tea. Reb Mordecai Meir was not sure he should trust such a one even with the making of tea. It was one thing to be a Gentile cook, who, the Talmud presumed, would not damage his livelihood and so could be trusted, and something entirely different to be a renegade Jew. However, bread and sugar could not be made unclean. Fulie bought the cheese from David in the dairy store across the street. If Fulie looked for a Gentile shop on another street, it meant he was an apostate out of spite, of whom it is said, "He knows his master and wants to defy Him." But so low he had not fallen.

The Sabbath meal was prepared by another neighbor. Reb Mordecai Meir lit the Sabbath candles himself. He sat at the table alone, in his threadbare satin coat, worn-out fur hat, chanting Sabbath chants, dipping a piece of hallah into the glass of ritual wine. The boy (which was what Reb Mordecai Meir called Fulie) didn't show himself on the Sabbath. The neighbor's daughter brought in rice soup, meat, carrot pudding. Reb Mordecai Meir half sang, half moaned.

If the old rabbi were still alive, Reb Mordecai Meir would have gone to live with him. But Reb Henokh was dead. The new rabbi was still a young man who cared more for the young Hasidim than the old. It was whispered that he was learned in worldly affairs. Many of the older Hasidim had died out and no new ones joined.

One Sabbath day, when Reb Mordecai Meir was sitting at the table murmuring, "I shall sing with praise," he heard the crack of a gun and a hideous scream. In the courtyard there was a din. Windows were thrown open. The sound of a police whistle pierced the air. A neighbor came in to tell Reb Mordecai Meir that the "comrades," the strikers, had shot one of their own, a bootmaker who was said to have denounced them to the police. Reb Mordecai Meir trembled.

"Who did it—Jews?"

"Yes, Jews."

"It is the end of the world." And Reb Mordecai Meir immediately regretted his words. It was not permitted to be sad or utter words of despair on the Sabbath.

Because Reb Mordecai Meir awoke for midnight prayers, he went to sleep early. At nine o'clock he was already in bed, often not undressed. He took off only his boots. That night he heard the kitchen door open and he recognized Fulie's steps. He fell asleep again, but at exactly twelve he awoke, got up, performed the ceremony of ritual hand washing, put on a housecoat and slippers, and began to lament on the destruction of the Temple. On his head he smeared a bit of ash, which he kept in a small jar. He intoned a plaintive melody. When Reb Mordecai Meir came to the verse "Rachel laments for her children," the door opened and Fulie entered barefoot, wearing a pair of dirty underpants, without a head covering. Reb Mordecai Meir raised his eyebrows and motioned to Fulie to leave and let him finish his supplications, but the boy said, "Grandfather, are you praying?"

Reb Mordecai Meir was not certain whether he was permitted to interrupt his prayers. After some hesitation he said, "I am reciting midnight prayers."

"What kind are they?"

"A Jew must never forget the destruction of the Temple."

"And what are you trying to accomplish by this?" Fulie asked.

Even though Reb Mordecai Meir understood every individual word, he did not grasp their meaning. He wanted to ask Fulie where his fringed undergarment was, but he realized that the question was pointless. He thought a moment and said, "One must pray. With God's help, the Messiah will come and there will be an end to the exile."

"If he hasn't yet come," Fulie asked, "why should he come now?"

"The Messiah wants to come to the Jews more than they want him to come, but the generation must be worth it. The Heavens send plenty of blessings, but we block the channels of mercy with our iniquities."

"Grandfather, I must talk to you."

"What do you want to talk about? One is not allowed to interrupt midnight prayers."

"Grandfather, the world won't get anywhere from all these prayers. People have prayed for nearly two thousand years, but the Messiah still did not get here on his white donkey. It's a battle, Grandfather, a bitter war between the exploiters and the exploited. Who incited the peasants to make pogroms on Jews? The Black Hundreds, the reactionaries. If the workers don't resist, we will be more enslaved. Grandfather, tomorrow there will be a big demonstration and I will be the speaker. If something should happen to me, I want you to give this envelope to a girl by the name of Nekhama Katz."

Now, for the first time, Reb Mordecai Meir noticed the boy holding a stuffed envelope.

He said, "I don't know any girls. I am an old man. Why are you involved with mutineers? You may be arrested, God forbid, and you will bring suffering on all of us. The czar has many Cossacks and he is stronger than you. Since you don't believe in the soul and the hereafter, why put yourself in danger?"

"Grandfather, I don't want to begin the discussion all over again. All of Europe is free and here the czar is a tyrant. We have no parliament. What he and his satraps want, they do. The war with Japan cost millions. Thousands of soldiers were lost. In the West they worry about the hygiene of the workers, but here a worker is worse than a dog. If we don't get a constitution, all of Russia will go down in blood."

Reb Mordecai Meir put down his prayer book. "Are you a worker?"

"What I am is not important, Grandfather. We are fighting for something, an ideal. Here is the letter. Put it in the drawer. Perhaps I will be back tomorrow. If not, a girl by the name of Nekhama Katz will come. Give it to her."

"Don't run, don't rush. He who is above governs the world. He determines that there will be wealthy and poor people. If there were no poor people, no one would want to do the ordinary work. One is a merchant and another a chimney sweeper. If everyone were a shopkeeper, who would sweep the chimneys?"

"We are striving to give chimney sweeps the same rights and the same means as merchants. Merchants aren't necessary. In a socialist world, production will be apportioned according to need. We won't let a middleman skim off the cream for himself."

"What! We Jews must not interfere. Whoever rules will persecute Jews."

"Anti-Semitism was created by the capitalists to divert the wrath of the masses against the regime. The Zionists want to run to Palestine, to the Tomb of Mother Rachel, but it's all just fantasy. We Jews must fight, together with all other oppressed people, for a better tomorrow."

"All right, all right, give me the letter. Leave me in peace. 'Except the Lord build a house, they labor in vain that build it.' It is written: 'No one should be punished before he is warned.' The Gemara says: 'If you go into a spice shop you smell good, and if you go into a tannery the stench stays with you.' "

"Grandfather, what are you calling a stench, the people's fight for their rights? Are you on the side of the exploiters?"

"Give me the envelope."

"Good night, Grandfather. We'll never understand each other."

Fulie left. Reb Mordecai Meir took hold of the envelope by one corner and put it into a drawer. He began to recite anew: "A voice was heard in Ramah, lamentation and bitter weeping, Rachel weeping for her children, refusing to be comforted." A kerosene lamp was burning and Reb Mordecai Meir's figure cast a large shadow on the wall. His head climbed the rafters. Reb Mordecai Meir grimaced and swayed back and forth. Can they possibly be made to understand the truth? he asked himself. They read a few books and repeat the gibberish. Constitution, schmonstitution! It's a battle between good and evil, God and Satan, Israel and Amalek. Esau and Ishmael refused to accept the Torah. The slave enjoys being abandoned. But when Jews cast away the Law, they become like pagans and maybe even worse. How could the Messiah come? Possibly, God forbid, the whole generation would become entirely guilty. He wiped his brow. "Oy, Father. The water reaches up to the very neck!"

After finishing prayers, Reb Mordecai Meir went back to bed. But this time he could not fall asleep. He heard the boy moving about in the kitchen. He banged the dishes, turned the faucet on. It seemed to Reb Mordecai Meir that he heard a sigh. Could that be Fulie? Who knows, perhaps he had thoughts of repentance. After all, on his mother's side, he stemmed from righteous men. Even among his Litvak forefathers there were probably some devout Jews. Reb Mordecai Meir could not remain in bed. Maybe the boy could be persuaded to stay home. What he said that evening was like a last testament. Reb Mordecai Meir got out of bed with trembling feet. Once again he put on his slippers and robe. When he opened the kitchen door he saw something so bizarre that he did not believe his own eyes. Fulie was standing completely dressed, holding a revolver in his hand. Reb Mordecai knew what it was. On the Feast of Omer children were given such guns, not real ones, only toys.

When he noticed his grandfather, Fulie laid the weapon on the kitchen table. "Grandfather, what do you want? Are you spying on me?"

"What kind of an abomination is this?" he asked. He began to shiver and his teeth chattered.

Fulie laughed. "Don't be afraid, Grandfather. It's not meant for you."

"For whom is it?"

"For those who want to hold back progress, to keep the world in darkness."

"What? *You* will sentence them to death? Seventy judges were required in the Sanhedrin to condemn anyone to die. There had to be admonition and at least two witnesses. The Gemara says that a court which sentenced anyone to death even once in seventy years was called a court of murderers."

"Grandfather, these people have sentenced themselves. Their time is past, but they refuse to give up peacefully. So they'll be made to leave by force."

"Fulie, Raphael, you are a Jew!" Reb Mordecai Meir choked on the words. "Esau lives by the sword. Not Jacob."

"Old wives' tales. Jews are made of the same stuff as Gentiles. It's all foolish chauvinism. This business about the Chosen People is sheer nonsense. Grandfather, I'm going."

"Don't leave! Don't leave! If they catch you, God forbid, they might . . ."

"I know, I know. I am not a child." Fulie put the revolver into the pocket of his pants. He took a package wrapped in newspaper with him. Probably some bread for a bite. He let the door slam as he left. Reb Mordecai Meir remained standing on unsteady feet. He leaned against the wall to keep from falling. "Have things gone so far?" he asked himself. Sleep was out of the question, but it was too early for morning prayers. The morning star was not yet in sight. Night and day still ruled in confusion.

On wobbling feet, Reb Mordecai Meir walked over to the window. To the right the sky was still black. But to the left, in the east, it had become like daylight. All the stores on the street were shut. A baker's apprentice passed by, barefoot, in white pants, carrying a tray of cakes or rolls on his head. "Well, baked goods are needed," Reb Mordecai Meir murmured.

He expected to see Fulie appear on the sidewalk, but he didn't come through. The gate was probably still locked. He must have friends here in the yard, Reb Mordecai Meir decided. Woe, woe, what has become of my people! For the first time he was envious of Beyle Teme—she had not lived to see these calamities. By now she was certainly in Paradise. Until today, Reb Mordecai Meir had seldom thought of his wife during prayers. A Jew was supposed to pray directly to God, not to any saintly man or woman. But now Reb Mordecai Meir began to talk to Beyle Teme's soul. "He is your grandchild. Intercede for him. Let nothing evil happen to him, and let him, God forbid, do no harm to others."

To the right, the moon was still visible and Reb Mordecai Meir looked up at it, the lesser light which, according to the Talmud, begrudged the greater light, and as compensation was given the stars. That meant that there was envy on high, Reb Mordecai Meir half asked, half stated. He could not bring himself to leave the window, hoping to see Fulie once more. The thought crossed his mind that Abraham also had an Esau for a grandchild. He had Ishmael for a son and the sons of Keturah. Even the saints couldn't bring forth only good seeds. Suddenly the street was flooded with a reddish glow. The sun had risen over the banks of the Vistula. There was a clatter of horseshoes on cobblestones and the twittering of birds could be heard. Reb Mordecai Meir saw soldiers, their swords gleaming, riding on horses. The riders kept glancing at the upper floors.

Is it against them that Fulie went to wage war? Reb Mordecai Meir pondered. He felt cold and shuddered. Never before had he wished to be rid of this world. But now he was ready to die. How much longer would he have to wander in the valley of tears? Better to go through the pains of Gehenna than to see this futile turmoil.

The shouting and confusion began in the early morning. Right here in the street, it seemed, the rebels tried to conquer the forces of the Russian czar. Youths stormed out of every gate, shouting, waving their fists, and singing. Policemen, their swords bared, chased them and fired shots. A red flag was raised with more singing and shouting. The stores remained shut. Gates were closed. The shrill sound of police whistles could be heard. First-aid wagons appeared, and for a while the street became empty. The red flag, which someone had just held aloft, now lay in the gutter, torn and dirty. The street soon began to fill up again. Another flag fluttered. There was renewed shouting and the stampeding of many feet.

Reb Mordecai Meir could not bear to watch any more. God's light certainly had to be dimmed and His face hidden before there could be free will, reward and punishment, redemption; but couldn't the Almighty find another way to reveal His power? These youths with their shaven beards and short coats bellowed like peasants. Once in a while the sound of female shrieks came through. A policeman was beaten up, a horse had fallen and lay on the pavement, apparently with broken legs. In what way was the poor animal guilty? Unless it was a soul in reincarnation, atoning for some transgression committed in a former life.

Reb Mordecai Meir began to pray. There was no possibility of going to the synagogue on such a day. He wrapped himself in his prayer shawl, kissed the fringes, placed the phylacteries on his arm and head. He could hardly stand through the Eighteen Benedictions. While he prayed, the din in the street grew louder. He heard the cries of those who were hit and injured. Blood was spattered on the wall across the way. Children, whom mothers had carried, borne, nursed, worried over their slightest whim, now lay in the mud writhing in the agonies of death. "Woe, my punishment is greater than I can bear!"

Usually after morning prayers Reb Mordecai Meir washed his hands, had a bite to eat: a piece of bread, a slice of cheese, sometimes a bit of herring, a glass of tea. But today he could not eat; the food would stick in his throat. He reminded himself of the passage in the Midrash: "When the Egyptians drowned in the Red Sea, the angels wanted to sing songs of praise, but the Almighty said to them, 'My creatures sink into the sea and you want to sing!'" The Creator had pity even on the Egyptian oppressors.

Reb Mordecai Meir felt dizzy and lay down on the couch. To keep the light of day out he put the hat with the big brim over his eyes. For a time he was neither awake nor asleep. Finally he fell into the deep sleep of those who have not rested for many nights and are utterly exhausted. He dreamed, but later could not recall his dreams.

The tumult from the outside became even wilder. He awoke with a start. Screams and shots reverberated. Reb Mordecai Meir imagined that multitudes of women were wailing and dogs were howling. During a moment's lull, Reb Mordecai Meir heard the singing of birds, which in the midst of this total madness fulfilled their mission. These creatures ignored the humans with their schemes and ambitions even while they built their nests under man's eaves, ate his leftovers, hopped about on his telephone wires. People too are helped by beings they cannot comprehend.

Reb Mordecai Meir got up with the intention of brewing himself a cup of tea. He went into the kitchen, found some matches, filled a kettle of water from the spout. There was a quarter of a loaf of bread which Fulie must have bought last night, as well as a piece of stale cake. The old man was about to strike a match when he suddenly remembered that he had decided to fast. "Today it is Tishe b'Av for me. I'll eat and drink nothing," and he put the match down.

The living room had a book closet and he began to rummage through it. He had no strength to study the Talmud, but he wanted to look through a Hasidic volume. Maybe *The Generations of Jacob Joseph*? He pulled out a thin little book, *The Waters of Shiloh*, written by the first of the Radzym dynasty. He was surprised; he didn't even know he owned this book. Reb Mordecai Meir turned to a page in the middle. There he read that the way to grasp the greatness of the Creator was to recognize one's own nothingness. As long as man considers himself important, his eyes are blinded to Heaven. Reb Mordecai Meir took hold of his beard. The flesh forgets. The Evil Spirit and the Lord of Forgetfulness band together. Perhaps they are one and the same?

Suddenly it occurred to him that it was strangely quiet outside.

Were they tired? He went to the window and saw that the street was empty, the shops still closed. Dusk was setting in. "Have they already gotten, what do they call it, the constitution?" he wondered. It was weird to see the stores closed on an ordinary weekday. The square, which was usually teeming with boys, girls, assorted peddlers, and urchins, was as empty as in the middle of the night.

Then he heard the tread of heavy steps on the stairs and in an instant knew that they were coming to him, and that it was with bad news. He trembled and his lips began to move in prayer, even though he realized that it was too late now to ward off what had already happened. For a few moments there was no sound and the thought flashed through his mind that maybe he was mistaken. Then the thumping on the door and the bang of a boot made his legs buckle. It seemed to him he would not be able to reach the door. But he opened it and saw what he expected to see: four men were carrying a body on a stretcher, a dead man—Fulie. They entered without speaking, with the sullenness of pall-bearers.

"The murderers killed him," one of them shouted. "Where should we put him down?" a second one asked. Reb Mordecai Meir pointed to the floor. The dead man was bleeding. A puddle of blood formed on the floor. A hand stuck out from under the cover—a lifeless hand, limp and pale, which no longer could take anything, no gift, no favor, no constitution . . .

Reb Mordecai Meir's belly swelled up like a drum. "Great God, I don't want to live any longer. Enough!" He was angry with God for the punishment which He had visited upon him in his old age. He had to vomit and dragged himself to the toilet, where he retched as if he had eaten and drunk all day and not fasted. Fires leaped before his eyes. Never in his life had he complained to God. He murmured, "I don't deserve this affliction!" And he knew that he was blaspheming.

Late that night there was again a knocking at his door. "Who is it, another corpse?" Reb Mordecai Meir asked himself in his anxiety. He was sitting beside Fulie's body reciting psalms. When he opened the door, first a policeman entered, followed by a civilian, and then by two more policemen and the janitor. They were saying something in Russian, but Reb Mordecai Meir did not understand their language. He pointed to the corpse but they turned away.

A search began. Drawers were opened, papers thrown around. From the dresser the person in civilian clothes took Fulie's thick envelope for Nekhama Katz. He opened it and removed several sheets of paper, a notebook, a nickel watch, other objects. He read a part of the letter to the others—in Russian. One of them smiled. Another stared silently. He then said to Reb Mordecai Meir in broken Yiddish, "Grandfather, come."

"What? Where?"

"Come."

"What will happen to the corpse?"

"Come, come."

Somewhere the janitor found Reb Mordecai Meir's coat. Reb Mordecai Meir wanted to ask the one in charge why he was being arrested, but he could speak neither Polish nor Russian. Anyway, what good would it do to ask? The civilian took him by one arm, a policeman by the other, and they led him down the dark staircase. The janitor lit matches. He opened the gate. A small carriage with barred windows was waiting outside. They helped Reb Mordecai Meir get in and sat him down on a bench. One of the policemen sat next to him. Slowly the carriage began to move.

"Well, let me imagine that it is my funeral," Reb Mordecai Meir said to himself. "No one will say Kaddish for me anyhow."

A strange calm came over him and the complete surrender that accompanies misfortune so great that one knows nothing worse can occur. Before, when they had brought Fulie's body, he had rebelled in his thought, but now he regretted his resentment. "Father in Heaven, forgive me." There came to his mind the saying from the Talmud: "No one is subject to penalty for words uttered in agony."

"What time is it?" he wondered. Suddenly he remembered that he had not taken his prayer shawl and phylacteries. Well, it was too late even for that. Reb Mordecai Meir started to confess his sins. "We have transgressed, we have betrayed, we have cheated, we have deceived . . ." He raised his hand and tried to make a fist to beat his breast, but his fingers were rigid. Well, he has probably already atoned for his mistakes, Reb Mordecai Meir was thinking about Fulie. His intentions were good. He wanted to help the poor. He pitied the hungry. Perhaps that was his salvation. In Heaven everything is judged according to intention. Maybe his soul is already cleansed.

It was not customary to say Kaddish without a quorum or for someone who had not yet been buried, but Reb Mordecai Meir knew that he had little time left. He mumbled the Kaddish. Then he recited a chapter from the Mishnah which he knew from memory. "At what time is it permissible to recite the Shema in the evening? From the time that the priests enter the Temple to eat their food offerings. So sayeth Rabbi Eliezer. And the sages say: Until midnight."

"Hey, you, Jew, old dog, who are you talking to, your God?" the policeman asked. Somehow Reb Mordecai Meir understood these few words. What does he know? How can he understand? Reb Mordecai Meir defended him in his thoughts. Since no evil can come from God, those created in His image can't be completely wicked. He said to the policeman, "Yes, I am Jew. I pray God."

Those were all the Gentile words Reb Mordecai Meir knew.

Old Love

HARRY BENDINER awoke at five with the feeling that as far as he was concerned the night was finished and he wouldn't get any more sleep. Actually, he woke up a dozen times every night. He had undergone an operation for his prostate years before, but this hadn't relieved the constant pressure on his bladder. He would sleep an hour or less, then wake up with the need to void. Even his dreams centered around this urge. He got out of bed and padded to the bathroom on shaky legs. On the way back he stepped out onto the balcony of his eleventh-story condominium. To the left he could see the skyscrapers of Miami, to the right the rumbling sea. The air had turned a bit cooler during the night, but it was still tropically tepid. It smelled of dead fish, oil, and perhaps of oranges as well. Harry stood there for a long while enjoying the breeze from the ocean on his moist forehead. Even though Miami Beach had become a big city, he imagined that he could feel the nearness of the Everglades, the smells and vapors of its vegetation and swamps. Sometimes a seagull would awake in the night, screeching. It happened that the waves threw onto the beach the carcass of a barracuda or even that of a baby whale. Harry Bendiner looked off in the direction of Hollywood. How long was it since the whole area had been undeveloped? Within a few years a wasteland had been transformed into a settlement crowded with hotels, condominiums, restaurants, supermarkets, and banks. The street lights and neon signs dimmed the stars in the sky. Cars raced along even in the middle of the night. Where were all these people hurrying to before dawn? Didn't they ever sleep? What kind of force drove them on? "Well, it's no longer my world. Once you pass eighty, you're as good as a corpse."

Translated by Joseph Singer

He leaned his hand on the railing and tried to reconstruct the dream he had been having. He recalled only that all those who had appeared in the dream were now dead—the men and the women both. Dreams obviously didn't acknowledge death. In his dreams, his three wives were still alive, and so was his son, Bill, and his daughter, Sylvia. New York, his hometown in Poland, and Miami Beach merged into one. He, Harry or Hershel, was both an adult and a cheder boy.

He closed his eyes for a moment. Why was it impossible to remember dreams? He could recall every detail of events that had happened seventy and even seventy-five years ago, but tonight's dreams dissolved like foam. Some force made sure that not a trace of them remained. A third of a person's life died before he went to his grave.

After a while Harry sat down on the plastic chaise that stood on the balcony. He looked toward the sea, to the east, where day would soon be dawning. There was a time when he went swimming the first thing in the morning, particularly during the summer months, but he no longer had the desire to do such things. The newspapers occasionally printed accounts of sharks attacking swimmers, and there were other sea creatures whose bites caused serious complications. For him it now sufficed to take a warm bath.

His thoughts turned to matters of business. He knew full well that money couldn't help him; still, one couldn't constantly brood about the fact that everything was vanity of vanities. It was easier to think about practical matters. Stocks and bonds rose or fell. Dividends and other earnings had to be deposited in the bank and marked down in an account book for tax purposes. Telephone and electric bills and the maintenance of the apartment had to be paid. One day a week a woman came to do his cleaning and press his shirts and underwear. Occasionally he had to have a suit dry-cleaned and shoes repaired. He received letters that he had to answer. He wasn't involved with a synagogue all year, but on Rosh Hashanah and Yom Kippur he had to have a place to worship, and because of this he received appeals to help Israel, yeshivas, Talmud Torahs, old-age homes, and hospitals. Each day he got a pile of "junk mail," and before he discarded it, he had to open and glance at it, at least.

Since he had resolved to live out his years without a wife or even a housekeeper, he had to arrange for his meals, and every other day he went shopping at the local supermarket. Pushing his cart through the aisles, he selected such items as milk, cottage cheese, fruit, canned vegetables, chopped meat, occasionally some mushrooms, a jar of borscht or gefilte fish. He certainly could have permitted himself the luxury of a maid, but some of the maids were thieves. And what would he do with himself if other people waited on him? He remembered a saying from the Gemara that slothfulness led to madness. Fussing over the electric stove in the kitchen, going to the bank, reading the newspaper—particularly the financial section—and spending an hour or two at the office of Merrill Lynch watching the quotations from the New York Exchange flash by on the board lifted his spirits. Recently he had had a television set installed, but he rarely watched it.

His neighbors in the condominium often inquired maliciously why he did things himself that others could do for him. It was known that he was rich. They offered him advice and asked him questions: Why didn't he settle in Israel? Why didn't he go to a hotel in the mountains during the summer? Why didn't he get married? Why didn't he hire a secretary? He had acquired the reputation of a miser. They constantly reminded him that "you can't take it with you"—as if this were some startling revelation. For this reason he stopped attending the tenants' meetings and their parties. Everyone tried in one way or another to get something out of him, but no one would have given him a penny if he needed it. A few years ago, he boarded a bus from Miami Beach to Miami and found he was two cents short of the fare. All he had with him was twenty-dollar bills. No one volunteered either to give him the two cents or to change one of his bank notes, and the driver made him get off.

The truth was, in no hotel could he feel as comfortable as he did in his own home. The meals served in hotels were too plentiful for him and not of the kind that he needed. He alone could see to it that his diet excluded salt, cholesterol, spices. Besides, plane and train rides were too taxing for a man of his delicate health. Nor did it make any sense to remarry at his age. Younger women demanded sex, and he hadn't the slightest interest in an old woman. Being what he was, he was condemned to live alone and to die alone.

A reddish glow had begun to tinge the eastern sky, and Harry went to the bathroom. He stood for a moment studying his image in the mirror—sunken cheeks, a bare skull with a few tufts of white hair, a pointed Adam's apple, a nose whose tip turned down like a parrot's beak. The pale-blue eyes were set somewhat off-center, one higher than the other, and expressed both weariness and traces of youthful ardor. He had once been a virile man. He had had wives and love affairs. He had a stack of love letters and photographs lying about somewhere.

Harry Bendiner hadn't come to America penniless and uneducated like the other immigrants. He had attended the study house in his hometown until the age of nineteen; he knew Hebrew and had secretly read newspapers and worldly books. He had taken lessons in Russian, Polish, and even German. Here in America he had attended Cooper Union for two years in the hope of becoming an engineer, but he had fallen in love with an American girl, Rosalie Stein, and married her, and her father,

Sam Stein, had taken him into the construction business. Rosalie died of cancer at the age of thirty, leaving him with two small children. Even as the money came in to him so did death take from him. His son, Bill, a surgeon, died at forty-six, of a heart attack, leaving two children, neither of whom wanted to be Jewish. Their mother, a Christian, lived somewhere in Canada with another man. Harry's daughter, Sylvia, got the very same type of cancer as her mother, and at exactly the same age. Sylvia left no children. Harry refused to sire any more generations, even though his second wife, Edna, pleaded that he have a child or two with her.

Yes, the Angel of Death had taken everything from him. At first his grandchildren had called him occasionally from Canada and sent him a card for the New Year. But now he never heard from them, and he had cut them out of his will.

Harry shaved and hummed a melody—where it had come from he didn't know. Was it something he had heard on television, or a tune from Poland revived in his memory? He had no ear for music and sang everything off-key, but he had retained the habit of singing in the bathroom. His toilet took a long time. For years the pills he took to relieve constipation had had no effect, and every other day he gave himself an enema—a long and arduous process for a man in his eighties. He tried to do calisthenics in the bathtub, raising his skinny legs and splashing his hands in the water as if they were paddles. These were all measures to lengthen life, but even as Harry performed them he asked himself, "Why go on living?" What flavor did his existence possess? No, his life made no sense whatsoever—but did that of his neighbors make more sense? The condominium was full of old people, all well off, many rich. Some of the men couldn't walk, or dragged their feet; some of the women leaned on crutches. A number suffered from arthritis and Parkinson's disease. This wasn't a building but a hospital. People died, and he didn't find out about it until weeks or months afterward. Although he had been among the first tenants in the condominium, he seldom recognized anybody. He didn't go to the pool and he didn't play cards. Men and women greeted him in the elevator and at the supermarket, but he didn't know who any of them were. From time to time someone asked him, "How are you, Mr. Bendiner?" And he usually replied, "How *can* you be at my age? Each day is a gift."

This summer day began like all the others. Harry prepared his breakfast in the kitchen—Rice Krispies with skimmed milk and Sanka sweetened with saccharin. At about nine-thirty he took the elevator down to get the mail. A day didn't go by that he didn't receive a number of checks, but this day brought a bounty. The stocks had fallen, but the companies kept paying the dividends as usual. Harry got money from buildings on which he held mortgages, from rents, bonds, and all kinds of business ventures that he barely remembered. An insurance company paid him an annuity. For years he had been getting a monthly check from Social Security. This morning's yield came to over eleven thousand dollars. True, he would have to withhold a great part of this for taxes, but it still left him with some five thousand dollars for himself. While he totaled up the figures, he deliberated: Should he go to the office of Merrill Lynch and see what was happening on the Exchange? No, there was no point to it. Even if the stocks rose early in the morning, the day would end in losses. "The market is completely crazy," he mumbled to himself. He had considered it an iron rule that inflation always went along with a bullish market, not with a bearish market. But now both the dollar *and* the stocks were collapsing. Well, you could never be sure about anything except death.

Around eleven o'clock he went down to deposit the checks. The bank was a small one; all the employees knew him and said good morning. He had a safe-deposit box there, where he kept his valuables and jewelry. It so happened that all three of his wives had left him everything; none of them had made out a will. He didn't know himself exactly how much he was worth, but it couldn't be less than five million dollars. Still, he walked down the street in a shirt and trousers that any pauper could afford and a cap and shoes he had worn for years. He poked with his cane and took tiny steps. Once in a while he cast a glance backward. Maybe someone was following him. Maybe some crook had found out how rich he was and was scheming to kidnap him. Although the day was bright and the street full of people, no one would interfere if he was grabbed, forced into a car, and dragged off to some ruin or cave. No one would pay ransom for him.

After he had concluded his business at the bank, he turned back toward home. The sun was high in the sky and poured down a blazing fire. Women stood in the shade of canopies looking at dresses, shoes, stockings, brassières, and bathing suits in the store windows. Their faces expressed indecision—to buy or not to buy? Harry glanced at the windows. What could he buy there? There wasn't anything he could desire. From now until five, when he would prepare his dinner, he needed absolutely nothing. He knew precisely what he would do when he got home—take a nap on the sofa.

Thank God, no one had kidnapped him, no one had held him up, no one had broken into his apartment. The air conditioner was working, and so was the plumbing in the bathroom. He took off his shoes and stretched out on the sofa.

Strange, he still daydreamed; he fantasized about unexpected successes, restored powers, masculine adventures. The brain wouldn't accept old age. It teemed with the same passions it had in his youth. Harry often said to his brain, "Don't be stupid. It's too late for everything. You have nothing to hope for any more." But the brain was so constituted that it went on hoping nonetheless. Who was it who said, A man takes his hopes into the grave?

He had dozed off and was awakened by a jangling at the door. He became alarmed. No one ever came to see him. "It must be the exterminator," he decided. He opened the door the length of the chain and saw a small woman with reddish cheeks, yellow eyes, and a high pompadour of blond hair the color of straw. She wore a white blouse.

Harry opened the door, and the woman said in a foreign-accented English, "I hope I haven't wakened you. I'm your new neighbor on the left. I wanted to introduce myself to you. My name is Mrs. Ethel Brokeles. A funny name, eh? That was my late husband's name. My maiden name is Goldman."

Harry gazed at her in astonishment. His neighbor on the left had been an old woman living alone. He remembered her name—Mrs. Halpert. He asked, "What happened to Mrs. Halpert?"

"The same as happens to everybody," the woman replied smugly.

"When did it happen? I didn't know anything about it."

"It's more than five months already."

"Come in, come in. People die and you don't even know," Harry said. "She was a nice woman . . . kept herself at a distance."

"I didn't know her. I bought the apartment from her daughter."

"Please have a seat. I don't even have anything to offer you. I have a bottle of liqueur somewhere, but—"

"I don't need any refreshments and I don't drink liqueur. Not in the middle of the day. May I smoke?"

"Certainly, certainly."

The woman sat down on the sofa. She snapped a fancy lighter expertly and lit her cigarette. She wore red nail polish and Harry noticed a huge diamond on one of her fingers.

The woman asked, "You live here alone?"

"Yes, alone."

"I'm alone, too. What can you do? I lived with my husband twenty-five years, and we didn't have a bad day. Our life together was all sunshine without a single cloud. Suddenly he passed away and left me alone and miserable. The New York climate is unhealthy for me. I suffer from rheumatism. I'll have to live out my years here."

"Did you buy the apartment furnished?" Harry asked in businesslike fashion.

"Everything. The daughter wanted nothing for herself besides the dresses and linens. She turned it all over to me for a song. I wouldn't have had the patience to go out and buy furniture and dishes. Have you lived here a long time already?"

The woman posed one question after another, and Harry answered them willingly. She looked comparatively young—no more than fifty or possibly even younger. He brought her an ashtray and put a glass of lemonade and a plate of cookies on the coffee table before her. Two hours went by, but he hardly noticed. Ethel Brokeles crossed her legs, and Harry cast glances at her round knees. She had switched to a Polish-accented Yiddish. She exuded the intimate air of a relative. Something within Harry exulted. It could be nothing else but that heaven had acceded to his secret desires. Only now, as he listened to her, did he realize how lonely he had been all these years, how oppressed by the fact that he seldom exchanged a word with anyone. Even having her for a neighbor was better than nothing. He grew youthful in her presence, and loquacious. He told her about his three wives, the tragedies that had befallen his children. He even mentioned that, following the death of his first wife, he had had a sweetheart.

The woman said, "You don't have to make excuses. A man is a man."

"I've grown old."

"A man is never old. I had an uncle in Wloclawek who was eighty when he married a twenty-year-old girl, and she bore him three children."

"Wloclawek? That's near Kowal, my hometown."

"I know. I've been to Kowal. I had an aunt there."

The woman glanced at her wristwatch. "It's one o'clock. Where are you having lunch?"

"Nowhere. I only eat breakfast and dinner."

"Are you on a diet?"

"No, but at my age—"

"Stop talking about your age!" the woman scolded him. "You know what? Come over to my place and we'll have lunch together. I don't like to eat by myself. For me, eating alone is even worse than sleeping alone."

"Really, I don't know what to say. What did I do to deserve this?"

"Come, come; don't talk nonsense. This is America, not Poland. My refrigerator is stuffed with goodies. I throw out more than I eat, may I be forgiven."

The woman used Yiddish expressions that Harry hadn't heard in at least sixty years. She took his arm and led him to the door. He didn't have to go more than a few steps. By the time he had locked his door she had opened hers. The apartment he went into was larger than his and brighter. There were pictures on the walls, fancy lamps, bric-a-brac. The windows looked out directly at the ocean. On the table stood a vase of flowers. The air in Harry's apartment smelled of dust, but here the air was fresh. "She wants something; she has some ulterior motive," Harry told himself. He recalled what he had read in the newspapers about female cheats who swindled fortunes out of men and out of other women, too. The main thing was to promise nothing, to sign nothing, not to hand over even a single penny.

She seated him at a table, and from the kitchen soon issued the bubbling sound of a percolator and the smell of fresh rolls, fruit, cheese, and coffee. For the first time in years Harry felt an appetite in the middle of the day. After a while they both sat down to lunch.

Between one bite and the next, the woman took a drag from a cigarette. She complained, "Men run after me, but when it comes down to brass tacks they're all interested only in how much money I have. As soon as they start talking about money I break up with them. I'm not poor; I'm even—knock wood—wealthy. But I don't want anyone to take me for my money."

"Thank God I don't need anyone's money," Harry said. "I've got enough even if I live a thousand years."

"That's good."

Gradually they began to discuss their finances, and the woman enumerated her possessions. She owned buildings in Brooklyn and on Staten Island; she had stocks and bonds. Based on what she said and the names she mentioned, Harry decided that she was telling the truth. She had, here in Miami, a checking account and a safe-deposit box in the very same bank as Harry. Harry estimated that she was worth at least a million or maybe more. She served him food with the devotion of a daughter or wife. She talked of what he should and shouldn't eat. Such miracles had occurred to him in his younger years. Women had met him, grown instantly intimate, and stuck with him, never to leave again. But that such a thing should happen to him at his age seemed like a dream. He asked abruptly, "Do you have children?"

"I have a daughter, Sylvia. She lives all alone in a tent in British Columbia."

"Why in a tent? My daughter's name was Sylvia, too. You yourself could be my daughter," he added, not knowing why he had said such a thing.

"Nonsense. What are years? I always liked a man to be a lot older than me. My husband, may he rest in peace, was twenty years older, and the life we had together I would wish for every Jewish daughter."

"I've surely got forty years on you," Harry said.

The woman put down her spoon. "How old do you take me for?"

"Around forty-five," Harry said, knowing she was older.

"Add another twelve years and you've got it."

"You don't look it."

"I had a good life with my husband. I could get anything out of him—the moon, the stars, nothing was too good for his Ethel. That's why after he died I became melancholy. Also, my daughter was making me sick. I spent a fortune on psychiatrists, but they couldn't help me. Just as you see me now, I stayed seven months in an institution, a clinic for nervous disorders. I had a breakdown and I didn't want to live any more. They had to watch me day and night. He was calling me from his grave. I want to tell you something, but don't misunderstand me."

"What is it?"

"You remind me of my husband. That's why—"

"I'm eighty-two," Harry said and instantly regretted it. He could have easily subtracted five years. He waited a moment, then added, "If I were ten years younger, I'd make you a proposition."

Again he regretted his words. They had issued from his mouth as if of their own volition. He was still bothered by the fear of falling into the hands of a gold digger.

The woman looked at him inquisitively and cocked an eyebrow. "Since I decided to live, I'll take you just as you are."

"How is this possible? How can it be?" Harry asked himself again and again. They spoke of getting married and of breaking through the wall that divided their two apartments to make them into one. His bedroom was next to hers. She revealed the details of her financial situation to him. She was worth about a million and a half. Harry had already told her how much he had. He asked, "What will we do with so much money?"

"I wouldn't know what to do with money myself," the woman replied, "but together, we'll take a trip around the world. We'll buy an apartment in Tel Aviv or Tiberias. The hot springs there are good for rheumatism. With me beside you, you'll live a long time. I guarantee you a hundred years, if not more."

"It's all in God's hands," Harry said, amazed at his own words. He wasn't religious. His doubts about God and His providence had intensified over the years. He often said that, after what had happened to the Jews in Europe, one had to be a fool to believe in God.

Ethel stood up and so did he. They hugged and kissed. He pressed her close and youthful urges came throbbing back within him.

She said, "Wait till we've stood under the wedding canopy."

It struck Harry that he had heard these words before, spoken in the same voice. But when? And from whom? All three of his wives had been American-born and wouldn't have used this expression. Had he dreamed it? Could a person foresee the future in a dream? He bowed his head and pondered. When he looked up he was astounded. Within those few seconds the woman's appearance had undergone a startling transformation. She had moved away from him and he hadn't noticed it. Her face had grown pale, shrunken, and aged. Her hair seemed to him to have become suddenly disheveled. She gazed at him sidelong with a dull, sad, even stern expression. Did I insult her or what? he wondered. He heard himself ask, "Is something wrong? Don't you feel well?"

"No, but you'd better go back to your own place now," she said in a voice which seemed alien, harsh, and impatient. He wanted to ask her the reason for the sudden change that had come over her, but a long-forgotten (or a never-forgotten) pride asserted itself. With women, you never knew where you stood anyhow. Still, he asked, "When will we see each other?"

"Not today any more. Maybe tomorrow," she said after some hesitation.

"Goodbye. Thanks for the lunch."

She didn't even bother to escort him to the door. Inside his own apartment again, he thought, Well, she changed her mind. He was overcome with a feeling of shame—for himself and for her, too. Had she been playing a game with him? Had malicious neighbors arranged to make a fool of him? His apartment struck him as half empty. I won't eat dinner, he decided. He felt a pressure in his stomach. "At my age one shouldn't make a fool of oneself," he murmured. He lay down on the sofa and dozed off, and when he opened his eyes again it was dark outside. Maybe she'll ring my doorbell again. Maybe I should call her? She had given him her phone number. Though he had slept, he woke up exhausted. He had letters to answer, but he put it off until morning. He went out onto the balcony. One side of his balcony faced a part of hers. They could see each other here and even converse, if she should still be interested in him. The sea splashed and foamed. There was a freighter far in the distance. A jet roared in the sky. A single star that no street lights or neon signs could dim appeared above. It's a good thing one can see at least one star. Otherwise one might forget that the sky exists altogether.

He sat on the balcony waiting for her to possibly show up. What could she be thinking? Why had her mood changed so abruptly? One minute she was as tender and talkative as a bride in love; a moment later she was a stranger.

Harry dozed off again, and when he awoke it was late in the evening. He wasn't sleepy, and he wanted to go downstairs for the evening edition of the morning paper, with the reports of the New York Exchange; instead he went to lie down on his bed. He had drunk a glass of tomato juice before and swallowed a pill. Only a thin wall separated him from Ethel, but walls possessed a power of their own. Perhaps this is the reason some people prefer to live in a tent, he thought. He assumed that his broodings would keep him from sleeping, but he quickly nodded off. He awoke with pressure on his chest. What time was it? The luminous dial on his wristwatch showed that he had slept two hours and a quarter. He had dreamed, but he couldn't remember what. He retained only the impression of nocturnal horrors. He raised his head. Was she asleep or awake? He couldn't hear even a rustle from her apartment.

He slept again and was awakened this time by the sound of many people talking, doors slamming, footsteps in the corridor, and running. He had always been afraid of a fire. He read newspaper accounts of old people burning to death in old-age homes, hospitals, hotels. He got out of bed, put on his slippers and robe, and opened the door to the hall. There was no one there. Had he imagined it? He closed the door and went out onto the balcony. No, not a trace of firemen below. Only people coming home late, going out to nightclubs, making drunken noise. Some of the condominium tenants sublet their apartments in the summer to South Americans. Harry went back to bed. It was quiet for a few minutes; then he again heard a din in the corridor and the sound of men's and women's voices. Something had happened, but what? He had an urge to get up and take another look, but he didn't. He lay there tense. Suddenly he heard a buzzing from the house phone in the kitchen. When he lifted the receiver, a man's voice said, "Wrong number." Harry had turned on the fluorescent light in the kitchen and the glare dazzled him. He opened the refrigerator, took out a jug of sweetened tea, and poured himself half a glass, not knowing whether he did this because he was thirsty or to buoy his spirits. Soon afterward he had to urinate, and he went to the bathroom.

At that moment, his doorbell rang, and the sound curtailed his urge. Maybe robbers had broken into the building? The night watchman was an old man and hardly a match for intruders. Harry couldn't decide whether to go to the door or not. He stood over the toilet bowl trembling. *These might be my final moments on earth* flashed through his mind. "God Almighty, take pity on me," he murmured. Only now did he remember that he had a peephole in the door through which he could see the hall outside. How could I have forgotten about it? he wondered. I must be getting senile.

He walked silently to the door, raised the cover of the peephole, and looked out. He saw a white-haired woman in a robe. He recognized her; it was his neighbor on the right. In a second everything became clear to him. She had a paralyzed husband and something had happened to him. He opened the door. The old woman held out an unstamped envelope.

"Excuse me, Mr. Bendiner, the woman next door left this envelope by your door. Your name is on it."

"What woman?"

"On the left. She committed suicide."

Harry Bendiner felt his guts constrict, and within seconds his belly grew as tight as a drum.

"The blond woman?"

"Yes."

"What did she do?"

"Threw herself out the window."

Harry held out his hand and the old woman gave him the envelope.

"Where is she?" he asked.

"They took her away."

"Dead?"

"Yes, dead."

"My God!"

"It's already the third such incident here. People lose their minds in America."

Harry's hand shook, and the envelope fluttered as if caught in a wind. He thanked the woman and closed the door. He went to look for his glasses, which he had put on his night table. "I dare not fall," he cautioned himself. "All I need now is a broken hip." He staggered over to his bed and lit the night lamp. Yes, the eyeglasses were lying where he had left them. He felt dizzy. The walls, the curtains, the dresser, the envelope all jerked and whirled like a blurry image on television. Am I going blind or what? he wondered. He sat and waited for the dizziness to pass. He barely had the strength to open the envelope. The note was written in pencil, the lines were crooked, and the Yiddish words badly spelled. It read:

> Dear Harry, forgive me. I must go where my husband is. If it's not too much trouble, say Kaddish for me. I'll intercede for you where I'm going.
>
> Ethel

He put the sheet of paper and his glasses down on the night table and switched off the lamp. He lay belching and hiccuping. His body twitched, and the bedsprings vibrated. Well, from now on I won't hope for anything, he decided with the solemnity of a man taking an oath. He felt cold, and he covered himself with the blanket.

It was ten past eight in the morning when he came out of his daze. A dream? No, the letter lay on the table. That day Harry Bendiner did not go down for his mail. He did not prepare breakfast for himself, nor did he bother to bathe and dress. He kept on dozing on the plastic chaise on the balcony and thinking about that other Sylvia—Ethel's daughter— who was living in a tent in British Columbia. Why had she run away so far? he asked himself. Did her father's death drive her into despair? Could she not stand her mother? Or did she already at her age realize the futility of all human efforts and decide to become a hermit? Is she endeavoring to discover herself, or God? An adventurous idea came into the old man's mind: to fly to British Columbia, find the young woman in the wilderness, comfort her, be a father to her, and perhaps try to meditate together with her on why a man is born and why he must die.

The Admirer

FIRST she wrote me a long letter full of praise. Among other things, she said that my books had helped her "find" herself. Then she called and arranged a meeting. Soon afterward she called again, since it turned out she already had an engagement that day, and she proposed another. Two days later a long telegram came. It seemed that she would be visiting a paralyzed aunt on the new meeting day. I had never received such a long telegram, with such fancy English words. A call followed, and we settled on a new date. During an earlier telephone conversation I had mentioned that I admired Thomas Hardy. In a few days a messenger brought a luxuriously bound set of Thomas Hardy's works. My admirer's name was Elizabeth Abigail de Sollar—a remarkable name for a woman whose mother, she told me, came from the Polish town of Klendev, the daughter of the local rabbi.

On the day of the visit I cleaned my apartment and put all my manuscripts and unanswered letters in the laundry hamper. My guest was due at eleven. At twenty-five past eleven the phone rang and Elizabeth Abigail de Sollar shrieked, "You gave me a phony address! There is no such building!"

It seemed she had mistaken East Side for West. I now told her precisely how to find me. Once she got to my street on the West Side, she should enter a gate bearing the number she had. The gate opened onto a courtyard. There she would find an entrance with a different number, which I gave her, and I explained that I lived on the eleventh floor. The passenger elevator happened not to be working and she would have to use the service elevator. Elizabeth Abigail de Sollar repeated all my directions and tried to find a pencil and a notebook in her handbag

Translated by Joseph Singer

to write them down, but at that moment the operator demanded a nickel. Elizabeth Abigail de Sollar didn't have a nickel, and breathlessly she uttered the number of the phone booth from which she was calling. I called her at once, but no one answered. I must have dialed the wrong number. I picked up a book and began to read from where I opened it in the middle. Since she had my address and phone number, she would show up sooner or later. I hadn't managed to get to the end of the paragraph when the telephone rang. I picked up the receiver and heard a man cough, stammer, and clear his throat. After a while he regained his voice and said, "My name is Oliver Leslie de Sollar. May I speak to my wife?"

"Your wife made a mistake and went to a wrong address. She should be here soon."

"Excuse me for disturbing you, but our child has suddenly got sick. She started coughing violently and choking, and I don't know what to do. She suffers from asthma, Elizabeth has drops for these emergencies, but I can't find them. I'm distraught."

"Call a doctor! Call an ambulance!" I shouted into the mouthpiece.

"Our doctor isn't in his office. One second, excuse me . . ."

I waited a few minutes, but Oliver Leslie de Sollar didn't come back and I hung up the receiver. "That's what happens when you deal with people—right away complications arise," I said to myself. "The deed itself is a sin," I mentally quoted an Indian sacred book—but which one? Was it the Bhagavad Gita or the Dhammapada? If the child choked to death, God forbid, I would be indirectly responsible.

My doorbell rang in a long and insistent summons. I hurried to open it and saw a young woman with blond hair falling to her shoulders, a straw hat, with flowers and cherries, of the kind worn when I was still a cheder boy, a white blouse with lace at the neckline and sleeves, a black embroidered skirt, and buttoned shoes. Although it was sunny outside, she carried an umbrella with ribbons and bows—all in all, a photograph come to life from an album. Before she could even close the door behind her, I said, "Your husband just called. I don't wish to alarm you, but your child is having an attack of asthma and your husband can't get a doctor. He wants to know where the drops are."

I was sure my visitor would dash to the telephone, which stood on a table in the hall, but instead she measured me with her eyes from head to toe, then back again, while a sweet smile spread across her face. "Yes, it's you!" She held out a hand in a white glove reaching to the elbow and presented me with a package wrapped in shiny black paper and tied in a red ribbon. "Don't be concerned," she said. "He does this every time I go somewhere. He can't stand my leaving the house. It's pure hysteria."

"What about the child?"

"Bibi is as stubborn as her father. She doesn't want to let me out of the house, either. She's his child from a former wife."

"Please come in. Thank you for the present."

"Oh, you filled a gap in my life. I've always been a stranger to myself. By chance I discovered one of your novels in a bookstore and from then on I've read everything you've written. I believe I've told you that I'm the Klendev rabbi's grandchild. That's on my mother's side. On my father's side I stem from adventurers."

She followed me into the living room. She was short and slim, with a smooth white skin seldom seen in adults. Her eyes were pale blue tinged with yellow, and somewhat squinty. Her nose was narrow and on the long side, her lips thin, her chin receding and pointed. She had on no cosmetics. Usually I form a concept of a person from the face he presents, but I couldn't form a clear one of this young woman. Not healthy, I thought: sensitive, aristocratic. Her English seemed to me not American but foreign. As I chatted with her and asked her to have a seat on the sofa, I unwrapped the package and took out a ouija board with a planchette, obviously handmade, of costly wood and edged in bone.

She said, "I gather from your stories that you're interested in the occult, and I hope this is a fitting gift."

"Oh, you give me too many gifts."

"You've earned them all."

I asked her questions, and she responded willingly. Her father was a retired lawyer. He was separated from Elizabeth's mother and was living with another woman in Switzerland. The mother suffered from rheumatism and had moved to Arizona. She had a friend there, an old man of eighty. Elizabeth Abigail had met her husband in college. He had been her philosophy professor. He was also an amateur astronomer and used to sit up with her half the night at the observatory studying the stars. A Jew? No, Oliver Leslie was a Christian, born in England but descended from Basques. Two years after she married him he became sick, fell into a chronic depression, quit his job, and settled in a house a few miles from Croton-on-Hudson. He had isolated himself completely from people. He was writing a book on astrology and numerology. Elizabeth Abigail smiled the smile of those who have long since discovered the vanity of all human endeavors. At times her eyes grew melancholy and even frightened.

I asked her what she did in that house in Croton-on-Hudson and she replied, "I go crazy. Leslie doesn't speak for days or weeks at a time except to Bibi. He tutors her—she doesn't go to school. We do not live as man and wife. For me, books have become the essence of my being.

When I find a book that speaks to me, this is a great event in my life. That's why—"

"Who takes care of the household?"

"No one, really. We have a neighbor, an ex-farmer who left his family, and he brings us food from the supermarket. At times he cooks for us, too. A simple man, but in his own fashion a philosopher. He is also our chauffeur. Leslie can't drive the car any more. Our house stands on a hill that's awfully slippery, not only in winter, but whenever it rains."

My visitor grew silent. I was already accustomed to the fact that many of those who wrote me or came to see me were eccentrics—odd, lost souls. Elizabeth Abigail happened to resemble my sister slightly. Since she came from Klendev and was a rabbi's grandchild, she might have been my relative. Klendev isn't far from the towns where generations of my ancestors lived.

I asked, "How is it that Bibi is with her father, not her mother?"

Elizabeth replied, "The mother committed suicide."

The telephone rang and I heard the same stammering and throat clearing I had heard earlier. I immediately called Elizabeth, who approached slowly and with the reluctance of one who knows what's coming. I heard her tell her husband where the drops were and order him sharply not to annoy her again. He spoke at length and she responded with an occasional brief phrase. "What? Well, no." Finally she said, "That I don't know," in a tone of impatience. She came back into the room and resumed her seat on the sofa.

"It's become a system with them—the moment I go somewhere, Bibi gets these chest spasms and her father calls to alarm me. He can never find the drops, which don't help in any case, because her asthma is deliberately brought on by him. This time I didn't even tell him where I was going, but he eavesdrops on me. I wanted to ask you a number of questions, but he has driven them from my mind. Yes, where in heaven's name is this Klendev? I couldn't find it on any map."

"It's a village in the Lublin area."

"Were you ever there?"

"It just so happens that I was. I had left home and someone recommended me for a teaching position there. I gave a single lesson, and the school authorities and I agreed at once that I am no teacher. The very next day I left."

"When was this?"

"In the twenties."

"Oh, my grandfather was no longer living then. He died in 1913."

Although what my visitor had to say held no special interest for me,

I listened closely. It was hard for me to believe that only one generation separated her and the Klendev rabbi, his milieu, and his way of life. Her face had in a mysterious fashion molded itself to that of the Anglo-Saxons whose culture she had absorbed. I detected within her traces of other lands, other climates. Could it be that Lysenko was right after all?

The clock showed twelve-thirty and I invited my guest to go downstairs with me for lunch. She said that she didn't eat lunch. The most she might have was some tea, but if I wanted to have lunch, she'd go along with me. After a while we went into the kitchen and I brewed tea. I put cookies on a plate for her and for myself fixed bread with cottage cheese. We sat at a card table, facing each other like a married couple. A cockroach crawled across the table, but neither Elizabeth nor I made any effort to disturb it. The cockroaches in my apartment apparently knew that I was a vegetarian and that I felt no hatred for their species, which is a few hundred million years older than man and which will survive him. Elizabeth had strong tea, with milk, and I had mine weak, with lemon. When I drank, I held a cube of sugar between my teeth as had been the custom in Bilgoray and Klendev. She didn't touch the cookies, and gradually I finished them off. There had evolved between us a familiarity that requires no preliminaries.

I heard myself ask, "How long is it since you've stopped sleeping with him?"

Elizabeth began to blush, but when the blood had colored half her face it receded. "I'll tell you something, though you won't believe it."

"I'll believe anything you say."

"I'm physically a virgin." She blurted out the words and seemed astonished to have said them.

To show that she had not shocked me, I said casually, "I thought this was an extinct breed already."

"There is always a Last Mohican."

"You never asked a doctor about the situation?"

"Never."

"What about psychoanalysis?"

"Neither Leslie nor I believe in it."

"Don't you need a man?" I asked, bewildered by my daring.

She raised her glass and took a sip of tea. "Very much so, but I've never met a man I wanted to be with. That's how it was before I met Leslie and that's how it's been since. When I first knew him, I figured that Leslie would be a man to me, but he said that he wanted to wait for marriage. This seemed foolish to me, but we waited. When we were married we made several attempts, but they didn't work out. At times I imagined that the Klendev rabbi wouldn't let it happen because Leslie was a Gentile. After a while we both developed a revulsion toward the whole thing."

"You are both ascetics," I said.

"Eh? I don't know. I indulge in passionate affairs in my daydreams. I've read Freud, Jung, Stekel, but I'm convinced that they cannot help me. I'm amazed at my frankness with you. I've never written to an author before. I generally don't write letters. It's even hard for me to write to my father. Suddenly I write you and phone you. It's as if one of your dybbuks had entered me. Now that you seem to have opened, so to say, a sealed source within me, I'll tell you something else. Since I've started reading you, you've become the lover in my fantasies—you have driven off all the others."

Elizabeth took another sip of tea. She smiled and added, "Don't get scared. This isn't the purpose of my visit."

I felt a dryness in my throat and had to strain to make my voice emerge clearly. "Tell me about your fantasies."

"Oh, I spend time with you. We take trips together. You take me along to Poland and we visit all the villages you describe. Strange, but in my imagination your voice is the same as your voice is now and I can't conceive how this can be. Even your accent is as I imagined it. This is something really irrational."

"Every love is irrational," I said, embarrassed by my own assumption.

Elizabeth bowed her head and gave this some thought.

"At times I go to sleep with these fantasies and they are transformed into dreams. I see towns full of movement. I hear Yiddish spoken, and although I don't know the language, I understand everything in the dream. If I didn't know that these places have been destroyed, I would go there to see if everything matches my dreams."

"Nothing matches any more."

"My mother always spoke to me of her father, the rabbi. She came to America with her mother—my grandmother—when she was eight. My grandfather was married for the second time when he was seventy-five to a girl of eighteen, and my mother was the result of this marriage. Six years later, my grandfather died. He left many exegeses. The whole family perished under the Nazis, and all his manuscripts were burned. My grandmother brought along a small Hebrew book he had published and I have it in my purse in the foyer. Would you like to see it?"

"Absolutely."

"Let me wash the dishes. You wait here. I'll get Grandfather's book and you can look it over in the time I do them."

I remained at the table and Elizabeth brought me a slim book entitled *The Outcry of Mordechai*. On the title page the author listed his genealogy, and as I studied it I saw that my visitor and I were actually related by a connection many centuries back. We were both descended from Rabbi Moses Isserles and also from the author of *The Revealer of Profundities*. The book by the Klendev rabbi was a pamphlet against the Radzyn rabbi, Reb Gershon Henoch, who believed that he had found in the Mediterranean Sea the murex whose secretion was used in ancient Israel to dye the ritual fringes blue, although it was traditionally accepted that the murex had been concealed after the destruction of the Temple and would be found again only when the Messiah came. Reb Gershon Henoch hadn't reckoned on the storm of protest from the other rabbis, and he directed his followers to wear the blue fringes. This aroused great controversy in the rabbinical world. Elizabeth's grandfather called Reb Gershon Henoch "betrayer of Israel, apostate, messenger of Satan, Lilith, Asmodeus, and their evil host." He warned that the sin of wearing these sham fringes could bring dire punishment from heaven. The pages of *The Outcry of Mordechai* had grown yellow and so dry that pieces flicked off the margins when I leafed through them.

Elizabeth washed the plates and our glasses in the sink with a sponge. "What's written there?" she asked me.

It wasn't easy to explain to Elizabeth de Sollar the dispute between the Radzyn rabbi and the other rabbis and Talmudic scholars of his generation, but I somehow found the words. Her eyes sparkled as she listened. "Fascinating!"

The telephone rang and I left Elizabeth to answer it. It was Oliver Leslie de Sollar again. I told him that I would fetch his wife, but he said, "Wait. May I have a few words with you?"

"Yes, of course."

Oliver Leslie began to cough and clear his throat. "My daughter, Bibi, nearly died from her attack today. We barely saved her. We have a neighbor here, a Mr. Porter, who is a friend, and he found some medicine that another doctor had once prescribed. She's asleep now. I want you to know that my wife is a sick woman, both physically and spiritually. She has tried to commit suicide twice. The second time she took so many sleeping pills she had to be kept three days in an iron lung. She has an enormously high opinion of you and is in love with you in her own fashion, but I want to warn you not to encourage her. Our marriage is extremely unhappy, but I'm like a father to her because her own father deserted her and her mother when Elizabeth was only a child. Her father's indifference instilled in her a puritanism that has made our existence a nightmare. Don't promise her anything, because she lives entirely in a world of illusions. She needs psychiatric care, but she refuses it. I'm sure that you understand and that you will act like a responsible person."

"You may be completely sure."

"She exists on tranquillizers. I used to be a philosophy professor, but after we married I could no longer hold my position. Fortunately, I have wealthy parents, who help us. I've suffered so much from her that my own health has deteriorated. This is the type of woman who robs a man of his potency. If, heaven forbid, you became involved with her, your talent would be the first casualty. If she lived in the sixteenth century, she would have been surely burned at the stake as a witch. In the years I've known her, I've come to believe in black magic—as a psychological phenomenon, naturally."

"I hear you're writing a book on astrology."

"Is that what she told you? Nonsense! I'm doing work on Newton's last thirty years and his religious convictions. You undoubtedly know that Newton considered gravity a divine force—the purest expression of godly will. The greatest scientist of all times was also a great mystic. Since gravity controls the universe, it follows that the celestial bodies influence the organic and spiritual world in every manner and form. This is aeons removed from the usual astrology with its horoscopes and other folderol."

"Shall I get your wife?"

"No. Don't tell her I called. She is capable of causing me terrible scandals. She once attacked me with a knife . . ."

During the time Oliver Leslie had been talking to me, Elizabeth didn't appear. I wondered why it was taking her so long to dry two plates and glasses, but I assumed that she hadn't wanted to disturb my conversation. The moment I hung up I went into the kitchen, but Elizabeth wasn't there. I guessed what had happened. A narrow passage led from the kitchen to my bedroom, where an extension telephone stood on a night table. I opened the door to the passage and Elizabeth was standing on the threshold.

She said, "I had to go to the bathroom."

From the manner in which she said this—quickly, guiltily, in a defensive tone—I knew that she was lying. She might have been on the way to the bathroom (although how could she know that this door led to it?) and spied the extension phone. Her eyes reflected a blend of anger and mockery. So that's the kind of baggage you are, I thought. Every trace of restraint I might have felt toward her vanished. I put my hands on her shoulders. She trembled, and her face assumed the mischievous expression of a little girl caught stealing or dressing up in her mother's clothes.

"For a virgin, you're a shrewd piece," I said.

"Yes, I heard everything, and I'll never go back to him," she said in a voice grown firmer and younger as well. It was as if she had thrown off a mask she had worn a long time and in that split second become someone else—someone youthful and frolicsome. She pursed her lips as if about to kiss me. I was overcome with desire for her, but I remembered Oliver Leslie's warning. I bent toward her and our eyes came so close I saw only a blueness like that within a grotto. Our lips touched but didn't kiss. My knees pressed against hers and she began to move backward. While I pushed her slightly and playfully, a solemn voice admonished me: "Beware! You're falling into a trap!"

At that moment the phone rang again. I lurched with such force that I nearly knocked her over. A ringing telephone evokes a reaction of wild expectations in me—I often compare myself to Pavlov's dogs. For a moment I wavered between hurrying forward into the bedroom or back to the hall; then I ran to the hall with Elizabeth at my heels. I took up the receiver and she tried to wrest it from me, obviously convinced that her husband was calling again. I thought so myself, but I heard a firm, middle-aged female voice ask, "Is Elizabeth de Sollar with you? I'm her mother."

At first I didn't grasp the meaning of the words—in my confusion I had forgotten my visitor's name. But soon I recovered. "Yes, she is here."

"My name is Mrs. Harvey Lemkin. I just received a call from my son-in-law, Dr. Leslie de Sollar, telling me that my daughter is paying you a visit and that she left her sick little stepdaughter and all the rest of it. I want to warn you that my daughter is an emotionally ill and irresponsible person. My son-in-law, Professor de Sollar, and I have spent a fortune to help her—with negative results, I am sorry to say. At thirty-three she is still a child, although she is highly intelligent and writes poems that in my opinion are remarkable. You are a man and I can well understand that when a pretty and greatly gifted young woman demonstrates her admiration you should be intrigued, but don't let yourself become involved with her. You'll fall into a mess from which you'll never escape. Because of her, I've left New York, a city I love with all my heart and soul, and I've buried myself away out here in Arizona. My daughter spoke so much of you and praised you so highly that I began to read what you write in English and in Yiddish too. I am the Klendev rabbi's daughter and my Yiddish is pretty good. I could tell you a lot and I would be more than glad to meet you in New York—I come there from time to time—but I beseech you by all that's holy: Leave my daughter alone!"

The whole time her mother was speaking, Elizabeth stood apart and looked at me sidelong, inquisitively, half frightened and half ashamed. She made a gesture as if to come closer, but I motioned her away with my left hand. She made me think of a schoolgirl listening to a teacher or principal accuse her in front of her parents and unable to restrain herself from denying the charges. Her mother's voice was so loud she must have heard every word. Just when I was about to make some reply, Elizabeth jumped forward, tore the receiver from my hand, and exclaimed in a wailing voice, "Mother, I'll never forgive you! Never! Never! You're no longer my mother and I'm no longer your child! You sold me to a psychopath, a capon . . . I don't need your money and I don't need *you*! Whenever I might snatch a moment's happiness you spoil it all for me. You're my worst enemy. I'll kill you! I'll leave you a corpse for what you're doing to me . . . Bitch! Whore! Thief! Criminal! You sleep with an eighty-year-old gangster for money! I spit on you! I spit, spit, spit, spit!"

I stood there and watched foam bubble from her mouth. She bent over and writhed in pain. She clutched at the wall. I reached out to help her, but at that moment she fell with a crash, dragging the telephone down with her. She lay cramped and tossing, while one hand beat rapidly against the floor as if she were trying to signal the tenant below. Her mouth twisted and I heard a gasping growl. I knew what was happening —Elizabeth had suffered an epileptic fit. I lifted the phone and yelled into the mouthpiece, "Mrs. Lemkin, your daughter is having a seizure!" But the connection was broken. Should I call an ambulance? How did one go about doing that? My telephone had apparently stopped working. I wanted to open the window and call for help, but in the clamor and clang of Broadway no one would hear me from the eleventh floor. Instead, I ran into the kitchen, filled a glass with water, and poured it on Elizabeth's face. This caused her to bellow weirdly, and saliva sprayed my forehead. I rushed out into the corridor and began to pound on my neighbor's door, but no one answered. Only now did I notice that a stack of magazines and envelopes lay on his threshold. I turned to go back to my apartment and to my consternation saw that I had let the door slam shut. I didn't have the key on me. I pushed the door with all my might, but I'm not one of those bruisers who can break down a door.

In all my desperation I remembered that a duplicate key to my apartment hung in the office in the courtyard. I could also ask there that an ambulance be called. I realized full well what charges Elizabeth's husband and mother could bring against me in the event she died in my apartment. They might even accuse me of murder . . . I pressed the button for the service elevator and the pointer showed that it was standing on the seventeenth floor. I ran down the stairs, and in my mind— perhaps even aloud—I cursed the day I was born. As I ran, I heard the service elevator descending. I reached the lobby, and two moving men had the exit blocked with a sofa. Someone on the seventeenth floor was moving out. The lobby was filled with furniture, flower urns, stacks of books. I asked the men to let me pass, but they pretended not to hear. Well, I thought, this visit will be the death of me. Then I remembered that on the sixth floor lived a typesetter from the newspaper of which I was a staff member. If anyone in the family was home, he would help me call an ambulance and phone the office about a duplicate key. I started to run up the stairs to the sixth floor. My heart pounded and I broke out in a sweat. I rang the doorbell of the typesetter's apartment, but no one answered. I was prepared to run downstairs again when the door parted the length of the chain. I saw an eye, and a female voice asked, "What do you want?"

I began to explain to the woman what had happened. I spoke in clipped sentences and with the frenzy of one in mortal danger. The woman's single eye bored through me. "I'm not the lady of the house. They're abroad. I'm a cousin."

"I beg you to help me. Believe me that I'm no thief or robber. Your cousin sets all my manuscripts. Maybe you've heard my name?"

I mentioned the name of the newspaper, I even cited the titles of several of my books, but she had never heard of me. After some hesitation she said, "I can't let you in. You know how it is these days. Wait here, I'll call the office on the house phone. Tell me your name again."

I repeated my name for her, gave her the number of my apartment, and thanked her profusely. She closed the door. I expected that any minute she would inform me she had called the office and help was on the way, but seven minutes went by and the door didn't open. I stood there, tense and miserable, and took a quick reckoning of man and his existence. He is completely dependent, a slave to circumstance. The slightest mishap and everything goes to pieces. There is one solution—to free oneself totally from making for oneself the Sabbath that is called life and turn back to the indifference of causality, to death, which is the substance of the universe.

Five more minutes passed and still the door didn't open. I began to skip down the stairs again, my mind churning with images of how I would punish this heartless woman if I possessed unlimited power. I reached the lobby and the sofa was standing outside. I saw Mr. Brown, the superintendent, and frantically told him my predicament. He gazed at me in astonishment. "No one called. Come. I'll give you the key."

The service elevator was free, and I rode up to the eleventh floor, opened the door, and found Elizabeth Abigail de Sollar lying on the sofa in the living room, her hair wet and disheveled, her face pale, her shoes off. I barely recognized her. She seemed to me much older—almost middle-aged. She had placed a towel under her head. She looked at me with the silent reproof of a wife whose husband has left her sick and alone and gone off somewhere for his own pleasure. I half shouted, "My dear Elizabeth, you must go home to your husband! I'm too old for such goings on."

She considered my words; then she said in a dull tone, "If you order me to go, I will go, but not back to him. I'm finished with him and with my mother, too. From now on, I am alone in the world."

"Where will you go?"

"To a hotel."

"They won't let you into a hotel without luggage. If you don't have any money, I can—"

"I have my checkbook with me, but why can't I stay here with you? I'm not altogether well, but it's nothing organic—only functional. It's *they* who made me sick. I can type. I know a little stenography, too. Oh, I forgot that you write in Yiddish. This I don't know, but I would learn it in time. My mother used to speak Yiddish with my grandmother when she didn't want me to understand what they were saying, and I picked up quite a number of words. I once bought a vegetarian cookbook, and I'd cook vegetarian meals for you."

I looked at her in silence. Yes, she was my relative—the genes of our ancestors reached out directly to both of us. The notion that it might be incest for us to be together flashed through my mind—one of those uninvited ideas that emerge, God knows from where, and shock with their ridiculous irrelevance.

"That sounds like paradise, but unfortunately it cannot be," I said.

"Why not? You probably have someone else. Yes, I understand. But is there any reason you can't have a maid? I'll be everything to you—a maid and a cook as well. Your apartment is neglected. You probably eat in cafeterias. I do nothing in my own house because I have no interest in it, but my mother made me take a course in housekeeping. I would work for you and you wouldn't have to pay me anything. My parents are both filthy rich and I'm their only daughter. I'm not interested in your money . . ."

Before I could answer her, I heard a sharp ring at the door. At the same time the telephone rang. I grabbed the receiver, told whoever was calling that there was someone at the door, and ran to open it. I saw a man who could have been no one but Oliver Leslie de Sollar—tall, lean, with a long face and neck, a ruff of faded blond hair around a bald skull, wearing a checked suit, a stiff collar, and a narrow tie with a still narrower knot of the type that reminded me of the Warsaw dandies. I nodded and returned to the telephone. I was sure that it was Elizabeth's mother calling, but a rough masculine voice spoke my name and demanded acknowledgement that it was really I. Then the caller said slowly and with the tone of an official, "My name is Howard William

Moonlight and I represent Mrs. Harvey Lemkin, the mother of Mrs. Elizabeth de Sollar. I am sure that you know whom—"

I interrupted him to shout, "Mr. de Sollar is here! He'll talk to you!"

I dashed to the door, where my visitor still stood erectly, politely, waiting to be invited inside. I cried out, "Mr. de Sollar, it's not two hours since your wife came to visit me and hell is loose here! I've already received threatening calls from you, from your mother-in-law, and now from a lawyer. Your wife has managed to have an epileptic fit and only God knows what else. I'm sorry to say this, but I'm not interested in your wife, your mother-in-law, her lawyer, or in the whole crazy affair. Do me a favor and take her home. If not, I will . . ."

I was left momentarily speechless. I was about to say that I would call the police, but the words didn't come out. I glanced at the telephone and saw to my amazement that Elizabeth was mumbling into the mouthpiece with her eyes fixed on me and my visitor. He said in a thin voice that didn't match his stature, "I'm afraid there's been some misunderstanding. I'm not the person who called you. My name is Dr. Jeffrey Lifshitz. I'm an assistant professor of literature at the University of California and a great admirer of your writing. I have a friend in this building who also happens to be a devoted reader of yours, and when I visited him today we got to talking about you and he told me that you are his neighbor. I wanted to phone you, but I couldn't find your name in the directory and I thought I'd ring your doorbell. Forgive me for disturbing you."

"You haven't disturbed me. I'm pleased to have you as a reader, but there has been a considerable commotion going on in my house. Will you be staying in the city for long?"

"I'll be here the whole week."

"Would it be convenient for you to come to see me tomorrow?"

"Certainly."

"Let us say tomorrow at 11 a.m.?"

"It will be a pleasure and an honor. Again, excuse me for dropping in on you in such a—"

I assured Professor Lifshitz that I would be happy to meet with him, and he left.

Elizabeth had put down the receiver. She stood by the telephone as if waiting for me to come to her. I stopped a few paces away and said, "I'm sorry. You're a great woman, I understand your plight, but I can't get into a battle with your husband, your mother, and now with a lawyer, too. What did he want? Why did he call?"

"Oh, they're all mad. But I heard what you told your guest you mistook for my husband, and I swear I'll trouble you no more. What happened today proves to me that only one way remains for me to set myself free. I just want to point out that your diagnosis was incorrect. I'm not an epileptic."

"Then what is it?"

"The doctors themselves don't know. A kind of hypersensitivity that I inherited from who knows where, maybe from our common ancestor. What was his book?"

"The Revealer of Profundities."

"What kind of profundities did he reveal?"

"That no love of any kind is lost," I said, although I had never read a word by this ancestor of mine.

"Does he say where all the loves, all the dreams, all the desires go?"

"They're somewhere."

"Where? In the profundities?"

"In a celestial archive."

"Even heaven would be too small for such an archive. I will go. Oh, it's ringing again! Please don't answer! Don't answer!"

I picked up the receiver, but there was no one on the line. I hung up and Elizabeth said, "That's Leslie. That's one of his antics. What did the Revealer of Profundities say about madness? I must go! If I don't lose my mind, you'll hear from me. Maybe today, from the hotel."

Elizabeth de Sollar never called or wrote me again. She left behind and never claimed her ornate umbrella and her grandfather's book, *The Outcry of Mordechai*, which was supposed to be the only existing copy, so precious to her, and this has remained a mystery to me. But another mystery connected with her visit was soon unraveled. I met my neighbor the typesetter and told him about his cousin who promised to call the office and never showed herself again.

He smiled, shook his head, and said, "You knocked on the wrong door. I live on the fifth floor, not on the sixth."

The Yearning Heifer

I

IN those days I could find great bargains in the small advertisements in my Yiddish press newspaper. I was in need of them because I earned less than twelve dollars a week—my royalties for a weekly column of "facts" gleaned from magazines. For example: a turtle can live five hundred years; a Harvard professor published a dictionary of the language spoken by chimpanzees; Columbus was not trying to discover a route to the Indies but to find the Ten Lost Tribes of Israel.

It was during the summer of 1938. I lived in a furnished room on the fourth floor of a walk-up building. My window faced a blank wall. This particular advertisement read: "A room on a farm with food, ten dollars weekly." After having broken with my girl friend Dosha "forever," I had no reason to spend the summer in New York. I packed a large valise with my meager belongings, many pencils as well as the books and magazines from which I extracted my information, and took the Catskill Mountain bus to Mountaindale. From there I was supposed to phone the farm. My valise would not close and I had bound it together with many shoelaces which I had purchased from blind beggars. I took the 8 a.m. bus and arrived in the village at three o'clock in the afternoon. In the local stationery store I tried to make the phone call but could not get connected and lost three dimes. The first time I got the wrong number; the second time the phone began to whistle and kept on whistling for minutes. The third time I may have gotten the right number but no one answered. The dimes did not come back. I decided to take a taxi.

When I showed the driver the address, he knitted his brows and shook his head. After a while he said, "I think I know where it is." And

Translated by the author and Ruth Schachner Finkel

he immediately began to drive with angry speed over the narrow road full of ditches and holes. According to the advertisement, the farm was situated five miles from the village, but he kept on driving for half an hour and it became clear to me that he was lost. There was no one to ask. I had never imagined that New York State had such uninhabited areas. Here and there we passed a burned-down house, a silo which appeared unused for many years. A hotel with boarded windows emerged from nowhere and vanished like a phantom. The grass and brambles grew wild. Bevies of crows flew around croaking. The taxi meter ticked loudly and with feverish rapidity. Every few seconds I touched the trouser pocket where I kept my money. I wanted to tell the driver that I could not afford to drive around without an aim over heather and through deserts, but I knew that he would scold me. He might even drop me off in the middle of the wilderness. He kept on grumbling and every few minutes I heard him say, "Sonofabitch."

When, after long twisting and turning, the taxi did arrive at the correct address, I knew that I had made a bad mistake. There was no sign of a farm, just an old ruined wooden house. I paid four dollars and seventy cents for the trip and I tipped him thirty cents. The driver cast a murderous look at me. I barely had time to remove my valise before he started up and shot away with suicidal speed. No one came out to meet me. I heard a cow bellowing. As a rule, a cow bellows a few times and then becomes silent, but this cow bellowed without ceasing and in the tone of a creature which has fallen into an insufferable trap. I opened a door into a room with an iron stove, an unmade bed with dirty linen, a torn sofa. Against a peeling wall stood sacks of hay and feed. On the table were a few reddish eggs with hen's dirt still stuck to them. From another room came a dark-skinned girl with a long nose, a fleshy mouth, and angry black eyes beneath thick brows. A faint black fuzz grew on her upper lip. Her hair was cut short. If she hadn't been wearing a shabby skirt, I would have taken her for a man.

"What do you want?" she asked me in a harsh voice.

I showed her the advertisement. She gave a single glance at the newspaper and said, "My father is crazy. We don't have any rooms and board, and not for this price either."

"What is the price?"

"We don't need any boarders. There is no one to cook for them."

"Why does the cow keep on screaming?" I asked.

The girl appraised me from head to foot. "That is none of your business."

A woman entered who could have been fifty-five, sixty, or sixty-five years old. She was small, broad, one shoulder higher than the other, with a huge bosom which reached to her belly. She wore tattered men's slippers, her head was wrapped in a kerchief. Below her uneven skirt I could see legs with varicose veins. Even though it was a hot summer day she had a torn sweater on. Her slanted eyes were those of a Tartar. She gazed at me with sly satisfaction as if my coming there was the result of a practical joke. "From the paper, huh, aren't you?"

"Yes."

"Tell my husband to make a fool of himself instead of others. We don't need boarders. We need them like a hole in the head."

"I told him the same thing," the girl added.

"I am sorry but I got here with a taxi and it has gone back to the village. Perhaps I could stay for one night?"

"One night, huh? We have for you neither a bed nor linen. Nothing," the woman said. "If you like, I will call you another taxi. My husband is not in his right mind and he does everything for spite. He dragged us out here. He wanted to be a farmer. There is no store or hotel here for miles and I don't have the strength to cook for you. We ourselves eat out of tin cans."

The cow did not stop bellowing, and although the girl had just given me a nasty answer, I could not restrain myself and I asked, "What's the matter with the cow?"

The woman winked at the girl. "She needs a bull."

At that moment the farmer came in, as small and broad-boned as his wife, in patched overalls, a jacket which reminded me of Poland, and a cap pushed back on his head. His sunburned cheeks sprouted white stubble. His nose was veined. He had a loose double chin. He brought in with him the smells of cow dung, fresh milk from the udder, and newly dug earth. In one hand he held a spade and, in the other, a stick. His eyes under bushy brows were yellow. When he saw me he asked, "From the paper, huh?"

"Yes."

"Why didn't you call? I would have come with my horse and buggy to meet you."

"Sam, don't make a fool of the young man," his wife interrupted. "There's no linen for him, no one to cook for him, and what are ten dollars a week? It would cost us more."

"This leave to me," the farmer answered. "I have advertised, not you, and I am responsible. Young man"—he raised his voice—"I am the boss, not they. It's my house, my ground. Everything you see here belongs to me. You should have written a card first or phoned, but since you are here, you are a welcome guest."

"I am sorry, but your wife and your daughter—"

The farmer didn't let me finish. "What they say is not worth more than the dirt under my nails." He showed me a hand with muddy fingers.

"I will clean up your room. I will make your bed, cook your food, and provide you with everything. If you receive mail I will bring it to you from the village. I go there every second or third day."

"Meanwhile, perhaps I can sleep here tonight? I'm tired from the trip and—"

"Feel at home. They have nothing to say." The farmer pointed at his family. I had already realized that I had fallen into a quarrelsome house and I did not intend to be the victim. The farmer continued, "Come, I will show you your room."

"Sam, the young man won't stay here," his wife said.

"He will stay here, eat here, and be satisfied," the farmer replied, "and if you don't like it, go back to Orchard Street together with your daughter. Parasites, pigs, *paskudas!*"

The farmer put the spade and the stick into a corner, grabbed my valise, and went outside. My room had a separate entrance with its own flight of stairs. I saw a huge field overgrown with weeds. Near the house was a well and an outhouse like in a Polish shtetl. A bedraggled horse was nibbling on some grass. Farther away there was a stable, and from it came the plaintive cry of the animal, which had not stopped in all this time. I said to the farmer, "If your cow is in heat, why doesn't she get what she needs?"

"Who told you that she's in heat? It is a heifer and I just bought her. She was taken from a stable where there were thirty other cows and she misses them. She most probably has a mother or a sister there."

"I've never seen an animal that yearns so much for her kin," I said.

"There are all kinds of animals, but she will quiet down. She's not going to yell forever."

I I

The steps leading into my room squeaked. One held on to a thick rope instead of a banister. The room smelled of rotting wood and bedbug spray. A stained, lumpy mattress with the filling sticking out of the holes was on the bed. It wasn't especially hot outside but inside the room the heat immediately began to hammer at my head and I became wet with perspiration. Well, one night here will not kill me, I comforted myself. The farmer set my valise down and went to bring linen. He brought a pillow in a torn pillowcase, a coarse sheet with rusty spots, and a cotton-filled blanket without a cover. He said to me, "It's warm now, but the moment the sun sets, it will be deliciously cool. Later on you will have to cover yourself."

"It will be all right."

"Are you from New York?" he asked me.

"Yes, New York."

"I can tell from your accent that you were born in Poland. What part do you come from?"

I mentioned the name of my village and Sam told me he came from a neighboring village. He said, "I'm not really a farmer. This is our second summer here in the country. Since I came from Poland I was a presser in New York. I pulled and pushed the heavy iron so long that I got a rupture. I always longed for fresh air and, how do you call it—Mother Earth—fresh vegetables, a fresh egg, green grass. I began to look for something in the newspapers and here I found a wild bargain. I bought it from the same man who sold me the heifer. He lives about three miles from here. A fine man, even though he's a Gentile. His name is Parker, John Parker. He gave me a mortgage and made everything easy for me, but the house is old and the earth is full of rocks. He did not, God forbid, fool me. He told me everything beforehand. To clean up the stones would take twenty years. And I'm not a young man any more. I'm already over seventy."

"You don't look it," I complimented him.

"It's the good air, the work. I worked hard in New York, but only here I started to work for real. There we have a union, it should live long, and it did not allow the bosses to make us slaves like the Jews in Egypt. When I arrived in America, the sweatshops were still in existence, but later on things got easier. I worked my eight hours and took the subway home. Here I toil eighteen hours a day and, believe me, if I did not get the pension from the union I could not make ends meet. But it's all right. What do we need here? We have our own tomatoes, radishes, cucumbers. We have a cow, a horse, a few chickens. The air itself makes you healthy. But how is it written in Rashi? Jacob wanted to enjoy peace but the misfortune with Joseph would not allow it. Yes, I studied once; until I was seventeen I sat in the study house and learned. Why do I tell you this? My wife, Bessie, hates the country. She misses the bargains on Orchard Street and her cronies with whom she could babble and play cards. She's waging war on me. And what a war! She went on strike. She doesn't cook, she doesn't bake, she doesn't clean the house. She refuses to budge and I do everything—milk the cow, dig in the garden, clean the outhouse. I should not tell you, but she refuses to be a wife. She wants me to move back to New York. But what will I do in New York? We have given up the rent-controlled apartment and gotten rid of the funiture. Here we have something like a home—"

"How about your daughter?"

"My Sylvia takes after her mother. She's already over thirty and she should have gotten married, but she never wanted to become anything.

We tried to send her to college and she refused to study. She took all kinds of jobs but she never stuck with them. She has quite a good head, but no *sitzfleisch*. She tires of everything. She went out with all kinds of men and it always ended in nothing. The moment she meets one, she immediately begins to find fault with him. One is this way, the other one is that way. For the past eight months she's been with us on the farm, and if you think she helps me much, you are mistaken. She plays cards with her mother. That's all she does. You will not believe me, but my wife still has not unpacked her things. She has, God only knows, how many dresses and skirts, and everything is packed away like after a fire. My daughter, too, has a lot of rags but hers are also in her trunk. All this is to spite me. So I decided, Let some people move in here and I will have someone to talk to. We have two other rooms to rent. I'm not trying to get rich by offering a room and three meals a day for ten dollars weekly. I won't become a Rockefeller. What is your business? Are you a teacher or something?"

After some hesitation I decided to tell him the truth, that I write for a Yiddish newspaper as a free-lancer. The man's eyes immediately lit up.

"What is your name? What do you write there?"

"*A Bundle of Facts.*"

The farmer spread out his arms and stamped his feet. "You are the writer of *A Bundle of Facts?*"

"It's me."

"My God, I read you every week! I go to the village Friday especially to get the paper, and you won't believe me, but I read *A Bundle of Facts* before I even read the news. The news is all bad. Hitler this, Hitler that. He should burn like a fire, the bum, the no-good. What does he want from the Jews? Is it their fault that Germany lost the war? From just reading about it one could get a heart attack. But your facts are knowledge, science. Is it true that a fly has thousands of eyes?"

"Yes, it's true."

"How can it be? Why does a fly need so many eyes?"

"It seems that to nature everything comes easy."

"If you want to see the beauty of nature, stay here. Wait a minute. I must go and tell my wife who we have here."

"What for? I'm not going to stay here anyhow."

"What are you saying? Why not? They are bitter women, but when they hear who you are, they will be overjoyed. My wife reads you too. She tears the paper out of my hand because she wants to read *A Bundle of Facts* first. My daughter also knows Yiddish. She spoke Yiddish before she knew a word of English. With us she speaks mostly Yiddish because—"

The farmer dashed out. His heavy shoes pounded on the steps. The heifer kept howling. There was frenzy in her voice, an almost-human rebellion. I sat down on the mattress and dropped my head. Lately I had been committing one folly after another. I had quarreled with Dosha over a foolishness. I had already spent money to get here and tomorrow I would have to take a taxi and a bus to get back to New York. I had begun to write a novel but I got bogged down and I couldn't even decipher my own scribbling. As I sat there, the heat roasted my body. If only there were a shade to cover the window! The heifer's lamenting drove me mad. I heard in it the despair of everything that lives. All of creation was protesting through her. A wild idea ran through my mind: Perhaps during the night I should go out and kill the heifer and then myself. A murder followed by a suicide like this would be something new in the history of humanity.

I heard heavy steps on the staircase. The farmer had brought his wife over. Then began the apologies and the strange exaggerations of simple people when they encounter their beloved writer. Bessie exclaimed, "Sam, I must kiss him."

And before I managed to say a word, the woman caught my face in her rough hands, which smelled of onion, garlic, and sweat.

The farmer was saying good-naturedly, "A stranger she kisses and me she lets fast."

"You are crazy and he's a scientist, greater than a professor."

It took but a minute and the daughter came up. She stood in the open door and looked on half mockingly at the way her parents fussed over me. After a while she said, "If I have insulted you, excuse me. My father brought us here to the wasteland. We have no car and his horse is half dead. Suddenly a man with a valise drops from the sky and wants to know why the heifer is yelling. Really funny."

Sam clasped his hands together with the look of a man about to announce something which will astound everyone. His eyes filled with laughter. "If you have so much pity on animals, I am going to give back the heifer. We can do without her. Let her go back to her mother, for whom she pines."

Bessie tilted her head to one side. "John Parker won't give you back the money."

"If he won't return the whole amount, he will return ten dollars less. It's a healthy heifer."

"I will make up the difference," I said, astonished at my own words.

"What? We will not go to court," the farmer said. "I want this man in my house all summer. He won't have to pay me. For me it will be an honor and a joy."

"Really, the man is crazy. We needed the heifer like a hole in the head."

I could see that husband and wife were making peace because of me.

"If you really want to do it, why wait?" I asked. "The animal may die from yearning and then—"

"He's right," the farmer called. "I'm going to take the heifer back right now. This very minute."

Everyone became silent. As if the heifer knew that her fate was being decided this minute, she let out a howl which made me shudder. This wasn't a yearning heifer but a dybbuk.

III

The moment Sam entered the stable the heifer became quiet. It was a black heifer with large ears and huge black eyes that expressed a wisdom which only animals possess. There was no sign that she had just gone through so many hours of agony. Sam tied a rope around her neck and she followed him willingly. I followed behind with Bessie near me. The daughter stood in front of the house and said, "Really, I wouldn't believe it if I hadn't seen it with my own eyes."

We walked along and the heifer did not utter a sound. She seemed to know the way back because she tried to run and Sam had to restrain her. Meanwhile, husband and wife argued before me the way couples used to argue when they came to my father's court for a Din Torah. Bessie was saying, "The ruin stood empty for years and nobody even looked at it. I don't think someone would have taken it for nothing. Suddenly my husband appears and gets the bargain. How does the saying go? 'When a fool comes to the market, the merchants are happy.' "

"What did you have on Orchard Street? The air stank. As soon as daylight began, the crash and noise started. Our apartment was broken into. Here you don't have to lock the door. We can leave for days and weeks and no one will steal anything."

"What thief would come to such a desert?" Bessie asked. "And what could he take? American thieves are choosy. They want either money or diamonds."

"Believe me, Bessie, here you will live twenty years longer."

"Who wants to live so long? When a day is over, I thank God."

After about an hour and a half I saw John Parker's farm—the house, the granary. The heifer again tried to run and Sam had to hold her back with all his strength. John Parker was cutting grass with a crooked scythe. He was tall, blond, lean, Anglo-Saxon. He raised his eyes, amazed, but with the quiet of a person who is not easily astounded. I even imagined I saw him smiling. We had approached the pasture where the other cows were grazing and the heifer became wild and tore herself out of Sam's hands. She began to run and jump with the rope still around her neck, and a few cows slowly raised their heads and looked at her, while the others continued to rip the grass as if nothing had happened. In less than a minute the heifer, too, began to graze. I had expected, after this terrible longing, a dramatic encounter between the heifer and her mother: much nuzzling, fondling, or whatever cows do to show affection to a daughter who was lost. But it seemed that cattle didn't greet one another that way. Sam began to explain to John Parker what had happened and Bessie too chimed in. Sam was saying, "This young man is a writer. I read his articles every week and he is going to be our guest. Like all writers, he has a soft heart. He could not stand the heifer's suffering. My wife and I cherish every line he writes. When he said that the heifer might disturb his thinking, I made up my mind, come what may. So I brought the heifer back. I am ready to lose as much as you will say—"

"You will lose nothing, it's a good heifer," John Parker said. "What do you write?" he asked me.

"Oh, facts in a Yiddish newspaper. I am trying to write a novel too," I boasted.

He remarked, "Once I was a member of a book club, but they sent me too many books and I had no time to read. A farm keeps you busy, but I still get *The Saturday Evening Post*. I have piles of them."

"I know. Benjamin Franklin was one of the founders." I tried to show erudition about American literature.

"Come into the house. We'll have a drink."

The farmer's family came out. His wife, a darkish woman with short black hair, looked Italian to me. She had a bumpy nose and sharp black eyes. She was dressed city-fashion. The boy was blond like his father, the girl Mediterranean-looking like her mother. Another man appeared. He seemed to be a hired hand. Two dogs dashed out of somewhere and, after barking for a few seconds, began to wag their tails and to rub up against my legs. Sam and Bessie again tried to explain the reason for their visit, and the farmer's wife scrutinized me half wondering and half with irony. She asked us in, and soon a bottle of whiskey was opened and we clinked glasses. Mrs. Parker was saying, "When I came here from New York I missed the city so much that I almost died, but I'm not a heifer and nobody cared about my feelings. I was so lonesome that I tried to write, even though I'm not a writer. I still have a few composition books lying around and I myself don't remember what I put down in them."

The woman looked at me hesitatingly and shyly. I knew exactly what she wanted and I asked, "May I look at them?"

"What for? I have no literary talent. It is kind of a diary. Notes about my experiences."

"If you have no objections, I would like to read them, not here, but back at Sam's farm."

The woman's eyes brightened. "Why should I object? But please don't laugh at me when you read the outpourings of my emotions."

She went to look for her manuscript and John Parker opened a chest drawer and counted out the money for the heifer. The men haggled. Sam offered to take a few dollars less than what he had paid. John Parker wouldn't hear of it. I again proposed to make good the difference, but both men looked at me reproachfully and told me to mind my own business. After a while Mrs. Parker brought me a bundle of composition books in an old manila envelope that smelled of moth balls. We said goodbye and I took their phone number. When we got back, the sun had already set and the stars shone in the sky. It was a long time since I had seen such a starry sky. It hovered low, frightening and yet solemnly festive. It reminded me of Rosh Hashanah. I went up to my room. I could not believe it but Sylvia had changed my linen: a whiter sheet, a spotless blanket, and a cleaner pillowcase. She had even hung up a small picture with a windmill.

That evening I ate supper with the family. Bessie and Sylvia asked me many questions and I told them about Dosha and our recent quarrel. Both wanted to know the reason for the quarrel, and when I told them they both laughed.

"Because of foolishness like this, a love should not be broken," Bessie said.

"I'm afraid it's too late."

"Call her this very moment," Bessie commanded.

I gave Sylvia the number. She turned the crank on the wall phone. Then she screamed into the phone as if the woman at the phone company were deaf. Perhaps she was. After a while Sylvia said, "Your Dosha is on the telephone," and she winked.

I told Dosha what I had done and the story about the heifer. She said, "I am the heifer."

"What do you mean?"

"I called you all the time."

"Dosha, you can come up here. There is another room in the house. These are kind people and I already feel at home here."

"Huh? Give me the address and phone number. Perhaps this coming week."

About ten o'clock Sam and Bessie went to sleep. They bid me good night with the gay anticipation of a young couple. Sylvia proposed that we go for a walk.

There was no moon, but the summer night was bright. Fireflies lit up in the thickets. Frogs croaked, crickets chirped. The night rained meteors. I could make out the whitish luminous band which was the Milky Way. The sky, like the earth, could not rest. It yearned with a cosmic yearning for something which would take myriads of light-years to achieve. Even though Sylvia had just helped me make peace with Dosha, she took my hand. The night light made her face feminine and her black eyes emitted golden sparks. We stopped in the middle of the dirt road and kissed with fervor, as if we had been waiting for each other God knows how long. Her wide mouth bit into mine like the muzzle of a beast. The heat from her body baked my skin, not unlike the glowing roof a few hours earlier. I heard a blaring sound, mysterious and otherworldly, as though a heavenly heifer in a faraway constellation had awakened and begun a wailing not to be stilled until all life in the universe shall be redeemed.

I · B · S

A Tale of Two Sisters

LEON, or Haim Leib, Bardeles poured cream into his coffee. He put in a lot of sugar, tasted it, grimaced, added more cream, and took a bite of the macaroon the waiter had brought him.

He said, "I like my coffee sweet, not bitter. In Rio de Janeiro they drink tiny little cups of coffee that's as bitter as gall. They serve it here, too—espresso—but I like a glass of coffee like you used to get in Warsaw. When I sit here with you, I forget that I'm in Buenos Aires. It seems to me we're in Lurs's in Warsaw. What do you say to the weather, eh? It took me a long time to get used to Sukkoth falling in the spring and Passover in the fall. I can't even begin to tell you the confusion this topsy-turvy calendar brings out in our people. Hanukkah comes during a heat wave and you can melt. On Shevuoth, it's cold. Well, at least the spring smells are the same—the lilac has the same aroma that used to waft in from the Praga woods and the Saxony Gardens. I recognize the smells, but I cannot identify them. The Gentile writers list every flower and plant, but how many names are there for flowers in Yiddish? I know only two kinds of flowers—roses and lilies. When I go to a florist's once in a while to buy someone a bouquet, I always rely on the clerk. Drink your coffee!"

"Tell the story," I said.

"Eh? Can it be told? Where shall I begin? I promised to tell you everything, the whole truth, but can you tell the truth? Wait, I'll have a cigarette first. Actually, one of your American cigarettes."

Leon Bardeles took out one of the packs of cigarettes I had brought him from New York. I had known him over thirty years. I had once even written an introduction for a book of his poems. He was fifty-three

Translated by Joseph Singer

or fifty-four and had survived the Hitler hell and the Stalin terror, but he still looked young for his age. He had a head of black curly hair, big black eyes, a thick lower lip, and a neck and shoulders that exuded masculine strength. He still wore a shirt with a *Slowacki* collar, just as in Warsaw. He blew smoke rings and gazed at me with narrowed eyes, like an artist at a model.

He said, "I'll begin in the middle. I beg you: Don't ask me for any dates, because when it comes to that I'm completely disoriented. It must have been 1946, or maybe it was still the end of '45. I had left Stalin's Russia and gone back to Poland. In Russia I was supposed to go into the Polish army, but I wormed my way out of it. I went through Warsaw and saw the ruins of the ghetto. You wouldn't believe this, but I actually went looking for the house where I had lived in 1939—maybe I'd find some of my manuscripts among the bricks. The chances of recognizing the house on Nowolipki Street and finding a manuscript after all the bombardments and fires were less than zero, but I recognized the ruins of the house and found a printed book of mine, actually the one with your introduction. Only the last page was missing. I was amazed, but not terribly so. So many incredible things have occurred in my life that I have become completely blasé. If I came home and found my dead mother tonight, I wouldn't blink an eye. I'd say, 'Mamma, how are you?'

"From Warsaw I stumbled on to Lublin and from there to Stettin. Most of the cities lay in ruins and we slept in stables, barracks, and in the street, too. They berate me here in Buenos Aires why I don't write about my experiences. First of all, I'm not a prose writer. Secondly, everything has grown jumbled in my mind, particularly the dates and names of towns, and I'm sure that I'd brew up such a stew of errors that they'd call me a liar and a fabricator. Some refugees were half-mad. One woman had lost a child and she looked for it in ditches, in haystacks, in the most unlikely places. In Warsaw a deserter from the Red Army took it into his head that there were treasures buried beneath the rubble. He stood in the bitter frost and dug with a spade among the bricks. Dictatorships, wars, and cruelty drive whole countries to madness. My theory is that the human species was crazy from the very first and that civilization and culture are only enhancing man's insanity. Well, but you want the facts.

"The facts, to make it brief, were these: In Stettin I met a woman who literally bewitched me on the spot. You know that I've had a good many women in my life. In Russia there was a lack of everything except so-called love. The way I am, no danger, crisis, hunger, or even sickness can rob me of that which is now called a libido, or whatever names the professors dream up for it. It was as far from the romantic love of our youth as we're now from Jupiter. All of a sudden, I'm standing in front of a woman and gaping as if I'd never seen a female before. Describe her? I'm not good at description. She had long black hair and skin white as marble. You must forgive me all these banalities. Eyes she had that were dark and strangely frightened. Fear was nothing unusual in those days. You risked your life every second. Russia wouldn't let us out and we were supposed to enter Palestine illegally, since England wouldn't let us in. False papers were arranged for us, but it was easy to tell that they weren't in order. Well, but those eyes reflected another kind of fear. It was somehow as if this girl had been dropped on earth from another planet and didn't know where she was. Maybe that's what the fallen angels looked like. But those were men. She wore cracked shoes and a magnificent nightgown that she mistook for a dress. The Joint Distribution Committee had sent underwear and clothes to Europe that rich American ladies had donated to the refugees, and she had received this costly nightgown. Besides fear, her face expressed a rare kind of gentility. All this somehow didn't jibe with reality. Such delicate creatures usually didn't survive the war. They dropped like flies. Those who made it were the strong, the resolute, and often those who walked over the corpses of others. For all my womanizing, I am somewhat bashful. I'm never the one to make the first move. But I virtually couldn't tear myself away. I mustered my courage and asked her if I could help her. I spoke to her in Polish. At first she was silent and I suspected that she was mute. She looked at me with the kind of helplessness often seen in a child. Then she replied in Polish, 'Thank you. You cannot help me.'

"Ordinarily, when someone gives me this kind of rebuff, I walk away, but this time something held me back. It turned out that she came from a Hasidic home and was the daughter of a Warsaw landlord, a follower of the Alexander Rabbi. Deborah, or Dora, was one of those Hasidic girls who are raised in an almost assimilated atmosphere. She attended a private girls' Gymnasium and studied piano and dancing. At the same time, a rabbi's wife came to her house to tutor her in prayers and Jewish law. Before the war, she had two older brothers, the elder of whom already had a wife in Bedzin, while the younger studied in a yeshiva. She also had an older sister. The war made a quick mess of the family. The father was killed by a German bomb, the older brother in Bedzin was shot by the Nazis, the younger brother was drafted into the Polish army and killed somewhere, the mother died of starvation and kidney disease in the Warsaw ghetto, and the sister, Ytta, disappeared and Dora didn't know where she was. Dora had a French teacher on the Aryan side, a spinster named Elzbieta Dolanska, and she saved Dora. How she did this would take too long to tell. Dora spent two years in a cellar and the teacher fed her with her last savings. A saint of a woman, but she perished during the Polish uprising. That's how the Almighty rewards the good Gentiles.

"I didn't get all this out of her at once but gradually, literally drawing out word after word. I said to her, 'In Palestine you'll get back on your feet. You'll be among friends.'

" 'I can't go to Palestine,' she said.

" 'Why not? Where, then?'

" 'I must go to Kuibyshev.'

"I couldn't believe my own ears. Imagine, a trip in those days from Stettin back to the Bolsheviks—and to Kuibyshev. The road was rife with danger.

" 'What business have you in Kuibyshev?' I asked her and she told me a story that, if I hadn't confirmed it myself later, I would have called the ravings of a sick mind. Her sister, Ytta, had jumped from the train taking her to the concentration camp and made her way through the fields and forests to Russia. There she lived with a Jewish engineer who had attained a high rank in the Red Army. This officer was later killed in the war and Ytta lost her mind. She was confined in an insane asylum in that area. Through wild chance, actually a miracle, Dora found out that her sister was still alive. I asked her, 'How can you help your sister when she is insane? There she at least gets medical care. What can you do for a deranged woman without money, an apartment, or a groschen to your name? You'll both die.'

"And she said, 'You are perfectly right, but she is the only one left of my family and I can't leave her to waste her years away in a Soviet asylum. It's possible that she'll get well when she sees me.'

"It's usually not my way to mix into other people's business. The war taught me that you can't help anybody. In essence, we were all walking on graves. When you spend years in camps and prisons and stare death in the face ten times a day, you lose all compassion. But when I heard what this girl proposed to do, I was filled with a kind of pity that I had never felt before. I tried to talk her out of it time and again. I offered a thousand arguments.

"She said, 'I know that you are right, but I must go back.'

" 'How will you get there?' I asked her, and she said, 'I'm ready to go even on foot.'

"I said, 'I'm afraid you're no less crazy than your sister.'

"And she replied, 'I fear that you're right.'

"After all his wanderings and tribulations, the person sitting here next to you gave up the chance to go to Israel, which was to me at that time the most beautiful dream, and I went off with a strange girl to Kuibyshev. It was actually an act of suicide. One thing I found out then was that pity is a form of love and, actually, its highest expression. I won't describe the trip to you—it was not a trip but an odyssey. I can only tell you that the Reds detained us twice along the way and it failed by a whisker that we didn't both end up in prison or in a slave camp. Dora behaved in a strangely heroic fashion during the trip, but I sensed that this was more resignation than bravery. I forgot to tell you—she was a virgin and underneath all that despair lay a passionate woman. I was used to women loving me, but this was different from anything I had ever known. She clung to me in a mixture of love and desperation that frightened me. She had an education and in the cellar where she had hidden for two years she had read a whole library in Polish, French, and German, but she lacked all experience. Every little thing frightened her. In her hiding place she had read many Christian books as well as the works of Madame Blavatsky, and occult and theosophic writings that had been left to Miss Dolanska by an aunt. Dora babbled on about Jesus and ghosts, but I had no patience for such things, even though I myself had become a mystic, or at least a fatalist, during the Holocaust. Oddly enough, she combined all this with the Jewishness of her home.

"There was no particular hardship in crossing the border into Russia, but the trains were jammed. In the middle of everything, the locomotive was uncoupled, hooked on to some other wagons, and we were left standing there for days on end. In the cars, the passengers fought constantly. A brawl would erupt and everyone would be shoved out of the wagons. Corpses lay scattered along the tracks. The cold inside the cars was frightful. Some people even rode on flatcars while the snow fell on them. In the closed cars you had to carry a chamber pot or a bottle in which to relieve yourself. A peasant sat on the roof of a car, and when the train entered a tunnel, he lost his head. And that's how we got to Kuibyshev. All the way there, I couldn't stop wondering at myself over what I had done. This thing with Dora was no simple affair. I had actually bound myself up with her for life. To abandon someone like that would have been like leaving a child alone in a forest. Even before we got there, we got into all kinds of conflicts, all of which had to do with the fact that Dora was afraid to leave me alone for even a minute. When the train stopped at a station and I tried to get some food or hot water, she didn't let me get off. She was always suspicious that I was trying to desert her. She would seize my sleeve and try to drag me back. The passengers, especially the Russians, had something to laugh at. A streak of insanity seemed to run through this family; it manifested itself in fear, suspicion, and a kind of mysticism that stemmed from the time when man still lived in caves. How this primitive heritage reached all the way to an affluent Hasidic family in Warsaw is a riddle. This whole adventure that I went through remains an enigma to me to this day.

"We got to Kuibyshev and it seemed all in vain. There was no sister and no insane asylum. That is to say, there was an asylum, but not for strangers. The Nazis destroyed hospitals, clinics, and asylums as they retreated. They shot or poisoned the patients. The Nazi murderers hadn't reached Kuibyshev, but the hospital was jammed with the heavily wounded. Who in those days worried about the insane? Well, but a woman had told Dora all the details. The Jewish officer's name was Lipman, the woman was Lipman's relative, and there was no reason for her to lie. Can you imagine the disappointment? We had endured the whole trek with all its miseries for nothing. But wait, we did find Ytta, not in an insane asylum, but in a village living with an old Jew, a shoemaker. The woman hadn't invented things. Ytta had suffered from depression and had been treated for it at some institution and after a while they had discharged her. I never learned all the facts, but even those that she told me I later forgot. The whole Holocaust is tied up with amnesia.

"The shoemaker was a Polish Jew, actually from one of your towns, Bilgoray or Janov, an old man nearly eighty but still active. Don't ask me how he got to Kuibyshev or why Ytta moved in with him. He lived in some dump, but he could patch boots and shoes and there is need for this everywhere. He sat there with his long white beard, surrounded by old shoes in a shack that was more like a chicken coop, and as he hammered tacks or drew the thread, he mumbled a verse of the Psalms. By a clay stove stood a red-haired woman—barefoot, ragged, disheveled, and half naked—cooking barley. Dora recognized her sister at once, but the other didn't know Dora. When Ytta finally realized that this was her sister, she didn't cry but started to bay like a dog. The shoemaker began to rock to and fro on his stool.

"There was supposed to be a communal farm, a kolkhoz, somewhere nearby, but all I could see was an old-fashioned Russian village with wooden huts, a little church, deep snow, and sleighs harnessed to dogs and skinny nags, just the way I used to see them in pictures in a Russian-language textbook. Who knows, I thought, maybe the whole Revolution had been only a dream. Maybe Nicholas still sat on the throne. During the war and afterward, I saw many reunions of people with their loved ones, but these two played out a shattering sisterly drama. They kissed, licked, howled. The old man mumbled through his toothless mouth, 'A pity, a pity . . .' Then he turned back to his shoes. He seemed to be deaf.

"There was nothing to pack. All that Ytta had were a pair of shoes with thick soles and heels and a sheepskin without sleeves. The old man took a black loaf of bread out of somewhere and Ytta tucked it away in her sack. She kissed the old man's hands, his brow and beard and commenced to bark anew, as if possessed by the spirit of a dog. This Ytta was taller than Dora. Her eyes were green and as fearsome as a beast's. Her hair was of an unusual shade of red. To describe to you how we made our way from Kuibyshev to Moscow and from there back to Poland again, I'd have to sit here with you till tomorrow. We dragged along and smuggled our way through, facing arrest, separation, or death at any moment. But summer had come, and after lengthy travails, we finally got to Germany, and from there to Paris. I make it sound so simple. Actually, we only got to France by the end of 1946, or maybe it was already 1947. One of the social workers on the Joint Distribution Committee was a friend of mine, a young man from Warsaw who went to America in 1932. He knew English and other languages as well. You can't imagine the power Americans wielded in those days. I could easily have obtained a visa to America through him, but Dora took it into her head that I had a sweetheart there. In Paris, the Joint—actually, that same young man—got us a small apartment, which was no easy task. We received a monthly stipend from this same organization.

"I know what you're about to ask me—have a little patience. Yes, I lived with them both. I married Dora officially in Germany—she wanted to stand under a canopy and she did—but, in actuality, I had two wives, two sisters, just like the patriarch Jacob. All I lacked was a Bilhah and a Zilpah. What would stop the likes of me? Not the Jewish and certainly not the Gentile laws. In the war, the whole human culture crumbled like a ruin. In the camps—not only in Germany but in Russia and later in the DP camps where the refugees lived for years—all shame vanished. I knew of one case where a woman had her husband on one side and her lover on the other and all three of them lived together. I've witnessed so many wild things that to me they've become normal. A Schicklgruber or a Dzhugashvili comes along and moves the clock back ten thousand years. Not completely, mind you. There were also instances of rare piety and of self-sacrifice for a minor law in the *Shulchan Aruch,* or even for some custom. This itself may be a bit of wildness, too.

"I didn't want all this. It's one thing to have an adventure—it's quite another to make a permanent institution out of it. But it was out of my hands. From the moment the two sisters met, I was no longer a free man. They enslaved me with their love for me, their love toward each other, and their jealousy. One minute they would be kissing and crying from great devotion and suddenly they would begin to slug away, pull hair, and curse each other with words you wouldn't hear in the underworld. I had never before seen such hysteria or heard such screams. Every few days one of the sisters, or sometimes both, tried to commit suicide. One moment it would be quiet. The three of us might be sitting

eating or discussing a book or picture—all of a sudden a horrible shriek
and both sisters would be rolling on the floor, tearing pieces from each'
other. I'd run up, trying to separate them, but I'd catch a slam in the
face or a bite and the blood would be dripping from me. Why they were
fighting I would never know. Fortunately, we lived on the upper story, a
garret, and we had no neighbors on our floor. One of the sisters would
run to the window and try to throw herself out, while the other seized a
knife and went for her own throat. I'd grab one by the leg and take the
knife away from the other. They'd howl at me and at each other. I'd try
to find out what caused the outburst, but I learned in time that they
didn't know the reason themselves. At the same time, I want you to
know that both of them were intelligent in their own fashion. Dora had
excellent taste in literature. She'd offer an opinion about a book and it
was accurate to the dot. Ytta was musically inclined. She could sing
whole symphonies. When they had the energy, they displayed great
capability. They had picked up a sewing machine somewhere and from
scraps and pieces they sewed dresses of which the most elegant ladies
would be proud. One thing both sisters shared, a complete lack of common sense. Actually, they shared many traits. At times it even seemed
to me that they were two bodies with one soul. If there had been a tape
recorder to take down the things they said, particularly at night, it
would make Dostoevsky seem trite. Complaints against God poured out
of them, along with laments for the Holocaust that no pen could trans-
cribe. What a person really is comes out only at night, in the dark. I
know now that both of them were born crazy, not the victims of any
circumstances. The circumstances, naturally, made everything worse. I
myself became a psychopath living with them. Insanity is no less contagious than typhus.

"Besides squabbling, brawling, telling endless stories of the camps
and of their home in Warsaw, and chattering about clothes, fashions,
and whatnot, the sisters had one favorite topic: my treachery. They
forged an indictment against me that made the Moscow trials seem like
pure logic by comparison. Even as they sat on the sofa, kissed me,
waged a playful competition over me, and indulged in a game that was
both childish and animalistic and therefore indefinable, they kept abus-
ing me. It boiled down to the fact that I had only one urge—to betray
them and carry on with other women. Each time the concierge called me
to the telephone, they ran to listen in. When I received a letter, they
promptly opened it. No dictator could have enforced such a strict censorship as these sisters did over me. They left no doubt that the mailman, the concierge, the Joint Committee, and I were all part of a
conspiracy against them, although what kind of conspiracy this was and
what was its purpose was something even their twisted minds couldn't

establish. Lombroso contended that genius is insanity. He forgot to say that insanity is genius. Their helplessness was genius too. I sometimes had the feeling that getting through the war had drained them of that specific power for survival that every human and animal possesses. The fact that Ytta hadn't been able to find another job in Russia besides that of a maid and mistress to that old shoemaker only accented her lack of initiative. They often toyed with the notion of becoming maids in Paris, governesses, or something in that vein, but it was clear both to me and to them that they couldn't hold any kind of job for more than a few hours. They were also the laziest creatures I had ever met, although from time to time they were seized by a burst of effort and energy that was as exaggerated as their usual laziness. Two women should have been able to keep house, but our apartment was always a mess. They would prepare a meal and argue as to who should wash the dishes until it came time to cook again. Sometimes days and even weeks went by and we ate only dry food. The bedding was often dirty, and we had cockroaches and other vermin. The sisters weren't physically dirty. They boiled pots of water at night and turned the apartment into a bathhouse. The water dripped down below, and the downstairs tenant, an old French cavalier, banged on our door and threatened us with the police. Paris was starving, but in my house food was thrown out in the garbage. The apartment was piled with rags. They hardly ever wore the dresses that they sewed or received from the Joint Committee, but they went around half naked and barefoot.

"As alike as the sisters were, so were they also different. Ytta possessed a brutality that was completely foreign to a girl from a Hasidic home. Many of her stories dealt with beatings and I knew that bloodshed and violence of any kind roused her sexually. She told me that, while she was still a girl in her father's house, she once sharpened a knife and slaughtered three ducks that her mother kept in a shed. Her father beat her for this severely and Dora used to throw this up to her when they quarreled. Ytta was unusually strong, but each time she tried to do something, she managed to hurt herself. She walked around covered with bandages and plasters. She often hinted that she would take revenge on me, even though I had rescued her from slavery and want. I suspected that somewhere inside her she would have been glad to remain with the old shoemaker; maybe because this would have allowed her to forget her family and especially Dora, with whom she maintained a love-hate relationship. This hostility used to come out in every quarrel. Dora was the one who screamed, wept, and scolded, while Ytta resorted to blows. I was often afraid that she might kill Dora in a rage.

"Dora was better educated, more refined, and possessed of a sick imagination. She slept fitfully and kept telling me her dreams, which were sexual, diabolical, tangled. She awoke quoting verses from the Bible. She tried to write poems in Polish and in Yiddish. She had formulated a sort of personal mythology. I often said that she was possessed by the dybbuk of a follower of Sabbatai Zevi or Jacob Frank.

"I had always felt a curiosity about the institution of polygamy. Could jealousy be rooted out? Could you share someone you loved? In a sense, the three of us were taking part in an experiment whose results we all awaited. The longer the situation lasted, the more obvious it became to us all that things couldn't remain the way they were. Something had to happen and we knew that it would be evil, a catastrophe. Each day posed a new crisis, each night carried the threat of some scandal or impotence. Although our neighbors on the lower floors had their own troubles and were accustomed to wild doings from the time of the German Occupation, they began to look at us suspiciously, to nose around, and to shake their heads in disapproval. As sinful as was our behavior, our religious upbringing soon began to make demands on our Jewishness. Dora made the benediction over the Sabbath candles every Friday and then sat around smoking cigarettes. She had formulated her own version of the *Shulchan Aruch* in which pork was forbidden but horsemeat was kosher, in which there was no God but you had to fast on Yom Kippur and eat matzo on Passover. Ytta had become an atheist in Russia, or so she said, but every night before going to sleep she mumbled a nightly prayer or some incantation. When I gave her a coin, she spat on it to ward off the evil eye. She would get up in the morning and announce, 'Today will be an unlucky day . . . something bad is going to happen . . .' Inevitably, what happened was that she hurt herself, or broke a dish, or a stocking tore on her.

"Dora kept the funds in our household. I always gave her more than she needed, since I received stipends from a few institutions and later money from relatives in America as well. After a while I noticed that she had accumulated a nest egg. Her sister apparently knew of this and received her share of the loot. I often heard them whispering and arguing about money.

"I forgot the main thing—children. Both sisters wanted a child by me and many arguments erupted because of this. But I was dead set against it. We were living on charity. Each time the conversation came around to children, I came up with the same answer: 'For what? So the next Hitler would have someone to burn?' I don't have a child to this day. As far as I'm concerned, I want to put an end to the human tragedy. I suspect that neither Dora nor Ytta was even capable of bearing children. Such females are like mules. I'll never understand how a

Hasidic Jew came to have two such daughters. We carry stray genes going back to the time of Genghis Khan, or the devil knows when.

"The calamity that we anticipated came in a quiet fashion. The arguments gradually subsided to be replaced by a depression that consumed the three of us. It began with Dora's getting sick. Exactly what was wrong with her, I never found out. She lost weight and coughed a lot. I suspected consumption and took her to a doctor, but he found no evidence of illness. He prescribed vitamins and iron, which didn't help. Dora became frigid, too. She no longer wanted to join in our nightly games and idle chatter. She even got herself a cot and set it up in the kitchen. Without Dora, Ytta soon lost interest in our sex triangle. She had never been the one to take the initiative; in fact, she did only what Dora told her. Ytta was a big eater and a heavy sleeper. She snored and snorted in her sleep. A situation soon developed in which, instead of having two women, I had none. Not only were we silent at night but during the day too; we became steeped in moroseness. Before, I used to get weary from all the babbling, endless wrangling, and extravagant praises the sisters heaped on me, but now I longed for those days. I talked the situation over with the sisters and we decided to put an end to the alienation that lay between us, but such things can't be changed with decisions. I often had the feeling that some invisible being lurked among us, a phantom who sealed our lips and burdened our spirits. Each time I started to say something, the words stuck in my throat. When I did say it, the words that came out required no answer. I looked on with amazement as the two chatterbox sisters became close-mouthed. All the speech seemed to have been drained from them. I became as taciturn as they. Before, I could babble on for hours without any thought or reflection, but suddenly I became diplomatic and careful to weigh every word, afraid that no matter what I said it would cause a commotion. I used to laugh when I read your stories about dybbuks, but I now actually felt myself possessed. When I wanted to pay Dora a compliment, it came out an insult. Oddly enough, the three of us couldn't stop yawning. We sat there, yawned, and looked at one another with moist eyes in astonishment, partners in a tragedy we could neither understand nor control.

"I became impotent too. I lost the urge for the two sisters. I lay in bed nights, and instead of lust, I felt something that can only be called anti-lust. I often had the uncomfortable feeling that my skin was icy cold and my body was shrinking. Although the sisters didn't mention my impotence, I knew that they were lying in bed with their ears cocked, listening to the strange process taking place within my organs—the ebbing of the blood and the cramping and shrinking of the limbs that seemed to degenerate to the verge of withering. I often imagined that in the dark I saw the silhouette of a figure that was as flimsy and transparent as a spider web—tall, thin, long-haired—a shadowy skeleton with holes instead of eyes, a monster with a crooked mouth that laughed soundlessly. I assured myself that it was nerves. What else could it be? I didn't believe in ghosts then and I don't to this day. I became convinced of one thing one night—thoughts and emotions can literally materialize and become entities of some substance. Even now, as I think about it, ants crawl up and down my spine. I've never spoken about this to anyone—you're the first and, I assure you, the last person to ever hear this.

"It was a spring night in 1948. A spring night in Paris can sometimes be bitter cold. We went to sleep separately—I on the cot, Dora on the sofa, and Ytta in bed. We put out the lights and lay down. I don't remember such a cold night even in the camps. We covered ourselves with all the blankets and rags we had in the house, but we still couldn't get warm. I put the sleeves of a sweater over my feet and threw my winter coat over the blanket. Ytta and Dora burrowed into their covers. We did all this without speaking and this silence lent our frantic efforts a brooding oppressiveness that defies description. I remember precisely lying there in bed and thinking that the punishment would come that night. At the same time, I silently prayed to God that it shouldn't. I lay there for a while half frozen—not only from the cold but from the tension too. I searched in the dark for the *shed* (as I called the creature of spider webs and shadows), but I saw nothing. At the same time, I knew that he was there, hovering in some corner or possibly even behind the bedboard. I said to myself, 'Don't be an idiot, there are no such things as ghosts. If Hitler could slaughter six million Jews and America sends billions of dollars to rebuild Germany, there are no other forces except the material. Ghosts wouldn't permit such an injustice . . .'

"I had to urinate and the toilet was out in the corridor. Usually I can hold myself in, if need be, but this time the urge was too insistent. I got up from the cot and went creeping toward the kitchen door, which led to the outside. I had taken only two steps when someone stopped me. Brother, I know all the answers and all the psychological flimflam, but this thing before me was a person and he blocked my path. I was too frightened to cry out. It's not in me to scream. I'm sure that I wouldn't scream even if it were killing me. Well, and who was there to help me, even if I did? The two half-mad sisters? I tried to push him aside and I touched something that might have been rubber, dough, or some sort of foam. There are fears from which you can't run away. A furious wrangling erupted between us. I pushed him back and he yielded a bit, yet offered resistance. I remember now that I was less afraid of the evil spirit than of the outcry the sisters might raise. I can't tell you how long this struggle lasted—a minute or perhaps only a few seconds. I thought I would pass out on the spot, but I stood there and stubbornly and silently wrestled with a phantom, or whatever it was. Instead of feeling cold, I became hot. Within a second, I was drenched as if standing under a shower. Why the sisters didn't scream is something I'll never understand. That they were awake I am sure. They were apparently terrified of their own fear. Suddenly I caught a blow. The Evil One vanished and I sensed that my organ was no longer there, either. Had he castrated me? My pajama bottoms had fallen. I felt around for my penis. No, he hadn't torn it out but had jammed it so deep into me that it had formed a negative indentation rather than a positive. Don't look at me that way! I'm not crazy now and I wasn't crazy then. During this whole nightmare, I knew that it was nerves—nervousness that had assumed substance. Einstein contends that mass is energy. I say that mass is compressed emotion. Neuroses materialize and take on concrete form. Feelings put on bodies or are themselves bodies. Those are your dybbuks, the sprites, the hobgoblins.

"I walked out into the corridor on wobbly knees and found the toilet, but I literally had nothing to urinate with. I read somewhere that in the Arab lands such things happen to men, especially to those who keep harems. Strange, but during the whole excitement I remained calm. Tragedy sometimes brings a kind of brooding resignation that comes from no one knows where.

"I turned back to the apartment, but neither of the sisters made a rustle. They lay there quiet, tense, barely breathing. Had they cast a spell over me? Were they themselves bewitched? I began to dress slowly. I put on my drawers, my pants, my jacket, and my summer coat. I packed some shirts, socks, and manuscripts in the dark. I gave the two sisters enough time to ask me what I was doing and where I was going, but they didn't utter a peep. I took my satchel and left in the middle of the night. Those are the bare facts."

"Where did you go?"

"What's the difference? I went to a cheap hotel and took a room. Gradually everything began to return to normal and I was able to function again. I somehow managed to overcome the nightmarish night and the next morning I caught a plane to London. I had an old friend there, a journalist on the local Yiddish newspaper, who had invited me to come a few times. The editorial office consisted of a single room and the whole paper went under soon afterward, but in the meantime I got some work and lodgings. From there, I left for Buenos Aires in 1950. Here I met Lena, my present wife."

"What became of the two sisters?"

"Do *you* know? That's as much as I know."

"Didn't you ever hear from them?"

"Never."

"Did you look for them?"

"Such things you try to forget. I hypnotized myself into thinking that the whole thing had been only a dream, but it really happened. It's as real as the fact that I'm sitting here with you right now."

"How do you explain it?" I asked.

"I don't."

"Maybe they were dead when you left."

"No, they were awake and listening. You can differentiate between the living and the dead."

"Aren't you curious to know what happened to them?"

"And if I am curious, what of it? They're probably alive. The witches are somewhere—maybe they've married. I was in Paris three years ago, but the house where we lived no longer exists. They put up a garage there."

We sat there silently; then I said, "If mass consisted of emotion, every stone in the street would be a skein of misery."

"Maybe they are. Of one thing I'm sure—everything lives, everything suffers, struggles, desires. There is no such thing as death."

"If that's true, then Hitler and Stalin didn't kill anyone," I said.

"You have no right to kill an illusion, either. Drink your coffee."

For a long while neither of us spoke; then I asked half in jest, "What can you learn from this story?"

Haim Leib smiled. "If Nietzsche's crazy theory about the exhaustion of all atomic combinations and the eternal return is true, and if there'll be another Hitler, another Stalin, and another Holocaust, and if in a trillion years you'll meet a female in Stettin—don't go with her to look for her sister."

"According to this theory, I will have no choice but to go and to experience everything that you did," I said.

"In that case, you'll know how I felt."

Three Encounters

I

I LEFT home at seventeen. I told my parents the truth: I didn't believe in the Gemara or that every law in the *Shulchan Aruch* had been given to Moses on Mount Sinai; I didn't wish to become a rabbi; I didn't want a marriage arranged by a matchmaker; I was no longer willing to wear a long gaberdine or grow earlocks. I went to Warsaw, where my parents had once lived, to seek an academic education and a profession. My older brother, Joshua, lived in Warsaw and had become a writer, but he wasn't able to help me. At twenty I came back home with congested lungs, a chronic cough, no formal education, no profession, and no way that I could see of supporting myself in the city. During the time I was away, my father had been appointed rabbi of Old-Stikov in Eastern Galicia—a village of a few dozen crooked shacks, with straw-covered roofs, built around a swamp. At least, in the fall of 1924 that's how Old-Stikov appeared to me. It had rained all October, and those shacks lay reflected in the swamp as if it were a lake. Ruthenian peasants, stooped Jews in gaberdines, women and girls wearing shawls over their heads and men's boots waded in the mud. Clouds of mist swirled in the air. Crows soared overhead, cawing. The sky hung low, leaden, heavy with storms. The smoke from chimneys didn't rise but drifted downward toward the soaked earth.

The community had assigned Father a semi-ruin of a house. In the three years I was away, his beard, red when I left, had become streaked with strands of white. Mother had discarded her wig for a kerchief. She had lost her teeth and her sunken cheeks made her nose hooked, her chin receded. Only her eyes remained youthful and sharp.

Father warned me, "This is a pious community. If you don't conduct yourself as you should, they'll drive us out of here with sticks."

Translated by Joseph Singer

"Father, I'm giving in. My only hope is that the army won't take me."

"When do you have to report for conscription?"

"In a year."

"We'll arrange a match for you. God willing, your father-in-law will ransom you. Put aside your foolishness and study the Yoreh Deah."

I went to the study house but no one was studying there. The congregation, mostly artisans and dairymen, came to pray early in the morning and returned for the evening services; in between time, the place was deserted. I found an old volume on the Cabala there. I had brought along from Warsaw an algebra book and a Polish translation of Baudelaire's poems.

Abraham Getzel the matchmaker came to look me over—a little man with a white beard ranging nearly to his loins. He was also the village beadle, the cantor, and the Talmud teacher. He measured me up and down and sighed. "These are different times," he complained. "Girls want a husband who's a provider."

"I can't blame them."

"The Torah has lost its value in our generation. But don't you worry, I'll find you a bride."

He proposed a widow who was six or seven years older than I and had two children. Her father, Berish Belzer, managed a brewery owned by an Austrian baron. (Before the war, Galicia had been ruled by Emperor Franz Josef.) When the weather cleared somewhat during the day, one could see the brewery chimney. Black smoke sat on it like a hat.

Berish Belzer came to the study house to have a chat with me. He had a short beard the color of beer. He wore a fox coat and a derby. A watch on a silver chain dangled from his silk vest. After we had talked for a few minutes, he said, "I see you're no businessman."

"I'm afraid you're right."

"Then what are you?"

And the match was off.

All of a sudden the mail brought news from Warsaw. My brother had become co-editor of a literary weekly and I was offered the job of being its proofreader. He said that I could publish my stories there if they proved good enough. The moment I read the letter my health improved. From then on I didn't cough once during the night. I regained my appetite. I ate so much that my mother grew alarmed. Enclosed with the letter was the first issue of the magazine. It discussed a new novel by Thomas Mann, *The Magic Mountain*, and it contained poems in free verse, illustrated with Cubistic drawings. It reviewed a book of poetry entitled *A Boot in the Lapel*. Its articles spoke of the collapse of the old world and the emergence of a new man and a new spirit that would reappraise all values. It printed a chapter of Oswald Spengler's *The Decline of the West*, as well as translations of poems by Alexander Blok, Mayakovsky, and Esenin. New writers had appeared in America during the war years, and their work was beginning to be published in Poland. No, I could not while away my days in Old-Stikov! I waited only for the train fare to be sent me from Warsaw.

Now that I was about to return to modern culture, I began to observe what was happening in Old-Stikov. I listened to the women who came to consult Father on ritual matters and to gossip with Mother. We had a neighbor, Lazar the shoemaker, and his wife brought us the good tidings that their only daughter, Rivkele, was marrying her father's apprentice. Soon afterward Rivkele herself came to invite us to the engagement party. I looked at her with amazement. She reminded me of a Warsaw girl. She was tall, slim, with unusually white skin, black hair, dark-blue eyes, a long neck. Her upper lip drew back slightly to reveal white teeth without a blemish. There was a watch on her wrist and earrings dangled from the small lobes of her ears. She wore a fancy shawl with fringe and boots with high heels. She glanced at me shyly and said, "You are invited!"

We both blushed.

The next day I went with my parents to the party. Lazar the shoe-maker's house had a bedroom and a big room where the family cooked, ate, and worked. Scattered on the floor around the worktable were shoes, boots, heels. Rivkele's fiancé, Yantche, was short, broad, and dark, with two gold front teeth. The nail of his right index finger was deformed. For the party he had put on a paper collar and dickey. He passed cigarettes to the male guests. I heard him say, "Marry and die are two things you must do."

Warsaw was in no rush to send me train fare. Snow had fallen and a frost gripped Old-Stikov. Father had gone to the house of prayer to study and warm himself at the stove. Mother went to pay a call on a woman who had slipped on the ice near the well and broken a leg. I sat alone at home, going over my manuscripts. Although it was daytime, a cricket chirped, telling of a story as old as time. It stopped, listening to its own silence, then commenced again. The upper panes of the window were covered with frost flowers, but through the lower panes I could see a water carrier with icicles in his beard carrying two pails of water on a wooden yoke. A peasant in a sheepskin hat, his feet wrapped in rags, followed a sledge loaded with logs and pulled by an emaciated horse. I could hear the tinkling of the bell on its neck.

The door opened and Rivkele entered. "Your mother isn't here?" she asked me.

"She went to pay a sick call on somebody."

"I borrowed a glass of salt from her yesterday and I'm giving it back." She put a glass of salt on the table, then looked at me with a bashful smile.

"I didn't get the chance to wish you good luck at the engagement party, so I'm doing it now," I said.

"Thank you kindly. God willing, the same to you." After a pause, she added, "When it's your turn."

We talked, and I told her that I was going back to Warsaw. This was supposed to remain a secret, but I boasted to her that I was a writer and had just been made a staff member on a periodical. I showed her the magazine, and she gazed at me in astonishment. "You must have some brain!"

"To write, what you need most is an eye."

"What do you write—your thoughts?"

"I tell stories. They call it literature."

"Oh yes, things happen in the big cities," Rivkele said, nodding. "Here time stands still. There used to be a fellow here who read novels, but the Hasidim broke in on him and tore them all to shreds. He ran away to Brody."

She sat down on the edge of the bench and glanced toward the door, ready to spring up the moment anyone might come in. She said, "In other towns they put on plays, hold meetings, and whatnot, but here everyone is old-fashioned. They eat and they sleep, and that's how the years go by."

I realized that I was doing wrong to say this, but I said it anyway: "Why didn't you arrange to marry someone from a city?"

Rivkele thought it over. "Do they care around here what a girl wants? They marry you off and that's that."

"So it wasn't a love match?"

"Love? In Old-Stikov? They don't know the meaning of the word."

I am not an agitator by nature, and I had no reason to praise the Enlightenment that had disenchanted me, but somehow, as if against my will, I began to tell Rivkele that we lived in the twentieth century, not in the Middle Ages; that the world had awakened and that villages like Old-Stikov weren't merely physical quagmires but spiritual ones as well. I told her about Warsaw, Zionism, socialism, Yiddish literature, and the Writers' Club, where my brother was a member and to which I held a guest pass. I showed her pictures in the magazine of Einstein, Chagall, the dancer Nijinsky, and of my brother.

Rivkele clapped her hands. "Oy, he resembles you like two drops of water!"

I told Rivkele that she was the prettiest girl I had ever met. What would become of her here in Old-Stikov? She would soon begin bearing children. She would go around like the rest of the women in coarse boots and a dirty kerchief over a shaved head and take old age upon herself. The men here all visited the Belzer rabbi's court and he was said to perform miracles, but I heard that every few months epidemics raged in town. The people lived in filth, knew nothing about hygiene, science, or art. This was no town—I spoke dramatically—but a graveyard.

Rivkele's blue eyes with the long eyelashes gazed at me with the indulgence of a relative. "Everything you say is the pure truth."

"Escape from this mudhole!" I cried out like a seducer in a trashy novel. "You are young and a beauty, and I can see that you're clever, too. You don't have to let your years waste away in such a forsaken place. In Warsaw you could get a job. You could go out with whoever you please and in the evenings take courses in Yiddish, Hebrew, Polish —whatever you wish. I'll be there, too, and if you want we'll meet. I'll take you to the Writers' Club, and when the writers get a glimpse of you they'll go crazy. You might even become an actress. The actresses who play the romantic parts in the Yiddish theater are old and ugly. Directors are desperate to find young, pretty girls. I'll get a room and we'll read books together. We'll go to the movies, to the opera, to the library. When I become famous, we'll travel to Paris, London, Berlin, New York. There they're building houses sixty stories high; trains race above the streets and under the ground; film stars earn a thousand dollars a week. We can go to California, where it's always summer. Oranges are as cheap as potatoes . . ."

I had the odd feeling that this wasn't I talking but the dybbuk of some old enlightened propagandist speaking through my mouth.

Rivkele threw frightened glances toward the door. "The way you talk! Suppose someone hears—"

"Let them hear. I'm not afraid of anybody."

"My father—"

"If your father loved you he should have found you a better husband than Yantche. The fathers here are selling their daughters like the wild Asiatics. They're all steeped in fanaticism, superstition, darkness."

Rivkele stood up. "Where would I spend the first night? Such a fuss would break out that my mother couldn't endure it. The outcry would be worse than if I converted." The words stuck in Rivkele's mouth; her throat moved as if she were choking on something she couldn't swallow. "It's easy for a man to talk," she mumbled. "A girl is like a—the slightest thing and she is ruined."

"That's the way it used to be, but a new woman is emerging. Even here in Poland women already have the right to vote. Girls in Warsaw study medicine, languages, philosophy. A woman lawyer comes to the Writers' Club. She has written a book."

"A woman lawyer—how is this possible? Someone's coming." Rivkele opened the door. My mother was standing at the threshold. It wasn't snowing, but her dark kerchief had turned hoary with frost.

"Rebbitsin, I brought over the glass of salt."

"What was the hurry? Well, thank you."

"If you borrow, you have to pay back."

"What's a glass of salt?"

Rivkele left. Mother looked at me suspiciously. "Did you talk to her?"

"Talk? No."

"As long as you're here, you must behave decently."

I I

Two years passed. The magazine of which my brother was editor and I the proofreader had failed, but in the meantime I managed to publish a dozen stories and no longer needed a guest pass to the Writers' Club, because I had become a member. I supported myself by translating books from German, Polish, and Hebrew into Yiddish. I had presented myself before a military board, which had deferred me for a year, but now I had to go before another. Although I often criticized Hasidic conscripts for maiming themselves in order to avoid being accepted for service, I fasted to lose weight. I had heard horrible stories about the barracks: young soldiers were ordered to fall in muck, to leap over ditches; they were wakened in the middle of the night and forced to march for miles; corporals and sergeants beat the soldiers and played malicious tricks on them. It would be better to sit in jail than to fall into the hands of such hooligans. I was ready to go into hiding—even to kill myself. Pilsudski had ordered the military doctors to take only strong young men into the army, and I did everything I could to make myself weak. Besides fasting, I went without sleep; I smoked steadily, lighting one cigarette from the butt of the last; I drank vinegar and herring brine. A publisher had commissioned me to do a translation of Stefan Zweig's biography of Romain Rolland, and I spent half my nights working on it. I rented a room from an old physician, a onetime friend of Dr. Zamenhof, the creator of Esperanto. The street was named after him.

That night I had worked until three o'clock. Then I lay down on the bed in my clothes. Every time I fell asleep I woke up with a start. My dreams had become strangely vivid. Voices spoke to me from all sides, bells rang, choirs sang. When I opened my eyes I could still hear their reverberations. My heart palpitated, my hair pricked my skull like wires. My hypochondria had returned. My lungs felt compressed and about to collapse. The day was rainy. Whenever I looked out the window I saw a Catholic funeral cortege on its way to Powązek Cemetery. When I finally sat down to work on the translation, Yadzia, the maid, knocked on my door and announced that a young woman was asking for me.

My caller turned out to be Rivkele. I didn't recognize her immediately. She was smartly dressed in a coat with a fur collar, and a modish hat. She carried a purse and an umbrella. Her hair was cut *à la garçon,* and her dress was stylishly short; it came just to her knees. I felt so addled I forgot to be surprised. Rivkele told me what had happened to her. An American had come on a visit to Old-Stikov. He was a former tailor who said he had become a ladies'-clothing manufacturer in New York. He was a distant relative of her father's. He assured the family that he had divorced his wife in America and began to court Rivkele. She broke her engagement to Yantche. The visitor from America bought her a diamond ring, went with her to Lemberg, took her to the Yiddish theater, to the Polish theater, to restaurants, and generally behaved like a prospective bridegroom. Together they visited Crakow and Zakopane. Her parents demanded that he marry her, but he came up with all kinds of excuses. He had divorced his wife according to Jewish law, he said, but he still needed a civil decree. On the road, Rivkele began to live with him. Rivkele talked and cried. He had seduced and deceived her. He owned no factory; he worked for someone else. He had not divorced his wife. He was the father of five children. All this came out when his wife suddenly arrived in Old-Stikov and made a scandal. She had family in Jaroslaw and Przemyśl—butchers, draymen, tough fellows. They warned Morris—that was his name—that they would break his neck. They turned him in to the police. They threatened to report him to the American consul. The result was that he went back to his wife and they sailed together to America.

Rivkele's face was drenched with tears. She trembled, convulsed by hiccuplike sobs. Soon the truth came out. He had made her pregnant; she was in her fifth month. Rivkele moaned. "Nothing is left me but to hang myself!"

"Do your parents know that—"

"No, they don't know. They'd die of shame."

This was another Rivkele. She bent down to take a draw on my cigarette. She had to go to the bathroom, and I took her through the living room. The doctor's wife—a small, thin woman with a pointed face, many warts, and popping eyes that were yellow as if from jaundice —glared at her. Rivkele lingered in the bathroom for such a long time that I feared she had taken poison.

"Who is that creature?" the doctor's wife demanded. "I don't like the looks of her. This is a respectable house."

"Madam, you have no reason to be suspicious."

"I wasn't born yesterday. Be so good as to find lodgings somewhere else."

After a while Rivkele came back to my room. She had washed her face and powdered it. She had put on lipstick.

"You are responsible for my misfortune," she said.

"*I* am?"

"If it weren't for you, I wouldn't have let myself go with him. Your words stuck in my mind. You spoke in such a way that I wanted to leave home right then and there. When he came, I was—as they say—already ripe."

I had the urge to scold her and tell her to be on her way, but she started to cry again. Then she began to sing a tune as old as the female sex: "Where do I go now and what do I do? He has slaughtered me without a knife . . ."

"Did he leave you some money at least?" I asked.

"There is a little left."

"Maybe something can still be done."

"Too late."

We sat without speaking, and the lessons of the moral primers came back to me. No word goes astray. Evil words lead to iniquitous deeds. Utterings of slander, mockery, and profanity turn into demons, hobgoblins, imps. They stand as accusers before God, and when the transgressor dies they run after his hearse and accompany him to the grave.

As if Rivkele guessed my thoughts, she said, "You made me see America like a picture. I dreamed of it at night. You made me hate my home—Yantche, too. You promised to write me, but I didn't get a single letter from you. When Morris arrived from America, I clutched at him as if I were drowning."

"Rivkele, I have to report for conscription. I'm liable to be sent to the barracks tomorrow."

"Let's go away somewhere together."

"Where? America has closed its gates. All the roads are sealed."

III

Nine years went by. It was my third year in New York. From time to time, I published a sketch in a Yiddish newspaper. I lived in a furnished room not far from Union Square. My room was dark. I had to climb four stories to get to it, and it stank of disinfectant. The linoleum on the floor was torn, and cockroaches crawled from beneath it. When I turned on the naked bulb that hung from the ceiling, I saw a crooked bridge table, an overstuffed chair with torn upholstery, and a sink with a faucet that dripped rusty water. The window faced a wall. When I felt like writing—which was seldom—I went to the Public Library at Forty-second Street and Fifth Avenue. Here in my room, I only lay on the sagging bed and fantasized about fame, riches, and women who threw themselves at me. I had had an affair, but it ended, and I had been alone for months. I kept my ears cocked to hear if I was being summoned to the pay phone below. The walls of the house were so thin that I could hear every rustle—not only on my floor but on the lower floors as well. A group of boys and girls who called themselves a "stock company" had moved in. They were getting ready to put on a play somewhere. In the meantime, they ran up and down the stairs, shrieking and laughing. The woman who changed my bedding told me that they practiced free love and smoked marijuana. Across from me lived a girl who had come to New York from the Middle West to become an actress, and for whole days and half the nights she sang wailing melodies that someone told me were called the "blues." One evening, I heard her sing over and over again in a mournful chant:

> *He won't come back,*
> *Won't come back,*
> *Won't come back,*
> *Never, never, never, never.*
> *Won't come back!*

I heard footsteps and my name being called. I sat up so hastily that I nearly broke the bed. The door opened and by the dim light of the hall I saw the figure of a woman. I didn't put on my light because I was ashamed of the condition of my room. The paint on the walls was peeling. Old newspapers lay scattered around, together with books I had picked up along Fourth Avenue for a nickel each, and dirty laundry.

"May I ask who you are looking for?" I said.

"It's you. I recognize your voice. I'm Rivkele—Lazar the shoemaker's daughter from Old-Stikov."

"Rivkele!"

"Why don't you put on the light?"

"The light is broken," I said, baffled by my own lie. The blues singer across the way became quiet. This was the first time that I had ever had a visitor here. For some reason her door stood always ajar, as if deep inside her she still hoped that he who wouldn't come back would one day come back after all.

Rivkele mumbled, "Do you at least have a match? I don't want to fall."

It struck me that she spoke Yiddish in an accent that wasn't exactly American but no longer sounded the way they had spoken back home. I got off the bed carefully, led her over to the easy chair, and helped her sit down. At the same time I snatched one of my socks from the back of the chair and flung it aside. It fell into the sink. I said, "So you're in America!"

"Didn't you know? Didn't they write you that—"

"I asked about you time and again in my letters home, but they never answered."

She was silent for a time. "I didn't know that you were here. I only found out about it a week ago. No, it's two weeks. What a time I had finding you! You write under another name. Why, of all things?"

"Didn't they tell you from home that I'm here?" I asked in return.

Rivkele didn't reply, as if she were thinking the question over. Then she said, "I see you know nothing. I'm no longer Jewish. Because of this, my parents have disowned me as a daughter. Father sat shivah for me."

"Converted?"

"Yes, converted." Rivkele made a sound that was something like laughter.

I pulled the string and lit the naked bulb that was half covered with paint. I didn't know myself why I did this. My curiosity to see Rivkele in the role of a Gentile must have outweighed any shame I felt about my poverty. Or maybe in that fraction of a second I decided her disgrace was worse than mine. Rivkele blinked her eyes, and I saw a face that wasn't hers and that I would never have recognized on the street. It seemed to me broad, pasty, and middle-aged. But this unfamiliarity lasted only an instant. Soon I realized that she hadn't really changed since the last time I had seen her in Warsaw. Why, then, had she seemed so different at first glance? I wondered.

Apparently Rivkele went through the same sensations, because after a while she said, "Yes, it's you."

We sat there, observing each other. She wore a green coat and a hat to match. Her eyelids were painted blue and her cheeks were heavily rouged. She had gained weight. She said, "I have a neighbor who reads the Yiddish paper. I had told her a lot about you, but since you sign your stories by another name, how could she know? One day she came in and showed me an account of Old-Stikov. I knew at once that it was you. I called the editorial office, but they didn't know your address. How could that be?"

"Oh, I'm here on a tourist visa and it's expired."

"Aren't you allowed to live in America?"

"I must first go to Canada or to Cuba. Only from the American consul in a foreign country can I get a permanent visa to return."

"Then why don't you go?"

"I can't go on a Polish passport. It's all tied up with lawyers and expenses."

"God in heaven!"

"What happened to you?" I asked. "Did you have a child?"

Rivkele placed a finger with a red, pointed nail to her lips. "Hush! I had nothing. You know nothing!"

"Where is it?"

"In Warsaw. In a foundling home."

"A boy?"

"A girl."

"Who brought you to America?"

"Not Morris—somebody else. It didn't work out. We split up and I went to Chicago, and there I met Mario . . ." Rivkele began to speak in a mixture of Yiddish and English. She had married Mario in Chicago and adopted the Catholic faith. Mario's father owned a bar that was patronized by the Mafia. Once, in a quarrel, Mario stabbed a man and he was serving his second year in prison. Rivkele—her name was now Anna Marie—was working as a waitress in an Italian restaurant in New York. Mario had at least a year and a half left to serve. She had a small apartment on Ninth Avenue. Her husband's friends came by, wanting to sleep with her. One had threatened her with a gun. The owner of the restaurant was a man past his sixties. He was good to her, took her to the theater, the movies, and to nightclubs, but he had an evil wife and three daughters, each one more malicious than the next. They were Rivkele's mortal enemies.

"Are you living with him?"

"He is like a father to me." Rivkele changed her tone. "But I never forgot you! Hardly a day goes by that I don't think of you. Why this is I don't understand. When I heard that you were in America and read that article about Old-Stikov, I became terribly excited. I called the paper maybe twenty times. Someone told me that you sneak into the press-room at night and leave your articles there. So I went there late one night after work, hoping to find you. The elevator man told me that you had a box on the ninth floor where I could leave a letter for you. I went up and all the lights were on, but no one was there. Near the wall a machine was writing by itself. It frightened me. It reminded me of what they recite on Rosh Hashanah—"

"The Heavenly Book that reads itself and everyone inscribes his own sins in it."

"Yes, right. I couldn't locate your box. Why are you hiding from the newspapermen? They wouldn't denounce you."

"Oh, the editor adds all kinds of drivel to my pieces. He spoils my style. For the few dollars he pays me, he makes me look like a hack."

"That article about Old-Stikov was good. I read it and cried all night."

"Do you miss home?"

"Everything together. I've fallen into a trap. Why do you live in such a dump?"

"I can't even afford this."

"I have some money. Since Mario is in jail, it would be easy for me to get a divorce. We could go to Canada, to Cuba—wherever you ought to go. I'm a citizen. We'll marry and settle down. I'll bring my daughter over. I didn't want any children with him, but with you . . ."

"Idle words."

"Why do you say that? We are both in trouble. I got myself into a mess and was feeling hopeless. But when I read what you wrote everything came back to me. I want to be a Jewish daughter again."

"Not through me."

"You are responsible for what has happened to me!"

We grew silent, and the girl across the way who had stopped singing and seemed to be listening to her own perplexity, like the cricket in Old-Stikov, resumed her mournful song:

> *He won't come back,*
> *Won't come back,*
> *Won't come back,*
> *Never, never, never, never.*
> *Won't come back . . .*

Passions

"WHEN a man persists he can do things which one might think can never be done," Zalman the glazier said. "In our village, Radoszyce, there was a simple man, a village peddler, Leib Belkes. He used to go from village to village, selling the peasant women kerchiefs, glass beads, perfume, all kinds of gilded jewelry. And he would buy from them a measure of buckwheat, a wreath of garlic, a pot of honey, a sack of flax. He never went farther than the hamlet of Byszcz, five miles from Radoszyce. He got the merchandise from a Lublin salesman, and the same man bought his wares from him. This Leib Belkes was a common man but pious. On the Sabbath he read his wife's Yiddish Bible. He loved most to read about the land of Israel. Sometimes he would stop the cheder boys and ask, 'Which is deeper—the Jordan or the Red Sea?' 'Do apples grow in the Holy Land?' 'What language is spoken by the natives there?' The boys used to laugh at him. He looked like someone from the Holy Land himself—black eyes, a pitch-black beard, and his face was also swarthy.

"Once a year a messenger used to come to Radoszyce, a Sephardic Jew. He was sent to collect the alms that were given in the name of Rabbi Meir the Miracle Worker, that he should intercede for them in the next world. The messenger wore a robe with black and red stripes and sandals that looked as though they were of ancient times. His hat was also outlandish. He smoked a water pipe. He spoke Hebrew and also Aramaic. His Yiddish he had learned in later years. Leib Belkes was so fascinated by him that he went with him from house to house to open the alms boxes. He also took him to his home, where he ate and slept. While the messenger stayed in Radoszyce, Leib Belkes did no work. He kept on asking questions like 'What does the Cave of Machpelah look

Translated by the author and Dorothea Straus

485

like?' 'Does one know where Abraham is buried and where Sarah?' 'Is it true that Mother Rachel rises from her grave at midnight and weeps for her exiled children?' I was still a boy then, but I too followed the messenger wherever he went. When could one see such a man in our region?

"Once, after the messenger left, Leib Belkes entered a store and asked for fifty packs of matches. The merchant asked him, 'What do you need so many matches for? You want to burn the village?' And Leib said, 'I want to build the Holy Temple.' The storekeeper thought that he had lost his mind. Just the same, he sold him all the matches he had.

"Later, Leib went into a paint store and asked for silver and gold paint. The storekeeper asked him, 'What do you need these paints for? Do you intend to make counterfeit money?' And Leib answered, 'I am going to build the Holy Temple.' The messenger had sold Leib a map, a large sheet of paper showing the Temple with the altar and all the other objects of ritual. At night when Leib had time he sat down and began to build the Temple according to this plan. There were no children in the house. Leib Belkes and his wife had two daughters but they had gone into domestic service in Lublin. His wife asked him, 'Why do you play with matches? Are you a cheder boy again?' And he replied, 'I am building the Temple of Jerusalem.'

"He managed to build everything according to this plan: the Holy of Holies, the Inner Court, the Outer Court, the Table, the Menorah, the Ark. When the people of Radoszyce learned what he was doing, they came to look and admire. The teachers brought their pupils. The whole edifice stood on a table, and it couldn't be moved, because it would have collapsed. When the rabbi had word of it, he too came to Leib Belkes, and he brought some yeshiva boys with him. They sat around the table and they were dumfounded. Leib Belkes had constructed out of matches the Holy Temple exactly as it was described in the Talmud!

"Well, but people are envious and begrudge others their accomplishments. His wife began to complain that she needed the table for her dishes. There were firemen in Radoszyce, and they were afraid that so many matches would cause a fire and the whole town might go up in flames. There were so many threats and complaints that one day when Leib returned from his travels his temple was gone. His wife swore that the firemen came and demolished it. The firemen accused the wife.

"After his temple had been destroyed, Leib Belkes became melancholic. He still tried to do business, but he earned less and less. He often sat at home and read Yiddish storybooks that dealt with the land of Israel. At the study house he bothered the scholars and yeshiva boys by asking them questions about the coming of the Messiah. 'Will one huge cloud take all the Jews to the Holy Land, or will a cloud descend for each town separately?' 'Will the Resurrection of the Dead take place immediately, or will there be a waiting period of forty years?' 'Will there still be a need to plow the fields and to gather the fruit from the orchards, or will manna fall from the sky?' People had something to scoff at.

"Once, late in the evening, when his wife told him to close the shutters, he went outside and did not return. There was an uproar in Radoszycc. Some people believed that the demons had spirited him away. Others thought that his wife nagged him so much that he ran away to his relatives on the other side of the Vistula. But what man would run away at night without his overcoat and without a bundle? If this had happened to a rich man, they would have sent out searchers to find him. But when a poor man disappears, there is one pauper less in town. His wife—Sprintza was her name—was deserted. She earned a little from kneading dough in wealthy houses on Thursday. She also got some support from her daughters when they married.

"Five years passed. Once on a Friday, when Sprintza was standing over the oven and cooking her Sabbath meal, the door opened, and in came a man with a gray beard, dusty and barefooted. Sprintza thought it was a beggar. Suddenly he said, 'I was in the Holy Land. Give me some prune dessert.'

"The town went wild. They all came running, and Leib was taken to the rabbi. The rabbi questioned him, and he learned that Leib had gone on foot to the Holy Land."

"On foot?" Levi Yitzchok asked.

"Yes, on foot," Zalman said.

"But everyone knows that to get to the Holy Land one must travel by ship."

Meyer Eunuch clutched his chin where a beard should have grown and said, "Perhaps he lied?"

"He brought letters from many rabbis, as well as a sack of holy earth that he dug himself at the Mount of Olives," Zalman said. "When someone died he placed a handful of it under the corpse's head. I saw it myself; it was as white as crumbled chalk."

"How long did the trip take him?" Levi Yitzchok asked.

"Two years. On the way back he went by boat. The rabbi asked him, 'How can a man do a thing like that?' And he answered, 'I yearned so much that I could not bear it any more. That night when I went out to close the shutters and I saw the moon running among the clouds I began to run after it. I kept running until I reached Warsaw. There, kind people showed me the road. I wandered over fields and forests, mountains and wasteland, until I arrived at the land of Israel.' "

"I am astonished that the beasts did not devour him," Levi Yitzchok half asked, half stated.

"It is written that the Lord preserves the simple," Meyer Eunuch said.

For a while all three were silent. Levi Yitzchok took his blue glasses off his nose and began to wipe the lenses with his sash. He suffered from trachoma. One of his eyes was milky white, and he could not see with it at all. Levi Yitzchok owned a cane that once belonged to the preacher of Kozienice. Levi Yitzchok never parted with it even on the Sabbath. He limped, and a crutch is not forbidden. For a long while he rested his chin on this cane. Then he straightened himself and said, "Stubbornness is a power. In Krasnystaw there was a tailor by the name of Jonathan. He sewed for women, not men. As a rule, a women's tailor is a frivolous person. When one sews a garment for a female, one has to take her measurements, and sometimes she may be in her unclean days. Even if she is in her clean days, it is not proper to touch a woman, especially if she is married. Well—but there must be tailors. You cannot make all garments by yourself. This Jonathan happened to be a pious man but uneducated. However, he loved Jewishness. On the Sabbath he read the Yiddish Bible with his wife, Beila Yenta. When a book sales-man came to town, Jonathan bought from him all the tomes and story-books in Yiddish. There was in Krasnystaw a congregation of psalm reciters and a society of Mishnah students. Jonathan belonged to both of these groups. He listened to the lectures, but he was afraid to say any-thing, because whenever he uttered a word in Hebrew he mangled it and the scholars made fun of him. I see him before my eyes: tall, lean, pockmarked. Gentleness looked out from his eyes. It was said that one couldn't find a better tailor even in Lublin. When he made a dress or a cape, it fitted like a glove. He had three unmarried daughters. When I was a boy I used to see him often, because a friend of mine, Getzel, an orphan, was his apprentice. Other masters mistreated their apprentices, beat them, and did not give them enough to eat. Instead of teaching them the trade, they sent them on errands, and ordered them to rock the babies or to carry the slops so that they should never learn the skill properly and have to be paid a salary. But Jonathan taught the orphan the trade, and, from the day he learned to make a buttonhole and to sew on a button, Jonathan paid him four rubles a year. Getzel had studied at a yeshiva before he became a tailor's helper, and Jonathan used to ask him all kinds of impossible questions—like 'What was the name of the mother of Og the King of Bashan?' 'Did Noah take flies into the Ark?' 'How many miles between paradise and Gehenna?' He wanted to know everything.

"Now, listen to this. Everyone knows that on the day of the Rejoicing over the Law the honored citizens, the learned, the affluent are called to carry the scrolls first—before the laborers, the simple people, those of little income. This is the way it is all over the world. But in our town the head of the synagogue was not a native. He knew very few people, and someone had to give him a paper listing the order of those to be called. There was another Jonathan in town, a scholar and a rich man, and the head of the synagogue confused the two men and he called Jonathan the tailor first. In the study house there was murmuring and giggling. When Jonathan the tailor heard that he had been called first, along with the rabbi and the elders, he couldn't believe his own ears. He realized that it was a mistake, but when a man is summoned to carry the scroll he dare not refuse. Among the workers and the apprentices praying at the west wall there was laughter. They began to push Jonathan and to pinch him good-naturedly. It was in the time before the government took over the sale of vodka, and vodka was cheaper than borscht. In every half-decent home, one could find a keg of vodka, with straws for drinking, and over it hung a side of dried mutton to munch afterward. On the day of the Rejoicing over the Law, people allowed themselves to take a sip before prayers, and almost everyone was tipsy. Jonathan the tailor came over to the reading table and was given the scroll. Everybody stared, but only one person said anything—Reb Zekele, a usurer. He exclaimed, 'Who calls up an ignoramus to carry the scroll first?' And he returned his own scroll to the beadle. It was beneath his dignity to carry the scroll with Jonathan the tailor.

"In the study house a commotion arose. To give back a scroll was sacrilege. The head of the synagogue was bewildered. To shame a person in the presence of a whole community is a terrible sin. No one sang and danced with the scrolls this time. The same simple people who had laughed at Jonathan and the honor given to him now cursed Reb Zekele and gnashed their teeth. When the ceremony was over, Jonathan the tailor approached Reb Zekele and said in a loud voice that all could hear, 'It is true that I am ignorant, but I swear to you that in a year from now I will be a greater scholar than you are.'

"The usurer smiled and said, 'If this happens, I will build you a house in the marketplace for nothing.' Reb Zekele the usurer dealt in lumber. He owned mortgages on half the houses in town.

"Jonathan stood for a while in perplexity. Then he said, 'If I am not a greater scholar than you are, I will sew for your wife—and for nothing —a fox-fur coat reaching to the ankles, lined in velvet and with ten tails.'

"What went on in the town that day is indescribable. In the women's section of the synagogue they heard about the bet and there was bedlam.

Some women laughed, others cried. Still others quarreled and tried to snatch the bonnets off each other's head. There were many poor people in town and a few rich ones, but in those times no one skimped on a holiday. Every third citizen invited guests to his house for a drink. There was dancing in the marketplace. The women had cooked huge pots of cabbage with raisins and cream of tartar. They had baked strudels, tarts, all kinds of fruitcakes. The Burial Society gave a banquet and mead was poured like water. One of the elders who had special merit in the eyes of the community was honored by having a pumpkin with lighted candles placed on his head, and being carried on the shoulders of the people to the synagogue yard. Bevies of children, the holy sheep, ran after him baaing. There was in town a he-goat that was not allowed to be slaughtered because he was first-born, and urchins put a fur hat on his horns and led him into the ritual bath. On that particular day there was only one topic of conversation—Jonathan the tailor's oath and the usurer's promise. Reb Zekele the usurer could easily afford to build a house for nothing, but how could Jonathan become a scholar in one year? The rabbi immediately announced that such an oath was not valid. In times of old, the rabbi said, Jonathan would have been hit thirty-nine times with a belt for breaking the commandment 'Thou shalt not take the name of the Lord thy God in vain.' But what could be done today? The town became divided into two parties. The scholars maintained that Jonathan should be fined and that he must come in his stocking feet to the synagogue to repent in public for giving a false oath. And if he refused, he should be excommunicated and his shop should not be patronized. The rabble threatened to burn the usurer's house and drive him out of town with sticks. Thank God, there are no Jewish robbers. In the evening of the holiday everybody became sober. It began to rain, and everyone returned to his bundle of troubles."

"Did they forget the whole thing?" Zalman the glazier asked.

"Nothing was forgotten. Just wait," Levi Yitzchok said.

Levi Yitzchok took out his wooden snuffbox, opened it, sniffed, and sneezed three times. His snuff was famous. He put into it smelling salts used at the Day of Atonement to revive the fasters. He wiped his red nose with his large kerchief and said, "If Getzel the apprentice had not been my friend I would not have known all the details. But Getzel boarded at Jonathan's, and he told me everything. When Jonathan came home that evening, the moment he opened the door he exclaimed, 'Beila Yenta, your husband has died! From today on you are a widow! My daughters, you are all orphans!' They began to cry, as on the ninth day of Ab, 'Husband—Father—how can you leave us?' And Jonathan answered, 'From today until the day of the Rejoicing over the Law next year, you have no provider.'

"He had hidden behind his Passover dishes a nest egg of one hundred guldens saved as a dowry for his oldest daughter, Taube. He took the money and left the house. There was in town a man called Reb Tevele Scratch-me. Scratch-me was of course a nickname. In his young years he had been a Talmud teacher. Like all teachers, he had in front of him on the table a hare's leg attached to a leather thong. Yet he did not use it to whip the children but to scratch himself. He suffered from eczema on his back. When it began to itch he handed the hare's leg to one of his pupils and ordered, "Scratch me." That is how he got his name. In his old age he gave up teaching and lived with his daughter. His son-in-law was a pauper, and Tevele Scratch-me lived in dire poverty. Jonathan the tailor went to Reb Tevele and asked him, 'Do you want to earn some money?' 'Who doesn't want money?' Tevele asked back. And Jonathan said, 'I will pay you a gulden a week if you will teach me the whole Torah!' Tevele burst out laughing. 'The whole Torah —even Moses did not know that! The Torah is like tailoring, without an end!' They spoke a long time, and finally it was decided that Tevele would teach Jonathan for a whole year and make him a greater scholar than Zekele. Jonathan calculated that if one studied seven pages of the Talmud each day of the year, all the thirty-seven tractates would be learned. It was said that Zekele had not gone through even half of this. Well—but the Talmud isn't enough. One had also to study Midrash, the commentaries. Why draw it out? Jonathan the tailor became a yeshiva boy. He sat at a table in the study house day and night and studied with Tevele. In the middle of the week, when the women's section was empty, they carried their volumes up there in order not to be disturbed. If I tell you that they studied eighteen hours a day, this is no exaggeration. All week long Jonathan slept on a bench in the study house. He went home to sleep only on the Sabbath and holidays."

"What happened to his family?" Zalman asked.

"What happens to all families when the provider goes? They did not die of hunger. The girls all went into service. Beila Yenta was a seamstress and she accepted light work. My friend Getzel slowly became the master. Jonathan did one thing—he studied. Such diligence the world has never beheld! Two or three nights a week he didn't sleep at all. The story soon spread to neighboring villages, and people came to stare at Jonathan as though he were a miracle worker. At the beginning, Reb Zekele laughed at the whole business. He said, 'If this simpleton can become a scholar, hair will grow on the palms of my hands.' Later on, toward the end of the year, people began to speak of the wonders of Jonathan's acquired knowledge. He recited by heart whole sections from the Gemara. He could anticipate the questions of such commentators as Rabbi Meir of Lublin and Rabbi Shlomo Luria.

"Now Zekele the usurer grew frightened. He too began to burn the midnight oil to overtake Jonathan. But it was already too late. Besides, he was up to his neck in business, and he was in the middle of a lawsuit to boot. His wife, Slikka, a greedy creature with a big mouth, was terribly eager for Jonathan to make her a fox coat with ten tails without cost, and for the first time in her life she drove her husband to study. But it did not work. I will make it short. On the eighth day of Sukkoth, the seven elders of the town and a number of other scholars gathered at the house of the rabbi, and they examined Zekele and Jonathan as if they were yeshiva boys. Zekele had forgotten a lot. For years he had studied only on the Sabbath—and there is a proverb that says, 'He who studies only on the Sabbath is only a seventh part of a scholar.' As for Jonathan, he remembered almost all of the Talmud by heart. His teacher, Tevele, had remarked that in teaching Jonathan he himself became erudite. Not only did Jonathan show knowledge but he showed astuteness as well. The rabbi's house was jammed with people. Others had to stand outside to hear Jonathan discuss the Law with the rabbi. At the beginning, Zekele tried to discover flaws in Jonathan's answers, but soon the tables were turned and Jonathan corrected Zekele. I wasn't there, but those who saw Zekele wrangle with Jonathan the tailor about some difficult passage of Maimonides or about the meaning of an obscure sentence of Rabbi Meir Schiff swore that it was like the fight between David and Goliath. Zekele screamed and gasped and scolded his opponent, but to no avail. No, Jonathan the tailor did not swear falsely. The rabbi and the seven elders unanimously gave the verdict that Jonathan was more of a scholar than Zekele. Jonathan's wife and daughters were sitting in the kitchen, and when they heard the verdict they fell upon each other wailing. The town seethed like a kettle. Synagogue Street was full of tailors, shoemakers, combers of pig bristles, coachmen, and such. It was their victory.

"The next day, Jonathan was called to take the scroll first—not by error this time. The most honored people invited him for a drink. There was talk that now Jonathan could become a rabbi or an assistant rabbi, or at least a ritual slaughterer. But Jonathan let it be known that he was returning to his scissors and iron. Zekele tried to avoid payment by contending that he did not swear but only promised, and a promise does not have to be kept. But the rabbi ordered him to build a house for Jonathan, quoting from Deuteronomy: 'That which is gone out of thy lips thou shalt keep.' Zekele procrastinated as long as he could, but after the Feast of Shevuoth the house already had a roof. Only then did Jonathan make it known that he didn't want the house for himself but as an inn for yeshiva boys and poor travelers. He signed a document giving the house away to the community."

"He remained a tailor, eh?" Zalman the glazier asked.

"To the end."

"Did he marry off his daughters?"

"What else? There is no Jewish cloister."

All the time Levi Yitzchok was speaking, Meyer Eunuch was making gestures. His yellow eyes filled with laughter. Then he closed them, lowered his head, and seemed as though he was dozing. Suddenly he straightened up, clutched his beardless chin, and asked, "How did the village peddler know the road to the Holy Land? Most probably he asked. I guess he wandered over the Turkish lands, Egypt, and Istanbul. How did he manage to eat? Most probably he begged. There are Jews everywhere. Most likely he slept in the poorhouse. In warm countries one can even sleep in the streets. As for Jonathan the tailor, I assume that from his childhood he craved for learning, and the power of will is strong. There is a saying, 'Your will can make you a genius.' When you are idle, a year is nothing, but if you study day and night with diligence, you sop it up like a sponge. He did well not to accept the house from Reb Zekele, because it is forbidden to make a spade for digging from the Torah. As it was, he gained in addition the virtue of hospitality. Leib Belkes and Jonathan were both simple people—though not completely so. But it also happens with great men that they get an obsession in their minds. There is a saying, 'Greatness too has its share of insanity.'

"In Bechtev there was a Cabalist, Rabbi Mendel. He was descended from the renowned Hodel, who used to dance in a circle with the Hasidim. She did not, God forbid, hold their bare hands directly. She kept a kerchief over each hand, and the Hasidim held on to the kerchief. Rabbi Mendel could have had a large following, but he disliked crowds and discouraged them. Even in the High Holy Days he didn't get more than a few score in his study house. His wife died young, and she didn't leave him a child to take his place after his death. Many matches were proposed, but he refused to remarry. His followers argued with him: What about the commandment 'Be fruitful and multiply'? But the rabbi answered, 'I am going to get so many whips in Gehenna that a few more won't matter. Why are they so afraid of Gehenna? Since the Almighty created it, it must be paradise in disguise.' He should forgive me, but he was a devious kind of saint—but a great spirit just the same. There was much gossip about him, but he didn't care a fig. It even happened that he uttered sharp words against the Lord of the Universe. Once when he was reciting the psalms, he came to the passage 'He that sitteth in the heavens shall laugh.' Rabbi Mendel exclaimed, 'He shall laugh—but I am crushed!' When those who opposed him heard of this blasphemy, they almost managed to have him excommunicated.

"The disciples of the Baal Shem did not believe in fasting. Hasidism was exhilaration, not sadness. But Rabbi Mendel indulged in fasting. He began by fasting only on Mondays and Thursdays. Then he started to fast from one Sabbath to the next. He also immersed himself in cold baths. He called the body the enemy, and he would say, 'You don't have to appease an enemy. Of course, you are not allowed to kill him, but neither are you obliged to pamper him with marzipans.' His old Hasidic followers died out gradually. The younger men joined the courts of Gora and Kotzk. There remained in Rabbi Mendel's court only twenty or thirty persistent followers, in addition to a few hangers-on who stayed with him all year and ate from the common pot. An old beadle, stone-deaf, cooked porridge for them every day. A charitable woman went from house to house for them and collected potatoes, groats, flour, buckwheat, and whatever else she was offered.

"One Rosh Hashanah the rabbi had no more than twenty people in his study house. The following Yom Kippur he had only a quorum, including himself, the beadle, and the hangers-on. At the pulpit Rabbi Mendel recited all the prayers—Kol Nidre, the morning prayer, the midday prayer, and the closing prayer. It was already late when they finished the night prayer, and they blessed the new moon. The beadle offered the fasters some stale bread with herring and some chicken soup. None of them had any teeth left, and their stomachs had shrunk from undernourishment. Rabbi Mendel was older than any of them, but his voice remained young. His hearing, too, was good. The rabbi sat at the head of the table and spoke: 'Those who run after the pleasures of the world don't know what pleasure is. For them gluttony, drinking, lechery, and money are pleasures. There is no greater delight than the service of Yom Kippur. The body is pure and the soul is pure. The prayers are a joy. There is a saying that from confessing one's sins one does not get fat. It's completely false. When I confess my sins I become alive and vigorous. If I could have my say in heaven, every day would be Yom Kippur.' "

"After the rabbi said these words he rose from his chair and exclaimed, 'I have no say in heaven, but in my study house I do. From today on for me it will be a perpetual Yom Kippur—every day except for the Sabbath and Feast Days!' When the people of the village heard what the rabbi was about to do, there was pandemonium. The scholars and the elders came to the rabbi and asked, 'Isn't this breaking the Law?' And the rabbi replied, 'I do it for purely selfish reasons, not to please the Creator. If they punish me high up, I will accept the punishment. I also want to have some pleasure before I go!' The rabbi called out to his beadle, 'Light the candles; I am going to recite Kol Nidre.' He ran over to the pulpit and started to sing Kol Nidre. I wasn't there, but those who were present declared that such a Kol Nidre had not been heard since the world began. All of Bechtev came running. They thought that Rabbi Mendel had lost his mind. But who would dare to tear him away from the pulpit? He stood there in his white robe and prayer shawl and recited, 'It shall be forgiven' and 'Our supplications shall rise.' His voice was as strong as a lion's, and the sweetness of his singing was such that all apprehensions ceased. I will make it short. The rabbi lived two and a half years more, and those two and a half years were one long Yom Kippur."

Levi Yitzchok took off his dark glasses and asked, "What did he do about phylacteries? Didn't he put on phylacteries on weekdays?"

"He put them on," Meyer Eunuch answered, "but the liturgy was that of Yom Kippur. Toward evening he read the Book of Jonah."

"Didn't he eat a bite at night?" Zalman the glazier asked.

"He fasted six days of the week unless a holiday fell in the middle of it."

"And the hangers-on fasted with him?"

"Some left him. Others died."

"So did he pray to the bare walls?"

"There were always people who came to look and wonder."

"And the world allowed something like this?" Levi Yitzchok asked.

"Who was going to wage war against a holy man? They dreaded his irritation," Meyer Eunuch said. "One could clearly see that heaven approved. When a man fasts so long, his voice grows weak, he doesn't have the strength to stand on his feet. But the rabbi stood for all the prayers. Those who saw him told how his face shone like the sun. He slept no longer than three hours—in his prayer shawl and robe, with his forehead leaning on the Tractite Yoma, exactly like at Yom Kippur. At midday prayer he kneeled and intoned the liturgy concerning the service in the Holy Temple of Jerusalem."

"What did he do when it actually was Yom Kippur?" Zalman the glazier asked.

"The same as any other day."

"I never heard this story," Levi Yitzchok said.

"Rabbi Mendel was a hidden saint, and of those one hears little. Even today Bechtev is a forsaken village. In those times it was far away from everything—a swamp among forests. Even in the summer it was difficult to reach it. In the winter the snow made the roads impassable. The sleighs got stuck. And there was the danger of bears and wolves."

It became quiet. Levi Yitzchok took out his snuffbox. "Nowadays something like this would not be permitted."

"Greater transgressions than that are allowed in our day," Meyer said.

"How did he die?"

"At the pulpit. He was standing up reciting, 'What can man attain when death is all he can gain?' When he came to the verse 'Only charity and prayer may mitigate death's despair,' the rabbi fell down and his soul departed. It was a kiss from heaven—a saint's death."

Zalman the glazier put some tobacco into the bowl of his pipe. "What was the sense of it?"

Meyer Eunuch pondered for a while, and then said, "Everything can become a passion, even serving God."

Brother Beetle

I

I BEGAN to dream about this trip when I was five years old. At that time my teacher, Moses Alter, read to me from the Pentateuch about Jacob crossing the Jordan while carrying only his staff. But a week after my arrival in Israel, at the age of fifty, there were few marvels left for me to see. I had visited Jerusalem, the Knesset, Mount Zion, the kibbutzim in Galilee, the ruins of Safad, the remains of the fortification of Acre, and all the other sights. I even made the at-that-time dangerous trip from Beersheba to Sodom, and on the way saw camels harnessed to the plows of Arabs. Israel was even smaller than I had imagined it to be. The tourist car in which I traveled seemed to be going in circles. For three days wherever we went we played hide-and-seek with the Sea of Galilee. During the day, the car was continually overheating. I wore two pairs of sunglasses, one on top of the other, as protection against the glare of the sun. At night, a hot wind blew in from somewhere. In Tel Aviv, in my hotel room, they taught me to maneuver the shutters, but in the one moment it took me to get out on the balcony, the thin sand carried by the khamsin wind managed to cover the linens of my bed. With the wind came locusts, flies, and butterflies of all sizes and colors, along with beetles larger than any I had ever seen before. The humming and buzzing was unusually loud. The moths beat against the walls with unbelievable strength, as if in preparation for the final war between man and insect. The tepid breath of the sea stank of rotten fish and excrement. That late summer, electricity failures were frequent in Tel Aviv. A suburban darkness covered the city. The sky filled with stars. The setting sun had left behind the redness of a heavenly slaughter.

On a balcony across the street, an old man with a small white beard, a silken skullcap partly covering his high forehead, half sat, half reclined

---

Translated by the author and Elizabeth Shub

on a bed, reading a book through a magnifying glass. A young woman kept bringing him refreshments. He was making notes in the book's margins. On the street below, girls laughed, shrieked, picked fights with boys, just as I had seen them do in Brooklyn, and in Madrid, where I had stopped en route. They teased one another in Hebrew slang. After a week of seeing everything a tourist must see in the Holy Land, I had my fill of holiness and went out to look for some unholy adventure.

I had many friends and acquaintances from Warsaw in Tel Aviv, even a former mistress. The greatest part of those who had been close to me had perished in Hitler's concentration camps or had died of hunger and typhoid in Soviet Middle Asia. But some of my friends had been saved. I found them sitting in the outdoor cafés, sipping lemonade through straws and carrying on the same old conversations. What are seventeen years, after all? The men had become a little grayer. The women dyed their hair; heavy makeup hid their wrinkles. The hot climate had not wilted their desires. The widows and widowers had remarried. Those recently divorced were looking for new mates or lovers. They still wrote books, painted pictures, tried to get parts in plays, worked for all kinds of newspapers and magazines. All had managed to learn at least some Hebrew. In their years of wandering, many of them had taught themselves Russian, German, English, and even Hungarian and Uzbek.

They immediately made room for me at their tables, and began reminding me of episodes I could not possibly forget. They asked my advice on American visas, literary agents, and impresarios. We were even able to joke about friends who had long since become ashes. Every now and then a woman would wipe away a tear with the point of her handkerchief so as not to smear her mascara.

I didn't look for Dosha, but I knew that we would meet. How could I have avoided her? That evening I happened to be sitting in a café frequented by merchants, not artists. At the surrounding tables the subject was business. Diamond merchants brought out small bags of gems and their jeweler's loupes. A stone passed quickly from table to table. It was inspected, fingered, and then given to another, with a nod of the head. It seemed to me that I was in Warsaw, on Krolewska Street. Suddenly I saw her. She glanced around, looking for someone, as if she had an appointment. I noticed everything at once: the dyed hair, the bags under her eyes, the rouge on her cheeks. One thing only had remained unchanged—her slim figure. We embraced and uttered the same lie: "You haven't changed." And when she sat down at my table, the difference between what she had been then and what she was now began to disappear, as if some hidden power were quickly retouching her face to the image which had remained in my memory.

I sat there listening to her jumbled conversation. She mixed countries, cities, years, marriages. One husband had perished; she had divorced another. He now lived nearby with another woman. Her third husband, from whom she was separated, more or less, lived in Paris, but he expected to come to Israel soon. They had met in a labor camp in Tashkent. Yes, she was still painting. What else could she do? She had changed her style, was no longer an impressionist. Where could old-fashioned realism lead today? The artist must create something new and entirely his own. If not, art was bankrupt. I reminded her of the time when she had considered Picasso and Chagall frauds. Yes, that was true, but later she herself had reached a dead end. Now her painting was really different, original. But who needed paintings here? In Safad there was an artists' colony, but she had not been able to adjust herself to the life there. She had had enough of wandering about through all kinds of godforsaken villages in Russia. She needed to breathe city air.

"Where is your daughter?"

"Carola is in London."

"Married?"

"Yes, I'm a *sabta*, a grandmother."

She smiled shyly, as if to say: "Why shouldn't I tell you? I can't fool you, anyhow." I noticed her newly capped teeth. When the waiter came over, she ordered coffee. We sat for a while in silence. Time had battered us. It had robbed us of our parents, our relatives, had destroyed our homes. It had mocked our fantasies, our dreams of greatness, fame, riches.

I had had news of Dosha while I was still in New York. Some mutual friends wrote to me that her paintings were not exhibited; her name was never mentioned in the press. Because she had had a nervous breakdown, she had spent some time in either a clinic or an asylum.

In Tel Aviv, women seldom wear hats, and almost never in the evening, but Dosha had on a wide-brimmed straw hat which was trimmed with a violet ribbon and slanted over one eye. Though her hair was dyed auburn, there were traces of other colors in it. Here and there, it even had a bluish cast. Still, her face had retained its girlish narrowness. Her nose was thin, her chin pointed. Her eyes—sometimes green, sometimes yellow—had the youthful intensity of the unjaded, still ready to struggle and hope to the last minute. How else could she have survived?

I asked, "Do you have a man, at least?"

Her eyes filled with laughter. "Starting all over again? The first minute?"

"Why wait?"

"You haven't changed."

She took a sip of coffee and said, "Of course I have a man. You know I can't live without one. But he's crazy, and I am not speaking figuratively. He's so mad about me that he destroys me. He follows me on the street, knocks at my door in the middle of the night, and embarrasses me in front of my neighbors. I've even called the police, but I can't get rid of him. Luckily, he is in Eilat at the moment. I've seriously thought of taking a gun and shooting him."

"Who is he? What does he do?"

"He says he is an engineer, but he's really an electrician. He's intelligent, but mentally sick. Sometimes I think that the only way out for me is to commit suicide."

"Does he at least satisfy you?"

"Yes and no. I hate savages and I'm tired of him. He bores me, keeps everybody away from me. I'm convinced that someday he'll kill me. I'm as certain of that as that it's night now. But what can I do? The Tel Aviv police are like the police everywhere. 'After he kills you,' they say, 'we'll put him in jail.' He should be committed. If I had somewhere to go, I would leave, but the foreign consulates aren't exactly handing out visas. At least I have an apartment here. Some apartment! But it's a place to sleep. And what can I do with my paintings? They're just gathering dust. Even if I wanted to leave, I don't have the fare. The alimony I get from my former husband, the doctor, is a few pounds, and he's always behind in his payments. They don't know what it's all about here. It's not America. I'm starving and that's the bitter truth. Don't grab your wallet; it's not really that bad. I've lived alone and I'll die alone. I'm proud of it, and besides, it's my fate. What I'm going through and what I've been through, nobody knows, not even God. There's not a day without some catastrophe. But suddenly I walk into a café and there you are. That's really something."

"Didn't you know that I was here?"

"Yes, but how did I know what you'd be like after all these years? I haven't changed a bit, and that's my tragedy. I've remained the same. I've the same desires, the same dreams—the people persecute me here, just as they did twenty years ago in Poland. They are all my enemies, and I don't know why. I've read your books. I've forgotten nothing. I've always thought about you, even when I lay swollen from hunger in Kazakhstan and looked into the eyes of death. You wrote somewhere that one sins in another world, and that this world is hell. For you, that may have been just a phrase, but it's the truth. I am the reincarnation of some wicked man from another planet. Gehenna is *in* me. This climate sickens me. The men here become impotent; the women are consumed with passion. Why did God pick out this land for the Jews? When the khamsin begins, my brains rattle. Here the winds don't blow; they wail like jackals. Sometimes I stay in bed all day because I don't have the strength to get up, but at night I roam about like a beast of prey. How long can I go on like this? But that I'm alive and seeing you makes it a holiday for me."

She pushed her chair away from the table, almost overturning it. "These mosquitoes are driving me crazy."

I I

Although I had already had dinner, I ate again with Dosha and drank Carmel wine with her. Then I went to her home. On the way, she kept apologizing for the poorness of her apartment. We passed a park. Though lit by street lamps, it was covered by darkness which no light could penetrate. The motionless leaves of the trees seemed petrified. We walked through dim streets, each bearing the name of a Hebrew writer or scholar. I read the signs over women's clothing stores. The commission for modernizing Hebrew had created a terminology for brassières, nylons, corsets, ladies' coiffures, and cosmetics. They had found the sources for such worldly terms in the Bible, the Babylonian Talmud, the Jerusalem Talmud, the Midrash, and even the Zohar. It was already late in the evening, but buildings and asphalt still exuded the heat of the day. The humid air smelled of garbage and fish.

I felt the age of the earth beneath me, the lost civilizations lying in layers. Somewhere below lay hidden golden calves, the jewelry of temple harlots, and images of Baal and Astarte. Here prophets foretold disasters. From a nearby harbor, Jonah had fled to Tarshish rather than prophesy the doom of Nineveh. In the daylight these events seemed remote, but at night the dead walked again. I heard the whisperings of phantoms. An awakening bird had uttered a shrill alarm. Insects beat against the glass of the street lamps, crazed with lust.

Dosha took my arm with a loyalty unprofaned by any past betrayal. She led me up the stairway of a building. Her apartment was actually a separate structure on the roof. As she opened the door, a blast of heat, combined with the smell of paint and of alcohol used for a primus stove, hit me. The single room served as studio, bedroom, kitchen. Dosha did not switch on the lights. Our past had accustomed us both to undress and dress in the dark. She opened the shutters and the night shone in with its street lamps and stars. A painting stood propped against the wall. I knew that in the daylight its bizarre lines and colors would have little meaning for me. Still, I found it intriguing now. We kissed without speaking.

After years of living in the United States, I had forgotten that there could be an apartment without a bathroom. But Dosha's had none.

There was only a sink with running water. The toilet was on the roof. Dosha opened a glass door to the roof and showed me where to go. I could find neither switch nor cord to turn on the light. In the dark I felt a hook with pieces of torn newspaper stuck to it. As I was returning, I saw through the curtains of the glass door that Dosha had turned on the lamp.

Suddenly the silhouette of a man crossed the window. He was tall and broad-shouldered. I heard voices and realized immediately what had happened. Her mad lover had returned. Though terrified, I felt like laughing. My clothes were in her room; I had walked out naked.

I knew there was no escape. The house was not attached to any other building. Even if I managed to climb down the four stories to the street, I could not return to my hotel without clothes. It occurred to me that Dosha might have hidden my things quickly when she heard her lover's steps on the stairs. But he might come outside at any minute. I began to look around the roof for some stick or other object with which to defend myself. I found nothing. I stood against the outside wall of the toilet, hoping he wouldn't see me. But how long could I stay there? In a few hours it would be daybreak.

I crouched like an animal at bay waiting for the hunter to shoot. Cool breezes from the sea mingled with the heat rising from the roof. I shivered and could barely keep my teeth from chattering. I realized that my only way of escape would be to climb down the balconies to the street. But when I looked, I saw that I could not even reach the nearest one. If I jumped I might break a leg or even fracture my skull. Besides, I might be arrested or taken to a madhouse.

Despite my anxiety, I was aware of the ridiculousness of my situation. I could hear them giggling at my ill-fated tryst in the cafés of Tel Aviv. I began to pray to God, against whom I had sinned. "Father, have mercy on me. Don't let me perish in this preposterous way." I promised a sum of money for charity if only I could get out of this trap. I looked up to the numberless stars that hovered strangely near, to the cosmos spreading out with all its suns, planets, comets, nebulae, asteroids, and who-knows-what-other powers and spirits, which are either God Himself or that which He has formed from His substance. I imagined that there was a touch of compassion in the stars as they gazed at me in the midst of their midnight gaiety. They seemed to be saying to me, "Just wait, child of Adam, we know of your predicament and are taking counsel."

For a long time I stood staring at the sky and at the tangle of houses which make up Tel Aviv. An occasional horn, the bark of a dog, the shout of a human being erupted from the sleeping city. I thought I heard the surf and a ringing bell. I learned that insects do not sleep at night. Every moment some tiny creature fluttered by, some with one pair of wings, others with two. A huge beetle crawled at my feet. It stopped, changed its direction, as if it realized it had gone astray on this strange roof. I had never felt so close to a crawling creature as in those minutes. I shared its fate. Neither of us knew why he had been born and why he must die. "Brother Beetle," I muttered, "what do they want of us?"

I was overcome by a kind of religious fervor. I was standing on a roof in a land which God had given back to that half of his people that had not been annihilated. I found myself in infinite space, amid myriads of galaxies, between two eternities, one already past and one still to come. Or perhaps nothing had passed, and all that was or ever will be was unrolled across the universe like one vast scroll. I apologized to my parents, wherever they were, against whom I had once rebelled and whom I was now disgracing. I asked God's forgiveness. For instead of returning to His promised land with renewed will to study the Torah and to heed His commandments, I had gone with a wanton who had lost herself in the vanity of art. "Father, help me!" I called out in despair.

Growing weary, I sat down. Because it was getting colder, I leaned against the wall to protect myself. My throat was scratchy, and in my nose I felt the acrid dryness that precedes a cold. "Has anyone else ever been in such a situation?" I asked myself. I was numbed by that silence that accompanies danger. I might freeze to death on this hot summer night.

I dozed. I had sat down, placing my chin on my chest, the palms of my hands against my ribs, like some fakir who has vowed to remain in that position forever. Now and then I tried to warm my knees with my breath. I listened, and heard only the mewing of a cat on a neighboring roof. It yowled first with the thin cry of a child and then with that of a woman in labor. I don't know how long I slept—perhaps a minute, perhaps twenty. My mind became empty. My worries vanished. I found myself in a graveyard where children were playing—they had come out of their graves. Among them was a tiny girl in a pleated skirt. Through her blond curls, boils could be seen on her skull. I knew who she was, Jochebed, our neighbor's daughter at 10 Krochmalna Street, who had caught scarlet fever and had been carried out to a children's hearse one morning. The hearse was drawn by a single horse and had many compartments that looked like drawers. Some of the children danced in a circle, others played on swings. It was a recurring dream which began in my childhood. The children, seeming to know that they were dead, neither talked nor sang. Their yellowish faces wore that otherworld melancholy revealed only in dreams.

I heard a rustling and then felt someone's touch. Opening my eyes, I saw Dosha wearing a housecoat and slippers. She was carrying my clothes. My suspenders dragged along the rooftop together with a sleeve of my jacket. She put my shoes down and, placing her finger on her lips, indicated silence. She grimaced and stuck out her tongue in mockery. She backed away and, to my amazement, opened a trapdoor leading to the stairway. I almost stepped on my glasses, which had fallen out of my pocket. In my confusion, I wasn't aware of Dosha leaving. I saw a booklet lying near me—my American passport. I began to search for my money, my traveler's checks. I dressed quickly, and in my haste I put my jacket on inside out. My legs became shaky. I climbed through the trapdoor and found myself on the steps.

On the ground floor, I found the door chained and locked. I tried to force it like a thief. At last, the latch opened. Having closed it quietly behind me, I walked rapidly away, without once looking back at the house where I had so recently been imprisoned.

I came to an alley which seemed to be newly constructed because it was not yet paved. I followed whatever street I came to just to get as far away as possible. I walked and I talked to myself. I stopped an elderly passer-by, addressing him in English, and he said to me, "Speak Hebrew," and then showed me how to reach my hotel. There was fatherly reproach in his eyes, embedded in shadow, as if he knew me and had guessed my plight. He vanished before I could thank him.

I remained where he left me, meditating on what had happened. As I stood alone in the stillness, shivering in the cold of dawn, I felt something moving in the cuff of my pants. I bent down, and saw a huge beetle which ran out and disappeared in an instant. Was it the same beetle I had seen on the roof? Entrapped in my clothes, it had managed to free itself. We had both been granted another chance by the powers that rule the universe.

I · B · S

The Betrayer of Israel

WHAT could be better than to stand on a balcony and be able to see all of Krochmalna Street (the part where the Jews lived) from Gnoyna to Ciepla and even farther, to Iron Street, where there were trolley cars! A day never passed, not even an hour, when something did not happen. One moment a thief was caught and then Itcha Meyer, the drunkard— the husband of Esther from the candy store—became wild and danced in the middle of the gutter. Someone got sick and an ambulance was called. A fire broke out in a house and the firemen, wearing brass hats and high rubber boots, came with their galloping horses. I stood on the balcony that summer afternoon in my long gaberdine, a velvet cap over my red hair, with two disheveled sidelocks, waiting for something more to happen. Meanwhile, I observed the stores across the street, their customers, and also the Square, which teamed with pickpockets, loose girls, and vendors running a lottery. You pulled a number from a bag, and if good luck was with you, you could win three colored pencils, or a rooster made of sugar with a comb of chocolate, or a cardboard clown that shook his arms and legs if you pulled a string. Once a Chinaman with a pigtail passed the street. In an instant it became black with people. Another time a dark-skinned man appeared in a red turban with a tassel, wearing a cloak that resembled a prayer shawl, with sandals on his bare feet. I learned later that he was a Jew from Persia, from the town of Shushan—the ancient capital where King Ahasuerus, Queen Esther, and the wicked Haman lived.

Since I was the rabbi's boy, everybody on the street knew me. When you stand on a balcony you are afraid of no one. You are like a general. When an enemy of mine passed I could spit on his cap and all he could do was shake a fist and call me names. Even the policeman didn't look so tall and mighty from above. Flies with violet bellies, bees and butterflies landed on the rail of the balcony. I tried to catch them or I just admired them. How did they manage to fly to Krochmalna Street, and where did they get their flamboyant colors? I had tried to read an article about Darwin in the Yiddish newspaper but I hardly understood it.

Suddenly a tumult broke out again. Two policemen were leading a little man, and screaming women ran after him. To my amazement, they all entered our gate. I could barely believe it: the policemen led this little man to our home, into my father's courtroom. He was accompanied by Shmuel Smetena, an unofficial lawyer, a crony of both the thieves and the police. Shmuel knew Russian and often served the Jews of the street as an interpreter between them and the authorities. I soon discovered what had happened. That little man, Koppel Mitzner, a peddler of old clothes, was the husband of four wives. One lived on Krochmalna Street, one on Smocza Street, one on Praga, and one on Wola. It took quite a while for my father to orient himself to the situation. The senior policeman, with a golden insignia on his cap, explained that Koppel Mitzner had not married the women legally, with a license from the magistrate, but only according to Jewish law. The government could hardly prosecute him since the women had only Jewish marriage contracts, not Russian certificates. Koppel Mitzner contended that they were not his wives but his lovers. On the other hand, the officials could not allow him to break the law without punishment. So the head of the police had ordered the culprit brought to the rabbi. How strange that I, a mere boy, caught on to all these complications more quickly than my father. He was busy with his volumes of the Talmud and commentaries when Koppel, his wives, and the whole crowd of curious men and women burst into our apartment. Some of them laughed, others rebuked Koppel. My father, a small man, frail, wearing a long robe and with a velvet skullcap above his high forehead, his eyes blue, and his beard red, reluctantly put away pen and paper on his lectern. He sat down at the head of the table and asked others to be seated. Some sat on chairs, others on a long bench along the wall, which was lined to the ceiling with books. Between the windows stood the Ark of the Holy Scrolls with its gilded cornice, on which two lions held the tablets with the Ten Commandments between their curled tongues.

I listened to every word and observed each face. Koppel Mitzner, as small as a cheder boy, skin and bones, had a narrow face, a long nose, and a pointed Adam's apple. On his tiny chin grew a sparse little beard the color of straw. He wore a checked jacket and a shirt which closed at the collar with an ornate brass button. He had no lips, only a crevice of a mouth. He smiled cunningly and tried to outscream the others with his thin voice. He pretended that the whole event was nothing but a joke or a mistake. When my father finally grasped what Koppel had done, he asked, "How did you dare to commit a sin like this? Don't you know that Rabbi Gershom decreed a penalty of excommunication for polygamy?"

Koppel Mitzner signaled with his index finger for everyone to be quiet. Then he said, "Rabbi, first of all, I didn't marry them of my own free will. They caught me in a trap. A hundred times I told them I had a wife, but they attached themselves to me like leeches. The fact that I didn't end up in the insane asylum on Bonifrate Street proves that I'm stronger than iron. Second, I need not to be more pious than our patriarch Jacob. If Jacob could marry four wives, I am allowed to have ten, perhaps even a thousand, like King Solomon. I also happen to know that the ruling of Rabbi Gershom was made for one thousand years, and nine hundred of those thousand have already passed. Only one hundred years are left. I take the punishment upon myself. You, Rabbi, will not roast in my Gehenna."

There was an uproar of laughter. A few of the young men applauded. My father clutched his beard. "What will happen a hundred years from now we cannot know. For the time being the ruling of Rabbi Gershom is valid and the one who breaks it is a betrayer of Israel."

"Rabbi, I did not steal, I did not swindle. Rich Hasidim go bankrupt twice a year and then travel to their rabbi on holidays and sit at his table. When I buy something I pay cash. I don't owe anybody a penny. I provide for four Jewish daughters and nine good children."

His wives tried to interrupt Koppel but the police did not let them. Shmuel Smetena translated Koppel's words into Russian. Even though I did not understand the language it occurred to me that he shortened Koppel's arguments—he gesticulated, winked, and it seemed he did not want the Russians to understand all of Koppel's defenses. Shmuel Smetena was tall, fat, with a red neck. He wore a corduroy jacket with gilded buttons and on his vest a watch chain made of silver rubles. The uppers of his boots shone like lacquer. I kept glancing at Koppel's wives. The one from Krochmalna Street was short, broad like a Sabbath stew pot, and she had a potato nose and a huge bosom. She seemed to be the oldest of the lot. Her wig was disheveled and as black as soot. She cried and wiped the tears with her apron. She pointed a thick finger with a broken nail at Koppel, calling him criminal, pig, murderer, lecher. She warned him that she would break his ribs.

One of the women looked as young as a girl. She wore a straw hat with a green band and carried a purse with a brass clasp. Her red cheeks were like those of the streetwalkers who stood at the gates and waited for guests. I heard her say, "He is a liar, the greatest cheat in the whole world. He has promised me the moon and the stars. Such a faker and braggart you cannot find in the whole of Warsaw. If he will not divorce me this very moment he must rot in prison. I have six brothers and each of them can make mincemeat out of him."

As she said these angry words, her eyes smiled and she showed dimples. She seemed lovely to me. She opened her purse, took out a sheet of paper, and shoved it in front of my father's face. "Here is my marriage contract."

The third woman was short, blond, older than the one with the straw hat but much younger than the one from Krochmalna Street. She said she was a cook in the Jewish hospital, where she had met Koppel Mitzner. He introduced himself to her as Morris Kelzer. He came to the hospital because he suffered from severe headaches and Dr. Frankel told him to remain two days for observation. The woman said to my father, "Now I understand why his head ached. If I had cooked up such a kasha as he did, my head would have ruptured and I would have lost my mind ten times a day."

The fourth woman had red hair, a face full of freckles, and eyes as green as gooseberries. I noticed a golden tooth on the side of her mouth. Her mother, who wore a bonnet with beads and ribbons, sat on the bench, screaming each time her daughter's name was mentioned. The latter tried to quiet her by giving her smelling salts, which are used on Yom Kippur for those who are neither strong enough to fast nor willing to break the fast. I heard the daughter say, "Mother, crying and wailing won't help. We have got into a mess and we must get out of it."

"There is a God, there is," the old woman screeched. "He waits long, but He punishes severely. He will see our shame and disgrace and pass judgment. Such an evildoer, such a whoremonger, such a beast!"

Her head fell back as if she was about to faint. The daughter rushed to the kitchen and returned with a wet towel. She rubbed the old woman's temples with it. "Mother, come to yourself. Mother, Mother, Mother!"

The old woman woke up with a start, and began to yell again. "People, I'm dying!"

"Here, swallow this." The daughter pushed a pill between her empty gums.

After a while the policemen left, ordering Koppel Mitzner to appear at police headquarters the next day, and Shmuel Smetena began to scold Koppel. "How can a man, especially a businessman, do something like this?" My father told Koppel that he must divorce the three other wives without delay and keep the original wife, the one from Krochmalna Street. Father requested that the women approach the table, and he asked them if they agreed to a divorce. But somehow they did not answer clearly. Koppel had six children with the wife from Krochmalna Street, two with the cook from the Jewish Hospital, and one with the redhead. Only with the youngest one did he have no children. By now I had learned the names of the women. The one from Krochmalna Street was called Trina Leah, the cook Gutsha, the redhead Naomi. The youngest one had a Gentile name, Pola. Usually when people came for a Din Torah—a judgment—Father made a compromise. If one litigant sued for twenty rubles and the other denied owing anything, my father's verdict would be to pay ten. But what kind of compromise could be made in this case? Father shook his head and sighed. From time to time he glanced toward his books and manuscripts. He disliked being disturbed in his studies. He nodded to me as if to say, "See where the Evil One can lead those who forsake the Torah."

After much haggling Father sent the women to the kitchen to discuss their grievances and the financial details with my mother. She was more experienced than he in worldly matters. She had peered into the courtroom once or twice and threw Koppel a look of disdain. The women immediately rushed into the kitchen and I followed. My mother, taller than my father, lean, sickly white, with a sharp nose and large gray eyes, was, as always, reading some Hebrew morality book. She wore a white kerchief over her blond wig. I heard her say to Koppel's wives, "Divorce him. Run away from him like from the fire. I should be forgiven for my words, but what did you see in him? A debaucher!"

Gutsha the cook replied, "Rebbetzin, it's easy to divorce a man, but we have two children. It's true that what he pays for their support is a pittance but it's still better than nothing. Once we divorce, he will be as free as a bird. A child needs shoes, a little skirt, underpants. Well, and what should I tell them when they grow up? He used to come on Saturdays only, still to the girls he was Daddy. He brought them candy, a toy, a cookie. And he pretended to love them."

"Didn't you know that he had a wife?" my mother asked.

Gutsha hesitated for a while. "In the beginning I didn't know, and when I found out it was already too late. He said he didn't live with his wife, and they would be divorced any day. He dazzled me and bewitched me. He's a smooth talker, a sly fox."

"She knew, the whore, she knew!" Trina Leah called out. "When a man visits a woman on the Sabbath only, he's as kosher as pork. She's no better than he is. People like her only want to grab other women's husbands. She's a slut, an outcast." And Trina Leah spat in Gutsha's face.

Gutsha wiped off her face with a handkerchief. "She should spit blood and pus."

"Really, I cannot understand," my mother said to the women and to herself. Then she added, "Perhaps he could be ordered to pay for the children by the law of the Gentiles."

"Rebbetzin," Gutsha said, "if a man has a heart for his children, he doesn't need to be forced. This one came every week with a different excuse. He doled out the few guldens like alms. Today the policemen came to the hospital and took me away as if I were a lawbreaker. My enemies rejoiced at my downfall. I left my children with a nurse who must leave at four o'clock and then they will be alone."

"In that case, go home at once," my mother said. "Something will be done. There is still a remnant of order in the world."

"No order whatsoever. I dug my own grave. I must have been insane. I deserve all the blows I'm getting. I'm ready to die, but who will take care of my darlings? It is not their fault."

"She's as much of a mother as I'm a countess," Trina Leah hollered. "Bitch, leper, hoodlum!"

I had great compassion for Gutsha; nevertheless, I was curious about the men, and I ran back to the room where they were arguing. I heard Shmuel Smetena say, "Listen to me, Koppel. No matter what you say, the children should not be the victims. You will have to provide for them, and if not the Russians will put you into the cage for three years and no one would bat an eyelid. No lawyer would take a case like this. If you fall into a rage and stab someone, the judge may be lenient. But what you did day in and day out was not the act of a human being."

"I will pay, I will pay—don't be so holier-than-thou," Koppel said. "These are my children, and they will not have to go begging. Rabbi, if you permit me, I will swear on the Holy Scroll." And Koppel pointed to the Ark.

"Swear? God forbid!" Father replied. "First you have to sign a paper that you will obey my judgment and fulfill your obligations to your children. Woe is me!" My father changed his tone. "How long does a man live altogether? Is it worth losing the world to come because of such evil passions? What becomes of the body after death? It's eaten up by the worms. As long as one breathes, one can still repent. In the grave there is no longer free choice."

"Rabbi, I'm ready to fast and to do penances. I have one explanation: I lost my senses. A demon or evil spirit entered me. I got entangled like a fly in a spider's web. I'm afraid people will take revenge on me and no one will enter my store any more."

"Jews have mercy," my father said. "If you repent with all your heart, no one will persecute you."

"Absolutely true," Shmuel Smetena agreed.

I left the men and went back to the kitchen. The old woman, Naomi's mother, was saying, "Rebbetzin, I didn't like him from the very beginning. I took one look at him and I said, 'Naomi, run from him like from the pest. He's not going to divorce his wife. First let him divorce her,' I said, 'then we will see.' My dear lady, we are not just people from the gutter. My late husband, Naomi's father, was a Hasid. Naomi was an honest girl. She became a seamstress to support me. But he has a quick tongue that spouts sweet words. The more he tried to please me with his flattery, the more I recognized what a serpent he was. But my daughter is a fool. If you tell her that there is a horse fair in Heaven, she wants to go up and buy a horse there. She had bad luck in addition. She was married and became a widow after three months. Her husband, a giant of a man, fell down like a tree. Woe what I have lived to see in my old age. I wish I had died a long time ago. Who needs me? I just spoil bread."

"Don't say this. When God tells us to live, we must live," my mother said.

"What for? People sneer at us. When she told me that she was pregnant from that mooncalf I grabbed her hair and . . . People, I'm dying!"

That day, all three women agreed to divorce Koppel Mitzner. The divorce proceedings were to take place in our house. Koppel signed a paper and gave my father an advance of five rubles. Father had already written down the names of the three women. The name Naomi was a good Jewish name. Gutsha was a diminutive of Gutte, which used to be Tovah. But what kind of name was Pola? My father looked the name up in a book with the title *People's Names*, but there was no Pola there. He asked me to bring Isaiah the scribe and they talked it over. Isaiah had much experience in such matters. He told my father that he drew a circle in a notebook each time he wrote a divorce paper and recently his son counted over eight hundred such circles. "According to the law," Isaiah said, "a Gentile name is acceptable in a divorce paper."

Naomi was supposed to be divorced first. The ritual ceremony was to take place on Sunday. But that Sunday neither Koppel nor his wives showed up. The news spread on Krochmalna Street that Koppel Mitzner had vanished together with his youngest wife, Pola. He deserted the three other wives, and they would never be permitted to remarry. Where he and Pola went, no one knew, but it was believed that they had run away to Paris or to New York. "Where else," Mother said, "would charlatans like these run to?"

She gave me an angry look as if suspecting that I envied Koppel his journey, and, who knows, perhaps even his companion. "What are you doing in the kitchen?" she cried. "Go back to your book. Such depravities are not for you!"

The Psychic Journey

I

IT happened like this. I stood one hot day uptown on Broadway before a fenced-in plot of grass and began to throw food to the pigeons. The pigeons knew me, and ordinarily when they saw me with my bag of seed they surrounded me. The police had told me it was forbidden to feed pigeons outdoors, but that was as far as they went. One time a huge cop even came up to me and said, "Why is it everybody brings food for the pigeons and no one stops to think that they might need a drink? It hasn't rained in New York for weeks, and pigeons are dying of thirst." To hear this from a policeman was quite an experience! I went straight home and brought out a bowl of water, but half of it spilled in the elevator and the pigeons spilled the rest.

This day, on my way to the fenced-in plot I noticed the new issue of *The Unknown* at a newspaper stand and I bought a copy, since the magazine was snatched up in my neighborhood almost as soon as it appeared. For some reason, many readers on uptown Broadway are interested in telepathy, clairvoyance, psychokinesis, and the immortality of the soul.

For once, the pigeons did not crowd around me. I looked up and saw that a few steps away stood a woman who was also throwing out handfuls of grain. I started to laugh—under her arm she carried a copy of the new issue of *The Unknown*. Despite the hot summer day, she was wearing a black dress and a black, broad-brimmed hat. Her shoes and stockings were black. She must be a foreigner, I thought; no American would dress in such clothes in this weather, not even to attend a funeral. She raised her head and I saw a face that seemed young—or, at least, not old. She was lean and swarthy, with a narrow nose, a long chin, and thin lips.

Translated by Joseph Singer

I said, "Competition, eh?"

She smiled, showing long false teeth, but her black eyes remained stern. She said, "Don't worry, sir. There will be more pigeons. Enough for us both. Here they are now!" She pointed prophetically to the sky.

Yes, a whole flock was flying in from downtown. The plot grew so full that the birds hopped and fluttered to force their way to the food. Pigeons, like Ḥasidim, enjoy jostling each other.

When our bags were emptied, we walked over to the litter can. "After you," I said, and I added, "I see we read the same magazine."

She replied in a deep voice and a foreign accent, "I've seen you often feeding the pigeons, and I want you to know that those who feed pigeons never know need. The few cents you spend on these lovely birds will bring you lots of luck."

"How can you be sure of that?"

She began to explain, and we walked away together. I invited her to have a drink with me and she said, "Gladly, but I don't drink alcoholic beverages, only fruit juices and vegetable juices."

"Come. Since you read *The Unknown*, you're one of my people."

"Yes, my greatest interest is in the occult. I read similar publications from England, Canada, Australia, India. I used to read them back in Hungary, where I come from, but today for believing in the higher powers over there you go to jail. Is there such a magazine in Hebrew?"

"Are you Jewish?"

"On my mother's side, but for me separate races and religions don't exist, only the one species of man. We lost the sources of our spiritual energy, and this has given rise to a disharmony in our psychic evolution. The divisions are the result. When we emit waves of brotherliness, reciprocal help, and peace, these vibrations create a sense of identification among all of God's creatures. You saw how the pigeons flew in. They congregate around the Central Savings Bank on Broadway and Seventy-third Street, which is too far for pigeons to see what's happening in the Eighties. But the cosmic consciousness within them is in perfect balance and therefore . . ."

We had gone into a coffee shop that was air-conditioned, and we sat down in a booth. She introduced herself as Margaret Fugazy.

"It's remarkable," she said. "I've observed that you always feed the pigeons at one o'clock when you go out for lunch, while I feed them in the mornings. I fed them as usual this morning. All of a sudden a voice ordered me to feed them again. Now, at six o'clock pigeons aren't particularly eager to eat. They're starting to adjust to their nightly rhythm. The days are growing shorter and we're in another constellation of the solar cycle. But when a voice repeats the same admonition over and over, this is a message from the world powers. I came out and found you too about to feed the pigeons. How is it you were late?"

"I also heard a voice."

"Are you psychic?"

"I was only fooling."

"You mustn't fool about such things!"

After three-quarters of an hour, I had heard a lot of particulars. Margaret Fugazy had come to the United States in the nineteen-fifties. Her father had been a doctor; her parents were no longer living. Here in New York she had grown close to a woman who was past ninety, a medium, and half blind. They had lived together for a time. The old lady had died at the age of a hundred and two, and now Margaret supported herself by giving courses in Yoga, concentration, mind stimulation, bio-rhythm, awareness, and the I Am.

She said, "I watched you feeding the pigeons a long time before I learned that you're a writer and a vegetarian. I started reading you. This led to a telepathic communication between us, even if it has been one-sided. I went so far as to visit you at home several times—not physically but in astral form. I would have liked to catch your attention, but you were sound asleep. I leave my body usually around dawn. I found you awake only once and you spoke to me about the mysteries of the Cabala. When I had to go back I gave you a kiss."

"You know my address?"

"The astral body has no need of addresses!"

Neither of us spoke for a time. Then Margaret said, "You might give me your phone number. These astral visits involve terrible dangers. If the silver cord should break, then—"

She didn't finish, apparently in fear of her own words.

II

On my way home at one o'clock that morning, I told myself I could not risk getting mixed up with Margaret Fugazy. My stomach hurt from the soybeans, raw carrots, molasses, sunflower seeds, and celery juice she had served me for supper. My head ached from her advice on how to avoid spiritual tension, how to control dreams, and how to send out alpha rays of relaxation and beta rays of intellectual activity and theta rays of trance. It's all Dora's fault, I brooded. If she hadn't left me and run off to the kibbutz where her daughter Sandra was having her first baby, I'd be together with her now in a hotel in pollen-free Bethlehem, New Hampshire, instead of suffering from hay fever in polluted New York. True, Dora had begged me to accompany her to Israel, but I had no intention of sitting in some forsaken kibbutz near the Syrian border waiting for Sandra to give birth.

I was afraid walking the few blocks from Columbus Avenue and Ninety-sixth Street to my studio apartment in the West Eighties, but no taxi would stop for me. Riding up in the elevator, I was assailed by fears. Maybe I had been burglarized while I was away? Maybe out of spite for not finding any money or jewelry the thieves had torn up my manuscripts? I opened the door and was struck by a wave of heat. I had neglected to lower the venetian blinds and the sun had baked the apartment all day. No one had cleaned here since Dora left, and the dust started me sneezing. I undressed and lay down, but I couldn't fall asleep. My nose was stuffed up, my throat scratchy, and my ears felt full of water. My anger at Dora grew, and in fantasy I worked out all kinds of revenges against her. Maybe marry this Hungarian miracle worker and send Dora a cable announcing the good tidings.

Day was dawning by the time I dropped off. I was wakened by the phone ringing. The clock on the bedside table showed twenty past ten. I picked up the receiver and grunted, "*Nu?*"

I heard a deep female voice. "I woke you, eh? It's Margaret, Margaret Fugazy. Morris—may I call you Morris?"

"You can even call me Potiphar."

"Oh, listen to him! What I want to say is that this morning a sign has been given that our meeting yesterday wasn't simply some coincidence but an act of fate, ordained and executed by the hand of Providence. First let me tell you that after you left me I was deeply worried about you. You promised me to take a cab but I knew—don't ask me how—that you didn't. Just before daybreak I found myself in your apartment again. What a mess. The dust! And when I saw your pale face and heard your choked breathing I decided that you absolutely cannot remain in the city. On the other hand, it would not be good that our relationship should start off with a long separation. Well, early this morning an old friend of mine called—Lily Wolfner, also a Hungarian. I hadn't heard from her in over a year, but last night before going to sleep I suddenly thought about her and this to me is always a signal I will soon be hearing from that individual. Precisely at nine my phone rang, and I was so sure I answered with 'Hello, Lily.' Lily Wolfner is a travel agent. She arranges tours to Europe, Africa, Japan, and Israel, too. Her tours always have a cultural program. The guides are psychologists, psychiatrists, writers, artists, rabbis. I was twice the guide of such tours interested in psychic research, and some other time I'll tell you of my remarkable experiences with them.

"I said, 'Lily, what made you think of me?' and she told me she had a group that wanted to combine a visit to the State of Israel on the High Holidays with an advanced course in awareness. She offered me the job as guide. I don't remember how, but I mentioned your name to her and the fact that you had promised to give me an esoteric insight into the Cabala. I beg you, don't interrupt me. As soon as she heard your name, she became simply hysterical. 'What? He really exists? He lives right here in New York City and you had supper with him?' I'll cut it short— she proposed that we both be guides for this tour. She'll accede to your every demand. These are rich women, many of them probably your readers. I told her I'd speak with you, but first she had to check with the women. A half hour didn't go by when she called me back. She had already reached her clients and they were as excited by the idea as she was. My dear, one would have to be blind not to see the hand of destiny in all this. Lily is a businesswoman, not some mystic, but she told me that you and I together would make a fantastic pair! I want you to know that in the past months I've faced deep crises in my life—spiritual, physical, financial. I was closer to suicide than you can imagine. When I came up next to you yesterday, I knew somehow that my life was in your hands, strange as this may sound. I beg you therefore and plead on my knees—don't say no, because this would be my death sentence. Literally."

Margaret had not let me get a word in edgewise. I wanted to tell her that I wasn't a specialist in the Cabala and that I had no urge to wander around Israel with a flock of women who would try to combine sightseeing with mysticism, but somehow I hesitated, bewildered by my own weakness.

Margaret exclaimed, "Morris, wait for me. I'm coming to you!"

"Astrally?" I asked.

"Cynic! With my body and soul!"

III

Who said it—perhaps no one: every person's drama is a melodrama. I both performed in this melodrama and observed it as a spectator.

I sat in an air-conditioned bus speeding from Haifa to Tel Aviv. We had spent Rosh Hashanah in Jerusalem. We had visited Sodom, Elath, Safad, the occupied regions around the Suez Canal and the Golan Heights, a number of kibbutzim. Wherever we stopped, I lectured about the Cabala and Margaret gave advice on love, health, and business; on how to use the subconscious for buying stocks, betting on horses, finding jobs, husbands; on how to meditate. She spoke about the delta of the brain waves and the resonance of the Tantrist personality, the dimensions of the Shambala and the panorama of cybertronic evocations. She conducted astrochemical analyses, showed how to locate the third eye, the pineal eye, revealed the mysteries of Lemuria and Mt. Shasta. I attended séances at which she hypnotized the ladies, most of whom went to sleep—or at least pretended to. She swore that my mother had revealed herself to her and urged her to keep an eye on me; I had been born a Sagittarian and a Scorpio might start a fatal conflict with me.

I was enmeshed in a situation that made me ashamed of myself. Thank God, until now I hadn't met Dora or anyone else I knew, but the tour was to be in Israel almost another full week. It could easily happen that someone might recognize me. Also, the group had become quarrelsome—disappointed in the hotels, the meals, the merchandise for sale in the gift shops—and increasingly critical of its guides. Many had turned cool toward Margaret and her lessons, and their enthusiasm for the Cabala had diminished. One woman suggested that my interpretation of the Cabala was too subjective and was actually a kind of poetic hodgepodge.

According to schedule, we were to stop over a few days in Tel Aviv to give the women time to shop. They would observe Yom Kippur in Jerusalem and on the next day fly from Lod airport for America. I had intended to surprise Dora at the end of the tour, and before leaving New York I had demanded from Lily Wolfner an open ticket so that I would not have to return with the group. I told her I had some literary business to take care of in Israel. To avoid complications, I had not mentioned this to Margaret.

Following breakfast on the day before the group was to go to Jerusalem to pray at the Wailing Wall, I had to reveal my secret. I wanted to remain in Tel Aviv for the holiday, at the very hotel where we were now registered. I was weary from the constant traveling and the company of others, and I yearned for a day by myself.

I had been prepared for resentment, but not for the scene that Margaret kicked up. She wept, accused Lily Wolfner and me of hatching a plot against her, and threatened me with retributions by the higher powers. A mighty catastrophe would befall me for my duplicity.

Suddenly she cried, "If you stay in Tel Aviv I'm staying, too! I don't have to pray at the holy places on Yom Kippur. My job is finished as much as yours is!"

"You must go along with the group; otherwise you'll forfeit your ticket," I pointed out to her.

"The morning after Yom Kippur I'll take a taxi to Lod straight from here."

When the women heard that their two guides would be in Tel Aviv for Yom Kippur, they made sarcastic remarks, but there was no time for lengthy explanations; the bus was waiting in front of the hotel. Margaret assured the women that she would meet them at the airport early on the day after Yom Kippur, and she saw them off. I was too embarrassed even to apologize. I had done damage not only to my own prestige but to the Cabala's as well.

Afterward, I showed Margaret my contract, which stated that my job had ended the night before; I had every right to stay on in Israel for as long as I wanted.

Margaret refused to look at it. "You've got some female here," she pronounced, "but your plans will come to naught!" She pointed a finger at me, mumbled, and I sensed that she was trying to bring the powers of evil down upon me. Baffled by my own superstition, I tried to soothe her with promises, but she told me she had lost all trust in me and called me vile names. When she finally went off to unpack her things, I used the time trying to call the kibbutz near the Golan Heights where Dora was staying. I wasn't able to make the connection.

So many guests had gone to Jerusalem that no preparations for the pre-holiday feast were being made at the hotel. Margaret and I had to find a restaurant. Although I am not a synagogue-goer, I do fast on Yom Kippur.

"I will fast with you," Margaret announced when I told her. "If God has chosen to castigate me with such humiliations, I have surely sinned grievously."

"You say you're half a Gentile, yet you carry on like a complete yenta," I chided her.

"I'm more Jewish in my smallest fingernail than you are in your whole being."

We had in mind to buy provisions to fill up on before commencing our fast, but by the time we finished lunch the stores were closed. The streets were deserted. Even the American Embassy, which stood not far from the hotel, appeared festively silent. Margaret came into my room and we went onto the balcony to gaze out to sea. The sun bowed to the west. The beach was empty. Large birds I had never seen before walked on the sand. Whatever intimacy had existed between Margaret and me had been severed; we were like a married couple that has already decided on a divorce. We leaned away from each other as we watched the setting sun cast fiery nets across the waves.

Margaret's swarthy face grew brick-red, and her black eyes exuded the melancholy of those who estrange themselves from their own environment and can never be at home in another. She said, "The air here is full of ghosts."

I V

That evening we stayed up late over the Ouija board, which told one woeful prophecy after another. From sheer boredom, or perhaps once and for all to end our false relationship, I confessed to Margaret the truth about Dora. She was too weary to make a scene all over again.

The next morning we went for a walk—along Ben-Yehuda Street; on Rothschild Boulevard. We considered going into a synagogue, but those we passed were packed with worshippers. Men stood outside in their prayer shawls. Around ten o'clock we returned to the hotel. We had talked ourselves out, and I lay down to read a book on Houdini, who I had always considered possessed mysterious powers despite the fact that he opposed the spiritists. Margaret sat at the table and dealt tarot cards. From time to time she arched her brows and gave me a dismal look. Then she said that because of my treachery she had had no sleep the night before, and she left to go to her room. She warned me not to disturb her.

In the middle of the day I heard a long-drawn-out siren, and I wondered at the military's conducting tests on Yom Kippur. I had had nothing to eat since two the afternoon before and I was hungry. I read, napped, and indulged in a bit of Day of Atonement introspection. All my life I had chased after pleasure, but my sweethearts became too serious and acquired the bitterness of neglected wives. This last journey had degraded and exhausted me. Not even my hay fever had been alleviated.

I fell asleep and wakened after the sun had set. According to my reckoning, the Jews in the synagogues would be concluding the services. One star appeared in the sky and soon a second and then a third, when it is permitted to break the fast. The door opened and Margaret slithered in like a phantom. We had fasted not twenty-four hours but thirty. Margaret looked haggard. We took the elevator down. The lobby was half dark, the glass door at the entrance covered by a black sheet. Behind the desk sat an elderly man who didn't look like a hotel employee. He was reading an old Yiddish newspaper. I went over to him and asked, "Why is it so quiet?"

He looked up with annoyance. "What do you want—that there should be dancing?"

"Why is it so dark?"

The man scratched his beard. "Are you playing dumb or what? The country is at war."

He explained. The Egyptians had crossed the Suez Canal, the Syrians had invaded the Golan Heights. Margaret must have understood some Yiddish, for she cried, "I knew it! The punishment!"

I opened the front door and we went out. Yarkon Street lay wrapped in darkness; every window was draped in sheets. Far from the usual gay end of Yom Kippur in Tel Aviv, when restaurants and movie houses are jammed, it was more like the night of the ninth day of Ab in some Polish shtetl. Headlights of the few cars that moved by slowly were either turned off or covered with blue paint. We walked the few steps to Ben-Yehuda Street hoping to buy food, but the stores were closed. We went back to my room and Margaret discovered a radio set into the night table. The news was all of war; civilian communication had been suspended. The armed forces had been mobilized. The broadcaster appealed to the people not to give in to panic. I found a bag of cookies and two apples in my valise, and Margaret and I broke our fast. Margaret had engaged a taxi to take her to Lod airport at five this coming morning, but would the taxi come? And would there be a plane leaving for America? Based on the news from the Golan front, I had a feeling that the kibbutz where Dora was now lay in Arab hands. Who knew if Dora was alive? There was a possibility that the Syrians or Egyptians would reach Tel Aviv tomorrow. Margaret urged me to go with her to Lod if the taxi showed up, but I wasn't about to while away my days and nights at an airport where thousands of tourists would have congregated from every corner of the land.

Margaret asked, "And to perish here would be better?"

"Yes, better."

We listened to the radio until two o'clock. Margaret seemed to be more shocked by what she called my base conspiracy than by the war. Her only comfort, she told me, was the fact that she had known it in the depths of her soul. She now forecast that Dora and I would never meet again. She even maintained that this war was one of the calamities Providence had prepared for me. Since time is an illusion and all events are predetermined, she argued, judgment often precedes the transgression. Her life was filled with examples—enemies prevented from accomplishing their evil aims by circumstances her guardian angel had arranged months or years in advance. Those who did succeed in hurting her were later killed, maimed, or afflicted with insanity. Before going to her room, Margaret said she would pray that I be forgiven. She kissed me good night. She hinted that though the Day of Atonement was over, the doors of repentance were left open to me.

I had fallen into a deep sleep. I opened my eyes as someone shook my shoulder. It was dark, and for a moment I didn't know where I was or who was waking me.

I heard Margaret say in a solemn voice, "The taxi is here!"

"What taxi? Oh!"

"Come with me!"

"No, Margaret, I'm staying here."

"In that case, be well. Forgive me!"

She kissed me with rusty lips. Her breath smelled of the fast. She closed the door behind her and I knew that we had parted forever. Only after she had gone did I realize the motives behind my decision. I didn't have a reservation, as she had, but an open ticket. Besides, I had told the women of the tour that I would be staying on; it would not be right in their eyes or mine to flee like a coward. Once, Dora and I had toyed with the notion that we were stranded together on a sinking ship. The other passengers screamed, wept, and fought to get to the lifeboats, but she and I lingered in the dining hall with a bottle of wine. We would relish our happiness and go under rather than push, scramble, and beg for a bit of life. Now this fantasy had assumed a tinge of reality.

It was dawn. The sun had not yet risen, but several men and women were performing calisthenics on the beach. In the dim light they looked like shadows. I wanted to laugh at these optimists who were developing their muscles on the day before their deaths.

I thrust my hand into the pocket of my jacket hanging on the chair and tapped my passport and traveler's checks. I had had no special reason to bring along a large amount of money, but I had—more than two thousand dollars in traveler's checks and a bankbook besides. No one had stolen them, and I went back to bed to catch up on my sleep. I had a number of acquaintances in Tel Aviv and some who could even be described as friends, but I was determined to show myself to nobody. What could I say I was doing there? When had I arrived? It would only entangle me in new lies. I turned on the radio. The enemy was advancing and our casualties were severe. Other Arab nations were preparing to invade.

I tried again to put through a call to Dora's kibbutz and was told that this was impossible. The fact that the telephone and electricity were working and that there was hot water in the bathroom seemed incredible.

I rode in the elevator down to the lobby. The day before, it had been my impression that the hotel was empty, but here were men and women conversing among themselves in English. All the male employees of the hotel had been called up and their places had been taken by women. Breakfast was being served in the dining room. Bakeries had baked rolls during the night—they were still warm from the oven. I ordered an omelette, and the waitress who brought it to me said, "Eat as long as the food is there." Even though the day was bright, I imagined that layers of shadows were falling from above as at the beginning of a solar eclipse. I did not approach the other Americans. I had no urge to speak to them or listen to their comments. Besides, they talked so loudly I could hear them anyhow—at Lod airport, they were saying, people hovered outside with their luggage and no help was available. I could see Margaret among them, murmuring spells, conjuring up the spirits of revenge.

After breakfast I strolled along Ben-Yehuda Street. Trucks full of soldiers roared by. A man with a white beard, wearing a long coat and a rabbinical hat, carried a palm branch and a citron for the Sukkoth holiday. Another old man struggled to erect a Sukkoth on a balcony. Emaciated newspapers had been printed during the night. I bought one, took a table at a sidewalk café, and ordered cake with coffee. All my life I had considered myself timid. I was constantly burdened with worries. I was sure that if I were in New York now reading about what was happening in Israel I would be overcome by anxiety. But everything within me was calm. Overnight I had been transformed into a fatalist. I had brought sleeping pills from America; I also had razor blades I could use to slit my wrists should this situation become desperate. Meanwhile, I nibbled at the cake and drank the thick coffee. A pigeon came up to my chair and I threw it a crumb. This was a Holy Land pigeon—small, brown, slight. It nodded its tiny head as if it were assenting to a truth as old as the very land: If it is fated to live, you live, and if it is fated to die, it's no misfortune, either. Is there such a thing as death? This is something invented by human cowardice.

The day passed in walking aimlessly, reading the book about Houdini, sleeping. The supermarket on Ben-Yehuda Street had opened and was crowded with customers. Waiting lines stretched outside; housewives were buying up everything in sight. But I was able to get stale bread, cheese, and unripe fruit in the smaller stores. During the day, peace seemed to reign, but at night the war returned. Again the city was dark, its streets empty. At the hotel, guests sat in the bar watching television in tense silence. The danger was far from over.

About eleven I rode up to my room and went out onto the balcony. The sea swayed, foamed, purred the muffled growl of a lion that is sated briefly but may grow ferocious any moment. Military jets roared by. The stars seemed ominously near. A cool breeze was blowing. It smelled of tar, sulphur, and Biblical battles that time had never ended. They were all still here, and hosts of Edom and Amalek, Gog and Magog, Ammon and Moab—the lords of Esau and the priests of Baal— waging the eternal war of the idolaters against God and the seed of Jacob. I could hear the clanging of their swords and the din of their chariots. I sat down in a wicker chair and breathed the acrid scent of eternity.

Sirens wailing a long and breathless warning wakened me from a doze. The sound was like the blast of a thousand rams' horns, but I knew that the hotel had no shelter. If bombs fell on this building there would be no rescue. The door to my room opened as if by itself. I went in and sat on my bed, ready to live, ready to die.

V

Eight days later, I flew back to the United States. The following week Dora arrived. How strange, but on Yom Kippur Dora had escaped with her daughter and the newborn baby to Tel Aviv, and they had stayed in a hotel on Allenby Road only a few blocks from my hotel. The circumcision had been performed the day before Sukkoth. I told Dora that I had spent a few weeks as writer-in-residence at some college in California. Dora had the habit of questioning me closely whenever I returned from a trip, probing for contradictions. She believed that my lectures were nothing but a means to meet other women and deceive her. This time she accepted my words without suspicion.

I went back to feeding the pigeons every day, but I never met Margaret. She neither called nor wrote, and as far as I knew she did not visit me astrally.

Then one day in December when I was walking with Dora on Amsterdam Avenue—she was looking for a secondhand bookcase—a young man pushed a leaflet into my hand. Although it was cold and snow was falling, he was coatless and hatless and his shirt collar was open. He looked Spanish to me or Puerto Rican. Usually I refuse to accept such leaflets. But there was something in the young man's appearance that made me take the wet paper—an expression of ardor in his black eyes. This was not just a hired distributor of leaflets but a believer in a cause. I stopped and glanced down to see the name Margaret Fugazy in large letters above her picture as she might have looked twenty years ago. "Are you lovelorn?" I read. "Have you lost a near and dear relative? Are you sick? Do you have business trouble, family trouble? Are you in an inextricable dilemma? Come and see Madame Margaret Fugazy, because she is the only one who can help you. Madame Margaret Fugazy, the famous medium, has studied yoga in India, the Cabala in Jerusalem, specializes in ESP, subliminal prayers, Yahweh power, UFO mysteries, self-hypnosis, cosmic wisdom, spiritual healing, and reincarnation. All consultations private. Results guaranteed. Introductory reading $2."

Dora pulled my sleeve. "Why did you stop? Throw it away."

"Wait, Dora. Where has he gone?" I looked around. The young man had disappeared. Was he waiting just for me?

Dora asked, "Why are you so interested? Who is Margaret Fugazy? Do you know her?"

"Yes, I do," I answered, not understanding why.

"Who is she—one of your witches?"

"Yes, a witch."

"How do you know her? Did you fly with her to a Black Mass on a broomstick?"

"You remember Yom Kippur when you went to the Golan kibbutz? While you were there I flew with her to Jerusalem, to Safad, to Rachel's Tomb, and we studied the Cabala together," I said.

Dora was used to my playful chatter and absurdities. She chimed in, "Is that so? What else?"

"When the war broke out the witch got frightened and flew away."

"She left you alone, eh?"

"Yes, alone."

"Why didn't you come to me? I am something of a witch myself."

"You too had vanished."

"You poor boy. Abandoned by all your witches. But you can get her back. She advertises. Isn't that a miracle?"

We stood there pondering. The snow fell dry and heavy. It hit my face like hail. Dora's dark coat turned white. A single pigeon tried to fly, flapping its wings but falling back. Then Dora said, "That young man seemed strange. He must be a sorcerer. And all this for two dollars! Come, let's go home—by subway, not by psychic journey."

The Manuscript

We sat, shaded by a large umbrella, eating a late breakfast at a sidewalk café on Dizengoff Street in Tel Aviv. My guest—a woman in her late forties, with a head of freshly dyed red hair—ordered orange juice, an omelette, and black coffee. She sweetened the coffee with saccharine, which she plucked with her silvery fingernails from a tiny pillbox covered with mother-of-pearl. I had known her for about twenty-five years —first as an actress in the Warsaw Variety Theater, Kundas; then as the wife of my publisher, Morris Rashkas; and still later as the mistress of my late friend, the writer Menashe Linder. Here in Israel she had married Ehud Hadadi, a journalist ten years younger than herself. In Warsaw, her stage name was Shibtah. Shibtah, in Jewish folklore, is a she-demon who entices yeshiva boys to lechery and steals infants from young mothers who go out alone at night without a double apron—one worn front and back. Her maiden name was Kleinmintz.

In Kundas, when Shibtah sang her salacious songs and recited the monologues which Menashe Linder wrote for her, she made the "very boards burn." The reviewers admired her pretty face, her graceful figure, and her provocative movements. But Kundas did not last longer than two seasons. When Shibtah tried to play dramatic roles, she failed. During the Second World War, I heard that she died somewhere, in the ghetto or a concentration camp. But here she was, sitting across from me, dressed in a white mini-skirt and blouse, wearing large sunglasses and a wide-brimmed straw hat. Her cheeks were rouged, her brows plucked, and she wore bracelets and cameos on both wrists, and many rings on her fingers. From a distance she could have been taken for a young woman, but her neck had become flabby. She called me by a nickname she had given me when we were both young—Loshikl.

She said, "Loshikl, if someone had told me in Kazakhstan that you and I would one day be sitting together in Tel Aviv, I would have thought it a joke. But if one survives, everything is possible. Would you believe that I could stand in the woods sawing logs twelve hours a day? That is what we did, at twenty degrees below zero, hungry, and with our clothes full of lice. By the way, Hadadi would like to interview you for his newspaper."

"With pleasure. Where did he get the name Hadadi?"

"Who knows? They all give themselves names from the Haggadah. His real name is Zeinvel Zylberstein. I myself have already had a dozen names. Between 1942 and 1944, I was Nora Davidovna Stutchkov. Funny, isn't it?"

"Why did you and Menashe part?" I asked.

"Well, I knew that you would ask this question. Loshikl, our story is so strange that I sometimes don't believe it really happened. Since 1939 my life has been one long nightmare. Sometimes I wake up in the middle of the night and I don't remember who I am, what my name is, and who is lying next to me. I reach out for Ehud and he begins to grumble. '*Mah at rotzah?* ('What do you want?') Only when I hear him talk in Hebrew do I recall that I am in the Holy Land."

"Why did you part with Menashe?"

"You really want to hear it?"

"Absolutely."

"No one knows the whole story, Loshikl. But I will tell you everything. To whom else, if not to you? In all my wanderings, not a day passed that I did not think of Menashe. I was never so devoted to anyone as I was to him—and I never will be. I would have gone through fire for him. And this is not just a phrase—I proved it with my deeds. I know that you consider me a frivolous woman. Deep in your heart, you have remained a Hasid. But the most pious woman would not have done a tenth of what I did for Menashe."

"Tell me."

"Oh, well, after you left for America, our few good years began. We knew that a terrible war was approaching and every day was a gift. Menashe read to me everything he wrote. I typed his manuscripts and brought order into his chaos. You know how disorganized he was, he never learned to number his pages. He only had one thing on his mind— women. I had given up the struggle. I said to myself, 'That's how he is and no power can change him.' Just the same, he became more and more attached to me. I had gotten myself a job as a manicurist and was supporting him. You may not believe me, but I cooked for his para- mours. The older he became, the more he had to convince himself that he was still the great Don Juan. Actually, there were times when he was completely impotent. One day he was a giant and the next day he was an invalid. Why did he need all those sleazy creatures? He was nothing but a big child. So it went on until the outbreak of the war. Menashe seldom read a newspaper. He rarely turned on the radio. The war was not a complete surprise to anyone—they were digging trenches and piling up barricades on the Warsaw streets already in July. Even rabbis took shovels and dug ditches. Now that Hitler was about to invade them, the Poles forgot their scores with the Jews and we all became, God help us, one nation. Still, when the Nazis began to bombard us, we were shocked. After you left, I bought some new chairs and a sofa. Our home became a regular *bonbonnière*. Loshikl, disaster came in a matter of minutes. There was an alarm, and soon buildings were crumbling and corpses lay strewn in the gutters. We were told to go into the cellars, but the cellars were no safer than the upper stories. There were women who had sense enough to prepare food, but not I. Menashe went to his room, sat down in his chair, and said, 'I want to die.' I don't know what happened in other houses—our telephone stopped functioning immediately. Bombs exploded in front of our windows. Menashe pulled down the shades and was reading a novel by Alexandre Dumas. All his friends and admirers had vanished. There were rumors that journalists were given a special train—or perhaps special cars on a train—to flee from the city. In a time like this, it was crazy to isolate yourself, but Menashe did not stir from the house until it was announced on the radio that all physically able men should cross the Praga bridge. It was senseless to take luggage because trains were not running and how much can you carry when you go on foot? Of course, I refused to remain in Warsaw and I went with him.

"I forgot to tell you the main thing. After years of doing nothing, in 1938, Menashe suddenly developed an urge to write a novel. His muse had awakened and he wrote a book which was, in my opinion, the best thing he had ever written. I copied it for him, and when I did not like certain passages, he always changed them. It was autobiographical, but not entirely. When the newspapers learned that Menashe was writing a novel, they all wanted to start publishing it. But he had made up his mind not to publish a word until it was finished. He polished each sentence. Some chapters he rewrote three or four times. Its tentative title was *Rungs*—not a bad name since every chapter described a different phase of his life. He had finished only the first part. It would have become a trilogy.

"When it came to packing our few belongings, I asked Menashe, 'Have you packed your manuscripts?' And he said, 'Only *Rungs*. My other works will have to be read by the Nazis.' He carried two small valises and I had thrown some clothes and shoes, as much as I could carry, into a knapsack. We began to walk toward the bridge. In front of us and behind us trudged thousands of men. A woman was seldom seen. It was like a huge funeral procession—and that is what it really was. Most of them died, some from bombs, others at the hands of the Nazis after 1941, and many in Stalin's slave camps. There were optimists who took along heavy trunks. They had to abandon them even before they reached the bridge. Everyone was exhausted from hunger, fear, and lack of sleep. To lighten their loads, people threw away suits, coats, and shoes. Menashe could barely walk, but he carried both valises throughout the night. We were on the way to Bialystok because Stalin and Hitler had divided Poland and Bialystok now belonged to Russia. En route, we met journalists, writers, and those who considered themselves writers. They all carried manuscripts, and even in my despair I felt like laughing. Who needed their writings?

"If I were to tell you how we reached Bialystok, we would have to sit here until tomorrow. Menashe had already discarded one of the valises. Before he did, I opened it to make sure his manuscript wasn't there, God forbid. Menashe had fallen into such a gloom that he stopped talking altogether. He started to sprout a gray beard—he had forgotten his razor. The first thing he did when we finally stopped in a village was to shave. Some towns were already obliterated by the Nazi bombings. Others remained untouched, and life was going on as if there was no war. Strange, but a few young men—readers of Yiddish literature—wanted Menashe to lecture to them on some literary topic. This is how people are—a minute before their death, they still have all the desires of the living. One of these characters even fell in love with me and tried to seduce me. I did not know whether to laugh or cry.

"What went on in Bialystok defies description. Since the city belonged to the Soviets and the dangers of the war were over, those who survived behaved as though they had been resurrected. Soviet–Yiddish writers came from Moscow, from Kharkov, from Kiev, to greet their colleagues from Poland in the name of the party, and Communism became a most precious commodity. The few writers who really had been Communists in Poland became so high and mighty you would think they were about to go to the Kremlin to take over Stalin's job. But even those who had been anti-Communists began to pretend they had always been secret sympathizers or ardent fellow travelers. They all boasted of their proletarian origins. Everyone managed to find an uncle who was a shoemaker; a brother-in-law a coachman; or a relative who went to prison for the cause. Some suddenly discovered that their grandparents were peasants.

"Menashe was, in fact, a son of working people, but he was too proud to boast about it. The Soviet writers accepted him with a certain respect. There was talk of publishing a large anthology, and of creating a publishing company for these refugees. The editors-to-be asked Menashe if he had brought some manuscripts with him. I was there and told them about *Rungs*. Although Menashe hated it when I praised him—we had many quarrels because of this—I told them what I thought of this work. They all became intensely interested. There were special funds to subsidize such publications. It was decided that I was to bring them the manuscript the next day. They promised us a big advance and also better living quarters. Menashe did not reproach me for lauding his work this time.

"We came home, I opened the valise, and there lay a thick envelope with the inscription *Rungs*. I took out the manuscript, but I recognized neither the paper nor the typing. My dear, some beginner had given Menashe his first novel to read, and Menashe had put it into the envelope in which he had once kept his own novel. All this time, we had been carrying the scribblings of some hack.

"Even now when I speak about it, I shudder. Menashe had lost more than twenty pounds. He looked wan and sickly. I was afraid that he would go mad—but he stood there crestfallen and said, 'Well, that's that.'

"Besides the fact that he now had no manuscript to sell, there was danger that he might be suspected of having written an anti-Communist work which he was afraid to show. Bialystok teemed with informers. Although the NKVD did not yet have an address in Bialystok, a number of intellectuals had been arrested or banished from the city. Loshikl, I know you are impatient and I will give you the bare facts. I did not sleep the whole night. In the morning, I got up and said, 'Menashe, I am going to Warsaw.'

"When he heard these words, he became as pale as death, and asked, 'Have you lost your mind?' But I said, 'Warsaw is still a city. I cannot allow your work to get lost. It's not only yours, it's mine, too.' Menashe began to scream. He swore that if I went back to Warsaw, he would hang himself or cut his throat. He even struck me. The battle between us raged for two days. On the third day, I was on my way back to Warsaw. I want to tell you that many men who left Warsaw tried to return. They missed their wives, their children, their homes—if they still existed. They had heard what was going on in Stalin's paradise and they decided that they could just as well die with their dear ones. I told myself: To sacrifice one's life for a manuscript, one has to be insane. But I was seized with an obsession. The days had become colder and I took a sweater, warm underwear, and a loaf of bread. I went into a drugstore and asked for poison. The druggist—a Jew—stared at me. I told him that I had left a child in Warsaw and that I did not want to fall alive into the hands of the Nazis. He gave me some cyanide.

"I didn't travel alone. Until we reached the border, I was in the company of several men. I told them all the same lie—that I was pining away with longing for my baby—and they surrounded me with such love and care that I was embarrassed. They did not permit me to carry my bundle. They hovered over me as if I were an only daughter. We knew quite well what to expect from the Germans if we were caught, but in such situations people become fatalistic. At the same time, something within me ridiculed my undertaking. The chances of finding the manuscript in occupied Warsaw, and returning to Bialystok alive, were one in a million.

"Loshikl, I crossed the border without any incident, reached Warsaw, and found the house intact. One thing saved me—the rains and the cold had started. The nights were pitch dark. Warsaw had no electricity. The Jews had not yet been herded into a ghetto. Besides, I don't look especially Jewish. I had covered my hair with a kerchief and could easily have been taken for a peasant. Also, I avoided people. When I saw someone from a distance, I hid and waited until he was gone. Our apartment was occupied by a family. They were sleeping in our beds and wearing our clothes. But they had not touched Menashe's manuscripts. The man was a reader of the Yiddish press and Menashe was a god to him. When I knocked on the door and told them who I was, they became frightened, thinking that I wanted to reclaim the apartment. Their own place had been destroyed by a bomb and a child had been killed. When I told them that I had come back from Bialystok for Menashe's manuscript, they were speechless.

"I opened Menashe's drawer and there was his novel. I stayed with these people two days and they shared with me whatever food they had. The man let me have his bed—I mean my bed. I was so tired that I slept for fourteen hours. I awoke, ate something, and fell asleep again. The second evening, I was on my way back to Bialystok. I had made my way from Bialystok to Warsaw, and back to Bialystok, without seeing one Nazi. I did not walk all the time. Here and there a peasant offered me a ride. When one leaves the city and begins to hike through field, woods, and orchards, there are no Nazis or Communists. The sky is the same, the earth is the same, and the animals and birds are the same. The whole adventure took ten days. I regarded it as a great personal victory. First of all, I had found Menashe's work, which I carried in my blouse. Besides, I had proved to myself that I was not the coward I thought I was. To tell the truth, crossing the border back to Russia was not particularly risky. The Russians did not make difficulties for the refugees.

"I arrived in Bialystok in the evening. A frost had set in. I walked to our lodgings, which consisted of one room, opened the door, and lo and behold, my hero lay in bed with a woman. I knew her quite well: an atrocious poetess, ugly as an ape. A tiny kerosene lamp was burning. They had got some wood or coal because the stove was heated. They were still awake. My dear, I did not scream, I did not cry, I did not faint as they do in the theater. Both gaped at me in silence. I opened the door of the stove, took the manuscript from my blouse, and put it in the fire. I thought that Menashe might attack me, but he did not utter a word. It took a while before the manuscript caught fire. With a poker, I pushed the coals onto the paper. I stood there, watching. The fire was not in a hurry and neither was I. When *Rungs* became ashes, I walked over to the bed with the poker in hand and told the woman, 'Get out or you will soon be a corpse.'

"She did as I told her. She put on her rags and left. If she had uttered a sound, I would have killed her. When you risk your own life, other people's lives, too, are worthless.

"Menashe sat there in silence as I undressed. That night we spoke only a few words. I said, 'I burned your *Rungs*,' and he mumbled, 'Yes, I saw.' We embraced and we both knew that we were doing it for the last time. He was never so tender and strong as on that night. In the morning, I got up, packed my few things, and left. I had no more fear of the cold, the rain, the snow, the lonesomeness. I left Bialystok and that is the reason I am still alive. I came to Vilna and got a job in a soup kitchen. I saw how petty our so-called big personalities can be and how they played politics and maneuvered for a bed to sleep in or a meal to eat. In 1941, I escaped to Russia.

"Menashe, too, was there, I was told, but we never met—nor would I have wanted to. He had said in an interview that the Nazis took his book from him and that he was about to rewrite it. As far as I know, he has never rewritten anything. This really saved his life. If he had been writing and publishing, he would have been liquidated with the others. But he died anyhow."

For a long while we sat in silence. Then I said, "Shibtah, I want to ask you something, but you don't have to answer me. I am asking from sheer curiosity."

"What do you want to know?"

"Were you faithful to Menashe? I mean physically?"

She remained silent. Then she said, "I could give you a Warsaw answer: 'It's none of your leprous business.' But since you are Loshikl, I will tell you the truth. No."

"Why did you do it, since you loved Menashe so much?"

"Loshikl, I don't know. Neither do I know why I burned his manuscript. He had betrayed me with scores of women and I never as much as reproached him. I had made up my mind long ago that you can love one person and sleep with someone else; but when I saw this monstrosity in our bed, the actress in me awoke for the last time and I had to do something dramatic. He could have stopped me easily; instead, he just watched me doing it."

We were both silent again. Then she said, "You should never sacrifice yourself for the person you love. Once you risk your life the way I did, then there is nothing more to give."

"In novels the young man always marries the girl he saves," I said.

She tensed but did not answer. She suddenly appeared tired, haggard, wrinkled, as if old age had caught up with her at that very moment. I did not expect her to utter another word about it, when she said, "Together with his manuscript, I burned my power to love."

The Power of Darkness

THE doctors all agreed that Henia Dvosha suffered from nerves, not heart disease, but her mother, Tzeitel, the wife of Selig the tailor, confided to my mother that Henia Dvosha was making herself die because she wanted her husband, Issur Godel, to marry her sister Dunia.

When my mother heard this strange story she exclaimed, "What's going on at your house? Why should a young woman, the mother of two little children, want to die? And why would she want her husband to marry her sister, of all people? One mustn't even think such thoughts!"

As usual when she became excited, my mother's blond wig grew disheveled as if a strong wind had suddenly blown up.

I, a boy of ten, heard what Tzeitel said with astonishment, yet somehow I felt that she spoke the truth, wild as it sounded. I pretended to read a storybook but I cocked my ears to listen to the conversation.

Tzeitel, a dark, wide woman in a wide wig, a wide dress with many folds, and men's shoes, went on, "My dear friend, I'm not talking just to hear myself talk. This is a kind of madness with her. Woe is me, what I've come to in my old age. I ask but one favor of God—that He take me before He takes her."

"But what sense does it make?"

"No sense whatever. She started talking about it two years ago. She convinced herself that her sister was in love with Issur Godel, or he with her. As the saying goes—'A delusion is worse than a sickness.' Rebbetzin, I have to tell someone: Sick as she is, she's sewing a wedding dress for Dunia."

Mother suddenly noticed me listening and cried, "Get out of the kitchen and go in the other room. The kitchen is for women, not for men!"

Translated by Joseph Singer

I started to go down to the courtyard, and as I was passing the open door to Selig the tailor's shop I glanced inside. Selig was our next-door neighbor at No. 10 Krochmalna Street, and his shop was in the same apartment where he lived with his family. Selig sat at a sewing machine stitching the lining of a gaberdine. As wide as his wife was, so narrow was he. He had narrow shoulders, a narrow nose, and a narrow gray beard. His hands were narrow too, and with long fingers. His glasses, with brass rims and half lenses, were pushed up onto his narrow forehead. Across from him, before another sewing machine, sat Issur Godel, Henia Dvosha's husband. He had a tiny yellow beard ending in two points.

Selig was a men's tailor. Issur Godel made clothes for women. At that moment, he was ripping a seam. It was said that he had golden hands, and that if he had his own shop in the fancy streets he would make a fortune, but his wife didn't want to move out of her parents' apartment. When she got pains in the chest and couldn't breathe, her mother was there to take care of her. It was her mother—and occasionally her sister Dunia—who eased her with drops of valerian and rubbed her temples with vinegar when she grew faint. Dunia worked in a dress shop on Mead Street, wore fashionable clothes, and avoided the pious girls of the neighborhood. Tzeitel also watched over Henia Dvosha's two small children—Elkele and Yankele. I often went into Selig the tailor's shop. I liked to watch the machines stitch, and I collected the empty spools from the floor. Selig didn't speak like the people in Warsaw—he came from somewhere in Russia. He often discussed the Pentateuch and the Talmud with me, and he would speculate about what the saints did in Paradise and how sinners were roasted in Gehenna. Selig had been touched by Enlightenment and often sounded like a heretic. He would say to me, "Were your mother and father up in Heaven, and did they see all those things with their own eyes? Maybe there is no God? Or, if there is, maybe He's a Gentile, not a Jew?"

"God a Gentile? One mustn't say such things."

"How do you know one mustn't? Because it says so in the holy books? *People* wrote those books and people like to make up all kinds of nonsense."

"Who created the world?" I asked.

"Who created God?"

My father was a rabbi and I knew wouldn't want me to listen to such talk. I would cover my ears with my fingers when Selig began to blaspheme, and resolve to never enter his place again, but something drew me to this room where one wall was hung with gaberdines, vests, and trousers and the other with dresses and blouses. There was also a dressmaker's dummy with no head and wooden breasts and hips. This time I felt a strong urge to peek into the alcove where Henia Dvosha lay in bed.

Selig promptly struck up a conversation with me. "You don't go to cheder any more?"

"I've finished cheder. I'm studying the Gemara already."

"All by yourself? And you understand what you read?"

"If I don't, I look it up in Rashi's Commentary."

"And Rashi himself understood?"

I laughed. "Rashi knew the whole Torah."

"How do you know? Did you know him personally?"

"Know him? Rashi lived hundreds of years ago."

"So how can you know what went on hundreds of years ago?"

"Everyone knows that Rashi was a great saint and a scholar."

"Who is this 'everybody'? The janitor in the courtyard doesn't know it."

Issur Godel said, "Father-in-law, leave him alone."

"I asked him a question and I want an answer," Selig said.

Just then a small woman round as a barrel came in to be fitted for a dress. Issur Godel took her into the alcove. I saw Henia Dvosha sitting up in bed sewing a white satin dress that fell to the floor on both sides of the bed. Tzeitel hadn't lied. This was the wedding dress for Dunia.

I raced out of the shop and down the stairs. I had to think the whole matter out. Why would Henia Dvosha sew a dress for her sister to wear when she married Issur Godel after she, Henia Dvosha, died? Was this out of great love for her sister or love for her husband? I thought of the story of how Jacob worked seven years for Rachel and how her father, Laban, cheated Jacob by substituting Leah in the dark. According to Rashi, Rachel gave Leah signs so that she, Leah, wouldn't be shamed. But what kind of signs were they? I was filled with curiosity about men and women and their remarkable secrets. I was in a rush to grow up. I had begun watching girls. They mostly had the same high bosom as Selig's dummy, smaller hands and feet than men's, and hair done up in braids. Some had long, narrow necks. I knew that if I should go home and ask Mother what signs girls had and what Rachel could have given to Leah, she would only yell at me. I had to observe everything for myself and keep silent.

I stared at the passing girls, and thought I saw something like mockery in their eyes. Their glances seemed to say, "A little boy and he wants to know everything . . ."

Although the doctors assured Tzeitel that her daughter would live a long time and prescribed medicines for her nerves, Henia Dvosha grew worse from day to day. We could hear her moans in our apartment. Freitag the barber-surgeon gave her injections. Dr. Knaister ordered her taken to the hospital on Czysta Street, but Henia Dvosha protested that the sick were poisoned there and dissected after they died.

Dr. Knaister arranged a consultation of three—himself and two specialists. Two carriages pulled up before the gates of our building, each driven by a coachman in a top hat and a cloak with silver buttons. The horses had short manes and arched necks. While they waited they kept starting forward impatiently, and the coachmen had to yank on the reins to make them stand still. The consultation lasted a long time. The specialists couldn't agree, and they bickered in Polish. After they had received their twenty-five rubles, they climbed into their carriages and drove back to the rich neighborhoods where they lived and practiced.

A few days later Selig the tailor came to us in his shirtsleeves, a needle in his lapel and a thimble over the index finger of his left hand, and said to my father, "Rabbi, my daughter wants you to recite the confession with her."

My father gripped his red beard and said, "What's the hurry? With the Almighty's help, she'll live a hundred and twenty years yet."

"Not even a hundred and twenty hours," Selig replied.

Mother looked at Selig with reproof. Although he was a Jew, he spoke like a Gentile; those who came from Russia lacked the sensitivity of the Polish Jew. She began to wipe away her tears. Father rummaged in his cabinet and took out *The Ford of the Jabbok*, a book that dealt with death and mourning. He turned the pages and shook his head. Then he got up and went with Selig. This was the first time Father had been to Selig's apartment. He never visited anyone except when called to officiate in a religious service.

He stayed there a long time, and when he came back he said, "Oh, what kind of people are these? May the Almighty guard and protect us!"

"Did you recite the confession with her?" Mother asked.

"Yes."

"Did she say anything?"

"She asked if you could marry right after shivah, the seven days of mourning, or if you had to wait until after sheloshim, the full thirty."

Mother made a face as if to spit. "She's not in her right mind."

"No."

"You'll see, she'll live years yet," Mother said.

But this prediction didn't come true. A few days later a lament was heard in the corridor. Henia Dvosha had just passed away. The front room soon filled with women. Tzeitel had already managed to cover the sewing machines and drape the mirror with a black cloth. The windows had been opened, according to Law. Issur Godel appeared among the throng of women. He was dressed in a vented gaberdine cut to the knee, a paper dickey, a stiff collar, a black tie, and a small cap. He soon was on his way to the community office to arrange for the funeral. Then Dunia walked into the courtyard wearing a straw hat decorated with flowers and a red dress and carrying a bag in ladylike fashion. Dunia and Issur Godel met on the stairs. For a moment they stood there without speaking, then they mumbled something and parted—he going down and she up. Dunia wasn't crying. Her face was pale, and her eyes expressed something like rage.

During the period of mourning, men came twice a day to pray at Selig the tailor's. Selig and Tzeitel sat on little benches in their stocking feet. Selig glanced into the Book of Job printed in Hebrew and Yiddish that he had borrowed from my father. His lapel was torn as a sign of mourning. He chatted with the men about ordinary matters. The cost of everything was rising. Thread, lisle, and lining material were all higher. "Do people work nowadays?" Selig complained. "They play. In my time an apprentice came to work with the break of day. In the winter you started working while it was still dark. Every worker had to furnish a tallow candle at his own expense. Today the machine does everything and the worker knows only one thing—a new raise every other month. How can you have a world of such loafers?"

"Everyone runs to America!" Shmul the carpenter said.

"In America there's a panic. People are dying of hunger."

I went to pray each day at Selig the tailor's, but I never saw Issur Godel or Dunia there. Was Dunia hiding in the alcove or had she gone to work instead of observing shivah? As soon as this period of mourning was over, Issur Godel trimmed his beard, and exchanged his traditional cap for a fedora and the gaberdine for a short jacket. Dunia informed her mother that she wouldn't wear a wig after she was married.

The night before the wedding, I awoke just as the clock on the wall struck three. The window of our bedroom was covered with a blanket, but the moonlight shone in from each side. My parents were speaking softly, and their voices issued from one bed. God in Heaven, my father was lying in bed with my mother!

I held my breath and heard Mother say, "It's all their fault. They carried on in front of her. They kissed, and who knows what else. Tzeitel told me this herself. Such wickedness can cause a heart to burst."

"She should have got a divorce," Father said.

"When you love, you can't divorce."

"She spoke of her sister with such devotion," Father said.

"There are those that kiss the Angel of Death's sword," Mother replied.

I closed my eyes and pretended to be asleep. The whole world was apparently one big fraud. If my father, a rabbi who preached the Torah and piety all day, could get into bed with a female, what could you expect from an Issur Godel or a Dunia?

When I awoke the next day, Father was reciting the morning prayers. For the thousandth time he repeated the story of how the Almighty had ordered Abraham to sacrifice his son Isaac on an altar and the angel shouted down from Heaven, "Lay not thy hand upon the lad." My father wore a mask—a saint by day, a debaucher at night. I vowed to stop praying and to become a heretic.

Tzeitel mentioned to my mother that the wedding would be a quiet one. After all, the groom was a widower with two children, the family was in mourning—why make a fuss? But for some reason all the tenants of the courtyard conspired to make the wedding noisy. Presents came pouring in to the couple from all over. Someone had hired a band. I saw a barrel of beer with brass hoops being carried up the stairs, and baskets of wine. Since we were Selig's next-door neighbors, and my father would officiate at the ceremony besides, we were considered part of the family. Mother put on her holiday dress and had her wig freshly set at a hairdresser's. Tzeitel treated me to a slice of honey cake and a glass of wine. There was such a crush at Selig's apartment that there was no room for the wedding canopy, and it had to be set up in my father's study. Dunia wore the white satin wedding gown her sister had sewn for her. The other brides who had been married in our building smiled, responded to the wishes offered them in a gracious way, laughed and cried. Dunia barely said a word to anyone, and held her head high with worldly arrogance.

It was whispered about that Tzeitel had had to plead with her to get her to immerse herself in the ritual bath. Dunia had invited her own guests—girls with low-cut dresses and clean-shaven youths with thick mops of hair and broad-brimmed fedoras. Instead of shirts they wore black blouses bound with sashes. They smoked cigarettes, winked, and spoke Russian to each other. The people in our courtyard said that they were all socialists, the same as those who rebelled against the czar in 1905 and demanded a constitution. Dunia was one of them.

My mother refused to taste anything at the affair: some of the guests had brought along all kinds of food and drinks, and one could no longer be sure if everything was strictly kosher. The musicians played theater melodies, and men danced with women. Around eleven o'clock my eyes closed from weariness and Mother told me to go to bed. In the night I awoke and heard the stamping, the singing, the pagan music—polkas, mazurkas, tunes that aroused urges in me that I felt were evil even though I didn't understand what they were.

Later I woke again and heard my father quoting Ecclesiastes: "I said of laughter, It is mad, and of mirth, What doeth it?"

"They're dancing on graves," Mother whispered.

Soon after the wedding, scandals erupted at Selig's house. The newlyweds didn't want to stay in the alcove, and Issur Godel rented a ground-floor apartment on Ciepla Street. Tzeitel came weeping to my mother because her daughter had trimmed Yankele's earlocks and had removed him from cheder and enrolled him in a secular school. Nor did she maintain a kosher kitchen but bought meat at a Gentile butcher's. Issur Godel no longer called himself Issur Godel but Albert. Elkele and Yankele had been given Gentile names too—Edka and Janek.

I heard Tzeitel mention the number of the house where the newlyweds were living, and I went to see what was going on there. To the right of the gate hung a sign in Polish: ALBERT LANDAU, WOMEN'S TAILOR. Through the open window I could see Issur Godel. I hardly recognized him. He had dispensed with his beard altogether and now wore a turned-up mustache; he was bareheaded and looked young and Christian. While I was standing there, the children came home from school—Yankele in shorts and a cap with an insignia and with a knapsack on his shoulders, Elkele in a short dress and knee-high socks. I called to them, "Yankele . . . Elkele . . ." but they walked past and didn't even look at me.

Tzeitel came each day to cry anew to my mother: Henia Dvosha had come to her in a dream and shrieked that she couldn't rest in her grave. Her Yankele didn't say Kaddish for her, and she wasn't being admitted into Paradise.

Tzeitel hired a beadle to say Kaddish and study the Mishnah in her daughter's memory, but, even so, Henia Dvosha came to her mother and lamented that her shrouds had fallen off and she lay there naked; water had gathered in her grave; a wanton female had been buried beside her, a madam of a brothel, who cavorted with demons.

Father called three men to ameliorate the dream, and they stood in front of Tzeitel and intoned, "Thou hast seen a *goodly* vision! A goodly vision hast thou seen! Goodly is the vision thou hast seen!"

Afterward, Father told Tzeitel that one dared not mourn the dead too long, or place too much importance in dreams. As the Gemara said, just as there could be no grain without straw, there couldn't be dreams without idle words. But Tzeitel could not contain herself. She ran to the community leaders and to the Burial Society demanding that the body be exhumed and buried elsewhere. She stopped taking care of her house, and went each day to Henia Dvosha's grave at the cemetery.

Selig's beard grew entirely white, and his face developed a network of wrinkles. His hands shook, and the people in the courtyard complained that he kept a gaberdine or a pair of trousers for weeks, and when he finally did bring them back they were either too short or too narrow or the material was ruined from pressing. Knowing that Tzeitel no longer cooked for her husband and that he lived on dry food only, Mother frequently sent things over to him. He had lost all his teeth, and when I appeared with a plate of groats, or some chicken soup or stuffed noodles, he smiled at me with his bare gums and said, "So you're bringing presents, are you? What for? It's not Purim."

"One has to eat the year round."

"Why? To fatten up for the worms?"

"A man has a soul, too," I said.

"The soul doesn't need potatoes. Besides, did you ever see a soul? There is no such thing. Stuff and nonsense."

"Then how does one live?"

"It's Breathing. Electricity."

"Your wife—"

Selig interrupted me. "She's crazy!"

One evening Tzeitel confided in my mother that Henia Dvosha had taken up residence in her left ear. She sang Sabbath and holiday hymns, recited lamentations for the Destruction of the Temple, and even bewailed the sinking of the *Titanic*. "If you don't believe me, rebbetzin, hear for yourself."

She moved her wig aside and placed her ear against Mother's.

"Do you hear?" Tzeitel asked.

"Yes. No. What's that?" Mother asked in alarm.

"It's the third week already. I kept quiet, figuring it would pass, but it grows worse from day to day."

I was so overcome by fear that I dashed from the kitchen. The word soon spread through Krochmalna Street and the surrounding streets that a dybbuk had settled in Tzeitel's ear, and that it chanted the Torah, sermonized, and crowed like a rooster. Women came to place their ears against Tzeitel's and swore that they heard the singing of Kol Nidre. Tzeitel asked my father to put his ear next to hers, but Father wouldn't consent to touch a married woman's flesh. A Warsaw nerve specialist became interested in the case—Dr. Flatau, who was famous not only in Poland but in all Europe and maybe in America, too. And an article about the case appeared in a Yiddish newspaper. The author borrowed its title from Tolstoy's play *The Power of Darkness*.

At just about that time, we moved to another courtyard in Krochmalna Street. A few weeks later, in Sarajevo, a terrorist assassinated the Austrian Archduke Ferdinand and his wife. From this one act of violence came the war, the shortages of food, the exodus of refugees from the small towns to Warsaw, and the reports in the newspapers of thousands of casualties.

People had other things to talk about than Selig the tailor and his family. After Sukkoth, Selig died suddenly, and a few months later Tzeitel followed him to the grave.

One day that winter, when the Germans and Russians fought at the Bzura River, and the windowpanes in our house rattled from the cannon fire and the oven stayed unheated because we could no longer afford coal, a former neighbor from number 10, Esther Malka, paid a call on my mother. Issur Godel and Dunia, she said, were getting a divorce.

Mother asked, "Why on earth? They were supposed to be in love."

And Esther Malka replied, "Rebbetzin, they *can't* be together. They say Henia Dvosha comes each night and gets into bed between them."

"Jealous even in the grave?"

"So it seems."

Mother turned white and said words I've never forgotten: "The living die so that the dead may live."

The Bus

WHY I undertook that particular tour in 1956 is something I haven't
figured out to this day—dragging around in a bus through Spain for
twelve days with a group of tourists. We left from Geneva. I got on the
bus around three in the afternoon and found the seats nearly all taken.
The driver collected my ticket and pointed out a place next to a woman
who was wearing a conspicuous black cross on her breast. Her hair was
dyed red, her face was thickly rouged, the lids of her brown eyes were
smeared with blue eyeshadow, and from beneath all this dye and paint
emerged deep wrinkles. She had a hooked nose, lips red as a cinder, and
yellowish teeth.

She began speaking to me in French, but I told her I didn't understand the language and she switched over to German. It struck me that
her German wasn't that of a real German or even a Swiss. Her accent
was similar to mine and she made the same mistakes. From time to time
she interjected a word that sounded Yiddish. I soon found out that she
was a refugee from the concentration camps. In 1946, she arrived at a
DP camp near Landsberg and there by chance she struck up a friendship
with a Swiss bank director from Zurich. He fell in love with her and
proposed marriage but under the condition that she accept Protes-
tantism. Her name at home had been Celina Pultusker. She was now
Celina Weyerhofer.

Suddenly she began speaking to me in Polish, then went over into
Yiddish. She said, "Since I don't believe in God anyway, what's the
difference if it's Moses or Jesus? He wanted me to convert, so I converted a bit."

"So why do you wear a cross?"

Translated by Joseph Singer

"Not out of anything to do with religion. It was given to me by someone dying whom I'll never forget till I close my eyes."

"A man, eh?"

"What else—a woman?"

"Your husband has nothing against this?"

"I don't ask him. There he is."

Mrs. Weyerhofer pointed out a man sitting across the way. He looked younger than she, with a fair, smooth face, blue eyes, and a straight nose. To me he appeared the typical banker—sober, amiable, his trousers neatly pressed and pulled up to preserve the crease, shoes freshly polished. He was wearing a panama hat. His manner expressed order, discipline. Across his knee lay the *Neue Zürcher Zeitung*, and I noticed it was open to the financial section. From his breast pocket he took a piece of cloth with which he polished his glasses. That done, he glanced at his gold wristwatch.

I asked Mrs. Weyerhofer why they weren't sitting together.

"Because he hates me," she said in Polish.

Her answer surprised me, but not overly so. The man glanced at me sidelong, then averted his face. He began to converse with a lady sitting in the window seat beside him. He removed his hat, revealing a shining bald pate surrounded by a ruff of pale-blond hair. "What could it have been that this Swiss saw in the person next to me?" I asked myself, but such things one could not really question.

Mrs. Weyerhofer said, "So far as I can tell, you are the only Jew on the bus. My husband doesn't like Jews. He doesn't like Gentiles, either. He has a million prejudices. Whatever I say displeases him. If he had the power, he'd kill off most of mankind and leave only his dogs and the few bankers with whom he's chummy. I'm ready to give him a divorce but he's too stingy to pay alimony. As it is, he barely gives me enough to keep alive. Yet he's highly intelligent, one of the best-read people I've ever met. He speaks six languages perfectly, but, thank God, Polish isn't one of them."

She turned toward the window and I lost any urge to talk to her further. I had slept poorly the night before, and when I leaned back I dozed off, though my mind went on thinking wakeful thoughts. I had broken up with a woman I loved—or at least desired. I had just spent three weeks alone in a hotel in Zakopane.

I was awakened by the driver. We had come to the hotel where we would eat dinner and sleep. I couldn't orient myself to the point of deciding whether we were still in Switzerland or had reached France. I didn't catch the name of the city the driver had announced. I got the key to my room. Someone had already left my suitcase there. A bit later, I

went down to the dining room. All the tables were full, and I didn't want
to sit with strangers.

As I stood, a boy who appeared to be fourteen or fifteen came up to
me. He reminded me of prewar Poland in his short pants and high
woolen stockings, his jacket with the shirt collar outside. He was a
handsome youth—black hair worn in a crewcut, bright dark eyes, and
unusually pale skin. He clicked his heels in military fashion and asked,
"Sir, you speak English?"

"Yes."

"You are an American?"

"An American citizen."

"Perhaps you'd like to join us? I speak English. My mother speaks a
little, too."

"Would your mother agree?"

"Yes. We noticed you in the bus. You were reading an American
newspaper. After I graduate from what you call high school, I want to
study at an American university. You aren't by chance a professor?"

"No, but I have lectured at a university a couple of times."

"Oh, I took one look at you and I knew immediately. Please, here is
our table."

He led me to where his mother was sitting. She appeared to be in her
mid-thirties, plump, but with a pretty face. Her black hair was combed
into two buns, one at each side of her face. She was expensively dressed
and wore lots of jewelry. I said hello and she smiled and replied in
French.

The son addressed her in English: "Mother, the gentleman is from
the United States. A professor, just as I said he would be."

"I am no professor. I was invited by a college to serve as writer-in-
residence."

"Please. Sit down."

I explained to the woman that I knew no French, and she began to
speak to me in a mixture of English and German. She introduced herself
as Annette Metalon. The boy's name was Mark. The waiters hadn't yet
managed to serve all the tables, and while we waited I told the mother
and son that I was a Jew, that I wrote in Yiddish, and that I came from
Poland. I always do this as soon as possible to avoid misunderstandings
later. If the person I am talking to is a snob, he knows that I'm not
trying to represent myself as something I'm not.

"Sir, I am also a Jew. On my father's side. My mother is Christian."

"Yes, my late husband was a Sephardi," Mrs. Metalon said. Was
Yiddish a language or a dialect? she asked me. How did it differ from
Hebrew? Was it written in Latin letters or in Hebrew? Who spoke the

language and did it have a future? I responded to everything briefly. After some hesitation, Mrs. Metalon told me that she was an Armenian and that she lived in Ankara but that Mark was attending school in London. Her husband came from Saloniki. He was an importer and exporter of Oriental rugs and had had some other businesses as well. I noticed a ring with a huge diamond on her finger, and magnificent pearls around her neck. Finally, the waiter came over and she ordered wine and a steak. When the waiter heard I was a vegetarian he grimaced and informed me that the kitchen wasn't set up for vegetarian meals. I told him I would eat whatever I could get—potatoes, vegetables, bread, cheese. Anything he could bring me.

As soon as he had gone, the questions started about my vegetarianism: Was it on account of my health? Out of principle? Did it have anything to do with being kosher? I was accustomed to justifying myself, not only to strangers but even to people who had known me for years. When I told Mrs. Metalon that I didn't belong to any synagogue, she asked the question for which I could never find the answer—what did my Jewishness consist of?

According to the way the waiter had reacted, I assumed that I'd leave the table hungry, but he brought me a plateful of cooked vegetables and a mushroom omelette as well as fruit and cheese. Mother and son both tasted my dishes, and Mark said, "Mother, I want to become a vegetarian."

"Not as long as you're living with me," Mrs. Metalon replied.

"I don't want to remain in England, and certainly not in Turkey. I've decided to become an American," Mark said. "I like American literature, American sincerity, democracy, and the American business sense. In England there are no opportunities for anyone who wasn't born there. I want to marry an American girl. Sir, what kind of documents are needed to get a visa to the United States? I have a Turkish passport, not an English one. Would you, sir, send me an affidavit?"

"Yes, with pleasure."

"Mark, what's wrong with you? You meet a gentleman for the first time and at once you make demands of him."

"What do I demand? An affidavit is only a piece of paper and a signature. I want to study at Harvard University or at the University of Princeton. Sir, which of these two universities has the better business school?"

"I really wouldn't know."

"Oh, he has already decided everything for himself," Mrs. Metalon said. "A child of fourteen but with an old head. In that sense, he takes after his father. He always planned down to the last detail and years in advance. My husband was forty years older than I, but we had a happy life together." She took out a lace-edged handkerchief and dabbed at an invisible tear.

The bus routine required that each day passengers exchanged seats. It gave everyone a chance to sit up front. Most couples stayed together, but individuals kept changing their partners. On the third day, the driver placed me next to the banker from Zurich, who was apparently determined not to sit with his wife.

He introduced himself to me: Dr. Rudolf Weyerhofer. The bus had left Bordeaux, where we had spent the night, and was approaching the Spanish border. At first neither of us spoke; then Dr. Weyerhofer began to talk of Spain, France, the situation in Europe. He questioned me about America, and when I told him that I was a staff member of a Yiddish newspaper his talk turned to Jews and Judaism. Wasn't it odd that a people should have retained its identity through two thousand years of wandering across the countries of the world and after all that time returned to the land and language of its ancestors? The only such instance in the history of mankind. Dr. Weyerhofer told me he had read Graetz's *History of the Jews* and even something of Dubnow's. He knew the works of Martin Buber and Klausner's *Jesus of Nazareth*. But for all that, the essence of the Jew was far from clear to him. He asked about the Talmud, the Zohar, the Hasidim, and I answered as best I could. I felt certain that shortly he would begin talking about his wife.

Mrs. Weyerhofer had already managed to irritate the other passengers. Both in Lyons and in Bordeaux the bus had been forced to wait for her—for a half hour in Lyons and for over an hour in Bordeaux. The delays played havoc with the travel schedule. She had gone off shopping and had returned loaded down with bundles. From the way she had described her husband to me as a miser who begrudged her a crust of bread, I couldn't understand where she got the money to buy so many things. Both times she apologized and said that her watch had stopped, but the Swiss women claimed that she had purposely turned back the hands of her gold wristwatch. By her behavior Celina Weyerhofer humiliated not only her husband, who accused her in public of lying, but also me, for it was obvious to everyone on the bus that she, like me, was a Jew from Poland.

I no longer recall how it came about but Dr. Weyerhofer began to unburden himself to me. He said, "My wife accuses me of anti-Semitism, but what kind of anti-Semite am I if I married a Jewish woman just out of concentration camp? I want you to know that this marriage has caused me enormous difficulties. At that time many people in financial circles were infected with the Nazi poison, and I lost important connections. I was seriously considering emigrating to your America or even to

South Africa, since I had practically been excommunicated from the Christian business community. How is this called by your people . . . cherem? My blessed parents were still living then and they were both devout Christians. You could write a thick book about what I went through.

"Though my wife became converted, she did it in such a way that the whole thing became a farce. This woman makes enemies wherever she goes, but her worst enemy is her own mouth. She has a talent for antagonizing everyone she meets. She tried to establish a connection with the Jewish community in Zurich, but she said such shocking things and carried on so that the members would have nothing to do with her. She'd go to a rabbi and represent herself as an atheist; she'd launch a debate with him about religion and call him a hypocrite. While she accuses everyone of anti-Semitism, she herself says things about Jews you'd expect from a Goebbels. She plays the role of a rabid feminist and joins protests against the Swiss government for refusing to give women the vote, yet at the same time she castigates women in the most violent fashion.

"I noticed her talking to you when you were sitting together and I know she told you how mean I am with money. But the woman has a buying mania. She buys things that will never be used. I have a large apartment she's crowded with so much furniture, so many knickknacks and idiotic pictures that you can barely turn around. No maid will work for us. We eat in restaurants even though I hate not eating at home. I must have been mad to agree to go on this trip with her. But it looks as if we won't last out the twelve days. While I sit talking here with you, my mind is on forfeiting my money and leaving the bus before we even get to Spain. I know I shouldn't be confiding my personal problems like this, but since you are a writer maybe they can be of use to you. I tell myself that the camps and wanderings totally destroyed her nerves, but I've met other women who survived the whole Hitler hell, and they are calm, civilized, pleasant people."

"How is it that you didn't see this before?" I asked.

"Eh? A good question. I ask myself the same thing. The very fact that I'm telling you all this is a mystery to me, since we Swiss are reticent. Apparently ten years of living with this woman have altered my character. She is the one who allegedly converted, but I seem to have turned into almost a Polish Jew. I read all the Jewish news, particularly any dealing with the Jewish state. I often criticize the Jewish leaders, but not as a stranger—rather as an insider."

The bus stopped. We had come to the Spanish frontier. The driver went with our passports to the border station and lingered there a long time.

Dr. Weyerhofer began talking quietly, in almost a mumble, "I want to be truthful. One good trait she did have—she could attract a man. Sexually, she was amazingly strong. I don't believe myself that I am speaking of these things—in my circles, talk of sex is taboo. But why? Man thinks of it from cradle to grave. She has a powerful imagination, a perverse fantasy. I've had experience with women and I know. She has said things to me that drove me to frenzy. She has more stories in her than Scheherazade. Our days were cursed, but the nights were wild. She wore me out until I could no longer do my work. Is this characteristic of Jewish women in Eastern Europe? The Swiss Jewish women aren't much more interesting than the Christian."

"You know, Doctor, it is impossible to generalize."

"I have the feeling that many Jewish women in Poland are of this type. I see it in their eyes. I made a business trip to the Jewish state and even met Ben-Gurion, along with other Israeli leaders. We did business with the Bank Leumi. I have a theory that the Jewish woman of today wants to make up for all the centuries in the ghetto. Besides, the Jews are a people of imagination, even though in modern literature they haven't yet created any great works. I've read Jakob Wassermann, Stefan Zweig, Peter Altenberg, and Arthur Schnitzler, but they disappointed me. I expected something better from Jews. Are there interesting writers in Yiddish or Hebrew?"

"Interesting writers are rare among all peoples."

"Here is our driver with the passports."

We crossed the border, and an hour later the bus stopped and we went to have lunch at a Spanish restaurant.

In the entrance, Mrs. Weyerhofer came up to me and said, "You sat with my husband this morning and I know that the whole time he talked about me. I can read lips like a deaf-mute. You should know that he's a pathological liar. Not one word of truth leaves his lips."

"It so happens he praised you."

Celina Weyerhofer tensed. "What did he say?"

"That you are unusually interesting as a woman."

"Is that what he said? It can't be. He has been impotent several years, and being next to him has made me frigid. Physically and spiritually he has made me sick."

"He praised your imagination."

"Nothing is left me except my imagination. He drained my blood like a vampire. He isn't sexually normal. He is a latent homosexual—not so latent—although when I tell him this he denies it vehemently. He only wants to be with men, and when we still shared a bedroom he spent whole nights questioning me about my relationships with other men. I had to invent affairs to satisfy him. Later, he threw these imaginary sins up to me and called me filthy names. He forced me to confess that I had relations with a Nazi, even though God knows I would sooner have let them skin me alive. Maybe we can find a table together?"

"I promised to eat with some woman and her son."

"The one I saw you with yesterday in the dining room? Her son is a beauty, but she is too fat and when she gets older she'll go to pieces. Did you notice how many diamonds she wears? A jewelry store—tasteless, disgusting. In Lyons and Bordeaux none of us had a bathroom, but she got one. Since she is so rich, why does she ride in a bus? They don't give her a plain room but a suite. Is she Jewish?"

"Her late husband was a Jew."

"A widow, eh? She's probably looking for a match. The diamonds are more than likely imitations. What is she, French?"

"Armenian."

"Foolish men kill themselves and leave such bitches huge estates. Where does she live?"

"In Turkey."

"Be careful. One glance was enough to tell me this is a spider. But men are blind."

I couldn't believe it, but I began to see that Mark was trying to arrange a match between his mother and myself. Strangely, the mother played as passive a role in the situation as some old-time maiden for whom the parents were trying to find a husband. I told myself that it was all my imagination. What would a rich widow, an Armenian living in Turkey, want with a Yiddish writer? What kind of future could she see in this? True, I was an American citizen, but it wouldn't have been difficult for Mrs. Metalon to obtain a visa to America without me. I concluded that her fourteen-year-old son had hypnotized his mother—that he dominated her as his father had probably done before him. I also toyed with the notion that her husband's soul had entered into Mark and that he, the dead Sephardi, wanted his wife to marry a fellow Jew. I tried to avoid eating with the pair, but each time Mark found me and said, "Sir, my mother is waiting for you."

His words implied a command. When it was my turn to order my vegetarian dishes, Mark took over and told the waiter or waitress exactly what to bring me. He knew Spanish because his father had had a partner with whom he had conversed in Ladino. I wasn't accustomed to drinking wine with my meals, but Mark ordered it without consulting me. When we came to a city, he always managed that his mother and I were left alone to shop for bargains and souvenirs. On these occasions he warned me sternly not to spend any money on his mother, and if I had already done so he demanded to know how much and told his mother to pay me back. When I objected, he arched his brows. "Sir, we don't need gifts. A Yiddish writer can't be rich." He opened his mother's pocketbook and counted out whatever the amount had been.

Mrs. Metalon smiled sheepishly at this and added, half in jest, half in earnest, that Mark treated her as if she were his daughter. But she had obviously accepted the relationship.

Is she so weak? I wondered. Or is there some scheme behind this?

The situation struck me as particularly strange because the mother and son were together only during vacations. The rest of the year she remained in Ankara while he studied in London. As far as I could determine, Mark was dependent on his mother; when he needed something he had to ask for money.

At first, the two of them sat in the bus together, but one day after lunch Mark told me that I was to sit with his mother. He himself sat down next to Celina Weyerhofer. He had arranged all this without the driver's permission, and I doubted if he had discussed it with his mother.

I had been sitting next to a woman from Holland, and this changing of seats provoked whispering among the passengers. From that day on, I became Mrs. Metalon's partner not only in the dining room but in the bus as well. People began to wink, make remarks, leer. Much of the time I looked out of the window. We drove through regions that reminded me of the desert and the land of Israel. Peasants rode on asses. We passed an area where gypsies lived in caves. Girls balanced water jugs on their heads. Grandmothers toted bundles of wood and herbs wrapped in linen sheets over their shoulders. We passed ancient olive trees and trees that resembled umbrellas. Sheep browsed among cracked clods of earth on the half-burned plain. A horse circled a well. The sky, pale blue, radiated a fiery heat. Something Biblical hovered over the landscape. Passages of the Pentateuch flashed across my memory. It seemed to me that I was somewhere in the plains of Mamre, where presently would materialize Abraham's tent, and the angel would bring Sarah tidings that she would be blessed with a male child at the age of ninety. My head whirled with stories of Sodom, of the sacrifice of Isaac, of Ishmael and Hagar. The stacks of grain in the harvested fields brought Joseph's dreams to mind. One morning we passed a horse fair. The horses and the men stood still, congealed in silence like phantoms of a fair from a vanished time. It was hard to believe that in this very land, some fifteen years before, a civil war had raged and Stalinists had shot Trotskyites.

Barely a week had passed since our departure, but I felt that I had been wandering for months. From sitting so long in one position I was overcome with a lust that wasn't love or even sexual passion but something purely animalistic. It seemed that my partner shared the same feelings, for a special heat emanated from her. When she accidentally touched my hand, she burned me.

We sat for hours without a single word, but then we became gabby and said whatever came to our lips. We confided intimate things to one another. We yawned and went on talking half asleep. I asked her how it happened that she had married a man forty years older than herself.

She said, "I was an orphan. The Turks murdered my father, and my mother died soon after. We were rich but they stripped us of everything. I met him as an employee in his office. He had wild eyes. He took one look at me and I knew that he wanted me and was ready to marry me. He had an iron will. He also had the strength of a giant. If he hadn't smoked cigars from early morning till late at night, he would have lived to be a hundred. He could drink fifteen cups of bitter coffee a day. He exhausted me until I developed an aversion to love. When he died, I had the solace that I would be left in peace for a change. Now everything has begun to waken within me again."

"Were you a virgin when you married?" I asked in a half dream.

"Yes, a virgin."

"Did you have lovers after his death?"

"Many men wanted me, but I was raised in such a way I couldn't live with a man without marriage. In my circle in Turkey a woman can't afford to be loose. Everyone there knows what everyone else is doing. A woman has to maintain her reputation."

"What do you need with Turkey?"

"Oh, I have a house there, servants, a business."

"Here in Spain you can do what you want," I said, and regretted my words instantly.

"But I have a chaperon here," she said. "Mark watches over me. I'll tell you something that will seem crazy to you. He guards me even when he is in London and I'm in Ankara. I often feel that he sees everything I do. I sense it isn't he but his father."

"You believe this?"

"It's a fact."

I glanced backward and saw Mark gazing at me sharply as if he were trying to hypnotize me.

When we stopped for the night at a hotel, we first had to line up for the toilets, then wait a long time for our dinner. In the rooms assigned to us, the ceilings were high, the walls thick, and there were old-fashioned washstands with basins and pitchers of water.

That night, we stopped late, which meant that dinner was not served until after ten. Once again, Mark ordered a bottle of wine. For some reason I let myself be persuaded to drink several glasses. Mark asked me if I had had a chance to bathe during the trip, and I told him that I washed every morning out of the washbasin with cold water just like the other passengers.

He glanced at his mother half questioningly, half imperatively.

After some hesitation, Mrs. Metalon said, "Come to our room. We have a bathroom."

"When?"

"Tonight. We leave at five in the morning."

"Sir, do it," Mark said. "A hot bath is healthy. In America everyone has a bathroom, be he porter or janitor. The Japanese bathe in wooden tubs, the whole family together. Come a half hour after dinner. It's not good to bathe immediately following the evening meal."

"I'll disturb both of you. You're obviously tired."

"No, sir. I never go to sleep until between one and two o'clock. I'm planning to take a walk through the city. I have to stretch my legs. From sitting all day in the bus they've become cramped and stiff. My mother goes to bed late, too."

"You're not afraid to walk alone at night in a strange city?" I asked.

"I'm not afraid of anybody. I took a course in wrestling and karate. I also take shooting lessons. It's not allowed boys my age, but I have a private teacher."

"Oh, he takes more courses than I have hairs on my head," Mrs. Metalon said. "He wants to know everything."

"In America, I'll study Yiddish," Mark announced. "I read somewhere that a million and a half people speak this language in America. I want to read you in the original. It's also good for business. America is a true democracy. There you must speak to the customer in his own language. I want my mother to come to America with me. In Turkey, no person of Armenian descent is sure of his life."

"My friends are all Turks," Mrs. Metalon protested.

"Once the pogroms start they'll stop being your friends. My mother tries to hide it from me but I know very well what they did to the Armenians in Turkey and to the Jews in Russia. I want to visit Israel. The Jews there don't bow their heads like those in Russia and Poland. They offer resistance. I want to learn Hebrew and to study at Jerusalem University."

We said goodbye and Mark wrote the number of their room on a small sheet he tore from a notebook. I went to my room for a nap. My legs wobbled as I climbed the stairs. I lay down on the bed in my clothes with the notion of resting a half hour. I closed my eyes and sank into a deep slumber. Someone woke me—it was Mark. To this day I don't know how he got into my room. Maybe I had forgotten to lock it or he had tipped the maid to let him in.

He said, "Sir, excuse me but you've slept a whole hour. You've apparently forgotten that you are coming to our room for your bath."

I assured Mark that I'd be at his door in ten minutes, and after some hesitation he left. Getting undressed and unpacking a bathrobe and slippers from my valise wasn't easy for me. I cursed the day I had decided to take this tour, but I hadn't the courage to tell Mark I wouldn't come. For all his delicacy and politeness Mark projected a kind of childish brutality.

I threw my spring coat over my bathrobe and on unsteady legs began climbing the two floors to their room. I was still half asleep, and for a moment I had the illusion that I was on board ship. When I got to the Metalons' floor, I could not find the slip of paper with the room number. I was sure that it was number 43, but the tiny lamp on the high ceiling was concealed behind a dull shade and emitted barely any light. In the dimness I couldn't see this number. It took a long time of groping before I found it and knocked on the door.

The door opened, and to my amazement I saw Celina Weyerhofer in a nightgown, her face thickly smeared with cream. Her hair looked wet and freshly dyed. I grew so confused that I could not speak. Finally I asked, "Is this 43?"

"Yes, this is 43. To whom were you going? Oh, I understand. It seems to me that your lady with the diamonds is somewhere on this floor. I saw her son. You've made a mistake."

"Madam, I don't wish to detain you. I just want to tell you they invited me to take a bath there, that's all."

"A bath, eh? So let it be a bath. I haven't had a bath for over a week myself. What kind of tour is this that some passengers get privileges and others are discriminated against? The advertisement didn't mention anything about two classes of passengers. My dear Mr.—what is your name?—I warned you that that person would trap you, and I see this has happened sooner than I figured. Wait a minute—your bath won't run out. Since when do they call it a bath? We call it by a different name. Don't run. Because you've forgotten the number, you'll have to knock on strangers' doors and wake people. Everyone is dead tired. On this tour, before you can even lie down you have to get up again. My husband is a good sleeper. He lies down, opens some book, and two minutes later he's snoring like a lord. He carries his own alarm clock. I've stopped sleeping altogether. Literally. That's my sickness. I haven't slept for years. I told a doctor in Bern about this—he's actually a professor of medicine—and he called me a liar. The Swiss can be very coarse when they choose to be. He had studied something in a medical book or he had a theory, and because the facts didn't jibe with his theory this made me a liar. I've been watching you sitting with that woman. It looks as if you're telling her jokes from the way she keeps on laughing. My husband sat next to her one time before she monopolized you, and she told him things no decent woman would tell a stranger. I suspect she is a madam of a whorehouse in Turkey. Or something like that. No respectable woman wears so much jewelry. You can smell her perfume a mile away. I'm not even sure that this boy is her son. There seems to be some kind of unnatural relationship between them."

"Madam Weyerhofer, what are you saying?"

"I'm not just pulling things out of the air. God has cursed me with eyes that see. I say 'cursed' because this is for me a curse rather than a blessing. If you absolutely must take a bath, as you call it, do it and satisfy yourself, but be careful—such a person can easily infect you with God knows what."

Just at that moment the door across the hall opened and I saw Mrs. Metalon in a splendid nightgown and gold-colored slippers. Her hair was loose; it fell to her shoulders. She was made up, too. The women glared at each other furiously; then Mrs. Metalon said, "Where did you go? I'm in 48, not 43."

"Oh, I made a mistake. Truly, I'm completely mixed up. I'm terribly sorry—"

"Go take your bath!" Mrs. Weyerhofer said and gave me a light push. She muttered words in French I didn't understand but knew to be insulting. She slammed her own door shut.

I turned to Mrs. Metalon, who asked, "Why did you go to her, of all people? I waited and waited for you. There is no more hot water anyhow. And where has Mark vanished to? He went for a walk and hasn't come back. This night is a total loss to me. That woman—what's her name? Weyerhofer—is a troublemaker, and crazy besides. Her own husband admitted that she's emotionally disturbed."

"Madam, I've made a terrible mistake. Mark wrote down your room number for me, but while changing my clothes I lost the slip. It's all because I'm so tired—"

"Oh, will that red-haired bitch malign me before everyone on the bus now! She is a snake whose every word is venom."

"I truly don't know how to excuse myself. But—"

"Well, it's not your fault. It was Mark who cooked up this stew. The driver told me to keep it secret that we're getting a bathroom. He doesn't want to create jealousy among the passengers. Now he'll be mad at me and he'll be right. I can't continue this trip any longer. I'll get off with

Mark in Madrid and take a train or plane back to the border or maybe even to Paris. Come in for a moment. I'm already compromised."

I went inside, and she took me to the bathroom to show me that the hot water was no longer running. The bathtub was made of tin. It was unusually high and long. On its outside hung a kind of pole with which to hold in and let out the water. The taps were copper. I excused myself again and Mrs. Metalon said, "You're an innocent victim. Mark is a genius, but like all geniuses he has his moods. He was a prodigy. At five he could do logarithms. He read the Bible in French and remembered all the names. He loves me and he is determined to have me meet someone. The truth is, he's seeking a father. Each time I join him during vacations he starts looking for a husband for me. He creates embarrassing complications. I don't want to marry—certainly not anyone Mark would pick out for me. But he is compulsive. He gets hysterical. I shouldn't tell you this, but I have a good reason to say it—when I do something that displeases him, he abuses me. Later he regrets it and beats his head against the wall. What can I do? I love him more than life itself. I worry about him day and night. I don't know exactly why you made such an impression on him. Maybe it's because you're a Jew, a writer, and from America. But I was born in Ankara and that's where my home is. What would I do in America? I've read a number of articles about America, and that's not the country for me. With us, servants are cheap and I have friends who advise me on financial matters. If I left Turkey, I would have to sell everything for a song. I tell you this only to point out there can never be anything between us. You would not want to live in Turkey any more than I want to live in New York. But I don't want to upset Mark and I therefore hope that for the duration of the trip you can act friendly toward me—sit with us at the table and all the rest. When the tour ends and you return home, let this be nothing more for you than an episode. He's due back soon. Tell him that you took the bath. You'll be able to have one in Madrid. We'll be spending almost two days there, and I'm told the hotel is modern. I'm sure you have someone in New York you love. Sit down awhile."

"I've just broken up with a woman."

"Broken up? Why? You didn't love her?"

"We loved each other but we couldn't stay together. This past year we argued constantly."

"Why? Why can't people live in peace? There was a great love between my husband and me, though I must admit I had to give in to him on everything. He bullied me so that I can't even say no to my own child. Oh, I'm worried. He never stayed away this long. He probably wants you to declare your love for me so that when he comes back everything will be settled between us. He is a child, a wild child. My greatest fear is that he might attempt suicide. He has threatened to." She uttered these last words in one breath.

"Why? Why?"

"For no reason. Because I dared disagree with him over some trifle. God Almighty, why am I telling you all this? Only because my heart is heavy. Say nothing about it, God forbid!"

The door opened and Mark came in. When he saw me sitting on the sofa, he asked, "Sir, did you take your bath?"

"Yes."

"It was nice, wasn't it? You look refreshed. What are you talking about with my mother?"

"Oh, this and that. I told her she's one of the prettiest women I've ever met," I said, astonished at my words.

"Yes, she is pretty, but she mustn't remain in Turkey. In the Orient, women age quickly. I once read that an actress of sixty played an eighteen-year-old girl on Broadway. Send us an affidavit and we'll come to you."

"Yes, I'll do that."

"You may kiss my mother good night."

I stood up and we kissed. My face grew moist and hot. Mark began to kiss me, too. I said good night and started down the stairs. Again it seemed to me that I was on board ship. The steps were running counter to my feet. I suddenly found myself in the lobby. In my confusion I had gone down an extra floor. It was almost dark here; the desk clerk dozed behind the desk. In a leather chair sat Mrs. Weyerhofer in a robe, legs crossed, veiled in shadow. She was smoking a cigarette.

When she saw me, she said, "Since I don't sleep anyway, I'd rather spend the night here. A bed is to sleep in or make love in, but when you can't sleep and have no one to love, a bed becomes a prison. What are you doing here? Can't you sleep, either?"

She drew the smoke in deeply and the glow of the cigarette temporarily lit up her eyes. They reflected both curiosity and malaise.

She said, "After that kind of bath, a man should be able to sleep soundly instead of wandering around like a lost soul."

Mark began telling everyone on the bus that his mother and I were engaged. He planned that when the bus came back to Geneva I should ask the American consul for visas for himself and his mother so that all three of us could fly to America together. Mrs. Metalon told him several times that this would be impossible—she had a business appointment in Ankara. I made up the lie that I had to go to Italy on literary business. But Mark argued that his mother and I could postpone our business affairs temporarily. He spoke to me as if I were already his stepfather.

He enumerated his mother's financial assets. His father had arranged a trust fund for him, and he had left the remainder of his estate to his wife. According to Mark's calculations she was worth no less than two million dollars—maybe more. Mark wanted his mother to liquidate all her holdings in Turkey and transfer her money to America. He would go to America to study even before he graduated from high school. The interest on his mother's capital would allow us to live in luxury.

Mark had decided that we would settle in Washington. It was childish and silly, but this boy cast a fear over me. I knew that it would be hard to free myself from him. His mother had hinted that another disappointment could drive him to actually attempt suicide. She suggested, "Maybe you'd spend some time with me in Turkey? Turkey is an interesting country. You'd have material to write about for your newspaper. You could spend two or three weeks, then go back to America. Mark wouldn't want to come along. He will gradually realize that we're not meant for each other."

"What would I do in Turkey? No, that's impossible."

"If it's a matter of money, I'll be glad to cover the expenses. You can even stay with me."

"No, Mrs. Metalon, it's out of the question."

"Well, something is bound to happen. What shall I do with that boy? He's driving me crazy."

We had two days in Madrid, a day in Córdoba, and we were on our way to Seville, where we were scheduled to stop for two days. The tour program promised a visit to a nightclub there. Our route was supposed to take us through Málaga, Granada, and Valencia to Barcelona, and from there to Avignon, then back to Geneva.

In Córdoba, Mrs. Weyerhofer delayed the bus for nearly two hours. She vanished from the hotel before our departure and all searching failed to turn her up. On account of her, the passengers had already missed a bullfight. Dr. Weyerhofer pleaded with the driver to go on and leave his lunatic wife alone in Spain as she deserved, but the driver couldn't bring himself to abandon a woman in a strange country. When she finally showed up loaded down with bundles and packages, Dr. Weyerhofer slapped her twice. Her packages fell to the floor and a vase shattered. "Nazi!" she shrieked. "Homosexual! Sadist!" Dr. Weyerhofer said aloud so that everyone could hear, "Well, thank God, this is the end of my martyrdom." And he raised his hand to the sky like a pious Jew swearing a vow.

The uproar caused an additional three-quarters of an hour delay. When Mrs. Weyerhofer finally got into the bus, no one would sit next to her, and the driver, who had seen us speaking together a few times, asked me if I would, since there were no single seats. Mark tried to seat me next to his mother and take my place, but Mrs. Metalon shouted at him to stay with her, and he gave in.

For a long while Mrs. Weyerhofer stared out the window and ignored me as if I were the one responsible for her disgrace. Then she turned to me and said, "Give me your address. I want you to be my witness in court."

"What kind of witness? If it should come to it, the court would find for him, and—if you'll excuse me—rightly so."

"Eh? Oh, I understand. Now that you're preparing to marry the Armenian heiress, you're already lining up on the side of the anti-Semites."

"Madam, your own conduct does more harm to Jews than all the anti-Semites."

"They're my enemies, mortal enemies. Your madam from Constantinople was glowing with joy when those devils humiliated me. I am again where I was—in a concentration camp. You're about to convert, I know, but I will turn back to the Jewish God. I am no longer his wife and he is no longer my husband. I'll leave him everything and flee with my life, as I did in 1945."

"Why do you keep the bus waiting in every city? This has nothing to do with Jewishness."

"It's a plot, I tell you. He organized the whole thing down to the last detail. I don't sleep the whole night, but comes morning, just as I'm catching a nap he turns back the clock. Your knocking on my door the other night—what was the name of the city?—when you were on your way to take a bath at that Turkish whore's, was also one of his tricks. It was a conspiracy to let him catch me with a lover. It's obvious. He wants to drive me out without a shirt on my back, and he has achieved his goal, the sly fox. I won't be allowed to remain in Switzerland, but who will accept me? Unless I can manage to make my way to Israel. Now I understand everything. You'll be the witness for *him*, not for me."

"I'll be a witness for no one. Don't talk nonsense."

"You obviously think I'm mad. That's his goal—to commit me to an asylum. For years he's been talking of this. He's already tried it. He keeps sending me to psychiatrists. He wanted to poison me, too. Three times he put poison in my food and three times my instinct—or maybe it was God—gave me a warning. By the way, I want you to know that this boy, Mark, who wants so desperately for you to sit next to that Turkish concubine, is not her son."

"Then who is he?"

"He is her lover, not her son. She sleeps with him."

"Were you there and saw it?"

"A chambermaid in Madrid told me. She made a mistake and opened the door to their room in the morning and found them in bed together. There are such sick women. One wants a lapdog, and another a young boy. Really, you're crawling into slime."

"I'm not crawling anywhere."

"You're taking her to America?"

"I'm not taking anyone."

"Well, I'd better keep my mouth shut." Mrs. Weyerhofer turned away from me.

I leaned my head back against the seat and closed my eyes. I knew well that the woman was paranoid; just the same, her last words had given me a jolt. Who knows? What she told me might have been the truth. Sexual perversion is the answer to many mysteries. I was almost overcome with nausea. Yes, I thought, she is right. I'm crawling into a quagmire.

I had but one wish now—to get off this bus as quickly as possible. It occurred to me that for all my intimacy with Mrs. Metalon and Mark, so far I hadn't given them my address.

I dozed, and when I opened my eyes Mark informed me that we were in Seville. I had slept over three hours.

Despite our late start, we still had time for a fast meal. I had sat as usual with Mrs. Metalon and Mark. Mark had ordered a bottle of Malaga and I had drunk a good half of it. Vapors of intoxication flowed from my stomach to my brain.

The topic of conversation at the tables was Dr. and Mrs. Weyerhofer. All the women concluded that Dr. Weyerhofer was a saint to put up with such a horror.

Mrs. Metalon said, "I'd like to think that this is her end. Even a saint's patience has to burst sometime. He is a banker and a handsome man. He won't be alone for long."

"I wouldn't want him for a father," Mark said.

Mrs. Metalon smiled and winked at me. "Why not, my son?"

"Because I want to live and study in America, not in Switzerland. Switzerland is only good for mountain climbing and skiing."

"Don't worry, there's no danger of it."

As she spoke, Mrs. Metalon did something she had never done before—she pressed her knee against mine.

Coaches waited in front of the hotel to take us to a cabaret. Candles flickered in their head lanterns, casting mysterious designs of light and shadow. I hadn't ridden in a horse-drawn carriage since leaving Warsaw. The whole evening was like a magic spell—the ride from the hotel to the cabaret with Mrs. Metalon and Mark, and later the performance. Inside the carriage, driving through the poorly lit Seville streets Mrs. Metalon held my hand. Mark sat facing us and his eyes gleamed like some night bird's. The air was balmy, dense with the scents of wine, olive oil, and gardenias. Mrs. Metalon kept on exclaiming, "What a splendid night! Look at the sky, so full of stars!"

I touched her breast, and she trembled and squeezed my knee. We were both drunk, not so much from wine as from fatigue. Again I felt the heat of her body.

When we got out of the coach Mark walked a few paces in front and Mrs. Metalon whispered, "I'd like to have another child."

"By whom?" I asked.

"Try to guess," she said.

I cannot know whether the actors and actresses and the music and the dancing were as masterly as I thought, but everything I saw and heard that evening enraptured me—the semi-Arabic music, the almost Hasidic way the dancers stamped their feet, their meaningful clicking of the castanets, their bizarre costumes. Melodies supposed to be erotic reminded me of liturgies sung on the night of Kol Nidre. Mark found an unoccupied seat close to the stage and left us alone. We began to kiss with the ardor of long-parted lovers. Between one kiss and the next, Mrs. Metalon (she had told me to call her Annette) insisted that I accompany her to Ankara. She was even ready to visit America. I had scored one of those victories I could never explain except by the fact that in the duel of love the victim is sometimes as eager to surrender as the attacker is to conquer. This woman had lived alone for a number of years. She was accustomed to the embraces of an elderly man. As I thought these things, I warned myself that Mark would not allow our relationship to remain an affair.

From time to time he glanced back at us searchingly. I didn't believe Mrs. Weyerhofer's slanderous tale of mother and son, but it was obvious that Mark was capable of killing anyone he considered to be dishonoring her. The woman's words about wanting another child portended danger. However strong my urge for her body, I knew that I had no spiritual ties with her, that after a while misunderstandings, boredom, and regrets would take over. Besides, I had always been afraid of Turks. As a child, I had heard in detail of Abdul-Hamid's savageries. Later, I read about the pogroms against the Armenians. There in faraway Ankara they could easily fabricate an accusation against me, take away my American passport, and throw me in prison, from which I would not emerge alive. How strange, but when I was a boy in cheder I dreamed of lying in a Turkish prison bound with heavy ropes, and for some reason I had never forgotten this dream.

On the way back from the nightclub, both mother and son asked if I had a bathtub in my room. I told them no, and at once they invited me to bathe in their suite. Mark added that he was going to take a stroll through town. The fact that we were scheduled to stay in Seville through the following night meant that we did not have to get up early the next morning.

Mrs. Metalon and Mark had been assigned a suite of three rooms. I promised to come by and Mrs. Metalon said, "Don't be too late. The hot water may cool soon." Her words seemed to carry a symbolic meaning, as if they were out of a parable.

I went to my room, which was just under the roof. It exuded a scorching heat. The sun had lain on it all day and I switched on the ceiling lamp and stood for a long time, stupefied from the heat and the day's experiences. I had a feeling that soon flames would come shooting from all sides and the room would flare up like a paper lantern. On a brass bed lay a huge pillow and a red blanket full of stains. I needed to stretch out, but the sheet seemed dirty. I imagined I could smell the sperm that who knows how many tourists had spilled here. My bathrobe and pajamas were packed away in my valise, and I hadn't the strength to open it. Well, and what good would it do to bathe if soon afterward I had to lie down in this dirty bed?

In the coach and in the cabaret everything within me had seethed with passion. Now that I had a chance to be alone with the woman, the passion evaporated. Instead, I grew angry against this rich Turkish widow and her pampered son. I made sure that Mark wouldn't wake me. I locked the door with the heavy key and bolted it besides. I put out the light and lay down in my clothes on the sprung mattress, determined to resist all temptation.

The hotel was situated in a noisy neighborhood. Young men shouted and girls laughed wantonly. From time to time, I detected a man's cry followed by a sigh. Was it outside? In another room? Had someone been murdered here? Tortured? Who knows, remnants of the Inquisition might still linger here. I felt bites and scratched. Sweat oozed from me but I made no effort to wipe it away. "This trip was sheer insanity," I told myself. "The whole situation is filled with menace."

I fell asleep and this time Mark did not come to wake me. By dawn it turned cold and I covered myself with the same blanket that a few hours earlier had filled me with such disgust. When I awoke, the sun was already burning. I washed myself in lukewarm water from the pitcher on the stand and wiped myself with a rusty towel. I seemed to have resolved everything in my sleep. Riding in the carriage through the city the night before, I had noticed branches of Cook's Tours and American Express. I had a return ticket to America, an American passport, and traveler's checks.

When I went down with my valise to the lobby, they told me that I had missed breakfast. The passengers had all gone off to visit churches, a Moorish palace, a museum. Thank God, I had avoided running into Mrs. Metalon and her son and having to justify myself to them. I left a tip for the bus driver with the hotel cashier and went straight to Cook's. I was afraid of complications, but they cashed my checks and sold me a train ticket to Geneva. I would lose some two hundred dollars to the bus company, but that was my fault, not theirs.

Everything went smoothly. A train was leaving soon for Biarritz. I had booked a bedroom in a Pullman car. I got on and began correcting a manuscript as if nothing had happened.

Toward evening, I felt hungry and the conductor showed me the way to the diner. All the second-class cars were empty. I glanced into the diner. There, at a table near the door, sat Celina Weyerhofer struggling with a pullet.

We stared at each other in silence for a long while; then Mrs. Weyerhofer said, "If this is possible, then even the Messiah can come. On the other hand, I knew that we'd meet again."

"What happened?" I asked.

"My good husband simply drove me away. God knows I've had it up to here with this trip." She pointed to her throat.

She proposed that I join her, and she served as my interpreter to order a vegetarian meal. She seemed more sane and subdued than I had seen her before. She even appeared younger in her black dress. She said, "You ran away, eh? You did right. You would have been caught in a trap you would never have freed yourself from. She suited you as much as Dr. Weyerhofer suited me."

"Why did you keep the bus waiting in every city?" I asked.

She pondered. "I don't know," she said at last. "I don't know myself. Demons were after me. They misled me with their tricks."

The waiter brought my vegetables. I chewed and looked out the window as night fell over the harvested fields. The sun set, small and glowing. It rolled down quickly, like a coal from some heavenly conflagration. A nocturnal gloom hovered above the landscape, an eternity that was weary of being eternal. Good God, my father and my grandfather were right to avoid looking at women! Every encounter between a man and a woman leads to sin, disappointment, humiliation. A dread fell upon me that Mark would try to find me and exact revenge.

As if Celina had read my mind, she said, "Don't worry. She'll soon comfort herself. What was the reason for your taking this trip? Just to see Spain?"

"I wanted to forget someone who wouldn't let herself be forgotten."

"Where is she? In Europe?"

"In America."

"You can't forget anything."

We sat until late, and Mrs. Weyerhofer unfolded to me her fatalistic theory: everything was determined or fixed—every deed, every word, every thought. She herself would die shortly and no doctor or conjurer could help her. She said, "Before you came in here I fantasized that I was arranging a suicide pact with someone. After a night of pleasure, he stuck a knife in my breast."

"Why a knife, of all things?" I asked. "That's not a Jewish fantasy. I couldn't do this even to Hitler."

"If the woman wants it, it can be an act of love."

The waiter came back and mumbled something.

Mrs. Weyerhofer explained, "We're the only ones in the dining car. They want to close up."

"I'm finished," I said. "Gastronomically and otherwise."

"Don't rush," she said. "Unlike the driver of our ill-starred bus, the forces that drive us mad have all the time in the world."

A Night in the Poorhouse

I

AT nine in the evening the poorhouse attendant extinguished the kerosene lamp. He left burning a single tallow candle, which soon began to flicker. Outside, the frost glistened, but inside the poorhouse it was warm. The gravely ill lay in beds. The others slept on straw pallets on the floor.

Next to the oven lay Zeinvel the thief, whom peasants had crippled when they caught him stealing a horse, and Mottke the beadle, who for a long time had served as beadle to a bogus rabbi named Yontche, a cobbler who donned a Hasidic rabbi's attire and traveled through the Polish towns allegedly performing miracles. They had gone as far as Lithuania together. Yontche was subsequently caught in the act with a servant girl and fled to America. Mottke, too, tried to escape to America, but he was detained on Ellis Island and then deported because of trachoma. Later he became half blind. Both Mottke the beadle and Zeinvel the thief had lived in the poorhouse for years, although in separate rooms most of the time.

Zeinvel was tall, and as black as a gypsy, with slanted eyes, a head of black hair, and a mouth full of white teeth. Besides being lame, he suffered from consumption. As a young man he had had the reputation of being a dandy. He managed to trim his beard even in the poorhouse. Mottke was small, round like a barrel, with tufts of flax-blond hair around his scabby skull and with a yellow beard that grew on one cheek only. His eyes were always swollen and half closed. He was something of a scholar, and it was said that he and Yontche used to switch roles. One month Yontche would be the rabbi and Mottke the beadle; the next month it was the other way around.

Translated by Joseph Singer

After a while the tallow candle went out. A full moon was shining outside and its light reflected up from the snow upon the poorhouse walls. Zeinvel and Mottke never went to sleep before midnight. They chatted and told stories.

Mottke was saying, "Cold outside, eh? It's going to get even colder. Here in Poland the cold is still bearable, but when a frost comes up in Lithuania oaks burst in the forests. One thing is good there—wood is cheap. The villages are tiny, but almost all the men are learned. You meet a carpenter or a blacksmith—by day he planes a board or pounds his hammer on the anvil, but after the evening services he reads a chapter of the Mishnah to a group in the study house. They don't set much store by Hasidic rabbis. You can travel half of Lithuania without seeing a Hasid. The men avoided us, but the women used to come to us on the sly, and brought whatever they could—a chicken, a dozen eggs, a measure of buckwheat, even a garland of garlic. There's no lack of sickness anywhere, and we gave them all kinds of remedies—cow's eggs with duck milk, as well as various amulets and talismans we both invented. When we were in Lithuania, a thing happened that turned a village topsy-turvy."

"What happened?" Zeinvel asked.

"Something with a dybbuk."

"A dybbuk in Lithuania?"

"Yes, in Lithuania. I had been told that the Litvaks didn't believe in dybbuks. The Vilna Gaon didn't believe in such things, and from the Vilna Gaon to God is but one step. But what the eyes see can't be denied. The name of the village was Zabrynka. When Yontche and I got there, the ritual slaughterer invited us for the Sabbath repast. In Lithuania a Sabbath guest doesn't sleep in the poorhouse. A bed is made up for him at his host's house. The slaughterer's name was Bunem Leib, and his wife's Hiene—a name not heard in our parts. They had only one daughter, Freidke, a short girl with red hair and freckles. She was already engaged to a youth who was studying slaughtering under her father. His name was Chlavna. In Lithuania they have the queerest names. He was a handsome young man—tall, dark, well dressed. In Lithuania no one wears a satin robe on the Sabbath, unless maybe a rabbi. Nor are their earlocks as long as here in Poland. Everything with them is different. We put sugar into gefilte fish, they put pepper.

"Yontche was a glutton. The moment he entered a house, he took right to the food. I like to look around. I noticed that Freidke was madly in love with Chlavna. She never took her eyes off him. Her eyes were blue, sharp, and kind of melancholy. Why? It's in my nature that I notice things whether they concern me or not. A healthy young fellow should have an appetite, but it struck me that Chlavna hardly ate a thing. Whatever was served him, he left over—the Sabbath loaf, the soup, the meat, even the carrot stew. When Hiene served him a glass of tea, his hand trembled so that he spilled it on the tablecloth. Eh, I thought, a slaughterer's hand shouldn't tremble. That won't do.

"Yontche and I celebrated the Sabbath there, and after the Sabbath we went our way. We didn't know it then, but that winter was our last together. We hadn't had much luck in Lithuania, and Yontche acted more like a coachman than like a rabbi. Usually when I left a town I soon forgot everyone there, but I sat in the sleigh thinking about Freidke and Chlavna and I knew somehow that I'd be coming back to Zabrynka. But why? What did these strangers mean to me?

"We came to another town and there I really quarreled with Yontche, and told him that he was an outcast and that he should go to blazes. I felt so downhearted I went to a tavern. I sat down, took a shot of vodka, and someone came up to me—a little shipping agent—and said, 'You don't recognize me, but we met in Zabrynka. You are the beadle.'

" 'What's happening in Zabrynka?' I asked, and he said, 'You haven't heard the news? A dybbuk has entered the slaughterer's daughter.'

" 'A dybbuk?' I said. 'In Freidke?'

"And he told me this story: That Sabbath night, soon after we had left town, the butchers brought to Bunem Leib a large black bull with spiral horns, a tough beast. Since Freidke's fiancé, Chlavna, had learned the craft, with all its laws, and had already slaughtered several calves, Bunem Leib decided to let him slaughter it. When a bull is slaughtered, the butchers tie him with ropes, throw him to the ground, and hold him until he bleeds to death. But when Chlavna made the benediction and slashed the bull's throat the animal tore loose, lunged to its feet, and began to run round with such fury that he nearly brought down the slaughterhouse. He went racing across the marketplace and cracked a lamppost and overturned a wagon. All this time, the blood gushed from him as if from a tap. After a long chase, the butchers caught him and dragged him back to the slaughterhouse, already a carcass. Only then did they discover that Chlavna had vanished. Someone said that he was seen leaning over the well. Others saw him running toward the river. They searched with poles, but he wasn't found. The rabbi examined the knife Chlavna used and he found the blade jagged. The bull was declared unkosher. The butchers fell into such a rage against Bunem Leib for turning the job over to Chlavna that they shattered his windowpanes.

"That night was to Bunem Leib and to his household one long turmoil. At dawn, when he and his wife had finally dozed off, they were roused by a strange wail—not human but animal. Freidke stood naked in the center of the room bellowing like an ox. She was shaking, jerking, and lowing, as if she were the very bull her fiancé had botched. Then a terrible human voice tore itself out from her mouth. All Zabrynka came running, and it became clear that a dybbuk had entered Freidke. The dybbuk cried that he had been a man in life—an evildoer, a drunk, a lecher. When he died, his soul hadn't been allowed into Heaven but had been sentenced to be reincarnated as a bull. The Angel of Death told him that when this bull was slaughtered according to the ritual law and pious Jews ate his flesh after reciting the right benediction, he, the sinner, would be redeemed. Now that Chlavna had rendered the meat impure, the sinner's forsaken soul had entered Freidke.

"I was so taken aback by what the shipping agent told me that I left Yontche bag and baggage, grabbed my bundle, and headed back to Zabrynka. A deep snow had fallen and a bitter frost had settled in. I couldn't get a sleigh and I had to walk halfway there. The wind nearly blew me away. I was sure that my end had come and I began to say my confession."

"You fell in love with that Freidke, eh?"

"In love? You talk nonsense."

"What happened next?" Zeinvel asked.

"I came to Zabrynka in the middle of the night. The shutters were locked everywhere, but Bunem Leib's house was lit up and there were people inside. They seemed to have stayed to listen to the dybbuk instead of going to sleep. No one took notice of me when I entered. I learned later that Freidke's mother had become ill from grief and had been taken to some relative. I barely recognized Bunem Leib. He had become emaciated, yellow, and drained in the few days since I was there. Freidke stood there barefoot, half naked, with straggly red hair over her shoulders, her face as white as that of a corpse and her eyes bulging. She screamed with a voice I could never have believed could come out of a girl's tender throat. This was not a human voice but that of an ox. I heard her bellow, 'Slaughter me, Bunem Leib, slaughter me! I am the bull you caused to be *tref* and so doomed to eternal torment. You don't see them, but hordes of demons, hobgoblins, and devils are lurking right here waiting to tear me to pieces and carry me away to the wastelands behind the Dark Mountains. Neither your mezuzah nor the talismans and amulets you hung in all the corners of the house can help me. Look, if you are not completely blind: monsters with noses to their navels, with snakes instead of hair, with snouts of boars, as black as pitch, as red as fire, as green as gall! They dance and howl like the mad. Is it my fault, Bunem Leib, that you have chosen for your son-in-law a schlemiel, a mollycoddle who cannot wield a knife? He could as much be a slaughterer as you could be a wet nurse. His hands were shaking

like those of a man of ninety. He was such a weakling that when he saw
a drop of blood on the white of an egg he was ready to faint. A slaughterer cannot be afraid of blood. A real man doesn't run away from his
bride-to-be when things go wrong. You picked a mama's boy for your
daughter, a pampered little brat, a eunuch. He was more afraid of me,
the bull, than I was of his knife! Slaughter me, Bunem Leib, and save
me from all these vicious spirits. If not, I will catch you on my horns
and gore you and carry you away to swamps from which there can never
be any rescue.'

"'My daughter, what are you talking about? You are my child,'
Bunem Leib said to her. 'Let this evil fiend only free you, and if Chlavna
is not your destined one, I will find another spouse for you, God willing,
and we will lead you to the wedding canopy. Merciful God, help me! I
can't take any more of this anguish.'

"Bunem Leib was crying. But Freidke answered, 'I'm not your
daughter but the bull you have given into the hands of a bungler. Take
out your knife and slaughter me! Shed my blood! You, Bunem Leib, are
a male, not a neuter. No ox, no cow, no sheep or rooster ever ran away
from your knife. Kill me, Bunem Leib, kill me!' "

"You heard all this?" Zeinvel asked.

"May I hear the Messiah's ram's horn as clearly."

"Go on."

"It is impossible to tell it all. Toward dawn Bunem Leib became so
tired and haggard that he had to go to sleep, but the town's rowdies took
over the show. For them it was fun. Imagine, an only daughter, a quiet
little dove, stands in the middle of the night, her breasts uncovered, her
red hair wild as a witch's, and she confesses sins that make your head
swim. I heard her say, 'While alive, I did everything to spite God. I
shaved my beard, I ate pork on Yom Kippur, I fornicated with Gentile
wenches and Jewish whores. I denied God, and I thought I would live to
be a hundred and indulge in all my abominations. But suddenly I got
sick with pox and saw that I was done for. Still, to my last breath I
blasphemed God and served the idols. When I finally expired, the Burial
Society wouldn't cleanse my body and they buried me without shrouds,
at midnight, without anyone saying Kaddish. Even before the gravediggers had thrown the last spadeful of dirt over me, the Angel Dumah
opened my grave, spat at me, pierced me with his fiery rod, and dragged
me to the very gates of Gehenna. He tried to hurl me inside, but Satan
slammed the door and shouted, "It is a disgrace to Gehenna to allow
such scum to enter into it." '

"You can be the world's biggest heretic, Zeinvel, but when you see
and hear a thing like this, you must admit that there is a God."

"No, you mustn't."

"Then what was all that?"

"Nerves."

"How do nerves know what goes on in the netherworld?" Mottke asked.

"The nerves know everything."

"What are they—prophets?"

"Even better than that," Zeinvel said. "Good night."

"Well, you are talking nonsense."

Zeinvel had fallen asleep and was snoring, but Mottke lay awake. He talked to himself: "Gone to sleep, eh? A dunce, a boob . . . Thinks he knows it all, but to me he's still a fool."

"Mottke, shut up."

"You're not asleep?"

"I am asleep, but I hear every word anyway. I learned this trick in jail. There, if you fall asleep for real they'll strip the shirt right off your back. What became of Freidke?"

"How should I know? I stayed there for three days, then I went my way. I haven't told you everything yet. Neighbors swore to me that Freidke had never sung before. True, a well-brought-up girl doesn't let her voice be heard, so as not to arouse us males; nevertheless, if a girl has a voice she'll sing while rocking a child, or she will join in the Sabbath chants. All of a sudden Freidke started singing droll songs in Yiddish, Polish, even in Russian. She serenaded a bride and made wedding jests, all in rhyme. She mocked the women haggling in the butcher shops, and their splashing in the ritual bath. The hoodlums made snide remarks to her, and she answered each one on his own terms. She fast-talked them so, they were left speechless. All the neighbors said the same—this wasn't Freidke but a wag, a rascal, with a tongue like a razor. His profanities left you rolling with laughter. Brother, I stood by and watched a female turn both into a bull and into a man. Nerves can't do this."

"What can do it?"

"Only God."

"There is no God."

"How did the world form?" Mottke asked.

"It grew from itself like a scab."

II

Zeinvel dozed off again, but Mottke still lay awake. The sick in the poorhouse sighed and mumbled in their sleep. Wasn't Zeinvel right, Mottke reflected. A merciful God wouldn't allow so much misery. People die like flies here. Each day the Burial Society comes with the ablution board to carry out a body.

For a while Mottke listened to a cricket chirping behind the stove. It jingled as if with little bells. It told a tale without a beginning or an end. How was it that it chirped the whole night, Mottke wondered. Don't crickets need sleep, too? Or do they sleep during the day? And what do they find to eat among the rags? It was crazy to think that this cricket had a father, a mother, a grandfather, a grandmother, and maybe children, too. I'm all befuddled, Mottke mused. I'm dead tired all day, but at night my brain works like a churn.

Sometimes during the day, when Mottke wanted to show off his erudition, he forgot everything, jumbled passages like some ignoramus. But in the middle of the night his brain opened up. He recalled whole chapters of the Scripture, sections of the Gemara, even the liturgies of Rosh Hashanah and Yom Kippur. People who had died so long ago that he no longer remembered their names materialized seemingly alive before him. He remembered names of villages in which he had stayed with Yontche. Chants of cantors and songs of Hasidim came back to his mind. Mottke had been raised in a religious home. His father had taken him along to the wonder rabbi at Turisk. As a boy, he had read Hasidic books, had even dreamed of becoming a rabbi. But his father had died of typhus, his mother had married some boor, and Mottke had slipped into the confidence game with Yontche.

Now Mottke began droning a song that he had heard in Turisk at the Sabbath meal:

> I'll sing with praise
> To open the gates
> Of the Heavenly orchards
> For their sacred mates.

Zeinvel got to coughing and sat up. "Why are you singing in the middle of the night? Are you hungry?"

"I'm not hungry."

"You've got a burr in your saddle, eh?"

"Wasted away a life for nothing," Mottke said, shocked at his own words.

"You want to become a penitent like that musician who blindfolded himself so that he couldn't look at women?"

"Too late for that."

"Yes, brother, for us it might have been too late when we were born," Zeinvel said. "That business with Freidke was all stuff and nonsense. It's all made up—the Jewish God, the Christian God. That Chlavna was a clumsy dolt and a miserable coward. Freidke, on the other hand, was putting on an act because he deserted her. Young girls hear old wives' tales, absorb every trifle, and then they mimic them.

"I had a wild female once, a Talmud teacher's daughter. Mindle was her name. She looked like a kosher virgin. I could have sworn she couldn't count to two—a pale little face, big black eyes. It all started when I met her at the pump and filled a pail of water for her. She gave me a pretty thank you and threw in a sweet smile. I was already a thief by then and I had had more women than you have hairs on your head. At that time, it wasn't easy to get a Jewish girl—not in our parts, anyway—but there was no shortage of shiksas. They don't know any pretenses. They've got Uncle Esau's blood in their veins. Well, but I saw fire in Mindle's eyes. Each time I saw her going with her pail, I ran outside with my pail. I must have pumped a hundred pails for her. I began thinking that it was a waste of time. Suddenly I hand her the pail and she slips a note into my hand. I ran so fast with my own pail that I spilled half of it. I walk into the house and I read, 'Meet me in the cemetery at midnight.'

"One line, that's all—fancy handwriting. I had tasted everything— girls, matrons, young, old—but I grew as rattled as a yeshiva boy. I was scared, too. In those days I still believed in the creatures of the night. What kind of girl would meet a fellow in the cemetery at midnight? It was said that corpses prayed in the synagogue at night and that if someone walked by they would call him inside to read from the Torah. Also, a carpenter's daughter had hanged herself in our town because some tramp made her pregnant, and it was said that she climbed out of her grave in the nights and wandered among the tombstones. Just the same, I couldn't wait for night to fall and, later, for the clock on the town hall to toll eleven-thirty. My piece of goods had figured out everything in advance. Her father, a fervent Hasid who wore two skullcaps, one in front and one in back, went to bed with the chickens. He got up before dawn to bewail the Destruction of the Temple. The mother traveled to fairs to support her older daughter, a penniless widow who lived in Krasnystaw with three children. She sold jackets that she padded herself.

"I'll cut it short. Mindle had scheduled our meeting for the end of the month, when the moon wasn't shining and when the mother was off to some fair. The night was hot and dark. The road to the cemetery led through Church Street. The Jews lived close to the marketplace. Farther along, only Gentiles lived—tiny houses and huge dogs. I walked by and they attacked me like a pack of wolves. With one dog you can manage, but with fifty you don't stand a chance. Besides, when the Gentiles hear their dogs bark, they come running outside with cudgels. I thought I was going to be martyred, but somehow I made it to the cemetery. I tapped, feeling my way like a blind man. I was still a believer then, and in my mind I donated eighteen groschen to charity. I stretched out my arms and there she was, as if she had emerged from the ground. When you're scared, all desire leaves you, but the moment I touched her she burned me like a hot coal. She whispered a secret in my ear. There was no need for talk. How can such a firebrand grow up in a pious teacher's house?"

"She satisfied you, eh?" Mottke asked.

"That's not the word," Zeinvel said. "We fell on each other and we couldn't break apart. I took it for granted she was a virgin, but that would be the day!"

"A tasty piece, eh?"

"We lay for hours among the headstones and I couldn't get enough. As hot as fire and as sharp as a dagger. Whenever I began to cool off she said something so spicy that I shuddered and the game started all over again. Where she had learned such talk in our little village I'll never know."

"How is it you didn't marry her?" Mottke asked.

"Eh? I wanted a respectable girl, not a slut. She spoke frankly: one man to her was like an appetizer. She needed many, always new ones. I'm no saint, but I wished a wife like my mother. In my trade, you've got to be ready to do time. To sit in prison and worry that your wife is running around with every bum is scant pleasure. Even as I fondled and kissed her and promised her the moon and the stars, I longed for my Malkele, may she rest in peace. I already knew her by then. She was a friend of my sister Zirel. I wasn't planning to remain a thief. I wanted to amass a stake and become a horse dealer. But man proposes and God disposes."

"That means you *do* believe in God," Mottke said.

"It only sounds this way. What is God? Who is He? No one has gone up to Heaven and come to an understanding with Him. It's all written in the Torah, but what's the Torah? Parchment and ink. Whoever holds the pen writes what pleases him. For nearly two thousand years Jews have been waiting for the Messiah, but he's in no hurry to show up."

"So the world is lawless, eh?"

"Whoever can, grabs. And whoever can't lies six feet under."

"Still, if good people didn't send us groats and soup here we would long since have been flat on our backs," Mottke said.

"They don't do it for us," Zeinvel said. "They think this will reserve them golden chairs in Paradise and large portions of the Leviathan."

"You once said yourself that you believe in fate," Mottke argued. "You said that the last time you went to steal a horse you knew in advance that you would come a cropper and that it was fated this way. Those were your very words."

"God is God and fate is fate. I had stolen a half-dozen nags within a few weeks, and the peasants had started sleeping in the stables. They stood guard with axes and rattles. My Malkele begged me: 'Zeinvel, enough!' She knelt before me and warned me to stay home. She spoke about opening a store or, if worst came to worst, of going to America. She demanded that I swear on the Pentateuch that I would begin a new life. But even as I took the holy oath I knew that it wasn't worth a pinch of snuff. It's not in me to stand in a store and weigh out two ounces of almonds or cream of tartar. I don't have the patience for such drivel. Nor was I drawn to the land of Columbus. Everyone who went there ended up pressing pants or peddling from door to door. Letters came telling of a depression in New York, of workers picking food out of garbage cans. I loved Malkele, but she wasn't Mindle. I was faithful to her, God is my witness, but to sit with her days and nights and have her chip away at me didn't appeal to me. She had miscarried twice. She was constantly bewailing her lot and mine, too. I wanted once and for all to test my luck."

"You believe in luck?"

"Yes. In good luck and bad luck."

"There is a God, there is!" Mottke said.

"And if there is, what of it? He sits in the seventh Heaven, the angels flatter Him with their hymns, and He cares as much about us as about last year's frost."

"What became of Mindle?" Mottke asked.

"Oh, her father married her off to some dummy, a son of a rich Hasid, a follower of his rabbi's. My little kitten stood with him under the canopy pure and veiled as if she had never been touched. Why she would allow herself to be used this way is a riddle to me. Such females sometimes marry a fool so that they'll have someone to dupe easily. There is a great thrill in cheating—almost as much as in stealing. But you pay for everything. She died two years later in childbirth."

"So that's how it turned out?"

"Yes. Her husband, the lummox, had gone to his rabbi's and he lingered there for months. I was doing time in the Janov jail. Later, they transferred me to Lublin. That time I was innocent. I had been falsely accused. When I finally got out, Mindle was already in the other world."

"It was surely a punishment from God," Mottke said.

"No."

It grew silent. Even the cricket had ceased its chirping. After a while Zeinvel said, "I haven't forgotten her. If there is a Gehenna, I want to lie next to her on one bed of nails."

Escape from Civilization

I BEGAN to plan my escape from civilization not long after learning the meaning of the word. But the village of Bilgoray, where I lived until I was eighteen, didn't have enough civilization to run away from. Later, when I went to Warsaw, all I could do was run back to Bilgoray. The idea took on substance only after I arrived in New York. It was here that I started to suffer from some kind of allergy—rose fever, hay fever, dust, who knows? I took pills by the bottleful, but they didn't do much good. The heat that early spring was as intense as in August. The furnished room where I lived on the West Side was stifling. I am not one to consult with doctors, but I paid a visit to Dr. Gnizdatka, whom I knew from Warsaw and who faithfully read anything that I managed to get published in the Yiddish press.

Dr. Gnizdatka inserted a speculum into my nostrils and a tongue depressor into my mouth and said, *"Paskudno."* ("Bad.")

"What should I do?"

"Move somewhere near the ocean."

"Where is the ocean?"

"Go to Sea Gate."

The moment Dr. Gnizdatka spoke the name, I realized that the time had finally come to escape from civilization, and that Sea Gate could serve the same purpose as Haiti or Madagascar. The following morning, I went to the bank and withdrew my savings of seventy-eight dollars, checked out of my room, packed all my belongings into a large cardboard suitcase, and walked to the subway. In a cafeteria on East Broadway, someone had told me that it was easy to get a furnished room in Sea Gate. I carried a few books to be my spiritual mainstay while away from civilization: the Bible, Spinoza's *Ethics,* Schopenhauer's *The*

Translated by the author and Ruth Schachner Finkel

World as Will and Idea, as well as a textbook with mathematical formulas. I was then an ardent Spinozist and, according to Spinoza, one can reach immortality only if one meditates upon adequate ideas, which means mathematics.

Because of the heat in New York City, I expected Coney Island to be crowded and the beach lined with bathers. But at Stillwell Avenue, where I got off the train, it was winter. How surprising that in the hour it took me to get from Manhattan to the Island the weather had changed. The sky was overcast, a cold wind blew, and a needle-like rain had begun to fall. The Surf Avenue trolley was empty. At the entrance to Sea Gate there was actually a gate to keep the area private. Two policemen stationed there stopped me and asked who I was and what business I had in Sea Gate. I almost said, "I am running away from civilization," but I answered, "I came to rent a room."

"And you brought your baggage along?"

These interrogations in a country that is supposed to be free insulted me, and I asked, "Is that forbidden?"

One policeman whispered something to the other, and both of them laughed. I received permission to cross the frontier.

The rain intensified. I would have liked to ask someone where I could get a room, but there was no one to ask. Sea Gate looked desolate, still deeply sunk in its winter sleep. For courage I reminded myself of Sven Hedin, Nansen, Captain Scott, Amundsen, and other explorers who left the comforts of the cities to discover the mysteries of the world. The rain pounded on my cardboard suitcase like hail. Perhaps it *was* hailing. The wind tore the hat off my head, and it rolled and flew about like an imp. Suddenly through the downpour I saw a woman beckoning to me from the porch of a house. Her mouth moved, but the wind carried her voice away. She signaled me to come over and find protection from the wild elements. I found myself facing a fancy house with a gabled roof, columns, an ornate door. I walked onto the porch, dropped my suitcase (books and manuscripts can be as heavy as stones), wiped my face with a handkerchief, and was able to see the woman more clearly: a brunette who seemed to me in her thirties, with an olive complexion, black eyes, and classic features. There was something European about her. Her eyebrows were thick. There was no sign of cosmetics on her face. She wore a coat and a beret that reminded me of Poland. She spoke to me in English, but when I answered her and she heard my accent she shifted to Yiddish.

"Who are you looking for? I saw you walking in the rain with that heavy suitcase, and I thought I might . . ."

I told her I had come to rent a room and she smiled, not without irony.

"Is this the way you look for a room? Carrying your luggage? Please come inside. I have a house full of rooms that are to let."

She led me into a parlor, the like of which I had seen only in the movies—Oriental rugs, gold-framed pictures, and an elaborate staircase with carvings and a red velvet bannister. Had I entered an ancient palace? The woman was saying, "Isn't that odd? I've just opened the house this minute. It's been closed for the winter. The weather turned warm and I decided perhaps it's time. As a rule, the season here begins in late May or early June."

"Why is the house closed in the winter?" I asked.

"There's no steam. It's an old building—seventy or eighty years old. It can be heated, but the system is complicated. The heat comes through here." She indicated a brass grate in the floor.

I now realized it was much colder inside than outside. There was a staleness in the air characteristic of places that have been without sun for a long time. We stood silent for a moment. Then she asked, "Are you wanting to move in immediately? The electricity isn't turned on yet and the telephone hasn't been connected. Usually boarders come to make arrangements, pay a deposit, and move in when the weather has become really warm."

"I gave up my room in the city."

The woman looked at me inquisitively and after some hesitation said, "I could swear I've seen your picture in the newspaper."

"Yes, they printed my photograph last week."

"Are you Warshawsky?"

"That's me."

"God in Heaven!"

Darkness had fallen and Esther Royskes lit a candle in a copper candlestick. We were sitting in the kitchen eating supper, like man and wife. She had already told me her whole story: the trouble her ex-husband, a Communist poet, gave her; how she finally divorced him; and how he ran away with his lover to California and left Esther to take care of their two little girls. Two years ago, she had rented this house with the hope that she could earn a living from it, but it did not bring her enough income. People waited until after the Fourth of July and tried to get bargains. Last year, a number of her rooms remained empty.

I put my hand into my pocket, took out the seventy-eight dollars, and offered to give her a down payment, but she protested. "No, you are not going to do that!"

"Why not?"

"First, you have to see what you are taking. It is damp and dark here. You may, God forbid, get a cold. And where will you eat? I would

gladly cook for you, but since you tell me you plan to become a vegetarian it may be difficult."

"I will eat in Coney Island."

"You will ruin your stomach. All you get there is hot dogs. A man
who packs his valise and comes to Sea Gate without any forethought is
not practical. It's a miracle that brought you to me."

"Yes, it is a miracle."

Her black eyes gazed at me half mockingly, and I knew that this was
the beginning of a serious relationship. She seemed to be aware of it,
too. She spoke to me of things that are usually not told to a stranger.
The shadows cast on her face by the candlelight reminded me of a
charcoal sketch on a canvas. She said, "Last week I was lying in bed
reading your story in the paper. The girls were asleep, but I love to read
at night. Who writes about ghosts nowadays, I wondered, and in a
Yiddish newspaper to boot! You may not believe me but I thought that I
would like to meet you. Isn't that strange?"

"Yes, strange."

"I want to tell you that there is a romantic story connected with this
house. A millionaire built it for his mistress. Then Sea Gate was still a
place for the rich and American aristocrats. After his death, his mistress
remained here until she died. The furnishings are hers—even the library.
She seemed not to have left any will, and the bank sold everything
intact. For years it remained unoccupied."

"Was she beautiful?"

"Come, I will show you her portrait."

Esther picked up the candlestick. We had to pass through a number
of dark rooms to get from the kitchen to the parlor. I stumbled on the
thresholds and bumped into rocking chairs. I tripped over a bulge in a
rug. Esther took me by the wrist. I felt the warmth of her hand. She
asked me, "Are you cold?"

"No. A little."

In the flickering light of the candle, we stood and gazed at the
portrait of the mistress. Her hair was arranged in a high pompadour; her
low-cut dress exposed her long neck and the upper part of her breasts.
Her eyes seemed alive in the semidarkness. Esther said, "Everything
passes. I still find pressed flowers and leaves in her books, but there's
nothing left of her."

"I'm sure her spirit roams these rooms at night."

The candlestick in Esther's hand trembled and the walls, the pictures, and the furniture shook like stage props in a theater. "Don't say
that. I will be afraid to sleep!"

We looked at each other like two mind readers. I remember what I
thought then: A situation that a novelist would have to build up slowly,

gradually, through a number of chapters, over months or perhaps years, fate has arranged in minutes, in a few strokes. Everything was ready—the characters, the circumstances, the motivations. Well, but in a true drama one can never foresee what will happen the next instant.

The rain had stopped and we were back in the kitchen, drinking tea. I thought it was late, but when I looked at my wristwatch it showed twenty-five past eight. Esther glanced at her watch, too. We sat there for a while, silent. I could see that she was pondering something that required an immediate decision, and I knew what it was. I could almost hear a voice in her mind—perhaps it was the genius of the female species —saying, "It shouldn't come to him so easily. What does a man think when he's able to get a woman so quickly?"

Esther nodded. "The rain has stopped."

"Yes."

"Listen to me," she said. "You can have the best room in this house, and we will not haggle about money. I will be honored and happy to have you here. But it's too early for you to move in. I intended to spend the night here, but now I am going to lock up the house and go home to my children."

"Why don't you want to stay over? Because of me?" I asked, ashamed of my own words.

Esther looked at me questioningly. "Let it be so."

Then she said something that, according to the rules of female diplomacy, she should not have said: "Everything must ripen."

"Very well."

"Where will you sleep now that you've given up your room?"

"I will manage somehow."

"When do you intend to move in?"

"As quickly as possible."

"Will May 15th be too long for you to wait?"

"No, not too long."

"In that case, everything is decided."

And she looked at me with an expression of resentment. Perhaps she expected me to implore her and try to persuade her. But imploring and persuading have never been a part of my male strategy. In the few hours I spent with Esther I had become somewhat surer of myself. I figured that she was about ten years my senior. I had girded myself with the patience necessary to one prepared to give up civilization and its vanities.

Neither of us had removed our coats—it was too cold—so we didn't have to put them on. I took my suitcase, Esther her overnight bag. She blew out the candle. She said, "If you hadn't mentioned her spirit, I might have stayed."

"I'm sure that her spirit is a good one."

"Even good spirits sometimes cause mischief."

We left the house and Esther locked the door. The sky was now clear—light as from an invisible moon. Stars twinkled. The revolving beam from a nearby tower fell on one side of Esther's face. I didn't know why, but I imagined that it was the first night of Passover. I became aware that the house stood apart from other houses and was encircled by lawns. The ocean was only a block away. Because of the howling wind I couldn't hear its sounds earlier, but the winds had subsided and now I heard the waters churning, foaming, like a cosmic stew in a cosmic caldron. In the distance, a tugboat was towing three dark barges. I could barely believe that just an hour away from Manhattan one could reach such quiet.

Esther spoke haltingly. "You wanted to give me an advance before, but I refused to take it. If you are serious about the room, I will accept one, just to make sure that . . ."

"Will twenty dollars be enough?"

"Yes, enough. I ask for it only so that you won't change your mind," she said, and she laughed self-consciously.

In the night light, I counted out twenty dollars. We walked together to the gate. I recognized one of the policemen who had been on duty when I arrived. He looked at us and our suitcases knowingly, as if, like a wizard, he had guessed our secrets. He smiled and winked, and I heard him say, "Are you two going back to civilization?"

Vanvild Kava

IF a Nobel Prize existed for writing little, Vanvild Kava would have gotten it. During his lifetime he published one thin brochure and a few articles. Half of the brochure consisted of writer's names and titles of books. Just the same he was a member of the Yiddish Writers' Club in Warsaw and even belonged to the P.E.N. club.

When I acquired a guest card to the Writers' Club, Kava had already been there for many years. He was known as a strange character and the most severe critic possible. He declared such Yiddish classics as Sholom Aleichem and Peretz to be half-talents, and Mendele Mocher Sforim talentless. Sholem Asch he called a promising young man who didn't keep his promise. My brother, I. J. Singer, and my friend Aaron Zeitlin he considered barely beginners. Like a schoolteacher, Kava liked to grade achievements in numbers, and he gave them both two sevenths. I could not bargain with him about my brother, but I told him that Zeitlin was the closest thing to a master that I could think of. I compared him to such writers as Edgar Allan Poe, Lermontov, and Slowacki. But Kava's opinion of even these poets was not too high. He found faults in everyone. Kava maintained that since civilization and culture are only some five thousand years old, literature is still at the beginning of its development, actually in its infancy. It may take another five thousand years for a full-fledged literary genius to appear. I argued that every artist must start from the beginning; unlike science, art does not thrive on the information and qualities of others. But Kava replied, "Art has its mutations and selections, its own biological growth."

It seemed unbelievable that such an angry critic could exist in the Warsaw Yiddish Writers' Club. Every Friday in the book sections of the Yiddish newspapers, reviewers revealed at least half a dozen new talents. They were as lenient as Kava was strict. After he was willing to grant me .003 as my rating (quite lavish praise for a fledgling like myself), we had many conversations about literature. Kava pointed out to me that Tolstoy's *War and Peace* may be quite rich and accurate in description and dialogue, but is poor in construction. Dostoevsky had a greater vision than Tolstoy, but he had only a single accomplished work —*Crime and Punishment.* Shakespeare's value was in his poetry—not as much in his sonnets as in the few poems that appear in his plays. Kava admitted that, as a primitive, Homer was readable. He called Heine a jingle writer. In his brochure he listed all the literary and scientific works that needed to be translated into Yiddish in order for it to be more than a dialect. The Yiddishists attacked him as their worst enemy, but the professional translators praised him. Some literati felt that Kava should be thrown out of the Yiddish Writers' Club, and others defended him, saying that he was too ridiculous to be taken seriously.

Fate and Kava himself did their best to make him appear as a clown. He was small, emaciated, had a crooked mouth, and lisped out of its corner. The jokers in the Writers' Club specialized in mimicking him, his extreme understatements, his use of scientific phrases, and his pedantic style of talking. To Kava, Freud was a mere dilettante and Nietzsche a would-be philosopher. The literary wags gave Kava a nickname— Diogenes.

Kava lived on pennies. His only income came from substituting for the proofreaders of the Yiddish press when they went on their summer vacations. However, the typesetters completely ignored his corrections, since he had his own concepts about grammar and syntax. He brought entire encyclopedias, lexicons, and various dictionaries to the composing room. The editors maintained that if all of Kava's corrections were to be followed up, the daily newspapers could appear only once in three months.

Needless to say, Kava was an old bachelor. What woman would have married one such as Vanvild Kava? Summer and winter he wore a faded derby, a coat down to his ankles, a stiff collar which used to be called "father murderer." I was told that in his vest pocket he kept a chronometer instead of a watch. If someone asked him what time it was, he would say, "A minute and twenty-one seconds to five." When he read proofs, he used a watchmaker's eyepiece. Kava lived in a tiny fifth-floor walk-up attic room, all the walls of which were lined with books. On his visits to the Writers' Club he ordered nothing from the buffet, not even a glass of tea. He had discovered a bazaar where he could buy stale black bread, cheese, and fruit for next to nothing. It was said that he washed his own linen and pressed it by laying it under the heavy volumes of his library. Still, there was never a stain on his clothing. He had a system of sharpening razor blades on a glass. Vanvild Kava was an ascetic—not in the name of religion, but in the name of his version of worldliness.

Suddenly one day the Writers' Club was shaken by a sensation. Kava married. And whom? A young and beautiful girl. One had to know the Yiddish Writers' Club and its passion for gossip to realize the uproar this piece of news created. At first, everyone considered it a joke. But it soon became clear that it was no joke. The proofreaders and typesetters had already published their congratulations in their newspapers. One day Kava brought his new wife to the Writers' Club at exactly the time he came every day—seventeen minutes after eleven. She seemed in her late twenties, was dressed fashionably; had dark, short hair and polished nails. She spoke both Polish and Yiddish well. All that those who were present that day in the club could do was gape. Kava ordered two glasses of coffee for himself and his beloved and some cake. When the pair left, exactly seventeen minutes after twelve, the club began to buzz with excitement. A number of explanations and theories were created on the spot. I remember only one of them—that Kava was a kind of Yiddish Rasputin, a sexual miracle worker. But this theory was immediately dismissed as sheer nonsense. Every man in the Writers' Club considered all the other male members as impotent. Kava could not be the exception.

For days and weeks the Yiddish Writers' Club was busy solving this riddle, but as quickly as a solution was found, it collapsed. Some of the writers knew that I was friendly with Kava; I had also gone up in his ratings a few fractions of a point, and they insisted that I provide them with some insight. But I was just as bewildered as the others. No one would have dared to approach Kava and ask him any personal questions. There was a pride in this little man that did not allow for intimacy.

Then something happened. A girl whose home I visited had a friend from the town of Pulava. Pulava had a large printing shop where some Yiddish books were printed. The townspeople also boasted about having a few writers and translators. This girl from Pulava was a friend of Kava's wife, and one evening they both visited my girlfriend while I was there. It was an unexpected stroke of luck. I ate supper with a person who was part of a mystery. She seemed clever and tactful, and there was nothing enigmatic about her behavior. We discussed politics, literature, the literary group in Pulava. After supper, Mrs. Kava lit a cigarette and chatted with me while the other two girls washed the dishes. I said to her, "I would like to ask you something, but don't be offended if it is too personal. You really don't have to answer me if . . ."

"I know what you want to ask me," she interrupted. "Why I married Kava. Everybody is asking me the same thing. I will tell you why. I wasn't born yesterday, I know men, but all the men I had the misfortune of meeting bored me stiff. Not one of them had an opinion of his own. They all said the usual things that young men say to girls. They repeated the editorials in the newspapers almost verbatim and read all the books the reviewers recommended. Some of them offered to marry me, but how could I go and live with a man who made me yawn even at our first meeting? Conversation with a man is of high importance to me. Of course he must be a man, but this is not everything. Then I met Vanvild Kava and I found all the qualities in him I was looking for since I grew up—a person with knowledge and with opinions of his own. I began playing chess when I was twelve and I guess you know that Kava is a splendid chess player. He could have become a grand master if he had devoted his time to it. Of course he's older than I am, and poor, but I never looked for riches. I make a living as a teacher and don't need to be supported. I don't know what you think of his writing, but I consider him a mighty good writer. I hope that near me he will work on a regular basis and produce good works. That's all I can tell you."

Mrs. Kava's every word expressed decisiveness. It was the first time someone had spoken about Kava without laughing at him and mocking his mannerisms. I told her I knew Kava and admired his erudition and strong opinions, although they were overly extreme at times. She said to me, "He's original. Never banal. His trouble is that he writes in Yiddish. In another medium he would be highly appreciated, whether they agreed with him or not."

When I came to the Writers' Club the next day and told my cronies that I had met Kava's wife and repeated what she told me, they all looked disappointed. One of them asked, "How can you love someone like Kava?" And I gave him the usual answer: "No one has yet determined who can be loved and who cannot be."

After a while I stopped going to the house where I had met Kava's wife and Kava's visits to the Writers' Club became less frequent than in his bachelor years. The only news I heard about him was that he gave up his job as a substitute proofreader. I began to believe that he might mellow with this woman and perhaps write something of value. I had no doubt that the man possessed high literary potential. A person who demands so much from others might also demand much of himself under the right circumstances.

But then something so peculiar occurred that I'm still puzzled by it forty years later. A year or two had passed, and my friend Aaron Zeitlin, who had become the editor of a trimonthly magazine, offered me a position as an associate editor. We were looking for an important essay about Yiddish literature or literature in general for the first issue, and I proposed to Zeitlin that Kava write it. At first Zeitlin demurred. "Kava, of all people?" he said. "First of all, it would take him a year or two. Secondly, he will make mincemeat out of everybody. It will give us a bad name from the very beginning." But I answered, "Don't be so sure. My impression is that he has changed since he married. But even if he does tear everyone to pieces, we can always say in a footnote that we disagree with him. It might even help the magazine to come out with something totally negative."

After long haggling, I managed to persuade Zeitlin to give it a try, but he stipulated that Kava must agree to an eventual footnote of disagreement, and he must also give a definite date of delivery. I was happy that Zeitlin let himself be persuaded. Somehow I felt that Kava might surprise us.

It so happened that Kava came the next day to the Writers' Club, and when I made this proposition to him he seemed shaken. He said, "You ask me to write the leading article? I have been excommunicated from Yiddish literature for years. The name Kava was not kosher. Suddenly you choose me."

I assured Kava that both Zeitlin and I had a high opinion of him. I pleaded with him not to demand the impossible from writers and I also assured him that we would change nothing in his essay. If worst came to worst, we would add a footnote that we disagreed. That would be all.

After much hesitation Kava consented to write the essay and gave me a date of delivery. He promised that in no case would the essay be longer than fifty pages. I told Kava my premonition that this essay would be a turning point in his literary career. Kava shrugged, and said in his laconic way, "Time will tell."

The time to deliver the manuscript was close but we had not heard a word from Kava. He stopped coming to the Writers' Club altogether, and this was a sign for me that he was busy working on the essay. One day I got a telephone call from him. He asked for an extension of two weeks on the delivery of the manuscript. I asked him how the work was going and he said, "I'm afraid it may be somewhat longer than fifty pages."

"How much longer?" I asked.

"Nine and a half pages."

I knew that Zeitlin would be angry with me. Even fifty pages was too long. But I also knew that if a work is good the reader and the critics will accept any length. There was a moment when I wanted to ask Kava to let me have a fragment of his work but I decided not to show impatience. When I told Zeitlin what had happened he said, "I'm afraid

Kava will bring us not fifty-nine and a half pages but fifty-nine and a half lines."

The day came and I met Kava in the Writers' Club. He brought the manuscript. It was fifty-nine and a half pages. I could see that it had many erasures as well as quotations in German, French, and even in English, which could be a problem for a printer of a Yiddish magazine. Also his lines were written so close together that the fifty-nine and a half pages in Kava's longhand might make eighty pages in print. He said, "I'm giving this to you under the condition that you don't read it here, but go home and read it by yourself. Only then can you give it to Zeitlin."

I took the manuscript and ran home as quickly as I could. I was possessed with the desire to prove to Zeitlin that I was right. The moment I entered my furnished room, I threw myself on the sofa and began to read. I read three or four pages and everything pleased me. Kava began with a characterization of literature generally, and of Yiddish fiction specifically. The style was right, the sentences short and concise. I've never enjoyed reading a manuscript as much as I did those first five pages. On page 6, Kava wrote something about a "full-blooded writer." He had put the expression in quotation marks, noting that this term is used to categorize racehorses, not to evaluate talent. It is odd that in Yiddish, of all languages, this idiom should be applied to levels of the mind.

I read further and to my astonishment saw that Kava dwelled too long on the explanation of this borrowed idiom. It is certainly a digression that could be cut, I thought, if Kava wouldn't mind. But the further I read, the more perplexed I became. Kava had written an entire essay on horses—Arabian horses, Belgian horses, racehorses, Appaloosa horses. I read names I had never heard. I literally could not believe my own eyes. "Perhaps I'm dreaming," I said to myself. I pinched my cheeks to make sure that it was not a nightmare. Vanvild Kava had done excessive research, quoted scores of books, for an article on horses, their physiology, anatomy, and behavior, their various subspecies. He even added a bibliography. "Is he mad?" I asked myself. "Was this a game of spite?" The idea that I would have to bring this manuscript to Zeitlin made me shudder. There was no question that we could never publish it. I would have to break my word of honor and give the manuscript back to Kava. In all my anguish I felt like laughing.

After long brooding, I called on Zeitlin. I will never forget his grimaces when he reached the pages where Kava began to elaborate on the expression "full-blooded." He lifted his yellowish eyebrows and never let them down until he finished. For a while his face reflected a mixture of irony and disgust. Then I saw in his eyes something like the grief of a doctor when a patient comes to complain about a head cold and it turns out to be a malignant tumor. He said to me, "What did I tell you? How could you expect anything else from Kava?"

I had no choice. I had to return the manuscript. I asked Kava why he did what he did and pleaded with him to give me some explanation. He sat there motionless and pale. Then I heard him say, "I told you I was excommunicated from Yiddish literature. Don't come to me anymore with invitations to write. I will have to live out my years without your magazine." There was a moment when I was tempted to call Mrs. Kava and tell her of my predicament, but I was sure that she knew about this essay and that she would most probably defend her husband. Over the years a distorted outlook on things may become contagious.

It was kind of Kava that he did not stop speaking to me after that incident. Neither of us ever mentioned it. For many months I got up in the middle of the night and pondered: Was this an act of masochism? Was it some form of insanity? If so, what kind? Schizophrenia? Paranoia? Premature senility? One thing was clear: Kava had put a huge amount of work and study into this useless essay. No one in the Yiddish circle had the slightest interest in horses. Young as I was, I had already come to the conclusion that there are multitudes of human actions for which there is no motivation. As a matter of fact, in fiction motivations always spoil the story.

In 1935, when I left for America, the Yiddish section of the P.E.N. club published my first novel, *Satan in Goray*. The executive board hired Kava to do the proofreading and to write a preface. I was afraid that he would find myriads of errors in my book and use the preface for some of his freakish conceptions. But he made no special difficulties in the proofreading and his preface was short and to the point. No, Kava was not insane. I had the feeling his treatise on horses was his last spree into the absurd. Just then I left for America.

Once in a while I still try to fathom what might have been the meaning of Kava's bizarre act, but I know that if there was any, it dwells there where Vanvild Kava is now—in the so-called Great Beyond.

The Reencounter

THE telephone rang and Dr. Max Greitzer woke up. On the night table the clock showed fifteen minutes to eight. "Who could be calling so early?" he murmured. He picked up the phone and a woman's voice said, "Dr. Greitzer, excuse me for calling at this hour. A woman who was once dear to you has died. Liza Nestling."

"My God!"

"The funeral is today at eleven. I thought you would want to know."

"You are right. Thank you. Thank you. Liza Nestling played a major role in my life. May I ask whom I am speaking to?"

"It doesn't matter. Liza and I became friends after you two separated. The service will be in Gutgestalt's funeral parlor. You know the address?"

"Yes, thank you."

The woman hung up.

Dr. Greitzer lay still for a while. So Liza was gone. Twelve years had passed since their breaking up. She had been his great love. Their affair lasted about fifteen years—no, not fifteen; thirteen. The last two had been filled with so many misunderstandings and complications, with so much madness, that words could not describe them. The same powers that built this love destroyed it entirely. Dr. Greitzer and Liza Nestling never met again. They never wrote to one another. From a friend of hers he learned that she was having an affair with a would-be theater director, but that was the only word he had about her. He hadn't even known that Liza was still in New York.

Dr. Greitzer was so distressed by the bad news that he didn't remember how he got dressed that morning or found his way to the funeral parlor. When he arrived, the clock across the street showed twenty-five to nine. He opened the door, and the receptionist told him

that he had come too early. The service would not take place until
eleven o'clock.

"Is it possible for me to see her now?" Max Greitzer asked. "I am a
very close friend of hers, and . . ."

"Let me ask if she's ready." The girl disappeared behind a door.

Dr. Greitzer understood what she meant. The dead are elaborately
fixed up before they are shown to their families and those who attend
the funeral.

Soon the girl returned and said, "It's all right. Fourth floor, room
three."

A man in a black suit took him up in the elevator and opened the
door to room number 3. Liza lay in a coffin opened to her shoulders, her
face covered with gauze. He recognized her only because he knew it was
she. Her black hair had the dullness of dye. Her cheeks were rouged,
and the wrinkles around her closed eyes were hidden under makeup. On
her reddened lips there was a hint of a smile. How do they produce a
smile? Max Greitzer wondered. Liza had once accused him of being a
mechanical person, a robot with no emotion. The accusation was false
then, but now, strangely, it seemed to be true. He was neither dejected
nor frightened.

The door to the room opened and a woman with an uncanny resemblance to Liza entered. "It's her sister, Bella," Max Greitzer said to
himself. Liza had often spoken about her younger sister, who lived in
California, but he had never met her. He stepped aside as the woman
approached the coffin. If she burst out crying, he would be nearby to
comfort her. She showed no special emotion, and he decided to leave
her with her sister, but it occurred to him that she might be afraid to
stay alone with a corpse, even her own sister's.

After a few moments, she turned and said, "Yes, it's her."

"I expect you flew in from California," Max Greitzer said, just to
say something.

"From California?"

"Your sister was once close to me. She often spoke about you. My
name is Max Greitzer."

The woman stood silent and seemed to ponder his words. Then she
said, "You're mistaken."

"Mistaken? You aren't her sister, Bella?"

"Don't you know that Max Greitzer died? There was an obituary in
the newspapers."

Max Greitzer tried to smile. "Probably another Max Greitzer." The
moment he uttered these words, he grasped the truth: he and Liza were
both dead—the woman who spoke to him was not Bella but Liza herself. He now realized that if he were still alive he would be shaken with

grief. Only someone on the other side of life could accept with such indifference the death of a person he had once loved. Was what he was experiencing the immortality of the soul, he wondered. If he were able, he would laugh now, but the illusion of body had vanished; he and Liza no longer had material substance. Yet they were both present. Without a voice he asked, "Is this possible?"

He heard Liza answer in her smart style, "If it is so, it must be possible." She added, "For your information, your body is lying here too."

"How did it happen? I went to sleep last night a healthy man."

"It wasn't last night and you were not healthy. A degree of amnesia seems to accompany this process. It happened to me a day ago and therefore—"

"I had a heart attack?"

"Perhaps."

"What happened to *you*?" he asked.

"With me, everything takes a long time. How did you hear about me, anyway?" she added.

"I thought I was lying in bed. Fifteen minutes to eight, the telephone rang and a woman told me about you. She refused to give her name."

"Fifteen minutes to eight, your body was already here. Do you want to go look at yourself? I've seen you. You are in number 5. They made a *krasavetz* out of you."

He hadn't heard anyone say *krasavetz* for years. It meant a beautiful man. Liza had been born in Russia and she often used this word.

"No. I'm not curious."

In the chapel it was quiet. A clean-shaven rabbi with curly hair and a gaudy tie made a speech about Liza. "She was an intellectual woman in the best sense of the word," he said. "When she came to America, she worked all day in a shop and at night she attended college, graduating with high honors. She had bad luck and many things in her life went awry, but she remained a lady of high integrity."

"I never met that man. How could he know about me?" Liza asked.

"Your relatives hired him and gave him the information," Greitzer said.

"I hate these professional compliments."

"Who's the fellow with the gray mustache on the first bench?" Max Greitzer asked.

Liza uttered something like a laugh. "My has-been husband."

"You were married? I heard only that you had a lover."

"I tried everything, with no success whatsoever."

"Where would you like to go?" Max Greitzer asked.

"Perhaps to your service."

"Absolutely not."

"What state of being is this?" Liza asked. "I see everything. I recognize everyone. There is my Aunt Reizl. Right behind her is my Cousin Becky. I once introduced you to her."

"Yes, true."

"The chapel is half empty. From the way I acted toward others in such circumstances, it is what I deserve. I'm sure that for you the chapel will be packed. Do you want to wait and see?"

"I haven't the slightest desire to find out."

The rabbi had finished his eulogy and a cantor recited "God Full of Mercy." His chanting was more like crying and Liza said, "My own father wouldn't have gone into such lamentations."

"Paid tears."

"I've had enough of it," Liza said. "Let's go."

They floated from the funeral parlor to the street. There, six limousines were lined up behind the hearse. One of the chauffeurs was eating a banana.

"Is this what they call death?" Liza asked. "It's the same city, the same streets, the same stores. I seem the same, too."

"Yes, but without a body."

"What am I then? A soul?"

"Really, I don't know what to tell you," Max Greitzer said. "Do you feel any hunger?"

"Hunger? No."

"Thirst?"

"No. No. What do you say to all this?"

"The unbelievable, the absurd, the most vulgar superstitions are proving to be true," Max Greitzer said.

"Perhaps we will find there is even a Hell and a Paradise."

"Anything is possible at this point."

"Perhaps we will be summoned to the Court on High after the burial and asked to account for our deeds?"

"Even this can be."

"How does it come about that we are together?"

"Please, don't ask any more questions. I know as little as you."

"Does this mean that all the philosophic works you read and wrote were one big lie?"

"Worse—they were sheer nonsense."

At that moment, four pallbearers carried out the coffin holding Liza's body. A wreath lay on top, with an inscription in gold letters: "To the unforgettable Liza in loving memory."

"Whose wreath is that?" Liza asked, and she answered herself, "For this he's not stingy."

"Would you like to go with them to the cemetery?" Max Greitzer asked.

"No—what for? That phony cantor may recite a whining Kaddish after me."

"What do you want to do?"

Liza listened to herself. She wanted nothing. What a peculiar state, not to have a single wish. In all the years she could remember, her will, her yearnings, her fears, tormented her without letting up. Her dreams were full of desperation, ecstasy, wild passions. More than any other catastrophe, she dreaded the final day, when all that has been is extinguished and the darkness of the grave begins. But here she was, remembering the past, and Max Greitzer was again with her. She said to him, "I imagined that the end would be much more dramatic."

"I don't believe this is the end," he said. "Perhaps a transition between two modes of existence."

"If so, how long will it last?"

"Since time has no validity, duration has no meaning."

"Well, you've remained the same with your puzzles and paradoxes. Come, we cannot just stay here if you want to avoid seeing your mourners," Liza said. "Where should we go?"

"You lead."

Max Greitzer took her astral arm and they began to rise without purpose, without a destination. As they might have done from an airplane, they looked down at the earth and saw cities, rivers, fields, lakes —everything but human beings.

"Did you say something?" Liza asked.

And Max Greitzer answered. "Of all my disenchantments, immortality is the greatest."

Neighbors

THEY both lived in my building on Central Park West—he two floors below me, she one above. Greater contrast than those two would be hard to imagine. Morris Terkeltoyb, as I will call him, was a writer of "true stories" for the Yiddish newspaper to which I also contributed. Margit Levy was the former lover of an Italian count. One quality was common to the two of them: I could never learn the truth about either. Morris Terkeltoyb assured me that his stories were invented, but when I read them I realized they couldn't be all fantasy. They contained details and odd incidents that only life itself could devise. Besides, I often saw him with elderly people who looked like the characters out of his tales. Morris Terkeltoyb was far from being a man of literary skill. His style teemed with clichés. I once saw a manuscript of his at the newspaper. He had no notion of syntax. He used commas and hyphens indiscriminately. Each sentence ended with three dashes. But Morris Terkeltoyb wanted me to believe that he was a creative writer, not a reporter.

In the years I knew him, he told me many lies. Countless women threw themselves into his arms—socialites, stars of the Metropolitan Opera, famous authoresses, ballet dancers, actresses. Each time Morris Terkeltoyb traveled to Europe on vacation, he returned with a list of fresh amorous adventures. Once, he showed me a love letter in handwriting I recognized as his own. He wasn't even ashamed to include in his stories scenes taken from world literature. Actually, he was a lonesome old bachelor with a sick heart and one kidney. He himself seemed unaware of the missing kidney; I knew about it from a relative of his.

Morris Terkeltoyb was short, broad-shouldered, with remnants of

Translated by the author and Herbert R. Lottman

white hair that he combed into a bridge spanning his skull. He had large yellow eyes, a nose like a beak, and a mouth almost without lips—a gash revealing a large set of false teeth. He said he was descended from rabbis and merchants, and he must have studied the Talmud in his youth, because his conversation was filled with quotations from it. Yiddish was his language, but he also spoke a broken English, faulty Polish, and the kind of Yiddish-German that was used at Zionist congresses. Slowly, I managed to dig out some truths from his exaggerations. In Poland he had been engaged to the daughter of a rabbi; she died of typhoid fever a week before the wedding. He had studied in Hildesheimer's rabbinical seminary in Berlin but never graduated. He attended lectures on philosophy at a university in Switzerland. He had published a few poems in a Yiddish collection and some articles in the Hebrew newspaper the *Morning Star*. Of his mistresses I knew only one—the widow of a Hebrew teacher. I met her at a New Year's party, and after a few drinks she told me that she had been involved with Morris Terkeltoyb for years. He suffered from insomnia and had periods of impotence. She made fun of his boasting. He had bragged to her that he had had an affair with Isadora Duncan.

The other neighbor, Margit Levy, seemed not to be a liar, but the events of her life were so strange and complicated that I could never figure her out. Her father was a Jew; her mother belonged to the Hungarian aristocracy. Her father was supposed to have committed suicide when he learned that his wife was having an affair with a member of the Esterhazy nobility—a relative of the Esterhazy who was a major figure in the Dreyfus affair. Her mother's lover committed suicide when he lost his fortune at Monte Carlo. After his death, Margit's mother became insane and remained in a clinic in Vienna for twenty years. Margit was brought up by her father's sister, who was the paramour of the Brazilian owner of a coffee plantation. Margit Levy spoke a dozen languages. She had valises filled with photographs, letters, all kinds of documents that testified to the truth of her stories. She used to tell me, "From my life one could write not one book but a whole literature. Hollywood movies are child's play compared to what happened to me."

Now Margit Levy lived in a single room as the boarder of an old maid and survived on Social Security. She suffered from rheumatism and could barely walk. She took mincing steps, supporting herself on two canes. Though she claimed to be in her sixties, I calculated that she was well over seventy. Margit Levy existed in a state of confusion. Each time she visited me, she forgot something—her pocketbook, her gloves, her glasses, even one of her canes. Sometimes she dyed her hair red, sometimes black. She rouged her wrinkled face and used too much mascara. There were black bags under her dark eyes. The nails of her crooked fingers were painted bright red. Her neck made me think of a plucked chicken. I told her that I was poor at languages, but she tried again and again to talk to me in French, Italian, Hungarian. Though her name was Jewish, I noticed that she wore a little cross beneath her blouse, and I suspected that she had been converted. Margit Levy had one time borrowed a book of mine from the public library, and after that she became a reader of whatever I wrote. She assured me that she possessed all the powers I described in my stories—telepathy, clairvoyance, premonition, the ability to communicate with the dead. She owned a Ouija board and a small table without nails. Poor as she was, she subscribed to a number of occult magazines. After her first visit to me, she took my hand and said in a trembling voice, "I knew that you would come into my life. This will be my last great friendship."

And she brought me as a gift a pair of cuff-links that she had inherited from Count Esterhazy—the same Esterhazy who lost eighty thousand crowns in one night and then put a bullet through his head.

It didn't occur to me to bring my two neighbors together. The truth is that I didn't invite either one of them. They used to knock on my door, and if I wasn't too busy I would ask whoever it was to come in, and I would treat him or her to coffee and cookies. Morris Terkeltoyb received Hebrew newspapers from Tel Aviv. When he found a review of a book of mine or even an advertisement, he brought it to me. From time to time, Margit Levy would bake a cake in the oven of the old maid where she boarded, and she would insist on stopping by to give me a piece.

But once it happened that both came in at the same time. Margit found among her papers a letter she had spoken to me about. Morris had discovered a monthly magazine from South Africa that reprinted a sketch of mine. I introduced my guests to each other; though they had been living in the same building for years, they had never met. Margit had become partially deaf in recent months. For some reason she could not pronounce "Terkeltoyb." She pulled at her ear, frowned, mispronounced the name. At the same time she shouted into Morris Terkeltoyb's ear as if he were the one who was hard of hearing. Morris spoke to her in English, but she could not understand his accent. He shifted to German. Margit Levy shook her head and made him repeat each word. Like a demanding teacher, she corrected his grammar and pronunciation. He had the habit of swallowing words, and when he became excited his voice was shrill. Without finishing the coffee, he got up and went to the door. "Who is that crazy old woman?" he asked me. He slammed out as if I were to blame for his failure to impress Margit Levy.

When he had left, Margit Levy, who as a rule was exaggeratedly polite with everyone, going so far as to shower compliments on the neighbors' dogs and cats, called Morris Terkeltoyb an uneducated idiot, a ruffian. Though she knew that I came from Poland, she couldn't contain her rage and spoke of him as "a Polish schlemiel." She apologized immediately and assured me that I was an exception. The spots that came out on her cheeks were so red they could be seen through the rouge. She left the coffee I had placed before her. At the door she took both my wrists, kissed me, and pleaded, "Please, my dear, do not let me meet that creature again."

I imagined that I heard her cry as she made her way up the steps. Margit had a fear of elevators. She had been stuck in one for three hours. Also, an elevator door had closed on her hand, causing her to lose a diamond ring. She sued the building.

After this encounter, I decided never to let one of the two enter my apartment if the other was already there. I had lost patience with both of them. When Morris Terkeltoyb wasn't boasting of his successes with women or the brilliant offers he got from publishers and universities, he complained about the rudeness he met with from editors, reviewers, officials of the journalists' union, secretaries of the P.E.N. club. He was accepted nowhere; people were always doing him in. The proofreaders on our newspaper not only refused to correct the mistakes he marked in his stories but they intentionally crippled his text. Once, he caught a makeup man in the composing room reversing lines of type in an article. When Morris protested to the printers' union, he received no reply. He called Yiddish literature a racket. He accused playwrights of the Yiddish theater of stealing from his stories. He said to me, "You probably believe that I suffer from a persecution mania. You forget that people really do persecute one another."

"No, I don't."

"My own father persecuted me." And Morris Terkeltoyb recited in a plaintive voice a long monologue that could have been serialized as a dozen chapters on his true-story page. Whenever I tried to interrupt to ask for details, he rushed on with such intensity that there was no way to stop him. He dismissed my questions with an impatient wave of his hand. In the end, his stories left me utterly depressed.

I decided that with all their differences Margit Levy and Morris Terkeltoyb had much in common. Just as he did, Margit mixed up names, dates, episodes. Like him, she accused people who had died years before of innumerable offenses against her. All the evil powers had conspired to ruin Margit Levy. A broker who had invested her money became a devotee of race tracks and squandered her capital. A physician who was supposed to cure her rheumatism gave her an injection that brought out a rash on her body and caused an illness that almost killed her. Often she slipped on ice in winter, fell on escalators in department stores. Her pocketbook was snatched. Once, she was held up in the middle of the day in a street crowded with passers-by. Margit Levy swore that when she went on vacation the spinster who was her landlady wore her dresses and underwear, that she opened her letters, and even helped herself to her medicines.

"Who would use another person's medicine?" I asked her.

She replied, "If people could, they'd steal each other's eyes."

In the summer, I took a long holiday. I went to Switzerland, France, Israel. I left in the middle of August, when my hay fever begins, and came back at the beginning of December. I had paid my rent in advance, locking up my apartment before I left. There was nothing in it for thieves except books and manuscripts.

The day I returned, snow was falling in New York. When I got out of the taxi in front of my building, I was stunned by what I saw. Margit Levy was creeping along on a cane and a crutch, with Morris Terkeltoyb holding on to her arm. With his free hand he was pushing a cartful of food from the supermarket on Columbus Avenue. Margit's face was yellow from the cold and more wrinkled than ever. She wore a mangy fur coat and a black hat that reminded me of my childhood in Warsaw. She seemed ill, emaciated. Her eyes, too close together, had a piercing expression like those of a bird of prey. Morris Terkeltoyb had also aged. His beaked nose was red, and white whiskers sprouted on his face.

No matter how unusual an event may seem, my astonishment never lasts more than an instant. I approached them and asked, "How are you, my friends?"

Margit shook her head. "The facts speak for themselves."

Later a neighbor told me that the old maid in whose apartment Margit boarded had given up her place to go to Miami. Margit would have been thrown out into the street. Instead, she had moved in with Morris Terkeltoyb. How this came about my neighbor did not know. I noticed that the name of Margit Levy had been added on Morris Terkeltoyb's letter box.

A few days after my return, Margit visited me. She wept, mixed German with English, and told me at great length how the selfish spinster had decided without warning to move away, how all the neighbors had treated her misfortune with indifference. The only one who showed humanity was Morris Terkeltoyb. Margit acted as if he had taken her in as just a boarder. But the next day Morris knocked at my door, and from his unfinished sentences and gesticulations it became clear that their relationship was more than that of tenant and boarder.

He said, "One gets older, not younger. When you are ill, you need someone to bring you a glass of tea." He nodded, winked, smiled guiltily and sheepishly, inviting me to come see them in the evening.

I went down after supper. Margit received me as a hostess. The apartment looked clean, there were curtains at the windows, the table had a tablecloth and dishes that could only have belonged to Margit. I brought flowers; she kissed me and wiped away her tears. Margit and Morris continued to address each other as "you" instead of the familiar "thou," but I thought that I heard Margit forget herself once and use "thou." They talked to one another in a mishmash of German-English-Yiddish. When Morris Terkeltoyb ate herring with his fingers and started to wipe his hands on his sleeves, Margit said to him, "Use your napkin. This is New York, not Klimontow."

And Morris Terkeltoyb replied in a typical Polish Chassidic intonation, "*Nu*, so be it."

That winter Morris Terkeltoyb had a long spell of sickness. It started with the flu. Then the doctor discovered that he had diabetes and prescribed insulin. He stopped going down to the newspaper and sent his manuscripts by mail. Margit told me that Morris couldn't read his own articles in the paper, they contained so many errors. He got palpitations of the heart every time he read one. She asked me to bring proofs uptown for him. I was willing to help, but I rarely had time to go to the paper anymore. I lectured a lot, leaving the city for weeks. Once when I entered the composing room, I saw Margit Levy. She stood there waiting for proofs. She now took the subway downtown twice each week—first to pick up the proofs and the second time to return them. She said to me, "Aggravation does more damage to the health than any medicine can cure." She also said something that could only have come from Morris Terkeltoyb: "A writer doesn't die of medical errors, only of printing errors." Jake, the printer's devil, tossed the proofs to her hurriedly. Margit put on her glasses and began to look them over. Jake often ran off proofs so sloppily that letters were missing on the margins or lines were missing because the paper was too short to carry the whole column. Even though she didn't know Yiddish, she seemed to realize that some of the proofs were defective and she went to look for Jake among the humming linotype machines. The boy screamed at her and called her names, she complained when she came back. "Is this the way they treat literature in America?"

Toward spring, Morris Terkeltoyb began to go down to the newspaper again, but Margit had a gallstone attack and was taken to the hospital. Morris visited her twice a day. The doctors found all kinds of complications. They made many tests and took a good deal of blood for them. Morris claimed that American doctors had no respect for their patients; they cut them up as if they were already corpses. The nurses didn't come when they were called and the sick didn't get proper food. Morris had to prepare soup for Margit and bring her orange juice. He asked me, "In what way are doctors better than writers or theater directors? It's the same human species."

I left New York again for about three months. When I came back in the fall, I read in the newspaper that the Yiddish Writers' Union was having a memorial evening on the thirtieth day after the death of Morris Terkeltoyb. He had been stricken with a heart attack while reading proofs. Perhaps he died of a printing error. In the evening, I took Margit in a taxi to the hall. It was badly lit, half empty. Margit was wrapped in black. She did not understand the Yiddish speakers, but each time the name of Morris Terkeltoyb was mentioned she sobbed.

A few days after that, Margit knocked at my door. For the first time I saw her without cosmetics. She looked to me like a woman of ninety. I had to help her sit down on a chair. Her hands trembled, her head was shaking, and she spoke with difficulty. She said, "I don't want them to throw Morris's manuscripts into the garbage after my death." I had to give her a solemn promise that I would find an institution which would accept his manuscripts and books, the thousands of letters he kept in trunks and even in a laundry hamper.

Margit lived on for thirteen months. During that time she kept coming to me with projects. She wanted to publish a collection of Morris Terkeltoyb's best writing, but he had left so many manuscripts it would have taken years to choose among them. There was no chance of getting a publisher. She kept asking the same question: "Why didn't Morris write in an understandable language—Polish or Hungarian?" She wanted me to find a Yiddish grammar for her so that she could learn the language. Even though she had never read anything he had written, Margit called him a talent, possibly a genius. Another time Margit found a manuscript that looked like a play, and she urged me to offer it to a theater director or to find someone to translate it into English.

Margit Levy spent more of the last two months of her life in the hospital than at home. A few times I went to visit her. She was in the general ward, and her face had changed so much that on each visit I had trouble recognizing her. Her false teeth no longer fit her shrunken mouth. Her nose had become hooked, just like Morris's. She spoke to me in German, French, Italian. Once, I found her with another visitor—her lawyer, a German Jew. I heard her telling him that she had bought a plot in the cemetery of the Klimontow Society, near Morris's grave.

She died in January. It was a frosty day and the wind was blowing. Two people came to the chapel—the lawyer and myself. The rabbi quickly recited "God Full of Mercy," and delivered a brief eulogy. I heard him say, "The privilege of leaving a good name is for villagers only. In a city like New York, a person's name often dies before him." Then the coffin was put into a hearse and Margit Levy rode into eternity without anyone to accompany her.

I wanted to carry out my promise to find a place for Morris Terkeltoyb's packs of manuscripts, but the institutions I called all refused to take them. I kept in my apartment one valise filled with his writings and two albums that belonged to Margit Levy. All the rest the superintendent threw out into the street. That day I did not leave the house.

In Morris Terkeltoyb's valise I found, to my surprise, bundles of faded love letters that women had written him—all in Yiddish. One woman threatened that she would commit suicide if he did not return to her. No, Morris Terkeltoyb was not the psychopathic boaster I had thought him to be. Women did love him. I remembered Spinoza's saying that there are no falsehoods, there are only distorted truths. A strange idea ran through my mind: perhaps among these letters I would find one from Isadora Duncan. For a moment I had forgotten that Isadora Duncan did not know Yiddish.

A year after Margit Levy's death, I received an invitation from the Klimontow Society to attend the unveiling of a monument to Malkah Levy—the Society had given her a Hebrew name. But that Sunday a heavy snow fell, and I was sure that the unveiling would be postponed. Besides, I woke up with a severe attack of sciatica. I took a hot bath, but there was no one for whom to shave and dress. Neither did I miss anyone. After breakfast, I took out Margit's album, some of Morris's letters, looked at the pictures, and read the texts. I dozed, dreamed, and forgot my dreams the moment I wakened. From time to time I looked out the window. The snow descended sparsely, peacefully, as if in contemplation of its own falling. The short day neared its end. The desolate park became a cemetery. The buildings on Central Park South towered like headstones. The sun was setting on Riverside Drive, and the water of the reservoir reflected a burning wick. The radiator near which I sat hissed and hummed: "Dust, dust, dust." The singsong penetrated my bones together with the warmth. It repeated a truth as old as the world, as profound as sleep.

Moon and Madness

OUTSIDE, a thick snow was falling. It had begun at dawn and continued all day long and into the early evening. Then a frost set in. In the Radzymin study house it was warm. A pair of beggars with ropes around their loins sat by the oven roasting potatoes. Jeremiah, an old man, was reciting psalms. He had gone blind but had managed to learn the Book of Psalms by heart. At a long table across from the Ark of the Holy Scroll sat Zalman the glazier, Levi Yitzchok, who suffered from trachoma and wore dark glasses even at night, and Meir the eunuch, a Cabalist, who was known to be sane for half the month and insane the other half, after the moon became full. The conversation turned to pity, and Zalman the glazier said:

"Of course, pity is virtuous, but too much of it can do damage. Not far from our town of Radoszyce lived a Polish squire, Count Jan Malecki, the owner of big estates. Long before the czar had decreed the serfs to be free, the Count called all his peasants to a meeting and said to them, 'The earth belongs not to me but to those who work it. You're not my slaves any more. Elect an elder and divide the grounds among yourselves.' I can see this Malecki before my eyes—a big man, fat, with a red face and with a blond mustache that reached almost to his shoulders. He had no children, but his wife, the squiress, had five sisters and two brothers. They each had many children and Malecki provided for the whole impoverished family. It is peculiar that although he freed the peasants, Malecki himself worked the fields—plowed, sowed, and harvested. He had acquired a machine to cut straw, which he mixed with hay for feeding cattle. He could stand for hours at this machine working like a hired hand, while his brothers-in-law and sisters-in-law and their brats walked around idly, dressed up as if they were going to a ball. Once, his court Jew, Zelig, asked him what was the sense of allowing the others to behave this way and Malecki answered, 'Every man should do what he wants. I like to carry the burden, so I carry it. They like to be idle, so they should be.' By the way, all of Malecki's relatives indulged in quarrels and calumny. The young ones also stole. His nephews got drunk, walked around with pistols; they went hunting in the Count's forests and sometimes aimed at one another. The girls played the piano and went to parties. The people in Radoszyce gave the Count a nickname—Jan Schmatte, which means 'rag.'

"Since he was not a rebel and never quarreled with anyone, the Russians held no grudge against him and made him the judge of Radoszyce and the whole county. He refused to take a salary. I am told that on the day he became judge the thieves held a banquet. They knew that Malecki would never put anyone in prison. And so it was. When they brought him a thief who defended himself by claiming that his boots were torn, he had a headache, he was penniless, Malecki not only let him go free but gave him a few rubles as well. He was satisfied with a promise from the accused to become honest from that day on. The thugs and pickpockets had something to laugh about.

"There was a man in Radoszyce by the name of Maciek Sokal, and they called him the Lawyer. He was as much a lawyer as I am a doctor. He could barely read. Just the same, whenever someone was on trial he would engage Sokal as a defender. Sokal himself was a swindler, a drunk, a low creature. Before he began to appear in court as a defender, he was known as Sokal the Year-Round Witness. For anyone accused of a crime, he would invent an alibi, come as a witness, and swear falsely. Sokal knew that Malecki was gullible and he taught the criminals how to fool him. Things reached such a state that thieves began to come to Radoszyce from other villages.

"Yes, it soon came out that Malecki had created a lot of trouble with his leniency. The storekeepers in Radoszyce did not sleep nights. They hired a watchman to guard their stores with a stick and a rattle, but the toughs beat him up and he lay sick in the poorhouse for weeks. They began to steal horses in the surrounding villages. When the peasants caught a thief and brought him into Radoszyce, Malecki immediately freed him. Some merchants were robbed so often that they sold their stores for a song and moved to other towns. Others left for America. The peasants began to say there was only one way out—to get rid of Malecki. But the Russians were on his side. What did they care if Polish peasants suffered? People maintained that because of Sokal's shrewdness and Malecki's pity life had become more miserable than ever.

"Not far from Radoszyce was a hamlet by the name of Bojary. There was a rascal there named Wojtek—a drunk, a murderer, a thief, a rapist. He had no father. His mother bore him from a wandering gypsy.

He began to steal when he was five years old. After some time his mother died and Wojtek became a *parobek*, a field hand for a peasant who had acquired land of his own. This Wojtek used to come to the weekly fair at Radoszyce every Thursday, and he always created a scandal. He went into a store to buy a cap or a jacket and then refused to pay for it. He got drunk in the tavern, beat up the peasants, broke windowpanes, turned over tables and benches. He was known as an arsonist. Whenever he had a fight with somebody, he set fire to his house. Everyone knew about it. But when he was arrested and brought to trial there were never any witnesses against him.

"In Bojary there also lived a peasant, Stach Skiba, and he had a daughter, Stasia—a healthy lass, a good worker, able at home and in the fields. She had no mother. Many of the boys wanted her for a wife and came to her with gifts. More than anybody else, Wojtek ran after her. But the girl said to him, 'Sausage is not for a dog.' He threatened to stab her as well as her father and any man she married. But peasants are not easily frightened. Stasia finally got betrothed to a strong peasant boy, Stefan, and he told Wojtek that if he ever said a bad word to his fiancée he would break his neck. After a while there was a wedding, and all the peasants came to Stach Skiba's hut and they ate, drank, danced. In the middle of the celebration a scream and a lament broke out. The house had caught fire on all sides. Some of those who tried to push their way out through the narrow door were trampled to death. Somebody had piled big stones at the threshold. Over twenty people perished in the flames, among them the bride and the bridegroom. Some others were so burned that they remained crippled for life.

"This time there was a witness. An eight-year-old girl had seen Wojtek put rocks at Skiba's door. Also, a Jewish merchant from Radoszyce named Naphtali Gorszkower told the police that on the day before the fire Wojtek had bought an oversize can of kerosene from him. The peasants caught Wojtek, beat him, and took him on a cart to Radoszyce. Immediately Sokal emerged and began to scold the peasants for hurting an innocent lad. The only policeman in town put Wojtek in jail, but Sokal went directly to Count Malecki and told him that drunken peasants had attacked an innocent boy and broken his ribs. Sokal also told Malecki that Naphtali Gorszkower had been persuaded to bear false witness by the elder of the village, who had bought salt, kerosene, and axle grease from Gorszkower. Sokal demanded that His Excellency order the release of Wojtek at once and punish those who had beaten him. Why Sokal worked so hard for Wojtek was not clear, though people said that the thieves of Radoszyce paid a weekly salary to Sokal for defending every knave in town.

"While Sokal lingered in the courthouse, where the Count was sitting in his official robes, with a cross hanging from a golden chain around his neck, doing official business, a mob of peasants gathered outside waiting for news. Suddenly the door opened and Sokal appeared waving a paper. Malecki had given him a signed order releasing Wojtek immediately and compensating him for the abuse. When the peasants saw Sokal with the paper, they went mad. They began to scream in vile voices and threw themselves on him. I am told that in less than a minute Sokal was torn to pieces. The coffinmaker, a neighbor of ours, later told us that there was little left of the body to put in the coffin. From the courthouse to the jail was only two steps. The enraged peasants broke down the door and dragged out Wojtek; someone quickly got a rope, and they hanged him on a lamppost. With the noose on his throat, he managed to call, 'Brothers, remember that I am an orphan.' And one of the peasants called back, 'You will soon stop being an orphan.'

"When the Jews heard what was going on, they were frightened. The storekeepers in the market immediately closed their shops and everyone hid. It could easily have happened that the peasants in their fury would attack the Jews. Naphtali Gorszkower didn't even bother to close his store. He began to run and he kept on running until he reached America. I just say so. He disappeared, and his wife was considered a deserted woman. Only, a year later a letter came to her from New York. But I will make it short. One of the rabble called out, 'Let's get Malecki!' And that's all the peasants needed. They tore into the courthouse and killed the Count. All this took place in a matter of minutes.

"When the governor learned what the peasants had done, he sent a commission with a hundred Cossacks to Radoszyce, and an investigation began, which lasted months. First of all, they put the thieves in chains and sent them to the prison in Radom, or perhaps it was some other town. The merchants in Radoszyce were relieved. However, the Jews still had plenty to worry about. There were some county officials who incited the commission against them, saying that the Jews were the ones who had set fire to Stach Skiba's house and pointing out that this was the reason Naphtali Gorszkower had run away. They even put Naphtali's wife in jail for a few weeks.

"What could the Cossacks do? They rode back and forth on their small horses, waving their whips. Whoever happened to pass by on the street got whipped. About a dozen peasants in Bojary were sent to Siberia without a trial. One of them was the father of the little girl who saw Wojtek put stones before Skiba's door. He was accused of making his daughter bear false witness, because he had once quarreled with Wojtek about a pig Wojtek had stolen. How can a commission help? They cannot revive the dead. All I can say is, there was a lot of grief because of Count Malecki's misplaced pity. I once read in a Yiddish commentary on the Bible that those who pity the wicked end up by being cruel to the innocent."

"It's in the Gemara," Meir the eunuch corrected him.

It was quiet in the Radzymin study house, and one could hear the wick in the lamp sucking kerosene. Old Jeremiah happened to recite the chapter of the psalms which spoke of God's mercy in slaying Sihon the King of the Amorites and Og the King of Bashan and giving their land to Israel as a patrimony. The two beggars had opened the door of the oven, and with their bare fingers shoved out the roasted potatoes. Reb Levi Yitzchok removed the black glasses from his red eyes and wiped them with the hem of his coat. Meir the eunuch touched his hairless cheeks. He threw a glance toward the window and the sky. The moon was not yet full, but one could discern the missing crescent. After a while, Levi Yitzchok put his dark glasses back on and said:

"There was no lack of crazy squires in Poland. Some lost their minds from too much drinking, others from too much luxury. That Count Malecki had perhaps heard of the Jewish law that no one should be judged for a sin without the testimony of two people who had admonished the culprit and told him of his crime's punishment before he committed it. It is said in the Mishnah that a court that pronounced a death sentence once in seventy years was called a killing court."

"What murderer is going to kill someone in the presence of two witnesses and after admonishment?" Zalman the glazier asked. "A murderer waits for a time when he won't be seen. They attack mostly at dark, when no one is there."

"God sees," Levi Yitzchok replied. "He is in no need of witnesses. He is Himself the witness, the judge, the punisher. But since you are talking about misplaced pity I have also a story to tell."

"Let's hear."

"In Kozienice there was a landowner by the name of Stanislaw Karlowski, a little man. He was called Crazy Karlowski. All his adult years he was involved in litigations with other landowners and he lost in these protracted wranglings a lot of money as well as prestige. He had inherited from both his grandparents so many cattle, so many fields and forests that he could indulge all his whims. He had a habit of standing in court and calling the judge bad names, accusing him of being ignorant and a bribetaker. His lawyers begged him to keep quiet. But when a man is crazy he won't listen to advice. The neighboring landowners knew of his temper and they constantly laid claim to some of his land, and he was always the loser. He had a wife, who was immensely rich, too. She came from a family of Polish kings. I never saw her, but I am told she was most beautiful and a harlot. Everyone knew that she had dozens of lovers. She even had love affairs with the squires who took her mad husband to court.

"In our times, duels are forbidden, but in those days the nobles were always dueling. One noble said about another that his racehorse didn't run as fast as it should and he was immediately challenged to a duel. A duel could not take place without seconds, as they were called. Their mission was to make peace between the antagonists, but actually they provoked them to more hatred, eager to see combat and bloodshed. Once, some noble called Karlowski's wife promiscuous. Immediately Karlowski challenged him to a duel. As always, the seconds poured oil on the fire. Karlowski took one pistol, his opponent took another, and they went to a clearing in a forest to shoot it out. The seconds lurked on both sides and waited to see who would kill whom. This is what the Gentiles called an affair of honor. According to the rules, both parties were supposed to shoot simultaneously. But how can you know the exact moment to pull the trigger? The other fired first and wounded Karlowski in the knee. After a duel the former enemies were obliged to forgive one another, shake hands, and sometimes even kiss. So the two men apologized to one another and went through the entire ceremony. The one who shot first rode home on his horse to celebrate his victory. Karlowski was bandaged, put into a britska, and taken home.

"Now, listen. At the time when Karlowski was engaged in the duel, his faithless wife took one of her paramours up to a balcony on a tower from which one could see far away, and both looked through field glasses to where the duel took place, all the while kissing and embracing and having their pleasure. Both expected Karlowski to be killed, and when they saw through the field glasses that he was being loaded into a britska, they thought he was already a corpse. They went down to drink wine and to be comforted. Later on, when Karlowski was brought back alive, his wife instantly fell into a swoon, but after she was revived she kissed him, pretended to cry from joy, and thanked him profusely for defending her reputation. He later recovered, but he walked with a limp.

"You haven't heard everything yet. After a while, she became tired of him altogether. She packed her fancy garments and all her jewelry, grabbed all the money she could get her hands on, and went abroad with a young lecher—perhaps to Paris or some such place. Her husband sent armed riders after her with warrants for her arrest, but the couple had already crossed the frontier and there was nothing their pursuers could do. Karlowski railed to the few friends he had that the young charlatan had seduced his innocent wife and made her leave the path of righteousness. Since he was embroiled in lawsuits up to his neck, he had not much time to brood about his disgrace. Every few months he had to sell another forest or piece of land to pay his litigants and advocates, as well as his penalties for contempt of court. He had to borrow money at high interest. He even became indebted to the Jew who managed the business of his ever-diminishing estates. Three years passed like this. One day a carriage approached Karlowski's castle, and who do you think was inside? His wife—not alone but with a small child, a bastard. The people who saw her arriving were sure Karlowski would come out with a gun or a sword and kill her. What can be worse than a wife who comes back to a husband with a child born of whoredom? But he forgave her. I wasn't there, but I am told that she fell on his throat, lamented, and swore that she had been yearning for him all the time. It was the fault of that young stallion who bewitched her, seduced her, and brought her to shame. How is it written? 'And thou hadst a whore's forehead, thou refusedst to be ashamed . . .' She ate and wiped her mouth and said, 'I have done no harm.' She kept crying and Karlowski tried to soothe her. It didn't last long, and she again became ruler of the castle. She found other sinners, or perhaps the old ones returned. Karlowski, because of his litigations, had often to go to Lublin or Warsaw. He even appealed to the synod in Petersburg, hoping to find justice there. His debts had become so huge that he was on the verge of bankruptcy. But then a hundred-year-old aunt of his died and left him a small fortune. So he paid his debts and could afford new litigations.

"Don't think that you have heard the whole story. One day another carriage came to the castle, and who do you think was there? The father of the baby. He had committed some crime for which he could go to jail. He made believe he had come to see his child, but it was only a pretext to ask its mother for money. It seems that she could not forget him. I am told that she pawned her pearls to pay his debts. If I am not mistaken, he had played with marked cards and his parents had disowned him. I think he was also ill, from drunkenness or from bawdiness. Well, and what do you think Karlowski did? He became an ardent friend of his wife's debaucher, took him into his castle, called doctors to cure him. Even the priests in the surrounding villages condemned Karlowski and his insane behavior. However, Karlowski had a private chapel on his estate and his own deacon, who preached that his lord behaved as a pious Christian should, forgiving his enemy and turning the other cheek."

"What happened then?" Zalman the glazier asked.

"What could have happened?" Levi Yitzchok said. "That rake remained in the castle for a long time, rested, became healthy and fat. The wife was not young enough for him any more, and he was looking for younger prey. He soon found some governess or stewardess who was ready to put herself at his disposal. One day he broke open Karlowski's safe, took out everything of value, even his mistress's jewels, and ran away with that other woman. I think she was a distant relative of the wife's. Karlowski himself continued with his litigations. One day, when the judge brought a verdict against him, he became so shocked that he dropped dead. His wife tried to find solace with her coachman or some other servant, but meanwhile creditors seized the estate and evicted her. She died soon after."

"What happened to the illicit child?" Zalman the glazier asked.

"I really don't know," Levi Yitzchok said. "But what ever happens to the wicked and their seeds? As the psalmist says, they are like chaff driven by the wind."

For a long while it was quiet again in the study house. One of the beggars had stretched out on a bench and fallen asleep. He was snoring, murmuring, and from time to time a whistling came from his nostrils. The other beggar sat down to listen to the stories. He had a little yellow beard and large eyes, like those of a calf. He kept on nodding to every one of Levi Yitzchok's words until he, too, dozed off. Meir the eunuch wiped the frost off the windowpane with his palm and gazed toward the sky, as if to make sure that the moon was not yet completely full. He turned and said:

"What Squire Malecki was doing had nothing to do with pity. Ecclesiastes has said, 'In the place of justice even there was wickedness.' All these judges and lawyers need criminals, just as a doctor needs patients. From the honest who were wronged they will not draw any profit. As for the other squire, what was his name—Karlowski—he knew quite well what his shrew was doing, but he enjoyed letting her have her rotten ways. What does the Gemara say? 'The slave exults in disorder.' When a man sinks in the Forty-nine Gates of Defilement, his nature turns topsy-turvy. Bad becomes good, shame becomes honor. They wallow in slime and are proud of it. What was Sodom? What was the generation of the Flood? Nothing but perversity. And what happened to Rabbi Joseph della Reina? He had already managed to fetter Satan in chains and was about to bring Redemption. But he was suddenly overcome with mistaken pity and offered Satan a sniff of tobacco. This gesture of compassion for the Archfiend was incense to the idols, and all Rabbi Joseph's efforts collapsed. Immediately the Evil One freed himself from his shackles, regained his malign powers, and the Redemption was obstructed. Rabbi Joseph could have repented, because the doors of repentance are always open, but he had fallen into resignation. Since he could not bring the End of Days, he tried to bring the end of the world. Just as he had invoked holy names before, so he now turned to the names of the Evil Hosts. There is only one step from light to darkness.

" 'The greater a man is, the greater is his passion,' says the Talmud. Rabbi Joseph was born with blood of fire. In those times, Spain belonged to the sons of Ishmael. Rabbi Joseph had heard that there was a caliph whose wife was the greatest beauty of all lands, and her name was Ptima. She was utterly lustful, a reincarnation of Cozbi, the daughter of Zur. Since Rabbi Joseph had thrown off the yoke of holiness and given up the goal of becoming totally righteous, he chose total guilt. He uttered a Satanic name and bade two demons bring him this Ptima. He was still living in a cave, as in the times when he was fasting and doing penance in order to bring the Messiah. It was said that he descended from Joseph the Righteous and was as graceful as his ancestor. No wonder that when he and Ptima met they indulged in all possible abominations.

"There is a proverb: 'In time one gets tired even of kreplech.' After some months Rabbi Joseph was told that the Grand Vizier's wife was even more voluptuous than Ptima. Her name was Grisha. Since he had given up the rewards of the soul, there was nothing to impede him from tasting this one, too. He bade the demons bring Grisha to him, and when they did he was overwhelmed by her carnal beauty. From then on, the evil spirits brought him both these females each night—Ptima from sunset to midnight, and after he sent Ptima back to her bed, a journey that lasted an instant, he enjoyed Grisha until dawn.

"Once when Ptima spent her hours with Rabbi Joseph, she found in the bed a cameo with the name Grisha engraved on it. She became jealous and asked Rabbi Joseph who this Grisha was. Just as Delilah coaxed Samson, Ptima pestered Rabbi Joseph so long that he finally divulged to her that she was the wife of the Grand Vizier. Ptima knew that Rabbi Joseph worked all these miracles by the force of an unholy name, and after she lulled him to sleep she began to search for this name. She found it inscribed on a piece of parchment that he kept in a little bag at his throat. Once she found the ungodly name, she had the upper hand. She bade the demons bind Rabbi Joseph with a sash and bring her the mightiest males in all the kingdoms of man.

"I wonder if you know that the Fallen Angels—as well as the descendants of Anak, who were seen by the spies Moses sent to Canaan— are still alive today. They're hiding behind the Black Mountains, or perhaps on the other side of the River Sambatyon. The Angel of Death has no dominion over them, since they are not of this world. Ptima ordered the demons to bring these giants to her. They did so, and she copulated with them in the presence of Rabbi Joseph for three days and three nights. You can imagine what anguish Rabbi Joseph suffered, but since she was in possession of the impure name, he could not free himself. The caliph searched for his wife, but she had disappeared.

"The first time Ptima told her evil messengers to bring her the Fallen Angels and the sons of Anak, she whispered the name so that Rabbi Joseph could not hear it. Before dawn on the fourth day, she had become so fatigued from her loathsome game that she ceased being careful and uttered the name out loud. Rabbi Joseph seemed to be asleep but he awoke at that moment. He had forgotten the name and was helpless, but now that he knew it he regained his power and commanded the messengers of the night to do his will instead of hers. Since both sides applied the same incantation for different purposes, they canceled each other's spell and the evil ones flew back to Mount Seir and stayed in equilibrium. Slowly Rabbi Joseph managed to unbind himself, and he clutched Ptima's throat, about to strangle her. How far is adultery from murder?

"When the cunning Ptima realized her end was near, she began to plead and speak sweet words to Rabbi Joseph and to defend herself by saying that she actually loved him, and that she surrendered to the celestial monsters only because of her jealousy. She said to him, 'What could you gain by killing me? You'll never find anyone more passionate.' When Rabbi Joseph answered that Grisha's flesh was even more gratifying than hers, Ptima said, 'Grisha is not among the living any more. I told my devils to do away with her, and they did. She was buried yesterday.' She went on, 'You let me live, and we two can conquer the world. You will conjure the most beautiful women, and I the richest men. We will put them to sleep and rob them of their diamonds, their medals, and all their possessions. You will become the king of the netherworld and I will be your loving queen. In gratitude for your mercy I will overcome my jealous nature and build a harem for you with more wives and concubines than King Solomon could ever boast of. We will revive the Queen of Sheba, Rahab the Harlot, and give loose rein to all our hearts' desires.'

"It is known that those who can persuade others are easily incited themselves. Rabbi Joseph asked her if she would consent to reviving Grisha and she replied, 'Your delight would be mine. Bring her back to life and we all three will rejoice together.' 'What would happen to your husband?' Rabbi Joseph asked, and she answered slyly, 'For your sake, I will make myself a widow.'

"Not only did Rabbi Joseph give in to aberrant pity but he made a fatal misjudgment. Those who study the Cabala know that with witchery one can accomplish anything but the resurrection of the dead. Once Rabbi Joseph and Ptima attempted to reanimate Grisha, they lost their potency. A wild laugh came down from Mount Seir. Satan and Lilith were laughing with such abandon that the blare echoed over all the deserts. Rabbi Joseph della Reina was deprived of both the power of holiness and the power of the diabolic. He became sick with contamination. Ptima was now more than willing to return to the caliph, but he was four hundred miles away. Besides, the guards wouldn't have let her into the palace, because her beauty had vanished and she had become nothing but a sack of bones. No one would have recognized her."

"What did they do then?" Zalman the glazier asked.

"Rabbi Joseph spat on her and left her to her own devices. She became a beggar at the mosque and died soon after. Rabbi Joseph was too proud to repent and he expired in rebellion. He was reincarnated as a dog."

"I've never heard of this," Levi Yitzchok remarked.

"So you hear it now," Meir said.

"Have you read it in some book?" Levi Yitzchok asked.

"I am the book," Meir answered.

He got up and began to pace from wall to wall. He rubbed his hands one against the other. The kerosene lamp flickered. The wick wavered and smoked. The Radzymin study house became full of shadows. Zalman the glazier said, "Really, I will be afraid to walk home."

Meir the eunuch seemed to have heard his words, because he stopped, laughed, and cried out, "Don't be a fool, Reb Zalman. The moon is shining. The heavens are bright. Evil is nothing but a coil of madness."